"Time itself is but a shadow of eternity,
and the angels stand as guardians at its edges."
~ John Dee

To all the Star Twins

Across the infinity of space and time,
May you find your match.
For when you do, you will feel more deeply,
love more fiercely,
and shine brighter than ever before.

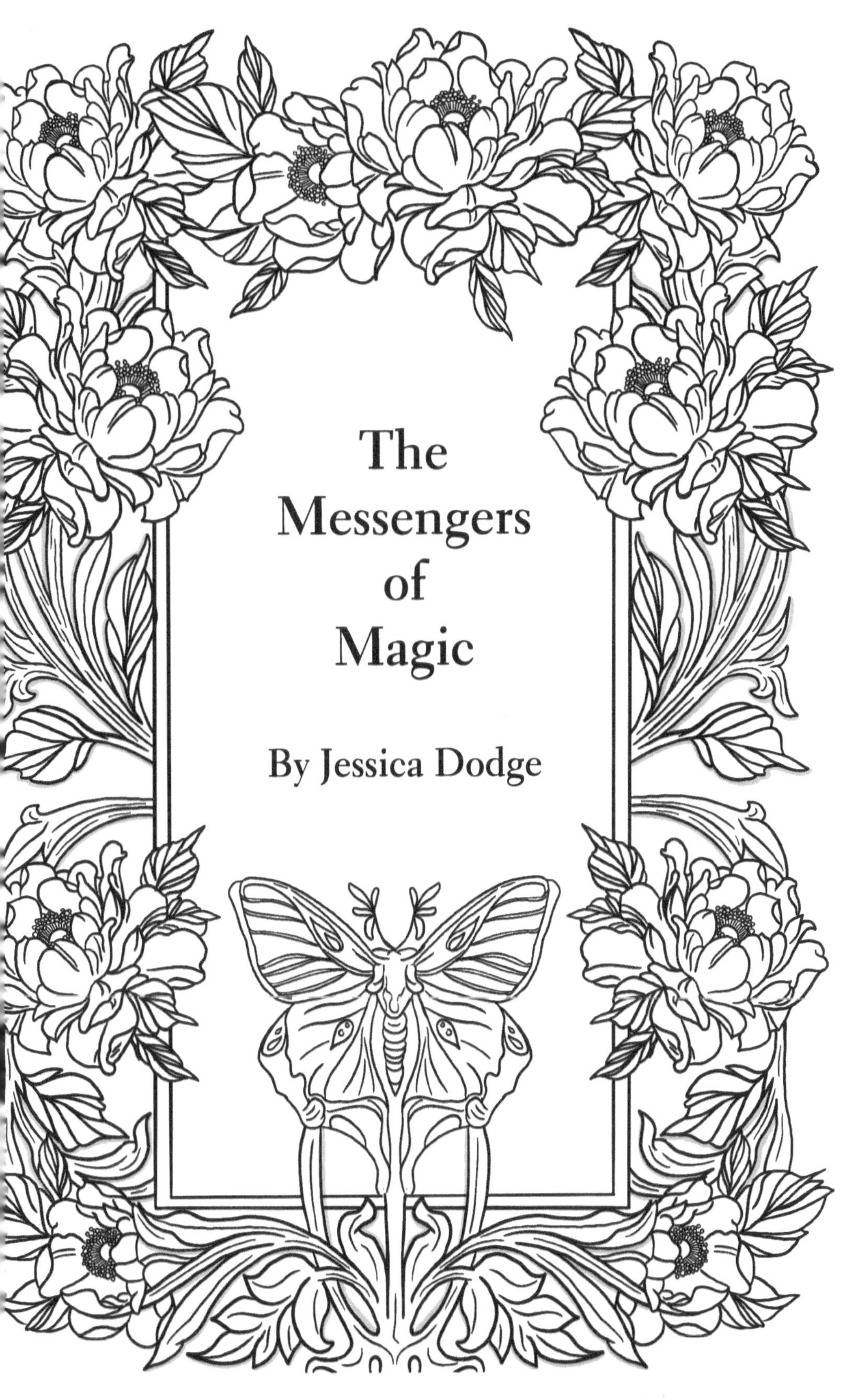

The Messengers of Magic

By Jessica Dodge

Editors: Rosie McCaffrey, Jennifer Bottum,
Anamchara Editing

Proofreader: Chelsea McKenna, Jenny Barroso
Formatter: DRStudio

Cover Design: Miblart & Dark Quill Creations
Page Art: Francesca Scillia & Jessica Dodge

Published by Wizard Supply Co VT
Newbury, Vermont, USA

ISBN:

Paperback: 978-1-965409-03-9

Hardcover: 978-1-965409-04-6

Ebook : 978-1-965409-05-3

For permissions, inquiries, or bulk purchase information, please
contact: Theforgottenwitch@gmail.com

Special Thanks:

Jennifer Bottum for being by my side through every rough draft.
You are my guiding light.
My books are better because of you.

Natalie Banks for always believing in me and cheering me on
through the good and bad. For helping me believe in myself and
my work. I'm so grateful.

Angelic Alphabet

P	Pa		O	Mals
B	Veh		Q	Gisg
C	Ged		R	Drux
D	Gal		F	Fen
A	Char		X	Med
G	Graph		Y	Don
H	Tal		Y	Ceph
N	Gon		Z	Van
S	Ur		Z	Fam
IJ	Ur		J	Gisg

TABLE OF CONTENTS

JOHN DEE

John Dee, the famed mathematician, astrologer, and adviser to Queen Elizabeth I, was a British scholar who straddled the worlds of science and mysticism. Born on July 13, 1527, in London, he was the son of Rowland Dee, a gentleman server to Henry VIII, and Johanna Wild. Dee traced his lineage to Welsh nobility, claiming descent from Rhodri the Great, a ninth-century ruler of Gwynedd. He was a pioneer in

both navigation and astronomy, but his deeper fascination lay in uncovering the secrets of the universe through alchemy, divination, and angelic communication.

His works, particularly his Enochian magic (angel magic) and theories of universal harmony, left a mark on Western esotericism. He believed the universe was woven with hidden patterns, a grand design that could only be decipherable through divine wisdom. His conversations with angels, spoken in a language not of this world, shared secrets of power and knowledge lost since the days of Eden. Even now, centuries later, his influence can be seen in the writings of Aleister Crowley, who incorporated elements of Dee's practices into his own occult philosophies. His influence stretched well beyond his lifetime, and even to this day, his name lingers in the shadows of the occult world.

In 1582, Dee began collaborating with Edward Kelley, a scryer who claimed to communicate with angels. Together, they conducted numerous spiritual séances, during which they believed they received messages in a divine language, now known as Enochian. These communications were meticulously documented by Dee and Kelley, and with the knowledge they gained from their talks with angels they created the Enochian alphabet.

Dee's personal life was marked by both scholarly pursuits and personal challenges. He was married three times and had eight children. His third wife, Jane Fromond, whom he married in 1578, bore him several children, including Arthur Dee, who later became an alchemist and physician. Despite his close association with the Elizabethan court, Dee faced periods of hardship, especially in his later years. After returning to England from his travels in Europe, he found his home and extensive library at Mortlake vandalized and many of his valuable books and instruments stolen. He died in poverty in late 1608 or early 1609, with his gravesite remaining unknown.

The hidden journal of John Dee was uncovered within a stone wall in a bookshop in Helensburgh, Scotland, in the early 1930s. After centuries exposed to the damp and cold, only a few of its final pages remained legible. The events described within those pages have baffled scholars, hinting at an unlikely collaboration with Giordano Bruno, the Italian philosopher and mathematician. The pair had collaborated on a device they called the *Astral Synchronum*, a mechanism designed to open a gateway between the realms of Heaven and Earth. Yet, what became of their final experiment, and whether Dee and Bruno ever succeeded, remains a mystery to this day.

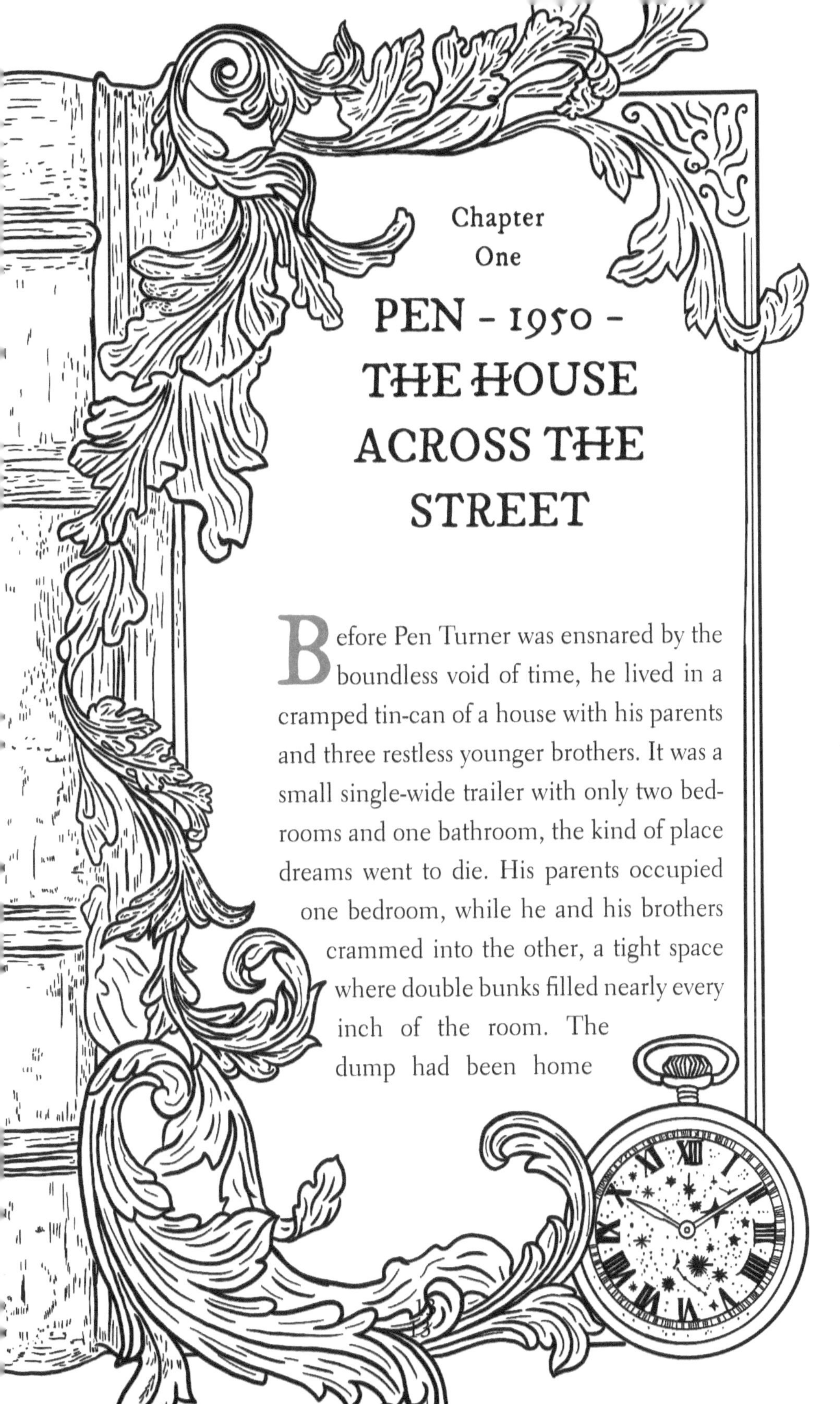

PEN
- 1950 -
THE HOUSE ACROSS THE STREET

Before Pen Turner was ensnared by the boundless void of time, he lived in a cramped tin-can of a house with his parents and three restless younger brothers. It was a small single-wide trailer with only two bedrooms and one bathroom, the kind of place dreams went to die. His parents occupied one bedroom, while he and his brothers crammed into the other, a tight space where double bunks filled nearly every inch of the room. The dump had been home since the day he was born; now, at eighteen, he had outgrown not only the bed he slept in but also the house itself.

The trailer sat on the smallest lot on Haward Street in Oak Ridge, West Virginia, an undeniable eyesore. All the other homes were stick-built houses, not trailers, owned by lower-middle-class Americans. Pen always thought it looked as if the trailer had fallen from the sky and no one had bothered to remove it. Most people who walked past turned their heads, pretending it didn't exist, and he couldn't blame them.

Across the street was a modest two-story house owned by Ward Richardson, a retired high school history teacher. Pen mowed Mr. Richardson's lawn every Thursday afternoon. Afterward, he would go inside and have iced tea with the old man and talk for hours, sometimes staying late into the evening.

Pen liked Ward. He was a nice man who had an endless supply of stories of his travels and adventures. Ward had been to Europe after the war, taking a ship over to France in '47, once travel restrictions were lifted. He spoke of riding steam trains through England, seeing the ruins of bombed-out cities, and walking the streets of Paris. Scenes that, to Pen, sounded like something out of a Hemingway novel.

Pen wished he could have been adopted by him, as his own father was an abusive drunk who had nothing to offer the world other than brake jobs and oil changes. He was happy working a dead-end job and living in a crappy old tin-can of a house. That was not how Pen planned to spend his life. He wanted to travel and see the world, chase adventure, and get as far away from Oak Ridge as he could possibly get.

He was smart, one of the brightest students in his entire high school, but that didn't matter to his father, whose head was as empty as the old well on Sycamore Lane. Ward was the only person he could share his academic achievements and awards with, the only person in his life who genuinely cared.

The heat was already creeping in on that mid-May morning in 1950, so Pen grabbed the mower and headed out to cut Ward's lawn before the worst of it settled in. Cicadas droned in the trees, and down the street, a neighbor's AM radio crackled out Perry Como's "Wanted."

When he'd finished, Ward was waiting with a pitcher of iced tea. "I think we're in for a hot summer this year," Ward said as he poured Pen a tall glass.

"It's looking that way. Graduation is in two weeks, and they've already decided to have it in the gymnasium," Pen told him.

"Have you told your parents about the letter from Bates yet?" Ward asked.

"No. Not sure they'd even care."

"Oh, I'm sure that's not true," Ward replied in his polite tone.

Ward had helped Pen fill out an application to Bates College and had even written a letter of recommendation on his behalf. Pen, despite his homelife, had worked hard throughout high school and had almost gotten straight A's. It was thanks to Ward's tutoring and the quiet refuge of his den that Pen had been able to focus, to read, to think.

The acceptance letter had come just last week, sent to Ward's address. Pen had been awarded the grant he'd applied for, covering nearly all his tuition. Without it, he would have never been able to afford to go. This was his way out. Bates College was his escape plan. He knew if he stayed in Oak Ridge, his future would mirror his father's. And that was the worst fate he could imagine.

Ward had been thrilled when they read the letter together; however, Pen knew convincing his parents that college was a good idea wouldn't be easy. His father wanted him to get his head out of the clouds and "be a man," which meant working with his hands, not his mind.

"Why don't I go over and have a talk with them?" Ward suggested as he refilled Pen's glass. "Maybe if they heard it from me and knew there was little obligation on their part, they might feel differently about it."

"I'm not sure that would do much good," Pen said. "Other than tick the old man off even more."

Pen's father didn't like Ward Richardson. He labeled him as a pompous old man who thought he was better than everyone else, which wasn't the case. Deep down, Pen knew the real reason: his father hated Ward, not for anything he had done, but because Pen looked up to *him* instead of his own father.

"You're probably right," Ward responded. "But I don't want you giving up on that just because he can't see past the edge of Oak Ridge. It's your life and you need to live it the way you want."

They spent the rest of the afternoon talking and paging through old books about New England that Ward kept on a large old bookshelf in his den. Pen felt a flicker of excitement as he imagined visiting the historic places pictured in the worn pages, places he'd see for himself when he was at Bates.

As the sky darkened, Pen headed back across the street to the tin-can. Somewhere a few blocks over, an ice cream truck jingled its tune, and the distant laughter of kids echoed down the street as they chased after it.

When he arrived home, his mother was cooking dinner, and the youngest of his brothers, Val, was playing with a set of wooden

Lincoln Logs that had once been Pen's. The older boys, Dave and Will, were in the tiny backyard kicking a ball around and making all kinds of racket. His father was sitting in an old pea-soup-colored chair, drinking a beer and smoking. The whole place reeked of baked beans, cat piss, and stale cigarette smoke. After coming from the crisp scent of Ward's house, the stench hit Pen so hard, he almost retched as he stepped inside.

"Where the hell have you been? You should've been home an hour ago to help your mother. Were you over there with that old windbag again?" his father snapped, a spray of beer spitting from his lips.

"I mowed his lawn. It's Thursday, remember?"

His father lurched to his feet and grabbed Pen's shirt, twisting the fabric into a knot within his fists before landing a hard slap across his face.

"Don't you talk to me like that, boy. I've got no problem putting you in your place." He let go, shoving Pen to the floor. He caught himself with one arm, elbow dragging across the worn carpet, leaving a raw burn.

Pen stayed there on the floor, looking up at his father, a balding, overweight mechanic who had to push his own kid around just to feel like more of a man. Pen almost felt sorry for him; this was the only semblance of authority he would ever have.

As Pen pulled himself to his feet, he glanced at his mother. She didn't say a word, just kept stirring a pot of beans and franks on the stove. His father settled back into his chair, cracked open another beer, and tuned in to an evening radio program.

This was Pen's life. Every day, the same as the last.

The day Pen graduated from high school, he handed the Bates acceptance letter to his mother. A glimpse of pride flashed across her eyes before it faded as his father snatched it from her hands and began to read.

"You think you're so much better than all of us, don't you? There ain't no way you're getting out of this town. And if you think I'm gonna give you even a cent to send you to some pansy-ass school so you can read books and sit on your ass all day, you have another thing coming," he spat, throwing the letter on the ground and making sure to step on it as he walked off.

"I think it's wonderful, honey. But we just don't have the money to send you to school," his mother said, patting him on the shoulder as she picked up the letter, now emblazoned with his father's footprint.

Pen watched as she smoothed the letter out in her hands. Her face looked drawn, her skin paler than usual, and there was a hollowness in her eyes he hadn't noticed before. Maybe it was just the moment, but she looked more worn down than normal.

"Remember," she added gently, handing it back to him, "you can still have plenty of adventures in those books you love. With a good imagination, you'll never be trapped in one place."

He understood what she meant.

He knew it was how she had survived all these years with his father, trapped in a life that allowed little escape. It was the one thing she had taught him, the one thing they had in common. Despite her lack of education, she could read, and she did so in every spare moment, fleeing into worlds far beyond the one that confined her. Pen had often woken in the night to find her at the kitchen table, a tattered library book open beside a half-drunk glass of Coca-Cola, the bubbles long gone.

Determined not to be trapped like his mother, Pen decided he would get a job and save whatever he could to cover the rest of his tuition money for Bates in the fall. He applied for a few jobs in town, but as fate would have it, the only place that would hire him was the gas station attached to the garage where his father worked. Thankfully, they were on opposite sides of the building, and he rarely had to see his old man.

One day, however, Pen was asked to fill in for George, an older man who had worked in the garage for as long as he could remember, doing oil changes with his father. George had fallen ill and never returned, and before Pen realized it, his temporary role had become a permanent one.

The summer days were long and hot and his hands were perpetually stained with oil. By the time fall was nearing, he was more than ready to leave, ready to head north, where the weather was cooler and a new life awaited him. He had saved all but fifty dollars of what he needed for his first year's tuition, and by the end of the month, he would have that and enough for a bus ticket.

After a long day in the garage, Pen walked home through a fine mist of rain. The heat had been so relentless, one of those days when it was so hot that even the rain turned to steam before it hit the pavement. Humidity clung to everything; the air was thick, heavy, sour with the scent of sweat and hot metal. Fans buzzed from every window he passed, trying in vain to chase away the weight of the day.

By the time he reached his parents' trailer, the sun was dipping low, and the night air finally descended, offering a slight reprieve from the sweltering heat.

Pen stepped into the tin-railed kitchen and found his mother preparing cold-cut sandwiches for his father and the boys, her hair piled in a high bun to keep her neck cool.

"Hi, honey. How was your day?" she inquired, just as she always did.

"Same old, same old," Pen replied.

She called the younger boys in for dinner, and they gathered around the aluminum-rimmed table, eating in near silence. Val and Will wolfed down their food and quickly returned to their game. Dave, the next oldest after Pen, stayed behind, eager to talk with their father about the garage. Fascinated by everything mechanical, he was fixing to walk in his father's shoes someday.

Pen's mother stood to clear the plates when suddenly her legs went limp, and down she went, crashing to the floor with force. Pen sprang from his chair and rushed to his mother's side, finding her unconscious on the linoleum of the cramped kitchen. His father rose slowly and wandered over, squinting down at her.

"Damn woman passed out again. It's the third time this week."

"What?" Pen asked.

"She doesn't drink enough water. I keep telling her, she needs to drink more water."

Pen lifted his mother's head and noticed a small drop of blood slipping from the corner of her mouth. Her eyes started to flutter, and slowly, she began to come to. With Pen's help, she sat up, then let out a small, weak cough that sprayed a fine mist of blood across Pen's shirt. The red speckles stood in stark contrast against the pale blue cotton.

"Oh my God, Mom. We need to get you to a doctor," Pen said, fear filling each word.

"I've already been to a doctor," she replied with sorrow in her eyes as she placed her hand on his shoulder. "It's my lungs." A single tear ran down her cheek. Pen's father turned without a word and went into the living room. He dropped into his chair and lit a cigarette.

"Cancer?" Pen was stunned and confused. He turned and yelled at his father. "How long have you known about this?"

"Since April," his mother answered quietly, getting up off the kitchen floor.

Pen stared at his mother as she went back to cleaning up the kitchen like nothing had happened. "Are the doctors treating you?"

"They told me there's no point. The cancer has too much of a hold on me for anything to help."

"How long?"

She didn't answer. Just kept washing the dishes, wiping down the table, as if the heaviness of it all could be scrubbed away.

Pen glanced at Dave, who was still at the table doing his best to disappear behind the local paper. The front page had some headline about the Korean War, something about Truman sending more troops overseas. But in that moment, nothing seemed more dire than his mother's situation.

He didn't have to wait long for his question to be answered. His mother passed away within a month. His father carried on as if indifferent to the situation; Pen never saw him shed a tear. Pen, though, spent many quiet nights with tear-filled eyes, grieving not just for his mother, but for the life she hadn't got to live. He missed her deeply. And the boys, God, they were lost without her. He couldn't abandon them now. Couldn't walk away and leave them with that man. He wouldn't do that to them.

There was no funeral, just a simple graveside prayer with the boys and their father. The coffin was pine, the cheapest they could afford. If it had been left to his father, she would have been cremated, but Pen knew that wasn't what she wanted. So, he had taken every penny he'd earned over the summer for Bates and bought her a proper casket.

His dreams of escaping Oak Ridge and heading to Bates were just that now, dreams.

Pen continued to work at the garage and take care of his brothers. He stepped into his mother's role, cooking, cleaning, doing what needed to be done as his father showed absolutely no intention of doing any of it.

Not having many friends, Pen found himself spending more of his free time at Ward's house. Ward understood grief; he had lost his wife, Emily, years earlier, and he knew how to talk about sorrow in a way that made it easier to bear. With Ward, he didn't have to pretend to be strong.

Ward also understood why Pen needed to stay in Oak Ridge, but he never let him lose sight of his dreams. He encouraged him to keep learning, to hold on to the hope that one day, he might still find his way to Bates.

But weeks turned into months, and months rolled into years.

By 1955, five years had passed since his mother's death. The boys were nearly grown, now nineteen, seventeen, and fifteen. Each had learned how to take care of themselves. Val was the only one still in school. Pen was still grinding away at the garage, the days blurring together, with Thursday afternoons at Ward's house the only small amount of pleasure in his life now.

He could see where his life was headed with painful clarity: a lifetime at the Gas 'n' Go, marrying some local girl, raising two point five kids in the same kind of dive trailer he had grown up in. It was his worst nightmare, and it was slowly coming true before his eyes. His outlook on life had gone from Prismacolor to a bleak black-and-white photo in a matter of years.

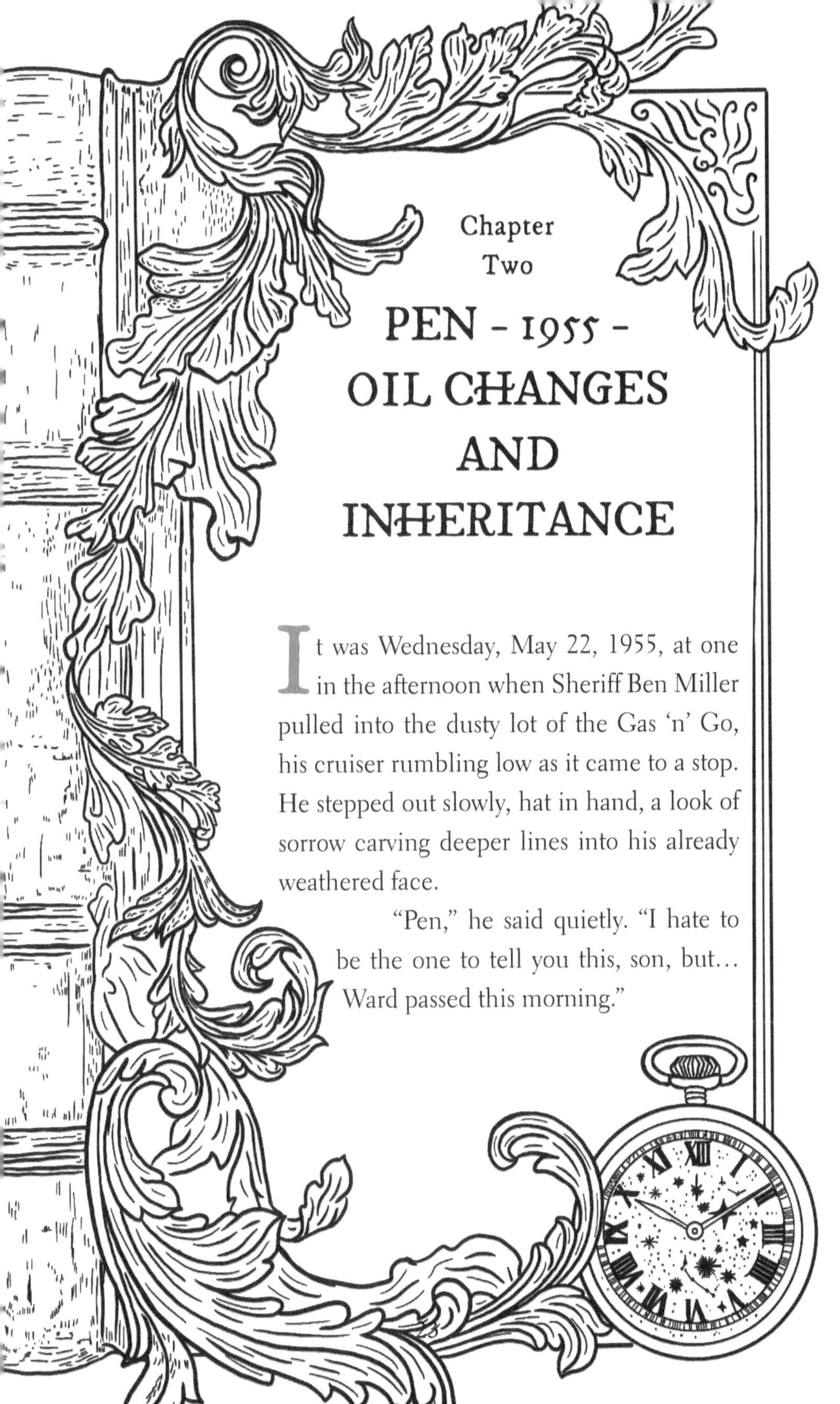

PEN - 1955 -
OIL CHANGES
AND
INHERITANCE

It was Wednesday, May 22, 1955, at one in the afternoon when Sheriff Ben Miller pulled into the dusty lot of the Gas 'n' Go, his cruiser rumbling low as it came to a stop. He stepped out slowly, hat in hand, a look of sorrow carving deeper lines into his already weathered face.

"Pen," he said quietly. "I hate to be the one to tell you this, son, but… Ward passed this morning."

Pen stared at him, the words hanging in the air like smoke. "What?"

The sheriff gave a slow nod. "He called the station earlier, said he wasn't feeling right. Asked if I could drive him to the doctor." He paused, swallowing hard. "By the time I got over there, he was already gone."

Pen's breath caught. His hands, which had been sorting through a box of spark plugs, stilled. "No," he muttered. "No, we… we had plans. He was fine yesterday. We were gonna play chess tomorrow."

Ben rested a heavy hand on his shoulder, the kind of touch meant to steady, though it barely registered.

Pen dropped everything he was doing and took off running down the road, his feet pounding the dirt like he could outrun the truth. Ward was old, near eighty-three, he knew that, but he hadn't felt old. Not to Pen. He was still sharp. Still telling stories. Still part of the fabric of Pen's days.

He didn't remember the run. Only that, somehow, he was standing in front of Ward's front porch, hands on his knees, chest heaving.

Ward was gone.

He stepped onto the porch, unsure what to do. The house sat quiet, too quiet. The screen door was shut tight, the curtains still drawn. The porch swing, Ward's favorite spot, creaked gently in the thick, heavy air. Pen sat on the steps at first, his legs too unsteady to go any farther. Then, without thinking, he rose and collapsed into the swing. And there, in the hush of early afternoon, he wept, long and hard. As hard as he had for his mother. Harder than he ever would for his father.

With Ward gone, the last bit of joy in his life had gone with him. Nothing remained but the hollow ache in his chest.

He stayed on the porch as day faded into night and the stars fully bloomed in the sky. Going inside felt impossible; he couldn't bear to see what it would feel like without Ward's presence. So, he sat there, letting the darkness settle over him like a cloak, and eventually, the motion of the swing lulled him into restless sleep.

For days afterward, he followed the same pattern: work, then over to Ward's house, where he spent the night on the porch swing. At first, he tried to convince himself that Ward was just away on one of his adventures. But no matter how much he tried to trick his mind, the sadness kept growing, blooming into something uncontainable, like a full-blown garden of grief rooted deep in his chest.

By the fourth or fifth day, Pen couldn't say which, as the days seemed to blur together into one long, continuous stretch, he woke to the sound of a car door shutting. Sitting up, he peered over the old porch railing and saw a man in a light blue suit approaching the steps.

"Hello, sir. Are you Mr. Turner? Pen Turner?" the man inquired.

"Yes," Pen replied, rubbing the sleep from his eyes.

"My name is Jensen Ross. I was Mr. Richardson's attorney. I'm sorry for your loss. I've got some paperwork here I need your John Hancock on," he said, stepping up onto the porch and pulling a thick stack of papers from his briefcase.

"Why do you need my signature?" Pen said, still groggy and not quite understanding what was going on.

"Oh, yes, of course. I'm sorry. Let me explain. Mr. Richardson had no living family, and what he had, he left to you in his will."

Pen's eyes grew wide. He stared at the man, completely baffled. Ward had never said a word about this. Not even a hint.

"Are you sure? That can't be right."

"He had no living relatives, and I assure you, he was of sound mind when he wrote the will many years ago."

"How many years ago?" Pen asked.

"Oh, I don't know. Maybe fifteen, maybe longer. I can't quite remember, but I can check the records if you want an exact date."

"No, that's not necessary," Pen mumbled.

Fifteen years ago. He would have been eight. That was the year he started mowing Ward's lawn. All this time, Ward had planned to leave him everything.

"He left you the deed to the house and all within it," Mr. Ross said, breaking his thoughts. "His car, what was left in his bank account, which is five hundred dollars, oh, and the bookstore in Helensburgh. Now, if you can sign here, I'll get this all filed and bring you the finalized paperwork within a week."

"Bookstore?" Pen looked up from the papers, eyebrows raised.

"Yes. It belonged to his wife's family. It's been collecting cobwebs and dust ever since they inherited it nearly twenty-five years ago."

"I'm not sure I know Helensburgh. Is it in Massachusetts?"

"Oh, I'm sorry, no. It's in Scotland."

Pen froze, stunned into silence.

"Now, if you can just sign here, I can get all of this processed."

Still in a daze, Pen signed and handed the documents back. Mr. Ross packed them into his briefcase and left without another word.

Pen stood there, head swimming with questions. Why hadn't Ward told him? Why had he never mentioned this bookstore in Scotland? Why leave it all to him?

Pen pulled a loose board up from the porch floor and grabbed the old brass key Ward had hidden there in case he ever needed a place to escape when Ward wasn't home. He slipped the key into the lock, turned it, and stepped inside. The house looked and smelled as it always had. But something essential was missing. Ward.

He walked over to the old velvet chair where Ward had spent every evening reading. The headrest had been rubbed bare, worn down to the backing. On the left arm, a dark stain lingered from the time when he was twelve and he'd spilled his hot cocoa on it. He'd spent the best days of his youth in this house. He'd always dreamed of what it would be like to live in a place such as this, but now that it was his, he didn't want it. Without Ward, it wasn't a home; it felt cold and lifeless, just an empty shell of a house.

Pen entered the den and approached the oak desk, where Ward's typewriter sat proudly in the center. He eased into the chair, running his fingers gently across the cool metal keys. On countless summer nights, he'd heard their rhythmic tapping drift through the open window.

He pulled open the large center drawer. Inside lay a scattering of papers and notes, loose and disorganized. His gaze landed on a thick envelope, his name written across it in Ward's handwriting. His heart stopped. He slowly lifted it out of the drawer and turned it over. For a long moment, he just held it. Then, carefully, he popped the seal. Inside was a white lined piece of paper with a note.

Dear Pen,

If you are reading this, then my time here on Earth has come to an end. I have left you all my worldly possessions. Do with them what you will, but promise me you will follow your dreams with what I have gifted you. My only wish is that you live up to your potential and be free of this town. Go explore, have adventures, fall in love. Believe in things beyond your reach. Be free.

Do you remember the story I once told you of the museum in Edinburgh where I met Emily? Go to places like that. Experience the art and culture of other countries. There is a big world out there with lots of places to see and people to get to know. I want you to find the kind of happiness I did. I want you to be the man I know you are, a man far too big for this small town.

Thank you for being the son I never had, and thank you for keeping an old man company. I will be forever grateful.

With all my best for you in this life, Pen. Until we meet again.

~Ward

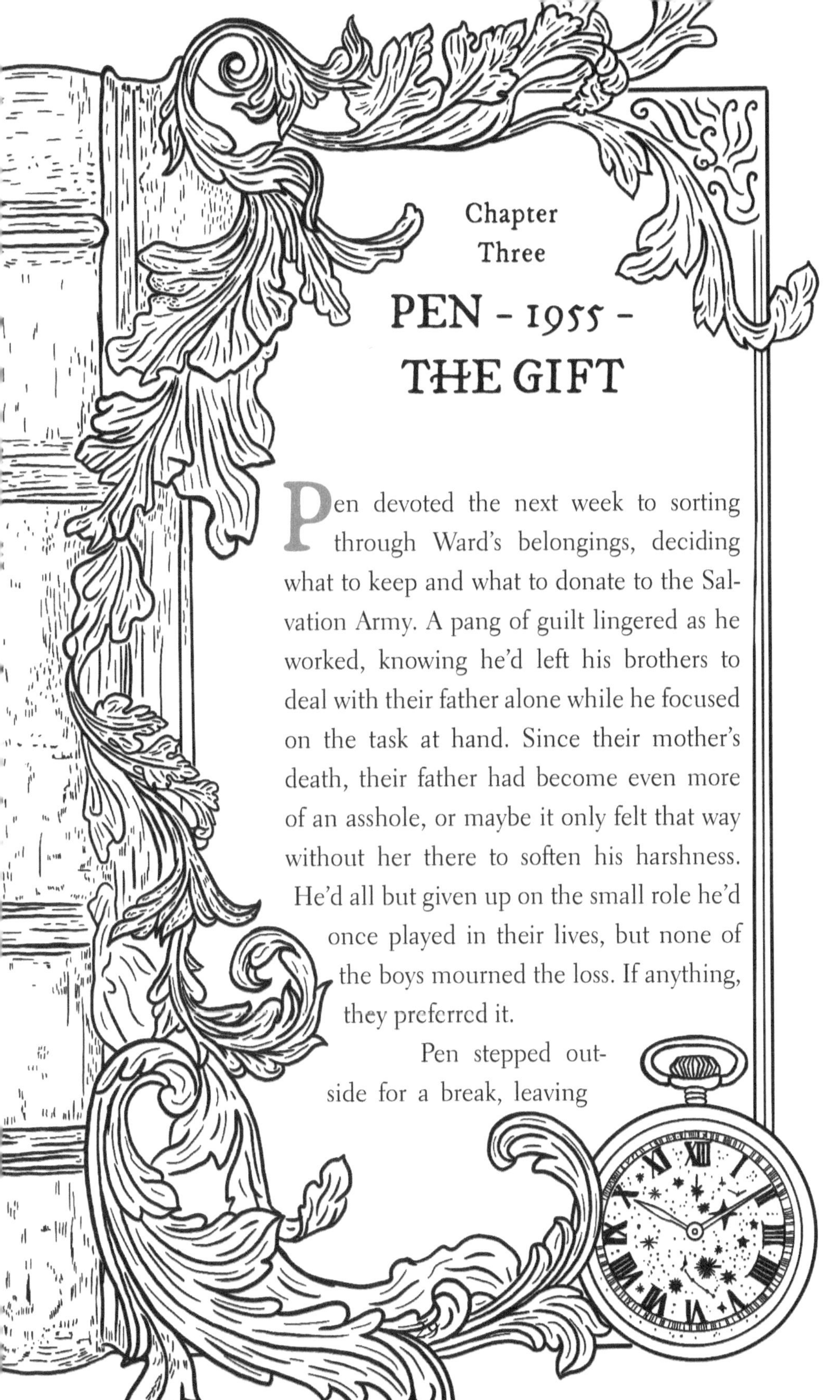

Chapter
Three

PEN - 1955 - THE GIFT

Pen devoted the next week to sorting through Ward's belongings, deciding what to keep and what to donate to the Salvation Army. A pang of guilt lingered as he worked, knowing he'd left his brothers to deal with their father alone while he focused on the task at hand. Since their mother's death, their father had become even more of an asshole, or maybe it only felt that way without her there to soften his harshness. He'd all but given up on the small role he'd once played in their lives, but none of the boys mourned the loss. If anything, they preferred it.

Pen stepped outside for a break, leaving

half-folded clothes and open donation boxes behind. The day was unseasonably crisp for late summer, the air already hinting at early autumn. A northern wind tugged at his shirt, and the thought of cooler days ahead lifted his spirits, if only a little. Just as he turned to head back inside, a large black Buick pulled into the driveway.

Mr. Ross, true to his word, had returned. The sound of the car door shutting echoed off all the surrounding houses, cutting through the quiet on the street.

"Hello, there, Mr. Turner. How are you today?" he asked as he walked up to the porch, briefcase in hand.

"As well as I can be," Pen replied.

"I have all the paperwork in order for you. The bank account has been closed, and I have a check here for five hundred dollars. The title to the car will need to be transferred and registered in your name. I also have the deed to the house."

He handed Pen a pen, a stack of papers, and two sets of keys, one for the house, the other for the car parked in the garage. Mr. Ross turned and walked back to his Buick. He opened the passenger-side door and reached inside, pulling out what looked to be a small clay pot with a fitted lid. Walking back up onto the steps, he held the pot out to Pen, who took it hesitantly.

"He had me handle everything after his passing," Mr. Ross said, nodding toward the clay urn. "But he specifically requested that you spread his ashes. Now, do you have any questions before I go?"

Pen stood there, stunned. He hadn't expected to be the one to take Ward's remains. But of course it made sense. Ward had no one else.

"Actually… yes, I do. I'd like you to take the deed back with you and add my brothers' names to it. I want them to have a place to call home if I decide to travel. Can you do that?"

"Are you sure? It's a bit risky signing a house over to a bunch of teenage boys, don't you think?"

"Well, it's riskier leaving them in that trailer with my asshole father. This way, they'll have a place of their own when I'm not here to help them."

Mr. Ross looked over his shoulder toward the tin-can across the street, gave a small nod, then took back the top envelope from the stack.

"I'll bring the revised paperwork for you to sign by the end of the week," he said, tipping his head in farewell.

As the Buick rolled away, Pen looked over at his childhood home. He shook his head in disgust, then glanced down at the urn in his hands, at his beloved friend.

Since Ward's death, Pen hadn't gone back home. He'd made up his mind not to tell his father about the inheritance. The old man would find a way to twist it, make him feel bad, or worse, try to claim some part of it for himself. If his father so much as said a bad word about Ward, Pen wasn't sure he could stop himself from knocking him out. Better to stay quiet. Better to stay in Ward's spare bedroom until everything was in order.

He stepped back inside the house. The silence pressed in thick. He walked into the kitchen, placed the urn carefully on the old table, and pulled out one of the two worn chairs. The other chair sat empty. Pen rested his hand on the urn. Its surface was sharp and cold, too cold for the warm man Ward had been.

Aside from his brothers, he had no one now. No friends. No girl. Just this empty house and a choice Ward had left him with. He could stay. Or he could leave. And now, he wasn't sure which was the right thing to do.

Over the next two days, he sat at Ward's desk with a giant folding map of the United States he'd picked up at the Gas 'n' Go. He'd decided on a road trip. With a pen in hand, he'd begun circling all the places he wanted to visit. Before long, he'd traced out a route, a long sweeping loop that connected every mark.

He'd start in Oak Ridge, heading south through Georgia, then over to Alabama and New Orleans. From there, he'd cut across Texas, wind up through the Midwest, trace the northern edge of the country, and finally land in New England to visit Bates before heading home. And somewhere along the way, he'd find the perfect place to spread Ward's ashes.

He was determined to live out a small part of his dreams, even if that just meant a summer trip in an old car by himself. He wouldn't be gone too long, a few months at the most. Just enough time to see the country, breathe, and feel like life was still his own. He didn't quite trust leaving the house in his brothers' hands for too long unsupervised, but this he had to do.

It was a Friday afternoon when Mr. Ross came back with the papers once again. Pen thanked him and then waited on the edge of his old driveway for his youngest brother, Val, to arrive home.

Pen and Val shared a special bond rooted in their mutual hatred for their father. As the firstborn and the last, their father had decided to name them after Pennzoil and Valvoline motor oils. Their mother protested, and the final compromise landed them with Pen and Val. Thank God for her. The two middle boys had more ordinary names and escaped the worst of the schoolyard jokes. Pen and Val, on the other hand, picked up the nickname "grease monkey," partly because of their names, partly because they weren't the cleanest of children. Living in a trailer with a barely functioning shower meant going to school with yesterday's dirt still on them. It had been a rough childhood, and Pen hoped that sharing a real house together might ease that pain, even if ever so slightly.

When Val returned from school, Pen greeted him and asked if he'd come across the street to Ward's old house.

"Where've you been? Dave took off yesterday with some girl he's been dating, and Will's been pulling overtime all week at the textile mill," Val demanded, irritation creeping into his voice as he followed Pen up the steps. "What's this all about, Pen? Why are we at Mr. Richardson's house?"

"You know Ward died a week ago, right?" Pen said, opening the weathered door. "Well, he left me his house. I had your name, Dave's, and Will's put on the deed. It's our home now." The floorboards creaked beneath their feet as they stepped inside, the clean scent of a well-kept home welcoming them.

"You're kidding me, right? No way this is ours?" Val said, eyes wide as he took in the space.

"I'm not pulling your leg, I promise. Whatever awful stuff Dad said about Ward wasn't true. I wish he'd let you guys get to know him. The only reason he ever let me come over here was for the money. Helped pay for his beer every week."

"Wait, Dad took the money Ward paid you to mow his lawn?"

"Yup, every time. But it wasn't about the money. Ward was nice to me, told me stories, helped me with school. And in turn, I was able to help you guys. He was like the father ours wasn't."

"Well, that doesn't take much," Val said.

"You can move in whenever you want. I'm leaving in a few days on a road trip and won't be back for a month or so. I'm hoping Will and Dave will move in too."

"Dad's going to go off the deep end when he finds out."

"He won't. I'll talk to him. I'm sure it won't be any sweat off his back if you come to stay here."

Val didn't wait. He raced home, threw some clothes and the few belongings he had into a bag, and was back at Ward's before his father returned from work. He sprinted through the house, calling dibs on a room. After all, he had arrived first. Pen watched him with a quiet smile. This was the happiest he'd seen Val since their mother passed away. Giving him this, freedom from their father, was the best gift Pen could offer.

Later, when the light flickered on in the trailer across the road, Pen ventured over to face his father. Stepping off the curb felt like walking into a different neighborhood. Ward's house had tall oaks, flowering plants, a well-manicured lawn. The trailer sat surrounded by gravel and weeds, a half-dead pine tree slouched beside it like it had given up too.

Inside, his father was sitting at the kitchen table, eating a cold-cut sandwich and drinking a beer. He glanced up, then went back to picking his crust off.

"What the hell are you doing here?" he muttered. "Thought you were too good for this family now."

"I'm just here to let you know that Val's going to be living with me."

"Oh really? And who the hell made you his father?"

"No one, but I've been more of one to him than you ever were. He's just another mouth to feed to you."

"Whatever," his father scoffed. "Never wanted him anyway. Accident, just like you. Less shit for me to deal with. He's all yours."

This was exactly what Pen expected. If given an easy way out, his father would always take it. There was nothing left to say. Pen turned and walked to the door. As he stepped outside, he glanced back, hoping it would be the last time he ever saw the old man.

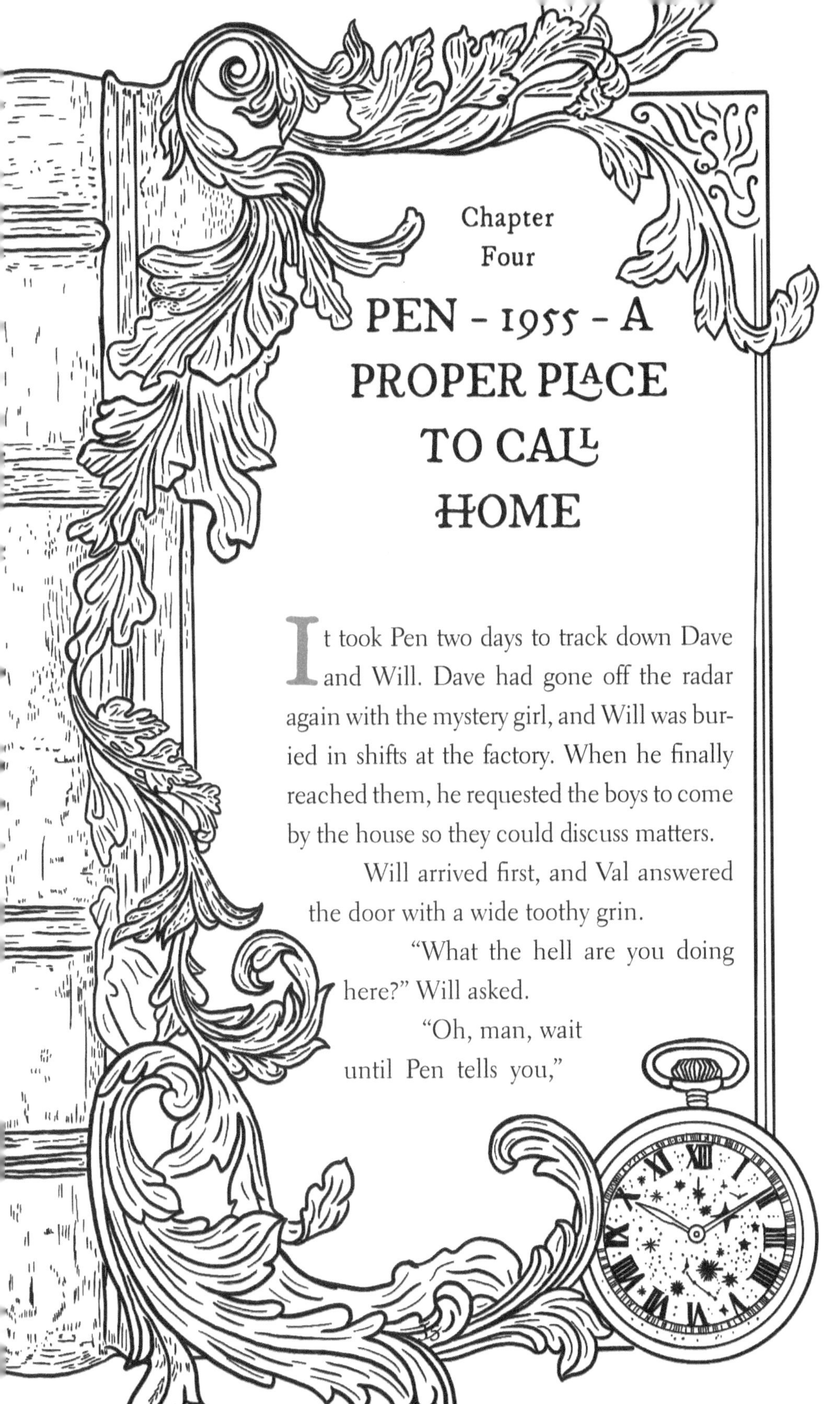

PEN - 1955 - A PROPER PLACE TO CALL HOME

It took Pen two days to track down Dave and Will. Dave had gone off the radar again with the mystery girl, and Will was buried in shifts at the factory. When he finally reached them, he requested the boys to come by the house so they could discuss matters.

Will arrived first, and Val answered the door with a wide toothy grin.

"What the hell are you doing here?" Will asked.

"Oh, man, wait until Pen tells you,"

Val said, practically bouncing on his heels as he led him into the kitchen.

Pen was cooking over the old gas stove, steam billowing from a large pot as he stirred pasta in wide, sweeping circles.

"Pen, what's this all about?" Will asked, stopping just inside the doorway.

"I'll explain when Dave gets here. I don't want to have to go over it twice. Grab a soda pop. Fridge is on your right." He nodded toward the baby-blue appliance humming in the corner.

"Where's Ward?"

The question hit Pen like a weight. Of course. Will had been working so much, he hadn't heard. Pen didn't answer, not with words, anyway. The grief must have been written across his face, and that was enough.

"Oh, Pen." Will's voice softened. "I'm sorry. I know how close you were with him."

Before Will could say more, a knock sounded from the front door.

"Stir that, will ya," Pen said, handing off the spoon to Will as he left the kitchen.

Outside, silhouetted by the glow of the streetlights, was Dave. He pulled Pen into a fierce hug when he opened the door.

"I'm so sorry, Pen. I just heard about Ward when I got back into town today."

"It's okay. Come in. I cooked us dinner."

For the first time in a long while, all four boys were together. After their mother's death, none of them had wanted to spend much time at the trailer. Without her, the place had fallen even further into disrepair.

In the kitchen, Pen drained the pasta and ladled rich meat sauce over the steaming spaghetti. The boys gathered around the dining table, and Val passed around the bread and butter.

"Alright, Pen, are you going to tell us what the hell we're doing here?" Dave finally asked.

Pen put down his fork. "When Ward died, he left this house and everything in it to me. I had all your names added to the deed. It's ours now."

Dave and Will exchanged stunned glances.

"Ward gave you his house?" Dave asked.

Pen nodded. "Yes. And now it belongs to all of us. A real home. You're welcome to stay as long as you want."

After a long pause, Will finally spoke. "I just got an apartment with a buddy from work a few weeks ago. I can't leave him high and dry. We're supposed to move in next week."

"That's okay. I just hoped one of you could stay here for the next month or so. I'm going on a road trip and want someone to stay with Val."

"I'll be fine. Pretty much live on my own now anyway. Dad's never around, always at work or the bar," Val rebutted.

Pen met his gaze. "I know. But I'd still feel better knowing someone's here. Just in case."

"Where are you going?" Will questioned, twirling pasta onto his fork.

"Just making a loop around to a few spots I've always wanted to see."

"Bates?" Val asked, and Pen's heart sank.

"Yeah, that's one of the stops." A silence settled over the table. They all knew what Pen had given up for them. He'd been their lifeline, his dreams set aside so they might have a chance at their own.

"I can stay," Dave said at last. "As long as you don't mind Mary moving in too."

All heads turned toward him. "And who's Mary?" they asked in unison.

"Well, my wife," Dave answered, looking down at his food and pushing it around on his plate while trying to avoid his brothers' glares.

"Wife?" Pen asked.

"I've been seeing her for a while now," Dave continued, his eyes alight with a spark Pen hadn't seen before. "This past weekend, we decided to get out of Oak Ridge. We ended up at a small church three towns over and had the reverend marry us on the spot. I know it sounds crazy, but I really love her."

Pen smiled and patted his brother on the shoulder. "Congratulations." And he was happy for him. His brother was almost twenty, and it was a normal age to marry someone, after all. "Of course she's welcome here." He lifted his soda pop. "To Dave and Mary."

Val and Will echoed the toast, clinking their bottle necks together.

They spent the next hour swapping stories, teasing one another, and laughing in the way only brothers can. Pen sat back, letting it wash over him, the voices, the warmth. This place was already feeling like the home they'd never had.

THE HIDDEN JOURNAL
OF JOHN DEE

September 5th, 1582

Today, after a most intense scrying session with Edward, he received word that the device Giordano and I have labored upon these many years must be completed before the Pope enacts his new Gregorian calendar come the next month. Once the calendar shifts forward by ten days, each of our carefully wrought calculations shall need altering. Edward relayed to me that these celestial alignments will remain sound only if bound to the Julian calendar.

Through Edward's communion with the angelic hosts, we have been exhorted to press forward with haste, for time grows short. Yet here I labor alone, as Giordano has been summoned to the court in Paris, the King insisting upon his presence to discourse on matters of philosophy and religion. Alas, there is neither time nor means for him to lend his hand in this final hour; thus, the Astral Synchronum's completion falls solely upon me. Though only a few remaining adjustments are needed, they are of utmost importance if the device is to function as intended and open the portal between realms.

For should even the smallest calculation be flawed, the consequence could be most dire. The angels warned that an error, however slight, might do more than simply disrupt the device; it could bring chaos to the heavens themselves, tearing asunder the delicate bonds of space and time. Therefore, I must ensure that all is in perfect order before the device is set into motion, lest we risk a calamity that no man may reverse.

By my reckonings, just one final astrological setting remains to be secured, along with an amendment to a prior alignment wherein I miscalculated the original calibration of its inner workings. These last tasks, though within my ability to accomplish alone, would greatly benefit from Giordano's sure hand, so well-suited to such delicate refinements. Yet I shall press on, guided by the counsel received, that all may be finished in due course, and without any errors that could unravel more than my own life's work.

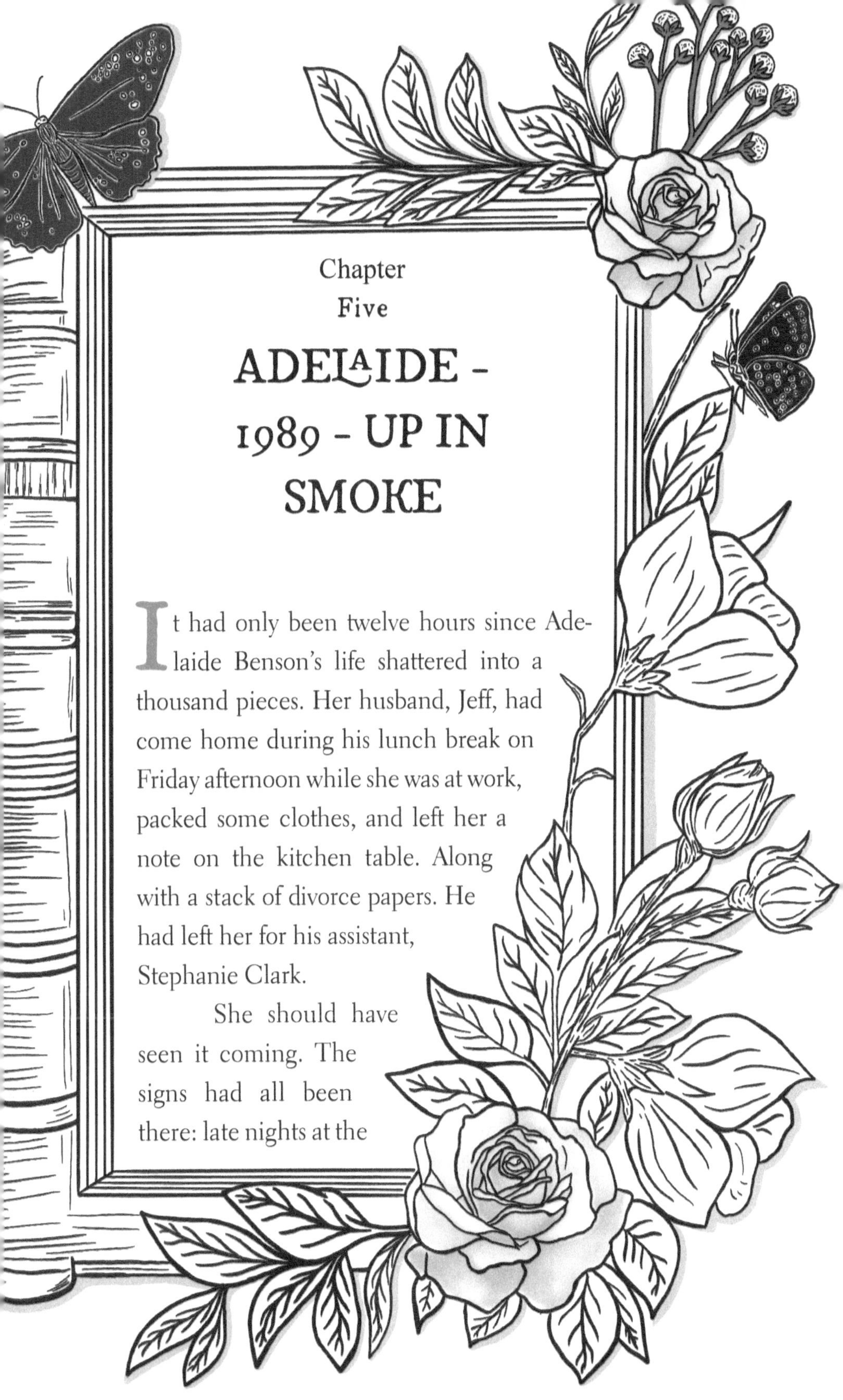

ADELAIDE – 1989 – UP IN SMOKE

It had only been twelve hours since Adelaide Benson's life shattered into a thousand pieces. Her husband, Jeff, had come home during his lunch break on Friday afternoon while she was at work, packed some clothes, and left her a note on the kitchen table. Along with a stack of divorce papers. He had left her for his assistant, Stephanie Clark.

She should have seen it coming. The signs had all been there: late nights at the office, too many "work trips" to London over the past few months, and a growing distance she hadn't wanted to name. But after nine years of marriage, it had completely blindsided her.

Adelaide had silenced the whispers of doubt floating in her head, dismissing them as paranoia. There was no way Jeff would be so brazen as to cheat on her with his assistant. That kind of shit only happened in books, not in real life. But here she was; her life had fallen into the depths of an all-too-familiar trope, casting her as the pitiful wife weeping over a clichéd breakup letter in her kitchen.

In it, Jeff declared his love for Stephanie, the pretty young blonde she'd met numerous times at his office. She'd even baked her cookies at Christmas. In that painful moment, Adelaide couldn't help but feel like a side character in her own life, destined to play the role of the forsaken spouse in someone else's love story.

She had known theirs wasn't the happiest of marriages, not finding much in common as they matured, but she'd believed he still loved her, as she did him. It might not have been the passionate, all-consuming love of their teenage years, but wasn't that the way of marriage? It softened, settled, grew quieter with time.

They'd tied the knot straight out of uni, ignoring her mother's pleas to wait. That summer, just after she turned twenty-one, they eloped. If her mother were alive today, she would have looked to the heavens and muttered, *This is precisely why you should always listen to your mother.*

But maybe her mother had been right about more than just Jeff. Maybe she'd been right about Adelaide never quite knowing how to stand on her own, always leaning too heavily on a man. It had been easier to settle into the life Jeff provided than to carve out something for herself.

Now, at nearly thirty, Adelaide found herself sitting alone

at the kitchen table, her gaze fixed on Jeff's note. She still couldn't believe he'd ended their marriage with a letter. *A coward's way out,* she thought. She picked it up again, trying to read it, but her tears kept blurring the words, forcing her to start over.

I need passion. Someone who challenges me, who keeps me on my toes. Someone with drive, who knows exactly where they're going and what they want in life.

That was as far as she ever got before the ache in her chest became too much. Eventually, she gave up and cried herself to sleep.

The next morning, she shuffled into the bathroom and flicked on the light. Her reflection stared back, puffy eyes, tear-stained cheeks. The headache that throbbed behind her temple could rival even the worst of her teenage hangovers. But none of it dulled the rage boiling inside her. As the sun rose, she found herself dragging the belongings Jeff had left behind out into the garden to burn. She started with the easy things: his clothes, his pillow, every last pair of his loafers. Then she moved on to bigger, more expensive items, his golf clubs, his carefully painted model airplanes, his records, that smug little new stack of cassette tapes he'd brought back from London last week, still in their Woolworths bag. Then she hauled out his new prized stereo system, giant speakers and all, and tossed them onto the pile.

Every item that hit the flames felt like shedding another layer of the life she'd built around Jeff, instead of one she'd built for herself. The truth was, she had relied on him, not just for love, but for stability. He had the career. He had the plan. And she'd molded herself into what he had wanted her to be, the perfect wife. And now, without him, she was nothing, had nothing, no security net to catch her. How had she been so stupid, so naive?

Once she started, she couldn't stop. She dragged out her own belongings next. Her wedding dress went first. Then half her closet, dresses, tops, shoes, she'd worn because *he* liked them, not because she did. She didn't want any of it. No reminders. No keepsakes. It was best if she destroyed it all. Better to leave nothing behind.

She stood as all traces of the life she once had went up in flames, literally and metaphorically. It was exhilarating, even freeing, as she watched the sparks from what had once been her favorite end table reach high above the treetops. A horrible stench lingered in the smoke billowing from the pile, and she coughed, eyes watering. The smell, noxious as it was, felt fitting. It mirrored how she felt about her life, rancid and ruined.

The last to go were their photos, starting with their wedding album; she tossed it into the hungry fire without a second glance. One by one, the memories burned, curling at the edges, turning to ash.

She sank onto the grass, watching as the flames devoured everything that had once made their house a home. But soon the rising wail of sirens in the distance jolted her back to reality.

The fire brigade burst through the side gate minutes later, boots thudding against the path, hoses uncoiling behind them as they shouted over one another, expecting to find the back of the house engulfed in flames. But when they reached the garden and saw it was just a bonfire of memories, their tone shifted, first relieved, then sharp with annoyance.

"You can't just set a fire like that, love. Not in a residential area. You're lucky no one's called the council."

She tried to answer back, but the smoke caught at the back of her throat, bitter and thick, and instead she just nodded in compliance. One of them turned the hose on the smoldering heap, steam rising in angry hisses, leaving her old life nothing more than a pile of smoldering muddy black ash with bits of half-burned things she used to love. It was fitting, she thought.

After they left, she went inside and packed what little clothing she hadn't burned, a photo of her parents, a few of her favorite paperbacks, a toothbrush, then headed out the door, not bothering to close it behind her. She never wanted to set foot in their house again. If someone decided to loot it, let them.

The first thing she did was stop at Brightwood Bank and drain their joint savings account. It was her inheritance, left to her in her mother's will, and there was no way she was going to let him have even a penny of it.

After that, everything blurred. She was on autopilot, having no idea where she was going, only knowing she needed to get away. So, she took the motorway and drove aimlessly, her mind reeling with everything that had happened in the past twenty-four hours.

How had she been so stupid?

She'd known, deep down, that something wasn't right. He'd started dressing better, bought a new car, and even started using some overpriced hair growth tonic for the thinning patch on the crown of his head. The signs were all there. But she'd ignored them, just as Jeff had told her to do. *You're overthinking again, Adelaide. You always do.*

And she'd believed him.

Amy, her best friend and coworker at the Ladd Library, had warned her years ago, after catching Jeff flirting with a young blonde at the annual library banquet. Adelaide had brushed it off at the time, thinking all men did things like that. Now she wondered how many women had come before Stephanie Clark. The idea made her stomach churn. She gripped the steering wheel, suddenly lightheaded, and felt as if she might actually throw up.

Pulling off the road at the next service exit, she stopped at a small petrol station tucked behind the lorry bays. She filled her tank, then walked over to a phone box to call Amy; she didn't want her to worry. By now, Amy surely would have noticed her absence from work. It was already afternoon, and she hadn't shown up. Adelaide was always punctual and rarely called out sick; disappearing like this would have Amy worried. But she wasn't ready to talk about what had happened. Not with anyone. Instead, she rang the archive line that went straight to a message machine. It was easier that way.

"Hey, Amy, I'm going to be out for the rest of the week, can you please cover for me. Sorry for the late notice. Will call you in a few days and explain."

Even though Glastonbury wasn't exactly a small town, she knew that by mid-afternoon, word of the fire, and Jeff leaving her, would have reached Amy via her and Jeff's mutual friends. She'd have to call her back later, once she had her mind sorted out and this damn headache was gone.

She paid for the petrol, grabbed a bottle of Coke, climbed into her old Volkswagen Golf, and pulled back onto the motorway. The sun sat starkly behind a thick blanket of clouds, which was not abnormal for England in the late-summer months, but today it felt more dreary and dark than normal. Adelaide turned on the radio and began twisting the dial, searching for something to drown out her thoughts. Yet, it seemed like every station was playing nothing but love songs. Come to think of it, she wasn't sure there were any songs that weren't about love, in one way or another. Either wanting it, having it, or losing it.

She stopped when she heard the opening riff of one of her favorite bands, Def Leppard. "Love Bites." It felt fitting. She cranked up the volume, despite her lingering headache, and screamed the lyrics at the top of her lungs.

Once the song ended and U2's "With or Without You" came on, she promptly turned the radio off and drove in silence. She chewed on her thumbnail, lost in the labyrinth of her thoughts, as she traveled further on the unfamiliar road. She hadn't been paying much attention to where she was going, her mind too tangled in what came next, what her future would hold without Jeff.

She had no plan. No map. No idea how to navigate the chaos of her shattered life. All she could do was keep driving, feeling utterly adrift in a world suddenly devoid of the stability she once knew.

When the digital clock on the dashboard read quarter past seven, the harsh reality of her situation hit her. She'd fled in a daze of anger, sadness, and betrayal, leaving without a word to anyone about what had happened or where she was going.

When she saw the *Welcome to Scotland* sign, a strange kind of relief washed over her. Crossing into another country felt like crossing some invisible threshold, one that put distance, real, physical distance between herself and the mess she'd left behind.

But the feeling didn't last.

With each mile, the weight slowly crept back in. She still had no destination, only the compulsion to keep moving away from her old life. And now, after hours on the road, the petrol gauge was edging toward empty again.

She began scanning for a place to stop for the night as her car coasted into a small village, dotted with modest stone houses and lichen-covered stone walls. A flicker of recognition tugged at her as she drove on. It wasn't until she saw the sign, *Helensburgh*, that she realized where she was. This wasn't random. This was where her subconscious had been leading her all along.

ADELAIDE –
1989 –
HELENSBURGH

As if pulled by an invisible thread, she'd driven to the town of Helensburgh, home to her only surviving relative, Great-Aunt Carolyn. Her father's aunt, an eccentric old woman who lived alone in the Scottish countryside. Adelaide hadn't thought about her in years.

She'd visited Helensburgh a handful of times during the summer holidays as a child, and remembered loving it. Picnics by the waterfront, chasing butterflies in her aunt's field, hunting for fairies in the forest near Carolyn's home.

Her father had always called their annual trip to Helensburgh their journey to Starfell. He'd told her a star had tumbled from the sky millennia ago, carving out the River Clyde as it fell, a great waterway that carried the land's stories to the sea. He'd made the whole thing up, of course, but because *he* told the story, she believed it. He had a way of turning the ordinary into something enchanted, as if each place had its own unique tale to be told.

The visits ended when her father got sick with cancer. He died just a month before she turned thirteen, and after that, Adelaide and her mother stopped going. It hurt her mother too much to do anything that reminded her of him, so the traditions were quietly abandoned. And with them, Carolyn. Her great-aunt had tried to reach out for a short time after his death, but it had slowed over the years until they lost contact.

It had to have been at least fifteen years since she'd seen Aunt Carolyn. She wasn't even sure she was still alive. And even if she had been pulled here by some invisible force, Adelaide couldn't just show up on her doorstep at eight o'clock at night. No, she'd find a place to stay and assess the situation in the morning, once the effects of this horrible day had worn off.

The town felt like a foggy memory; some parts stood out in sharp detail, while others blurred into unfamiliarity. She had almost passed through it completely when she spotted a sign for a bed and breakfast, pointing down a narrow side street. She followed it to a tall stone house with a sign out front that read: *Emperor Moth Inn.*

The place looked inviting, a warm glow spilling through white wooden-trimmed windows fitted with small panes of old glass. Tiny air bubbles lay within them, causing the lights inside to look like sparks. *Sparks of magic*, Adelaide thought, as she pulled into the small gravel driveway.

Weary, she turned off her engine, grabbed her bag, and walked through a rusty iron gate and up to the pale green door. She paused, then knocked.

A few seconds later, the weathered door creaked open, and a petite older woman with salt-and-pepper hair appeared in the frame.

"Good evening," the woman greeted in her gentle Scottish brogue.

"Hello, do you happen to have any rooms available?"

The woman swung the door wide open, and a gust of air, rich with the scent of cinnamon and nutmeg, blew past her and out into the damp night. "Yes, come in," she said, ushering Adelaide inside. "I'm Ellen, the owner of the inn." She stuck out a frail hand.

"Adelaide," she replied, taking it and giving it a gentle shake. Ellen smiled, warm and kind, but there was something else behind her eyes, something that almost resembled pity. Was it that obvious? Could she tell that she'd been crying for most of the day?

The inside of the house looked crisp and clean, almost like a museum with its antique furniture and framed art lining the walls. Ellen led her past a large staircase and into a sitting room, where a sizable fireplace dominated the far wall. Above the mantel hung two large glass frames, housing what must have been twenty or more different species of moths. Their delicate bodies were pinned in place, wings spread wide, tiny silver pins anchoring them at perfect angles. Adelaide found it a bit morbid, all those little dead bodies encased in glass. Still, it wasn't really any different from people who mounted heads of deer and other wild game on their walls.

She hadn't realized she'd been staring until Ellen spoke.

"Those are all the species of moths we have here in Scotland. My husband was an entomologist," Ellen explained with a smile. "He loved all insects, but moths were his favorite, particularly the emperor. He used to say they were the messengers of magic." She chuckled.

"Hence the name of your bed and breakfast?"

"Right you are, well spotted. After Ben passed, I was quite lonely, you know? It's a big house and just me to fill it. My friend suggested I turn it into a B&B to keep me busy and help me meet people, and, well, here we are."

"I'm sorry for your loss. The house is very beautiful," Adelaide said. An ache formed in her chest, partly for Ellen, for having to live out her years in the company of strangers because she missed her husband so much. And partly for herself, because she didn't know that kind of love and loyalty.

"Ah, you're too kind, dear. I was lucky to share it with my Ben for more than forty years. I don't get many guests, but keeping up the place gives me a sense of purpose, you know?"

She opened a door on the right and stepped inside, flipping the switch beside the doorframe. A warm light filled the space, revealing a wide chamber centered around a four-poster bed, draped in rich navy-blue bedding. The walls were covered in floral wallpaper in an almost overwhelming pattern of hyacinths, roses, and hydrangeas, a tiny bee on every other flower. Two large windows overlooked the back garden, and a tall six-drawer dresser sat neatly between them. In the corner was a chair and a small table, just big enough for a quiet cup of tea. But the true focal point was the large painting above the bed: a lunar moth set against a dark, star-speckled sky. The room was a peculiar mix, part classic "old lady" decor, part insectarium, no doubt a tribute to her late husband.

Ellen crossed to a narrow door, just left of the bed, and opened it. "This here is the bathroom," she said over her shoulder, "so you can wash up before bed." A tiny window above the sink framed a view of the garden. A delicate moth, a real one, fluttered gently against the pane, drawn to the light. "I'm just down the hall on the right if you need me." Ellen paused in the doorway. "Breakfast is served at eight sharp." She offered a sweet smile, then began to walk out of the room.

"Wait, don't you want my name, or a deposit?" Adelaide asked.

Ellen paused with her hand on the doorknob. "You look like you need to wash up and get some rest. We can figure all that out in the morning," she said with a wink, then gently shut the door.

Adelaide walked into the small bathroom and over to the mirror above the pedestal sink. The face staring back at her stopped her cold. Her blonde hair was a mess, matted in places, frizzing wildly in others, looking as if she hadn't run a brush through it in days. Dark circles hung beneath her eyes, so dark it looked like she had gotten in a fistfight and lost, badly. But the worst part was the black streak of soot smudged across the edge of her cheek.

No wonder Ellen had looked at her the way she had when she first arrived. Like she'd just escaped imprisonment. In a way, she kind of had. She'd loved Jeff so fiercely in the beginning that giving up her degree hadn't felt like a sacrifice. He'd scoffed at her studies, Oral Storytelling and Folklore, calling it a joke, a dead-end pursuit that would get her nowhere. And she'd believed him. When their love began to fade, she found comfort in the library, doing the next best thing, surrounding herself with books. But even then, Jeff hadn't taken her seriously, dismissing it as a hobby rather than a real job. Something to keep her busy.

She'd all but lost herself in becoming the woman he wanted, cooking dinners, keeping a spotless house, and throwing dinner parties for his colleagues. She'd cut and dyed her hair the way he liked, worn the clothes he approved of, even endured a perfume she hated just because he loved the scent. In the end, she'd been a prisoner of her own making, letting a man decide everything for her. And for what? So he could trade her in for a younger, shinier model?

How had she been so stupid? Why had she let Jeff dictate everything in her life? She'd been strong-willed when they met, she'd had dreams, ambitions, a voice. Maybe it was the fear of losing him, born from the abandonment she'd felt when her father died. Or maybe she'd never been as strong as she thought. Somewhere along the way, she'd faded, piece by piece, until all that remained of who she once was were shadows and memories.

She stared at the broken mess of a person staring back from the mirror, and she didn't recognize herself at all.

With a sigh, she took a washcloth from the small shelf beside the sink. Damping it with warm water, she wiped away the traces of soot, and with it the remnants of a life she no longer wanted.

Back in the bedroom, she lay down, pulled the covers over her, and as soon as she closed her eyes, she drifted off to sleep. No dreams came, just a quiet, blissful nothingness.

Adelaide woke to the soft glow of early morning light filtering through the gauzy white curtains lining the windows. For a moment, she stared blankly at the ceiling. Then it came to her, where she was and why she was here.

She sat up, her hair sticking to the sides of her face, still faintly smelling of the burnt remnants of her old life. Her thoughts drifted to Jeff. To the note he'd left, his words moving sharp and uninvited in her mind. *You and I are just not cut from the same cloth. I need someone ready to take on the world with me, someone with dreams bigger than shelving books.*

What a pompous ass, she thought, wishing he'd not been the first thing to occupy her mind. She got out of bed and pulled her hair back in a low ponytail. She hated him. But even more than that, she hated that he wasn't entirely wrong. Somewhere along the way, she *had* lost her passion and her dreams. Her drive. Her direction.

They'd been struggling for a while, but they'd built a comfortable life. And stability has a way of making you stay. So she had, hoping they might find their way back to each other. The passionate love they'd once shared had faded within a year of their wedding. She'd told herself that was normal, that real love, once the honeymoon phase ended, would settle into something quieter. But, if she was truly honest, it wasn't just love she'd been clinging to, it was the security Jeff provided.

The spring trips to Paris. The jewelry on her birthday. The expensive wine. The beautiful home. Without him, she couldn't afford any of it. Not even rent. It wasn't love that had kept her wedding band on. It was fear. Fear of what life would look like without the security he gave her. Fear of stepping into a world she no longer knew how to navigate on her own.

She should have left years ago, when she first sensed their love waning, before she'd given up on the person she once wanted to be. If she'd left then, in her early twenties, she might have found her way back to herself, and she'd have still been young enough to navigate single life. But starting over at nearly thirty, when all her friends were married with children, that was something else entirely.

Trying her best to pull herself out of the well of self-pity she'd fallen into, Adelaide concentrated on getting ready for breakfast. In the small bathroom, she turned on the shower, letting the room fill with steam before she slipped off her clothes and stepped in.

Hot water streamed over her skin, and slowly, the tension of the past few days began to ease. Her shoulders slackened, her breath deepened. She imagined all the pain and anger washing away, sliding down the drain with the smoky residue that clung to her body. But it wasn't that easy. Hurt like this didn't vanish with hot water and soap.

Still, she resolved to try. Just live in the moment for the rest of the day. *Baby steps*, she told herself, as she turned the water off and reached for a towel.

She balled up the clothes she'd worn the day before and threw them in the rubbish bin near the sink. They still carried the smell of smoke and unhappy endings, best left in the trash, along with all the other memories of that day.

She unzipped her bag and peered inside at the haphazard collection she'd thrown together in her rush to leave. Her toothbrush lay on top of her clothing, wedged next to her books and the framed photo of her parents. She picked the toothbrush up, stared at it, then dropped it into the bin too. The thought of it, having once sat beside Jeff's, of him using his after those late nights with *her*, made her sick.

After dressing, she ran her fingers through her hair and headed down to the kitchen for breakfast.

Following the smell of eggs and bacon, Adelaide passed through the sitting room and entryway, arriving in a large kitchen with an attached sunroom. As soon as she opened the door, her stomach groaned.

Ellen stood at the stove, placing several strips of bacon on a plate already piled high with eggs, toast, and roasted tomatoes.

"Good morning," Adelaide greeted, taking a seat at a table set for breakfast. It was beautifully laid out, a porcelain teapot in a rich forest green adorned with tiny forget-me-nots, alongside a glass pitcher of orange juice and a coffee decanter. Ellen had left nothing out.

"Hello, dear, did you sleep well?" Ellen asked, carrying the plate over to her.

"Yes, very well, thank you. I hope you plan on helping me eat all of this," Adelaide said, looking at enough food to feed an army.

"I'll take my breakfast once you are done," Ellen replied, wiping a spot of grease off the counter.

Adelaide hesitated. "I would love for you to join me, if you'd like, that is."

Ellen smiled as she made her way over, pulled out a chair across from Adelaide, and settled in with a quiet sigh. "So, what brings you to Helensburgh?" Ellen inquired as she buttered a slice of toast.

"I'm not entirely sure. I suppose I'm here to visit someone."

"Oh, do you have relatives here?"

"Yes, my great-aunt, Carolyn McGregor."

Ellen's head tilted, surprised. "Carolyn? Goodness. She and I go way back. She was in my book club for years."

Adelaide paused, fork halfway to her mouth, thoughts turning to where Great-Aunt Carolyn lived. It had been so long, she couldn't remember exactly how to get to her house, only that it was a little way outside the village.

"She still lives nearby, doesn't she?"

Ellen looked up from her tea. "Of course. If you take a right out of here, follow the main road out of the village, you'll see Hemlock Lane on your left. Her house is at the end of it."

"I haven't seen her in a long time, fifteen years or more. Is she well?"

"Quite. She'll probably outlive us all, that one, with all her teas and tinctures." Ellen laughed, taking a bite of her toast.

Adelaide smiled at Ellen as she finished her last bite of eggs and got up.

"What time is check out?" she asked as she put her plate in the old wash basin sink.

"Eleven, but stay as long as you need," Ellen said in a light tone.

As Adelaide passed through the sitting room, she paused in front of the fireplace, drawn to look at the collection of moths above it again. Stepping closer, she noticed small brass nameplates beneath each specimen. She scanned the names, searching for the emperor, which was impossible to miss. It was the largest in the case, looking as if it might fit snugly in her palm. Its wings resembled an autumn sunset: deep oranges, burgundies, and browns, but what caught her attention were the markings, two spots on each wing, shaped like a pair of eyes staring back at her. It made her uneasy, the way they seemed to follow her as she walked past.

Escaping into her room, away from the prying eyes of the moth, she shut the door behind her and decided that she would avoid looking at them on the way out.

She collapsed onto the bed and glanced at the small digital alarm clock on the nightstand: quarter past nine. She lay there, watching the minutes tick by, biting her thumbnail as her mind wandered.

Was it really fair to show up at Carolyn's unannounced after all these years? They hadn't spoken in so long. What if she didn't remember her, or worse, didn't want to? Maybe she should just pack her bags and head back to Glastonbury. But what was there to return to? Every bit of her life there was laced with memories of Jeff. Even her favorite bookshop was across the street from his office. She couldn't so much as browse without risking a glimpse of him through the window.

She rolled onto her back and stared at the old plaster ceiling, with its long crack that spanned the length of the room, separating it into two halves. It reminded her of her life now, split in two, before the affair and the after.

What would happen if she went back? She could picture it too clearly: the house, half-empty, the looming silence, the endless forms and meetings, the slow, suffocating process of untangling their lives. She wasn't ready for that. Not yet.

The thought of a *new* life felt impossible. But as she looked up at the broken ceiling, she realized she didn't need to rebuild everything at once. She just needed to get through one day at a time right now.

And today, she would show up on Great-Aunt Carolyn's doorstep and hope she remembered her.

Her subconscious had brought her here for a reason, maybe because Carolyn was the only family left on her father's side. Or maybe, deep down, she was reaching for the joy she'd known in this place, hoping that some small part of her father still lingered in Starfell.

He'd told her this place was built on stardust and magic. Maybe, if she was lucky, there was still a little bit of that magic left here that might help her move forward.

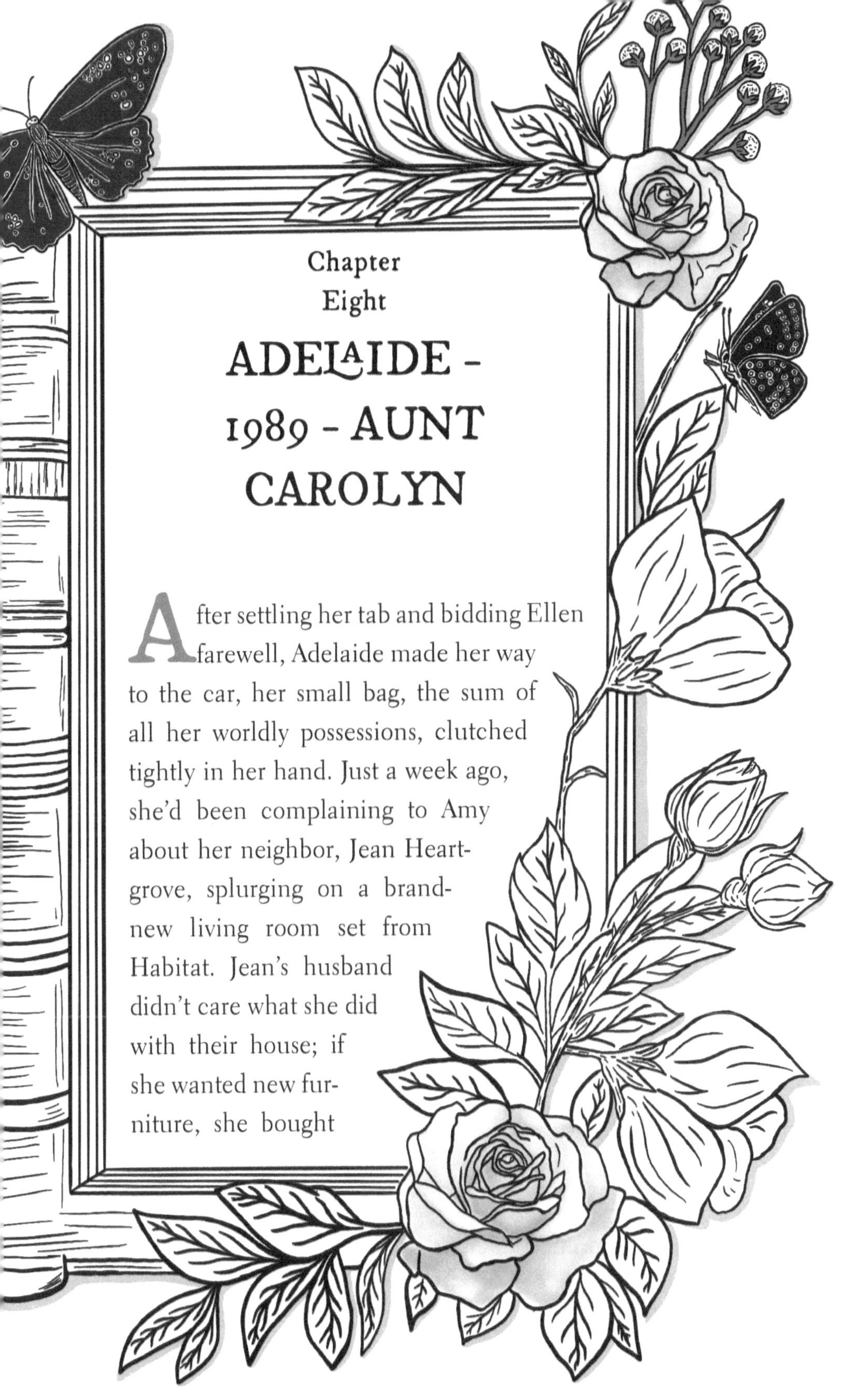

ADELAIDE – 1989 – AUNT CAROLYN

After settling her tab and bidding Ellen farewell, Adelaide made her way to the car, her small bag, the sum of all her worldly possessions, clutched tightly in her hand. Just a week ago, she'd been complaining to Amy about her neighbor, Jean Heartgrove, splurging on a brand-new living room set from Habitat. Jean's husband didn't care what she did with their house; if she wanted new furniture, she bought it. Jeff wouldn't even consider letting her buy a new coffee table without his approval.

It was his way of control, a constant reminder that he was the one who made the money and that she depended on him for the lifestyle she'd grown accustomed to. Playing along had been her sacrifice: nodding in agreement, letting him make the decisions. Because in the end, she didn't really have a leg to stand on. Her small wage from the library was barely enough to pay even a quarter of their bills.

How trivial it all seemed now, when everything she owned fit inside one single bag.

It's a strange irony, she thought, *how we spend our lives collecting things to build a comfortable life with someone, only to lose it all in the span of a few hours when something goes wrong.* The things she'd burned in the backyard, items she once thought she couldn't live without, like her Jane Hopkinson bag or her collection of Fleetwood Mac cassette tapes, meant nothing now. They were just things.

As she pulled out of the narrow driveway of the Emperor Moth Inn, something shifted in her. The idea of starting with nothing no longer felt as frightening. It felt liberating, like a blank canvas upon which she could find herself again. After so many years of being Jeff's wife, she'd lost sight of who she truly was. Now she had the space to find out.

As she left the village and headed toward Carolyn's, Adelaide spotted a small pharmacy beside a post office. She almost drove past, but something made her slow down, and before she could talk herself out of it, she pulled into the parking space out front.

Inside, the harsh fluorescent lights hummed overhead as she stood staring at the shelves. Rows of boxed hair dyes stared back at her, each promising a "New You." Her eyes drifted over each one, golden blonde, black, auburn, soft chestnut. Her eyes landed on one: Warm Medium Brown. It was close to her natural color, or at least what she remembered of it.

She picked it up, turned it over in her hands, second-guessing herself for only a moment before walking to the front of the store and checking out.

When she got back to the car, she tossed the box of Clairol onto the passenger seat, and slid behind the wheel.

It wasn't much. Just a box of dye. But if she was truly going to embark on this journey of self-discovery, she needed to look like herself again, not the glossy, bleached blonde Jeff had favored but the authentic Adelaide she had almost forgotten.

She started the engine, and she eased onto the road, the village fading behind her. The road grew narrower as it wound away from the village, overhung with oak trees and skirted by wild gorse. At first, the route seemed unfamiliar, stretching out longer than she'd expected. Worry crept in. She eased off the accelerator, scanning the roadside, fearing she might have missed her turn. Though the landscape hadn't changed, the trees had grown taller, the shrubs wilder, fogging her memory. *Perhaps this is a sign*, she thought. Maybe it would be best to go back to the bed and breakfast.

Just as she resolved to turn back, an old weathered road sign, partially obscured by a vine of ivy, came into view, its rusty letters spelling out Hemlock Lane.

She bit her bottom lip as she turned left, nerves fluttering as the car bumped down the lane. Her fingers tightened on the steering wheel, and she tried to recall what little she could remember about her great-aunt.

Adelaide's father had been an only child, and Carolyn, born from her mother's second marriage, was only eight years older than him. They'd grown up more like siblings than aunt and nephew, their bond remaining strong over the years.

Carolyn had to be close to seventy-six by now. The thought brought a pang of sadness; her father would have been sixty-eight at the end of the year, if he were still alive. And if he were, she was certain he'd be here, visiting Carolyn, just as he always had at this time of year.

Adelaide remembered her aunt as delightfully eccentric, with her flowy, mismatched dresses that seemed to change with the seasons, her long silver-streaked hair always braided with wildflowers or twigs she'd picked up on her walks. As a child, Carolyn had whisked her into the woods in search of fairy circles and wishing rocks, or to concoct some mysterious brew from her garden. Her house had always been filled with the scent of herbs and incense.

She blinked and the memories gave way to the view ahead. Hemlock Lane seemed more like a well-traveled path than a proper road, flanked by gorse and thistles so thick she could scarcely see anything beyond them. Then, just as the road curved, the old thatched roof came into view. As she pulled into the driveway, familiarity washed over her. The stone cottage looked untouched by the hands of time. The wide flower bed still encircled the house, and the massive oak still stood sentinel in the side garden, its branches heavy with age. Even the small stone birdbath remained, its base hadn't even a touch of moss on it.

Adelaide pulled up next to the same old Morris Minor she remembered Carolyn having years ago and shut off the engine. She sat, drawing in a long, deep breath. She glanced at the cottage. A warm inviting glow spilled from the windows as she tried to muster up the courage to barge in on her aunt's afternoon.

She absently bit at her thumbnail, trying to steady her

nerves, then reached for the door handle and got out of the car.

Wind chimes softly tinkled above the porch, and the scent of dozens of flowers drifted on a westward breeze.

Adelaide made her way up the small slate path and paused at the door, hand poised to knock. But before her knuckles could meet the dark blue wood, the door swung open. There stood Carolyn, dressed in an overly floral dress that looked straight out of the 1960s, paired with bright pink leggings, every bit as eccentric as Adelaide remembered. Her long hair, now completely white, was braided into a thick plait that draped over one shoulder. Her eyes, still as clear and sharp as a crystal-blue sky, were now framed by the fine lines of age.

For a moment, Carolyn simply stared, her eyes shining with recognition. Then she stepped forward and pulled Adelaide into a fierce embrace.

"My God, Adelaide. It's been years," she exclaimed, pulling back just enough to look her niece up and down. "Look at you! You've grown into a fine woman."

"You remember me?" Adelaide asked, her voice tinged with a hint of shyness.

"Oh, of course I do. You're the spitting image of your father. Well, the female version, that is," Carolyn remarked with a chuckle.

"I'm sorry for just showing up like this, without calling first," Adelaide began.

"Nonsense. You're family, and family is always welcome," Carolyn interrupted with a wave of her hand. "Come in, lass." Despite her roots in York, Great-Aunt Carolyn had acquired a subtle Scottish lilt over the years.

As Adelaide stepped inside, she was enveloped by the sweet, earthy scent of dried herbs and the lingering musk of years' worth of incense. The smell was so familiar, stirring something deep inside her. Memories came rushing in, warm afternoons in the garden, whispered spells in the woods, and with them an unexpected rush of emotions. She tried to blink them back, but the tears came anyway. One fell, then another, until the floodgates opened. Everything she'd held in, grief, anger, relief, spilled out all at once.

"Oh, pet, come here," Carolyn said, pulling Adelaide into another hug. "Go on, sit yourself down over there, and I'll make us some tea. Then you can tell me everything." She gestured to an overstuffed floral chair nestled near the fireplace.

Adelaide moved to the chair and sank into its worn cushions. She bit at her thumbnail, willing herself to get it together. She hadn't seen Carolyn in almost two decades, and here she was, showing up unannounced, blubbering like a damn fool.

She watched as Carolyn moved about the kitchen, her footsteps soft on the wooden floor. She set a kettle on the stove, then reached up into the large oak cupboard, retrieving a few jars filled with dried herbs. The house was modest, consisting of one large room that housed the kitchen, dining area, and sitting room all in one. A gentle *pop* of a jar lid coming off broke the quiet, releasing a sharp, spicy aroma. The scent curled through the space, rich with cinnamon and allspice, pulling Adelaide from her sorrows and offering a brief escape from her memories.

"Do you take milk in your tea?" Carolyn asked as she poured boiling water over a tea strainer filled with a fragrant blend of herbs.

"Yes, please," Adelaide replied, her voice muffled by a sniffle as she wiped her nose on the sleeve of her flannel shirt.

Carolyn continued her bustling before returning with a tray. On it were two steaming cups of tea and a small plate of biscuits.

"Drink this. It will help lift your spirits. Then you can tell me what's brought you here," she said gently.

Adelaide took a tentative sip, discovering its sweet yet slightly tangy flavor. She picked up a biscuit and smiled at the taste, lavender shortbread. Carolyn had often made them for her when she was a child.

It was then that something struck her. She looked around, noticing that the table was set for two.

"Did I come at a bad time? Are you expecting someone?" Adelaide asked, nodding toward the two place settings.

Carolyn glanced at the table, a flicker of confusion crossing her face. Then she smiled. "I was."

Adelaide set her cup down, her stomach sinking. "Oh, I'm so sorry. I didn't mean to intrude." She stood, already reaching for her bag. "I'll get out of your hair."

"Come now, sit down, pet," Carolyn insisted, patting the arm of Adelaide's chair. "It was you I was expecting."

Adelaide stopped, then slowly sat back down. "Me?" she asked. "But... how?"

"Let's just call it a woman's intuition," Carolyn smiled with a wink.

Adelaide wasn't sure what to make of this, but figured she'd been joking. Carolyn was old, maybe she kept the table set all the time, just in case she had visitors.

Adelaide leaned back into the armchair and lifted her tea, taking another slow sip. She let the warmth chase away the strangeness of Carolyn's words, or at least soften them for now.

"Now," Carolyn said, settling into the matching armchair across from Adelaide. "Tell me everything."

Adelaide took a deep breath. "Well... it all started with a letter on the kitchen table."

THE HIDDEN JOURNAL OF JOHN DEE

September 12, 1582

After filling more than a quarter of this notebook with meticulous calculations and rigorously double- and triple-checking every detail of the work Giordano and I have undertaken, I am convinced that the Astral Synchronum is finally complete. Giordano is expected to return to Mortlake within the week, and upon his arrival, he will conduct the final inspection before we set off for Dunblane, Scotland, to test the device.

In his latest scrying session, Edward received urgent instructions: we are to operate the Astral Synchronum solely within the sacred walls of Dunblane Cathedral. Under the protection of Archangel Michael, this hallowed place serves as a focal point of divine energy. Built in the twelfth century, the cathedral was renowned for its tales of miraculous healings and sightings of the divine, such as the fourteenth-century weaver who rose from prayer to find his lifelong limp healed or the veiled figure seen in the stained-glass glow during a storm, after which the village's frozen crops were mysteriously spared. Making it no surprise that the angels have guided us to initiate our work here. Though the journey will be long, if we depart upon

Giordano's return, we shall arrive before the new calendar is set into motion.

When the idea first came to me in 1563, I was blissfully unaware of its significance. Yet, as I finalize the last calculations in the device, I am reminded that year marked the Great Conjunction of Jupiter and Saturn in Pisces, a cosmic alignment that sparked the vision imparted to me by the divine. It was only years later that the scattered notes and sketches I made began to reveal their true meaning. Now, with mere weeks remaining until we can witness the culmination of our greatest life's work, I see how the path has unfolded over the years. Each seemingly insignificant step has woven together, guiding us to this pivotal moment.

As we stand on the brink of discovery, I feel a swell of anticipation. This is not merely a test of a device; it is a moment that may forever alter our understanding of the cosmos itself, and if all goes as planned, open a pathway to communicate with the divine.

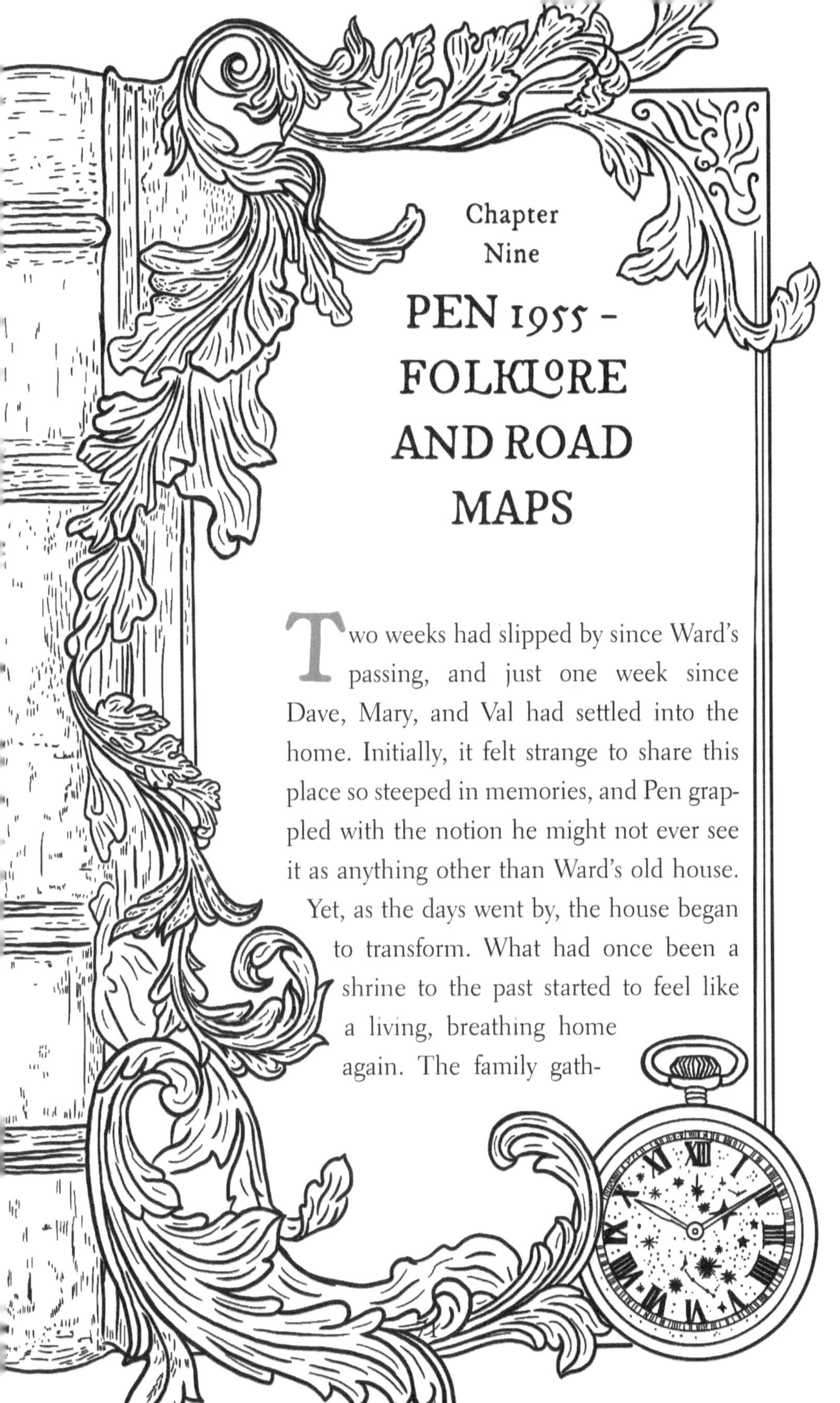

PEN 1955 – FOLKLORE AND ROAD MAPS

Two weeks had slipped by since Ward's passing, and just one week since Dave, Mary, and Val had settled into the home. Initially, it felt strange to share this place so steeped in memories, and Pen grappled with the notion he might not ever see it as anything other than Ward's old house. Yet, as the days went by, the house began to transform. What had once been a shrine to the past started to feel like a living, breathing home again. The family gathered around the table for meals, their laughter and conversations spilling onto the porch each evening. As the sun set behind the old sycamores that bordered the yard, the cool night air carried something within it, a quiet promise of new beginnings.

Pen had finally finished packing up and donating Ward's belongings, but he left Ward's study untouched, preserving everything within. He kept a few cherished items, like Ward's favorite hat, his typewriter, a baseball glove Pen had used as a child, and an old penny he'd found in the desk drawer, for luck. While most of Ward's clothing was sent to the Salvation Army, Pen held onto a few sweaters and two of his suits. Though they were a bit large, he hoped that one day, when he had the means, he might have them tailored to fit.

Almost every afternoon, Pen found himself in Ward's study, mapping out his route and scribbling down lists of things he wanted to do at each stop. The list grew, but the excitement never followed. He'd sit back, pencil in hand, staring at the circle around New Orleans, or the little star he'd scribbled beside Boston, waiting for the rush. But it didn't come. Despite his deep longing to leave, the road trip no longer held the allure it once had. He told himself it was guilt over leaving Val behind, but deep down, he knew that wasn't the real reason the excitement hadn't come. His eyes kept drifting to the corner of the study, to the envelope on the shelf marked *Helensburgh*. The more he planned his journey, the more his thoughts drifted to the mysterious bookstore in Scotland. Why had Ward never mentioned it? Not once, in all their years together?

Ward had always loved books, priding himself on being a well-read man. A bookstore would have been his dream come true. Pen could so easily picture him there, tucked behind a cluttered counter, lost in a novel, surrounded by shelves sagging with stories and wisdom. It seemed so fitting. Yet Ward had never said a word about it.

Mr. Ross had mentioned the store belonged to his wife Emily's family, but that only deepened the mystery. Why hold onto it all these years if they had no intention of running it? They surely could have sold the building years ago and turned a profit. It had been sitting abandoned for more than twenty-five years. Why keep it? The more Pen dwelled on it, the less sense it made. And the more the questions took up space his head.

As Pen's mind wandered, he sank into Ward's old desk chair, the leather creaking beneath him. He gazed at the long wall of books lining one side of the room. He rose from his seat and approached the shelves. His fingers lightly grazed the spines, feeling the worn edges and faded titles beneath his touch. He walked the wall's length without purpose, just aimlessly tracing the rows. Then he stopped. Tucked near the middle, partly hidden by thicker volumes, was a book he didn't remember seeing before. *Folklore of the Celtic Nations: Wales, Ireland, and Scotland.*

He tipped the book forward and eased it out of its snug resting place among the others. Back at the desk, he settled into the chair and opened the cracked leather cover. The title page revealed a medieval-style dragon, inked in red and gold, its wings curling across the parchment. It was reminiscent of those found on chapel ceilings. A thrill of excitement surged through Pen, the first he'd felt since Ward's passing, and he flipped through the pages, their edges soft with age. He discovered tales of creatures he'd never heard of before, Kelpies that lured wanderers into deep water, Afancs lurking in lakes, woven alongside more familiar legends of mermaids and fairies. Captivated, the light in the study shifted, and hours passed as he found himself lost in the strange, enchanted world of folklore.

"Mary made meatloaf," Dave said, interrupting as Pen neared the end of the book. "Thought it would be nice to have one last dinner together before you leave tomorrow." He motioned to him with a large sweeping of his arm toward the other room. "Come on and eat with us."

Pen looked up and gave Dave a nod, then closed the book with both hands, his fingers lingering before he set it aside. He stood up slowly, stretching until his spine popped, easing the stiffness from his neck and back after hours in the captain's chair. His gaze fell on the map sprawled on the desk, his route traced in red pen, like a newly formed scar stretching across the page. A growing sense of apprehension took hold as he stared at it, considering the adventure that lay ahead.

He glanced over at the globe resting on the bookshelf. He could still picture Ward pulling it down for him to spin. Pen would stick his finger out and stop it at random; wherever his finger landed, Ward would weave a story about that land. Now Pen realized he had likely made up those tales on the spot, drawn from imagination, not fact. As a child, he'd believed every word of Ward's magical adventures. He had always said, *One day you will have your own stories to tell*. Pen had clung to that promise until the day his mother died. Her loss had shattered his dreams, crushed whatever fragile hope he had of escaping this town. Even now, as those dreams resurfaced, they lacked the luster they once held, now just the idle wishes of a child.

"Pen, come on, food's getting cold," Dave yelled from the other room.

Pen paused in the doorway of the study, looking over his shoulder one last time. The book lay closed, resting next to the map, and he felt a niggling tug, like two competing voices.

The following day, the boys helped Pen load his belongings into Ward's old Chevrolet Fleetmaster. What few possessions he packed fit easily into the trunk: a battered suitcase filled with clothes, a stack of books for company, the road map marked with red ink, and the urn with Ward's remains.

The sky was overcast, and the air hung heavy with humidity, matching the unease Pen couldn't seem to shake. He stuck his hand into his pocket and flipped the old penny between his fingers, a nervous habit he'd picked up. Ward had kept that penny for a reason, and Pen decided it was for luck. As long as it stayed with him, things would turn out fine. At least that's what he told himself.

He had dreamed of leaving this place for years, but now that the day had arrived, all he felt was doubt. He had always been his brothers' anchor. Without him, who would they turn to? But they were grown now, he reminded himself, and they had each other, just as they always had. For their sake, Pen tried to summon a smile, projecting an air of confidence he didn't quite feel. They looked up to him, and it was his job to show them that there was a whole wide world waiting beyond the confines of Oak Ridge.

"Make sure you give us a ring when you reach Georgia," Will told Pen, stepping forward and giving him a hearty hug.

"I will," Pen replied, giving Will a solid pat on the back.

"How long do you reckon you'll be gone?" Val asked, his voice revealing a trace of the boy he once was, despite the new teenage facade.

"Not more than a few months," Pen answered, pulling Val into a warm embrace. "Dave and Mary will look after you just fine."

Dave draped an arm around Mary, pulling her close and grinning proudly. He seemed older now, more like a man, and Pen felt a sense of relief. Val would be in good hands.

"Keep in touch," Dave said, extending his hand.

"Count on it." Pen shook it firmly.

Mary smiled and hugged him. "I'll make sure these boys stay in line," she teased.

Pen walked over to the car and opened the door, then paused. "Do me a favor. Don't let Dad into the house. Now that I'm gone, I can just picture him trying to weasel his way in."

"There's no chance in hell he'll set foot in this house," Dave stated, puffing out his chest with resolve.

"Good. Well, I'll be seeing you," Pen said, waving as he shut the car door.

He backed down the driveway, eyes flicking to the rearview mirror. They stood waving on the porch, Will, Val, Dave, and Mary, smaller with each passing second.

He didn't know it yet, but it would be the last time he'd ever see them.

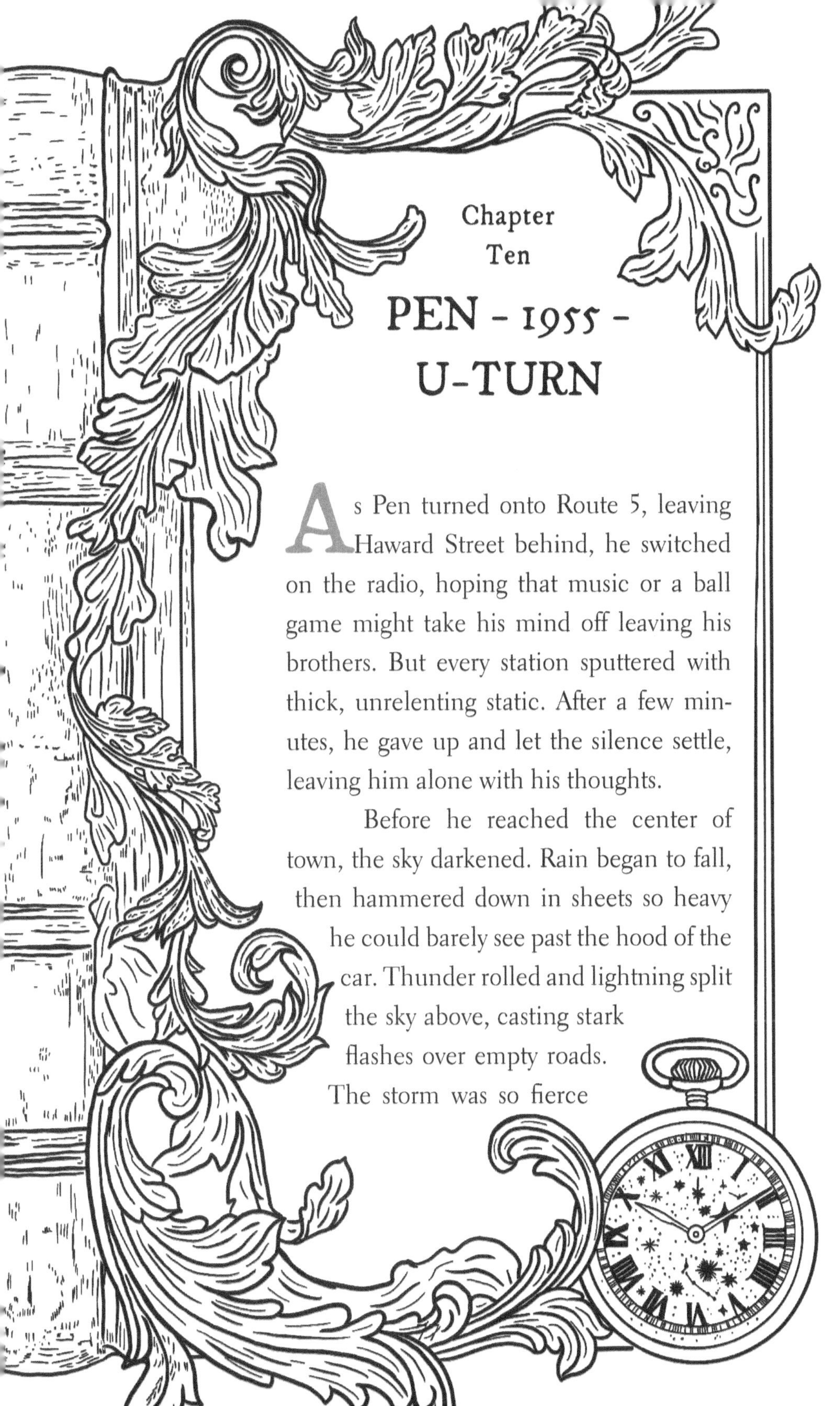

PEN - 1955 - U-TURN

As Pen turned onto Route 5, leaving Haward Street behind, he switched on the radio, hoping that music or a ball game might take his mind off leaving his brothers. But every station sputtered with thick, unrelenting static. After a few minutes, he gave up and let the silence settle, leaving him alone with his thoughts.

Before he reached the center of town, the sky darkened. Rain began to fall, then hammered down in sheets so heavy he could barely see past the hood of the car. Thunder rolled and lightning split the sky above, casting stark flashes over empty roads. The storm was so fierce he had to slow to a crawl, wipers flailing against the downpour. For a moment, it felt like the universe was trying to hold him back, trying to keep him in Oak Ridge. He pressed on, inching forward until the rain finally eased, allowing him to push past the town line. Trees flanked the roadside, their leaves dripping in the storm's wake, and up ahead, the turnoff to the southern highway came into view. He eased his foot off the gas, a flicker of doubt making him pause.

He'd dreamed of escaping to Bates, earning his degree, becoming a teacher like Ward, but those aspirations had faded over the years, worn down by the harsh realities of life since his mother's death.

This wasn't the future he'd imagined, but it was a new path, and one that still led him out of Oak Ridge. And he knew, deep down, it was the path Ward would have wanted him to take. Turning back now would feel like turning his back on everything Ward had hoped for him. He hadn't left Pen all his worldly possessions just so he could stay stuck in Oak Ridge. No, he had wanted him to go, to explore, to experience the world.

The doubt eased, not entirely gone, but softened by resolve. He gripped the wheel and pressed the gas, pushing through the last edge of his hesitation. He kept his mind on Ward, on the quiet certainty that this was what he would have wanted for him.

Before Pen left the county, he veered off onto a side road, tires crunching over gravel. He took a detour toward an old state park where Ward used to take him fishing. This was where he'd spread his ashes and say goodbye, in a place where the air still held echoes of their laughter. A place they'd both loved.

He shifted the car into park and grabbed the urn from the seat beside him. He followed a narrow, well-worn trail that led to the lake, tucked away within dense woods. Just as he remembered. At the water's edge, he stood for a long while, gripping the urn tightly.

Ripples danced across the lake's surface where insects skittered. His chest felt tight, his breath shallow. He had promised himself he would do this for Ward, but now the time had come, the finality of it left him rooted in place.

His eyes burned, and his fingers tightened around the cool surface of the urn.

Just open it. Scatter the ashes. Say goodbye.

But his body refused to move.

Out of the stillness, a cardinal appeared. It swooped past him, red wings cutting across the gray-green pines, and landed on a spindly branch beside him. For a heartbeat, it just watched him, its head tilting side to side, curious.

Ward had always believed cardinals carried the spirits of those who had passed. He used to say that when he saw one, he believed it was Emily, stopping by to say hello.

Pen swallowed hard. A single tear slipped free before he could stop it.

"Alright, Ward," he said. "I hear you."

He uncapped the urn and tipped it forward. A soft wind caught the ashes, lifting them into the air before they scattered across the surface of the water. Pen watched in silence as they sank, disappearing into the dark waters of the lake.

Then, the cardinal took flight.

"Goodbye, old friend," he whispered, his words carried off by the breeze, his heart still heavy with grief.

He stood there for a long time, not yet ready to let go. The memories of their time together here playing out like a movie in his mind.

It wasn't until the rain began to fall, soft and steady again, that Pen finally headed back to the car and the waiting road.

Two hours later, the rain had finally let up completely. He pulled into a small gas station in Wayne, West Virginia, a rundown old place with a single pump with peeling paint. A rusty Coca-Cola sign hung crookedly off the side of the building, squeaking in the wind left behind by the storm. A lanky teenage boy emerged from the garage, wiping his hands on a rag, before stuffing them into the front pocket of his stained overalls.

"What can I get ya?" the boy asked, squinting at him. The clouds were beginning to break, and sunlight pushed through in bright, hesitant streaks.

"Fill her up," Pen said, and he stepped out to stretch his legs.

The attendant began filling the tank while Pen walked to the back and popped the trunk. He glanced at the stack of books nestled beside his suitcase, the Celtic folklore volume perched on top. A spark of excitement surged through him at the sight of it. He unzipped his suitcase and pulled out the folder Mr. Ross had given him. Flipping through the papers, he stopped at the deed to the bookshop. His fingers traced the address. Something about it felt certain. Right. With care, he slid the deed back into the yellow envelope, tucked it between Ward's suits, and zipped the case shut.

Pen pulled the map from the passenger seat and spread it across the warm hood of the car. He stared at the red path he'd charted heading south. Then, with the edge of his thumb, he traced a new route north.

"Where ya headed?" the teenage boy asked, craning his neck to see the map.

Pen looked up, then back down at the map. "LaGuardia Airport," he answered, matter-of-fact, as if it had been the plan all along.

"New York, wow. Are you actually flying somewhere or are you picking someone up?" the boy asked, genuine curiosity in his voice as he finished fueling the car.

Pen paused, his gaze drifting to the trunk. "I'm headed to Scotland," he said, folding the map. Saying it out loud made it real, almost like signing a binding contract.

"Gee whiz, really? I've never met anyone who's been there. Maybe if I'm lucky, I'll get out of this place someday. See New York at least."

Pen studied him. Not long ago, he'd been that very kid, dreaming of escape but shackled to a gas pump.

"I'm sure you will," Pen replied, giving him a smile.

"That's four dollars and thirty-four cents," the kid said, tapping off the gas nozzle and slotting it back into the pump holder. Pen handed him a ten-dollar bill, climbed into the Fleetmaster, and started it up.

"Hold on, I'll get ya change," the boy told Pen as he put the car into gear.

"Keep it," Pen called out the window. "Save it for your trip to New York."

The boy grinned. "Thank you!" he yelled after him, waving with both hands, as Pen pulled away.

Pen smiled as the car rumbled onto the open road, heading north. The shift in direction felt sudden, but also right. He wasn't just driving from one tourist attraction to the next anymore; he was charting his own adventure. Writing the first page of his own story.

As the familiar landscape receded in the rearview mirror, a quiet thrill stirred through him. He was heading in the right direction. He could feel it in his bones. Then, as if Ward were sending him a sign, the radio crackled to life, landing on a station playing

Bing Crosby's "On the Road to Mandalay," one of Ward's favorites. Pen smiled, glancing at the empty urn. "Adventure, here I come!" he said, and he pressed his foot on the gas, the song carrying him toward a new dream.

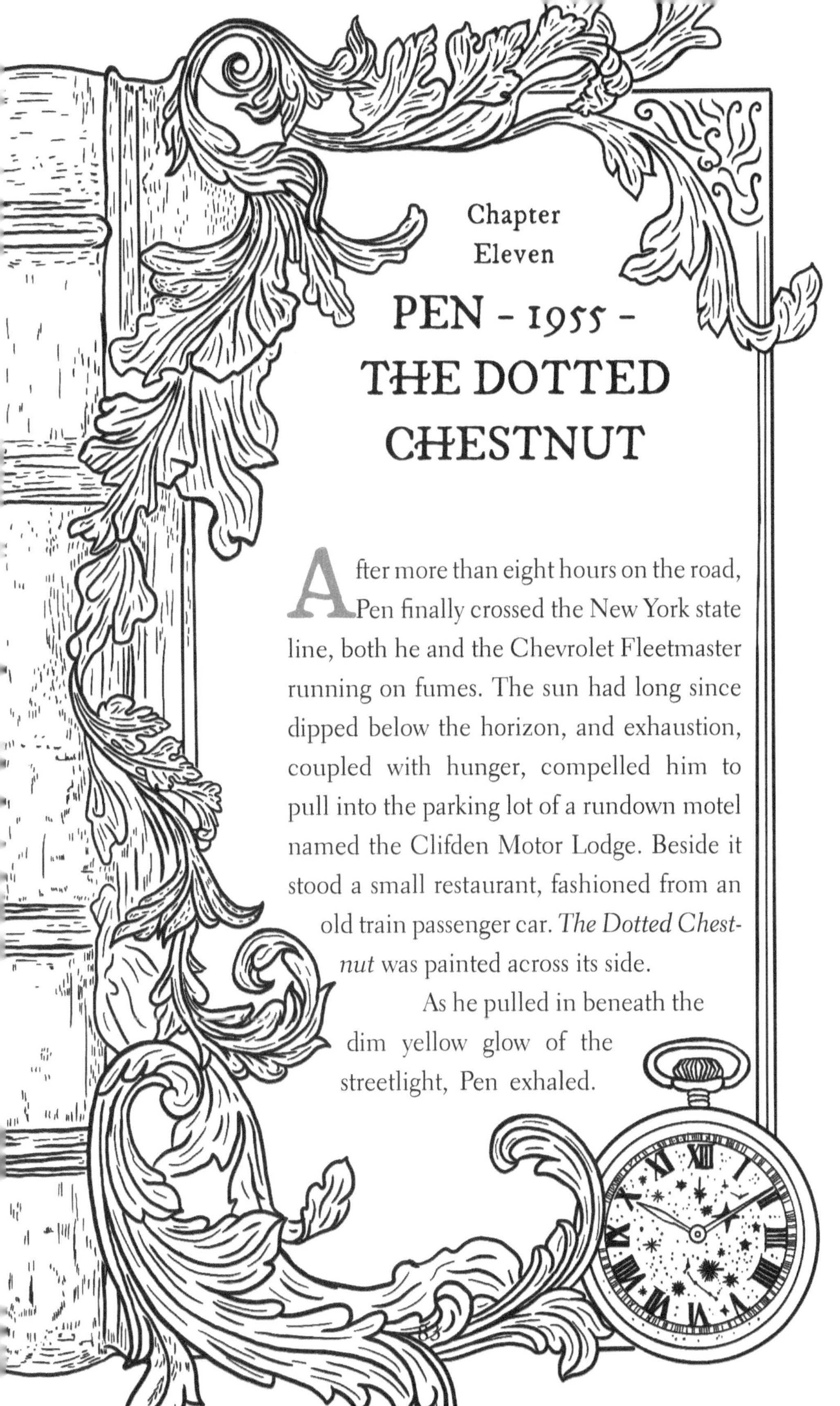

PEN - 1955 - THE DOTTED CHESTNUT

After more than eight hours on the road, Pen finally crossed the New York state line, both he and the Chevrolet Fleetmaster running on fumes. The sun had long since dipped below the horizon, and exhaustion, coupled with hunger, compelled him to pull into the parking lot of a rundown motel named the Clifden Motor Lodge. Beside it stood a small restaurant, fashioned from an old train passenger car. *The Dotted Chestnut* was painted across its side.

As he pulled in beneath the dim yellow glow of the streetlight, Pen exhaled.

His hands ached from gripping the wheel. He rolled his shoulders as the engine stilled, grateful to finally put the car in park. He'd never spent more than a few hours in a car before, and that had been years ago, on a trip to visit his grandmother in a nursing home in Sutton before she passed.

He stepped out into the thick night air and stretched his legs and back, both stiff and sore from the long drive. The moon was retreating behind a thick layer of clouds, and the air hung heavy with that electric feel that signaled rain wasn't far off.

Pen popped the trunk and grabbed his suitcase. The parking lot glistened, its fresh blacktop gleaming like newly formed ice on a frozen lake under the lights. The sharp tang of tar overpowered the sweetness of the blooming bushes that lined the motel's edge, their white petals catching the light like scraps of paper.

At the front entrance, a swarm of moths braided their way around the light fixed to the wall beside the door. He scurried past them, hoping none would get caught in his hair.

The motel's office was barely more than a box: a desk, a cigarette vending machine, and the low buzz of fluorescent lighting overhead. Behind the desk sat a woman who appeared to be in her mid-fifties. Her bleach-blonde hair was still twisted in pink curlers, and a plastic name tag on her shirt read *Janine*. Her cheeks were caked in rouge, so red and shiny they reminded Pen of a baked lobster.

"Good evening, Janine," Pen greeted politely. Janine didn't look up, her eyes fixed on a glossy magazine, the front-page headline blaring, "Scandal in High Society: Hidden Affairs Uncovered!"

Pen stood awkwardly, the silence stretching. It seemed as if she might finish the entire article before she acknowledged him. He cleared his throat.

She sighed, then slowly set the magazine aside, a look of annoyance spreading across her face.

"Must be a good read," he said. She rolled her eyes in reply. "Could I get a room for the night?"

Without answering, she flipped open a worn logbook and scanned its pages with a long painted fingernail.

"I'm puttin' you in Room 403," she rasped, pulling a registration card from under the desk. "Fill this out." She shoved it toward him. "That's gonna be six dollars."

Pen fished the money from his wallet, handed it to the woman, then grabbed a pen from the paper cup on the desk and began filling out the card. When he came to the line for his address, his hand hovered.

His home was no longer 66 Haward Street, where the tin-can was parked. Now, it was Ward's address. As he wrote it down, a flicker of warmth passed through him, followed by an ache. He had a real address now, a proper home. But it had come at the expense of his dearest friend.

"Here ya go," the woman said, her whiskey-laced voice cutting through his thoughts.

She handed him a brass key with 403 engraved into its top. It dangled from a keychain stamped with the motel's logo, a moth with a crown. *Fitting*, Pen thought, recalling the swarm fluttering madly by the light outside.

"You're gonna go out, turn right toward the diner. Room's second to the last," she told him, tossing his registration card onto a stack in a tray, and retreating behind her magazine again.

"Thanks," Pen replied, but he might as well have held his breath. She didn't hear, or didn't care.

Before heading to his room, Pen popped a quarter into the vending machine and watched as a pack of Lucky Strikes clunked into the tray. He pocketed the cigarettes and stepped out into the drizzle.

The moths had vanished, disappearing into dry crevices as the lamp continued to flicker. He lugged his suitcase down the concrete walkway until he reached his door. The number four was missing a nail and hung upside down. *Not promising*, he thought as he slid the key into the lock and turned the knob.

Running his hand along the side of the wall, he found the light switch and flicked it on. A bulb came on overhead, casting a tired glow over the room. It was modest: a double bed with a sunken middle, a single worn chair, and a scuffed-up table just big enough for one. The carpet was a disturbing shade of orange, and the walls were painted a shade of green that reminded Pen of his mother's pea soup.

He stepped inside and shut the door, then immediately opened the window. The air was thick with the stench of stale cigarette smoke, mildew, and a pungent perfume trying to cover it all. The combination was noxious. He shoved the window open wider and pulled back the curtain, hoping a breeze might cut through the stink. As the fresh air crept in, his stomach growled, a dull, hollow reminder that he hadn't eaten anything since the Coke and sandwich at the gas station hours ago.

Leaving the suitcase by the door, he turned and went back out into the drizzle.

The diner was only a few yards away, its windows glowing amber against the damp night. As Pen climbed the wooden steps, he took a moment to admire the old passenger car, candy-apple red with aluminum trim, the name *The Dotted Chestnut* painted in bold iron-black script across its side. Rain beaded along the roof and windows, catching the light.

Stepping inside, the warmth hit him immediately, along with the scent of grilled hamburgers and apple pie. His stomach responded with a loud, involuntary moan. The place was nearly empty, just an older gentleman hunched at the long counter that ran the length of the car. Opposite the counter, a row of small booths lined the wall, each one barely big enough for two.

A stocky man worked the grill, his white apron smeared with grease. A pretty young brunette moved behind the counter, her ponytail swaying as she placed a fresh pot of coffee on a warmer.

Pen slid onto a stool two down from the old man, the vinyl seat hissing beneath him. He glanced up at the oversized menu board above the grill, chipped letters spelling out the basics: burgers, dogs, eggs, pie.

The waitress ambled over, pulling a small white pad from her apron pocket. "What can I get for ya, honey?"

Pen glanced at her name tag. "Rose, can I get a cheeseburger and fries? Oh, and a chocolate shake, please."

"Well, aren't you a gentleman? You got it," she said with a smile, turning around to stick the order on the turnstile before spinning it over to the cook. She turned back, leaning slightly against the counter. "So, where are you from?"

"West Virginia."

"Aw," she said, her mouth quirking. "The South."

He gave a half-shrug. "Well, sort of, I suppose." He kept his tone polite, knowing full well West Virginia wasn't quite what you'd call the South.

"What's got you up this way?" she asked, her voice warming as she painted on the charm.

However, it was lost on Pen. He didn't have much experience with girls, and flirting wasn't his forte. Whatever signals she was sending went clean over his head.

"I'm actually headed to the airport in the morning," he told her.

Her eyes lit up. "Really? How exciting. Somewhere tropical, I hope?" Rose giggled as she flipped her hair.

"Scotland." The word left his mouth with a strange, swelling pride, and his stomach burned with anticipation.

"Oh," she said, faltering a little. "Not quite the Bahamas. So, what—"

"Order up," the cook called out, cutting Rose off. As she spun to grab the plate, the old man next to Pen leaned in.

"If you're headed to Scotland, you'd best watch out for the fairies and monsters lurking in that ancient land."

Pen smiled, unsure how to respond.

"Oh, don't mind Lenny," said Rose, dismissing him with a wave. "That old codger doesn't know his ass from his elbow."

"You listen here, Rose," Lenny barked, straightening on his stool. "I know what I'm talking about. I was stationed in Edinburgh during the war."

Rose rolled her eyes, handed Pen his plate of food then went into the back with the cook.

Pen looked over. "Were you really stationed there? Not to be rude, but you seem a bit long in the tooth for combat."

"I was. Of course, I was too old for the front lines by then, sure, but I worked with a team of engineers."

This piqued Pen's interest. Ward had often mentioned a friend who did similar work with the Brits during the war.

"What was it you worked on?" Pen asked, taking a bite of his burger.

"Can't say. It's classified," Lenny replied with a double raise of his eyebrows and a nod.

He was clearly pulling Pen's leg, the sharp tang of whiskey on his breath giving him away. Pen wasn't going to fall for it, but that comment about the monsters stirred something in him. It reminded him of the book tucked away in the trunk of Ward's car.

"So, do you really believe in fairies and monsters?" Pen questioned.

"You might think I've lost my marbles, but I do," Lenny said. "Maybe not fairies with wings and glitter, but magic? That's real. Seen it with my own two eyes, I have." Lenny took a long sip of his coffee, then pulled out a flask from his hip and added a generous splash to his cup.

Pen was unsure what to make of the man. He lit a Lucky Strike, then offered one to Lenny, who accepted it with a grateful nod.

"We got a package in the early spring of '44 at the base where I was stationed," Lenny began, exhaling a plume of smoke. "I worked in a team of three scientists, examining items the government couldn't make heads or tails of. One day, this crate shows up, and inside is a flat slab of black obsidian. The back was covered in strange carvings, letters, and symbols, but nothing we recognized. And dead center?" He tapped the air with a yellowed finger. "The Monas Hieroglyphica."

He paused, taking a long swig of his spiked coffee.

"We knew right away it had something to do with the occult. Ran every test we had, checked for radiation, traces of metal, even ran it through the X-ray machine. But far as we could tell, it was just what it looked like. A rock. None of it made a lick of sense. Then one night, we're working late. Clear night, with a full moon, rare for that place, usually rained all the time. Roger, one of the other Americans, was carrying the stone back to the locked closet where we kept classified stuff. As he passed the window, *bam*! Moonlight hit the surface." Lenny leaned in. "Poof, Roger vanished. I swear on my life. One second he's there, the next he's gone. Then just like that, he's back."

Lenny exhaled sharply, shaking his head. "I don't know what it was, but there's something in those hills. A strange kind of magic, I'm telling you."

Pen took a long drag of his cigarette, gaze fixed on the swirling smoke as Lenny's words echoed in his mind. The story had hooked him. It reminded him of *The Night of the Long Knives* by Felix H. L., his dog-eared copy. It was one of his favorites that Ward had gifted to him on his twelfth birthday. One of the first books to make his pulse quicken with possibility.

"I think you better get home to Marge, Lenny," Rose said sharply, swooping in and snatching his coffee cup away.

"Aw, come on now," he said, reaching for the cup. But Rose had already begun dumping its contents down the sink. Lenny grumbled, but didn't argue further. He pushed himself up from the stool and shuffled over to Pen, placing his old wrinkled hand on his shoulder. "You be careful over there, young man," he added.

Pen nodded as Lenny snuffed out his half-smoked cigarette in the ashtray next to him and ambled out into the night.

"Good riddance," Rose said as the door thudded shut behind him, wiping the counter with a force that made it clear she'd had that conversation before.

"How much do I owe you?" Pen asked, popping the last soggy french fry into his mouth.

"Seventy-five cents, handsome," Rose answered with a wink.

Pen handed her a dollar bill with a smile, missing, or maybe ignoring, the look of mild disappointment on Rose's face as he stood and headed for the door.

Outside, the rain had eased to a persistent mist. His shoes clopped against the wet pavement. Lenny's story looped in his mind. Obsidian stones, vanishing soldiers, strange magic. He told himself it was just an old drunk's tall tales, but a prickling of unease curled in his chest. Maybe this trip was a mistake. Maybe it was too spontaneous. Escape disguised as adventure.

"Ward, if you're up there, give me a sign," he said, looking up.

Just steps from his room, a moth drifted down from one of the lights in the parking lot and landed gently on his hand. Its wings were wide, the color of freshly tilled earth, with splotches of gray, tan, and orange, reminding him of the rug in his room.

The moth didn't flutter or twitch. It simply rested. Then, just as gently, it took flight, heading east, toward the Atlantic, toward Scotland.

"Thanks, Ward," he whispered.

He had his answer.

THE HIDDEN JOURNAL
OF JOHN DEE

October 2, 1589

After a full day spent meticulously reviewing our calculations and confirming that each detail was precisely in place, Giordano and I set off on our journey to Dunblane.

The trek took us just over a fortnight. We were fortunate, as the weather was surprisingly favorable, with unseasonably warm temperatures and only a few days of heavy rain. Arriving in Dunblane late in the evening, we decided it best to camp outside the village. We reasoned that making our appearance in the light of day would be more advantageous in gaining the Bishop's favor.

Our intent is to operate the Astral Synchronum in the crypt beneath the eastern end of the cathedral, as instructed by Edward during his scrying sessions. Gaining access to this sacred space will prove challenging, but I have devised a plan. I shall present myself as one of Queen Elizabeth's loyal advisors, dispatched to survey the tombs of the nobility buried there. My reputation as a trusted counselor ought to lend credibility to my request. After all, few would dare question the word of the queen. However, I must tread carefully, for if Her Majesty were to learn of my true purpose, I fear I would face her wrath.

Now, as I write by the flickering light of my candle, anticipation courses through me, mingled with an undercurrent of dread. We are mere hours away from discovering whether our years of toil and sacrifice will yield the results we seek. I pray we have completed our calculations correctly, for if we have not, Edward was warned by the divine that it could tear at the very fabric of our reality. We seek an audience with the angels, knowing they possess the knowledge of the divine principles that bind Heaven and Earth together, the very secrets by which the universe is ordered. And if we are correct and the synchronome opens the door to the divine, within hours, this knowledge will become ours. May the angels guide and protect us, and safeguard the world around us, should we falter. For in this pursuit of knowledge, we tread a dangerous line; even the smallest miscalculation could unleash dire consequences. We are but men, flawed and fallible; yet I hold hope that our work, forged in purpose and devotion, shall withstand the trials that lie ahead.

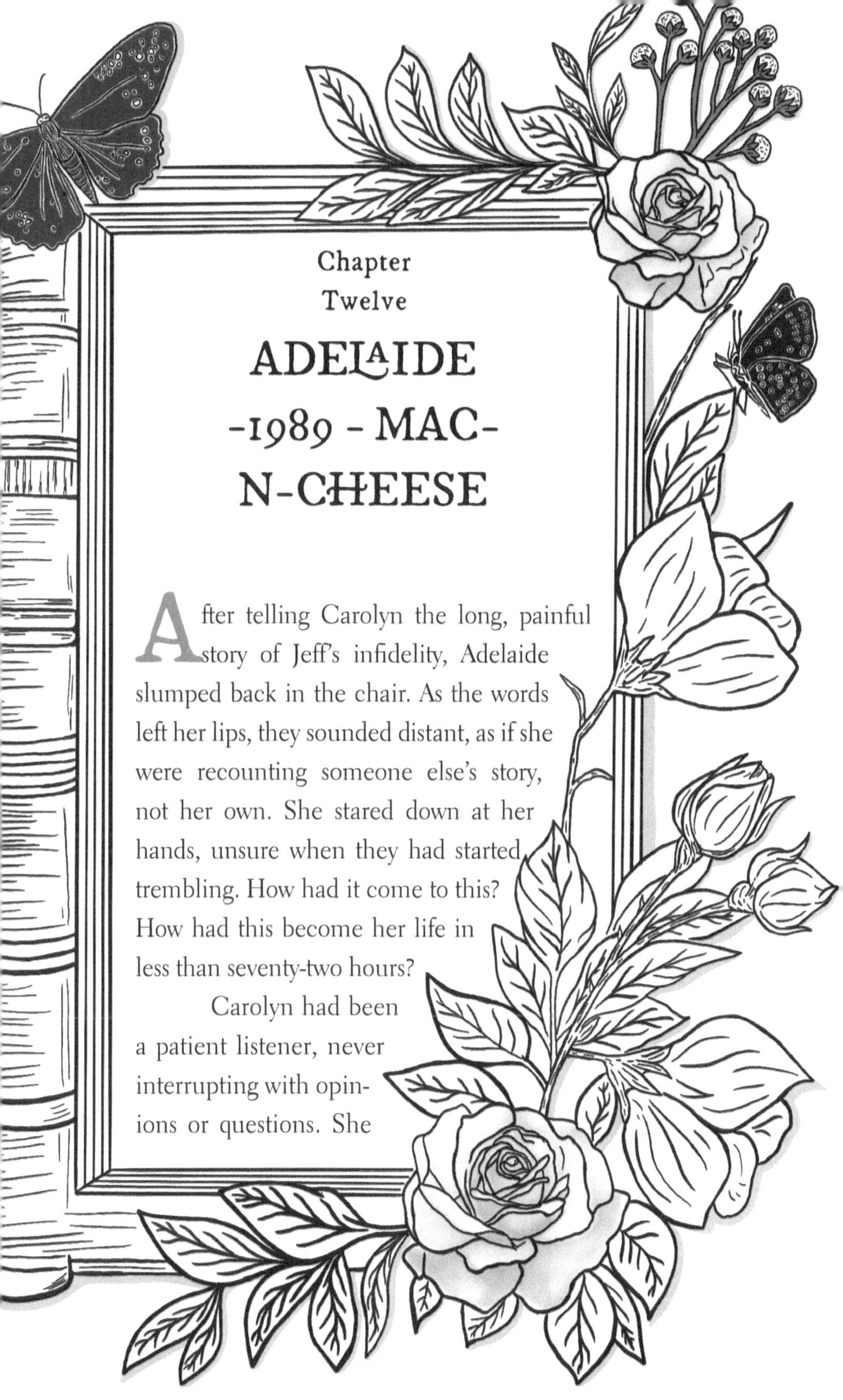

ADELAIDE -1989 - MAC-N-CHEESE

After telling Carolyn the long, painful story of Jeff's infidelity, Adelaide slumped back in the chair. As the words left her lips, they sounded distant, as if she were recounting someone else's story, not her own. She stared down at her hands, unsure when they had started trembling. How had it come to this? How had this become her life in less than seventy-two hours?

Carolyn had been a patient listener, never interrupting with opin- ions or questions. She simply let Adelaide speak, because sometimes the only way through heartbreak was to name it out loud. To say plainly, that Jeff had truly left her.

"You look exhausted. Why don't you rest your head while I cook us some dinner," Carolyn suggested, as she stood up, giving Adelaide a pat on the shoulder before she headed to the kitchen.

Adelaide sank deeper into the overstuffed armchair, letting out a deep breath. She wasn't sure if talking about it had helped, but there was a lighter feeling in her chest. Not quite relief, but maybe a little more space to breathe.

She looked around the room. It hadn't changed a bit since she was a child, still dressed in its wild mix of colors and styles. The blue-striped wallpaper, scattered with tiny roses, gave it a quaint, lived-in charm. By the fireplace, two armchairs in bold green-and-blue tartan stood like old friends, their sturdy frames grounded by a Persian rug woven with reds and golds. To the right of the hearth, a couch with a long, rounded back, shaped like a half-open clam-shell, rested in rich olive-green velvet. It looked like it belonged in a castle, not a modest cottage.

On the side table beside the couch sat a vase, but instead of flowers, it held a curious collection of feathers, each one different in size and color, fanning out like the plumage of an exotic bird. It was eclectic, but beautiful, just like Carolyn.

Adelaide smiled, longing to possess even a fraction of her great-aunt's free-spiritedness. Life with Jeff had been the opposite, a realm of bland conformity. Their living room, dining room, and bedroom sets had all been chosen straight from the Argos catalog, the most predict-able base models in shades of brown and cream. He had allowed her to select the wallpaper, but only from a narrow range of pre-approved styles he brought home. Now, with distance, she saw just how little control she'd truly had. Jeff had been the ultimate decision-maker on everything, from the color of her hair to the clothes she wore. How had she not seen it sooner? He'd kept her in a gilded cage, just enough space to stretch her wings, but never enough to truly fly.

Adelaide noticed the absence of a television; instead, a small radio perched on the mantel, and a record player sat on the side table next to the vase of feathers. Yet, there was no shortage of entertainment. The wall facing the stairs was dominated by a towering bookcase, packed from floor to ceiling with books. Carolyn's life, it seemed, was serene but full, unburdened by the distractions of modern life.

Jeff had always insisted on having the TV on, sports blaring, the news droning, always some kind of noise. Even when he was at work and she was home alone, the constant hum of the busy road outside their house left no room for quiet. But here, in the countryside, surrounded by nothing but the soft sounds of the wild, Adelaide felt a calm she hadn't known in a long time.

Standing, she wandered over to the wall of books as Carolyn continued bustling in the kitchen. She tipped a few volumes forward, inspecting their covers, her fingers tracing the worn spines. Like everything in the house, the collection was a vibrant, slightly chaotic mix. Half a row dedicated to gardening, a handful of history books from around the globe, a section devoted to religious books, and an extensive range of fiction and fantasy. Tucked among them was a surprisingly large selection of romance novels.

Adelaide smiled. Even Great-Aunt Carolyn had a soft spot for a little romance, it seemed. It made her wonder why she had never married. As far as Adelaide remembered, Carolyn had always lived alone. She glanced over at her now, stirring something fragrant on the stove. Still striking, and surely even more so in her youth. There seemed to be no reason why men wouldn't have sought her company. Yet, despite the curiosity gnawing at her, Adelaide felt it would be impolite to ask.

"Dinner's on," Carolyn announced a few minutes later, setting a large casserole dish down on a hot pad.

Adelaide walked over and took a seat at the small kitchen table. Once painted a deep teal, the table's surface was now worn down to bare wood in places, its edges softened by countless meals and conversations.

Carolyn scooped a generous serving of bubbling homemade macaroni and cheese onto Adelaide's plate. "I've got just the thing to mend a broken heart," she said with a warm smile. "This is my go-to comfort food."

Adelaide smiled back, accepting the plate with appreciation. "It's my favorite, too."

Carolyn sat down and reached across the table, resting her hand lightly on Adelaide's. "I think you should stay here for a little while, at least until things settle. There's no need to rush back," she added, giving her a gentle squeeze.

"I really don't want to impose. I just showed up out of nowhere after all these years. It doesn't seem fair to you."

"Nonsense," Carolyn replied with a smile. "I'd be thrilled to have you here."

They ate in shared silence for a while, the comfort of the meal and the simple presence of one another filling the space. Adelaide found herself wondering how long it had been since Carolyn had last shared a meal with someone. A pang of regret settled in her chest. She should have visited sooner, especially knowing how close Carolyn and her father had been. But life had gotten away from her, and she'd spent most of it preoccupied with whether she was doing adulthood right. Still, she was here now, and she would do her best to make up for lost time.

"Well, this old lady is ready for the land of nod," Carolyn stated, glancing at the clock on the stove that read 7:22.

Adelaide followed her gaze, surprised at how the day had slipped away so quickly. Carolyn got to her feet and started to clear the table. Adelaide followed, washing their two plates at the sink while Carolyn put away the leftovers.

"I'll make you up a bed on the couch for the night. There's an extra blanket in the hallway cupboard if you get cold. Now, you get some rest, we've work to do in the morning," she said with a mischievous smile. She walked over to the small cupboard beneath the stairs and pulled out a blanket and pillow, placing them neatly on the sofa.

"Thank you, Carolyn. Good night," Adelaide called out to her as she disappeared up the stairs.

For a moment, Adelaide wondered why Carolyn had her sleeping on the sofa when she had a guest room. Maybe it was just the surprise of her showing up unannounced, and the room wasn't clean.

Standing alone in the warm kitchen with a belly full of food, she should have felt tired, but instead, she felt quite the opposite. The idea of trying to sleep this early seemed futile. She turned toward the front door, drawn by the hush of the countryside and the coolness of the night, and walked to her car.

The sun had just dipped below the mountains, leaving their edges traced in a rim of deep gold. A light breeze carried the sweet melody of night birds, along with a symphony of insects. Out here, the dark was complete, no city glow, just stars beginning to pepper the sky. Adelaide stood, head tilted, breathing in the stillness. She couldn't remember the last time she'd seen the night like this, without the hazy veil of light pollution. At home, or what used to be her home, the streetlights never slept, always casting a faint glow that made it almost impossible to see the night sky.

After a long breath, she opened the car door. The warm glow of the interior light spilled into the darkness. She reached in, grabbed her bag and the box of hair dye off the front seat.

Just as she was about to close the door, a large moth flew into the car, drawn to the light. It dove at it again and again, wings tapping the bulb in a frantic motion. Adelaide watched, heart tightening, as it thudded against the plastic dome. She'd once read that moths use the moon to navigate, and when they mistake artificial lights for it, they become disoriented, chasing it in dizzying circles, until they eventually burn out. Was that what she'd done with Jeff? Chased something that looked like love, only to find herself lost in the glow of something false. Feeling a pang of sympathy for the creature, she reached up and turned off the light. Darkness folded back in. She waited, watching the moth hover for a moment before it drifted out of the car and into the night. Then she reached in and gently closed the door.

The moth glided above her as she walked back to the house, its wings brushing the air as it veered toward the kitchen window, chasing a new light. Adelaide knew then. She had spent too long chasing someone else's light. Jeff's ambitions, Jeff's desires, Jeff's vision of who she should be. No more. The only light she was willing to follow now was her own. Carolyn seemed content in her solitude, perhaps even happy. Maybe peace didn't come from being loved, but from learning to love your own company. The thought didn't seem so bad, and the idea no longer felt lonely.

Back inside, she made her way into the bathroom and opened the box of hair dye. It was time to find herself again, to strip away what wasn't hers, buried deep beneath layers of who she had become. She looked down at the box in her hands. Tonight, she would start by reclaiming a piece of herself, one strand at a time.

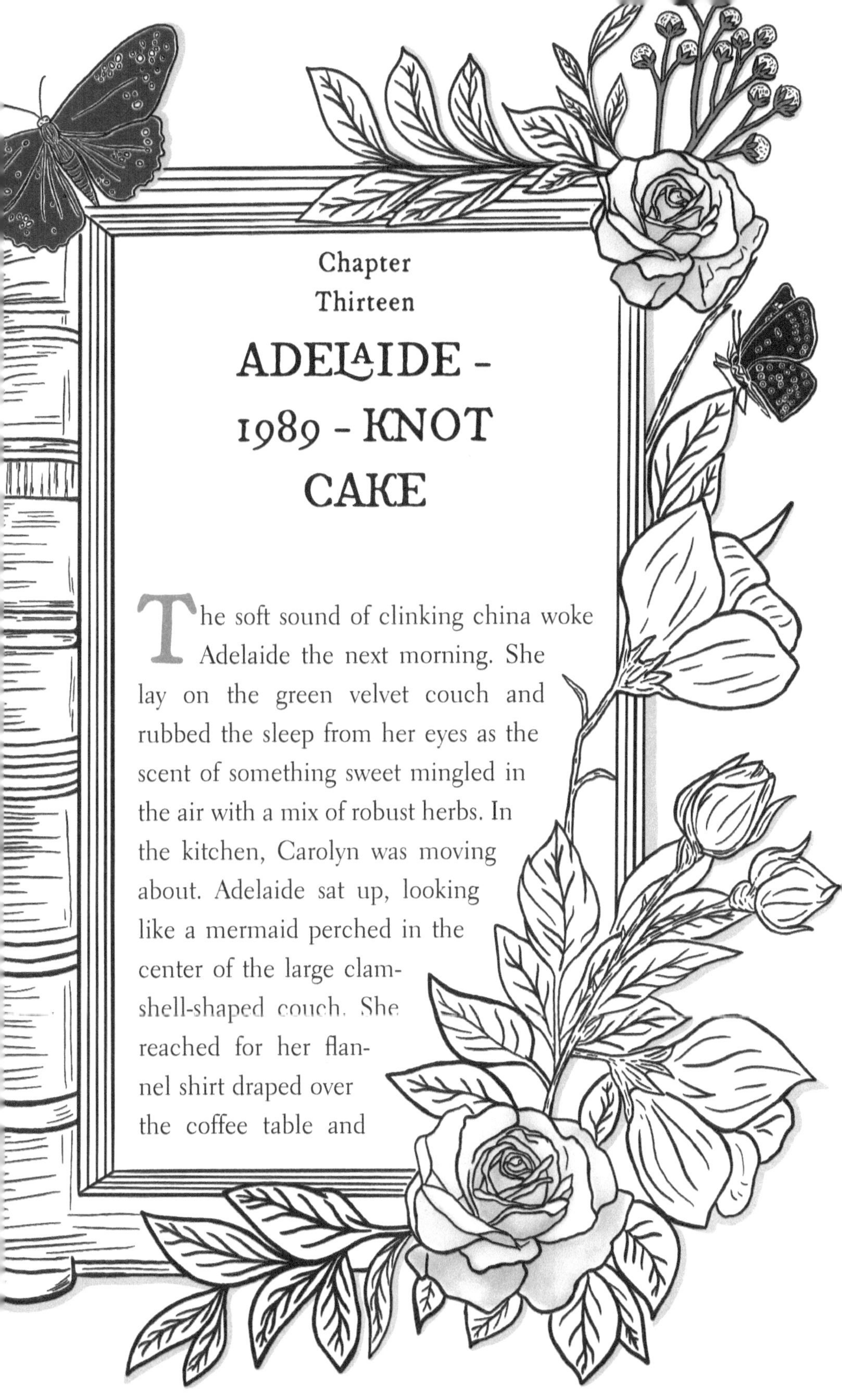

The soft sound of clinking china woke Adelaide the next morning. She lay on the green velvet couch and rubbed the sleep from her eyes as the scent of something sweet mingled in the air with a mix of robust herbs. In the kitchen, Carolyn was moving about. Adelaide sat up, looking like a mermaid perched in the center of the large clam-shell-shaped couch. She reached for her flannel shirt draped over the coffee table and slipped it on. The morning air inside the old stone house was cool and damp, and she wrapped the shirt tightly around her and padded into the kitchen.

"Morning," Adelaide said, yawning as she sat down.

"Good morning," Carolyn replied, her back turned as she rinsed a bowl in the sink. Adelaide stretched her legs out under the table and began absently picking at a loose thread dangling from her sleeve that tickled her wrist.

Carolyn turned, drying the bowl with a plaid dish towel, a warm smile deepening the lines on her face. "Well, there's the little Addie I remember," she said, her voice filled with fondness.

Adelaide froze, her fingers stilling on the thread. *Addie.* She hadn't been called that in years, not since she was a child. A small knot of worry tightened in her chest. Had Carolyn forgotten how old she was? She seemed so sharp yesterday, but now Adelaide wondered if age was beginning to cloud her memory.

"Umm," she was unsure how to respond.

Carolyn laughed, but the sound only deepened Adelaide's worry.

"Your hair," Carolyn pointed. "I do believe it was blonde yesterday."

Adelaide instinctively reached up and pulled a lock of hair forward. She'd almost forgotten she'd dyed it last night. The wavy strand in her fingers was no longer bleach-blonde but a light shade of brown, reminiscent of a fallen oak leaf, her natural color. The sight of it immediately pulled her thoughts to Jeff.

"Oh, yeah. I almost forgot I dyed it last night," she replied, forcing a laugh.

Carolyn chuckled. "Thought I was going nuts there for a minute, didn't you?"

Adelaide smiled, amused by her aunt's wit. But when she glanced out the kitchen window, her heart sank. The sky was a dull slate, heavy with clouds that threatened rain, mirroring the storm brewing inside her. What was she doing all the way in Scotland? She should probably call Amy, see if she could stay with her for a while. She was imposing here, wasn't she? The last thing her great-aunt needed was the burden of taking care of a broken-hearted mess. But the idea of going back made her stomach churn. The thought of returning to Glastonbury, of retracing the steps of her old life, filled her with a quiet kind of panic.

But then she looked back at Carolyn. Despite the years and distance, that quiet ease between them remained. It was the kind of comfort that didn't need catching up, the kind that only came with family.

Adelaide realized just how much she needed this connection, this guidance from someone she truly trusted. After her mother's death, it had been just her and Jeff, and then, when he left, it had been only her. She'd nearly forgotten she still had Carolyn until her grief stepped in and subconsciously pulled her here. It seemed fate had tugged an invisible thread, guiding her to the one person who might help her find her way again.

She blinked back the swell of emotion and forced a smile. "What are you cooking? It smells amazing."

"It's a knot cake."

Adelaide raised a brow. "If it's not a cake, then what's in the oven?"

Carolyn let out another laugh. "No, no. It's a *knot* cake. The kind used to heal a broken heart." She cracked the oven door and peeked inside.

"Never heard of it, but I'm willing to give it a try, especially if it tastes as good as it smells. What's in it?"

"You'll see," Carolyn told her, turning and pouring two mugs of steaming tea from a stout teapot wearing a knitted cozy that looked like a bumble bee.

"Thanks," Adelaide said as Carolyn handed her a mug and sat down next to her.

"So," Carolyn began, gesturing toward Adelaide's hair, "do you want to tell me about the sudden change of color?"

Adelaide gave a small shrug. "Yesterday, on the way here, I just… I decided I needed to find myself again. I've been Jeff's wife for so many years, I've forgotten who I am. Going back to my natural color seemed like a good start."

"Well, I like it much better. The blonde didn't suit you," Carolyn said, taking a sip of her tea.

"Jeff liked me blonde."

"I figured as much," Carolyn said gently.

Adelaide fell quiet, turning the mug in her hands. She wasn't sure when she had stopped choosing for herself. Maybe that's what growing up did, made you judge yourself against everyone's expectations.

The oven timer let out a long string of beeps, breaking Adelaide from her thoughts. Carolyn cracked the oven door once more, peeking inside before fully opening it. She pulled two quilted pot holders from a drawer, then carefully lifted the pan from the oven and set it on the old butcher block counter.

A wave of sweetness rolled through the room, a mix of sugar, honey, and something nutty. *Almond*, Adelaide guessed. Her mouth watered, and her stomach growled at the tempting aroma.

In the pan was a lightly browned sweet bread, its shape twisted into an elegant knot. Carolyn flipped the pan upside down and gave the bottom a hard thwack, and the cake landed with a soft flop. She nudged it upright, then reached for a small jar and began drizzling what looked to be honey over its top.

Crossing the kitchen, she opened a cupboard and pulled down two small china plates, each adorned with tiny pink roses. With a practiced hand, she cut a piece, then placed the knotted slice on one of the plates.

"Now," she started, handing Adelaide the plate, "I want you to do two things before you eat this. First, I want you to visualize unknotting yourself from Jeff. Imagine those ties snapping. The bonds that once held you together no longer exist, and you need to see those ties breaking. So, take your slice and pull it apart, separating the whole slice into two halves. One is you. The other is what you're leaving behind. The one you see as yourself, I want you to eat. The other you will toss in the bin. Second, as you eat, I want you to enjoy it, really taste it, focus on each flavor."

Adelaide took the plate and examined the misshapen dough, twisted and knotted in a rather chaotic fashion. It reminded her of something out of an old folktale, one of those pagan rituals whispered about in dusty old books. While she knew Carolyn meant well, the whole thing just felt a little too *new age* for her taste. She moved her hand to her mouth, biting down on her thumbnail, a nervous habit from childhood that seemed to have resurfaced since Jeff left her.

"I know, it sounds weird," Carolyn said with a knowing smile, as if reading Adelaide's thoughts, "but I promise it will help."

Adelaide looked at her great-aunt, whose steady gaze only held warmth. Whatever this ritual was, odd or not, her intentions were good. *What harm could it do,* she thought as she looked down at the misshapen piece of cake in front of her. She could see how Carolyn had braided the pieces together, and she found the spot where the strands met, the place she believed might unbind the two. But the pieces had baked together more tightly than she'd expected, and it took a bit of effort to ease them apart. As she worked, she imagined untangling herself from all of Jeff's expectations, his rules, his control, the quiet lies that had held their marriage together. When the knot finally split in two, she paused. One piece had been nestled below the other, shielded from the browning heat of the oven. That was the one she chose to keep. It reminded her of her own life spent in Jeff's shadow.

Pushing the other piece aside, Adelaide closed her eyes and took a small bite. At first, the flavors mingled into a simple sweetness, but as she kept her eyes shut and focused deeper, the taste began to unravel. She swallowed, then opened her eyes.

"And what was it you tasted?" Carolyn asked.

"The obvious things at first, the sugar and yeast. Then I think I caught lavender, maybe rose, along with a mix of honey, almonds, and cinnamon," Adelaide told her, the taste of the cake still lingering on her tongue.

"Good. Take another bite, you're missing something."

Adelaide picked up the piece and took another bite, closing her eyes again to concentrate. She knew there was something else there in the background, but she couldn't put her finger on it. Opening her eyes, she looked back at Carolyn and shrugged.

"I don't know. I know there's something there, but I can't figure out what it is."

"That's because it doesn't belong. Think about the sensations you're feeling, not just the flavors."

Adelaide sat still, letting the bite linger. And then she noticed it, a slight burning sensation on her tongue. It had been there all along, hidden beneath the sweetness, but she'd missed it. The other flavors had distracted her from it.

"Pepper," she burst out, a smile spreading across her face.

"Yes!" Carolyn beamed. "You didn't notice it at first because the other flavors were more pleasant. It was easier to let them mask the one that doesn't belong." She tilted her head, looking Adelaide in the eyes. "Sometimes, in life, we do the same thing. Even when deep down we know something's off, we often let the easier, more palatable things mask it. It's human nature, my darling." She gave Adelaide's shoulder a quick squeeze, then rose and gathered their plates, and threw all the cake in the trash.

Adelaide's eyes filled with tears. The analogy struck deep, more powerful than if Carolyn had simply said, *Oh darling, sometimes we don't want to see what's right in front of us.* It hit her in a way words alone never could. Carolyn's wisdom was subtle but profound, and it landed. Adelaide knew then she was exactly where she needed to be.

Carolyn opened the oven and pulled out another pan, flipping a second cake onto a plate. She added the glaze just as she had with the first.

"This one has no pepper," she said.

Adelaide watched her, then asked, "Have you ever needed to use the knot cake for yourself?"

Carolyn's smile faltered just slightly. "Many, many moons ago," she answered softly. "But some knots are harder to untie than others."

She let out a short laugh, but Adelaide could see the glint of old hurt in her eyes and immediately regretted asking. She stayed quiet, unsure how to respond.

"But you, my dear," Carolyn continued, brightening again, "are much stronger than I was at your age, I can tell. I've no doubt you'll keep your side unknotted."

She set down two fresh slices of cake.

"I hope you're right," Adelaide replied, her voice low. "I feel like a coward, running away like I did."

"That wasn't cowardice," Carolyn said, settling into her chair. "That was knowing when to step back and give yourself space. That takes a kind of wisdom most people don't find until it's too late." She reached for Adelaide's hand. "And I want you to know, you can stay here as long as you need. Truly."

She slid the plate toward her. This time, there was no knot, just a smooth, browned surface, like a clean slate.

Adelaide took a small bite, savoring the sweet, untangled flavors. As she swallowed, a quiet resolve took root within her. This was her clean slate, here with Carolyn, a chance to start anew, free from the knots of her past. And this time, she promised herself, she wouldn't ignore what was hidden beneath the surface.

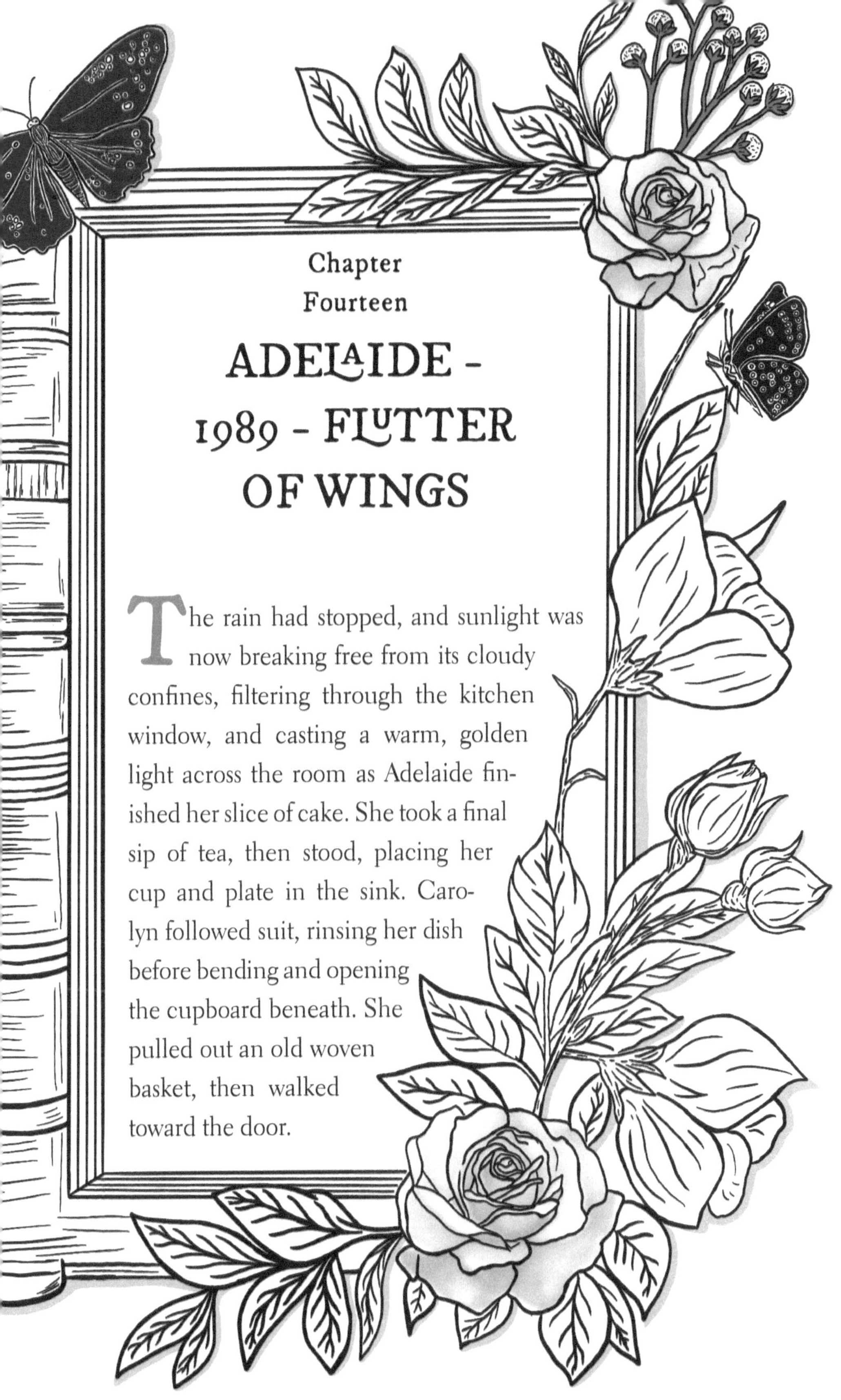

ADELAIDE – 1989 – FLUTTER OF WINGS

The rain had stopped, and sunlight was now breaking free from its cloudy confines, filtering through the kitchen window, and casting a warm, golden light across the room as Adelaide finished her slice of cake. She took a final sip of tea, then stood, placing her cup and plate in the sink. Carolyn followed suit, rinsing her dish before bending and opening the cupboard beneath. She pulled out an old woven basket, then walked toward the door.

"Come with me, I have something to show you," she said, pulling on her oversized raincoat and slipping on her leather boots. She picked up an old brass ring full of keys, hanging from a nail by the door, tucked it into her pocket, and stepped outside.

Adelaide slipped on her sneakers and followed her great-aunt out into the morning air. It bit at her cheeks, crisp and clean. Though it was only mid-August, the breeze carried a hint of autumn, her breath fogging faintly. Beneath her feet, the dew seemed heavier than usual after the rain, soaking through the tips of her shoes. She didn't know if this was typical for Scotland or if autumn was planning an early arrival this year.

Carolyn said nothing as she led the way along a well-trodden path through the overgrown grass in her back garden. Though tangled with weeds, the lawn was dotted with wildflowers that filled the thick, dewy air with their sweet fragrance. Beyond the garden lay a small field, a forest bordering its edges, the very one where Carolyn had once taken her to search for fairy circles as a child. At the end of the path, before the field's edge, stood a small stone cabin. Carolyn pulled the ring of keys from her pocket and stepped onto the small porch, where a wooden rocking chair sat, its slats warped and faded with age. She thumbed through the keys until she found a silver one, ornately etched and dulled by time. She slid it into the lock, turned the key, then pushed the door open, brushing aside a curtain of cobwebs as she stepped inside the dark space.

"I know it's not much, but if you want to stay here for a bit, I thought you might be able to make something of it," Carolyn told her, flipping on a switch. A soft yellow light blinked on overhead, spilling from a large tin light suspended from the open-beamed ceiling. The stone cabin was more spacious inside than Adelaide had expected. A single open room with a large fieldstone fireplace at one end, and a simple kitchenette tucked into one corner. In the back was a bed with a rusted iron frame beneath a dusty window. Another door, closed, stood to the right of the kitchen. The whitewashed walls had faded with time, giving the old gray stone a warmer, more inviting feel, although it was streaked in places with soot and grime.

Carolyn glanced at her. "Now, you don't have to stay here, of course. You're more than welcome to stay on the couch. But, this might be a bit more comfortable, though, pet, and give you some space to breathe."

Adelaide stepped further inside. "I love it," she said. "I don't think I ever came in here when I was a kid."

Carolyn laughed. "You were too busy chasing butterflies and pretending to be a fairy queen in the woods. Stone sheds didn't stand a chance against your imagination." She ran her finger across the window sill, leaving a crooked line in the dust.

"It's got water and electricity, but you're going to need this." Carolyn held out the basket. Adelaide peeked inside. An array of old rags, a few half-used cleaning products, an abalone shell, and a tightly bundled smudge stick. The smell of dried sage and something vaguely citrusy hit her as she lifted the edge of a rag.

"When you're done cleaning, make sure you clean the energy in the room too. Light the sage, blow it out, and walk the four corners of the space."

Adelaide smiled and gave a nod, but had no intention of performing that new-age weird ritual nonsense.

"Okay. I'm going to leave you to it. I'm off to the shop for a bit. I shouldn't be gone more than a few hours."

"Shop?" Adelaide asked.

"I have a small shop in town that sells herbs and teas," she handed Adelaide the ring of keys. "You must remember going there when you were little. You used to help me restock the herbs in big glass jars."

Adelaide paused, sifting through the fog of childhood memories. She didn't remember any shop, but the scent of dried lavender and the memory of mixing "magic potions" in tiny bottles drifted back.

"Vaguely," she replied.

"I'll take you there tomorrow, let you stock up on some tea for this place," Carolyn said as she opened the door. "Remember, let your hands be busy, and your mind will find peace. Oh, and don't kill the spiders, please."

She reached out and brushed her fingers gently across the broken web that floated in the doorway as she left.

Adelaide stood watching her great-aunt walk back through the sea of grass and flowers until she vanished from view. She shut the door and began to explore her new lodgings.

This cabin would be her transition place, the space that marked the shift from the life she had known to the one she had yet to build. Trading her warm, neatly curated middle-class house in the town she and Jeff had spent months searching for, for this cold, dark one-room shed seemed like a harsh contrast. But unlike her old house, this space was all hers to decorate and do as she pleased with. No compromises, no approvals needed. It was a lump of clay, waiting to be molded into whatever she dreamed up.

The furnishings were sparse, and a thick layer of dust coated every surface. Mouse droppings marked the counter and kitchen table, and cobwebs stretched across the windows and light fixtures like forgotten lace. It smelled of dust and old wood, of stillness left too long. It wasn't what you would call welcoming, at least not yet, but she could almost see what it might become with a little love.

The cabin had three windows: a small one above the wash-basin sink, another beside the door overlooking the path to Carolyn's house, and a large one at the back, framing the dense forest beyond. All three were draped with heavy navy-blue velvet curtains, which Adelaide drew open one by one, letting in the light and revealing even more dust than she had originally seen. At the final window, the one facing the forest, she paused. A spider's web stretched across the glass, a meticulously woven trap. At its center, a light green moth struggled, its delicate wings beating helplessly against the spider's silk.

It fluttered desperately, wings trembling, then stilled, as if gathering strength before trying again. Adelaide's heart ached for the trapped creature. The spider was nowhere to be seen, leaving the moth's fate in her hands. She reached out and began to carefully free the moth from the web, breaking the sticky strands around its paper-like wings.

"There you go, little guy," she said, as the moth broke free. It fluttered in mid-air for a moment, then flew so close to her cheek she felt the whisper of its wings brush up against her as if to say thank you.

She opened the door, letting in a rush of air, then waited for the moth to make its exit. It fluttered about the cabin, circling uncertainly, before finding its way back out into the wild. She stood in the doorway and watched until it disappeared out of sight.

Getting back to the task at hand, Adelaide began by wiping down all the surfaces in the cottage, starting with the kitchen. The first swipe of the rag came up brown, revealing the countertop's true color, a cheerful canary yellow with gold specks. From there, she moved to the windows, scrubbing away years of grime and sweeping down cobwebs. As the dust lifted, the light poured in, the room brightening with each pass of her rag. The work was oddly satisfying, mirroring how she felt about her life. Slowly wiping away the dark residue Jeff had left behind, hopefully to reveal her true light.

Pulling up the bottom corner of her flannel shirt, she wiped the sweat from her forehead, then looked at her watch. Just over an hour had passed, though it felt much longer. Still, the effort was paying off. The windows sparkled, and the cobwebs were gone. The cabin was beginning to feel less like a forgotten outbuilding and more like a place she could feel at home.

Adelaide eyed the door to the right of the kitchen. She suspected it led to the bathroom. She reached for the knob, bracing herself, half-expecting a dingy old outhouse-style toilet. Instead, the bathroom was quite normal and surprisingly clean. The air was musty, but not foul, and the surfaces were dust-free. *Likely spared by the shut door*, she thought. Still, she rolled her sleeves up further and got to work, scrubbing the toilet, rinsing the tub, spraying down the mirror until her reflection returned. She wiped the window, the windowsill, and the little counter above the sink, moving a little slower now, her arms starting to protest.

The room felt fresher, and she half considered filling the bath and soaking her sore limbs, but the dirt-caked floor still called. And she hadn't seen a mop anywhere.

She crossed to the cabin door, and her stomach let out a loud groan. The slice of cake she'd eaten for breakfast was long gone, burned off by a morning full of cleaning. Time to grab the mop from Carolyn's… and maybe find something to eat while she was there.

She set down the rag and spray bottle, grabbed the ring of keys from the table, and stepped out, pulling the door closed behind her.

As she stepped off the small sunken porch and returned to the path leading back to the main house, the tall grass and wildflowers danced in the wind, twisting and turning with each sweeping gust that blew in from the west. It stirred something inside her, and she stretched out her arms, letting her fingertips skim the grass, just as she had done as a child, running through open fields like a bird about to take flight. The soft blades brushed her fingers, awakening a long-forgotten energy. By the time she reached the gravel driveway, a quiet, genuine smile had found its way to her lips, the first since Jeff had left.

Carolyn's car was still gone, meaning she was likely still in town. Adelaide went inside and headed straight to the fridge. She cobbled together a quick meal: a few slices of cheese, a hunk of bread, and a generous smear of mustard. As she ate, she began her hunt for a mop and broom. Her first stop was the small closet in the entryway, but it was packed with jackets, hats, and an impressive collection of colorful, patterned umbrellas. Undeterred, she moved to the bathroom, remembering a cupboard there. It was stocked with neatly folded linens and a surprisingly large stash of Pears soap, but still no mop or broom.

Still searching, though now more out of curiosity than necessity, she wandered upstairs. The narrow hallway was shrouded in darkness, with no overhead light to guide her. The only sliver of light came from a thin beam escaping from the crack beneath Carolyn's bedroom door. Adelaide turned the old brass knob on the guest room door across the hall. It didn't budge. She tried again, this time giving it a gentle shove, in case the wooden frame had swollen with humidity, but still nothing. It was locked. Frowning, she bent and peered through the brass keyhole. All she could make out was a flicker of light, like a reflection shifting just out of view. Straightening, she turned to Carolyn's door and gave the doorknob a cautious test. It swung open easily, spilling daylight into the hallway and making her squint as her eyes adjusted to the brightness.

The bedroom was simply that, just a bed, a plain pine wood dresser, and a rocking chair set next to the large window that faced the woods. Adelaide hesitated on the threshold, knowing she probably shouldn't go any further. The door had been closed, after all. But curiosity got the better of her, and she stepped inside. Walking over to the window, she looked out across the field toward the dark treeline. She could see the tiny cabin nestled at the forest's edge. It looked almost forgotten, half-swallowed by the weeds, and she wondered what purpose it had served before it had become her refuge.

Turning back, she studied the room. Something felt off, though she couldn't quite say what. Everything was immaculate, the bed neatly made, the surfaces dust-free, the dresser drawers shut in perfect alignment. A braided rug spanned half the room, covering most of the aged wooden floor, but the weave looked too pristine. No indentations, no frayed edges. That was it. The room was too perfect, almost as if it were merely for show.

Adelaide glanced back across the hallway to the locked guest room door. A thin band of light peeked out from beneath, casting a faint golden streak across the dark floorboards.

Then, a shadow moved across the light.

Adelaide's heart leapt into her throat, and she froze, eyes locked on the gap beneath the door.

Had she just imagined that?

She stopped breathing, straining to hear past the hammering of her heart, a footstep, the creak of a floorboard, anything.

She stood there, seconds stretching into what felt like minutes, daring the shadow to move again but praying it wouldn't. Maybe it had just been a cloud passing in front of the sun, or some trick of the light.

Adelaide opened her mouth to call out when a car door slammed outside. The sound jolted her into motion. She exhaled sharply and shut Carolyn's bedroom door. Then quickly made her way downstairs, not wanting to be caught snooping where she didn't belong.

She'd barely made it into the living room when the front door opened and Carolyn walked in, with two large bags of groceries in her hands.

"Let me help you," Adelaide offered, quickly moving to grab the bags and carry them into the kitchen. Her heart was still racing, and she hoped Carolyn couldn't hear it pounding as she tried to compose herself.

"Thank you, dear," she replied, sitting down and taking off her boots. "Have you decided to stay on the sofa?" She took her jacket off and hung it on a hook by the door.

"No," said Adelaide, setting the bags down. "Just came in for a broom and mop. But, I didn't have much luck finding them." She'd tried to sound casual, but her voice wavered.

Carolyn's eyes flickered, just for a heartbeat, toward the stairs and something unreadable passed over her face. Walking over to an old beam in the kitchen she retrieved the mop and broom.

"Not only do these beams help support the house," Carolyn began with a smile, "but they also make great little nooks for hiding things."

"Thanks. I'm going to head back out and finish up what I can," Adelaide said, adjusting her grip on the mop and broom Carolyn passed to her.

"Okay, plan on coming back for dinner in a few hours. And there are some things in the garage that might make the place a bit cozier. Feel free to take whatever you like."

"Thank you, Carolyn. For everything. I hope it won't be too long before I get my feet back under me."

"Of course, Addie. You're welcome to stay as long as you like," Carolyn said with a warm smile as she began unpacking the bags.

Adelaide nodded and turned toward the door. As she stepped outside, she paused. Her gaze drifted up to the guest room window. She couldn't shake the feeling that Carolyn was hiding something, and though she knew she shouldn't stick her nose in where it didn't belong, her curiosity was piqued. There was something or someone there, lurking behind the guest room door.

THE HIDDEN JOURNAL
OF JOHN DEE

October 3, 1582

Calibration Log:

- Calibration 287 adjusted to 279.
- Gear 4 repositioned by 1 cm, aligning more precisely with Face Plate 3.
- Saturn shifted precisely a quarter of a cm to the right.
- Device wound with four full turns, quartz disc set facing due north.

One complete rotation of planetary alignments halted at north before reversing in a counterclockwise rotation.

We found the bishop easily convinced of our work for the queen and were led to the crypt without question. Once he left us, we got to work quickly, as there was little time and the window of opportunity was closing quickly.

As soon as the Astral Synchronum settled its alignment, the movement gradually slowed until it became nearly imperceptible. Then, as if stirred by the heavens themselves, the quartz disc began to glow, a soft white light at first, growing swiftly in intensity until every shadowed corner of the crypt was illuminated as if by daylight. We turned our faces away as the light grew blinding, each of us struck by the conviction that we had opened a gateway, a bridge to realms beyond our own.

In that moment, Giordano and I were certain we had succeeded in opening the portal. The light was unlike anything we had ever seen, a pure, holy brightness that seemed to pulse with life itself. With each second, it intensified, swelling to an almost unbearable brilliance. And then, in the stillness that followed, it felt as if the very essence of the angelic realm was descending upon us.

Then, with a single, sharp sound like glass shattering under immense force, the quartz disc fractured, casting shards of crystal and fragments of light across the crypt. We were thrown into darkness, our vision consumed by the lingering burst of light, gripping the darkness around us as our eyes struggled to adjust. When at last we could see again, I rushed to the Synchronum, inspecting every facet for damage. Though outwardly intact, the device now lay silent and unmoving, defying all attempts to coax it back to life. It was in that moment that our hearts froze with a chilling realization: if we had failed, we had done the unthinkable, disturbed the very fabric of time.

We stood there in the crypt, shadows lengthening around us, watching with dread for some sign, any sign, that our failed experiment might have set off unseen consequences. We waited, gripped by the silent terror that we might witness the unraveling of the natural order.

Chapter
Fifteen

PEN – 1955 – HELENSBURGH, SCOTLAND

The trip from New York to Scotland had been anything but smooth, with delayed flights, turbulence, and a bout of motion sickness Pen wouldn't soon forget. But somewhere between London Airport and Helensburgh, he'd found his footing.

He arrived in town a little after eight, stepping off the bus into the hush of the evening. The sun was setting behind the mountains, and the streets were painted in a thick layer of twilight. To his right, a vast river stretched wide, its surface shimmering with the last streaks of day. To his left, the streets of Helensburgh were quiet, shopfronts shuttered, shut up for the night, with only a few stragglers from the bus walking about.

Shops mingled with homes, woven between long hedgerows and thick, sturdy stone walls. It was just as he'd imagined, a quintessential Scottish village steeped in timeless charm.

He hoisted his suitcase off the sidewalk and started down the main street, scanning the dimly lit corners for road signs. He'd assumed the bookshop would be near the center of town, but that had been a mistake. Guided only by the sparse glow of a few stray lampposts, he finally spotted the worn, wooden sign for Camberwell Street.

His pulse quickened. After the dreadful plane ride and an equally uncomfortable bus journey, this was the moment he'd imagined for days, the first glimpse of the bookshop Ward had left him. He turned down the lane. The shops were nestled close, their windows dark; he followed the numbers along their doors, realizing they ran in reverse. The shop must be at the far end.

As he walked, he took note of the businesses lining the street: a leather shop with darkened windowpanes, a small wine and spirits store tucked behind ivy-covered brick, and a quaint little place called the Purple Thorn Apothecary. The name made him pause, it was so close to the name of the bookshop, the Feather Thorn, it felt more than a coincidence. He stepped closer.

The apothecary stood apart from the whitewashed shops on the street. Its stone walls remained bare, their deep blue-gray a rich addition to the buildings around it. Black shutters framed the windows, and a large mossy-green door sat square in the center, making it feel more like an enchanted cottage than a shop. In the wide front window, a wreath of dried vines, moss, and twigs hung, adding to the shop's strange allure. Pen stood there, transfixed. The storefront exuded a quiet, otherworldly charm, like something plucked straight out of a fairy tale. He'd never seen anything quite like it. His mind drifted to what Lenny had said at the diner about magic being in the air here. And standing here under the silver glow of the moon, the shop felt touched by it.

He glanced again. *The Feather Thorn. The Purple Thorn.* There had to be a connection. He made a mental note to look into it later and continued on in search of the bookshop.

He didn't have to go far; just two doors from the apothecary, nestled across from a small bakery, the Marbled Clover, he found it.

The Feather Thorn.

The weathered building rose taller than the others, its stonework worn by time but still solid beneath the layers of moss and vines that cloaked its exterior. Ivy had wound its way up the side and across the large-paned storefront window, as if nature itself was trying to reclaim the place. In the scant light, Pen could just make out the roof, a sturdy slate, by the looks of it. That, at least, gave him hope for what he'd find inside.

The once-rich navy-blue paint on the shutters, window frames, and door had cracked and begun to peel away, leaving behind patches of rotting wood. Damp had warped the lower panels, and the door itself looked as though one firm push might knock it from its hinges. Above, an old sign dangled from a single rusted bracket, creaking with a mournful cry as it swayed gently in the wind, its sound echoing the bookshop's forlorn appearance.

Pen slipped his hand inside his coat pocket and ran his fingers over the cold metal keys to the broken-down door, hesitating for a moment before pulling them out.

What was he doing here? He'd crossed an ocean to assess the shop he'd inherited, thinking he might sell it. Yet, as he stood before the Feather Thorn, he felt he might have bitten off more than he could chew. The shop wasn't just closed; it was crumbling. If the outside looked this bad, what would the inside be like? Perhaps he should have listened to the practical voice urging him to leave it to a real estate agent. Let someone else deal with the rot. Now, standing in the chilly night air, in a foreign street under a half-lit sky, he wondered if ignoring that voice had been a mistake.

He had come this far, and there really wasn't any turning back now. With barely a hundred dollars to his name, Pen needed to make this work if he wanted any hope of affording a ticket home.

Stepping up to the weathered door, he stuck the key into the lock and twisted. The mechanism resisted, forcing him to jiggle the key a few times before the rusty lock gave way with a reticent *click*.

As soon as the door opened, a wave of dust and the smell of aged paper and long-forgotten ink poured out, as if trying to escape its confines. It was oddly comforting, reminding him of the smell of Ward's den.

Inside was cloaked in shadow. The only light came from a lone streetlamp outside the shop's front window. Pen ran his hands along the wall, fingers brushing over peeling paint and cold plaster until they found a switch. He flipped it. Nothing. The room stayed dark, heavy with stillness. Of course, the power was off. Why had he expected anything else? It had been abandoned for over two decades. He pushed the door shut behind him, snuffing out the little light that remained, and darkness settled in.

Pen rummaged through the side pocket of his suitcase until he found his trusty Eveready flashlight. The beam flickered to life, dim, but steady, casting long, narrow shadows that danced across the floor. He swept the light slowly over the room. Shelves loomed around him, their books buried beneath layers of dust, crooked stacks leaning precariously, casting warped shadows on the walls.

He found a small counter with a cash register perched atop, and next to it a stack of yellowed newspapers. Beyond that were rows upon rows of bookcases stretched into the shadows, their contents whispering stories he had yet to explore. Pen's pulse kicked up a notch. He stepped further inside, the flashlight trembling slightly. These books, all of them, were his. For an avid reader, it was like stumbling into a forgotten temple. His inheritance. His treasure trove. Suddenly, the idea of selling the shop felt more complicated than he had imagined. Letting go might mean letting go of something more than just a building.

It was too dimly lit to make out the condition of the books or the space, but the air wasn't heavy with mold or mildew, and that had to be a good sign.

The bookshop, cloaked in darkness, carried an eerie stillness that stirred Pen's imagination. For a fleeting moment, he wondered if the monsters from those old stories might come to life and hide behind the shelves, waiting. It was absurd, of course, but something about the shadows and the silence seemed to breathe life into the books. He ran his hands along the dusty bookcases as he moved through the narrow aisles, letting them guide him to the back of the shop. There, he found a wide staircase that ran up the wall, like a secret path. Raising the flashlight, he cast its beam upward, the light catching motes of dust suspended in the air. Shaking off the ridiculous notion of monsters, Pen placed his hand on the rail and began to climb.

At the top of the stairs, an open loft area emerged, crammed with more books. Only a few feet of the space was visible, the rest swallowed by darkness. An iron railing ran along the edge, overlooking the shop floor below. Pen stepped closer and peered over. As he looked out over the sea of books, movement caught his eye. Did something just dart between the shelves? He stiffened as a jolt of adrenaline rushed through him. Frozen, he listened, but the shop had gone quiet again.

Probably just a stray cat, he told himself. *Or rats.* God, he hoped it wasn't rats.

Maybe it was the long journey, or being in a foreign country, but his imagination was beginning to wander. He shook his head, trying to dispel the tension prickling in his skin. Instead of venturing further, Pen turned his attention to a pair of large overstuffed chairs angled toward the open view below.

He lowered himself into one; it let out a groan, and a cloud of dust erupted, making him sneeze. The fabric carried that familiar musty scent of old upholstery, and it reminded him of the tin-can back in Oak Ridge. He winced at the thought. It made him think of his brothers and how they were faring without him. However, the idea of them at Ward's house, safe, warm, and no longer subjected to their father's wrath, gave him a small amount of comfort.

He looked out over his new world full of books. He'd come to Scotland with a plan: take stock, sell the shop, and have an adventure of his own along the way. But now, seated in the hush of the Feather Thorn, there was something about its atmosphere that made him pause. Ward, even in death, had altered the course of his life, setting him back on the path he had once hoped for Pen, and that Pen had hoped for himself.

He rested his head against the back cushion, meaning only to sit for a moment, to collect his thoughts. But the instant he closed his eyes, exhaustion claimed him. Within minutes, he was asleep, lost to the world.

And just beyond the edge of the light, mere feet away, a pair of eyes watched in silence.

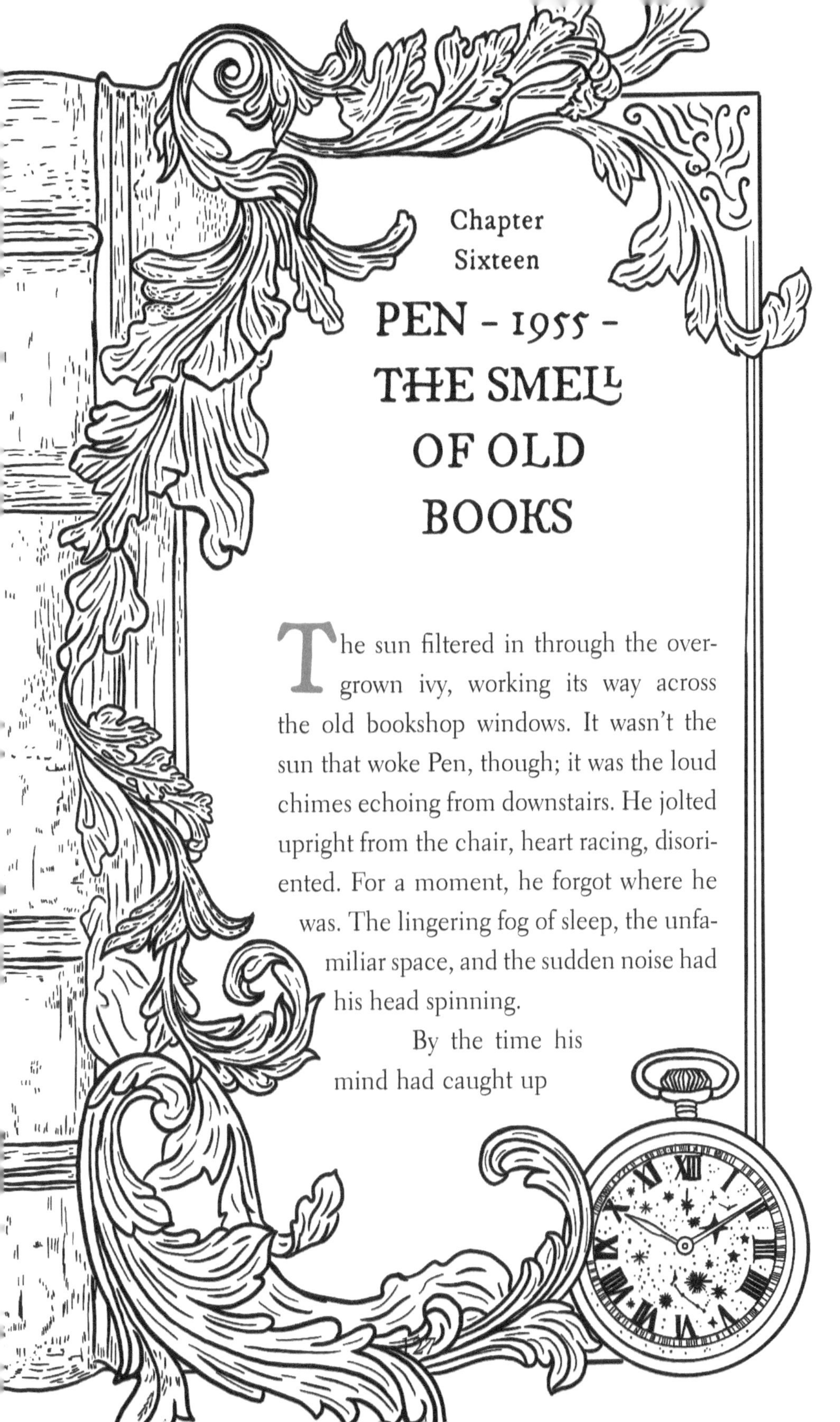

PEN - 1955 - THE SMELL OF OLD BOOKS

The sun filtered in through the overgrown ivy, working its way across the old bookshop windows. It wasn't the sun that woke Pen, though; it was the loud chimes echoing from downstairs. He jolted upright from the chair, heart racing, disoriented. For a moment, he forgot where he was. The lingering fog of sleep, the unfamiliar space, and the sudden noise had his head spinning.

By the time his mind had caught up

with reality, the sound that had woken him was gone. Pen leaned over the railing, rubbing the stiffness from his neck, and peered down into the shop below, expecting to see a grandfather clock responsible for the chimes. But there was nothing of the sort. He checked his watch, which was still set for Eastern Standard Time: 12:21. It couldn't have been a clock; the timing didn't match any logical hour to chime. Unsettled, Pen scanned the room again, more slowly this time, searching for anything that might have made the noise, but nothing stood out.

With the morning light now streaming in, it was the first time he'd truly seen the shop, and the sight stopped him in his tracks. Dust spiraled lazily in the splotchy rays filtering in. The place had an eerie, forgotten charm, as if it had been abandoned by time itself.

The room was painted white, a deep navy-blue trim framing each doorway and window, echoing the weatherworn shutters and front door. Dark walnut-stained bookcases lined the walls and formed orderly rows down the center of the shop. From his vantage point, he could see the massive storefront windows occupying nearly half the front wall, nestled snugly between the tallest shelves that almost reached the second story. Two long ladders clung to the cases, mounted on brass rails, their metal tarnished and dulled with age, yet they still looked sturdy, guardians of the uppermost shelves.

Suspended from the tall open ceiling, a wooden model airplane and a sailing ship hovered above the shop floor, as if forever in mid-voyage over a sea of stories. Cobwebs veiled most corners, and dust blanketed the shelves, but there was no sign of water damage. The books, too, appeared untouched by mold or decay. The shop's interior had held up better than its weathered exterior, almost as if time had forgotten to pass within its walls.

Turning, Pen surveyed the neatly labeled rows of books before him. He was standing in front of the Foreign Religions section, with Folklore & Fairy Tales to his right and Travel Guides & Atlases to his left. He picked up the first book his fingers touched, *Animal Totems*. Blowing off the dust, he cracked it open to a random page. A surge of excitement coursed through him as he read the first line:

In the Celtic tradition, a fox was seen as a symbol of wisdom, cunning, and guidance, often regarded as a clever spirit capable of moving between worlds, serving as a guide through the unseen or mystical realms.

He closed its leather cover and placed the book back on the shelf, a faint thrill still tingling in his veins. He made his way down the stairs, eager to explore the rest in the light of day.

Halfway down, he paused. The wall beside the staircase, which he'd overlooked last night, was a gallery of paintings and portraits. At its center hung a painting of a ship caught in a storm, sails torn, sky blackened, the swell of a furious sea. Just below was a sunlit wheat field, glowing warmly in the afternoon light. Another canvas showed a woman standing beneath an umbrella, her figure sharply rendered while the world beyond was blurred by a curtain of rain. The last of the large paintings depicted a man with a thick beard, an old-style telescope at his side. Smaller canvases filled the gaps: more abstract landscapes in muted hues and dreamlike brushstrokes. Each painting, regardless of style, bore the same initials—CM—etched in an elegant script at the bottom right, hinting at a single artist behind the collection.

Pen smiled as he reached the bottom of the stairs, taking in the bookshop's quiet charm. It felt as if magic lingered in the air, mingling with the dust and the comforting scent of old books. He walked across a patchwork of leafy shadows cast by the curtain of ivy outside, their shapes dancing across the worn wooden floor as he moved toward the front of the shop. On the front counter, an ornate brass cash register sat center stage. It looked to be a relic from the early 1920s, its intricate scrollwork and heavy keys now dull and veiled in a thick weave of webs. Behind it was a wooden stool with a mossy-green velvet seat, its plushness lost and powdered in dust. Like everything else, its true beauty was just beneath the surface, waiting patiently to be uncovered.

Drawn deeper into the space, Pen turned down the Fantasy aisle, its shelves packed tightly. Turning the corner, a sour, musky odor caught his attention, growing stronger with each step he took. It didn't take long to find the source: an animal's nest tucked into the shadows beneath a shelf labeled *Gardening*. It was a tangle of old newspapers, mismatched socks, and what appeared to be a knit cap, chewed and frayed. The hollow spot in the middle suggested something had curled there recently. Perhaps it was whatever creature he thought he'd seen skirting the shadows last night. Now, it was nowhere in sight, leaving only its scent and messy nest behind.

Pen furrowed his brow. How had an animal managed to get inside? The windows, though grimy, were intact, and the door, rickety as it was, had been shut and locked when he arrived. He glanced around, gaze sweeping the baseboards and corners, half-expecting to spot a hole in one of the walls or a large crack, but he saw no obvious entryway.

Following the back wall toward the staircase, something else caught his eye: a battered wooden door in the center of the wall, slightly ajar. A musty odor wafted through the gap as he slowly pushed it open. The hinges groaned in protest, and the smell grew stronger. He found a narrow stone stairwell spiraling upward. A small high window let in a shaft of light that barely touched the first few steps. From this angle, it looked like the stairs rose to a level above the loft, one he hadn't noticed from outside. The shop was already larger than it appeared from the street, and now there seemed to be even more to uncover.

He stepped through the doorway, letting the door swing shut behind him. A light breeze swept past, and he immediately spotted the source: a missing pane in the window. Damp morning air seeped in, and from the look of it, the little critter that had made the gardening section its home was using the window as its own personal entrance. The narrow ledge below it was strewn with dirt and dried grass, a trail of its comings and goings.

Pen climbed the winding staircase to the third floor. At the top, he found another door, painted in the same navy blue as the rest of the shop. Its fancy brass knob, gleamed in the low light, a rich amber color, worn smooth. He turned it slowly. The latch gave way with a soft click, and anticipation coursed through him. This place was a complete mystery, like a Christmas present waiting to be unwrapped.

The door opened into a large room that had clearly once served as a living space. From where he stood, Pen could see a compact kitchen with a table and a single chair tucked beside it. Just to his left, a small sofa faced an armchair positioned across the room near an old-style gramophone, with a worn coffee table resting between them. On the coffee table lay an open book, its corners bent, as if someone had set it down mid-chapter, and beside it was an ashtray, filled with half-smoked cigarettes.

Pen stood frozen on the threshold, studying the room, which looked lived in. He hesitated before stepping inside, feeling as though he were about to intrude on someone's home.

He walked into the kitchen and looked down at the table. A plate rested there, the toast on it now green with mold, edges curling inward like it had given up waiting. He bent over the cup beside it, frowning. Inside a puckered ring of dried tea clung to the porcelain.

To the left of the kitchen, a narrow hallway opened up, and Pen followed it, his footsteps soft on the worn floorboards. He passed a small bathroom, then stopped at the end of the hallway and pushed open the door, revealing a modest-sized bedroom. A single bed beneath a faded quilt. A small dresser with its drawers half closed. The closet door hung ajar, revealing an array of men's clothing and polished shoes. Pen ran his fingers over one of the collars. Everything was preserved, as if the man who'd lived here had left for work one day and never returned.

He turned slowly in the room, the eerie sense of abandonment giving him the creeps. "What happened to you?" he muttered into the quiet.

He leaned against the wall, arms folded tightly. He knew the shop had belonged to Ward's brother-in-law, but he didn't know what happened to him. Pen didn't even know the man's name. Just that Emily had inherited the bookshop years ago, and it had been abandoned ever since. Pen still couldn't understand why Ward hadn't wanted to manage it. Why keep a place that meant enough to pass down, but not enough to step foot in it again?

Pen noticed a photograph on the dresser and picked it up. The black-and-white image showed a woman beaming at the camera in front of the Feather Thorn's sign. Beside her stood a man, arm wrapped around her waist, looking at her as if she were the sun itself. Pen felt a pang deep in his chest. The frame was worn smooth at the edges, the kind of wear that only comes from years of being held, turned over, touched. Whoever kept this photo hadn't just looked at it; they'd cherished it. He set it back down gently and left the room.

In the kitchen again, Pen crossed to the three windows spanning the wall, overlooking the street below. Ivy had crept up to these windows as well, partially obscuring the view with its green tendrils, making him lean to see out.

The street was coming to life as the small shops opened their doors and turned over their *Open* signs. His gaze drifted to the apothecary. The door swung open, and a woman stepped outside. She looked to be in her forties, with long dark hair, and dressed in a green smock-like dress that brushed her calves. Pen watched as she unfolded a wooden sign that read *Tea Blends.*

There was something about her that reminded him of his mother, something quiet and sad around the eyes. She didn't look like his mother, but something in her expression mirrored what he'd seen in her for years: a muted grief for a life never fully lived. The ache for something unspoken. He wondered, just for a moment, what his mother's life might've been like if she hadn't married his father. Maybe she would've ended up doing something like this woman, running a roadside stand selling her famous blueberry pies or secondhand books. Happy and free. The idea left him with a heavy feeling in his chest.

After his mother's death, Pen hadn't grieved, not properly. He'd deliberately kept himself busy, burying himself in work and caring for his brothers to avoid confronting the void left by her absence. Ward had told him to slow down, to feel it, but Pen couldn't bring himself to face the silence she left behind. Instead, he threw himself into maintaining the tin-can, cooking for his brothers, and keeping the household running. He'd stepped into his mother's shoes so fully that he forgot to lace his own, skipping out on college at Bates, settling for the job at the gas station.

Now, standing alone in the stillness of the apartment, he found himself wondering if he was doing it again, running from the grief, this time from Ward. Perhaps he was. But this trip wasn't just an escape. It was a step toward the life Ward wanted for him. His wish for Pen to embrace adventure and forge his own path.

He turned from the window and made his way back down the stairs and into the heart of the bookshop. In the full light of day, the shop felt different. Less haunted. The shelves, though bowed with age, stood proud beneath their burdens. Books leaned together like old friends whispering secrets. The shop seemed to breathe, quiet and patient, like it was waiting to come alive again. Pen stood, listening. Maybe it wasn't some crumbling store filled with forgotten pages. Maybe, just maybe, the Feather Thorn was the start of a new chapter, the beginning of his own story.

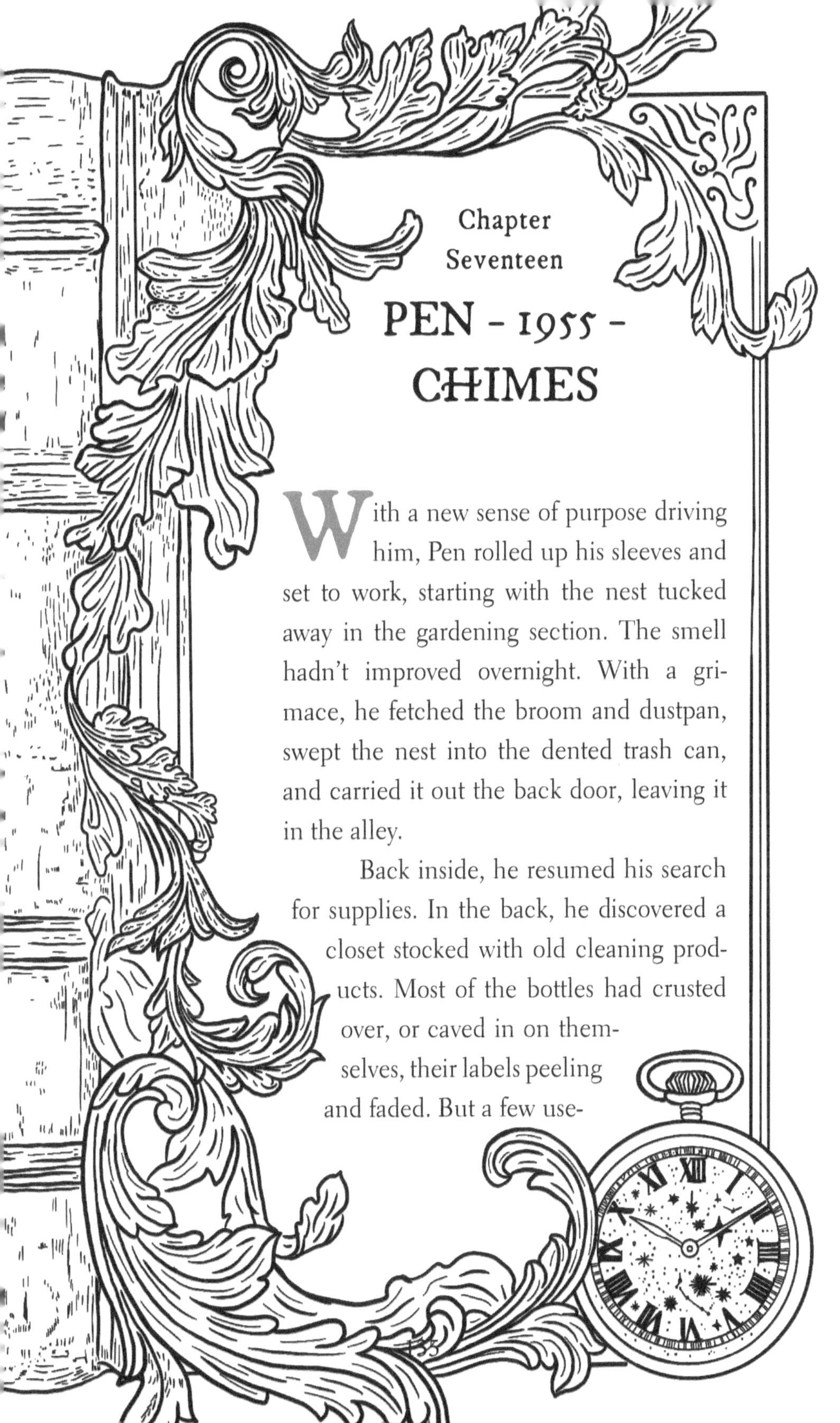

PEN – 1955 –
CHIMES

With a new sense of purpose driving him, Pen rolled up his sleeves and set to work, starting with the nest tucked away in the gardening section. The smell hadn't improved overnight. With a grimace, he fetched the broom and dustpan, swept the nest into the dented trash can, and carried it out the back door, leaving it in the alley.

Back inside, he resumed his search for supplies. In the back, he discovered a closet stocked with old cleaning products. Most of the bottles had crusted over, or caved in on themselves, their labels peeling and faded. But a few useful items still remained: a box of rags, a feather duster missing half its feathers, a glass bottle of bleach with the cork topper still intact, and half a jar of beeswax that still held its sheen. It was a start, but he made a note to buy some vinegar, as nothing else would cut through the film on the windows.

Supplies in hand, Pen filled a bucket with water in the cramped bathroom tucked in the back of the shop, adding just a touch of bleach. The scent bit his nose, sharp, clean, and strangely satisfying. He started at the front counter that housed the old cash register, and he lifted the stack of brittle newspapers, setting them on the stool, leaving a perfect dust-free rectangle in their wake. As he wiped away the years of dirt, the rich mahogany wood started to reveal itself. With each pass of the rag, the intricate wood grain emerged, swirling and shifting across the surface like a rolling wave.

Turning his attention to the first bookshelf, labeled *Children's Books*, Pen grabbed the worn feather duster. This shelf, along with the next one, was shorter than the others, thoughtfully designed for young readers. The rows were packed with children's books, including some from his own childhood, *The Little Engine That Could*, *Winnie-the-Pooh*, *Alice's Adventures in Wonderland*, *The Secret Garden*. Picking up *Babar the Elephant*, he smiled, remembering how it had been one of Val's favorites. Pen had read it so many times he was sure he could recite it line by line even now.

He paused, book in hand, as a knot of worry crept in. Val. The other boys were fine. Dave was married, Will lived on his own, but Val was still in school. He still needed someone and Pen had always been that someone. Val's rock. The one who made lunch, helped with homework, and stayed up with him during storms. Hell, he'd been more of a father to Val than their actual father ever had been.

As he dusted mindlessly, still caught in thoughts of home, Pen didn't hear the creak of the front door as it opened.

"Hello," a man's voice yelled out from behind him.

Pen jumped, spinning around to see a heavy-set man in a police uniform standing just inside the threshold. His stomach dropped. Even before the uniform registered, the tone of authority had triggered something instinctive, defensive. Growing up in the tin-can, cops had rarely meant safety. They were the ones who showed up after his father's drunken shouting matches or when the neighbors accused him and his brothers of trouble they hadn't started. They'd learned early to brace for blame when a policeman showed up at your door.

Pen wiped his hands on his jeans, set the feather duster down, then stepped forward.

"Hello. Can I help you?" Pen said, as he stuck his hand into his pants pocket in search of his lucky penny. He turned it over in his fingers, hoping it would help calm his nerves.

"I received a report of someone sneaking around in here. I'm afraid you're trespassing," the constable warned, his expression stern in a thick Scottish brogue.

"Oh, no, I mean, I'm sorry for the confusion. I inherited this place." Pen walked over to his suitcase and pulled out the yellow envelope with the paperwork inside. "Here. Deeds and all."

The constable took the envelope and began thumbing through the documents, silent as he read.

"Okay, all seems to be in order." He tucked the papers back into the envelope and returned it to Pen.

"My name's Pen Turner," Pen offered, extending his hand.

"Nice to meet you, Pen. I'm William MacDuff," the constable replied, shaking it.

Letting go, William glanced around the shop. "Used to be a fine place, this. Always busy when I were a lad."

Pen followed his gaze, trying to imagine the bookshop alive and bustling, customers chatting over books, children sitting cross-legged on the floor as their parents shopped. "Do you know why it closed?" he asked. "What happened to the man who ran it?"

William paused, as if uncertain whether he should tell Pen or not. "The fella just disappeared. One day he was here, the next, gone. No note, no word to anyone. Just up and vanished. Place was locked up tight, and no one ever heard from him again. His sister, Emily, inherited it, but she never touched it. It's sat like this for years."

Pen's brows lifted. "No one knows what happened to him?"

"Not a soul," William said, shaking his head. "Odd business, that."

The memory of the untouched breakfast, the book left open, suddenly it all made sense. It looked like someone had left for work one morning and simply never returned, because that's exactly what had happened. A shiver ran down his spine at the thought.

"So… do you plan to reopen it?" William asked, eyeing the pile of cleaning supplies on the counter.

"Oh, I hadn't really thought—"

"Looks to me like you're already on your way," William suggested, nodding toward the feather duster.

Pen glanced over his shoulder, then laughed softly. "I suppose you're right."

"Well, I'll leave you to it. Looks like you've got your work cut out," William observed, clapping Pen lightly on the shoulder before stepping toward the door. "Be nice to see this place open again."

Pen followed him outside into the cool mid-morning air. He pulled a cigarette from his pocket, struck a match, and shielded it from the breeze with his hand. The flame flared, then settled. He took a long drag, letting the smoke curl slowly from his lips as he watched constable MacDuff disappear around the bend.

Standing there, cigarette pinched between his fingers, his thoughts drifted back to the man who once owned the Feather Thorn. *How strange,* he thought, *that someone could just walk away from a place like this, vanish without a trace, leaving everything behind.*

Then his mind drifted to William's question. *Do you plan to reopen it?*

He hadn't come all this way thinking that was even a possibility. He only intended to sort things and sell the place, but maybe, just maybe, it wasn't such a far-fetched idea.

What if he did stay? What if he cleaned the place up, reopened the shop, and made a go of it? He turned, glancing back through the smudged front windows. Grime blurred the view, but beyond, shelves packed with books stood waiting to find homes.

But just as quickly as the excitement bloomed, it was chased away by guilt. *I can't just abandon my brothers... can I?* He took another drag, the smoke catching in his throat.

Maybe Val could come too. Maybe we could make something of it together.

A sudden whiff of freshly baked bread broke through his thoughts. His stomach gave a quiet protest, and he suddenly realized just how hungry he was. Tossing his cigarette to the ground, he crushed it beneath his shoe and patted his pocket for his wallet.

Across the street, the Marbled Clover looked warm and inviting. As he approached, he noticed someone peeking out from behind the lace curtain in the window. But as soon as their eyes met, the figure scurried away. *Must've been the one who called the police.*

Still, he didn't blame them. He probably looked like trouble, skulking around the shuttered old bookshop.

As he pushed open the door, a small set of brass chimes jangled overhead, interrupting Doris Day's "Whatever Will Be Will Be." The smell hit him instantly, yeast and spices with sweet undertones of sugar. Pen's mouth watered at the variety of pastries behind the glass display.

"Good Morning," a woman's voice echoed from behind the glass.

Pen looked up to see a woman in her thirties and a man not much older standing behind the counter. They wore matching aprons and curious expressions.

"Good morning," Pen replied.

"American, told ya," the woman muttered, nudging the man in his side.

"What can we get ye?" the man asked.

"Well, I don't know, everything looks so good. How about half a dozen of those donuts?" Pen pointed at a large square pan piled with golden-brown dusted rings.

"Right you are," the man said, grabbing a box and starting to fill it.

"I don't mean to pry," the woman started, as she tapped a few keys on the register, "but did we see you come out of the Feather Thorn?"

"Yes," Pen explained. "I inherited it a little while ago and decided to come over and have a look. Just got here last night."

"Really? Didn't think Rowland had any relatives," the man said, boxing the last donut. "That place's been abandoned since he disappeared back when we were wee yins."

Rowland, so that was the man's name, Pen thought.

"Yes, he had a sister, Emily, who lived back in the States," Pen told them.

"That's right. I'd forgotten about her. It's been a long time," the man remarked.

"That will be four shillings and five pence," said the woman.

Pen fished out a dollar bill from his wallet and handed it to her. "I hope this is okay, I forgot to exchange my money before I got here."

She blinked at the unfamiliar bill, then gave a kind smile. "That's American, isn't it? I'm afraid we can't take that, love."

"Oh, right," Pen said, fumbling for a backup. "Sorry, I should have sorted that first."

"Tell you what, consider this breakfast on us. But there's a bank just down the street if you want to sort out an exchange. You passed it when you came in on the bus, I expect."

"Thanks. My name's Pen, by the way. I'll come back later to settle up properly."

"Nice to meet you, Pen. This here's Dottie, my wife, and I'm Iain. And don't worry about it. We're just pleased to see someone at the bookshop again."

"I always loved that place as a bairn. Felt so magical in there. Are you going to reopen it?" Dottie asked, looking past Pen and out the window behind him.

"Well, to be honest, I'm kinda on the fence about it."

"Aye, you should," Iain insisted. "That shop was the heart of this street. Now, it's just a shell of what it used to be, sad wee thing."

"We thought it'd crumble into the ground before anyone came along to breathe life back into it," Dottie said, leaning onto Iain's shoulder. "Nice to see someone's taken a shine to it."

Pen turned and looked out of the bakery window. The Feather Thorn stood in stark contrast to the well-maintained buildings lining the street. Then that familiar spark ignited within him again. Maybe it was foolish. Maybe it was impossible. But he knew he needed to figure out a way to bring the bookshop back to life. The shop wasn't just filled with books. It was filled with thousands of stories waiting to be discovered and a mystery waiting to be solved. And if there was one thing Pen Turner couldn't resist, it was a good mystery.

THE HIDDEN JOURNAL OF JOHN DEE

October 10, 1582

We journeyed home after our failed attempt to open the gateway between Heaven and Earth. Still unsure why our calculations had failed, Giordano and I rode in shared silence, each consumed by the gravity of what we had attempted. Though nothing immediate seemed amiss, a lingering question gnawed at the edges of my thoughts: had we truly walked away unscathed, or were there consequences yet to reveal themselves?

A week has passed since that night in Dunblane, and at first, life appeared to carry on as normal. But now, subtle discrepancies have begun to emerge, each one hinting at a fissure in reality as we know it.

The first of these was the clock in my study, a trusted companion for years; it chimed thirteen times at midnight. This I could have dismissed as a malfunction or overwinding, perhaps. But when I stepped outside to observe the stars, I noticed that Polaris, a most reliable fixed point, a star I often used for navigation, had shifted. It no longer aligned with the constellation it had anchored for centuries, as though the heavens themselves had been rearranged. This was what first set my nerves on alert.

Then other peculiarities began to creep in, small at first but increasingly unsettling. A servant fetching water from the well came to me in distress, swearing he had seen his reflection in the rippling surface, but it was not his face as it is now. He described it as lined with wrinkles and his hair grayed with age, a version of himself decades older than he could possibly be. In Mortlake's square, a woman stopped me to speak of a feast day she insisted was to be celebrated on the coming Sabbath. Yet no such day exists upon any calendar I know of, and no record of it could be found. The final and most troubling sign came this morning as I reached for my journal to record these events.

Within its pages, I found a passage written in my own hand, yet I have no memory of composing it. The ink was fresh, the words clear, and yet they spoke of occurrences that have not come to pass.

Am I losing time? Is it madness? Or something else entirely? The handwriting is unmistakably mine, and yet the man who wrote those words feels like a stranger to me. I do not know which frightens me more, that I wrote them and have forgotten, or that another version of myself seems to have broken through into this reality.

These disturbances, faint though they are, seem to press against the edges of what is real. At first, they appeared as harmless oddities, but something darker lingers beneath them now. Giordano and I both sense it, though neither of us dares voice the thought aloud: in our failed experiment, have we torn something irreparable in the tapestry of time?

Each passing moment heightens my unease. I fear we may have shattered more than a quartz disc in that crypt. The world around us feels fragile, as if held together by mere threads that could unravel at any moment. It is as though the heavens themselves are holding their breath, waiting and watching for the moment when our mistake will demand its price.

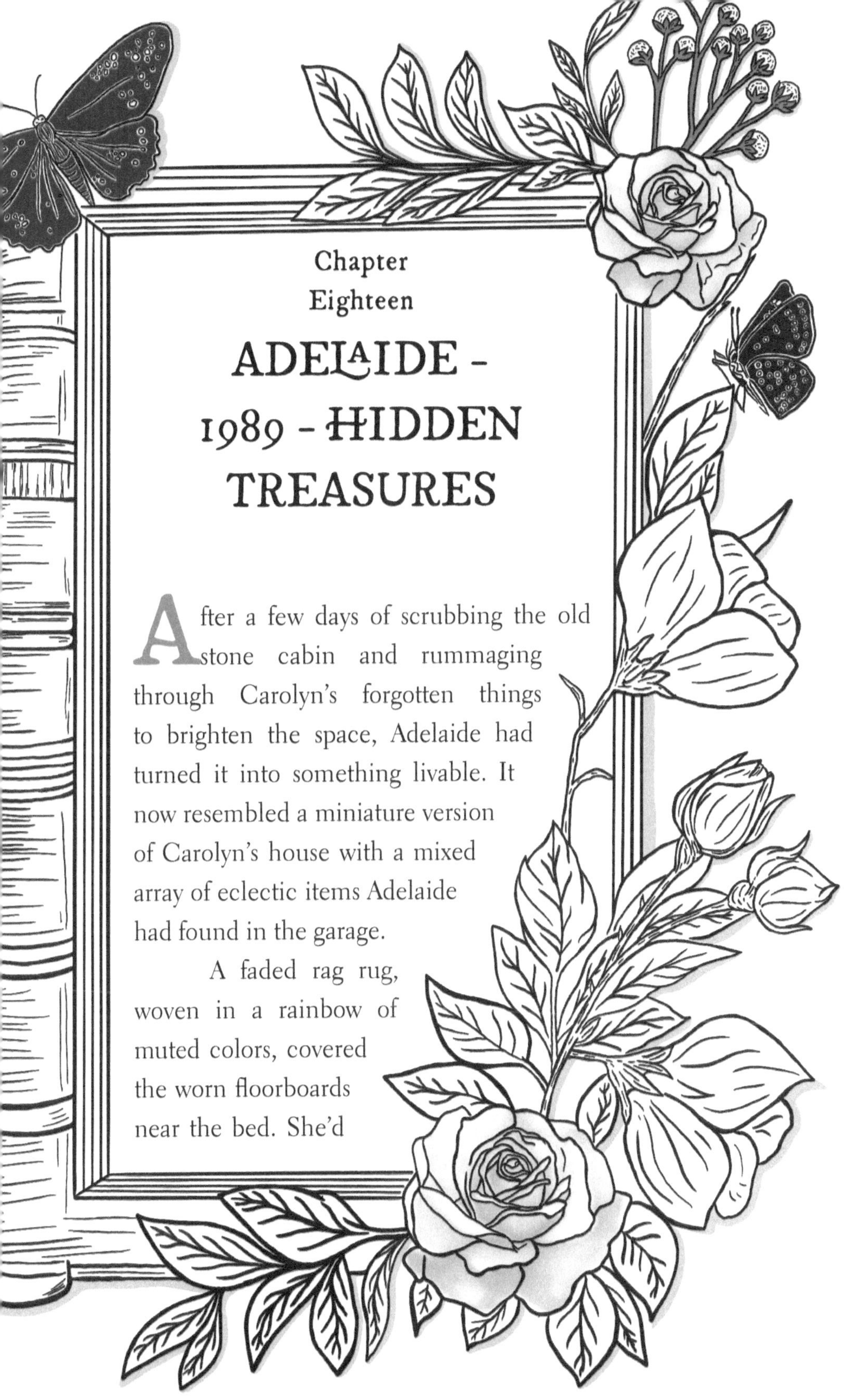

After a few days of scrubbing the old stone cabin and rummaging through Carolyn's forgotten things to brighten the space, Adelaide had turned it into something livable. It now resembled a miniature version of Carolyn's house with a mixed array of eclectic items Adelaide had found in the garage.

A faded rag rug, woven in a rainbow of muted colors, covered the worn floorboards near the bed. She'd placed a purple velvet armchair to face the fireplace, and propped an old wooden crate on its side as a makeshift end table next to it.

Tucked away in the corner of the garage, she found a box with a collection of paintings, lamps, and throw pillows. Most of the artwork was abstract, and she spent a while turning the canvases from side to side, trying to make sense of them. Finally deciding that abstract art was not her thing, she placed all but one back in the box. Figuring it was the only one she somewhat understood, she propped it up on the mantel beside a set of brass candle holders she'd found the day before.

She stepped back to inspect it. A field stretched across the canvas in golden strokes. A chapel rose faintly in the distance. It looked familiar, almost like the one outside town. She looked closer. She was sure she knew it. She just couldn't quite put her finger on it.

Moving back to the box, she pulled out two matching gold lamps, bases shaped like elephants, their trunks raised high to cradle their lampshades. They were hideous, but the cabin needed the light. She set one on the crate table and the other on the counter below the only cupboard in the house. The place had taken on the look of a patchwork quilt, layers of colors, textures, and cultures stitched together by necessity, but oddly charming all the same.

The box was empty now, except for two small throw pillows in a mix of colorful Indian silk. She tossed one onto the chair, and the other onto the bed, where it landed on a wool tartan blanket in deep reds and blues. Jeff would have hated it, and that thought alone made her smile. Gone were the days of matching decor and a well-kempt house. She didn't want mundane anymore. She wanted something new. Something that ignited a fire in her again.

She belted out the chorus to that old Queen song about breaking free, the words echoing off the walls as she scooped up the empty cardboard box. Jacket in one hand, purse in the other, she headed out the door toward Carolyn's house, still humming the tune under her breath.

She'd decided to walk into town today. It wasn't far, and she hadn't yet taken the time to explore. The day was beautiful, the sun playing peekaboo with fluffy white clouds, like those in a child's drawing, that dotted the sky.

At the bin by the garage, Adelaide lifted the lid and tossed the box in. But just as she was about to close it, she saw something peeking out from under the fold at the bottom of the box. She pulled it back out, lifted the flap, and fished out a black-and-white photo.

It took her a minute to recognize who she was looking at: a much younger Carolyn, probably in her twenties, standing next to a handsome man in the middle of a street. Adelaide smiled. She'd never seen a picture of her aunt at that age, and there was a striking resemblance between them, minus Adelaide's teased hair and bangs. She tucked the photo into her jacket pocket, tossed the box back into the bin, and began walking toward town.

Gravel crunched underfoot, scattering with each step. On either side of the road, tall grass and hedgerows formed a barrier, blocking her view beyond, so she focused on the pebbly path beneath her feet as it wound toward the paved road into town. Though it couldn't have been more than a mile or two, the walk felt much longer, and her feet were beginning to ache.

She must have missed the turn she'd taken on the way in. Now she stood at a fork in the road, trying to get her bearings, unsure which way to go. The irony wasn't lost on her. This, right here, was a perfect representation of her life, a crossroads with no clear direction. Hell, she didn't even know where any of the paths led. Staying put felt like the safest option. But unlike the metaphor, this one required a decision.

The loch must be to her left, and therefore, the town center was likely that way too. Just as she took a step, something flew past her face, startling her. A large moth, nearly the size of a small bird, flitted in front of her, wings fanned wide in their autumn palette, patterned like staring eyes. *The emperor*, she remembered. Just like the one encased at the bed and breakfast.

It fluttered toward the road on the right, then circled back. Again. And again. It almost seemed like it wanted her to chase after it. Ridiculous! It was a moth, not a puppy. Yet, she couldn't shake the feeling that maybe she should follow it.

What would Jeff have done? He wouldn't have noticed. Or if he had, he certainly wouldn't have followed it. That settled it. From now on, anything Jeff would have scoffed at or mocked her for wanting to do, she would embrace. She would fall into her own step, and her next one was to follow that moth.

As soon as Adelaide began walking toward it, the moth fluttered ahead, weaving down the street and occasionally circling back as if to ensure she was still following. It veered down an alleyway, leading her behind a row of homes and small shops. Then it stopped, settling on a rusty signpost, the sign long gone. Adelaide caught up, glancing past it. The moth had perched itself in front of an abandoned building, looking out of place on the busy street full of shops that were neatly kept. Vines twisted up its crumbling facade, and weeds crept across the stoop. Most of the front was hidden beneath a swath of ivy, but she could make out a weather-beaten door and a few panes of a window.

"Is this what you wanted to show me?" she asked the moth, which still rested on the signpost.

It lifted into the air, fluttered around her head in darting circles, then drifted up to the building and perched on its eave. Intrigued, Adelaide stepped off the pavement and pushed through the tangle of grass. At the window, she brushed the ivy aside, and, using the sleeve of her jacket, cleared off a pane and peered inside.

It was full of books, row upon row of them. She wiped off a second pane and looked in again. It was a bookshop. Abandoned, as if it had been locked away from time itself. Like a time capsule. Like a secret.

She stepped back. Why had it been left like this? What had happened to close its doors? It didn't make sense. The shopfronts beyond were well-kept, but this dilapidated shop looked as though it had been forgotten by everyone around it, darkening their prim and pretty street.

She stood there for a long moment, caught in the stillness, until a voice called out.

"Adelaide!"

She turned and spotted Carolyn waving cheerfully, her bright smile as warm as the sunlight spilling over the cobblestones. Adelaide lifted a hand in a small wave, then started toward her great-aunt. But she stilled, looking back to where the moth had been. It was gone, vanished, as if it had never been there at all.

Carolyn was busy propping up an open sign outside her shop. In bold, curling letters, it announced the Purple Thorn Apothecary. Adelaide smiled. The name was whimsical and entirely Carolyn.

"I didn't know you were coming into town today," Carolyn said as Adelaide approached.

"I finished up at the cabin and thought I'd get a little exercise and come see you."

"Well, you have impeccable timing. Jen's called in sick today, and I could use a little help."

"Sure, point the way," Adelaide replied as she took in the exterior of the shop. It looked like something out of a storybook: rich gray stone, black shutters and trim, and a moss-green door carved with curling vines and tiny flowers around its arched top. It was exactly how she pictured an apothecary to be.

Adelaide followed Carolyn inside through the door that looked like it could have been plucked from one of her favorite childhood books, *The Secret Garden*. Upon entering, the air wrapped around her, thick with the aroma of a thousand herbs and spices. It was a little overwhelming at first, but as she stood taking it in, the scents began to layer and soften, melding into something deeply familiar. It was Carolyn's scent. The one that clung to her jumpers and lingered in her hair. Adelaide had always chalked it up to some kind of hippy perfume or incense. But now she realized it was the essence of the shop itself, a rich blend of herbs and spices, with sharp notes of cinnamon and allspice.

The shop's interior was just as charming as its exterior. Tall shelves lined the walls, filled with large glass jars brimming with dried herbs. In the center of the room stood a massive oak table, crowded with an array of tinctures, teas, and herbal creams and salves. The shelves were stained a rich walnut color and sat in stark contrast against the whitewashed stone walls. From the rafters hung grapevine wreaths dressed with moss and dried flowers, giving the whole place an enchanted forest feel.

Toward the back, a long counter sat beneath a spray of wild-flowers in a green glass jar, and beside it, a vintage cash register. A radio hummed softly, Stevie Nicks's "Edge of Seventeen" filling the space.

Carolyn slipped a muslin apron over her head as she headed toward the rear of the shop. "Can you work the till while I fill a large tea order? Think you can handle that?"

"Um, I've never—"

But Carolyn was already gone, disappearing through a door behind the counter.

Adelaide began fiddling with the register, pressing buttons at random until one sprang the drawer open with a cheerful *ding*. Relieved she could at least make change, she stepped back into the shop, her gaze sweeping over the alphabetized wall of herbs in their neatly labeled jars. The song on the radio shifted to "Abracadabra" by the Steve Miller Band, and she smiled. The place certainly had a magical quality, like she'd stumbled back into some eccentric corner of time.

She reached for a jar labeled *Matricaria recutita* (Egyptian Chamomile). The lid popped off with a soft echo, and she raised it to her nose. A warm, honeyed scent wafted up, sweet and slightly grassy. She closed her eyes and took a deep breath, letting it settle her nerves.

The sudden jangle of chimes above the door brought Adelaide quickly back into the present and she screwed the lid back on and placed the jar back onto the shelf.

An older woman entered in a wide-brimmed sun hat, the kind you might wear to a garden party or the horse races.

Adelaide's heart rate picked up. She didn't have a clue how things worked here.

"Hello. Is there anything I can help you with?" she asked, watching as the woman wandered further in. Adelaide suspected her first customer might know far more about this place than she did, if she was local.

The woman studied her as she drew closer. "Oh, you must be Adelaide," she said with a kind smile as she stepped up beside her. "Carolyn's great-niece, isn't it? My word, the last time I saw you, your da had brought you up for a visit. You couldn't have been more than nine. I'm sure you don't remember me, I'm Susan."

Adelaide offered a polite, uncertain smile.

"I hear you're staying with Carolyn for a bit," she continued, a note of curiosity threading through her voice.

Adelaide's stomach gave a small twist. Of course word had already spread. Small towns had fast tongues. She kept smiling, but said nothing, wondering how much this woman knew. Had word already gotten out that her husband had replaced her with a younger model?

The silence stretched. "Well, I'm just here to pick up my arthritis cream."

Susan walked to the center table and grabbed a short brown glass jar labeled *Willow & Arnica Arthritis Balm*, then made her way to the counter. Setting her purse down, she rummaged through it while Adelaide turned the jar over in her hand, searching for a price.

"Do you happen to know how much this is?" she asked, looking over her shoulder toward the door Carolyn had disappeared through.

"Yes, of course," said Susan. "She charges me five pounds and one question."

Adelaide looked up, confused.

Susan let out a high-pitched cackle, eerily close to that of the Wicked Witch of the West's laugh in *The Wizard of Oz*.

"Carolyn always says pay what you can," Susan explained with a genuine smile. "And for me today, that's five pounds, and any question you would like to ask me. You must have one, being new here."

Well, that's certainly a different way to run a business, Adelaide thought. *And not a very profitable one.*

"Okay then, five pounds and a question it is," Adelaide stated as she mulled over her options. There were plenty of things she could ask, what people were saying about her sudden appearance here, for one, but her mind kept returning to the old building down the street.

"That abandoned building at the end of the street, what's its story?" She tucked the cash into the register and stepped back around onto the shop floor.

"Oh, the old Feather Thorn Bookshop," Susan said with a sigh. "Sad story, really. It's been abandoned for a long while now."

"But why? Other than the weeds, the inside looks like you could open the doors today and start selling books."

"The owner just vanished into thin air one day. Just gone. No note. No warning. Complete mystery." Susan shook her head. "Some folks tried to revive it over the years, but nothing ever stuck. The last owners finally sold it back to the town earlier this year after letting it sit empty for nearly a decade. It's actually going up for sale."

"Really?" Adelaide's heart ticked up at the words.

Susan tilted her head. "If you're curious, and it seems like you are, stop into the town clerk's office and see me." She gave Adelaide a kind pat on the shoulder. "I'll tell you what I can."

Adelaide followed her to the door and watched her go, a flicker of excitement blooming just beneath her ribs.

"Hope to see you soon," Susan called over her shoulder.

As Adelaide stepped outside, a flicker of movement caught her eye; it was the moth again, drifting past on a lazy current of air.

It dipped low, its wings flashing briefly in the sun before vanishing into the green veil of ivy that clung to the old bookshop. The air around her felt charged, like the moment before a storm. She looked toward the rundown building.

Yes, Susan would indeed be seeing her soon.

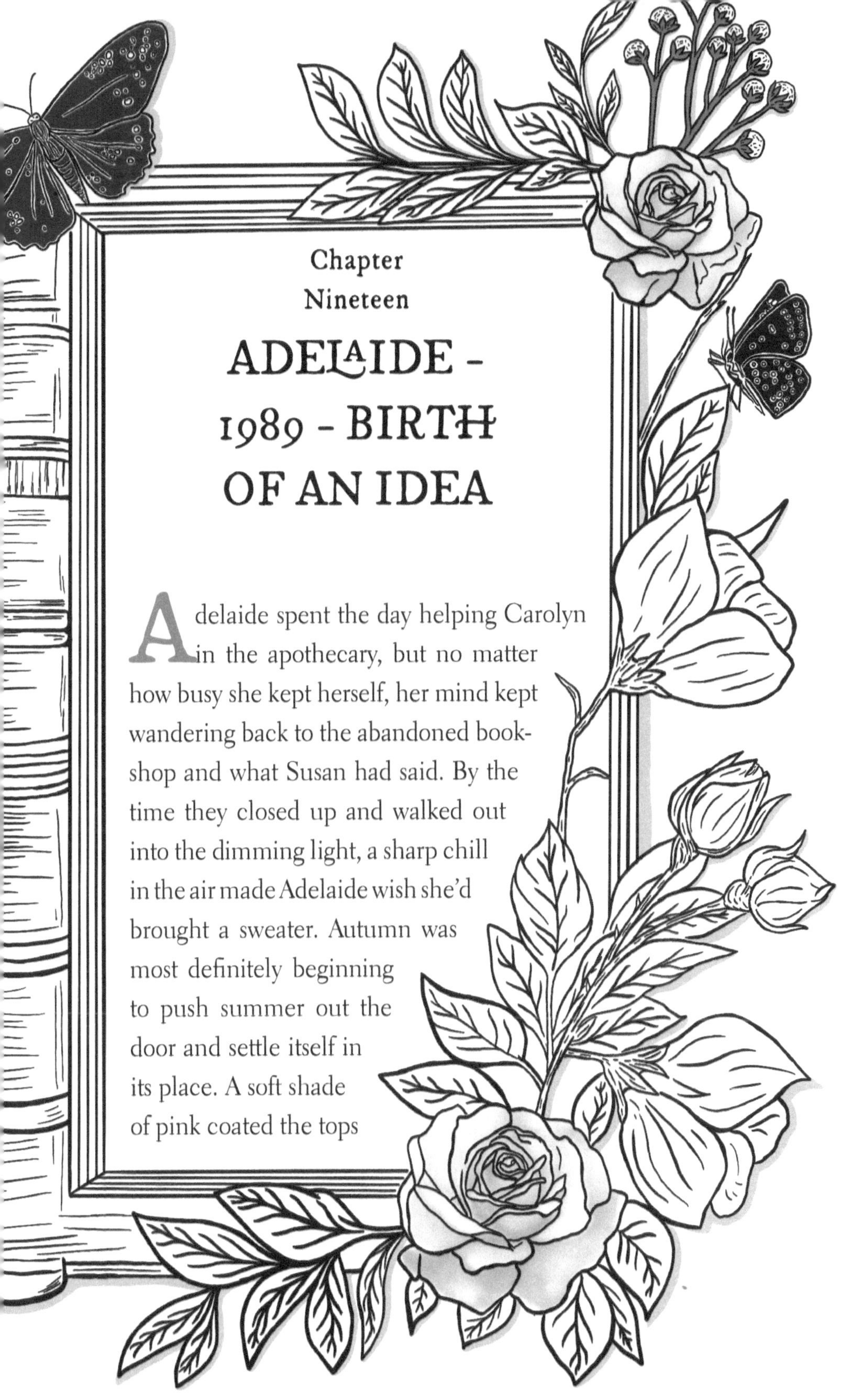

ADELAIDE – 1989 – BIRTH OF AN IDEA

Adelaide spent the day helping Carolyn in the apothecary, but no matter how busy she kept herself, her mind kept wandering back to the abandoned book-shop and what Susan had said. By the time they closed up and walked out into the dimming light, a sharp chill in the air made Adelaide wish she'd brought a sweater. Autumn was most definitely beginning to push summer out the door and settle itself in its place. A soft shade of pink coated the tops of the mountains, fading into an indigo sky where a crescent moon had just begun to glimmer. From the little shop's chimney, a thin plume of smoke spiraled upward, snaking its way into the darkening sky, looking like a lasso about to hook the moon.

A sweet smell wafted past, carried on the wind from the direction of the old bookshop. Adelaide turned her nose toward it, inhaling deeply.

"What's that amazing smell?" she asked as Carolyn locked up.

"That would be the Marbled Clover Bakery," Carolyn said with a smile as she turned to face the same direction.

"A bakery," Adelaide repeated as her mouth watered at the sweet smells filling the air around them.

"Shall we be bad tonight and have sweets for dinner?" Carolyn asked with a double raise of her eyebrow.

Adelaide grinned and nodded; her hungry stomach thought it was a marvelous idea. They strolled down the cobbled street toward the bakery. But as they drew closer, Adelaide's attention drifted, her gaze catching on the bookshop. Her thoughts twisted around an idea that had been brewing ever since Susan came into the shop, and she wondered how much the town would be selling the building for.

"Best chocolate puffs you've ever had," Carolyn declared, pulling open the bakery door and snapping Adelaide out of her reverie. A gust of warm sugary air swept out into the street, trailing behind the chime of the bell. Adelaide blinked, gave the bookshop one last look, and followed her aunt inside.

The bakery not only smelled divine, but it was one of the cutest little pastry shops she'd ever been in. A long polished wooden counter spanned the length of the room, dividing it in two. Behind it, the wall was dotted with an impressive display of vintage tea trays in a variety of colors and styles from the past. But underneath the counter, was where the real treasure lay.

A curved glass case showed off a dazzling spread of baked goods: empire biscuits topped with bright red cherries, golden Scotch pies with perfectly flaky crusts, glistening buttery rolls, sugar-dusted shortbread fingers stacked like timber, and fruit scones piled high like snow-capped peaks. A bundt cake drizzled with white frosting sat proudly on a pedestal plate next to a tray full of chocolate puffs.

Adelaide let her gaze wander over the sea of treats, and her stomach let out a groan.

Carolyn raised an eyebrow. "We'd better get you something quick before you decide to eat me," she teased.

A woman slightly younger than her great-aunt emerged from the back of the shop. She was a tiny thing, barely tall enough to peer over the counter, with a mop of ginger hair streaked with white, braided and flopped over one shoulder.

"Carolyn, how are you?" she said with a wide smile.

"Well. And how are you doing, Dottie?"

"Oh, we're good, keeping busy." She laughed, a sparkle in her eye that made her look younger than her years.

"This is my great-niece, Adelaide." Carolyn gestured between them.

"Yes, I heard you were in town. So nice to meet you," Dottie told Adelaide with a genuine smile.

Adelaide smiled back, though inwardly she cringed a little at the thought of being the town's latest gossip. She could only hope they assumed she was here visiting her great-aunt for a peaceful getaway and not running away from a bad breakup with her cheating husband.

"What can I get for ya?" Dottie slid open the long glass panel of the display case.

"Well, I can't very well come in here and leave without a half-dozen of your chocolate puffs. Though given how loudly this one's belly's talking, we might as well make it a full dozen," Carolyn said with a laugh, nodding toward Adelaide.

Adelaide's cheeks flushed red.

"And what about you, dear, what can I get for you?" Dottie asked as she started to fill a box with the puffs.

"Could I get two of those delicious-looking empire biscuits and two fruit scones, please," Adelaide requested, her mouth still watering.

Just as Dottie was closing the box, a man walked out from the back.

"Iain, nice to see you up and about. I was just about to ask Dottie how your leg's been," Carolyn said to the man as he limped over and stood beside Dottie.

"Much better, thanks to that salve you made me. Thank you."

"It was no problem. I'm happy it helped. Now, what do I owe you?" Carolyn reached into her oversized leopard-print purse, a bag so gaudy, it looked like it should belong to a punk rocker and not an old lady, and took out her wallet.

"No charge." Dottie smiled, handing her the box.

"Oh, no, please let me pay."

"You already did," Dottie replied. "You've paid me in full a hundred times over with that salve. If I'd had to hear him complaining another week about being laid up, I might have finished him off myself."

"You hear that, Carolyn? Ya saved my life from this brute of a woman," Iain joked, eyes twinkling as he looked down at Dottie, who was obviously his wife. Adelaide's breath caught, the warmth of the room suddenly turning cold around the edges. This, this was the future she'd once imagined with Jeff. The easy laughter, the playful banter, growing old side by side with someone who looked at you like that. She bit her thumbnail, trying to blink away the sting behind her eyes. Who was she kidding? They had never been that playful couple. There was no banter, no tenderness like this. Just a fantasy she'd held on to tighter than she'd realized. And now it was unraveling in a quiet village bakery, undone by a simple look. That was never going to be her and Jeff. Not in this lifetime.

"Well, thank you, and I'm glad I could help," Carolyn said with a chuckle, handing the box to Adelaide.

Adelaide offered the couple a thank you as she took the box and walked toward the door.

"We hope we see you again before you leave," Dottie said as Iain wrapped his arm around her.

"Oh, you will. Adelaide will be living with me for a little while," Carolyn told them.

Adelaide wasn't thrilled with her great-aunt's response. That little announcement would surely fuel the gossip fire that was already spreading throughout the town.

"Oh, how wonderful." Dottie beamed, deepening the creases on her face.

Adelaide edged closer to the door, desperate to avoid the next round of questions she could feel coming. Her hand closed around the door knob, ready to bolt, when something above the door caught her eye. A grouping of old black-and-white photos.

She froze.

There it was. The bookshop, the Feather Thorn, in its original glory. No vines. No rot. Just clean brickwork, tall windows, and a hand-painted sign arching above the door. A handsome man stood outside, hands tucked into his front pockets, smiling at the camera with a proud smile.

Adelaide felt her heart stop. The shop looked like a dream from another time, and a deep ache settled in her chest. *How could someone have just walked away from such a beautiful place*, she wondered.

"Those are pictures of all the shops on the street and their owners from 1955," Iain said.

"The one on the right is your aunt at the Purple Thorn," Dottie added, pointing.

"I remember the day these were taken. Iain bought you that camera for your birthday, and you went about town like an amateur photographer." Carolyn laughed at the memory.

"And a darn good one," Dottie rebutted with her own girlish laugh.

"Well, I think they're wonderful," Adelaide replied. She pulled open the door, letting the cool air rush in.

"You two have a good night," Carolyn said, following her outside.

The street had grown darker, and a nearby streetlight flickered to life, casting a soft golden glow over the front of the bookshop.

"What do you think happened to the guy who owned it?" Adelaide asked, even though Susan had already given her part of the story.

Carolyn shrugged. "Probably just gave up and went home. That's what people do when businesses don't turn a good profit." She turned briskly down the street. "Now, let's get going before I eat all these puffs without you."

Adelaide glanced back at the building. Maybe that was the answer. A failed venture. A quiet surrender. Still…

As she lingered, eyes fixed back on the bookshop, something moved, soft and delicate, just above the vines.

The moth.

It drifted from behind a shadowy corner and floated toward the eave, wings flashing briefly in the light. Her eyes followed its graceful dance.

Despite the chipped paint and weeds, the building called to her. Something about it pulsed with possibility. A-Ha's song "Take on Me" started playing in her mind, as she imagined what the place might look like if it were fixed up, warm lights in the windows, people inside. The idea she'd flirted with earlier was taking root, and she felt a growing desire to take it on, just like the song.

"Come on, Adelaide, or I'm eating these without you," Carolyn yelled from up the street.

"Coming," she shouted back.

The moth vanished into the shadows, its wings catching the last traces of light. Night had settled fully now, the town wrapped in a heavy cloak of darkness.

Adelaide turned to go, but paused.

A flicker. Just at the edge of her vision.

She spun back, eyes lifting to the second floor of the bookshop.

A shadow had crossed in front of one of the windows. She was sure of it.

Her heart thudded. She scanned each pane of glass, looking for proof. But they stared back blankly. Empty. Lifeless.

"Trick of the light," she whispered to herself, though her words held little conviction.

She finally turned away and jogged to catch up with Carolyn.

But had she looked back, just once more.
She would've seen it again.
A figure, half-hidden in the shadows, watching her from the upper window of the sad, forgotten Feather Thorn.

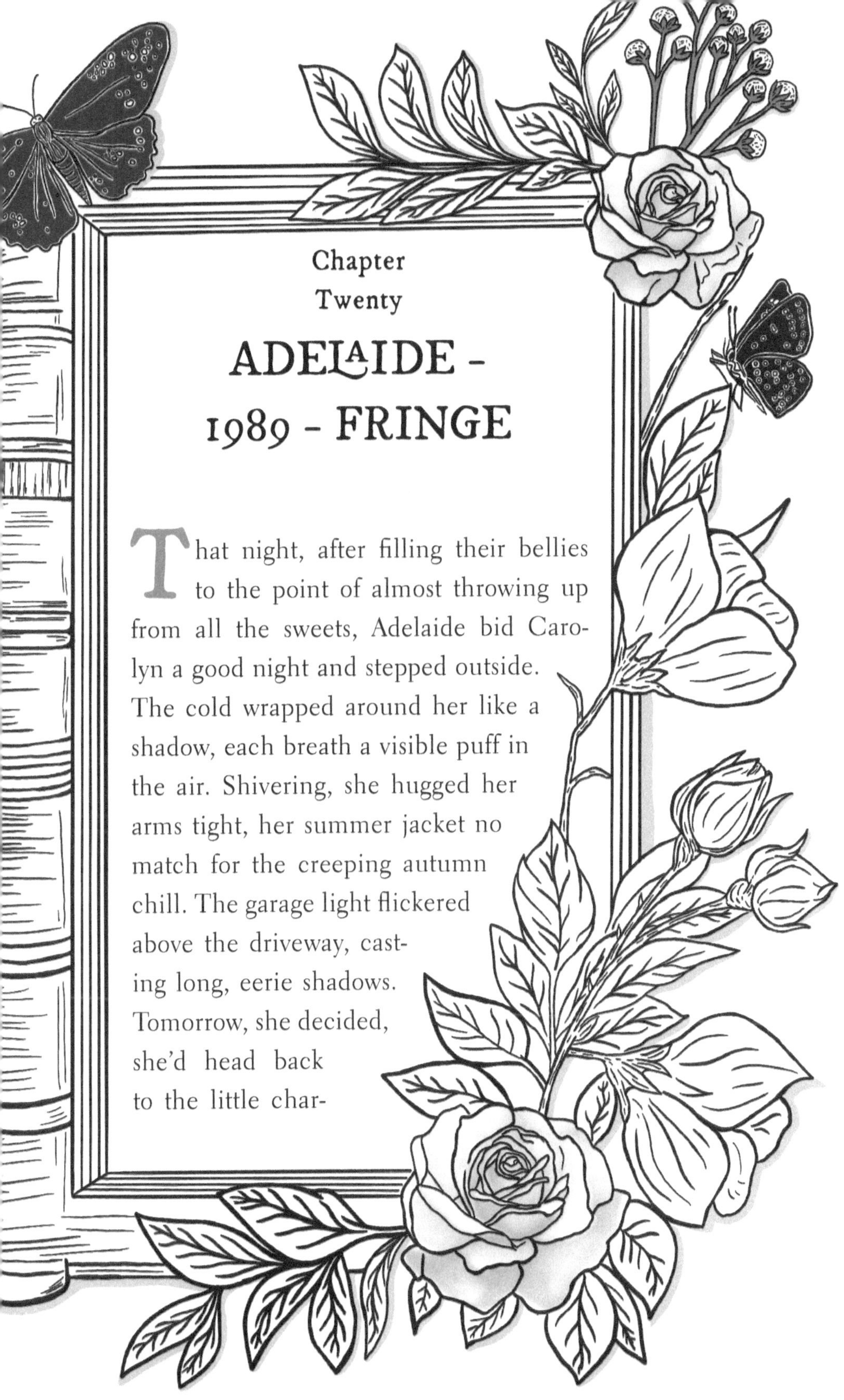

Chapter
Twenty

ADELAIDE –
1989 – FRINGE

That night, after filling their bellies to the point of almost throwing up from all the sweets, Adelaide bid Carolyn a good night and stepped outside. The cold wrapped around her like a shadow, each breath a visible puff in the air. Shivering, she hugged her arms tight, her summer jacket no match for the creeping autumn chill. The garage light flickered above the driveway, casting long, eerie shadows. Tomorrow, she decided, she'd head back to the little charity shop she'd noticed when she arrived in town, and get some warmer clothes.

As she rounded the back of the house, a beam of golden light spilled across the path from the guest room window above. Then, in a blink, it vanished, as if something had passed in front of it. She looked up quickly, heart ticking faster, but the glow returned, steady and undisturbed.

That was the locked room. The same one she'd seen a shadow slip beneath the door just days ago. Someone had just looked out the window, she was sure of it.

Maybe Carolyn had gone up there for something. Maybe. But the unease stuck like a burr, something about that room just felt off.

There was something up there, she could feel it.

She flipped on her torch and continued down the grassy path to the cabin. She wasn't fond of the dark, especially being outside in it. Every rustle of wind, every owl call set her nerves skittering. She quickened her pace, the darkness pressing closer, an unwelcome companion on her walk. As the path narrowed, tall grasses whispered on either side, shrubs loomed high, their tangled silhouettes swaying in the cold wind. She could barely see over them, and something childish and primal kicked in. She ran. Her shoes pounded against the earth, stomach rolling from too much sugar and the sprint. Ahead, the cabin's porch light blinked like a beacon, guiding her through the darkness and back to safety.

She doubled over when she reached the porch, pulling in long breaths. The stitch in her side throbbed, and she felt like she might throw up. After catching her breath, she fumbled the key into the lock, shoved the door open, and quickly secured it behind her. The torch's beam swept the room until it landed on the hideous elephant lamp. She grimaced but flicked it on, grateful for its warm, comforting light.

The eerie feeling clung to her, but only for a moment; the cabin, cozy and chaotic, offered a strange new comfort that set her nerves at ease. It was nothing like the pristine life she'd curated with Jeff. And maybe that was the best part.

Why was it that Jeff was still occupying her thoughts? She needed to stop thinking about him every time her mind stilled. The song "Little Lies" by Fleetwood Mac popped into her head, and she frowned. He was a complete ass, why should she even be thinking about whether or not he would have liked how she designed the cabin. God, he would have hated this place. The mismatched furniture. The clashing patterns. The joyful messiness of it all. But that thought made her smile. Stevie Nicks would have loved it, and from now on, Stevie was her new gold standard.

She wrapped herself in a knit blanket. It was growing colder with the autumn nights quickly approaching, and she didn't have wood yet for fires. That would be something else she would need to remedy soon.

She settled into bed, her gaze drifting to the abstract painting on the mantel, still trying to place the scene. Eventually, her eyes fluttered shut, and the image of the field followed her into sleep.

The next morning, Adelaide ventured back into town. She had two goals: buy a proper sweater and indulge in another of the delicious scones from the Marbled Clover Bakery. The cobbled streets were still damp from the overnight mist as she made her way toward the road that hugged the edge of the loch.

The charity shop came into view, nestled between a post office and an antiques store. A small hand-painted sign read, The

Common Blue Second Hand Goods. Odd name, given the shop's lavender door and purple trim, but who was she to judge?

A bell jingled as she stepped inside.

"Good mornin'," called a young woman from behind a mountain of dishes. She was elbow-deep in a battle to tame the shelves. Adelaide smiled and headed through a crooked doorway marked *Clothing*.

The room smelled like stale cigarette smoke and old lady perfume, making her stomach turn. Overwhelmed by the stench, she almost left until something caught her eye. Fringe!

Peeking out from behind a trench coat, she saw the edge of a caramel suede sleeve. Her breath hitched. She pushed the other coats aside, uncovering a vintage Schott NYC jacket with full fringe sleeves. Adelaide had wanted one since she was a teenager but never had the money. She let out a small squeal as she took the jacket off the hook and slipped it on. Perfect fit. She twirled in place, arms lifted, smiling as the fringe swung in the breeze.

"Class, isn't it?" a voice said from behind her.

Adelaide spun around. The shop girl stood there, smiling like she meant it, her eyes flicking from the jacket to Adelaide's face.

"It is," Adelaide replied, still beaming.

"I almost kept that one for myself, but my boyfriend would kill me if I brought another jacket home from this place." She laughed.

"Yeah, getting first dibs on everything is probably a blessing and a curse."

"Are you new in town?" the woman asked as she straightened out a row of trousers that were about to topple over.

"Just here for a visit with my aunt. I'm surprised you haven't heard. Seems like everyone I've met already knows me."

"Yeah, small town, most of these guys have nothing better to do than gossip about one another. I'm Camie, by the way." She stuck out her hand.

Adelaide took it. "Adelaide."

"So, were you looking for a jacket or did it just catch your eye?" Camie asked.

"I was actually hunting for warmer clothes. I didn't really pack for the cold, and autumn seems to be moving in quickly up here."

"Yeah, last few years the summers have been short. Looking like this one is shaping up to be the same. If you need some cozy stuff, come over here." Camie led her across the room and pointed at a cubby stuffed with thick woollen sweaters.

"Perfect," Adelaide said, crouching to look through the pile.

"I'll be at the till. If you need anything, just shout," Camie told her.

Adelaide eased the jacket off her shoulders and glanced at the tag. A tiny pang tugged at her chest as she hung it back on the hook. As much as she loved it, now wasn't the time for splurges and fringed sleeves. She was too old to pull those off. Wasn't she? Instead, she dug into the sweater pile. Colors spilled out like autumn leaves. Her hands landed on a classic Irish cream cable knit and a gray knit cardigan, clearly a man's, but its oversized warmth spoke of quiet, cozy mornings. She set them aside and found a few long-sleeved shirts, two pairs of jeans, and carried the modest haul back to the front to pay.

Camie stood behind a small makeshift counter, an old kitchen table polished to a sheen. Adelaide set her things on top.

"Nice choices," Camie said, neatly folding each item and placing them in a used Tesco bag. Her hands paused at the bottom of the stack. "Where's the jacket?"

Adelaide hesitated. "It's kind of young for me," she said, looking back toward the clothing room.

Camie's eyes widened, clearly scandalized. "Are you kidding me? You're not an old lady. That jacket looked amazing on you. Go grab it. That's an order!"

A smile broke across Adelaide's face as she turned and headed back. When she returned, Camie was tucking a small slip of paper into the bag.

"Okay, ring this up too," Adelaide said, handing the jacket over.

Camie slipped it into the bag. "The jacket's free of charge. A little welcome-to the-neighborhood gift from me to you. The rest is ten pounds."

"Oh, I couldn't. Won't you get in trouble?"

"Unlikely. Seeing as I own the place," Camie remarked, flashing a grin.

Adelaide smiled back. She hadn't been expecting that. "Camie, thank you so much."

"Us girls need to have each other's backs. And if that means keeping yours covered in a bloody brilliant suede jacket, I'm happy to do my part," she declared, handing over the bag.

Adelaide took it, smiling warmly. "Thanks again."

"Stop in and see me again. Maybe we can grab a pint?"

"That would be great."

As Adelaide exited the shop, she paused to look back. Camie was running the place solo and pulling it off with style. Her thoughts drifted to the bookshop and Susan. Hadn't Susan mentioned that the clerk's office was on this very street?

Adelaide began walking, scanning the row of stone buildings, looking at the hanging signs, until at the far end, she could make out a small wooden sign: *Town Clerk.*

Her pulse began to climb. She shouldn't. She should turn around. Go back to the apothecary. Let it go. But her feet were already moving. Before she knew it, she was standing at the clerk's door and stepped inside.

"Adelaide, nice to see you," Susan greeted, looking up from her desk, as she entered. "I was wondering if you were going to come and see me."

Adelaide smiled and shut the door behind her.

"Come," Susan said, pointing to the faded orange chair across from her desk.

The office was plain and functional, just two desks, a row of filing cabinets, and overhead fluorescent lights that cast a sterile blue-white wash over the space. The smell of old paper and burnt coffee lingered in the air.

Adelaide sat, placing her bag of clothing on the floor, nerves fraying at the edges.

"I see you've been to the Common Blue. Nice little place, isn't it?"

"Yes," Adelaide said, her mouth suddenly dry. What was she doing here? She should probably just say hello. Make some small talk and leave. But instead, the words tumbled out.

"I was wondering how much the town was selling that old bookshop for?" She couldn't believe she'd blurted that out; it was taking all her willpower not to bring her hand to her face and bite her nail as the nerves threatened to bubble over.

"I was hoping that's why you came," Susan told her. She opened a drawer and pulled out a stack of papers. "If you turn it back into a bookshop, the town is willing to sell it for twenty-three thou-sand pounds. If not, the price goes up to ninety-five thousand."

"What? Why so cheap?" Adelaide asked.

Susan leaned back in her chair. "So, it's always been a bit of a mystery, that place. Some say it's haunted, others say cursed, but really, it just has a strange history, what with the owner vanishing like he did. You know how stories grow legs around here. That's what happened, and now no one local wants it. But we don't want to see it torn down and turned into flats either. So we're offering a deal to whoever takes it on and turns it back into a bookshop that brings folks into town."

"Well, I ain't afraid of no ghost," Adelaide said.

"Loved that film." Susan laughed.

"But seriously, if I were to buy it and turn it back into a book-shop, it would only cost me twenty-three thousand pounds?"

"Yes, but are you sure this is something you want to take on? Do you have any business experience?"

Adelaide sat up straighter. "I actually work at the Ladd Library in Glastonbury."

"Well, isn't that mint! I think this just might be a perfect fit if you can get the finances."

Adelaide sat there. She had them. She'd transferred her inheritance into her personal account the day she left Glastonbury. Before Jeff could get his hands on it. She could pay in full. No loans. No strings. Who cared if there were ghosts? She'd take a haunted bookshop over a haunted marriage any day.

"I want it," she said before she could talk herself out of it.

Susan's eyebrows lifted slightly.

Adelaide's heart was racing now, but she didn't flinch. Jeff had walked out and left her in the ruins of a life they'd never really built together. But this, this was hers to claim. And she didn't need anyone's permission. No more what-ifs. No more waiting. This was her moment.

Her dream.

She would no longer be the one left behind.

THE HIDDEN JOURNAL OF JOHN DEE

October 17, 1582

This week, I encountered unsettling occurrences that led me to believe we have indeed torn the fabric of time itself.

A merchant arrived with a letter bearing a crest I did not recognize; inside was an invitation to a town in Britain that does not exist and to a wedding for people I have never met. At court, Sir Francis Walsingham spoke of a treaty with Spain, insisting it had been signed years ago. Yet I recall no such thing, and when I questioned him, he looked at me as though I were mad.

These discrepancies are not confined to people. A book I have kept in my study for years now bears a different title, and its contents have changed. Familiar passages have vanished, replaced with ones I do not recall. Last night, the moon seemed unnaturally large, its light casting an eerie, silvery glow over the landscape, and the sky was an unnatural shade of inky blue. Giordano insisted it looked as it always had, but to me, it was profoundly wrong, as if the heavens themselves had shifted.

I fear we have caused irreparable damage. Giordano and I have worked tirelessly to find a solution, yet the answers elude us. He believes the Astral Synchronum is the key to sealing the tear, but the device remains unresponsive. Our calculations have yielded nothing, and the celestial alignments we seek remain out of reach.

Time feels like an enemy, unraveling before our eyes. Each moment brings the weight of uncertainty and dread. If we cannot repair this tear, I fear the fabric of reality may collapse, and with it, all we know and are. What have we done? What will become of us if we fail?

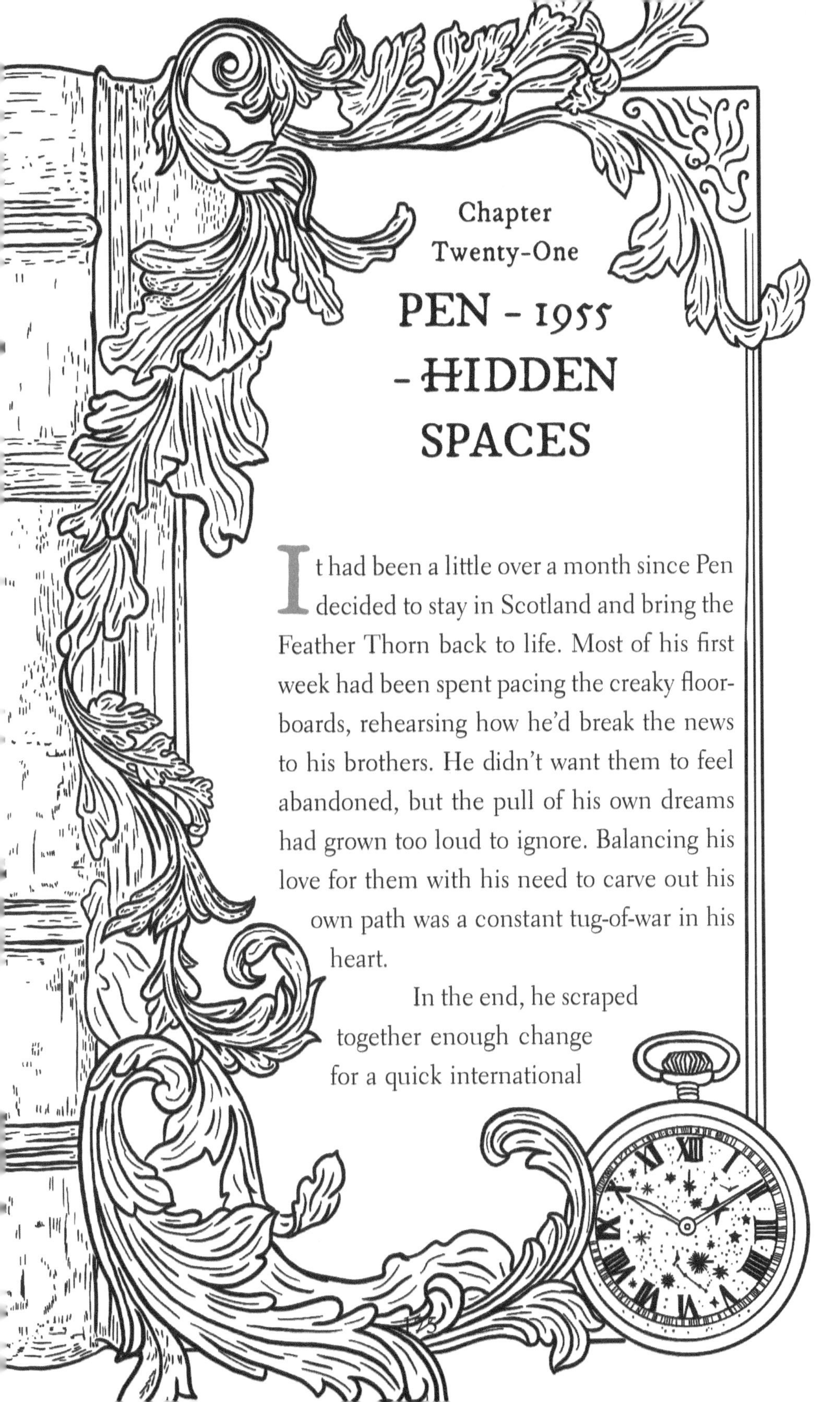

PEN - 1955 - H̶IDDEN SPACES

I t had been a little over a month since Pen decided to stay in Scotland and bring the Feather Thorn back to life. Most of his first week had been spent pacing the creaky floorboards, rehearsing how he'd break the news to his brothers. He didn't want them to feel abandoned, but the pull of his own dreams had grown too loud to ignore. Balancing his love for them with his need to carve out his own path was a constant tug-of-war in his heart.

In the end, he scraped together enough change for a quick international call, three minutes was all he could afford. His voice cracked as he spoke, rushed and shaky, but honest as the truth spilled out.

Dave and Will had taken it well, maybe even better than he'd hoped. They seemed proud of him, genuinely happy he was doing something for himself. Val, though, seemed more conflicted. Pen could tell his youngest brother missed him, so he'd made a promise: once the bookshop was up and running and Val turned sixteen, he would buy him a plane ticket to visit, and if he liked it here, he was welcome to stay.

Nearly three weeks had passed since that conversation, and Pen had thrown himself into the work like a man possessed. The front had been tamed, weeds yanked up by their stubborn roots, ivy peeled from the brick like old bandages. All that remained was one slender vine winding its way up the corner post. He'd left it there on purpose. It felt right, like a thread tying past to present.

Now, late August had settled over Helensburgh, and the days carried a crispness that warned of the autumn to come. Pen's fingers were growing numb as he tipped the last of the weeds into the rusting wheelbarrow he'd borrowed from Tim, the old man who lived at the end of the street.

"Looks like you're in need of this," a voice rang out behind him.

Pen turned to find Iain standing there, holding out a cup of steaming coffee and a donut. Over the past month, Iain and his wife, Dottie, had become fixtures in his life. They'd brought over tools and baked goods, helped haul debris, and invited him over for Gin Rummy nights. They were the first real adult friends he'd made, and he cherished their company and the sense of belonging they provided in this new Chapter of his life. But sometimes, when Dottie asked him a question or Iain laughed at something he said, a tight knot formed in his chest. He kept waiting for them to find out who he really was. Not Pen, the cheerful young man fixing up a quaint shop, but the poor kid from the tin-can in Oak Ridge, who had once lied about eating just so his brothers could have more. No matter how many coats of paint he applied to the outside, some part of him still felt like peeling wallpaper underneath. Like a fraud.

"Dottie and I've been watching you work for hours," Iain said. "Why don't you take a break?"

Pen pulled off his gloves and accepted the cup and donut. "Thanks. Is it always this cold here at the end of August?" he asked, as he took a tentative sip. The heat seeped through him, thawing the chill that had crept into his bones.

"Yeah, it can be." Iain shrugged. "But this year's a strange one."

"Back home in West Virginia, we don't usually get this kind of weather until late October," Pen replied, biting into the donut.

"It's looking great out here, Pen. How's the inside coming on?" Iain asked as he shoved his hands into the front pockets of his jeans.

Pen laughed. "Slow. I might be hiding out here to avoid the mess in there."

"Well, if you want a couple of extra sets of hands, Dottie and I can pop by Sunday, the bakery's closed then."

"I'm not going to say no to that," Pen said, taking another long swig from the cup. He handed it back with a nod. "Well, I better go dump this and get Tim's barrow back before dark."

As he lifted the wheelbarrow, Pen added, "Tell Dottie thanks, will you?"

"You got it," Iain replied, waving Pen off before he walked back across the street and into the bakery.

By the time Pen made it back to the bookshop, the sun was melting behind the mountains, painting their edges with a soft orange glow, as if they'd been set ablaze. He paused outside the Feather Thorn, admiring the way the light caught the fresh paint. It was finally beginning to look like an actual bookstore. All that was missing was the new sign, already commissioned from a woman named Carolyn, from the apothecary. The woman who reminded Pen so much of his mother.

Carolyn had been frosty when they first met, polite but distant when he introduced himself as the new owner of the Feather Thorn, but after several visits to her shop, mostly to buy tea, her coolness had softened.

Pen was starting to feel like he belonged, more than he ever had in Oak Ridge. The neighbors were warm, curious, and eager to see the shop come alive again. Even Susan MacDuff, the sheriff's wife and town clerk, had shown up with a pie during his first week in town.

It had been a long while since the Feather Thorn had last opened its doors, and the townsfolk seemed thirsty for the knowledge and adventures it had to offer, ready to step back into a world they hadn't visited in over two decades.

Pen walked inside. The bells above the door jingled, crisp and bright, a melody he'd grown fond of. He'd never owned much, just a battered bicycle he'd bought with money he'd secretly kept from mowing Ward's lawn. But now he had his own shop, a bookshop in Scotland, of all things. If he didn't know better, he might have believed Ward was his fairy godfather, pulling strings behind the scenes to nudge Pen toward his best life.

The shop had been thoroughly scrubbed during his first week, but there was still plenty to do. Every single book needed checking, dusting, and inspecting for mold or damage. He'd even learned that bookworms were real. He'd always thought it was just an endearing term for someone who loved to read, but no, they were tiny things that liked to eat the paper of old books, ruining the very things he loved most.

At the start of the week, Pen had tackled the children's book section, but the sheer volume had quickly overwhelmed him. So he'd shifted focus to the front of the shop, finishing the cleanup outside instead. With that task now complete, there was no escaping the mountain of books that awaited his inspection. He took a deep breath. At least Iain and Dottie were coming on Sunday to help, and six hands would be better than two.

Pen was making his way through the fiction section, nearing the door that led up to the apartment, when the strange chimes rang again. They'd done that on and off for weeks now, always without warning. No clock or watch he could find explained the sound. He'd searched the shop from top to bottom. Nothing.

Once the chimes had finished their solemn melody, Pen opened the door and climbed the stairs. The apartment hadn't changed much since he moved in. Aside from a thorough clean, he was hesitant to make any significant changes. The space felt too much like someone else's.

What if, one day, the previous owner came back and everything was different? He knew the odds of that were slim, nearly impossible even, but still the thought lingered. Instead, he lived among the relics of another's life, dented pans, a navy peacoat hanging by the door beside a pair of oversized boots. Some of it he'd started using himself, though the guilt of doing so occasionally prickled.

He sat at the small kitchen table and ate his makeshift dinner, eyes drifting toward the book that had been resting there since his arrival. *Beyond Space and Time: A Guide to General Relativity and Quantum Mechanics.* Not exactly light reading. He'd flipped through it a few times, more curious about the man who left it behind than the science inside. None of it made much sense to him, but the mystery of Rowland, the missing shop owner, only deepened.

Pen let the thought sit, then pushed the book aside and stood. His muscles ached from the day's work. Even stretching felt like a chore. He made his way to the sofa and turned on the radio, tuning it to his favorite comedy skit show, *Take It From Here.* The familiar voices and gentle crackle of static filled the room as he lay down.

He'd dozed off for a moment before he was jolted awake by the chimes ringing again, louder this time. Shrill, piercing, as if they were mere feet from his head. Pen jerked upright. Yet, as soon as his eyes opened, the sound began to fade, like someone was carrying away the source, descending the stairs.

He bolted for the door, throwing it open. The stairwell was empty, bathed in silver moonlight from the small window at the landing. Pen raced down the stairs, into the shop, feet pounding, following the sound through the aisles, between shelves of thrillers and biographies, each step bringing him closer, only for the chimes to retreat, like a ghost just out of reach.

Then he stopped. Dead in his tracks.

Under the stairs to the loft, two glowing yellow eyes stared back at him.

There was a chittering sound and then a scream. Not quite human, but close enough to freeze the blood in Pen's veins. It sounded like a child, startled or hurt, and it sent a jolt of fear racing through him, every hair on his body rising. His mind shot to the folklore book from Ward's house, to the creatures from its pages: the Kelpie, the Selkie, the beasts that didn't belong in the waking world. But reason kicked in, shaky though it was. This had to be the animal he'd suspected for weeks was living in the shop, the one that left muddy paw prints in the stairwell, the one he'd glimpsed once or twice from the corner of his eye.

Yet now that he was face-to-face with it, he wasn't so sure he wanted to confront it.

He stood rooted between the shelves, heart hammering, gaze locked on the hunched shadow beneath the stairs.

It shifted. Just a hair. And in that tiny movement, something strange flickered on the floor.

A faint glow, soft and golden, bleeding through a crack in the wood like candlelight.

Neither of them moved. Pen, holding his breath. The creature, crouched low in the shadows.

A silent standoff.

Slowly, Pen reached for a book on the shelf beside him, weighed it in his palm, and lobbed it toward the base of the stairs.

It landed with a loud thwack.

The critter bolted.

It streaked across the floor, a blur of limbs and claws, nail skittering against the old boards. For a breathless second, the moonlight caught it: a long, lean body and a bushy tail.

Definitely an animal.

Still, something in his gut wouldn't settle.

His eyes returned to the space beneath the stairs. The glow was still there, peeking from beneath a faded runner rug. A narrow table sat in front of it, stacked with a few old books, like props on a stage, as if nothing unusual lay just beyond it.

Pen crossed the room and flicked on a nearby lamp, hoping the light might ease the feeling in his chest.

It didn't.

Instead, the warm lamplight only made the glow more distinct, fading it into a fine line of gold slicing between the floorboards, steady and unnatural.

Shoving the table aside, he peeled back the rug. A trapdoor, set into the floor, the brass ring at its center dulled with age.

"There must be a basement," he muttered.

He grabbed the ring, pulled open the door. A narrow staircase descended into a pool of amber light. Looking above his head, he spotted a hook that fit the brass hoop perfectly, and he hooked it, propping the trapdoor open.

Pen walked down the stairs, every sense alert. The glow was coming from a stained-glass lamp, its panels orange and gold, dotted with dark brown moths in flight. Had it been left on all these years? Quietly waiting for the electricity to be restored.

The lamp rested on a broad oak desk, accompanied by a vintage typewriter, likely from the same era as the cash register upstairs. Aside from the desk and its chair, the room held a small shelf on the back wall with only a handful of books upon it.

That was it.

And yet the room felt… wrong.

A shiver ran down Pen's spine. It should have been unremarkable, just another space in the dusty old shop, but it felt hollow, haunted by a strange absence. He told himself it had probably been Rowland's office. But it didn't look like anyone had ever used it for bookkeeping.

Pen circled the desk, pulling at the drawers. All locked. The top one, the side drawers, nothing budged. He scanned the top of the desk for a key. Nothing except the old Underwood typewriter and a layer of dust so thick it could have been a blanket. He sighed and turned to the shelf on the back wall, running his fingers along the spines. Between the gaps. No luck.

He finally gave up and climbed back up the stairs, into the bookshop, lowering the trapdoor behind him.

The shop was still. Moonbeams streamed through the paned windows, throwing crosshatch shadows across the wooden floors.

The new clock he'd hung above the front counter read, quarter past eleven.

Still feeling the weight of the day, Pen walked back up to the apartment, to the bedroom, where he lay on the bed, staring at the ceiling. The moonlight danced across the walls, but his mind remained tethered to the hidden room, and sleep would not come.

Though the space was mostly empty, it wasn't void of presence. There was an energy in there that clung to him like damp clothes. There was something off about the room, something wrong in how it was hidden. The rug, the table, deliberate choices to keep that door out of sight.

But why? There was nothing down there but dust and locked drawers. Unless that was the point. Whatever was in those locked drawers, it wasn't meant to be found. Not easily, anyway.

He'd find the key. Tomorrow.

The drawers were the only part of that room still holding their secrets, and maybe, their contents would hold the answer to the biggest secret of all: What happened to Rowland all those years ago?

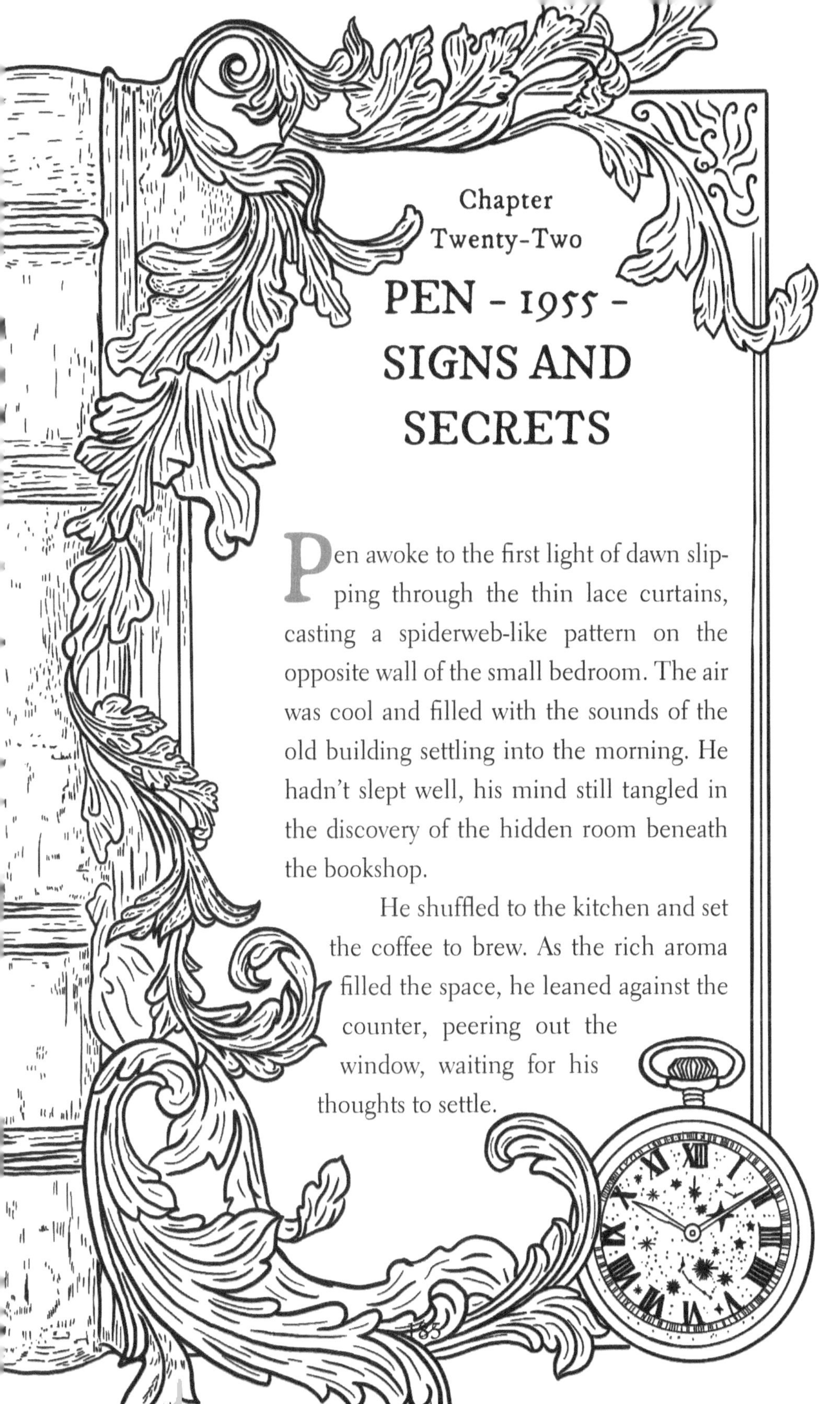

PEN - 1955 -
SIGNS AND SECRETS

Pen awoke to the first light of dawn slipping through the thin lace curtains, casting a spiderweb-like pattern on the opposite wall of the small bedroom. The air was cool and filled with the sounds of the old building settling into the morning. He hadn't slept well, his mind still tangled in the discovery of the hidden room beneath the bookshop.

He shuffled to the kitchen and set the coffee to brew. As the rich aroma filled the space, he leaned against the counter, peering out the window, waiting for his thoughts to settle.

Outside, the street was quiet, the windows of the shops still dark, not yet ready for the day ahead. Across the street, the apothecary sat, its green front door looking like something out of a storybook. He didn't quite know what to make of its owner, Carolyn. Everyone in town seemed to love her, but he hadn't seen the same joy and light in her that others had. To him, she carried a heaviness, one she hid beneath her charming smile and eccentric looks.

Turning his attention back to the kitchen, he made a simple breakfast of eggs over easy on toast and sat at the small table. He pushed his food around the plate, more lost in thought than hungry, turning over the strange puzzle that was the Feather Thorn. He had wanted a fresh start, a place to reinvent himself. What he hadn't counted on was becoming Joe Friday, solving a decade-old missing person case like something out of *Dragnet*. Yet, here he was, trying to understand all the strange and mysterious things that took place within the walls of the bookshop.

He picked up the old book still lying on the table, *Beyond Space and Time*. He'd flipped through the early chapters more than once, hoping something would stick, but nothing ever had. It read like a language he didn't speak. With a sigh, he decided that after dusting, he would find a book downstairs to replace this one, something he might actually enjoy reading.

After breakfast, he showered and shaved, then made his way downstairs. The morning light filtered through the windows, casting a warm, golden hue over the rows of books. As Pen walked through the history section, he ran his fingers along the tops of the books, leaving a clean trail in the dust. Halfway down the row, a title pulled him up short: *Liber Loagaeth* by John Dee. The name rang a bell. Maybe Ward must've mentioned it; it sounded exactly like something he would have devoured. Ward had always loved a mystery, especially the kind steeped in something older than science. Pen could still hear his voice, weaving tales of ancient marvels, Stonehenge, the Pyramids, the Nazca Lines, not just as wonders, but as pieces of a forgotten design. Ward believed in ley lines, those invisible threads binding sacred places across the world. Stonehenge, he said, rose with the sun. The Pyramids, arranged to echo the stars. Nothing at those places was by chance.

A small smile touched Pen's lips. Ward would have loved this place. But the thought brought back the question he couldn't shake. Why had he and Emily let the shop fall into neglect? Surely Rowland wouldn't have wanted that. Everything inside felt cared for, a labor of love, with shelves alphabetized and every item perfectly in its place. The shop had once mattered deeply to him, that was evident. And despite the years of abandonment, it had held up. Aside from the critter taking refuge in the gardening section.

That thought reminded him, the animal might still be hiding somewhere. He glanced over his shoulder, tucked the book under his arm, and headed toward the loft stairs, the place he'd seen it last night. As he approached the trapdoor, the unease surged back. Part of him wanted to avoid going down there, to leave whatever lay down there for another day. But his hand reached for the rug.

A knock at the front of the shop stopped him. He let go of the fabric, ensured it covered the hidden entrance, and moved the table back on top of it.

The knock came again, firmer this time. He hurried to the front of the shop. Standing on the other side of the paned glass was Carolyn, holding a large wrapped parcel.

"Good morning," Pen said, slightly out of breath as he opened the door.

Carolyn's eyes narrowed a little. "Good morning. I just wanted to drop this off. It's the sign."

Pen accepted the parcel and smiled. "Perfect timing. I'm hoping to open tomorrow. Iain and Dottie are coming over later to help with some last-minute tasks. Come in, and I'll get you the money for this."

He stepped aside, motioning her in, but Carolyn's gaze lingered on the shop's interior, a look of apprehension creasing her brow.

"Thanks, but I have errands to run. You can pay me later," she told him quickly, already turning away.

Pen watched as she hurried back down the street. It wasn't the first time she'd refused to step inside. He couldn't understand why. Was it the mess? The dust? Or was there something else about the Feather Thorn that made her wary?

Turning back to the parcel, he peeled back the wrapping to reveal a sign. It was beautiful. Painted in a deep navy blue that matched the door and trim of the shop, a single feather stretched across the center, delicate moth wings fanned out behind it. *Feather Thorn* arched in gold script across the top, with *Books* elegantly lettered below. Carolyn had clearly poured care into every detail. Pen frowned. The feather made sense, but the moth wings, why those? They felt out of place. He'd given her full creative freedom, though, so he wasn't going to nitpick now.

He leaned the sign gently against the wall and decided to do some dusting. As he reached the first shelf, that now-familiar sound broke the stillness, the soft, haunting chimes filling the air. He paused, listening. The sound shifted as he moved, almost as if it were following him. Or leading him. He stepped cautiously across the shop, weaving between shelves until he reached the trapdoor.

The chimes grew louder.

Of course. They had been coming from *there* this entire time.

He pushed the table aside, rolled the rug back, and grasped the brass ring. The trapdoor creaked open, revealing the narrow staircase leading into the dark room below. His heart raced as he descended, taking the stairs two at a time, chasing the melody before it disappeared again.

However, the chimes continued, louder now, more insistent. He stumbled through the dark, arms outstretched, groping for the desk. His fingers found the lamp's switch, and with a click, light chased the shadows back.

Rounding the back of the desk, he yanked at a drawer, the one the sound was coming from but it wouldn't budge. He'd forgotten it was locked. Frustrated but determined, Pen jogged upstairs and rummaged through the tin can of pens on the counter until his hand closed around a silver letter opener.

Back in the basement, he wedged it into the drawer seam and tried to pry it open.

The drawer held firm.

The chimes vibrated softly through the wood, taunting him, teasing him. So close, he was so close to finally figuring out what had been causing the incessant chiming all these weeks. But the letter opener was no match for the old-world craftsmanship.

With a sigh, he set it aside and began searching again. The key had to be here somewhere. He flipped through the books on the small shelf once again, then went back to the desk and lifted the typewriter, peering beneath.

Just then, the jingle of the shop's doorbells echoed from the room above.

Pen set the typewriter down. He headed up the stairs, tugged the trapdoor shut, and slid the rug back over it. For now, he wasn't ready to share this secret. Not yet.

Rounding the corner, he found Iain and Dottie by the door, slipping off their coats.

"Hey, you two," he greeted, a wide smile spreading across his face. It felt good to have company, especially after the maddening day he'd had so far.

"Okay, put us to work," Dottie said with a cheerful smile as she handed Pen a box. He flipped it open and grinned. Cinnamon donuts, his favorite.

"Thanks, guess I know what I'm having for dinner tonight," he joked, holding the box close as they walked farther into the shop. The sun was already dipping behind the buildings, shadows curling at the edges of the room. Pen turned on the overhead lights, flooding the shelves with light. Hopefully, whatever animal had been creeping around last night had made its exit; he didn't want to scare his help off.

"Right," Pen said, handing each of them a duster. "Every book needs to be pulled out, dusted off, and checked for mold or bookworms. If you find either, just put it on the stack by the counter."

"Got it. Where do you want us to start?" Iain asked, twirling his duster like a baton.

"I've almost finished this section down here," Pen replied, waving toward the large row of books under the loft area. "Still need to tackle the ones in the back and all the books in the loft."

"I'll take the loft, and the pair of ye work on the rest down here," Dottie called, heading for the stairs.

"You have no idea how much this means to me. I owe you guys, big time," Pen said.

"Yeah, you do." Iain laughed, clapping Pen on the back.

"Do ye have a radio in here?" Dottie yelled down from above. "This would be a damn sight easier with a little music."

Pen walked over to the large radio behind the desk, flipped it on, and turned the dial until he found a station playing "Rock Around the Clock" by Bill Haley. Cranking up the volume, he heard Dottie shout from above, "Now we're talking!"

They worked for what felt like hours, pulling books from shelves, dusting and inspecting them as the radio played the top one hundred hits of 1955. The pile of unsellable books grew slowly but steadily, and a knot of worry twisted in the pit of Pen's stomach; he didn't have the funds to replace them.

"I think you might have a problem here, Pen," Iain said, pointing to a stretch of biographies streaked with a thin layer of mold. Pen noticed a small hairline crack in the window nearby, just enough for the moisture to seep in.

"Thanks for catching those," Pen replied, gathering the books and carrying them to the discard pile. Among the casualties: Neville Chamberlain, Giordano Bruno, Michelangelo, and Robert Lewis Stevenson.

"I'm surprised the rest are in such good shape, all things considered," Iain observed, joining Pen at the front of the shop.

Pen opened the donut box and offered one to Iain.

"Don't mind if I do."

"Iain," Pen began, "can I ask you something?"

"Sure."

"What do you remember about Rowland, the guy who used to own this place?"

Iain chewed thoughtfully before answering. "Bits and pieces. I was still a bairn when he disappeared. He was around your age when he opened this place. His great-uncle left it to him. The building had been sitting empty for years, but Rowland brought it back to life by turning it into the Feather Thorn. Spent almost every waking hour here, unless he was with Carolyn."

"Carolyn from the apothecary?" Pen blinked. "Really?"

"Yes. They were madly in love," Dottie interjected as she joined them.

"So, what happened to him?" Pen asked.

"No one really knows," Iain answered. "Carolyn got sick with tuberculosis, nearly died. Some say Rowland ran away to avoid getting sick, others say he blamed himself for her sickness."

"The apartment upstairs looked like someone just stepped out for a moment and never came back." Pen's voice lowered. "There was still food on the table. Tea in the cup. Even a book open on the coffee table."

Iain gave a half-shrug. "People do strange things under pressure. Maybe he just snapped, packed up what he needed, and left."

Dottie shot him a look, then turned to Pen. "From what I remember hearing my parents say, Rowland wasn't the type to just leave. Not like that when Carolyn was so ill. They were inseparable. Even named their businesses after each other."

Pen nodded slowly. That explained the similar names and Carolyn's reluctance to set foot inside the shop. "She must have so many memories tied to this place," he murmured.

Dottie lowered her voice as her eyes swept the room. "I think something happened to him. Something strange."

"Oh, Dottie," Iain scolded, chuckling, "you need to stop reading those mystery novels. Sometimes the truth is hard, and sometimes people aren't as strong as we think."

"Nope. The truth is strange. No one saw him leave. Not even a goodbye. Didn't even take the cash from the till. That doesn't sound like someone who just gave up," Dottie countered.

Pen was quiet, a chill brushing the back of his neck. The idea of Rowland vanishing without a trace gnawed at him. He couldn't help thinking of the basement room. And felt a jolt of relief that he hadn't found Rowland's body down there.

"Alright," Dottie said, clapping. "Enough spooky talk. Let's get back to it. I'm almost done. I think you'll be able to open those doors tomorrow, after all," she added, climbing the stairs again.

Pen gave a small nod, about to reply, when the chimes began.

The sound rang through the shop, sharp, deliberate notes, each one more jarring than the last. They echoed off the walls and vibrated deep in his chest like a tuning fork struck too hard.

He looked at Iain. Then at Dottie.

Neither one so much as blinked.

"Do you—" he started. But they didn't look at him. Didn't react at all.

They just kept working. Like nothing was happening.

The chimes kept going. Loud. Clear. Unmistakable.

Pen's heart picked up speed, his mouth going dry. "Dottie?" he asked, louder now. "Iain?"

They both looked up, but only at the sound of his voice, not the chimes.

Dottie tilted her head. "Everything alright?"

Pen swallowed hard, scanning their faces for even the slightest recognition. "You don't hear that?" he asked. "The chimes?"

Iain raised a brow. "What chimes?"

Pen stared at them. The sound still ringing in his ears, echoing across the shop, as clear as day.

But they didn't hear it.

And he didn't know what was worse, that they hadn't heard the chimes, or the creeping thought that maybe they'd never been real to begin with.

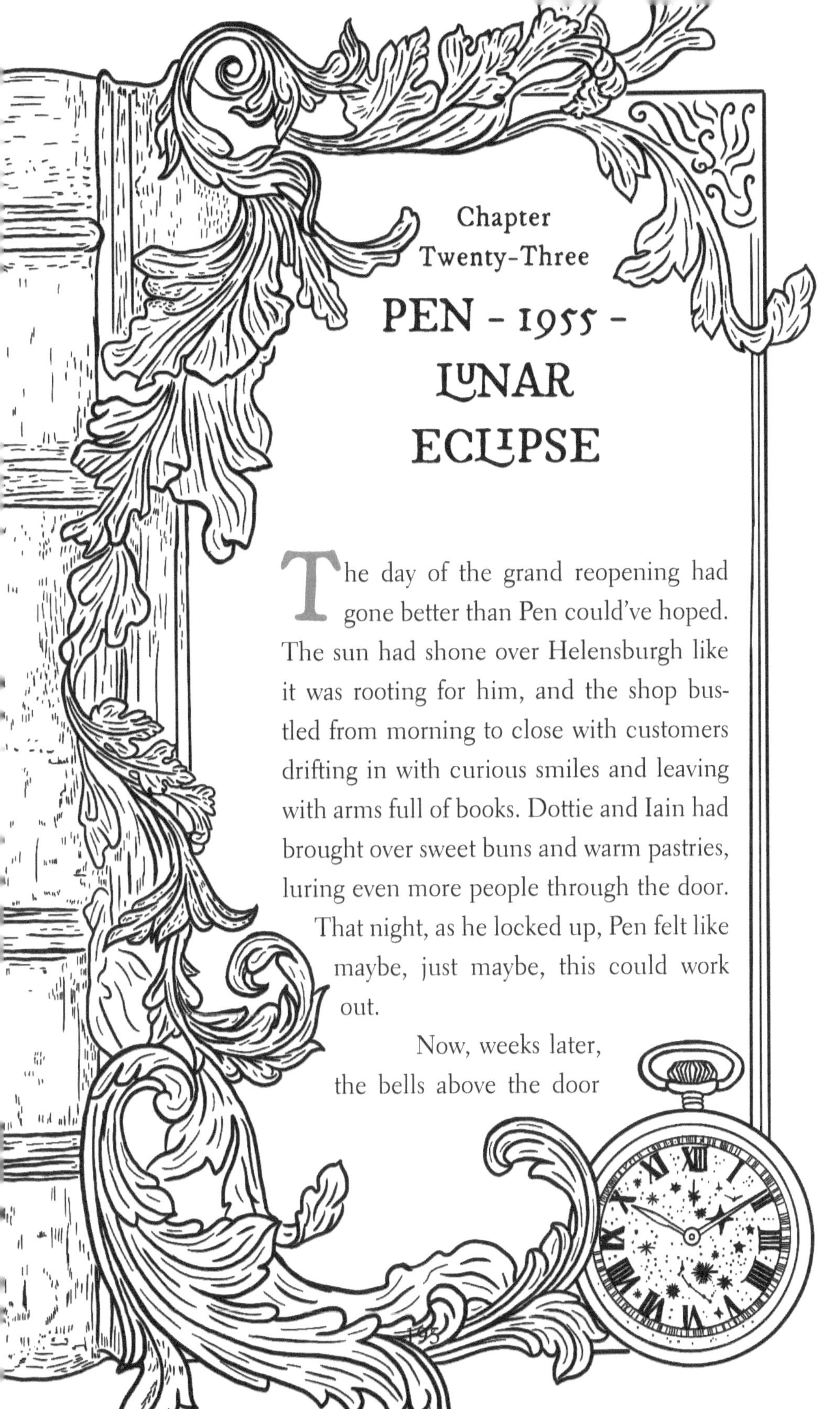

PEN - 1955 - LUNAR ECLIPSE

The day of the grand reopening had gone better than Pen could've hoped. The sun had shone over Helensburgh like it was rooting for him, and the shop bustled from morning to close with customers drifting in with curious smiles and leaving with arms full of books. Dottie and Iain had brought over sweet buns and warm pastries, luring even more people through the door.

That night, as he locked up, Pen felt like maybe, just maybe, this could work out.

Now, weeks later, the bells above the door

of the Feather Thorn still chimed steadily through the day, bringing with them a stream of customers, which kept him busy and brought in enough money to place his first order of new books. The townspeople, it seemed, had missed their bookshop.

Still, a thought needled at him. How many had come because of the books, and how many just wanted to stand in the shop where a man had vanished? Pen didn't blame them, though. Curiosity had its own gravity. But one absence was louder than all the chatter.

Carolyn. She hadn't come in. Not once. Not even when she passed by. After what Iain and Dottie had told him, it did make sense. Grief didn't always show up in tears; it sometimes just avoided doorways. Still, Pen found himself glancing toward the apothecary each morning, wondering.

As the days passed, the mysteries started to lose their grip. The drawers in the desk remained locked. The chimes, in their strange, solitary notes, hadn't rung since the day Dottie and Iain had helped clean the books. Maybe they'd been nothing. A trick of the mind from too much stress, or an overactive imagination. And that was for the best. Now, he had more important things to occupy his mind.

It was just past four when Pen began his usual end-of-day routine, shelving books, wiping down the counter, when the bells above the door rang out. He looked up and made his way to the front. There, standing in front of the fantasy section, was Carolyn.

"Carolyn, how are you?" Pen approached her with a tentative smile.

"Afternoon, Pen." Her tone was clipped, eyes moving quickly, brushing over bookshelves and the corners of the room, as though searching for something, or someone. Her gaze flicked toward the stairs, to the paintings, and then to him. An unreadable expression passed across her face.

"I'm sorry it's taken me this long to come by," she said, a sigh escaping her. "I expect you've heard all the tales by now." She looked tired in the golden light, and not the kind of tired that sleep cures. The kind that seeps in when years pass and questions outlast the people who can answer them. The lines on her face seemed to deepen, casting shadows that made her appear far older than her forty years.

Not knowing how to respond, Pen simply nodded.

"It's been a long time since I was last in here." Carolyn's gaze swept across the room once more. "You've done well."

Pen rubbed the back of his neck, glancing up at the model airplane and ship suspended from the ceiling above them. "Well, I kept most things the same, really. Just gave the place a good clean." He could only imagine how she must be feeling, stepping into this preserved time capsule, full of memories she probably didn't want to revisit.

"Feel free to have a look around," he offered, gesturing toward the shelves.

"Thank you, but I'm here for a book," she told him.

That caught him off guard. "Oh? Any book in particular?"

"*De Magia*' by Giordano Bruno." Her fingernail tapped against her thumbnail, a nervous tic betraying her cool demeanor.

"Hmm, not sure off the top of my head. Any idea which section it might be in?"

"Spirituality and religion."

"Right, that's just—" He swallowed the rest of his sentence as she brushed past him and began up the stairs.

"I know where it is," she snapped.

For a moment, Pen felt like he'd become the stranger here, an outsider occupying a place that hadn't really been his to begin with.

She paused halfway up, her gaze fixed on the paintings hanging along the wall. Her fingers lightly brushed the edge of a frame.

The paintings. They lined the stairwell, familiar to him now; he'd passed them every day without a second thought. Then his eyes shifted to the small initials in the corner of the nearest canvas: *CM.*

His breath caught. *Carolyn McGregor.*

She had painted them. All of them.

These weren't just fixtures, these paintings were hers. Her past. Her hands. Her history with Rowland, hanging on the walls of this place. He'd kept them on display, thinking them part of the shop's charm. Now they felt more intimate, a story that wasn't his to preserve.

He considered asking her if she'd like them taken down. Or moved to the apothecary. But the moment didn't seem right. She had made it through the door; that alone had probably taken more strength than she wanted anyone to notice. So he stayed quiet.

As she disappeared around the landing, Pen's gaze dropped instinctively to the trapdoor beneath the rug. Did she know about it? About the room below, and the locked desk? Did she know what the chimes were coming from? His curiosity stirred, but he tamped it down. Not now. Not tonight.

When Carolyn didn't immediately return with the book, he resumed closing up the shop and began logging the day's sales. The scratch of his pen was the only sound in the room. Until he heard her footsteps on the stairs.

"Did you find it?" Pen asked, glancing up from his writing as Carolyn approached the counter. He hadn't cataloged all the inventory yet, but he did remember seeing something of the sort up there.

"No," she said, placing a book on the counter, "but I'll take this." *The Principles of Astronomy* by George E. Hale and William W. Campbell.

Pen raised an eyebrow. "Interesting choice." He hadn't taken Carolyn for the scientific type; he'd imagined her leaning more toward the mystical, the unconventional. But astronomy did have its mysteries, too. Maybe that's what drew her in.

"I figured it would be a good read with the eclipse tonight and all."

"Eclipse?" Pen vaguely remembered reading about them back in high school, but he'd never actually seen one.

"Yes," she answered. "There's a lunar eclipse tonight." She spoke absently, gaze drifting, somewhere far beyond the bookshop walls. "How much do I owe you?"

"No charge," Pen said with a smile, wrapping the book and placing it into a paper bag.

"Pen, I insist on paying," Carolyn stated firmly.

He held up a hand. "Very well then, pay me with a piece of knowledge."

That earned him a small smile, the first he'd seen since she'd walked in. Carolyn glanced down at the book, then back at him.

"Did you know some sixteenth-century astronomers believed the sky could show you where the world thinned? Places where one reality bled into another, if you tracked the right alignments."

Pen blinked. "Like portals?"

"Sort of," she said. "But these didn't stay open, just a flicker and then gone, once the astral event ended."

He let out a quiet breath. "Sounds like something I should be shelving in the fiction section."

"Yes." Carolyn nodded, her smile widening. "Though I'd wager there's a few books here that cover that."

Pen laughed, glancing around the shop. "You're probably right."

"Goodnight, Pen, and thank you," Carolyn said, heading for the door.

"See you," Pen called after her, stepping out from behind the counter. He turned the brass lock, flipped the sign to *Closed,* and wandered to the front window. He watched as Carolyn walked away and wondered what thoughts trailed her steps. Across the road, he spotted Dottie and Iain in the bakery's large front window, packing up an order. Iain raised a hand. Pen waved back, smiling.

He still couldn't quite believe how different his life had become. It was everything he hadn't known he wanted and more. Though he missed his brothers back home, here in Helensburgh, something had settled inside him. Peace. Belonging. Purpose. Ward had given him a way out, a door into another kind of life. One where Pen wasn't just surviving under the shadow of his father's reputation. He was someone here. A bookshop owner. A neighbor. A friend. If he'd stayed in Oak Ridge, he'd probably still be elbow-deep in grease, dismissed before he'd even opened his mouth.

As he headed toward the stairs to the loft, ready to turn off the lights for the night, he paused and looked at the wall of paintings. Knowing now that Carolyn was the artist, he examined them with fresh eyes. It was as if the paintings were now coming into focus, and he was seeing them clearly. The woman in the rain; it was her. Younger, yes, but unmistakable now. He didn't know how he'd missed it before. It was the same person as in the photo that still rested on the dresser upstairs.

His attention shifted to the large portrait of the man with the long beard. He wondered if this might be Rowland. It was the most prominent of all the artworks, but it lacked the familiar *CM* signature. Cracks spidered across the canvas's edges, its surface older, more fragile. The eyes unsettled him, like they were watching him back. A chill crept over his shoulders as he reached up and unhooked the frame. Holding it wide, he carried it to the counter and turned it over.

His heart nearly stopped. Taped to the back of the frame was a small ornate silver key. Beside it, two words and a date had been engraved, *John Dee, 1559.*

Pen could hardly believe his eyes. The key. The desk. The name. John Dee, the same name on the spine of the book he'd pulled off the shelf weeks ago and never returned. Something had compelled him to keep it close, tucked behind the register. He hadn't known why. *What a remarkable coincidence!*

With a wave of excitement, Pen peeled the key free from the yellowed tape, grabbed the book, and headed to the hidden room.

Flipping the rug aside, he pulled open the door.

As he descended into the darkened room, Pen felt the air change. It was cooler. Goosebumps prickled down his arms, lifting the hairs. He switched on the lamp, pulled out the worn chair, and sat with the key clutched tightly in his hand.

He hesitated, then slid it into the top drawer lock. He felt resistance; it had to be the right key. He gave it a gentle jiggle, then with a soft, reluctant *click*, the drawer yielded.

Inside were stacks of papers. Pages covered in arcane symbols and cryptic, spidery handwriting. Mathematical equations curled between star charts and planetary maps. Nothing he recognized. Nothing he understood. With a slow exhale, he slid the drawer closed. Then he reached for the right-hand drawer.

This one opened more easily, the key turning smoothly in the lock. Inside, a neat stack of leather-bound journals nestled beside what appeared to be a handheld telescope, its brass exterior tarnished with age. Pen picked up one of the journals and flipped through its pages. More nonsensical writing, spiraling symbols, accompanied by meticulous drawings of celestial bodies and notations dated back to the sixteenth century. Tucked beneath the last journal lay another large celestial map with a line written along its edge that stopped him.

The Monad's influence courses through each celestial sphere, a silent architect shaping the destiny of worlds. In tracing these alignments, perhaps we touch the hem of creation itself.

Pen stared at the words. Something about *Monad* made his skin prickle. It felt familiar, yet he was sure he hadn't heard of it before. He studied the sprawling map, planets, stars, and alignments drawn in looping ink, before carefully setting it aside.

So, Rowland had been interested in astronomy too, he mused, stacking the journals on the desktop. He checked beneath them, half-hoping for something more valuable. There was nothing else.

A pang of disappointment washed over him. After all the buildup, this felt… underwhelming. Why go to such lengths to keep old maps and journals hidden away?

He turned to the final drawer, clinging to a last flicker of hope.

Pen inserted the key into the lock.

The moment it twisted, a sharp jolt surged up his arm like a crack of electricity. He gasped and dropped the key, clutching his wrist as the metal clattered against the wood.

His breath came in shallow bursts. Was it wired? Trapped, perhaps?

But a quick inspection revealed nothing unusual. No wires, no trick mechanisms, just an old desk and brass fittings worn from use.

Swallowing his nerves, Pen reached for the key again. This time, he turned it fast, half-expecting another shock.

Instead, the lock gave way with a loud click, then the drawer sprang open.

He froze.

For a long moment, he simply stared into the darkened space. A single chime broke his trance, clear, soft, close. Cautiously, he reached inside.

A small velvet pouch lay within, rich blue and faintly luminous in the lamplight. Pen lifted it carefully, its fabric soft in his fingers. Drawing the string open, he found a gold pocket watch resting against silk, its surface gleaming faintly.

It let out another soft chime, as if to say, *You found me.*

This was it. The source of the sound that had haunted the bookshop since he arrived.

Pen tipped the pouch and let the watch slip out into his palm. It was unlike anything he'd ever seen. There were no numbers on its face, only constellations, planets, the moon, and the sun, and three delicate golden hands, unmoving.

He turned it over, one side, then the other, marveling at its craftsmanship. Astrological symbols were etched along its rim. Could this be an astronomer's tool? Something for tracking celestial events? It certainly fit the theme of everything else he'd found in the desk.

Pen set the watch on top of the velvet bag and leaned back in the creaky chair. A hollow sigh escaped him. He'd imagined so much more. Treasures, letters, proof of Rowland's fate. He'd built up the mystery in his mind. But there was no stolen money, priceless jewels, or rare books that held secrets worth a fortune. The reality had fallen short. Just stacks of scribbled papers, faded star charts, old journals, and a celestial trinket that didn't even tick.

Still, the pocket watch gave him one small comfort.

He hadn't imagined the chimes. It proved he wasn't entirely mad.

He packed everything but the watch back into the drawers, locked them, then made his way back upstairs into the bookshop. The watch cradled in his hand.

Well, that was one mystery solved. Not the grand revelation he'd hoped for, but at least he now knew the source of the chimes.

He set the watch on the kitchen table and lit a cigarette. As the smoke curled above him, he tuned the radio to the nightly news and began making dinner.

"Today's broadcast highlights the growing military and economic support being provided to South Vietnam by the United States, as the region works to establish stability under Prime Minister Diệm amid rising tensions with the communist North and internal political unrest. In other news, tonight, skywatchers across the country will be treated to a spectacular lunar eclipse, as the moon enters the Earth's shadow, casting a dramatic reddish hue over the night sky, a rare and captivating celestial event for all to enjoy."

Pen sat down to eat as the broadcaster's voice faded into the background.

Later, feeling full, he picked up *Lord of the Flies*, the book Iain had convinced him to read. He'd resisted at first, but now hated to admit how much he was enjoying it. He sank into the sofa, turned on the side lamp, and let the hours slip by unnoticed until sleep finally claimed him.

He dreamed he was trapped in the hollow corridors of Oak Ridge High School. The school bell rang incessantly, shrill and urgent, signaling the end of class, but no one seemed to hear it. Students sat frozen, eyes vacant, staring at a stark, empty chalkboard. The bell's clang grew louder, a relentless, deafening noise. He covered his ears, but it didn't help.

Pen jolted awake, heart thudding, the sharp clang still ringing in his ears. But this time, it wasn't part of his dream. The bells were real. The chimes were no longer melodic, they blared from the kitchen in a harsh, metallic rhythm that rattled him. He staggered to his feet, disoriented, and stumbled toward the sound, hands clamped over his ears. Just like in the dream. The kitchen was bathed in an eerie reddish hue. Outside, the moon hung low and swollen, blood-red, mid-eclipse.

Shadows writhed across the floor, shifting with the faintest flicker of light, as if alive. The air crackled with electricity, like the moments before a lightning strike. He wasn't sure if he was awake or still trapped in the nightmare.

The chimes grew louder, each note vibrating in Pen's skull, as if he were being struck with a hammer. As he reached the table, the watch sat still and gleaming, ringing with a sound that seemed too big for its size.

His fingers fumbled over its smooth, cold surface. Desperate, he traced along the edge, finding a set of tiny inset buttons. One by one, he pressed them. Then all together.

Nothing changed. The chimes continued, louder, faster, their sound swelling with an intensity that set him clenching his jaw against the pressure in his head.

In a final surge of panic, Pen flipped open the glass top and moved the frozen golden hands around. Any direction. Every direction. Anything to make it stop.

The chimes still shrieked.

He slammed the glass top shut.

Click.

Silence.

Pen stood still. The moonlight, still tinged red, began to soften as the eclipse passed, the moon slowly slipping free from its shadow.

He let out a long breath, every part of him aching with relief, and set the watch back on the table. Without another glance, he shuffled into the bedroom and collapsed into bed, too shaken to think clearly.

In the kitchen, the watch sat untouched in the quiet.

Its hands started to move.

Not ticking.

Spinning.

And in that silence, something in the air shifted, just enough to be felt, if one were paying attention. A new stillness seeped through the room, cold and watchful, like a creeping fog.

Touching everything in its wake.

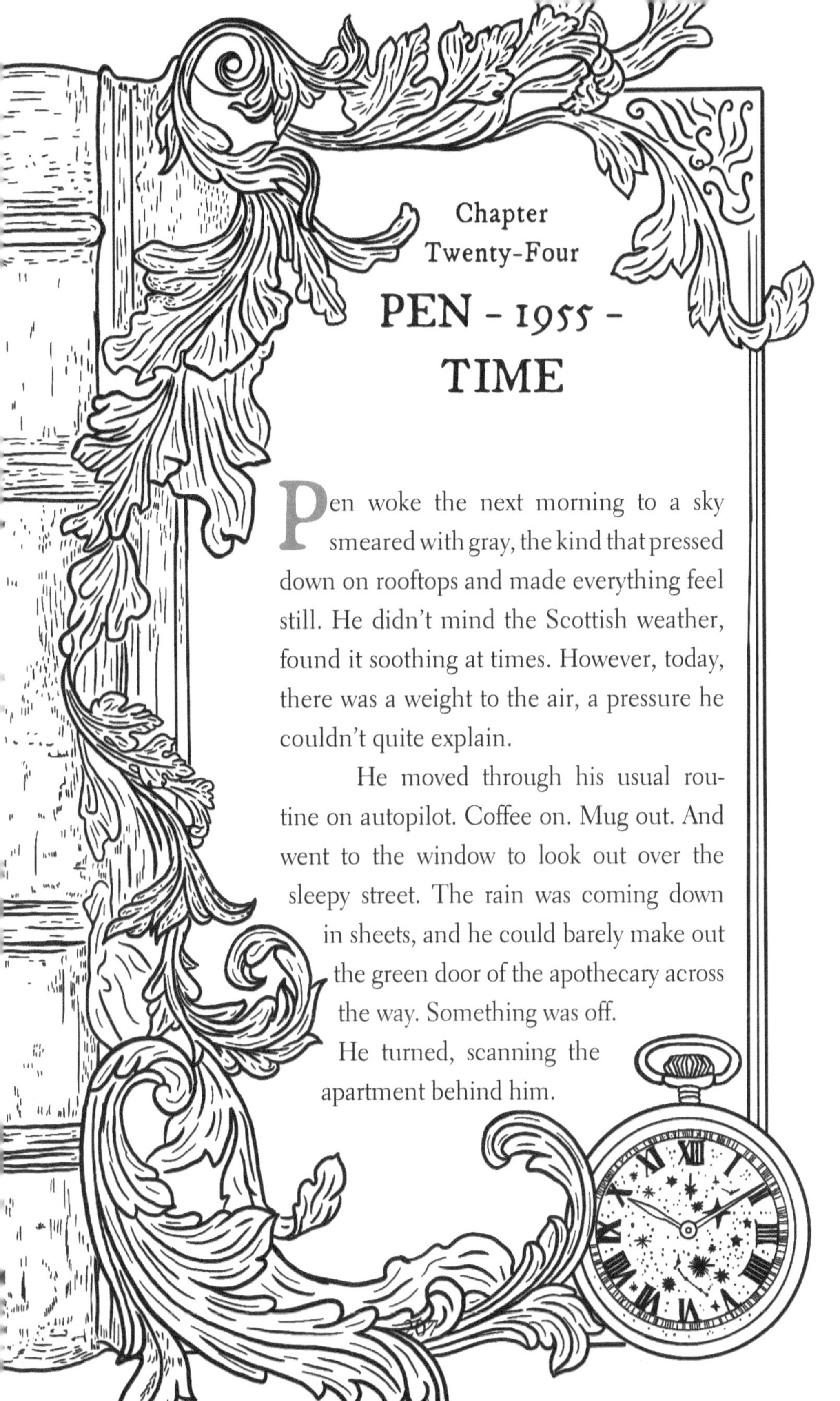

PEN – 1955 –
TIME

Pen woke the next morning to a sky smeared with gray, the kind that pressed down on rooftops and made everything feel still. He didn't mind the Scottish weather, found it soothing at times. However, today, there was a weight to the air, a pressure he couldn't quite explain.

He moved through his usual routine on autopilot. Coffee on. Mug out. And went to the window to look out over the sleepy street. The rain was coming down in sheets, and he could barely make out the green door of the apothecary across the way. Something was off.

He turned, scanning the apartment behind him.

On the table, the pocket watch sat exactly where he'd left it. He picked it up and turned it over. The hands now crept backward, *counter*clockwise, slow and steady, against the constellations etched into its face. Yesterday, they hadn't moved at all.

He must have wound it last night, just enough to spark it back to life. Its backward motion stirred a strange discomfort in him as he stared, unable to look away.

The rich aroma of roasting coffee filled the room, and he set the watch down. He poured a cup and stood at the window, cupping it in both hands. The heat warmed his palms, but did nothing for the chill threading down his spine.

Rain streamed in narrow rivulets across the cobblestones.

Something was missing. Something obvious.

Sound.

He couldn't hear the rain. No patter against the slate roof. No tap of rain on glass. Only silence, an eerie, all-encompassing silence.

Pen set the coffee down. The quiet filling the apartment wasn't natural. It wasn't peace. It was absence.

Had he somehow lost his hearing overnight? Or was he still trapped in a dream? He strained to listen, heart racing, but the stillness only deepened.

"Hello," he said aloud, relieved to hear his own voice. It was jarring, but he welcomed the sound. He reached for the book on the table and let it fall from his hands. The hardcover hit the wooden floor with a thud. Relief swelled in this chest. He could hear. The world hadn't gone completely silent. And yet, no rain. Maybe the storm had let up. Maybe the quiet was nothing more than a trick of the old windows and thick clouds. He clung to that thought, willing it to be true.

Shaking away his unease, Pen headed downstairs and prepared to open for the day.

It was Theodore Dreiser's birthday, and he'd planned a small tribute, *Sister Carrie* and *An American Tragedy* propped up on the front counter beside the small vase of sweet peas Dottie had dropped off the day before. He carried the books through the shop, their spines catching what little light came from the reading lamp glowing in the corner. At the counter, he set them in place, adjusting the covers to face outward. The soft ticking from the clock on the wall was a welcome sound this morning. He checked the time. 8:55. Almost time to open.

Across the street, the bakery had already sprung to life, its warm light spilling onto the slick cobblestones. Dottie and Iain would have been up for hours by now, shaping dough and boxing pastries, as they promptly opened at eight, an hour before the bookshop.

Pen watched the glow of the bakery for a moment, taking in the familiar rhythm of the morning, before turning back to his own tasks. He reached for the light switch, ready to bring the shop to life, but when he flicked it on.

Nothing.

He tried again. On. Off. On. Still nothing.

Frowning, he crossed to the next set of switches. Even the loft remained shrouded in gloom.

Could the storm have blown a fuse? He hurried back, flipped every breaker in the fuse box, and tried the lights again.

Still nothing. Except for the warm circle of light cast by the lamp in the reading corner.

Pen stared at it. How? If the power was out, how could it be working? It didn't make sense. Just like the absence of the rain's pitter-patter on the roof.

With the dreary weather and the scant light coming from the windows, opening today would be impossible. No one would want to browse books in near-darkness.

After another round of futile tinkering with the fuse box, Pen gave up. If he couldn't fix the lights, maybe Iain would know what was going on. He grabbed his rain slicker from the coat rack, pulled the large umbrella from its stand, and unlocked the door. As he pushed it open, the fresh scent of rain greeted him.

But as soon as Pen's foot hit the front step, the world shifted into a blur.

One moment he was stepping into the cool, damp air, and the next, he found himself back behind the front desk.

A bolt of fear shot through him; his heart thudded wildly, frantic and fast. He clutched the edge of the counter, breath shallow. *What the hell just happened?*

Trembling, Pen walked back to the door. His hand hovered over the knob, then he forced himself to open it again. He took one step forward. And he found himself sitting behind the front desk again.

His breath came in gasps, panic surging through him, hot and dizzying. "What the hell is going on here?" he whispered, staring down at his hands as the room swayed.

You're dreaming, he thought. *You must be.* What was it they said about dreams? You weren't supposed to be able to read in them. He grabbed the nearest book, turned to the first page, and read the text aloud. This wasn't a dream then, was it? Yet, it was too insane to be reality.

He scanned the counter. A small box of novelty pins sat beside the display. Bright blue buttons with the words, *Books are fun!* in cheerful yellow letters. He picked one up, pried open its back, and jabbed it into the soft flesh of his finger. Blood welled up in a small bead of crimson, then dripped onto the counter. A sharp sting radiated from its tip. The pain was real. He most definitely wasn't dreaming.

Pen moved to the door again, this time careful not to step on the threshold. Through the blur of rain, he could barely make out the door of the Marbled Clover. His eyes searched the bakery window. After what felt like an eternity, Dottie appeared with a stack full of bakery boxes in her arms.

"Dottie! Over here!" he yelled, voice raw with desperation. He waved both arms in wide arcs.

She didn't flinch. Didn't look up. Just continued folding boxes, calm and unaware.

When she did finally glance up, he began waving again. It was as if she couldn't see him at all. She just stood there, a far-off look on her face. How could she not see him? He was practically jumping up and down in the doorway.

Maybe it was too dark, maybe he was lost in the shadow of the doorframe. He slammed the door shut and ran to the front window. Grabbing the reading lamp, he dragged it closer, flooding the space around him with light.

Still nothing.

Moments later, Iain stepped into view, carrying a tray of scones to the front display cases. Pen's stomach leapt.

"Iain," he yelled, slamming his palms against the glass. "Hey, I'm right here!"

Iain looked up. Surely he had seen him. But Iain's eyes moved past the bookshop window, his expression blank. It was as if Pen didn't exist.

Panic clawed at his chest, heat rising to his face as nausea bubbled up in his throat. He needed to get out. Now. Then, it hit him: the back door. Without thinking, he bolted through the fantasy section. He fumbled with the lock, yanked the door open, and stepped into the alleyway…

Only to find himself back on the stool behind the counter. Again.

Head spinning, breath ragged, the room swam. His hands shook as he dropped his face into them, trying to make sense of a reality that defied logic.

His gaze fell to the brown leather dress shoes on his feet. Rowland's shoes. The ones he'd borrowed. What had he done? His mind reeled back through the past days, searching for anything that might explain this nightmare. Carolyn's unexpected visit, opening the drawers to the desk, the chimes, the watch…

It had to be the watch.

Pen tore up the stairs. The watch sat on the table, as if it hadn't just upended his world. He snatched it up. The hands were still moving, but more slowly now. So slow it almost looked as if they weren't moving at all. Turning it over in his hands, he inspected every inch of the gold casing, squinting at the surface for anything he might have missed. On the third rotation, he saw it. A faint, impossibly thin line of writing etched around the outer rim. He sprinted to the bedroom and pulled a magnifying glass from the nightstand. Back at the table, he hovered over the watch. Though the words were faded with wear, they came into focus: *The Order of the Monad.*

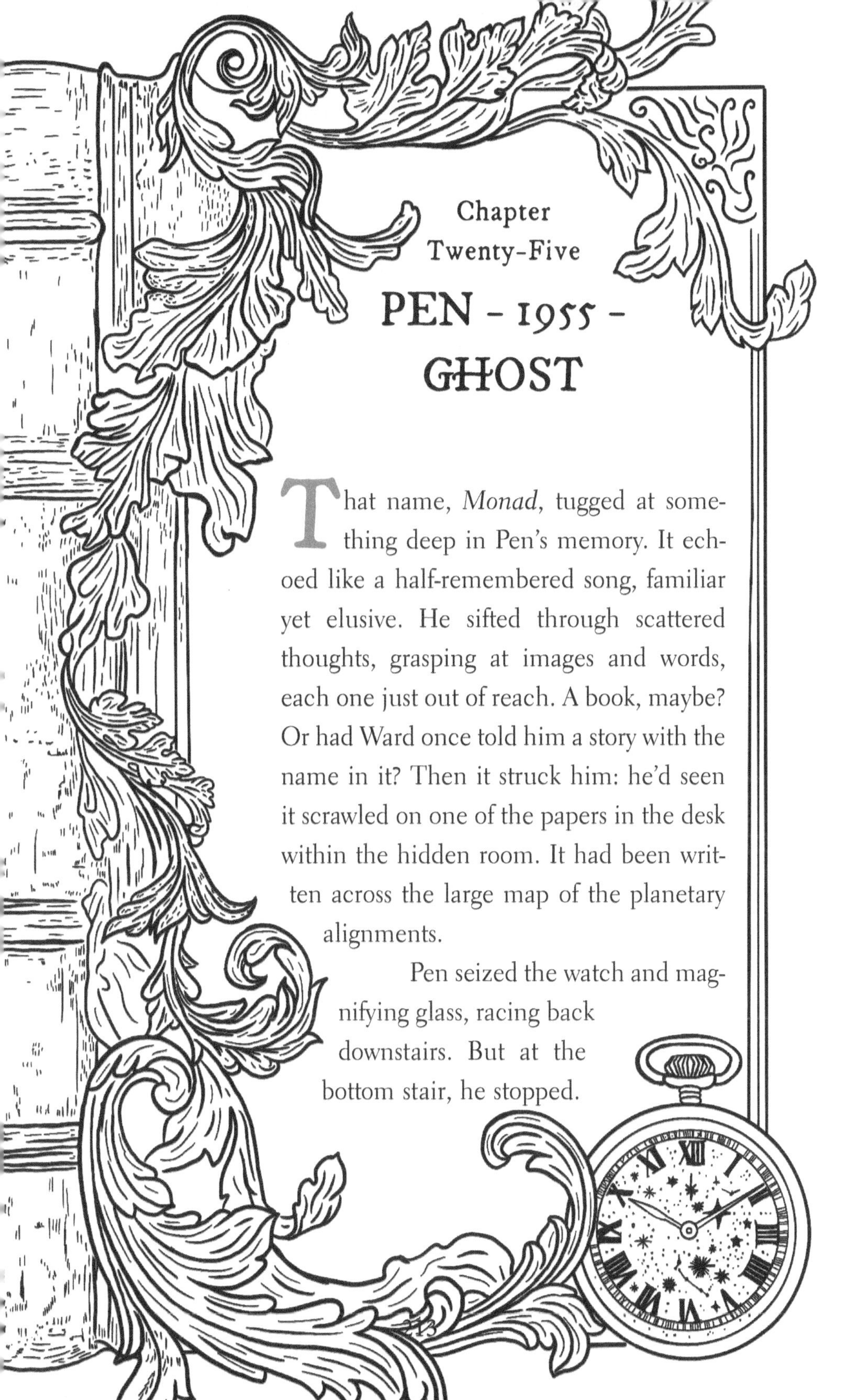

PEN - 1955 -
GHOST

That name, *Monad*, tugged at something deep in Pen's memory. It echoed like a half-remembered song, familiar yet elusive. He sifted through scattered thoughts, grasping at images and words, each one just out of reach. A book, maybe? Or had Ward once told him a story with the name in it? Then it struck him: he'd seen it scrawled on one of the papers in the desk within the hidden room. It had been written across the large map of the planetary alignments.

Pen seized the watch and magnifying glass, racing back downstairs. But at the bottom stair, he stopped.

There, blocking the doorway, was the squatter, a small fox, no bigger than a cat. It looked young, little more than a kit. Its russet fur was soaked, and its wide eyes darted from side to side, clearly calculating the best route of escape.

Pen felt a pang of sympathy for the creature, knowing what it was like to be trapped, and he took two steps back up the stairs, giving the little fox space to flee. The fox looked up at him. Their eyes met, a silent exchange, then it turned, darting through the cracked door and into the bookshop.

Pen stood there, stunned, the moment hanging like mist in the air. But the urgency of his task pulled him back. Shaking off his surprise, he followed the fox into the shop. As he made his way toward the hidden room, he glanced around, but the creature was nowhere in sight. It had vanished, slipping away into whatever new nook or cranny it had found for its hiding spot.

He yanked the rug aside and lifted the trapdoor, descending into the damp, shadowed space below. The scent of old wood and ink wrapped around him as he moved to the desk. He unlocked it, then slid open the drawer, set the journals aside, and pulled the map free. It was just as he remembered, a detailed sketch of planetary alignments, littered with scribbled equations and notes crowding the paper's margins. And there, three-quarters down the page, was the note. He read it aloud.

"The Monad's influence courses through each celestial sphere, a silent architect shaping the destiny of worlds. In tracing these alignments, perhaps we touch the hem of creation itself."

He pulled the watch from his pocket, its strange words catching the low light. Laying the celestial map flat across the desk, he held the watch beside it. The markings weren't random; they matched. Lines and curves mirrored the paths of stars inked into the page, a lattice of eerie precision. A chill went down his spine.

Lowering himself into the old captain's chair, Pen rubbed at his temples, thoughts spiraling. A hundred explanations for what might be happening to him raced through his mind, none of which were good. He wished he'd never found the trapdoor and this hidden room. Wished the mysterious chimes had remained just that, a mystery. If they had, he was quite certain he wouldn't be trapped inside the shop.

He needed to figure out what the hell was going on.

He began sifting through the rest of the papers in the desk. Most were dense with complex mathematical scribbles that left him feeling more lost than enlightened. Each line was a puzzle he lacked the skill to solve. Math had never been his strong suit in school. For all he knew, these equations held the secrets of the universe, but to him, they just looked like a mess of symbols that might as well have been in another language.

He leaned back in the chair, dragging his fingers through his hair. Reaching into his pocket, his fingers found the smooth curve of his lucky penny. He turned it over, grounding himself with the touch of the ordinary. The room felt closer than before. The shadows pressed against the walls, and a damp, earthy smell burned faintly in his nose.

He turned back to the stack of journals, searching for anything that might help him understand.

The first was more of the same: numbers, symbols, and lines of cramped, obsessive equations, meticulously penned in black ink. Certain numbers were circled in red, others were underlined in blue, creating a chaotic tangle that Pen had no idea how to decipher. He dropped it back on the desk and reached for the second.

This one opened differently. Page after page of flowing script, no equations, just words. A journal.

Pen's stomach turned when he saw the name pressed into the inner leather of the cover: Rowland. He flipped quickly, scanning pages of musings. Maybe Rowland had written about the watch. About halfway through, he came across a well-worn page, its edges bent and stained as if it had been read and reread countless times.

Pen leaned closer. Maybe this page held the answer.

September 12th, 1932

As I look back on the day I surprised Carolyn with a trip to Rosslyn Chapel just a few short weeks ago, my heart aches. I had never seen her so happy; the smile that graced her lips was more radiant than the summer sun, and her excitement was infectious. If I had only known the price of that joy, I might have thought twice before taking her away from the safety of home. It is my fault she now lies ill, her body wasting under the weight of an invisible enemy. I should have listened to Susan when she warned me it might not be wise to venture out while the TB outbreak was spreading. Yet, in my stubborn arrogance, I dismissed her advice, wanting so badly to impress my love.

If only we hadn't come across that group of children at the cathedral that day. Carolyn, with her generous heart, couldn't bear to see a small girl who had fallen behind, pale and coughing, struggling to keep up with the group. In a moment of compassion, she rushed to help, lifting the child in her arms and carrying her over to where the others had stopped to admire one of the cathedral's statues. She was completely unaware that this small kindness would cost her dearly.

The doctor's news today has left me with an ache in my chest that will not soon fade. Even if Carolyn survives this, she may never be able to bear a child. The infection has moved deep into her lungs, and they suspect, beyond. The thought of that crushing her spirit is unbearable. She would have made such a wonderful mother, nurturing and kind, just as she was to that little girl.

Now, I sit here, praying to a god I'm not sure exists, begging that the woman I love more than anything in this world will remain with me, earthside, and not be taken by this illness. Yet, prayer feels insufficient when I hold the key to a gateway that could take me back and change her fate. As the last keeper of the Astral Synchronum, I have sworn an oath never to use it, only to protect it and safeguard it from those who might wield it for harm. Yet I sit here, staring at the watch, waiting to hear a chime, to hear the sound that will allow me to save my love. Knowing I possess the means to go back in time and rewrite the past, yet being unable to do so is a torment no man should have to endure.

Pen set the journal down, his stomach twisting as he absorbed Rowland's words. His gaze drifted to the gold watch resting on the desk, quiet now, unmoving.

Was this it? The Astral Synchronum?

The hairs on the back of his neck rose.

Rowland had written as though the watch could transport him back in time. That was impossible. Wasn't it? He'd said he was waiting, listening for the chimes to sound so he could use it.

The watch had rung out in the middle of the night, waking Pen from a dead sleep. He'd fumbled with it, twisting knobs, pressing buttons in a desperate attempt to quiet it. Could that have triggered something? Had he somehow activated this device without realizing it? Had he traveled back in time? He shook his head. No, he couldn't have. It was too far-fetched. Besides, Dottie and Iain were still here. Everything looked the same.

And yet…

He hunched over, eyes tracing the symbols etched into the watch's face, then down at Rowland's words.

Something was happening. Something strange. It felt unreal, like he'd stepped into a story that wasn't his own. One that didn't belong in real life but in one of the science fiction books on the shelves.

Back in the bookshop, Pen moved to the window that looked toward the bakery. The clouds had begun to lift, casting a pale silver light into the shop. He watched, waiting, hoping Dottie or Iain might glance his way.

Time dragged on. Customers came and went. No one looked his way. But with the shop lights off and the closed sign still in the window, it was no wonder.

Evening settled in, the streetlights flickered on. Pen's legs ached from standing, but he didn't move.

His stomach twisted, his head felt cloudy.

He had almost given up hope when the bakery door swung open. Dottie stepped out, Iain close behind. They crossed the street, heading straight for the bookstore.

Pen's heart leapt into his throat. *Finally.* "One more minute in here, and I'd have gone completely mad, if I'm not already," he muttered, rushing to the door.

Dottie reached it first, giving the handle a turn, but it resisted. Confused, Pen looked down. He was sure he'd unlocked it.

"Come in, it's unlocked," he said.

Iain tried the handle as well, but it still wouldn't budge from the outside. Pen reached for the knob, but as soon as his hand met it, a force threw him backward, slamming him into the children's shelf. Books tumbled to the floor. Dazed, he staggered to his feet and turned back to the door. But Dottie and Iain weren't shocked or concerned. They had their hands pressed to the glass, peering in. Pen stepped up to the window, waving his hand wildly in front of Dottie's face. Nothing. Her gaze seemed to pass right through him.

A loud bang echoed against the shop door, and Pen heard Iain's muffled voice call out, "Pen, you in there?"

The room fell silent; the only sound was the relentless thud of his heartbeat in his ears, loud and frantic.

"Pen, are you okay?" Dottie's voice rang out, followed by another set of heavy knocks.

"I'm right here," he yelled back.

But neither of them reacted.

"Maybe he went somewhere for the day?" Iain suggested, stepping off the stoop.

Dottie frowned. "Don't you think he'd have mentioned it? We just had dinner two nights ago."

Iain sighed. "We're his friends, not his parents, Dottie."

She lingered at the door, glancing back through the window, inches from Pen's face, but her eyes drifted past him, empty of recognition. "I don't know, Iain. I have a bad feeling. Something isn't right."

"If he doesn't turn up in the next couple of days, we'll go talk to the police, okay?"

With one last worried look through the glass, Dottie turned and followed Iain back across the street. Pen had stood there, mere inches from her, as she looked straight through him, like he wasn't even there, like he was a ghost.

The thought struck him with a cold dread that sent him sprinting back to the apartment. He crashed into the bedroom, half-expecting, dreading, to find his own body lying on the bed. But it was empty. Just the usual tangle of sheets.

So he wasn't dead, at least not in the conventional sense. He wasn't sure if that was a blessing or a curse.

Pen made his way over to the window and gazed down at the street. The sign for the Purple Thorn Apothecary swayed gently. *Carolyn. She's right there, just across the road… and yet*, he thought grimly, *she might as well be a universe away.*

THE HIDDEN JOURNAL OF JOHN DEE

October 24, 1582

Giordano and I have yet to uncover a solution to mend the tear in time we so carelessly created. So I called upon Edward Kelley's assistance once more, hoping divine intervention might illuminate a path forward. Kelley brought with him an obsidian disc to scry for celestial guidance.

After several attempts, Kelley was used as a vessel, and a voice not of his own came through. It told me that an alignment of the stars within the next fortnight would provide the energy needed to reactivate the Astral Synchronum. This alignment, fleeting and rare, is our only chance to reverse the damage we have brought.

However, the celestial being also confirmed what Giordano had feared all along: the Astral Synchronum must not be used again for anything beyond this purpose. Its mechanisms are too delicate, the risk too great. To employ it in any other manner would surely worsen the tear, perhaps to the point of no return.

And so, we wait. The days feel endless as we prepare every component, every calculation, leaving no detail to chance. We gather rare materials, recalibrate the device, and ensure the crypt at Dunblane is ready to host our final attempt. Even as we toil, the world around us continues to fray; strange buildings have appeared off on the horizon that were not there before, and the sky has turned an unsettling shade of blue.

The weight of our actions bears heavily upon us, and we can only pray that when the celestial alignment comes, we will succeed in sealing the rift and restoring the natural order. Failure is not an option, for the alternative is chaos beyond comprehension.

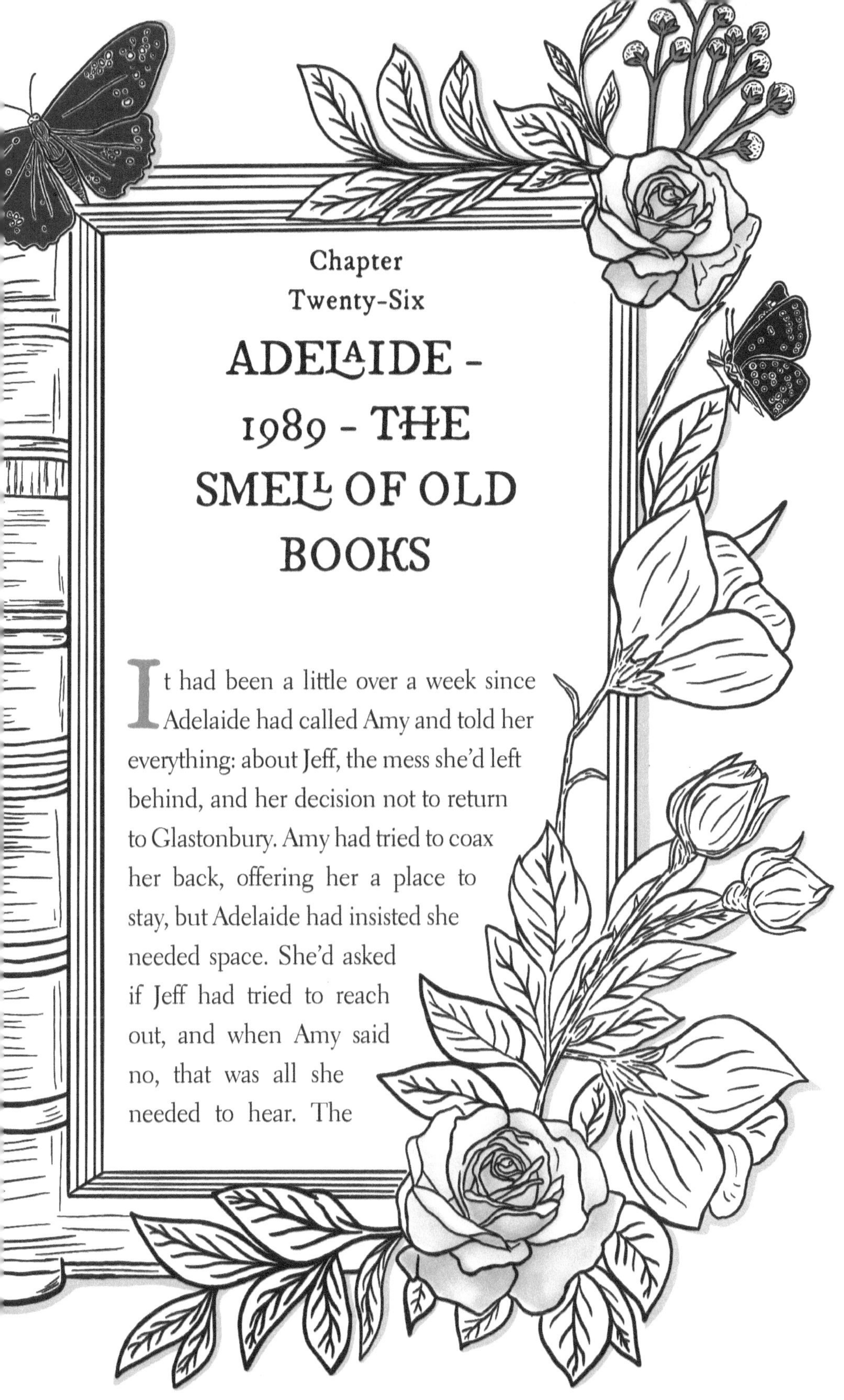

ADELAIDE - 1989 - THE SMELL OF OLD BOOKS

It had been a little over a week since Adelaide had called Amy and told her everything: about Jeff, the mess she'd left behind, and her decision not to return to Glastonbury. Amy had tried to coax her back, offering her a place to stay, but Adelaide had insisted she needed space. She'd asked if Jeff had tried to reach out, and when Amy said no, that was all she needed to hear. The fact he hadn't even bothered to find out where she was or if she was okay spoke volumes and sealed her decision to stay.

She'd emptied her savings and bought the old bookshop across from her great-aunt's apothecary. Susan had handed her the keys just yesterday and filed all the necessary papers. But Adelaide hadn't set foot inside; she hadn't even told a soul she'd bought it. Not even Carolyn.

She wasn't entirely sure why she was keeping it a secret, only that something inside her said she had to. That she needed to do this on her own, prove to herself that she could. Without anyone else's opinions in the mix.

Buying the bookshop was a monumental leap, one she'd never dream of before. For years, she'd poured everything into her marriage, nurturing Jeff's ambitions, sidelining her own until she'd forgotten she was allowed to have any. Now, the idea of chasing a dream felt strange, like she didn't quite deserve to. Maybe that's why she hadn't said a word about the shop. She was still questioning whether she deserved it.

She set her cup of tea aside and added another log to the crackling fire in the hearth. The flames hissed and popped, casting flickering shadows.

The chill had settled in early; the nights were sharp and bitter, and the cabin, charming as it was, offered little defense. Its drafty windows and thick stone walls seemed to trap the cold rather than keep it out. She had already burned through most of the stacked logs by the edge of the path near the woods, and was down to the last few. Carolyn had called for a wood delivery over a week ago, but nothing had arrived yet.

When winter came, this cabin wouldn't be livable. She'd either have to crash on Carolyn's sofa or find a place of her own.

Her stomach turned; it was too early for thoughts like these, too heavy to carry before the caffeine had worked its magic. She pushed them aside. First things first: find wood for tonight, and then head to the bookshop. She hadn't even asked for a tour before signing the papers. In hindsight, it had been impulsive, reckless, even. But she'd felt an urgency she couldn't explain, like if she hesitated, someone else might swoop in and claim it first. And she couldn't let that happen. From the first moment she'd seen it, with a lone moth settled atop the worn signpost, she'd known the Feather Thorn was meant to be hers. The pull toward it had been magnetic; even now, it hummed beneath her skin. Today, she would finally give in to that pull and unlock the doors to what she hoped would be her new beginning.

After finishing her morning chores, Adelaide tugged on her thrifted cream cable-knit sweater and suede jacket and stepped out into the brisk mid-morning air. The sky was a pale wash overhead, the kind of cool blue that made you breathe a little deeper. As she walked down the winding path to the main house, she stretched her arms, letting her fingertips skim the tops of the wildflowers as the soft grasses brushed against her thighs. The familiar rasp of seedheads and stalks against her skin grounded her, tethering her to this quiet patch of land. Every morning, she walked this same path. And every morning, it reminded her she wasn't in Glastonbury anymore.

Rounding the corner near the elder bush, she spotted Carolyn kneeling at the edge of the pathway, diligently pulling up weeds.

"Morning. Whatcha doing?" Adelaide called out, tucking her hands into her jacket pockets to warm them up.

Carolyn looked up, face flushed from exertion, gray hair sticking to her temples. "Trying to pull up this damn bishop's weed before it takes over the whole plot," she grumbled. She gave a satisfying tug and held up the scraggly root in triumph before tossing it onto a growing pile.

"Why don't you just let me mow it down?" Adelaide offered, eyeing the mess of stalks and stems around them.

Carolyn straightened slowly, using her stick to push herself upright. "Because then you'd mow everything. Including my crops." She waved her hand over what looked to Adelaide like a field of stubborn weeds. "And two, it will just grow back. Its roots need to be pulled up before it gets a hold on any more of this area."

"Crops?" Adelaide squinted at the field.

"Those may look like weeds to you, my dear, but this field is full of what I need to dry over the winter." Carolyn pointed her stick at a lanky plant. "This here's nettle. I use it in my teas to help settle the stomach, and it has antihistamine properties too. And this tall fellow is sorrel, an anti-inflammatory I use in my salves. Over there, dandelion, yarrow, plantain, mugwort, chickweed, shepherd's purse. All of it's useful. And there's more beyond, near your cabin."

Adelaide followed the line of the raised stick, newly aware of the wildly beautiful mess she'd meandered through each morning. "I had no idea you harvested all the herbs for the shop yourself."

"Oh, no, I don't," Carolyn said with a shrug. "I purchase most of my herbs in bulk for the teas and such, but when it comes to—" She paused as if searching for the right words. "Complex mixtures, I stick to what grows here on my land. These herbs have a special quality."

Adelaide didn't entirely understand, but she nodded anyway, letting the reverence in Carolyn's voice settle over her.

"Do you want any help?" she offered, watching as Carolyn knelt back down.

"No, no. You go enjoy the afternoon." She waved a gloved hand in dismissal, then immediately started muttering at another tangled root.

"Okay, if you're sure. I'm going to head into town; do you need anything?"

Carolyn didn't look up. "I have everything I need right here. Now shoo!"

Adelaide grinned. "Well, okay then. Good luck conquering the bishop's weed."

Her shoes crunched over the path as she turned toward the road. Her feet seemed to be carrying her into town much quicker than normal today, the excitement of exploring the shop fueling each footstep, and the jingle of the bookshop's keys in her pocket setting a steady rhythm.

By the time she reached the bookstore, the street was fully awake. Locals drifted in and out of shops, and the smell of fresh scones wafted through the air from the bakery.

The bookshop sat slightly back from the road, just far enough for the weeds to lay claim to the narrow path. Ivy had all but engulfed the flagstones, vines curling over the walkway in a tangled mass of green. She pushed forward, wading through the overgrowth until she reached the faded front door.

She paused, knee-deep in ivy and nettles, and tilted her head to take in the full, weary face of the shop. The windows were dim with grime and half covered in ivy, but in her mind, she saw it as it had been in the photograph above the bakery door, clean and inviting. Beneath the neglect lay a beautiful shop, just waiting to breathe again.

Heart fluttering, she slipped her hand into her pocket and drew out the keys. The brass lock was crusted with a thin layer of moss, as if nature was slowly reclaiming it. She scraped at it with the edge of the key, then slid it in and gave it a turn.

"Here we go," she muttered. The old lock groaned in protest. She jiggled it, turned it back and forth, but nothing happened.

"Crap," she said, twisting harder.

"I'm afraid it's locked," came a voice from behind her.

Adelaide jumped, then turned to see Dottie from the bakery standing just a few feet away, flour-dusted apron and all, looking at her with a mixture of curiosity and concern.

"Oh, hey," she said, brushing moss from her fingers.

"Adelaide! I thought that was you." Dottie glanced at the keys in Adelaide's hands. "What are you doing over here?"

"Trying to unlock this door. It's stuck."

Dottie's brow creased. "How'd you get the keys to the Feather Thorn?"

"I bought it last week," Adelaide answered, lowering her voice, "but please don't say anything. I haven't really told anyone yet, not even Carolyn."

"Oh," was all Dottie could say for a long moment as she gazed past Adelaide at the bookshop. "I didn't know the town was putting it back up for sale again."

"Yeah, Susan let me put a bid in before it was listed. She figured no one local would want it and thought it would be nice if someone connected to the town bought it. I also needed a change, and it felt right, so here I am." She hesitated. "Maybe a little impulsive, but, yeah."

Dottie's lips pressed together. "And you haven't told Carolyn?"

"I will. I just wanted to try and figure it out a bit on my own first, I guess."

"Well, she'll be surprised, that's for sure," Dottie stepped up beside Adelaide. "Here. There's a bit of a trick to it. First, grab the doorknob and pull the door closed. Tight as you can. Then, put the key in, not all the way. About three-quarters. Then turn."

Adelaide did as instructed, and sure enough, there was a satisfying click. The door creaked open an inch, and a breath of musty air spilled out, thick with the scent of leather bindings, timeworn paper, and a lingering trace of cologne. Her chest tightened with warmth and nostalgia. The smell hit like an old memory: library aisles, childhood afternoons, stories waiting in quiet corners.

"See!" Dottie grinned. "I guess the old trick still works!"

"Thanks, Dottie! I'd have been out here half the day wrestling with the thing if you hadn't come by."

"No trouble. I'll leave you to your exploring," she said, turning to walk back across the street. However, she turned back. "Adelaide, please make sure you tell your aunt before she hears it from someone else. I'd bet half the street's already clocked you out here, and you know how small towns talk."

Her tone made Adelaide pause. So Carolyn wouldn't be pleased to hear about the bookshop secondhand? Or she wouldn't be pleased to hear about it at all?

She opened her mouth to ask more, but a sound coming from inside the shop caught her attention. She turned for just a moment, looking through the crack of the open door, but when she looked back, Dottie had already disappeared into the bakery.

Adelaide faced the door again. Its once-rich navy-blue paint was now faded and chipped, the wood grain beneath peeking through. Another thing for her growing to-do list. She pushed the door open.

Stepping over the threshold, she gazed into the dimly lit space. A counter greeted her first, and beyond it, rows upon rows of books stretched into the shadows. Her heart raced as she took her first step into the shop, her shop. The shelves were brimming with books, far exceeding what she had anticipated. Not only had she snagged the building at a steal, but a hoard of stories, thousands of pounds worth of literary treasures.

As she moved further in, she marveled at a model ship and an airplane suspended from the ceiling, both softly lit by the sunlight trying to filter in through the high front window. When she turned, she saw the loft above, an inviting overlook accessed by a staircase lined with old paintings, their painted eyes seeming to follow her, as if curious about the new visitor.

She scanned for signs of rot or damp, but so far, so good. The roof seemed solid, no structural issues to speak of. A relief; she would have been way out of her depth if there had been.

Everything matched the picture she'd built in her mind, right down to the mahogany bookshelves, the loft overlooking the sea of books, and that hush of particular places where words slept on paper. She flipped the switch, expecting the power to be off, but a row of overhead tin lights sprang to life with a soft hum, bathing the space in a warm yellow glow.

She wandered to the fiction section and ran her fingers across the spines until they landed on *The Chronicles of Narnia*. She opened the worn cover and smiled. Her father had read it to her again and again; this was the book that had made her fall in love with stories. He would have loved this for her. But as she flipped through its pages, something gave her pause. The book was immaculate. No dust, no signs of age. How could that be? Susan had said no one had touched these books in over ten years. The last people who tried to revive the shop hadn't lasted even a month, claiming the place was haunted. Adelaide chuckled at the notion; weren't all the best libraries and bookshops?

She pulled out another book. Clean. Then another. Still nothing. She moved to a different section. Same story, dust-free. *How odd*, she thought, *but welcome*; it was one less chore she would need to tackle.

After exploring the loft area, Adelaide returned to the main level and ventured to the back. A door stood slightly ajar, a scattering of leaves at its base, and tiny muddy pawprints leading in and out. Curiosity piqued, she pushed it open and found a stairwell winding up to another floor. Halfway up, she spotted the culprit's entry, a cracked windowpane that let in a ribbon of cool late-summer air and a swirl of stray leaves. Another task for her list.

At the top, a door painted in the same rich navy blue as the front stood shut. She turned the knob, but it was locked. She fished out the keyring and tried each one, but none fit the door. She would have to stop by and see Susan later; she must have forgotten to give her a key to what was presumably the shop's storage area.

Just as she began to descend the stairs, a *click* echoed behind her. The unmistakable sound of a lock being turned.

She froze.

Was someone inside? That noise, when she had first opened the shop, had that been someone slipping away? Her heart raced. Slowly, she turned around. The door now stood open. Cool air drifted from the darkened room, heavy with the scent of old paper and something else. Like déjà vu wrapped in dust and shadows.

Then, from the gloom, a pair of yellow eyes slowly emerged.

ADELAIDE

- 1989 -

SHADOWS

Adelaide staggered back, her foot catching on the edge of the stairs. She grabbed the banister just in time. The creature's eyes, a bright, unnatural yellow, locked on hers, unblinking. They flicked left and then right, as if calculating an escape. Before she could move or call out, it bolted. A blur of motion, a rush of air, and bramble-scented musk. She let out a sharp scream, the sound ricocheting off the stone walls.

"What in the bloody hell?" She gasped, spinning around, but whatever it had been was already out of sight.

Was it a cat?

She looked back toward the open door at the top of the stairs, her breath still coming in quick, shallow bursts. But the stillness had returned, thick and undisturbed. No glowing eyes. No movement in the shadows. Nothing waiting in the dark.

Cautiously, she pushed the door open wider, the hinges creaking softly. The first time she'd tried, it hadn't moved at all. Now, it opened without resistance. She turned the knob back and forth, shut it, opened it, shut it again. *Just a door*, she told herself. *A stiff old door, probably swollen from damp.* But logic did little to quiet the unease sliding beneath her skin.

She opened the door again. Beyond it was not a storage room, but a flat. A whole flat. Small and self-contained. Susan hadn't mentioned anything about living quarters.

As she stepped inside, she ran her hand along the wall, looking for a light switch but found none; however, a lamp perched on a side table next to the sofa caught her eye, and she flicked it on.

An amber glow spread through the room, revealing a space frozen in time. The sofa, tufted and deep green. A gramophone nestled beside it. Everything was straight out of the 1930s. The faint smell of stale cigarette smoke and men's cologne hung in the air.

She drifted toward the small kitchen ahead of her. A single wooden chair sat pulled out from the table, angled toward a wide window that overlooked the street. Adelaide paused there, memory stirring.

The shadowy figure in the window.

In the quiet, she noticed the thick dust blanketing every surface, no smudges on the glass, no footprints. Just the kind of stillness that takes decades to settle. She frowned, the image of the figure at the window flickering in her mind again. Maybe she hadn't seen anything at all. Maybe it had just been a trick of the light.

Turning back toward the small living room, Adelaide noticed a narrow hallway off to the right. Following it, she stopped in the doorway of a bedroom. A double bed, neatly made, a pine dresser stood beside it, and a closet half-open, revealing a row of men's coats, tweed and wool, the kind from another time. A chill slipped down along her spine. It looked as if someone had simply stepped out for a walk one afternoon and never returned. Dottie's voice whispered in her mind: *No one ever came to collect or remove his things.*

As she turned to leave, something caught her eye. A silver frame. Inside, a black-and-white photograph, faded along its edges. A young woman in her early twenties smiled shyly at the camera, while the man beside her gazed at her lovingly. She reached for the frame with both hands.

Carolyn.

There was no mistaking the curve of her aunt's cheekbones, the wide, intelligent eyes. The man's face was unfamiliar, but the way he looked at her, like the world had stopped, sent a knot twisting in her stomach.

Why is there a photograph of Carolyn here?

Her heart thumped as she set the photo gently back on the dresser, fingers trembling. So Carolyn had known the man who lived here. More than known him, from the looks of it. Dottie's warning echoed louder: "Make sure she hears it from you."

A gust of wind rattled the loose pane in the bedroom window. Adelaide exhaled and walked back to the window overlooking the street. Carolyn's apothecary across the road sat shuttered for the day, its moss-green door calm and still. But Adelaide's thoughts churned.

If there was a story buried in this building, if Carolyn had once belonged to it somehow, Adelaide wasn't sure she wanted to disturb it yet. Secrets had weight in a small town. Sometimes, you need to carry them gently until the time was right.

She turned and took one last look around the flat. For all the questions it raised, it had solved one thing: Where she'd be living come winter. A roof over her head, solid walls, and a story she hadn't finished reading. *Two birds, one stone*, she thought, and smiled faintly as she pulled the door closed behind her.

Back downstairs in the bookshop, she scanned the edges of the room for the critter from the stairwell, but the shop lay still. Making her way to the front counter, she began forming a list in her head. First: pen and paper. She rooted around, finding a dusty jar of fountain pens and a stack of weathered ledgers. Underneath was a slim leather-bound book, its spine stamped with a name: *John Dee*. The pages crackled as she thumbed through them. Notes, strange symbols, faint smudges of ink. Something to dig into later. She set it aside, grabbed a notepad and pen and began scribbling.

Tame the overgrown weeds in front of the shop. With the way it looked now, it was a wonder someone hadn't gone missing in the thicket. *Fix the cracked window in the stairwell. Replace the broken spindle on the loft's banister. Toss those moth-eaten rugs.*

As the list grew, she paced the shop, footsteps echoing in the quiet.

By the time she'd finished, a page and a half stared back at her, repairs, updates, curiosities. But instead of dread, she felt a quiet thrill.

She tucked the list into her pocket and decided she would stop by the hardware store before heading home. Grab a few paint samples, maybe a new lock, and a hanging plant to cheer up the front. The idea of adding color brought with it a quiet warmth. The place needed it, needed life stirred back into its old bones.

Before flipping off the lights, she paused in the center of the room and turned in a slow circle, letting her gaze sweep across the shelves. Books. Her books now. Their spines winked at her from the shadows, stories waiting to be discovered. She inhaled deeply, old paper and something just a little sweet, like dried lavender.

"You're just what I needed," she sang out to the shop. The tune played in her head, "You Might Think" by The Cars, and she sang the lyrics aloud.

Just before she closed the door, she could have sworn she saw a shadow move behind the back row of bookcases. Hairs prickled on the back of her neck. It had to be another trick of the light. The door was open, the sun shifting angles. That's what it was.

Or maybe it was the ghost Susan had spoken of, come to welcome her. She chuckled… nervously, but it rang hollow.

Adelaide stepped outside, locking the door behind her, her laugh failing to mask the uneasy feeling coiling in her stomach, the feeling that someone, or something, was watching her.

That maybe, the bookshop wasn't as abandoned as it seemed.

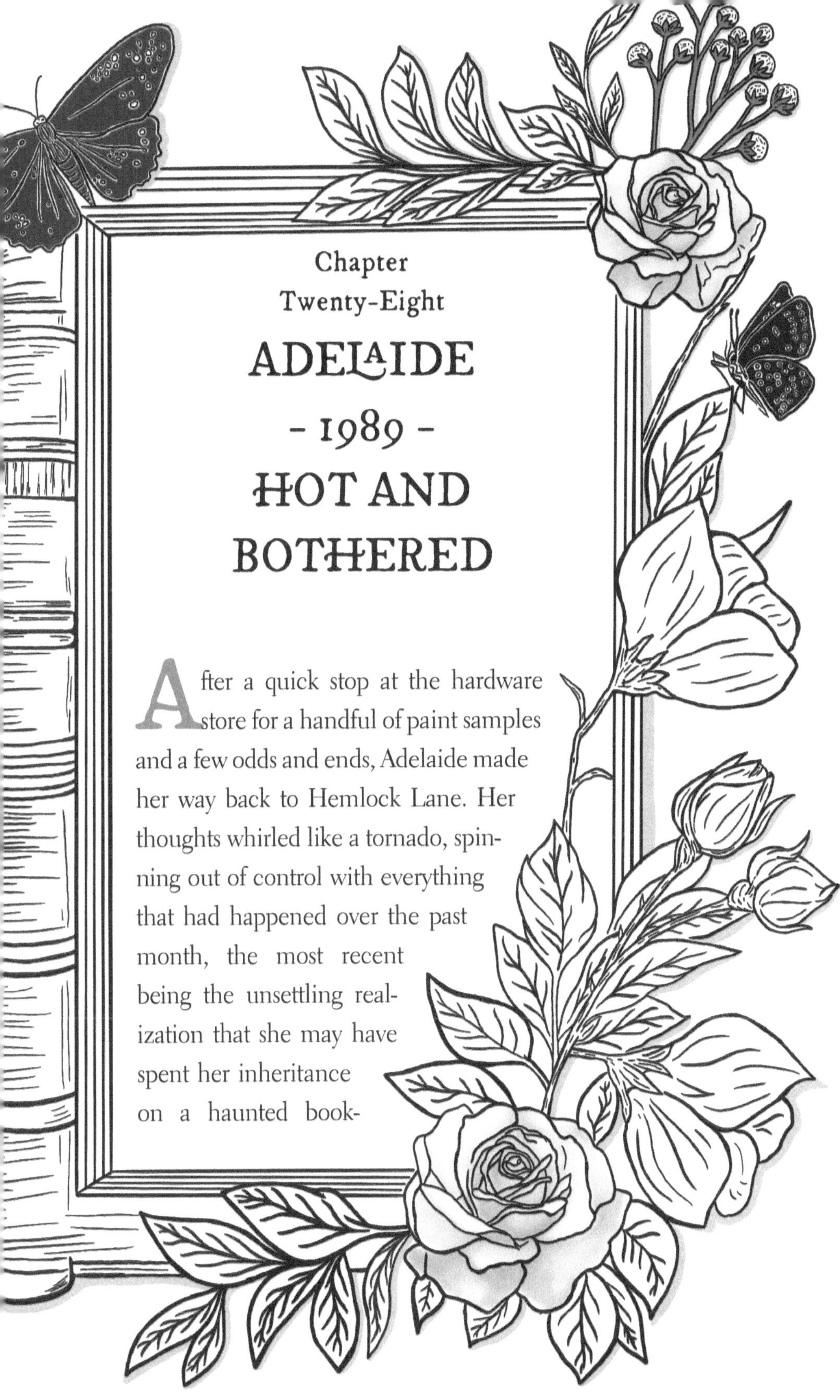

Chapter
Twenty-Eight

ADELAIDE

- 1989 -

HOT AND BOTHERED

After a quick stop at the hardware store for a handful of paint samples and a few odds and ends, Adelaide made her way back to Hemlock Lane. Her thoughts whirled like a tornado, spinning out of control with everything that had happened over the past month, the most recent being the unsettling realization that she may have spent her inheritance on a haunted bookshop. The jury was still out on that one. But even with the yellow eyes in the shadows, she didn't feel afraid. If anything, the Feather Thorn made her feel calm. As if something within its walls had been waiting for her, not to scare her off, but to welcome her home.

She wanted to ask Carolyn about the photo in the flat, but her intuition told her to wait. Better to tell her about the bookshop first, then maybe Carolyn would open up and share her story, and the connection she had to the Feather Thorn.

When she arrived at Carolyn's, a utility truck was parked in the driveway, its back piled high with firewood.

"Thank God," she muttered. The wood delivery had finally come. She was down to splinters and not in the mood to scavenge the woods this afternoon.

She rounded the path, distracted, and nearly collided with a man hauling a wheelbarrow.

"Oh, God! I'm sorry," she blurted, stumbling back. The man stopped short, his wheelbarrow squeaking to a halt.

He glanced up, dark curls damp with sweat, clinging to his forehead. His T-shirt clung to a broad chest, streaked with sawdust, and his moss-green eyes met hers with a blink of surprise.

"No bother," he replied, voice rich with a thick Scottish brogue.

Adelaide stared for half a second too long before catching herself. "Right, sorry again." She nodded and turned toward the cottage, her cheeks flushing.

When she reached the porch, she couldn't resist glancing back. He had lifted his shirt, wiping his brow, revealing a sculpted six-pack. A rush of heat tickled her neck, crept higher, and she quickly ducked inside, firmly closing the door. Leaning against it, she let the cool wood steady her racing pulse.

In the kitchen, she set the paint samples on the counter and filled the kettle. As it began to rumble, the scent of bergamot and black tea curled in the air just enough to calm her down.

Over the next hour, she tried to read, tried to focus, but every thump of wood landing on the growing pile outside the cabin made her ears perk. She forced herself to stay put, flipping pages more with tension than attention. Her eyes kept drifting to the window, without her permission, her heart ticking along to the rhythm of the logs.

A knock at the door jolted her back to reality.

She tossed the book into the chair, ran a quick hand through her hair, and tried to act normal as she approached the door. Her heart, naturally, refused to play along.

When she opened it, the man stood on the porch, not five feet away. A sweat-stained V darkening his T-shirt.

"Hello, there's a half-cord stacked there for you," he said, locking eyes with her. "Told Carolyn I'd bring another in a few days. Sorry, it took so long. Dave's been out for a week with a stomach bug, so it's just been me running the shop. I haven't had much time to chop and split this stuff."

She had no idea who Dave was or what shop he was talking about, but nodded along anyway.

"It's fine, really," she told him, hoping her voice sounded casual and not completely flustered. "There were a few logs left in a pile by the path. They did the trick over the past few days."

He offered his calloused hand. "Ewan."

"Adelaide." She shook it, firm but ladylike.

"Carolyn said you'd just moved here from Gaddesby?"

Not quite, but she let it slide. "Yup, needed a change of scenery."

"Well. Let me know if you need that other half, and I'll get it over to you next week." He flashed a smile, boyish, and maybe just a touch flirtatious.

"Okay, thanks, Ewan."

"Nice meeting you, Adelaide." He turned, pushing the wheelbarrow back down the path.

She watched him go, her pulse still skipping like a scratched record. She hadn't expected that. Then again, she hadn't expected any of this. Fresh out of an almost decade-long marriage, she was hardly in a place to be distracted by a guy, wasn't she?

Then again, they did say something about *getting back in the saddle*… Not that she was about to start entertaining reckless ideas.

But…

The old Adelaide wouldn't have bought a bookshop unseen. She wouldn't have wandered through overgrown paths or dared to climb creaking stairs alone. But the new Adelaide?

Well.

Maybe she didn't mind a little recklessness. Maybe it wasn't such a bad thing after all.

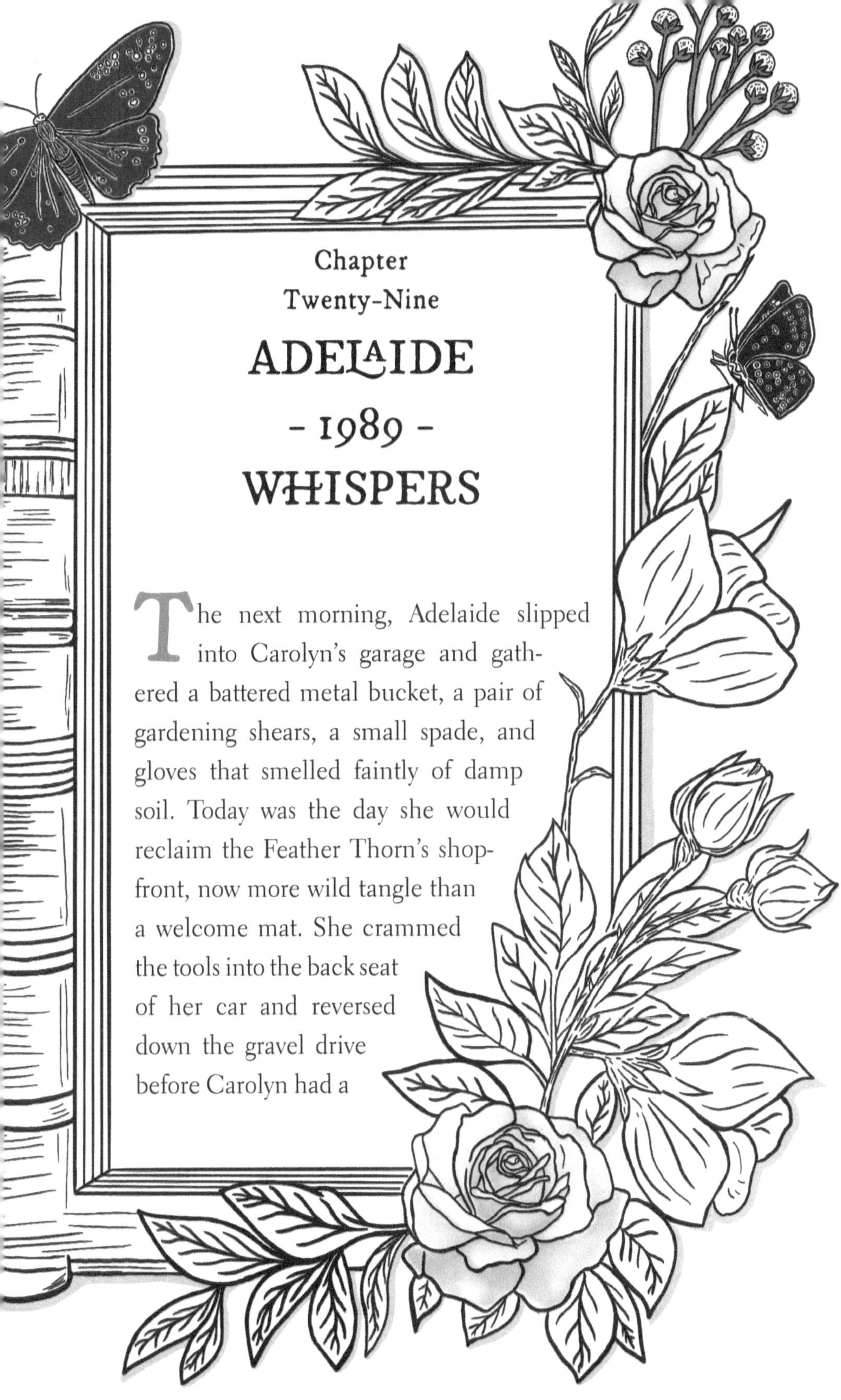

The next morning, Adelaide slipped into Carolyn's garage and gathered a battered metal bucket, a pair of gardening shears, a small spade, and gloves that smelled faintly of damp soil. Today was the day she would reclaim the Feather Thorn's shopfront, now more wild tangle than a welcome mat. She crammed the tools into the back seat of her car and reversed down the gravel drive before Carolyn had a chance to appear in the doorway, hands on hips and full of questions.

Since moving in, most of Adelaide's days had been spent settling into the cabin, tending the lawn, or helping with small chores while Carolyn was at the apothecary. Evenings were softer. She and her great-aunt shared simple dinners, reminiscing about her childhood visits. Carolyn spoke fondly of Adelaide's father and the mischief they'd gotten into as kids. It was the first time in years Adelaide had heard anyone speak his name without the hollow ache that used to fill her mother's silences.

Still, even as they grew closer, Adelaide hadn't breathed a word about the bookshop. It wasn't just the suspicion that Carolyn had a history with the place; it was something else that she didn't fully understand. A desire to keep it to herself just a little longer.

She'd tell her tomorrow. That was the plan. When Carolyn went to the apothecary, she'd join her and reveal the newly cleaned-up shopfront, and finally say it out loud. Plus, she still needed to pry more out of Dottie. That photograph upstairs hadn't left her thoughts.

As she drove into town, Adelaide's mind drifted, inevitably, maddeningly, to Ewan. *Good grief.* She gripped the steering wheel tighter. The way she'd flushed, tripped over her words, nearly melted into a puddle of nerves just because a man with sawdust on his T-shirt smiled at her. *Get a grip*, she scolded herself. What was she, seventeen? Still shaking her head at her own absurdity, she turned into the narrow alleyway beside the bookshop. The space was just tight enough to keep her car hidden from view, perfect, in case Carolyn wandered by.

Adelaide hauled the tools from the back seat, the metal bucket clanging against her knees, and made her way to the front door. She fitted the key into the lock, using Dottie's trick. A firm tug, then push. The old door groaned open.

Stepping inside, the familiar scent of cologne enveloped her, as if the shop had exhaled after being sealed shut for too long. The air stirred around her, brushing past her shoulders, spilling into the street like something half-alive, eager to stretch its limbs. The shadow she'd seen yesterday flickered in her mind.

She recalled a documentary she'd watched years ago about ghosts, people speaking in hushed voices about catching a whiff of perfume or aftershave, just before something strange happened. *Maybe that was it*, she mused. Why she kept smelling a man's cologne. Perhaps the scent clung to something in the shop, the old chair in the loft, the stool behind the desk, the fabric of time itself refusing to let go.

She flicked on the overhead lights. They buzzed to life, highlighting the endless rows of spines. It still felt unreal, this place, all of it, hers.

Pulling the paint sample cards from her pocket, she walked to the wall of the loft stairs, the one she wanted to accent with a splash of color. The current hue was a tired off-white, more the shade of dust and years gone by than any real design choice. She held up a rich navy blue and a deep emerald green, both catching the light in promising ways.

Returning to the counter, she placed the two paint strips side by side and stacked the others neatly beside them. Later, she'd decide which to use for the children's corner and the small reading nook in the loft. But first, the exterior.

And her first mission was obvious: clear the path to the door by cutting back the ivy and shrubs.

She rolled up her sleeves and got to work.

Next, she knelt beside the walkway and yanked the weeds from the narrow strip of earth between the pavement and the edge of the building. A trimmer would have made quick work of it, but her small spade would have to do. The rhythm of it, cut, tug, shake, toss, soon pulled her into a steady groove.

To her surprise, within an hour, a blue slate pathway emerged.

Tugging back a curtain of ivy near the steps, she unearthed something unexpected: an old wooden sign. She brushed it clean with her gloved hands. A large feather was painted in its center, with a pair of moth wings behind it. A *peculiar combination*, she thought, but strangely, perfectly fitting for how she had found the place.

She propped it up against the door. Despite the wear, it was beautifully well-preserved. With a little sanding and varnish, it could shine again.

As she finished trimming the last of the ivy obscuring part of the large front window, a man's voice called out from behind her.

"Wow, look at this! You've done a great job. It looks almost like a shop again."

Adelaide turned to see the older man from the bakery, Dottie's husband, Iain, walking toward her.

"Thanks," she said, brushing ivy clippings off her trousers. "I'll take that as a compliment."

"You should. It's been a long time since it looked this good."

Just then, Dottie strolled over, holding a lemonade and a muffin wrapped in a napkin.

"Thought you could use a pick-me-up," she added, handing them over.

Adelaide took them gratefully. "Thanks, I'm starving."

Dottie smiled, but there was a flicker of something quieter behind it. "It seems like just yesterday that Pen was over here doing the same thing."

Adelaide paused mid-sip. "Pen? Was he the owner who left because of the 'ghost?'"

"No, Pen was the second owner of the shop in 1955, the one in the photo you pointed out in the bakery a few weeks ago," Iain explained.

Adelaide stilled, her mind racing. The young man in that photo looked to be around the same age as Carolyn was in the picture on the dresser. A connection began to form, but she needed to be sure. "Can I ask you something?" she said, turning to Dottie. "Was Pen Aunt Carolyn's boyfriend?"

Dottie let out a soft laugh. "Heavens, no."

"Then why is there a photo of her in the flat above the bookshop with some guy? And why did you suggest she wouldn't take the news of me buying the shop well?"

Dottie exchanged a glance with Iain, her brow furrowed as if deciding how much she wanted to share. Finally, she spoke, her voice softening. "That picture belonged to Rowland, the original owner of the bookshop back in the thirties. He and your aunt were sweethearts, young and in love."

"What happened to them?" Adelaide probed, sensing Dottie's hesitation. "Don't you think I should know the whole story and how Carolyn is tied into the bookshop?"

Dottie sighed, her gaze drifting as if she were revisiting the past. "Rowland was everything to her. But then Carolyn fell ill with tuberculosis. Nearly died. Rowland said he knew of something that could help her, something that might save her. Then he vanished. Just disappeared. Carolyn filed a missing person report, hired a private investigator too. She was convinced something bad had happened to him." Her face grew weary as she went on. "She waited for him. Months turned into years. But he never came back. It shattered her heart, and she never truly recovered."

"That must have been so hard for her," Adelaide whispered, looking up at the window of the bookshop's flat.

"It was." Dottie nodded. "When Pen took over the shop years later, it reopened a wound that had barely begun to heal. And when he went missing too… She started saying this place was cursed. Haunted by ghosts, by grief. I didn't know how much she'd told you."

"She hasn't said anything about it," Adelaide replied. "Not a word."

"Rowland's absence stole something from her. She used to be so bright," Dottie said quietly, her voice barely above a whisper.

Iain stepped in gently. "Rowland was always a bit of a mystery, but as for Pen, he might've just returned to America; he had brothers over there."

Dottie's expression tightened. "Maybe. But Pen wouldn't have left without saying goodbye. That's not the kind of man he was."

A quiet fell between them. She shifted her weight, chilled by more than just the late-summer air. Two owners. Two disappearances. And now she stood where they once had, keys in hand.

"Have you told her yet?" Dottie asked, snapping Adelaide out of her trance.

"No," she admitted, biting her lip. "I planned to break the news tomorrow when she comes to town to open the apothecary. But now, I'm not so sure that's the best idea."

"Aye, you might want to think about telling her at home tonight instead," Iain suggested. "People in town have caught wind of it and are starting to talk. Word gets around these parts."

Adelaide nodded. "Thanks for sharing that story with me. At least now I know to approach it gently."

"Of course. If you need anything, just let us know," Dottie said, patting her on the shoulder. She glanced up at the bookshop, a look of sadness flickering across her face before she turned back toward the bakery.

"It really does look good," Iain called as he followed Dottie across the street.

Adelaide lingered in front of the door, the weight of the keys suddenly heavier. With the truth came a shift. The Feather Thorn didn't just belong to her; it belonged to a story written long before she arrived.

She stepped back inside. The light from the window seemed dimmer now, though the sun still hung high in the sky. At the counter, she reached for the paint strips, then paused. The two samples she'd set aside earlier had been moved.

She remembered placing them side by side: navy and emerald. Now, only the emerald strip remained on the counter. The navy one sat neatly atop the larger stack.

She stared at it, then picked it up. Had she moved it? She couldn't remember. But she didn't think so.

She stepped outside with the emerald-green sample still in her hand. Maybe it was nothing, just Dottie's story clinging to the edges of her thoughts and making her imagination run wild. Still, as she closed the door behind her, she couldn't quite shake the sense that something inside the shop had shifted since she found out its true history. And not just the paint strips.

THE HIDDEN JOURNAL OF JOHN DEE – NOTES ON THE RITUAL TO SEAL THE TEAR IN TIME

October 28, 1582

The celestial alignment necessary to mend the rip in time will occur on the night of the 12th of November. The stars themselves will create a configuration matching the sigil revealed during Kelley's scrying session. The ritual will depend on precise timing, calculations, and the flawless operation of the Astral Synchronum. The following outlines the necessary components and steps:

Location:

The ritual must take place in the crypt beneath the eastern end of Dunblane Cathedral. This site is a focal point of divine energy and is protected by Archangel Michael, as confirmed during the scrying session. The sacred ground will amplify the celestial alignment's energy and stabilize the tear.

Materials:

A purified quartz disc, newly crafted and imbued with oils of sage, frankincense and cinnamon, must replace the shattered one. The quartz will act as the conduit to channel the celestial alignment's energy into the Astral Synchronum.

Gold and silver filings mixed with blessed water to anoint the device and draw the Monas Hieroglyphica Sigil on the crypt floor. These elements symbolize the sun and moon, balancing the celestial forces.

Seven candles placed in alignment with the stars' positions, corresponding to the sigil's points, will maintain the flow of energy.

Astral Synchronum Preparation:
Calibrate the device according to the following settings:
Rotation: One full clockwise rotation followed by a half-counterclockwise turn.
Gears: Shift Gear 4 by two notches to the right to align with the planetary mechanisms.
Alignment Lever: Position Saturn's sphere at 12 degrees east.
Wind the device six full turns before placing the quartz disc into position. The sixth turn aligns with the planetary spheres' synchronization.

Ritual Sequence:
Begin the ritual exactly one hour after sunset when the stars begin to align. This timing ensures the celestial energy is at its peak.

Continuation of the Ritual Sequence:
Kelley is to recite the invocation to Archangel Michael, as dictated during the scrying session.

From the heaven, a silver thread
To mend the tear before it spreads
A gilded needle from heaven's door
To stop the shifting, to stand restored
Reverse the damage, set it right
By the alignment of the heavens
And their guiding light

These words must be spoken with clarity and unwavering faith to summon the celestial energies required for the repair. The invocation will act as a bridge between the divine forces and the mortal realm, ensuring their cooperation.

As the invocation is spoken, Giordano will activate the Astral Synchronum. The device must perform three complete rotations: two clockwise and one counterclockwise. This motion mirrors the celestial cycle revealed in our calculations and represents the unspooling and reweaving of the fabric of time.

The Sealing Process:
As the light from the quartz intensifies, the sigil on the crypt floor will absorb the energy, connecting the tear to the celestial alignment. This energy will knit the tear back together, restoring the natural order.

Once the ritual concludes and the device ceases its movement, the Astral Synchronum must be dismantled without delay. Should it remain whole, it bears the power to split the veil of time, splintering the fabric of our reality into fragments beyond all knowing.

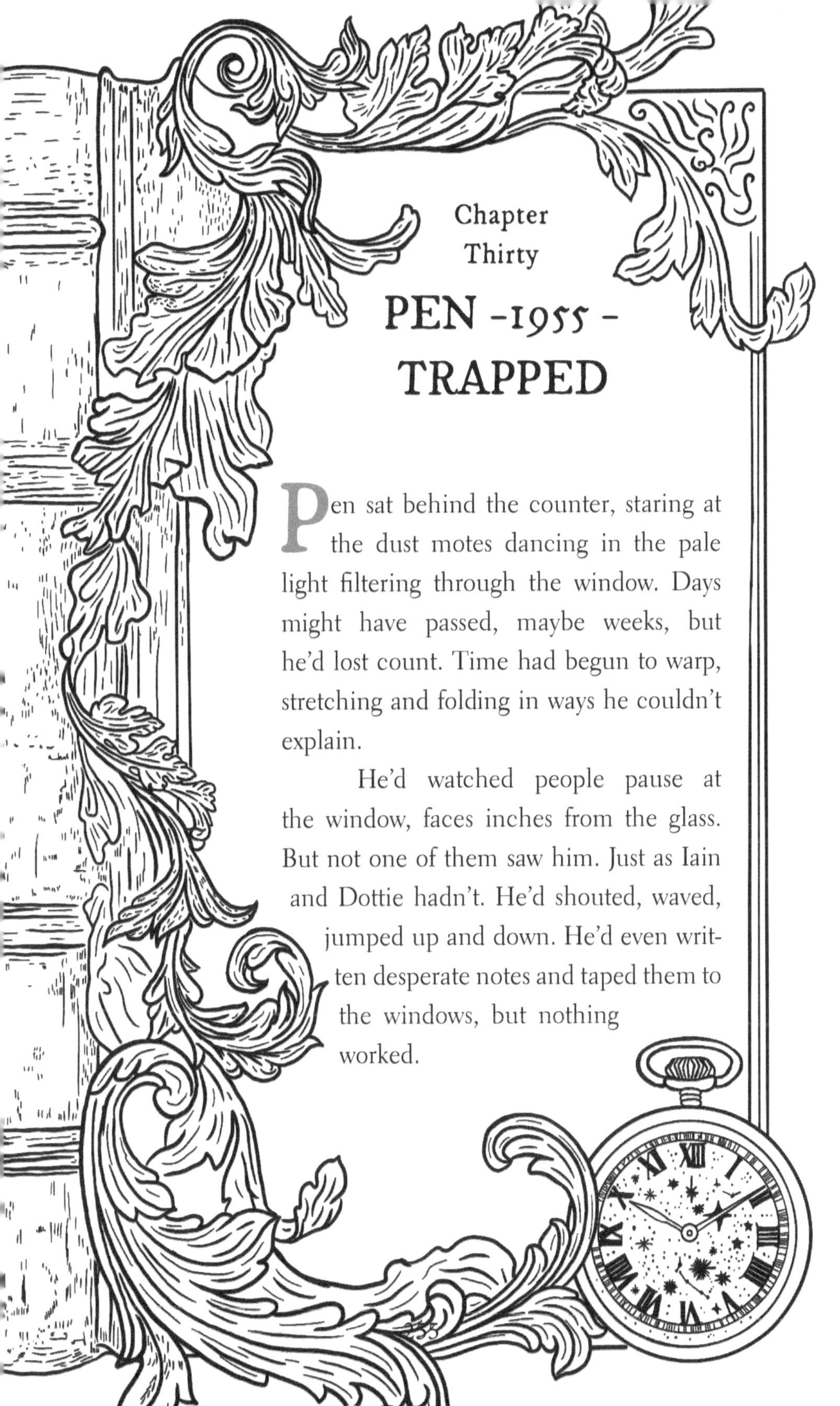

Chapter
Thirty

PEN –1955–
TRAPPED

Pen sat behind the counter, staring at the dust motes dancing in the pale light filtering through the window. Days might have passed, maybe weeks, but he'd lost count. Time had begun to warp, stretching and folding in ways he couldn't explain.

He'd watched people pause at the window, faces inches from the glass. But not one of them saw him. Just as Iain and Dottie hadn't. He'd shouted, waved, jumped up and down. He'd even written desperate notes and taped them to the windows, but nothing worked.

He'd tried phoning someone, anyone, but every call met him with static or silence. No dial tone. No voice.

There was a letterbox built straight into the front wall, just a square of weathered copper, its surface softened by age, streaked in places with green where time had crept in. The flap outside still faintly read *Feather Thorn*, the letters dulled but intact.

Inside, the slot led to a narrow copper chute, no wider than a shoebox. Pen had cleared out the spiderwebs weeks ago.

He slid a letter in, and it landed with the same soft tick it always did. This hadn't been the first letter he had tried to send. Despite the postman checking it each day, the letters piled up, untouched.

Even the radio offered nothing but a whispering void of white noise. It was like he'd been erased from the world, as though nothing he did could leave an impression.

At first, he'd tried to escape. The doors, the windows. But no matter how hard he fought to leave, he always ended up back behind the counter on his stool, as though he'd never moved at all.

Eventually, Pen came to accept the impossible: he was stuck in some kind of loop. Each day, the same half-bottle of milk reappeared in the fridge. The same eggs. The same ground beef and other staples he'd stocked up on the day of the eclipse. He was grateful for that, as the alternative would have been grim.

Without the books, he might have gone truly mad. They were his lifeline. His only companions. He looked up at the old model ship dangling above his head. He imagined drifting through fog, anchorless and forgotten. *At sea,* he thought, *at least there's a hope someone might find you.* But here? Even hope had begun to feel like fiction.

A faint metallic scrape broke the stillness.

The bell above the door gave a cheerful jingle as it swung open, and Dottie walked in, followed closely by Iain and the constable.

Pen shot to his feet, heart pounding against his ribs. Finally. Someone had come.

"Dottie!" Pen's voice cracked, hoarse from disuse. Relief flooded over him as he stepped toward her, ready to pour out everything he'd been holding in.

But she didn't turn to face him. None of them did.

Dottie walked right past him, her gaze sweeping the shop's interior, as if he weren't there, mere feet away.

His heart slowed, and a creeping cold settled over him as he watched her.

"Pen?" Dottie called, her tone laced with concern.

"I don't think he's here," Iain murmured, glancing at the constable. "Maybe he left a note?"

Constable MacDuff headed through the back door, up toward the apartment. Iain trailed after Dottie, deeper into the rows of books.

Pen followed, calling out, waving his hands, doing anything he could to break through. But it was like shouting underwater, his voice didn't reach. His presence didn't register. A ghost. That's what he'd become, a spectral echo, but made of skin and bone, invisible, intangible, trapped within the walls of the Feather Thorn.

The search continued. Dottie and Iain moved through the aisles, calling his name, voices laden with mounting worry. Each unanswered call twisted in Pen's gut like a knife.

The constable returned, shaking his head. "Nothing up there. Did you find anything?"

"No, nothing," Dottie said, her voice dropping with disappointment.

"Do you think he might have hurt himself?" the constable asked.

A look of concern washed over Dottie.

"Dottie, you know I wouldn't—" Pen began on reflex, then stopped. It was pointless. She couldn't hear him.

"No," she said at last. "There's no way. He wouldn't do that to his brothers."

She stepped closer to him, so close Pen could almost feel the warmth of her next to him. He reached out, placing his hand on her shoulder; it passed straight through, his fingers slipping through her like headlights cutting through thick fog. His chest tightened, breath catching in his throat. He stared down at his now-trembling hand. This wasn't strange anymore; it was terrifying.

"Maybe we should leave a note," Dottie suggested, glancing around the room again. "Just in case he comes back. Let him know to call us."

Iain nodded. "Maybe he's gone back to America."

Dottie pulled a pen and ledger pad from the front desk and began to write.

Pen,

Come over or give us a call when you get back.

We're worried about you.

Love, Dottie.

Pen hovered beside her, reading the message. Desperation gripped him in that moment, and he snatched up the pen as she set it down. He scrawled in the blank space beside her words.

I didn't leave. I'm still here. Please, help me. I don't know what's happening.

Dottie didn't react. Didn't pause. Didn't even glance at the fresh ink that now screamed from the page.

He watched them leave, one at a time. Dottie stopped in the doorway, one foot out and one still inside the shop. She looked back in, one last time, her eyes scanning the space as if she might catch a glance of him. For a heartbeat, Pen dared to hope. But then she stepped out, and the heavy oak door closed, shutting with unmistakable finality.

He paced the rows of books, his mind a blur of confusion. Nothing made sense. All the natural laws, time, space, reality had all buckled. He found himself sitting on the godforsaken stool again, but this time of his own volition, though the act felt no less futile. Dottie's note looked up at him, the familiar loops of her handwriting offering no comfort. Beside it lay *Liber Loagaeth*, the book by John Dee. It had been resting in that very spot for weeks. For some reason, he'd never put it away.

His eyes flicked to the painting of Dee on the wall. The key Rowland had taped to the back. Maybe none of it was random.

Pen picked up the book. He'd skimmed it before, but never fully read it. He'd never had time. Now, with nothing but time, he cracked the spine and began at the beginning.

It wasn't fiction; it was a record. Dee's documentation of an angelic language, received through the scrying of Edward Kelley. Page after page revealed the Enochian alphabet: symbols, rituals, invocations, each intended to unlock a piece of divine knowledge.

As he read on, a chill crawled across his skin, prickling the back of his neck. Rowland had known about this. That much was clear.

Nearly a quarter of the way through, Pen froze. He knew those symbols. He pulled the lucky penny from his pocket and flipped it over with his fingers as he thought. Where had he seen those markings? A book? No, a map? The celestial maps tucked away in the desk drawer of the hidden room.

Snapping the book shut, he clutched it tightly and hurried to the trapdoor. He descended the narrow staircase, stale air rushing to meet him as he entered the secret room below. At the desk, he set the book aside and pulled open the heavy drawers. The maps were there, just as he'd left them. He laid them out, opened the first one, and scanned the inked constellations and meticulous lines.

There, on the right-hand side. Tiny faded symbols. He reached for *Liber Loagaeth*, flipping feverishly until he found them. The three cryptic symbols. They matched exactly. He traced them with his fingertip. Then looked back at the translation in Dee's text. *Celestial Opening.*

Heart pounding, Pen pulled the next map into view. Two more symbols leapt out at him. He thumbed through the book again, cross-referencing the forms. *Time. Shift.*

The pieces were falling into place.

These weren't just celestial charts; they were a cipher, a hidden code interwoven with the Enochian language. Maps, yes, but to something far beyond the stars.

It was the third map that stole his breath. There, written across the parchment in careful ink, was the word he'd seen before. *Monad.* The very word etched onto the side of the watch.

His fingers trembled as he traced the string of symbols clustered above the name, symbols identical to those he had found in the book.

With painstaking care, Pen began to translate. *The portal's Key lies within the alignment of the heavens.*

The map slipped through his fingers.

He dashed up the stairs, footsteps thundering through the empty shop. At the counter, the watch waited. Its face glinted faintly in the dim light. Grabbing it, he rushed back to the hidden room and laid it beside the map and the open book.

His gaze fell to the back of the watch, where the metal had been delicately etched. There, almost invisible unless you knew what to look for, was the Enochian symbol for *Key*.

Pen tore open the drawers, pulling out every journal. Most were filled with mathematical equations and notes on cosmic events. But one held what he was looking for. A detailed drawing of the watch. Beneath it, a single line:

Astral Synchronum. Created by John Dee and Giordano Bruno. Designed to open a portal between Heaven and Earth.

He read on.

Rowland had believed the Synchronum could manipulate time itself. That under the right celestial conditions, it could create a rift, a wormhole, through which time could be bent or broken. He had hoped to use it. Not for fame or power. But to go back. To save Carolyn.

Pen's grip tightened on the old worn journal. The night he'd pressed the buttons… there had been an eclipse. He hadn't just wound the watch. He'd accidentally activated the watch. Opened a door. And stepped through. The horror of it settled like ice. He was trapped. Caught in a fracture of time.

And it was his fault.

He doubled over, pressing a hand to his mouth as nausea coiled in his gut. Not just a mistake. *His* mistake. Desperation had driven him to act before he understood the cost. And now, the world he'd known was gone.

But there was no time to dwell on it. If he was going to escape, the answers had to lie within the journals, within the complex equations and celestial charts, the symbology scrawled across every page.

He wasn't a mathematician. Not even close. But he had time. All the time in the world.

So he studied.

Bit by bit, night after night, the hidden room transformed. The walls bloomed with notes, observations, equations, and sketches. Pen tracked planetary paths, mapped celestial alignments, drew connections between Dee's rituals and Rowland's theories. Symbols danced across the damp stone walls, constellations stitched together, constellations of meaning.

He stopped keeping track of the days. They bled together into one long, sleepless pursuit. Each night, he climbed to the apartment, telescope in hand, and watched the skies. Mars. Venus. Jupiter. He learned them all. Waited for them to fall into place, like tumblers in a lock.

He was no longer waiting for a rescue. He was preparing for a release. The stars would align again. And when they did, he would be ready.

PEN - 1955 - BROKEN SILENCE

Pen had lost track of time, and time, it seemed, had lost track of him. The only thing tethering him to sanity was the sea of books that surrounded him. The days blurred together, marked only by the turning of pages. He'd read so many, he couldn't keep count; at some point, he'd stopped trying. The bookshop had become his entire world: dim light, musty air, and the rustle of paper his only constants. That, and the fox.

Pen first noticed the creature slinking around the gardening section, skittish and scrappy, where his old nest had been. The kit moved with a restless energy, as though searching for a way out. He couldn't help but wonder if the poor thing shared his fate, trapped here, caught in the same invisible loop.

He began leaving scraps: bits of ground beef, half a boiled egg, the items that reappeared in his refrigerator each morning. At first, the fox was cautious, only creeping in to eat once Pen was out of sight. But over time, the distance between them shrank. The fox began to appear during daylight hours, weaving through the stacks while Pen busied himself dusting and sorting the shelves.

Then, one day, as Pen sat in the loft with a book balanced across his knees, the fox appeared. Quiet yet unafraid. It padded toward him, then curled up at his feet and closed its eyes.

Pen stared at it, barely daring to breathe. "Frankie," he whispered. After Frankie Valli, his favorite singer. The name felt right. Familiar. A small thread tying him back to the world he'd known. A piece of home.

From that day on, the fox became his shadow. Frankie trotted beside him down the aisles, darting playfully between shelves. He was Pen's only companion, the only consistent rhythm in his otherwise monotonous days. The stillness felt less empty with Frankie. The fox's soft snores, the patter of paws on floorboards, the occasional yip or a sneeze, as Pen sifted through books or added new notes to the wall of the hidden room, made it feel less like a prison.

Together, they existed in the quiet pulse of the place until one day the silence broke.

The door to the bookshop creaked open, rousing the soft, sweet jingle of the bells, an unfamiliar sound after what Pen could only guess had been months. Frankie took off, vanishing into the shadows in search of a hiding place.

From his vantage point, Pen's gaze remained fixed on the entrance below. A young man in his thirties stepped in, followed by Susan, the town clerk. Her hair was grayer now, her features more lined. They moved beneath the model ship and airplane. The man looked around, his eyes full of wonder, the same kind of reverence Pen had felt the first time he stepped into the shop.

"Here it is," Susan said. "Probably needs a good dusting, but other than that, it's ready to go."

Hearing a voice that wasn't his own shook something loose in him, like the click of a long-seized cog. It felt strange, jarring.

"Great. Thank you," the man replied.

Susan handed him a ring of keys. "Well, I'll leave you to it."

There was something off about the man. His shoulder-length hair and trimmed beard didn't match. His jeans flared absurdly at the ankles, and his tunic-like shirt looked like something out of a costume box. Was Pen hallucinating? Had the silence finally pushed him over the edge? Or was this really happening? Was someone reopening the shop? The thought brought a jolt of hope. If the man was real, maybe there was a way to reach him. To tell him what this place really was. And maybe, just maybe, he could help Pen find a way out.

But as Pen watched, it felt unnervingly familiar. The way the man ran his fingers along the shelves, pausing to admire the books. The same sense of awe and discovery that Pen had once felt. Was it jealousy, seeing someone take over the very things he'd grown attached to? Or was it something deeper, a darker thought he hadn't dared name: that this stranger might end up just as he had, trapped?

Over the next few days, Pen tried everything to get the man's attention. He flipped the lights on and off, slammed doors, and even yelled in the man's face. Nothing. It was like being trapped behind a two-way mirror; Pen could see out, but no one could see in.

Then, one afternoon, it happened by accident, Pen tripped over Frankie, who was constantly underfoot now that they had a visitor, and bumped the painting of John Dee, tilting it askew. Not long after, the man rounded the corner and ascended the stairs with a small stack of books. Pen's heart leapt into his throat as the man paused at the crooked frame, frowned slightly, then straightened it as he passed.

He waited until the man disappeared into the autobiography section, then nudged the painting off-kilter again. Later, when the man came back down the stairs, he stopped just as before, frowned, and righted the painting once more.

Pen repeated this over the next day. Each time, the man fixed the painting, his frown growing deeper. Finally, murmuring, "Guess this one needs a new hook," he removed it from the wall and set it gently at the bottom of the stairs.

Pen stared, heart pounding. It wasn't much, but it was something. For the first time in what felt like an eternity, he'd left a trace, an impact in someone else's reality.

That evening, Pen sat on the bottom step, his gaze fixed on the painting now resting there.

"How can I move this in his reality?" he muttered to Frankie as he stared into John Dee's painted eyes.

An idea struck. He dashed to the hidden room and yanked *Liber Loagaeth* from the desk. Back by the painting, hands trembling, he flipped through the ancient text. Symbols scrolled past, but none leapt out. With a frustrated sigh, he set the book aside and returned his stare to the painting.

Exhausted, he left the book on the steps and retreated to bed, dread pooling. Maybe that had been his only chance to communicate with the man, and he'd failed.

The next morning, Pen descended the stairs just as the man unlocked the door, a box tucked under his arm. He set it on the counter and pulled out a neat stack of *Jonathan Livingston Seagull* books by Richard Bach. As he turned to shelve them, he paused, glancing over at the staircase. Pen followed his gaze. *Liber Loagaeth* was still lying where he'd left it.

Could he see it? First the painting, now this, it couldn't be a coincidence, could it? Pen's mind whirled. Both objects were connected to John Dee. Could that be the link?

The man set his stack down and picked up *Liber Loagaeth*. He cast a puzzled glance around the shop before placing it on the counter and returning to his task.

Pen didn't waste a second. He ran to the biography section, pulled out the thick leather-bound volume on John Dee, and placed it square in the center of the shop floor, impossible to miss.

Then, he waited.

The man rounded the fiction case and strolled right over the book without so much as a glance.

Pen's heart sank. He couldn't see it. So John Dee wasn't the connection after all. He slipped his hand into his pocket, fiddling with his lucky penny, thoughts spinning. The painting and the book, he'd touched both, the day time had stopped for him. Could *that* be the key?

Needing to test his theory, he went to the counter and pulled the silver letter opener from the can, the one he'd used to try to pry open the desk drawer that night. He dropped it to the floor. The sharp *clang* echoed through the shop.

The man whipped around, eyes wide, searching. *He heard it!*

Excitement rising, Pen picked up *Liber Loagaeth* again and flung it onto the floor.

The man jumped back, visibly shaken. "What the bloody hell?" he muttered, bending to retrieve it, eyes darting around the room.

Pen grinned. He'd gotten through.

This time, he lifted the book slowly, holding it at eye level. Right in front of the man's face. The man's jaw dropped. He stared at the floating volume, color draining from his cheeks. Pen let it fall.

The man backed away, grabbed his coat, and fled.

Pen winced. *Okay, maybe that was a bit much.*

Next time, Pen told himself, he'd try a gentler approach.

He waited. Surely the man would come back. But the next day came, and the next, and the shop remained empty.

"Maybe he needs a few days," Pen said to Frankie.

Days passed. Then weeks. Time blurred again into the same gray haze as before. The man never returned.

Then, one day, the silence was broken once again.

A couple entered the shop, wide-eyed and eager, their voices echoing off the shelves as they wandered around. Pen stood watching from the loft, Frankie curled at his feet. *This is my second chance,* he thought.

He pictured his brothers. If he could make this work, if he could get out, he could keep his promise to Val. He could go home. Hope surged. The story he would tell them. It seemed so unbelievable that he'd be lucky if they didn't think he was completely mad, but he wouldn't care; he'd hear their voices again.

This time Pen decided to try a different approach. He gathered every object he remembered touching the day of the eclipse:

books, the letter opener, a wooden spoon from the apartment, even his razor, and carefully arranged them on the floor to spell out a single word. *HELP.* Maybe they would understand.

The couple returned the next day, their conversation light as they unlocked the door, but the man stopped mid-sentence; the woman clutched at his arm. "What the…?"

They crept forward, studying the items on the floor. The woman nudged the spoon with her foot. They exchanged a look. Then a book slipped from Pen's hands and hit the floor with a thud. He hadn't meant to drop it, but he had. And they'd heard it.

They didn't run, but they didn't look back either. The door slammed shut behind them.

Pen stared at the word still on the floor. *HELP.* As stark and useless as before. He'd failed. Again.

The hope drained like the color from a bleached photograph. He wandered the shop aimlessly that afternoon, unable to focus on the wall of books or even Frankie's quiet steps trailing him.

That night, he didn't eat. He didn't write. He didn't plan.

He just sat.

One afternoon, something stirred, and he felt the urge of an old habit. He went upstairs to the apartment, cracked open the window, and looked out.

It was summer. The last time he'd looked out, snow covered the cobbled streets. Had that much time really passed? The street below buzzed with life, flowers in full bloom, a sky wide and blue, light glinting off car windshields. But not the boxy cars Pen remembered. Sleeker ones. Flashier ones. Then one passed with a glowing sign on top: Pizza Hut. What was a Pizza Hut? And why did it need a car to deliver it? He pressed his forehead to the glass as he watched it disappear down the street.

Over the next few days, he found himself back at the window. The clothing people wore was bright, almost fluorescent, and their hair was teased and wild, even the men's. Music thudded from a passing stereo with a strange, chaotic beat.

Everything had changed.

What is going on?

Then one afternoon he saw her. A pretty young woman following a moth as it fluttered its way toward his doorstep. She paused, peered at the sign, then wandered off toward the apothecary as the moth fluttered away. Moments later, Pen spotted an older woman. At first, Pen didn't grasp what he was seeing. But then, it hit him: it was Carolyn. Her once-dark hair was now white, her posture softened with age, her face lined with time. It was most definitely her, but a much older version.

He pressed a hand to the window. The last time he'd seen her, she'd been forty at most. Now she appeared to be in her *seventies. How long? How long have I been trapped in this hell?* His mind scrambled to piece together the years that had slipped away into decades, it seemed. Time outside the loop seemed to move faster; Pen hadn't aged even a day.

He watched as the two women disappeared into the Purple Thorn. Then he sat at the window and waited until they emerged again, walking down the street together, chatting as they stepped into the Marbled Clover. His gaze followed them through the glass, where Dottie and Iain stood behind the counter.

Dottie and Iain.

They had aged too, no longer in their thirties, but well into their sixties.

Pen swallowed hard. Everyone he'd ever known had aged, grown older, changed. He, too, would have been that old if he hadn't been trapped here in time.

He turned from the window, sinking to the floor as a cold realization gripped him. Years had passed. Not months. Not *a* year. Decades. He thought of his brothers, Val, Will, Dave. He'd imagined them waiting for him, confused by his disappearance. But now, they must have moved on, grown up, and had families of their own. Lived whole lives without him. What had they thought happened to him? That he'd died? He'd promised to come back. Promised to stay in touch. To keep them safe.

Pen clenched his fists, jaw tight.

No more waiting.

He had to find a way out. Before it was too late. Before everyone he'd ever known, everyone he'd ever loved, became nothing more than a memory he couldn't touch.

Because if he didn't, he would be left behind forever. Left in this endless loop. A stranger in a world that had long since forgotten his name.

PEN - 1955 - THIRD TIMES A CHARM

In the days that followed, Pen found himself standing by the window with Frankie at his side, watching, waiting, willing the mysterious woman he'd seen with Carolyn to reappear.

He was certain she'd looked straight up at him the other day as she and Carolyn left the bakery. Not just a glance, eye contact. But how could she have? No one had seen him since the day time stopped.

The moment had nested in his mind ever since. Maybe it meant something. Maybe she was different. Maybe she could be his new chance at escape.

Trying to keep the dangerous thread of hope from unraveling, he busied himself in the kitchen. Tugging open the fridge, he found the same few items as always. He pulled out the eggs and cracked one into the old cast-iron pan. Frankie yawned, then padded over to sit at his feet.

"I know, bud. Same old breakfast," he said, poking at the egg with a spatula. He'd taken to cooking even when he wasn't hungry. Just to fill the air with movement, smell, something real. He salted the egg, turned toward the kettle.

That's when he heard it.

The sound of the apartment's doorknob being turned.

Another rattle. The doorknob twisted again.

He moved quietly across the room, Frankie beside him, tail low and twitching. With breath held tight, he flicked the lock and slowly opened the door.

There, standing in the shadows on the stairs, was the outline of a woman.

He stepped back instinctively, half-hidden in the gloom. However, Frankie darted forward, slipping through the gap between Pen's legs, and bolted past the figure. There was a short gasp, followed by a short scream, unmistakably the sound of a woman.

She had seen Frankie. The fox was real to her. That meant the barrier wasn't absolute; there was still a way through. The woman stepped forward, and the light caught her face. It was her. The woman who followed the moth. The woman from the street. Peering into the half-lit room.

Pen held utterly still, unsure if she was seeing him or simply sensing something. Her gaze swept past him without landing, and his brief hope stuttered. She hadn't seen him.

She crossed the room, examining the bookshelves, pausing at the window. Pen drifted behind her, captivated. Up close, she was stunning, with that rare, natural beauty few possessed, entirely unaware of the storm her presence had stirred in him.

She turned abruptly, almost as if she had sensed him nearby. Her eyes met the space beside his face. But then she moved on, continuing her quiet exploration.

After taking a final look around, she left the apartment and headed downstairs into the shop. Pen couldn't help but follow.

Downstairs, she wandered the shop floor, notepad in hand, occasionally scribbling notes. Pen trailed behind her. When she finished, she set her notes aside, shrugged into her jacket, and left. But she glanced back, right as Pen stepped behind the Romance section.

Hope, fierce and unrelenting, surged through him.

He didn't sleep that night. He paced the shop. *What if she doesn't come back? What if I blink and six months have passed?*

Before dawn, Pen was back downstairs, pacing, muttering, eyes flickering to the door every few minutes. And then she returned. This time with a bucket filled with gardening supplies and a determined look on her face. He watched through the window as she trimmed the ivy away and cut back overgrown hedges. He hadn't noticed how worn and neglected the bookshop's exterior had become. The place, like everything outside the time loop, had aged. All his hard work from before, the paint, the polish, the careful curation, erased. Time had pulled at the edges like a loose thread, unraveling all he'd done until the shop looked untouched again.

Later, Dottie and Iain crossed the street to join her, arms full of treats and their usual bright smiles. Pen leaned closer to the window, straining to hear. Their voices were muffled, broken by laughter, but he caught her name, Adelaide, and that she was Carolyn's great-niece who'd bought the bookshop.

Pen straightened. This was it. This was his chance. They say the third time's a charm. But this time, he'd have to be careful. No more floating books. No more messages in objects.

He scanned the counter. A handful of paint sample cards lay piled up. He studied the colors she'd set aside, and an idea began to form. He reached for the letter opener and used it to lift the navy strip and place it atop the stack of samples, leaving his preferred choice, the emerald green, separate on the counter.

Then, he waited.

Adelaide entered the shop only moments later and made her way to the counter. Her brow furrowed. She looked at the single green paint strip, then at the stack. Pen sagged against the bookshelves.

It had worked. He'd managed to move something that wasn't directly tied to the day he'd disappeared. Granted, he'd used an item from that day to do it, but it was progress. This small success opened up a world of possibilities.

But before he could revel in his victory, she picked up the green paint strip, cast another puzzled look around, and left.

"Damn it," he mumbled. "Too much?"

That night, Pen paced again. Every idea he came up with to reach her felt like a dead end. Too cryptic, too eerie, too likely to send her running. He found himself in the hidden room, slouched in the captain's chair.

He ran his fingers over the Underwood typewriter keys as he stared off into space.

Then suddenly the familiar sound of chimes broke his

trance. Pen sat upright. Not the chimes of the front door.

They rang again. The unmistakable chime of the Astral Synchronum. The first time he'd heard them in what must have been years. Pen jumped to his feet, ready to race upstairs, but his shirt sleeve snagged on the Underwood's edge. He stopped to free it, and in that instant, realization struck.

The typewriter. He'd fiddled with it that day. Now *this* might work.

The chiming had stopped by the time he'd freed himself from the typewriter's grip, and instead of heading upstairs, he slid a sheet of paper in place, sat back down, and stared at the keys. What could he say? What wouldn't scare her? After several false starts and crumpled pages, he settled on something simple. A few quick taps and he was done.

He pulled the page free, folded it, and, with a silent prayer, walked upstairs. There, he slipped it into the letterbox next to the front door, half poking out, impossible to miss. Then he stepped back, heart hammering, and waited.

THE HIDDEN JOURNAL OF JOHN DEE

November 11, 1582

Tomorrow is the day. The day we either succeed or face the consequences of our actions. Giordano and I have reviewed the ritual again and again, ensuring that every step is executed precisely, for one misstep could doom us. The alignment we've waited for will not come again for another fourteen years, and we cannot afford to let time slip through our fingers. In that time, all we know could unravel completely.

I have seen more changes, small, seemingly insignificant at first, but each one pulling me further into doubt. The great apple tree that once stood proudly in our backyard, providing us with fruit for as long as I can remember, is now gone. It has simply vanished, as if it was never there at all. The neighbor's cottage, which I've known since my childhood, a solid landmark that has withstood the tests of time, now lies reduced to a mere shed, used only to house the neighboring farmer's sheep. It seems as though the world around us is shifting, crumbling into something unfamiliar.

I fear that it will not stop here. These are not mere coincidences. Reality itself is coming undone, and I can feel the tug of an alternate universe beckoning us, pulling us into something unknown. If the rip in time is not repaired tomorrow, there may be no other opportunity to repair it at all. We could slip completely into this new reality, one where we do not belong, one where everything we know ceases to exist.

I pray that the ritual will hold fast, that the universe will realign and restore itself. I pray that our reality will stay intact and that tomorrow's work will set things right. But there is a gnawing doubt in my mind, one I cannot shake. We have been playing with forces beyond our comprehension. Tomorrow, we will know whether we have been right in our efforts or whether our actions will lead to an irreversible collapse. I pray it is not too late.

Tomorrow, everything changes.

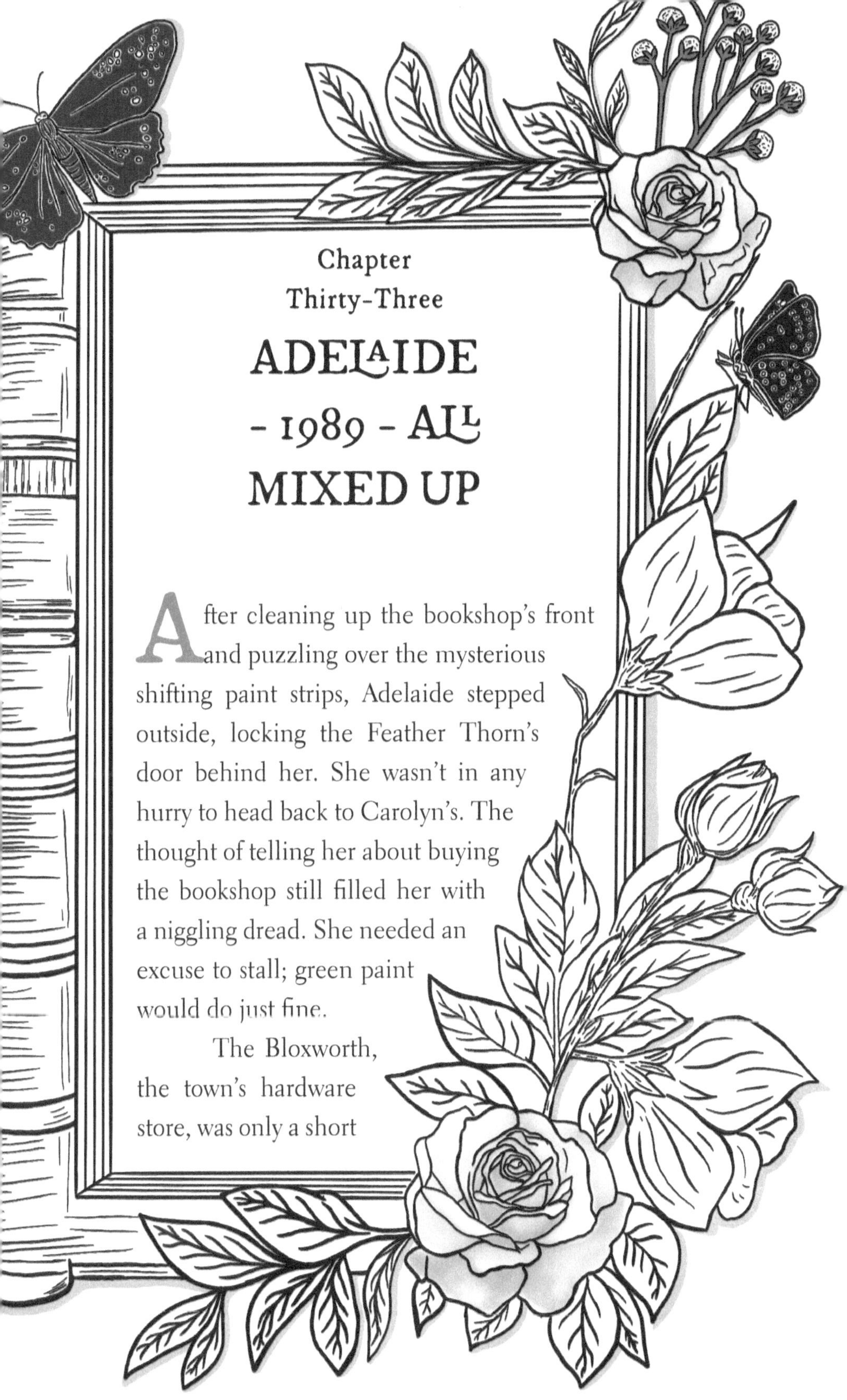

Chapter
Thirty-Three
ADELAIDE
- 1989 - ALL
MIXED UP

After cleaning up the bookshop's front and puzzling over the mysterious shifting paint strips, Adelaide stepped outside, locking the Feather Thorn's door behind her. She wasn't in any hurry to head back to Carolyn's. The thought of telling her about buying the bookshop still filled her with a niggling dread. She needed an excuse to stall; green paint would do just fine.

The Bloxworth, the town's hardware store, was only a short

walk away. She pushed open its heavy oak door, a cascade of chimes announcing her arrival. The shop was a small-town jumble of tools, homewares, and seasonal odds and ends. Rows of dark wooden shelves lined the walls, groaning under merchandise. It smelled like old nails and freshly cut timber, with a faint undertone of peppermint from the jars of sweets near the till. The worn black-and-white tiles underfoot gave the place an old-world charm that made her oddly nostalgic.

Adelaide made a beeline past coiled garden hoses and rows of padlocks, heading straight for the small paint counter at the back. It was empty. She leaned over it slightly, craning her neck to see into the dim storeroom behind, where paint cans lined old wooden shelves.

"Hello?" she called out. Her voice echoed, unanswered. Just as she was about to turn away, the sound of heavy footsteps thudded behind her. Adelaide turned to see Ewan approaching, sporting a green shop apron, covered in sawdust. Her heart gave a startled leap, and a warm flush spread over her cheeks.

"Adelaide, wasn't it?" he asked, swinging open the half-door and stepping behind the counter. His expression brightened. "What brings you in today?"

"Hi," she stammered, pulling the paint sample from the pocket of her suede jacket and holding it out. "I need paint."

As he took it, she glanced at his apron. So, this was the place he'd meant when he'd apologized about the timber delivery delay.

"Nice choice," he said, glancing at the sample. Then, with a grin, "And good taste in jackets, too."

She instinctively brushed the soft suede. She'd forgotten she was wearing it. Though she loved the jacket, it sometimes felt a little out of her old comfort zone.

"Oh, thanks," she managed, looking down at her shoes.

"Seriously," he added, a hint of amusement in his voice. "I mean it."

His words carried no pressure, just a quiet, pleasant confidence. Still, it flustered her. She found herself smiling, girlishly, before she turned away to browse a random aisle, pretending to look at something else while her pulse calmed. She wandered past latches and hinges, her hand trailing over the cold metal, until she paused at a display of sturdy bolt locks. A flash of the figure standing in the window of the flat flitted through her mind. The place had been abandoned for years; it wasn't unthinkable that someone had been squatting. Maybe they still were. It would explain the smell of men's cologne and the figure she'd seen. She picked two heavy-duty bolts off the rack and tucked them under her arm.

The sharp tang of pine and resin clung to the air as she wandered through the timber section looking for a board she could use to patch the broken stairwell window, but everything was too long or too thick. Perhaps Carolyn would have a scrap piece in the garage. She'd have to look later.

As she returned to the paint area, Adelaide pulled a roller and a wide-bristled brush from a wall rack. Ewan appeared just then, holding a fresh tin of paint with a green splotch on the lid that matched the swatch she'd brought in.

"Need a tray?" he asked, gesturing toward a stack of paint trays balancing on an old oak barrel.

"Yes, please," she replied, flashing a smile as she fumbled with the roller, brush, and locks, trying to free up a hand.

"No bother, I've got it." He grabbed a tray for her and walked to the front counter. "Helping Carolyn paint?"

She hesitated, then shook her head, placing the supplies down. "No, I've got a few projects of my own."

"The Feather Thorn?" he inquired, catching her off guard.

Part of her wanted to keep it quiet a little longer, admitting it felt like confirming the whispers going around town, but she was planning on telling Carolyn that evening.

"Yeah," she answered, trying to sound breezy. "Just giving it a fresh coat of paint in a few spots."

"It's nice to see someone taking an interest in it again," he said warmly, ringing up her items. "It's been sitting empty for far too long. This town could use a little more adventure, mystery… a touch of romance."

He lingered on that last word, his gaze holding hers a moment longer than necessary. Heat rose to her cheeks, and her mind immediately leapt into thoughts that had no business being entertained in a hardware store. Or anywhere else in public, for that matter.

"Right," she said quickly. "Yes, well, I hope to have it up and running soon."

"Good to hear. That'll be twenty-two pounds."

She dug out the cash from her back pocket, handed it over, then reached for the bag and paint, eager to bolt.

"Can I help you with all that?" Ewan asked, coming around the counter. He stepped close, too close, and she caught a hint of his aftershave, clean and woodsy, woodsmoke and pine, sending her thoughts down a path that was anything but clean and wholesome.

"Thanks, but I've got it," she squeaked, half an octave higher than normal. She pivoted toward the door, needing to put distance between herself and the man who seemed to bring out the teenage girl in her.

"Let me know if there's anything I can do to help!" he called after her.

She lifted the bag of supplies in a one-handed wave and threw him a quick smile, the kind that showed too many teeth, before practically bursting out the door.

She couldn't have been more awkward if she tried.

If this was what flirting looked like after nearly a decade of marriage, she was in trouble. Apparently, she had the social skills of a deer in headlights when it came to attractive men.

Back at the bookshop, she set down the purchases, locked up, and headed over to the bakery. If she was going to break the news to Carolyn, she figured a box of chocolate puffs might help sweeten the blow.

Dottie boxed up a dozen with a knowing smile, and Adelaide took them gratefully, climbing into her car just as the last of daylight faded. A cold dew was already frosting the pavement, and she guessed there'd be ice by morning.

It reminded her that her time at the stone cabin was nearly up. Though the thought no longer filled her with dread, now that she knew the Feather Thorn had a flat above it.

She'd miss it, of course. Over the past few weeks, the cabin had become her space, in a way nowhere else ever had. For the first time in her life, she had a place to breathe. But now, not only did she have a flat to live in, she had a bookshop to care for. A new Chapter of her life waiting to be written. And for once, it was a story she actually wanted to live. She'd never pictured her life without Jeff. But now, in the wake of everything, she was starting to discover who she was without him, and she liked the person she was becoming.

As she pulled into Carolyn's driveway, the warm glow from the kitchen windows that usually welcomed her home made her stomach twist. There was so much to explain. Carolyn's past with the shop wasn't simple, and if she believed the place was cursed, tonight wouldn't be easy. Adelaide was bracing for a storm.

She shut off the engine and lingered in the silence until the cold air began to creep into the car, forcing her out and toward the warmth of the house.

Clutching the box of chocolate puffs under one arm, she walked up the path and paused at the door.

The conversation would be uncomfortable, maybe even painful, but if she was ever going to stand on her own, it had to start now. Carolyn needed to understand why she'd bought the Feather Thorn. Why, no matter what anyone said, she couldn't walk away from it. It had called to her. And she was ready to answer.

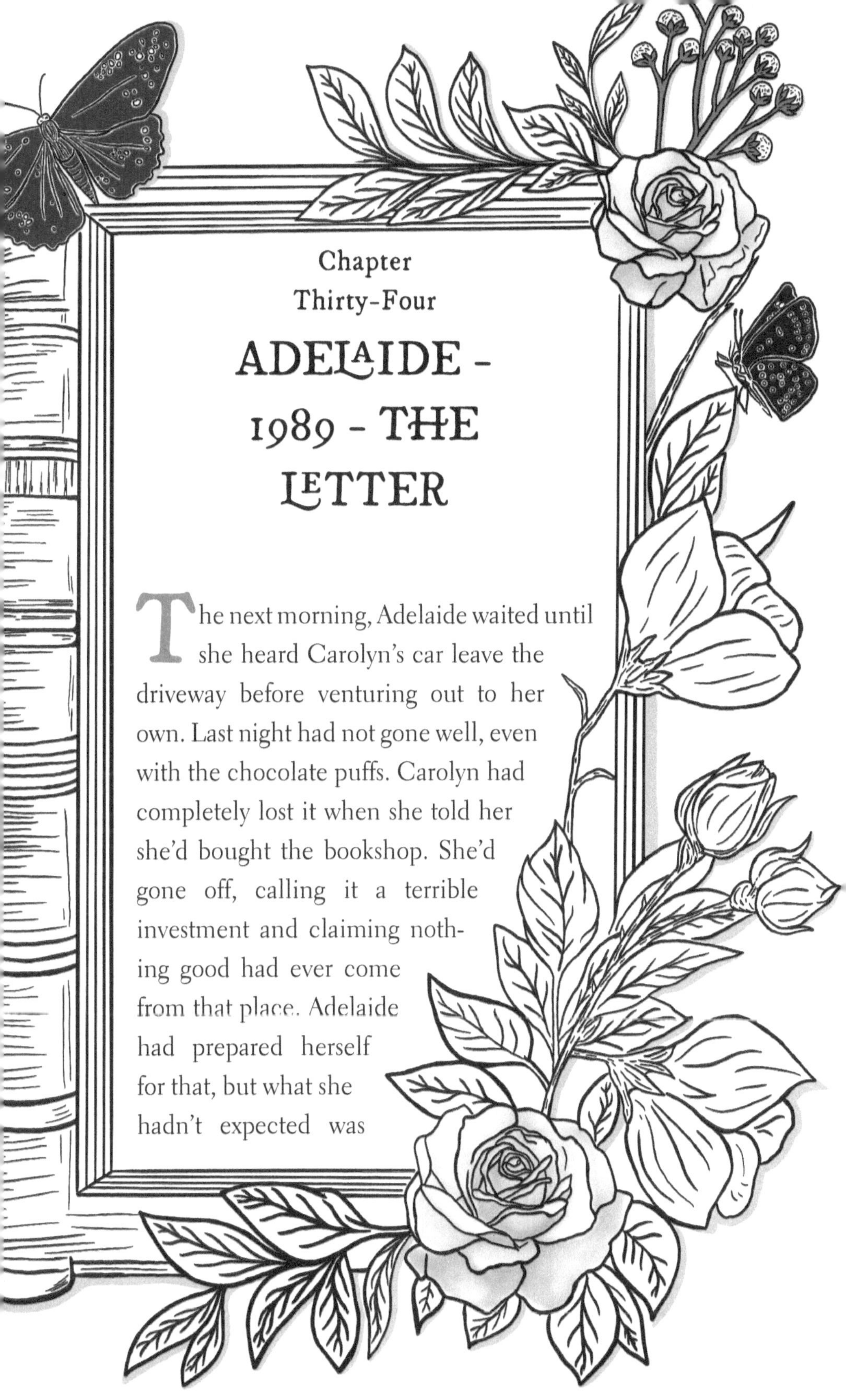

ADELAIDE - 1989 - THE LETTER

The next morning, Adelaide waited until she heard Carolyn's car leave the driveway before venturing out to her own. Last night had not gone well, even with the chocolate puffs. Carolyn had completely lost it when she told her she'd bought the bookshop. She'd gone off, calling it a terrible investment and claiming nothing good had ever come from that place. Adelaide had prepared herself for that, but what she hadn't expected was

Carolyn insisting she speak to Susan to "get her out of the contract."

When Adelaide told her that wasn't what she wanted, Carolyn's reaction intensified. She claimed the bookshop was cursed. That every owner failed. That it was doomed to bring more heartache than hope. Adelaide had spent the better part of the evening trying to reassure Carolyn that she would be just fine, that this was the new start she was looking for, that staying in Helensburgh, planting roots, was a good thing. But her words hadn't landed.

Adelaide knew Carolyn had a history with the Feather Thorn, and its original owner, Rowland, but she hadn't brought it up during their discussion, not even once. Her defenses were up, her eyes shadowed with something more than disapproval.

The conversation ended abruptly when Carolyn retreated to bed, still fuming, leaving Adelaide sitting alone with the untouched box of chocolate puffs.

This morning, Adelaide had decided it best to give her great-aunt a few days to cool off.

Outside, the air greeted her with a bite. Just as she'd predicted, the night's heavy dew had succumbed to the cold and coated everything within its grasp with frost. The fiery autumn colors were now muted, glazed in a thin shimmer of white. As she walked the path to the garage, she stretched out her hands like she always did, but the soft textures she loved had stiffened. Ice clung to every leaf and blade. She dragged her hand through the tall grass anyway, leaving a trail of ice crystals lingering in the air behind her, floating to the ground like sparks of magic in the early morning light.

It felt like a sign. Serendipitous, almost, that the first heavy frost had arrived on the very morning she'd woken up sure of what the Feather Thorn meant to her. After the fight with Carolyn, something had shifted. She didn't see the shop as a risk or an escape; it was a declaration, a commitment to herself. To her future. The old Adelaide would have caved. She would have let Carolyn talk to Susan, given in to keep the peace. But not now. This version of herself, the one who stood her ground, who knew she was responsible for her own happiness, would not give in.

Like the frost, harsh and biting, she was claiming what she wanted without asking permission.

As she started her car, Adelaide leaned back and watched the frost melt away from the windshield. She didn't bother turning on the radio; her thoughts were too loud. Plans for the Feather Thorn grew as she drove, one after another, and with each came a new rush of excitement. Hopefully, once she'd created her own version of the place, Carolyn would eventually come around.

She parked in the narrow side street next to the shop and shut off the engine. Gathering the basket of cleaning supplies she'd brought from the cabin, she headed to the front door. Unlocking it quickly, she stepped inside, eager to escape the bite of the chilly morning air. Though the bookshop wasn't much warmer than the outside, it was inviting in a way the damp air outside wasn't.

Flipping on the overhead tin lights, the shop came alive, golden pools sending down an inviting glow that settled over the rows of books. Adelaide breathed in. God, she loved that smell. She spotted the thermostat behind the counter and twisted the dial until it read twenty-one.

The bag of paint supplies she'd left by the door the night before sat waiting. She was excited to get to work, and today's job was to tackle the staircase wall. As she bent down to pick up the bag, a flash of white caught her eye. There, sticking out from the open top of the old letterbox, was a piece of paper. She was certain it hadn't been there yesterday; she would have noticed.

She pulled it free. Just a folded piece of paper, no envelope, no stamp, no name, no return address. It had most definitely not been left by the postman.

Inside a single sheet of typewritten paper read:

I am happy you are giving the Feather Thorn its second, or should I say third, chance. The emerald green is a great choice. I look forward to seeing what you do with it.

A slow smile crept over her face as she folded the letter and stuck it in her back pocket. She walked to the window and glanced down the street to the hardware store. Well, her flirting couldn't have been all that bad if Ewan had decided to leave her a note. She was surprised; she hadn't taken him for the type.

Grinning now, she twirled on her heel like a schoolgirl and marched toward the staircase wall. Today was painting day.

She stepped onto the first stair and flipped the switch for the overhead loft light. Nothing happened; it just hung dull and lifeless from its tin fixture. She clicked it on and off again; it appeared to have a blown bulb.

"We don't need that, plenty of natural light from these big windows," she said, turning back around to face them. "Now let's show him what we got, shall we?"

One by one, Adelaide began taking down the paintings and stacking them against the large window that faced the street. As she worked, she noticed the small landscape paintings scattered along the wall were done in a style strikingly similar to the wheat field painting that rested above the mantel in the cabin. She pulled one down for a closer look and found they did, in fact, bear the same signature as the one from the cabin: *CM.*

Strange, she thought, stepping closer to the large painting of the woman in the rain. She lifted it carefully from its hook and inspected it. From afar, she was anonymous, but now, with the painting in her hands, she saw it. The tilt of her chin. That smile. There was no mistaking who it was. Carolyn.

Her heart sank. This wall of paintings had been here since Rowland.

She cradled the frame, carried the portrait down the stairs, but before setting it with the rest, she flipped it around. Burned into the wood of the canvas was a single line:

For my Love.

Adelaide's heart ached. What should have been obvious from the beginning surged forth all at once. *CM* stood for Carolyn McGregor. Carolyn had painted these, all of them, for Rowland. Now, after last night's argument, she felt even worse. She had pushed, and she should have paused. Carolyn's warnings, her sharp protests, weren't about the business. They were about *him*. About the life she never got to live. A gallery of dreams left hanging on a staircase wall. She hadn't just bought a bookshop; she'd acquired part of Carolyn's story, her heartbreak, a place of shattered hopes and dreams.

If she was going to make the Feather Thorn her home, she knew she needed Carolyn's blessing.

She returned upstairs for the final painting, the largest of the group: a portrait of a man with an impressive beard. Stretching her arms wide, she struggled for a moment to lift it free from its hook on the wall. Finally she felt it give way, unhooking from its resting spot. It was surprisingly light for its size. As she navigated the stairs, her view obscured, the edge of the canvas bumped against the wall. At the last step, something clattered loudly onto the floor. Startled, she set the painting down against the others and went back to where she'd heard the object fall.

There, at the foot of the stairs, glinting in a patch of light, lay an old brass key.

She stooped to pick it up. "Did you drop this?" she asked, turning back to the portrait of the man.

She lifted the painting again and turned it around. A strip of yellowed tape clung loosely to the back, clearly too brittle to hold anything anymore, but the faint outline of the key was still impressed in its surface.

"Well, well, well. What have you been hiding, Mr. —" She squinted at the brass backplate. "Mr. John Dee."

Why did that name sound familiar? She'd seen it recently, she was sure of that, but she couldn't place where. Glancing around the room, she searched for something the key might unlock, but nothing stood out.

Tucking it into her back pocket, she resolved to go on that treasure hunt later; for now, she had a wall to paint.

Retrieving the paint can and bag of supplies, she set everything up. Pausing, she looked up into the loft. Her skin prickled. The air had turned still, and the familiar feeling of being watched swept over her again. The faint smell of men's cologne, with a hint of cigarette smoke, clung to the silence, lingering like a forgotten memory.

Shaking the feeling off, she pried open the tin of emerald paint and poured the thick, rich green into the tray, its glossy sheen catching the light. It flowed in smooth, heavy waves, reminding Adelaide of the ribbon sweeties her gran always bought her at Christmastime.

She made a quick pass with the roller in the tray, turning its white surface into a deep forest green.

The first swipe across the wall looked almost too dark, a

stark contrast to the soft off-white that had covered it for decades. She hesitated, the roller hovering midair. *Is this going to make the space too dark?*

Then, the stairwell light flickered, buzzed, and flared to life. The green came alive, rich and vibrant. Not overwhelming, just perfect.

She laughed. "Alright, then," she said to the light. "You win."

As she painted, she started to hum softly at first, then she broke into full voice, belting out "We Built This City" by Starship. Her voice bounced off the walls, lively and full of something she hadn't felt in years. Freedom.

When she finished the second coat, after a mildly terrifying wobble on the top rung of the ladder, she stood back and admired her work. It was the perfect accent for the space, standing out just enough to pull the eye to it but not overpowering the rich beauty of the shelves' wood grains. If anything, it made the bookcases stand out more.

She packed away the brushes and paints, then grabbed the bag of locks. Maybe she would take Ewan up on his offer to help. If the note in the letterbox really had been from him, then he'd already made the first move; maybe it was time she made the second. After nine years of seriousness, why not live a little? What did she have to lose? If it was nothing more than a little fun, she was one hundred percent okay with that; she was more than ready for a little bit of carefree fun.

THE HIDDEN JOURNAL
OF JOHN DEE

November 12, 1582

The ritual is complete. We performed every step with precision, moving in harmony with the celestial alignments as instructed. The planets shifted as planned, the Astral Synchronum chimed softly in response, and then gradually fell silent, its hands lying dormant.

Yet, as the final act passed, there was no rush of divine energy, no sudden burst of clarity. The light that had blazed so brightly during our first ritual did not show itself. However, I couldn't shake the feeling that we had merely applied a bandage to a wound that runs much deeper than we understand.

Giordano, ever the optimist, seems content with the outcome. He believes we have done what needed to be done, that the reality will settle, and the rip in time is now mended. I envy his conviction, but an unease still gnaws at me.

I have sent word to Edward Kelley. I must know if we succeeded. If there is even the slightest chance we missed something in our calculations, I fear the rip will only grow wider, dragging us further into a reality that does not belong to us. I will not rest until I can confirm, with divine guidance, whether we have truly repaired the tear or if our work was in vain.

Until then, I will wait. There is nothing more to be done for now. But in my heart, I fear that this is not over, that the changes will not stop, and that we have not yet averted the crisis we have unwittingly set in motion.

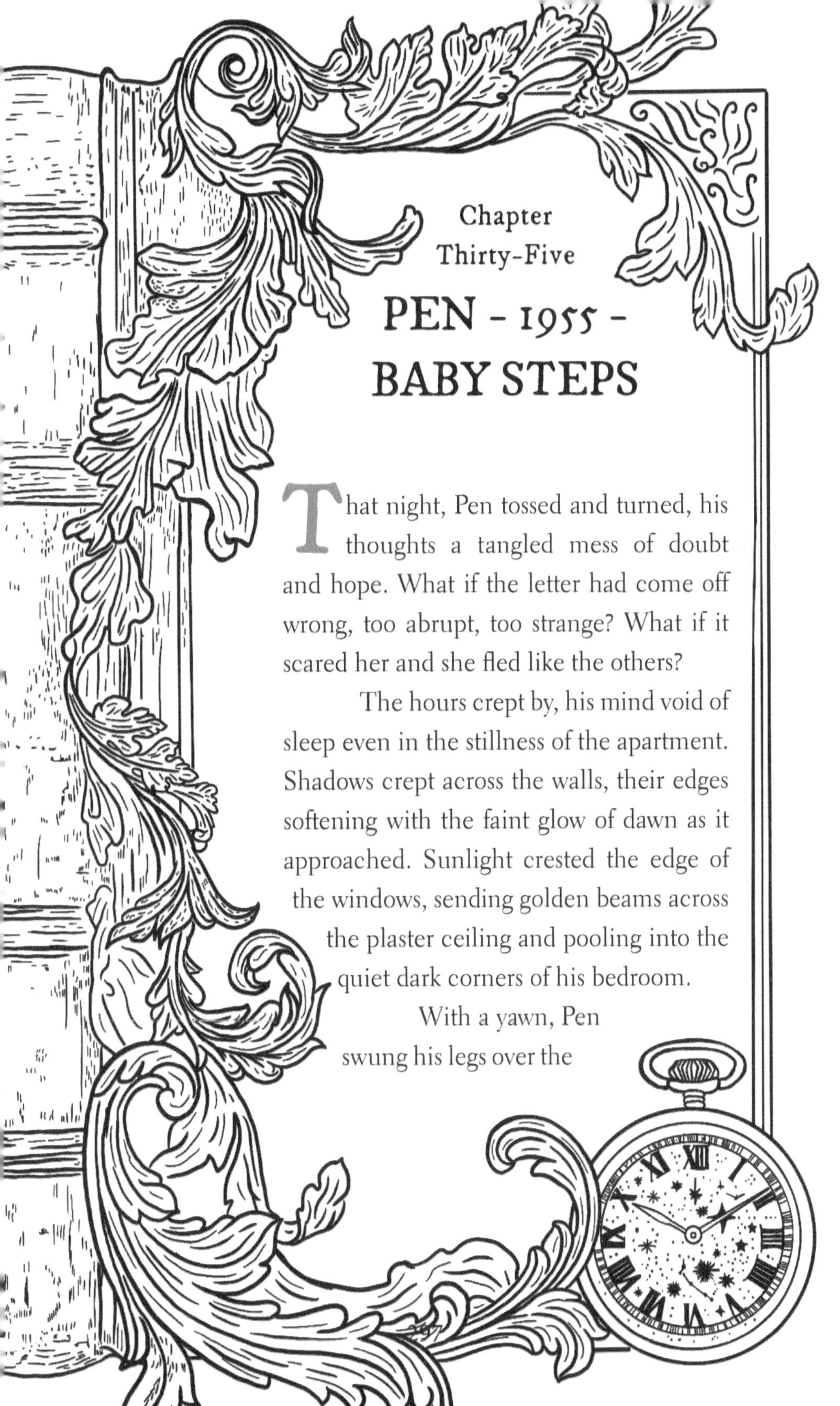

PEN - 1955 - BABY STEPS

That night, Pen tossed and turned, his thoughts a tangled mess of doubt and hope. What if the letter had come off wrong, too abrupt, too strange? What if it scared her and she fled like the others?

The hours crept by, his mind void of sleep even in the stillness of the apartment. Shadows crept across the walls, their edges softening with the faint glow of dawn as it approached. Sunlight crested the edge of the windows, sending golden beams across the plaster ceiling and pooling into the quiet dark corners of his bedroom.

With a yawn, Pen swung his legs over the

side of the bed, and the chill of the floor met his feet. He shuffled into the tiny kitchen, the scent of stale cigarette smoke and the old carpet settling around him. Frankie stirred in a corner of the living room, his rust-colored tail flicking, as he stretched. He padded over with a soft chitter, his bright eyes gleaming with the expectation of breakfast as he settled himself in front of the stove.

Pen, however, barely noticed. He drifted to the window, gaze falling on the apothecary door, its weathered facade a stark reminder of the time that had passed. The vision of Carolyn's aged face lingered in his mind still. Decades. She had aged decades, while he remained untouched.

He leaned closer to the glass; his own reflection stared back, his breath fogging the pane. Twenty-five, same as the day time stopped. No gray in his hair, no lines at the corners of his eyes. A phantom suspended in time. Behind his image, the street bustled on. He felt unmoored, neither part of the past nor part of the present but lost somewhere in between.

Frankie let out a sharp chitter, jolting Pen from his trance. He blinked, the image in the glass disappearing as he turned away from the window.

"Okay, I hear you," he relented, managing a tired smile.

He opened the refrigerator. Always the same. It didn't matter if he used the food or not, they always replenished overnight. No matter how many new dishes he tried to come up with, he was utterly sick of the combination. He longed for something different. A fresh apple. One of Dottie's cinnamon-sugar donuts. Anything other than ground beef and eggs.

Shaking off the thought, Pen heated a frying pan, cracked the eggs, and whisked them together. The kitchen soon filled with the smell of breakfast. He split the scrambled eggs between his own plate and a smaller bowl for Frankie.

"Here you go, sir," Pen said, bowing with mock formality.

Frankie bounded over, his soft yips brimming with delight as he dove headfirst into the bowl, tail wagging. Pen knelt to scratch behind his ears. "You don't know how lucky I am to have you," he murmured.

With a pot of coffee brewing, Pen dressed quickly and poured himself a steaming cup. Mug in hand, he made his way into the bookshop. Behind him, Frankie stretched lazily before curling back into his bed in the corner.

He felt a flicker of relief at the fox's choice. He didn't want to risk Adelaide seeing Frankie again, not yet.

Pen headed straight for the letterbox as soon as he stepped into the shop. His hand hovered over the paper, doubt creeping in. Maybe it was too much. Too soon. What if she thought it was creepy? The last thing he wanted was to make her afraid of the place. He couldn't afford to get this wrong. Not this time.

He bent down, fingers just grazing the edge of the letter, when the bells above the door rang.

The door creaked open beside him.

He froze.

Adelaide stepped inside, the chilly air following her in, a bucket swinging gently from one hand.

Pen pulled his hand away slowly, deciding a floating piece of paper might be enough to send her running. He stood motionless, caught between the impulse to run and the reality that it was pointless; she couldn't see him. Still, he held his breath as she walked in.

His heart did aerobics as she breezed past him, cheeks flushed pink from the cold. Setting the bucket down, she shrugged off her coat, then crossed to the thermostat and dialed up the heat.

Though her smile, bright and effortless, seemed to warm the entire shop on its own.

Then she turned and spotted the letter. Pen's heart thundered in his ears, drowning out everything around him. This was it. The moment of truth. She reached for the note, unfolded it slowly, and time seemed to snag. Then she smiled. Wide, radiant. Her cheeks deepening in color as she refolded the letter and tucked it into the back pocket of her jeans.

Pen finally exhaled, tension draining from his shoulders. She hadn't been frightened.

He followed her silently into the front of the shop, a shadow behind her. She flipped the switch to the stairwell light a few times with no result. Pen winced. That switch hadn't worked in years; it was the one at the top that controlled the bulb.

Unbothered, Adelaide moved to the paintings, removing them from the wall one by one. There was a grace to her movements, a fluidity, almost like a dancer, as she carefully lifted each frame and set it aside.

At the painting of Carolyn in the rain, she paused. Pen saw it, the recognition flicker across her face. He remembered that same jolt when he'd first understood its significance, and felt a strange pull of shared understanding. Her brows furrowed as she removed the frame from the wall and placed it alongside the others.

Drawn by something deeper than curiosity, Pen ascended the stairs and sat quietly at the top, his eyes fixed on her.

She returned for the last painting, the one of John Dee. It was large, and her petite frame struggled to lift it off the hook on the wall. Without thinking, Pen moved to her side. He leaned in, close enough to almost brush her arms, and eased the painting from its nail.

Lavender and honey.

He caught the faintest trace of it in her hair, and it nearly undid him. Not because it was strong, but because it was real. It was the first new scent he'd breathed in for as long as he could remember.

He hadn't realized how much he missed the presence of another person. The creak of floorboards under someone else's weight. The soft rustle of clothes that weren't his. The sound of another's voice. He'd been alone for so long, he'd almost forgotten what closeness felt like.

He clenched his jaw, trying to steady the flood of emotion, relief, sorrow, yearning, and awe. It wasn't just her presence. It was everything he hadn't let himself feel in years, breaking open at once.

She had no idea, of course. No idea how this small moment had knocked the breath from his lungs. He lingered in the warmth of her presence for as long as he dared, helping her balance the frame once or twice as she descended the stairs before letting go.

A sharp clatter broke through his thoughts. He blinked. At the foot of the stairs, something gleamed on the floorboards. The key.

He'd forgotten he'd returned it to the back of the painting. He watched, powerless, as she bent to retrieve it. Watched as she turned it over in her hand, curiosity already sparking in her eyes. Watched as she tucked it into her back pocket.

Pen paced back to the top of the stairs, his thoughts racing. Now that she had the key, it was only a matter of time. He knew how this would go. A mysterious key, hidden behind a centuries-old painting? No one could ignore that. She'd start searching, hunting for answers. It wouldn't be long before she stumbled upon the hidden room, just as he had.

With shaking hands, he lit a cigarette and leaned against the wall, the soft glow of the ember punctuating the dim light. Below him, Adelaide moved about the shop, unpacking painting supplies. Pen watched, a thousand thoughts pulling at him as she pried open the paint can. Then she paused. Her eyes lifted, right toward him. For one breathless second, he thought she saw him.

But just as quickly, she turned back to her work, not giving a second glance in his direction. Pen let out a sigh of relief, or disappointment, he wasn't sure. Then he saw it: the color of the paint as she poured it into the tray, a rich emerald green. His color. He smiled, but it was a fragile thing, trembling at the edges.

He watched as she dipped her roller into the paint, laying down a bold stripe across the wall, the deep green blooming against the aged white. She hesitated, the roller hovering mid-stroke as though second-guessing the color. Pen's gaze shifted to the light switch beside him. Closing his eyes, he concentrated, focused, and flicked the switch, willing it to respond in her time.

When he opened them, Adelaide was looking up, startled. But then her face softened into a smile. The glow in her expression began to unravel him, one heartbeat at a time.

His pulse quickened. How had he just done that? He must have flipped the switch the day he was trapped, but the other lights hadn't responded this way. The question looped in his mind. Was it her?

Adelaide rolled another stripe of emerald green across the wall.

She began to hum, a tune he didn't recognize, and soon her voice joined in, light and sweet, like rain on a hot summer's night.

There was something different about the shop since she'd arrived, a current in the air, like static before a storm. Could he have tapped into that energy to turn on the light?

The possibility sent a shiver through him.

He stayed there for hours, watching her paint, unable to pull away. When she propped a ladder against the wall to reach the highest points, he moved without thinking, steadying it from below, her invisible guardian.

He didn't know if it was helping in her timeline, but he had a strong feeling it was. Something was shifting, he could feel it, as though her presence was expanding his abilities to influence things in the shop, beyond what he had touched the day he became trapped. But how? A flicker of hope ignited as she made the final stroke upon the wall.

When she finally stepped back to admire her work, a smile spread across her face that sent a crackle of energy rippling through the room. It wasn't just the shop that felt charged; it was *him.*

Adelaide packed away her paint supplies, still smiling, and headed for the door with the bag from the hardware store. Pen watched from the top of the stairs as she left the Feather Thorn.

He went to the window, his heart racing with the possibilities as he watched her walk down the street toward the hardware shop. There was something undeniably magnetic about her, some kind of presence that seemed to shift the very gravity of the Feather Thorn.

Turning away from the window, something caught his attention; the top row of books in the first aisle of the fiction section was missing.

His brow furrowed. Had Adelaide moved them when he wasn't paying attention? No, he would have noticed. He hadn't been able to take his eyes off her the entire day. A wave of unease rippled through him, but he pushed it down. He wouldn't let it ruin the happiness she'd stirred in him. Not today.

He glanced down at the portrait of John Dee. He couldn't let her find the hidden room, at least not yet. If she discovered the watch, she might get trapped in this cycle with him. And while a selfish part of him thrilled at the thought of not being alone, he wouldn't wish that fate on anyone. Especially not her.

Pen turned toward the stairs, ready to head back to the apartment, when the sound of the bells from the door rang out. Adelaide stepped back inside, accompanied by a rugged-looking man. She pointed out the locks on the front and side doors, then smiled at him. A warm, easy smile. He envied that connection, that freedom of exchange he was no longer part of. A sharp frustration bubbled to the surface.

Pen watched as the man began tinkering, tools scraping against the wood. He told himself he wasn't spying, just observing, but he couldn't look away. Adelaide leaned on the counter, finger twirling in her hair as she chatted easily. There was a spark between them, and it gnawed at him.

Forcing himself to turn away, he wandered back to the apartment. Frankie trotted up, tail swishing, but Pen barely noticed. His thoughts were once again a tangled mess. *What just happened? What is this feeling?* This had been the best day he'd had in a long while, yet there was a deep ache in the pit of his stomach.

He heard the shop door close, then the clean click of a new lock engaging. He didn't look. Didn't dare. For all he knew, they were a couple and he was just a ghost lingering at the edge of something real. He had no business watching. No right to care.

But the thought scorched through him like fire.

Pen knew, in that moment, this woman might be his salvation.

Or his undoing.

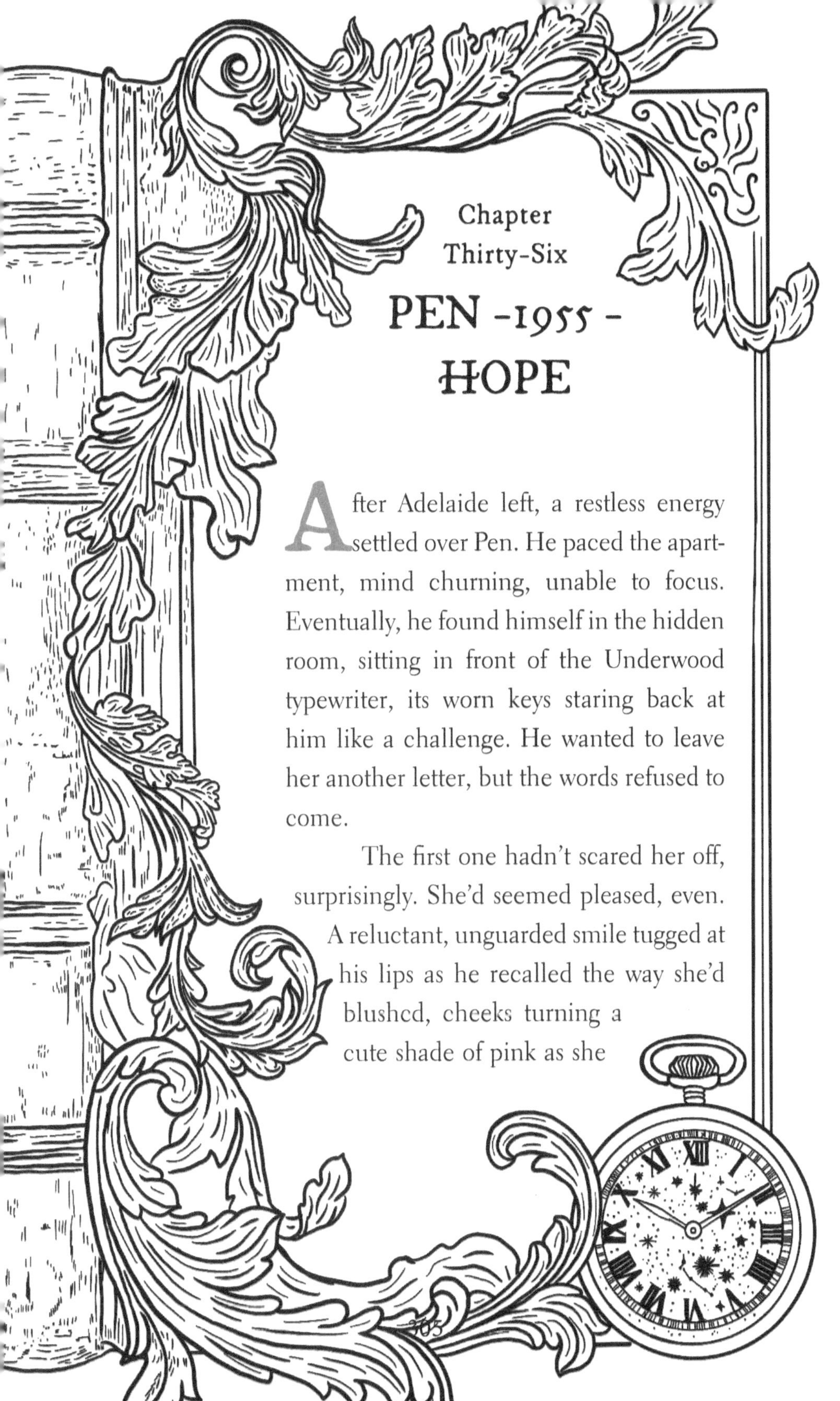

PEN – 1955 –
HOPE

After Adelaide left, a restless energy settled over Pen. He paced the apartment, mind churning, unable to focus. Eventually, he found himself in the hidden room, sitting in front of the Underwood typewriter, its worn keys staring back at him like a challenge. He wanted to leave her another letter, but the words refused to come.

The first one hadn't scared her off, surprisingly. She'd seemed pleased, even. A reluctant, unguarded smile tugged at his lips as he recalled the way she'd blushed, cheeks turning a cute shade of pink as she tucked the note into her back pocket.

Five failed drafts later, the waste bin overflowed with crumpled pages. He slouched back in the creaky captain's chair and closed his eyes, trying to push the image of her smile from his mind. This wasn't the time to get distracted. He needed a plan. An exit strategy. He needed his logical mind back. He couldn't be dreaming about some doe-eyed girl, as beautiful as she was.

He opened his eyes, straightened. Forced himself to focus solely on how she might help him escape. It wasn't as if he could come right out and tell her he was trapped in the bookshop, locked in some alternate reality. That would never go over well. No, he needed to ease into it, let her connect the puzzle pieces on her own. He began typing, his fingers clicking across the keys:

The wall looks great! The color really brings out the bookshelves. You've got impeccable taste. I can't wait to see what you do next to bring the bookshop back to life.

Short. Harmless. Encouraging.

He tore the page free, folded it and headed back up into the bookshop.

Frankie was darting around the main area, his paws skittering against the hardwood floor as he chittered excitedly. The little fox weaved between shelves and furniture, his energy boundless. *Poor guy,* Pen thought, watching as Frankie disappeared into the children's section. *No wild animal should be caged like this.*

The irony wasn't lost on him. He, too, was a caged animal, pacing the confines of this timeless prison, biding his time, waiting for a crack in the walls.

"I'm trying, boy," he muttered, his voice low, and almost pleading, as Frankie darted back out and circled his legs. He glanced down at the note he clutched, its edges already curling from the pressure of his grip.

He slipped the note into the old letterbox and let out a soft sigh that was swallowed by stillness.

Back upstairs, Pen dropped onto the sagging sofa and picked up *The Screwtape Letters* by C.S. Lewis from the worn side table. He'd found it misfiled in the folklore section, a hidden gem buried among tales of faeries and legends. He'd started it a week ago and had devoured the first half in just two nights. Lewis's writing always captivated him, offering an escape from the monotony of his days.

But things had changed since Adelaide had arrived. Now, the words couldn't hold his attention. He kept seeing her face. The way she laughed with the man fixing the locks. The way she brushed a stray hair from her face as she studied the shop like it might whisper its secrets to her, if only she listened carefully enough.

His thumb traced a line on the page: *"The present is the point at which time touches eternity."* He snorted softly. If that were true, then this, this time loop, must be his eternity. A stale, endless present he couldn't seem to escape. He tossed the book aside and leaned his head back, staring up at the cracked plaster ceiling as his thoughts began to spiral, shadows dancing in the corners, twisting like whispers he couldn't quite hear.

"I've had just about enough of this day," he whispered, his voice rough with exhaustion. He pushed himself off the couch and made his way to the bedroom.

The room was cloaked in darkness, save for the eerie silver light spilling through the window. Moonbeams stretched across the worn wooden floorboards, illuminating narrow paths of light while the rest of the room dissolved into deep, shadowy pools. Pen moved carefully, stepping only where the light touched, as if the darkness might swallow him whole.

It was a foolish, childish habit, one that reminded him of a game he used to play with Val: *Don't step on the crack, or you'll break your mama's back.* He smiled faintly at the memory, but it faded quickly.

Val. Dave. Will.

Their names struck a chord deep within him, and the ache of missing them tightened his throat. In his mind, they were still young, their faces frozen in time like the faded photograph tucked away in his wallet. But out there, beyond this cursed loop, they were grown now. Probably married with children who were the age they had been when he left.

Did they wonder what had happened to him? Had they searched for him, called around, checked hospitals? Or did they think he'd abandoned them? The thought churned his stomach, leaving him hollow and sick.

For the first time in his life, he longed to be back in Oak Ridge, back in the familiar chaos of his old life. He would have given anything to hear Dave's laugh again. To see Will's wide, boyish grin. To listen to one of Val's tall tales. But the past was lost, and the future wasn't coming. All he had was this, this aching, unchanging present.

Was this the cost of defiance? The price he had to pay for trying to create a future different from the one handed to him? Perhaps that was it.

Perhaps this was his punishment. His purgatory.

THE HIDDEN JOURNAL OF JOHN DEE

December 1, 1582

A grave discovery has been made today. Giordano came to me in great distress, his face pale, his voice trembling as he recounted what had just occurred. It seems our attempt to seal the rift has brought forth an unexpected and deeply troubling effect. The Astral Synchronum now possesses the power to turn back time itself.

Giordano, in his curiosity, and without fully grasping what was happening, unwittingly activated the device. As he described it, the Synchronum let out a series of chimes, three in total, before everything around him shifted. Moments later, he found himself days in the past. By sheer fortune, he did not encounter his former self, but the implications of what could have happened chilled us both to the core. Had he come face-to-face with himself, the consequences would have been catastrophic, time itself could have fractured, or worse, both timelines could have been destroyed entirely.

Giordano deduced that the number of chimes determines how many hours the device will keep the user in the past. However, once that time has elapsed, the user is snapped back to the exact moment they activated the device, like a tether pulling them through the fabric of time.

This new revelation comes with disturbing consequences. I feel it now, the signs are unmistakable. Objects have begun to shift in place, disappearing when no one has touched them, as if time is slipping through the cracks. I found earlier today that a book I had placed on the shelf last night after reading it was no longer there, vanished without a trace. I've witnessed the same events reoccurring, a bird repeatedly landing on a branch by my window, over and over in the exact same way; it's as though time itself is stuttering. The air feels charged, reality stretching at the seams. It is clear now that the Astral Synchronum is even more dangerous than we imagined. Not only does it threaten the stability of time itself, but each use seems to worsen the tear we have already created. The fabric of reality is fraying, and it is impossible to ignore.

If the Synchronum were to fall into the wrong hands, the consequences would be dire. Someone could easily misuse its power, rewinding time again and again, creating fractures that could never be repaired. I feel the world around me distorting, as though the past is bleeding into the present, and moments are slipping away, forgotten. It is a tool far beyond what we were ever prepared to control, a tool that could become a weapon of unimaginable destruction.

I do not yet see a solution, but I know one thing for certain: this device must be contained or destroyed before it tears the world apart. We have lost control, and now the danger grows with every passing day.

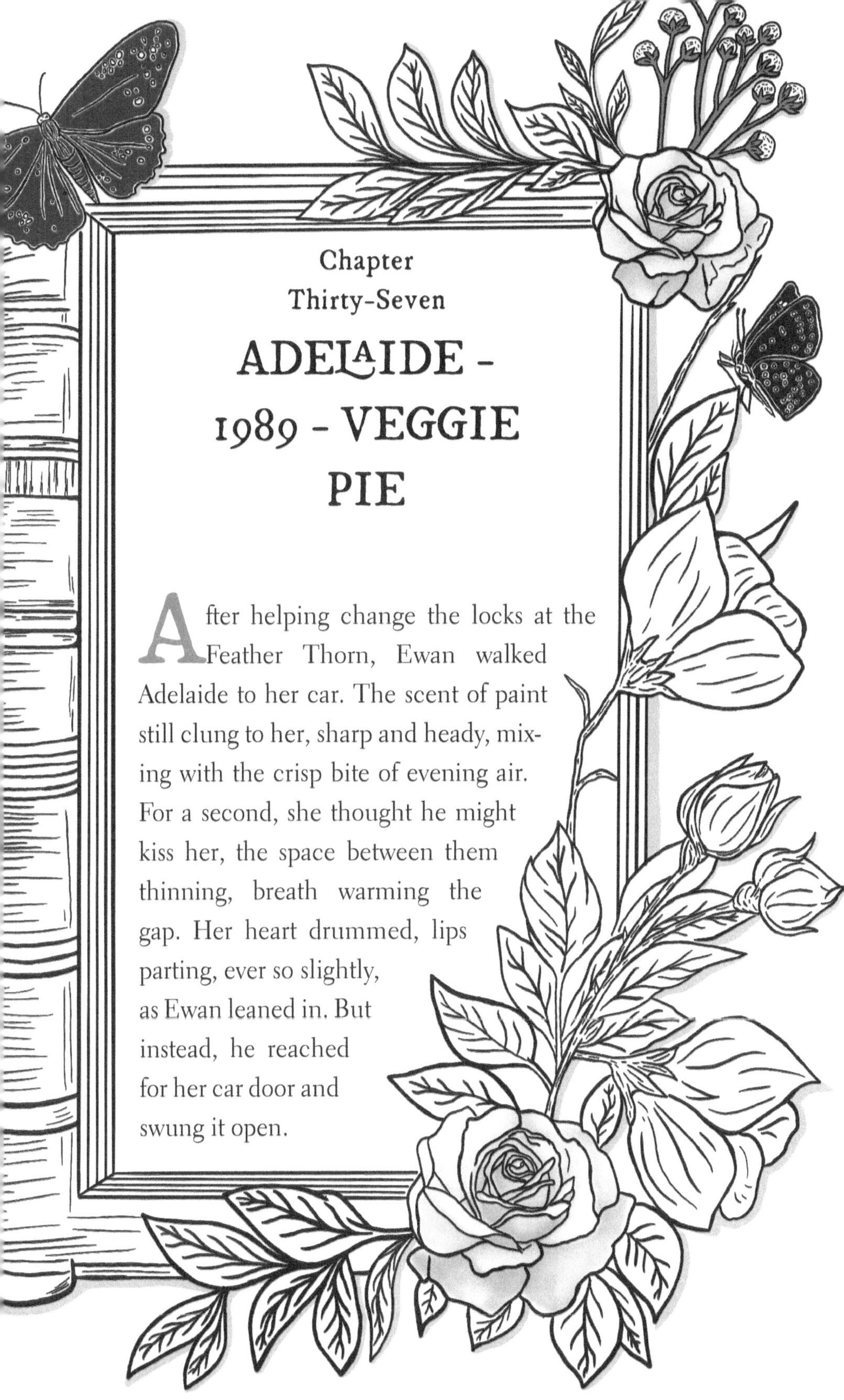

ADELAIDE –
1989 – VEGGIE
PIE

After helping change the locks at the Feather Thorn, Ewan walked Adelaide to her car. The scent of paint still clung to her, sharp and heady, mixing with the crisp bite of evening air. For a second, she thought he might kiss her, the space between them thinning, breath warming the gap. Her heart drummed, lips parting, ever so slightly, as Ewan leaned in. But instead, he reached for her car door and swung it open.

A pang of disappointment flickered, gone as quickly as it came when he spoke. "Would you like to have dinner with me tomorrow?"

"Yes," she answered, a little too quickly, her cheeks blooming with a quiet embarrassment. She considered mentioning the note, to ease out of the awkward moment, but the thought passed, replaced with excitement.

The idea buzzed in her veins as she drove home, thrilling and nerve-wracking all at once. She hadn't been on a proper date in years. What should she wear? What would they talk about? Was she even ready?

By the time she pulled into Carolyn's driveway, she'd already imagined their meal three different ways, each ending in a kiss. And she'd squirmed over how she might mess it up.

Her fantasies evaporated when she spotted Carolyn stepping out of her car, clutching her purple leopard-print bag like a shield.

Adelaide's heart sank. She'd hoped for a buffer, a few days to let the dust settle. But, of course, fate seemed to have other plans.

Drawing a steadying breath, she turned off the engine and stepped out of the car, already rehearsing excuses, apologies, explanations.

"Hey," Adelaide said, raising her hand in greeting, or perhaps surrender. She wasn't quite sure which.

"Adelaide, I'm glad you're here. Follow me."

That was it? No, *Hey, how are you?* Just the click of heels on the stone and the swish of her coat as Carolyn headed up the short pathway to the house.

Adelaide followed, the last of the sun setting the sky alight, orange melting into violet. The cold bit through her jeans, and her excitement from earlier had all but disappeared, replaced with a nervous anticipation.

Inside, Carolyn flipped on the light switch, flooding the open space with a warm, golden glow. Yet, despite the inviting light, Adelaide couldn't help but feel a little less welcome. The air still held the charge of things left unsaid, and she crossed her arms instinctively.

The wood stove crackled faintly, low embers glowing. Carolyn crouched to tend it, selecting a few logs from an ornate wrought-iron fire ring near the brick hearth. As she placed them on the coals, sparks danced up the chimney.

Adelaide hovered near the kitchen table, fingers nervously picking at its worn, chipped edge. Her tongue stuck to the roof of her mouth, nerves crowding her chest. She felt the need to make up an excuse to leave.

Carolyn, seemingly unaffected by the tension between them, moved to the sink, filled a large pot with water, and set it to boil on the stove. Then she opened the refrigerator. One by one, she gathered potatoes, carrots, turnips, a head of celery, and laid them all out in tidy rows. Without glancing up, she reached for two cutting boards and placed them on the center island.

"Come," Carolyn insisted, waving Adelaide over. "Chop this," she added, handing her the celery and a knife.

The routine broke something. The normalcy of it. Carolyn peeled the potatoes. Adelaide chopped slowly, the rhythm of the blade steadying her. For a few minutes, they worked in silence, save for the soft clack on the board and the hiss of water heating. Adelaide drew a breath, readying to break the ice when Carolyn's voice cut through the stillness first.

"I want you to know that I've had a long think about what we talked about last night," she began, her hands working quickly. Her voice was quieter than usual. "I know it's not my place to tell you what you should or shouldn't do with your own money and life. I'll be fully supportive of whatever choices you make, but before you commit to this, I think you should know the whole story behind the bookstore."

She scooped the chopped potatoes and celery into the pot of boiling water, the steam rising in soft clouds. Turning back, she handed Adelaide the carrots, then reached for the turnips.

"The bookstore had been in Rowland's family for centuries," Carolyn said. "He inherited it after his uncle passed in the summer of 1919. The building always went to the eldest male heir; that was Rowland. By the time he got it, the place was in shambles, just a dusty, neglected storehouse full of his uncle's belongings." Carolyn's knife moved against the chopping board, turnips soon joining the others in the pot with a gentle splash. "It had been more than a shop," she continued. "At different times, it was a home, a doctor's office, even a laboratory."

Adelaide kept her hands moving, slicing the carrots as the room filled with the scent of root vegetables and woodsmoke.

"There's a reason it passed down through the family for so many generations. They were never allowed to sell it. The shop holds more than memories. It holds… something else. A secret." She turned and met Adelaide's eyes. "An artifact. Created by John Dee, supposedly. Something that couldn't be destroyed. It was hidden in the building, and the family was entrusted to keep it safe, generation after generation."

Adelaide's pulse ticked up. *John Dee.* That name was burned into her memory. The brass plate on the back of the painting of the man with the large beard. The same painting that had hidden that key. Suddenly, its placement on the stairwell felt intentional. Like a watchman.

Carolyn stopped chopping. Her hands hovered just above the carrots as she studied Adelaide, eyes filled with apprehension, as if she was trying to choose her next words carefully. "I know how it sounds, all far-fetched, but I believe that artifact is connected to the disappearances of Rowland, and later, Pen Turner. What John Dee hadn't accounted for was that one day the family line would end, and someone else would own the shop. Pen Turner was that someone. Before the shop sat empty. Before you. Neither of them ran off or went mad, as people like to say. I think something happened to them in that building because of that artifact."

"The painting," Adelaide replied, swallowing. "The big one on the stairs. That's John Dee?"

Carolyn nodded, tipping more vegetables into the bubbling pot. "Yes. And it's quite old. Painted in the late sixteenth century, I believe."

"But, how do you know all this?"

"Rowland told me bits and pieces about his family and the history of the place, and over the years I eventually put it all together." She glanced up, just briefly, at the ceiling.

Adelaide followed her gaze. The guest room. Her suspicion surged again. Was Carolyn hiding something up there? That glance, it hadn't seemed accidental. But then again, maybe she was reading too much into it. All this talk of secrets and disappearances had her seeing them around every corner.

Her stomach growled loudly, breaking the tension. Carolyn cracked a small smile and pulled down a mixing bowl and a bag of flour from the shelf above the counter.

"Now you can see why I don't want you getting involved with that place," Carolyn stated, cracking an egg into the bowl. "I think it houses a very powerful source of energy, and God knows where, or what that is, but I've always had this feeling…" She poured in a splash of milk, then stirred. "I can't risk you picking up some mundane object only to find out it's part of the artifact and have you disappear like the others."

Adelaide lowered herself slowly into a chair at the table, her hands resting in her lap. "But how do you *know* it's the artifact?" she asked quietly. "That caused their disappearances?"

Carolyn paused, her gaze growing distant. "Rowland wasn't the first of his family to vanish in that place. There were stories, records, of relatives who disappeared long before him. I don't remember much from when Rowland went missing; I was very ill at the time. But I do remember Pen's story."

She reached up to a narrow wooden shelf above the stove and retrieved two small jars, each sealed with a cork top. Then, one by one, she opened them, and the rich, earthy scents of thyme and rosemary filled the room. She tapped a pinch of each into her palm, then sprinkled them into the boiling water, along with a single bay leaf.

Her voice softened, almost as if she was speaking to herself more than to Adelaide. "When Pen first arrived in town, we were all surprised. Rowland had been thought to be the last of his line. But it turned out that his sister Emily's husband gifted Pen the bookshop in his will." Carolyn stirred the pot, then turned back to the counter, hands working the dough. "Pen was full of life, so eager to make a name for himself, to forge his own path. Everyone loved him. He breathed new life into that place. And then, just like Rowland, he disappeared without a trace one day."

She floured the cutting board, then lifted the dough from the bowl and set it in the cloud of flour.

Adelaide's gaze lingered on her great-aunt's face. Carolyn's eyes were glassy. She didn't cry, she wouldn't, but her sorrow hung heavy in the room. Carolyn tore the dough into small balls, placing each one neatly on the counter.

"Do you really believe there's something in the shop causing people to disappear?" Adelaide asked. "Maybe Pen just went back to America, like Iain said." It sounded plausible enough. Perhaps Rowland had left, too, when things got too hard. She would never say that out loud, though.

Carolyn shook her head as she pulled a glass from the cupboard. "No," she said firmly, flipping the glass over and using its base to flatten the dough balls into discs. "There's no way Pen would have left like that. Not without a word. That wasn't who he was."

Her voice wavered slightly. "This is why I hesitated to tell you. I was afraid you'd think I was just some daft old woman with too many stories, like everyone else."

Adelaide's stomach knotted. "Of course I don't think that," she replied quickly, leaning forward and putting her hand on her aunt's. "I believe you."

Carolyn stilled, her eyes searching Adelaide's face. Whatever she found there seemed to satisfy her. She turned away and lifted the heavy pot from the stove, and drained the vegetables. Steam billowed up, curling into the ceiling, like ghosts escaping the past.

Adelaide believed her, at least, that Carolyn *believed* in what she was saying. It must be easier for her to accept the idea of a curse than to confront the idea that Rowland might have simply left her behind, choosing another life over the one they'd planned. And Pen's disappearance had only solidified that belief.

"So, now you can see why I don't want you making the Feather Thorn your new life." She tipped the steaming vegetables into a casserole dish, the colors vibrant against the pale porcelain. Then she turned her attention to the stove, where a fragrant sauce of chicken broth, milk, and spices bubbled in a saucepan.

"I do understand," Adelaide said. "But I also feel this is where I'm meant to be and what I'm meant to do." She paused. "How about this, I promise you, if I find anything strange or suspicious, I'll leave it well alone."

As she spoke, her hand drifted unconsciously to her back pocket, fingers brushing the outline of the key. Carolyn's warnings should have been enough to make her hesitate, but instead of caution, they sparked a deeper curiosity. *What could this key possibly unlock?*

Carolyn finished assembling the vegetable pot pie, laid the dough discs on top and slid it into the oven. The smell lingered, rich and savory, as she moved to a nearby cabinet and pulled down a bottle of whiskey and two small glasses. She poured a generous dram into each, carried them to the table and set one in front of Adelaide before settling into the chair across from her with a sigh that sounded equal parts tired and relieved.

"My sweet little Addie," Carolyn said with a dry laugh, swirling the whiskey in her glass. "You've always had a hard head. Stubborn as a mule." She took a swig of the amber liquid, her eyes twinkling with wry affection. "I suppose if that story didn't scare you off, not much else will, now will it?"

Adelaide chuckled lightly, meeting her aunt's gaze. "I suppose you're right. I'm pretty set on it." She hesitated for a moment, then decided to share what she'd done earlier that day. "I painted the stairway wall today… and found your paintings," she added after a beat, hoping to shift the mood. "I didn't know you painted."

For the first time that evening, a small, genuine smile broke across Carolyn's face. "Once upon a time, I did," she nodded, then took another sip.

"Why don't you anymore? You were good."

The smile faded. Carolyn's gaze drifted, unfocused, somewhere far beyond the kitchen walls. "After Rowland..." Her voice was quieter again. "I just couldn't find the inspiration. The world that used to feel so vibrant, so full of color, it all went dull and gray."

Adelaide felt the heaviness of those words settle over the room like a heavy blanket. She knew that feeling. How the light could fade so quickly to dark. She'd lived it, the slow fade after Jeff's betrayal, when her own world had seemed drained of life and purpose.

"I understand," Adelaide said gently. "Would you like me to bring the paintings to the apothecary? You should have them."

Carolyn shook her head, the empty glass still in her hand. "No. Keep them at the Feather Thorn. It's where they belong." She set the glass down. "What color did you paint the wall?"

"Emerald green," Adelaide replied, a faint smile forming at the memory. The tension in the room began to ease, the air lighter somehow. Carolyn had given up trying to change her mind. Surrender, it seemed, was simmering alongside the vegetable pie.

"Interesting choice," Carolyn said after a thoughtful pause. "I'll have to come by and see it sometime."

There it was. Not approval exactly, but a quiet acceptance. Carolyn wasn't fighting the current anymore. Instead, she seemed to be drifting with it, her resistance softening into reluctant acceptance. Adelaide wouldn't be giving up on the Feather Thorn or her dreams.

But acceptance wasn't the same as understanding. And silence settled over them again. Adelaide couldn't help but wonder:

Were her great-aunt's fears rooted in truth? Or were they just the shape grief took when left alone too long, the ghosts of loss?

Adelaide ran her thumb along the rim of her glass, caught between skepticism and curiosity. Was the Feather Thorn truly a keeper of dark secrets, or just the shadowed canvas of Carolyn's grieving heart?

Either way, there was a key in Adelaide's pocket. One that might just hold the answers. And something told her it was time to find out what it unlocked.

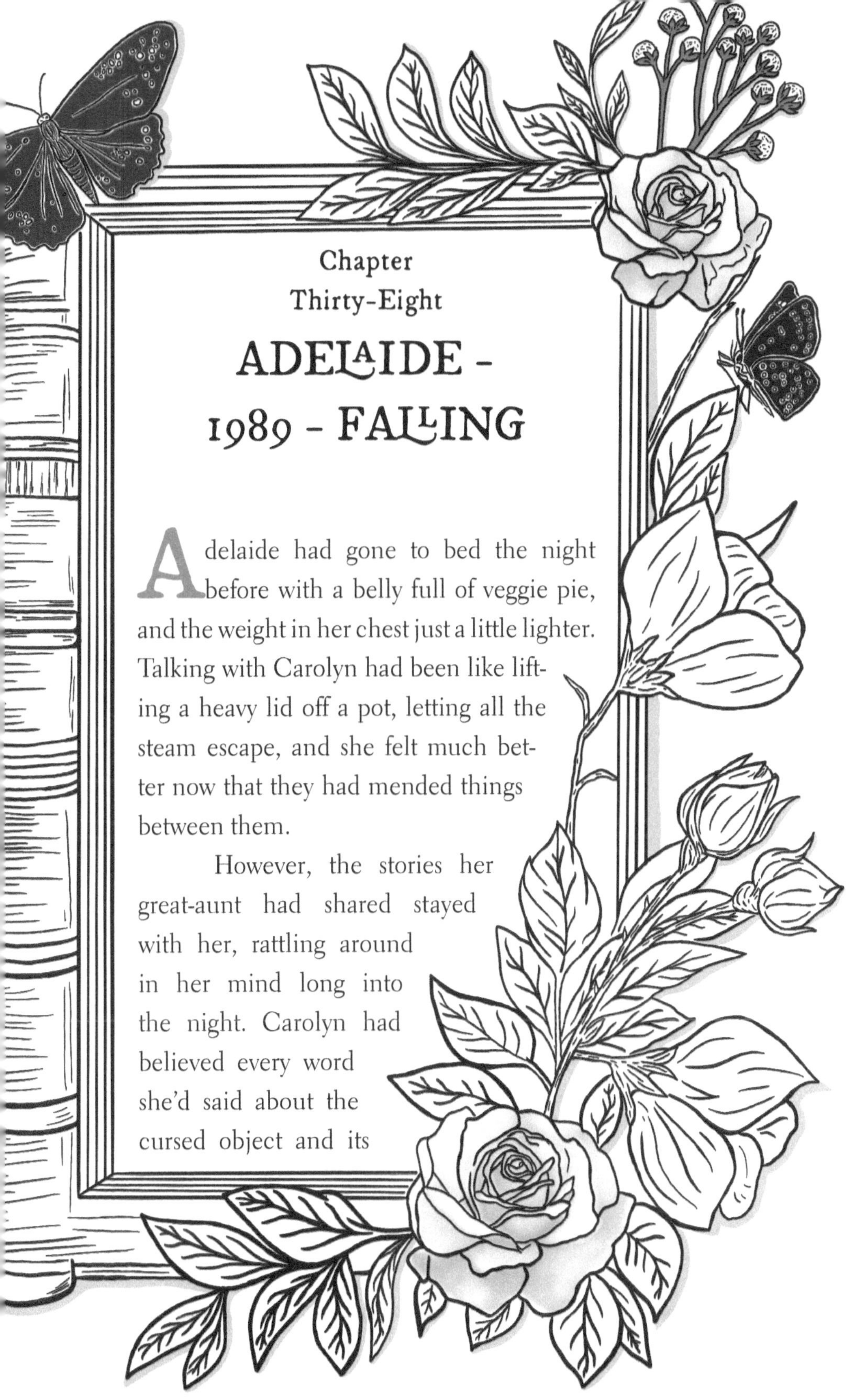

Chapter
Thirty-Eight

ADELAIDE –
1989 – FALLING

Adelaide had gone to bed the night before with a belly full of veggie pie, and the weight in her chest just a little lighter. Talking with Carolyn had been like lifting a heavy lid off a pot, letting all the steam escape, and she felt much better now that they had mended things between them.

However, the stories her great-aunt had shared stayed with her, rattling around in her mind long into the night. Carolyn had believed every word she'd said about the cursed object and its link to the disappearances. Adelaide had heard the conviction in her voice, but the whole thing felt impossible, desperate, even. A myth wrapped around old grief.

And yet.

There was the key taped behind the painting of John Dee. The strange energy humming through the Feather Thorn. The way the silence there felt watchful.

Now, bundled in her warmest sweater and jeans, with the tartan blanket wrapped around her shoulders, she stood at the hearth, staring at the painting above the mantel. The morning sunlight caught on its surface, making the golden wheat field glow, as if it were a window into another world. It was the first time she'd looked at it since realizing Carolyn had painted it. Now she saw it differently; there was love poured into every careful stroke. So why had this one ended up boxed away in the garage? It looked like it belonged with the others at the bookshop, as if it was part of the set there.

Taking a long sip of coffee, she studied the painting, trying to place its location. The scene tugged at something, some memory or half-remembered dream, but nothing came. With a sigh, she set her mug on the mantel and loaded the last of the firewood that she'd brought in the night before.

She'd made up her mind. Once that last stack of wood was gone, she'd move into the Feather Thorn. Judging how quickly she was burning through it, that might only be a week away. The cabin just couldn't keep up with the cold anymore, and winter was already starting to bite.

She rinsed her cup, left it in the sink, pulled on her jacket, and headed out.

Frost had feathered over the ivy crawling across the bookshop's windows, its muted minty green reminding her of her gran's old carnival glass sweet dish.

"That might not be a bad color for the kids' section," she muttered, fumbling with the keys. The door creaked open, and the familiar smell of the books greeted her like an old friend. As she reached for the light switch, her gaze snagged on the letterbox. Another letter poked from its lip. Her heart skipped, and a smile spread across her face.

She plucked it from its resting place and unfolded it, her eyes skimming eagerly across the words.

The wall looks great! The color really brings out the bookshelves. You've got impeccable taste. I can't wait to see what you do next to bring the bookshop back to life.

A flush crept up her neck and butterflies erupted in her stomach. A giggle slipped out, girlish and unguarded. She still couldn't believe Ewan was leaving her these sweet little notes, encouraging her to keep going. It was thoughtful, so thoughtful, the kind of thing you saw in films or read in novels. Was it real? Were men actually this romantic? Jeff certainly hadn't been. Not with her, at least.

The thought landed like a dropped stone. Her stomach twisted, but she refused to let it take hold. No. She wouldn't let memories of Jeff spoil this for her. He'd had his fun. Now it was her turn.

Trying to shake him off, she looked down at the note again, at the kind words, and realized with sudden, comical panic: she had nothing to wear for tonight. Nothing remotely date-appropriate. She'd need to pop into the Common Blue later and see if Camie could help her find something.

Folding the note carefully, she tucked it into her pocket and headed to the stairwell wall. She ran a hand along the surface. The green had deepened a shade overnight, but it still looked perfect, rich, warm and vibrant. She'd originally planned to paint the reading nook in the loft today, but her thoughts were already occupied with the date, her mind buzzing with what-ifs and outfit ideas. The nook could wait.

Instead of heading straight for the secondhand store, though, she opted to rehang the paintings first. The green wall called for it, like the space was waiting. Afterward, she'd swing by the shop, then head home for a hot bath, a face mask, maybe even shave her legs, for her first date in over nine years.

Nine years.

The thought stopped her. She stood in the middle of the shop, still holding a canvas, that number lodged in her chest. Had it really been that long since someone had looked at her like she mattered? She didn't know if she was ready, not really. It had only been a few weeks since her split with Jeff. Yet, it felt like so much longer. A lifetime, almost.

She was shedding the skin of her old life now, breath by breath, step by step, unsure where this new version of her would land, but more than willing to find out.

She started with the smaller paintings, lifting each one into place. Their gilded frames caught the light, making them stand out in sharp contrast to their new backdrop. Against the fresh color, the artwork seemed to wake up, details she'd not noticed before popping into view.

She reached for the last one, John Dee's portrait, and stared into his eyes. They seemed different now, kind but troubled, almost alive with unspoken knowledge. Like he was just waiting for someone to ask the right question. In his hands, he clutched what looked like a golden pocket watch. The longer she looked at it, the less like a painting it felt.

Picking it up, the weight, or lack of it, still baffled her. For its size and thick wooden frame, it should have been heavy. She'd thought the same thing yesterday when she'd taken it down.

She climbed the stairs, the canvas balanced awkwardly in her arms. A knot of tension tightened in her gut. Three steps from the top, she leaned forward, stretching onto her toes to catch the wire on the nail. It slipped. She tried again. Slipped. Shifting the frame higher, she squinted up, certain the nail had to be farther up the wall.

Just as she felt it catch, her foot slipped.

She tipped backward, one arm flailing in a desperate attempt to get her balance, the other held the edge of the frame.

The painting wobbled on the nail. Not strong enough to hold her. She let go, just as her weight tilted back.

And the world… stopped.

She didn't fall.

She hung there, suspended midair, not for a second, but for long enough to know something was wrong. Or right. Or impossible.

Her fingers found the railing. As if guided. She grabbed it, her foot scraping the edge of the stair, balance returning.

She gasped, chest heaving, legs shaking, clutching the railing with both hands, looking up, then down the staircase, half-expecting to see someone, or something, standing there. But she was alone. Carolyn's words whispered in her mind: *The place is cursed. It holds mysteries, centuries old. Things that hold great power.*

"Thank you," she whispered, unsure of to whom, or what, she was speaking. The words felt right, though.

She gathered herself, gripping the banister like a lifeline.

"Okay," she said, her voice trembling. "That's enough for today."

She descended the stairs slowly, both feet on each step, every nerve tingling.

At the front door, she collected her jacket and glanced up toward the top of the stairs. *There's no one there.*

But something was. The kind of presence you couldn't see, only sense, in the quiet spaces between heartbeats.

She turned and locked the door behind her, the key trembling slightly in her grip. Carolyn's words echoing louder now. *That place is cursed…*

Adelaide shook her head, trying to push the thoughts away. An invisible force had caught her. Saved her. She didn't want to believe Carolyn, but how could she not? Whatever it was, it didn't feel cursed. It didn't feel evil.

Outside, the wind cut sharp through her coat. She zipped it tighter and started toward the Common Blue. She could have driven, but she chose to walk. She needed air. Movement. Distance from whatever had just happened.

Two weeks ago, she would have rolled her eyes at talk of curses and unseen forces; now, she was whispering thank-you to empty staircases. Was she losing her mind? Maybe Jeff hadn't just broken her heart; maybe he'd broken something deeper. Perhaps this was how grief made sense of the senseless, the way it had for Carolyn when Rowland disappeared. But even as she walked faster, Adelaide could not shake the feeling that someone had caught her. And that whoever, or whatever it was, might still be watching.

"Get a grip," she mumbled, planting her feet a little firmer on the pavement. Whatever weirdness was going on, it had no place tonight. Tonight wasn't about ghosts or gut feelings; it was about living again.

A cheerful jingle rang out as she pushed open the door to the Common Blue. Warmth rushed to meet her, along with a swirl of overly floral perfume, candle wax, and stale cigarette smoke that made her nose wrinkle. She stepped farther in, scanning the delightful chaos of vintage bric-a-brac, secondhand clothes, and pastel-painted furniture.

At the back, Camie's brown curls bounced wildly as she danced to Duran Duran's "Hungry Like a Wolf." Adelaide smiled.

"Adelaide!" Camie spun round. "Do you read minds? I was literally just thinking about you!"

"If I did, I'd be charging for it," Adelaide said, laughing as she made her way over.

"I heard you bought the old Feather Thorn," Camie said, eyes wide. "I was going to stop by, see if you were around, maybe grab a pint later?"

"Yeah, jumped in feet first," Adelaide said, flipping through a rack of dresses. "Now I'm just trying to breathe a little new life into it. Been painting and all that this week."

Camie gave a low whistle. "You've got some guts. Nobody around here would've touched that place with a ten-foot pole after all the stories."

Adelaide raised a brow. "That bad, huh?"

Camie laughed. "So, what brings you in today?"

"I'm surprised you haven't already heard, with how gossip spreads like wildfire around here," Adelaide teased.

Camie shot her a knowing smile and shrugged.

"You're kidding me, right? Please tell me there isn't some town gossip hotline."

"No, just Ewan's mate Dan. Came in earlier and spilled the beans." Camie nudged her. "So? When's the big date?"

"Tonight. And I've got nothing to wear but old jeans and baggy sweaters."

"I think I can help you out there." Camie grabbed her hand. "Follow me." She led Adelaide to the back, where a long metal rod stretched the length of the room, jammed with dresses in every color, decade, and level of taste. Camie pushed hangers aside, searching for something in particular.

"There she is!" Camie yanked a black pencil skirt and a flouncy white blouse off the rack. "Add that kick-ass jacket I gave you to this, and you've got a winner. And it looks just your size," she added, handing the outfit to Adelaide with a grin.

Adelaide held them up. "Where's your changing room?"

"Right this way," Camie said, pointing to a curtained alcove. "And don't you hide in there. I need a full fashion show."

Adelaide slipped behind the curtain and changed quickly. The mirror was old and streaked, but the reflection staring back was startling. With her hair back to its natural color, she hardly recognized herself. She loved it. It felt daring and sexy, everything she hadn't felt in years.

She stepped out and twirled, the white blouse flaring.

Camie whooped. "Holy shit, you're a total knockout. Like, damn, you should be a backup dancer for Cyndi Lauper or something in that."

"Ha, hardly." Adelaide blushed. "But I love it. Do you think Ewan will?"

"He'd be a bloody fool not to."

Adelaide ducked back behind the curtain and changed. At the till, she pulled out her wallet, the clothes already folded on the counter. Camie's smile softened. "Hey, girl to girl, just be careful. Guys like Ewan? They're charming as hell, but they can also be heartbreakers.”

“Oh, believe me, I’m not looking for anything serious. I just need a bit of fun,” Adelaide replied with a wink.

Camie’s grin returned. “Well, in that case, this outfit is going to rock his bloody world.”

“Thanks, Camie,” Adelaide said, handing her the money. “How about I take you up on that pint tomorrow?”

“You’re on. And I expect all the juicy details.”

“Deal. Swing by the bookshop when you close tomorrow. I’ll be there painting.”

Camie passed over the crinkled Tesco bag. “Good luck tonight. Not that you’ll need it with that outfit.”

Adelaide stepped outside, clutching the bag, a thrill fizzing under her skin. The cool air felt good, and for a few minutes, everything felt wonderfully, blessedly normal. But as she turned the corner toward the Feather Thorn, her thoughts drifted. Back to the stairs. The painting of John Dee. The invisible pause before the near-fall. She shook her head, trying to clear it, but the memory clung like a cobweb. Fine and persistent.

Carolyn’s words whispered again: *That place is cursed.* Adelaide didn’t want to believe in curses. She *didn’t* believe in curses. But the Feather Thorn was definitely not an ordinary building; there was something unseen lurking within its walls.

THE HIDDEN JOURNAL
OF JOHN DEE

December 3, 1582

It has been over three weeks since the ritual to repair the rift in time was performed. The days drag on, heavy with the weight of uncertainty. Although there have been no more apparent distortions in the fabric of reality, the air feels thick with something I cannot yet name. The feeling that something is not right, that the consequences of our actions are yet to fully unfold. Even though the rip seems to be held in check at the moment.

I find myself growing restless as I wait for Edward Kelley to return from his trip to France. His absence has made the passing of time feel almost unbearable. Each day stretches on, each minute a small eternity as I wait for him to return with his ability to give me answers. His connection to the divine may offer me the clarity I so desperately need. Until then, I can do little but sit in silence, my mind preoccupied with the knowledge that we have meddled with forces beyond our comprehension, and that we may not yet have seen the full extent of the consequences. What if it's just a matter of time before it begins to unravel once again, and this time, we might not have a way to even slow it down, much less to fix it.

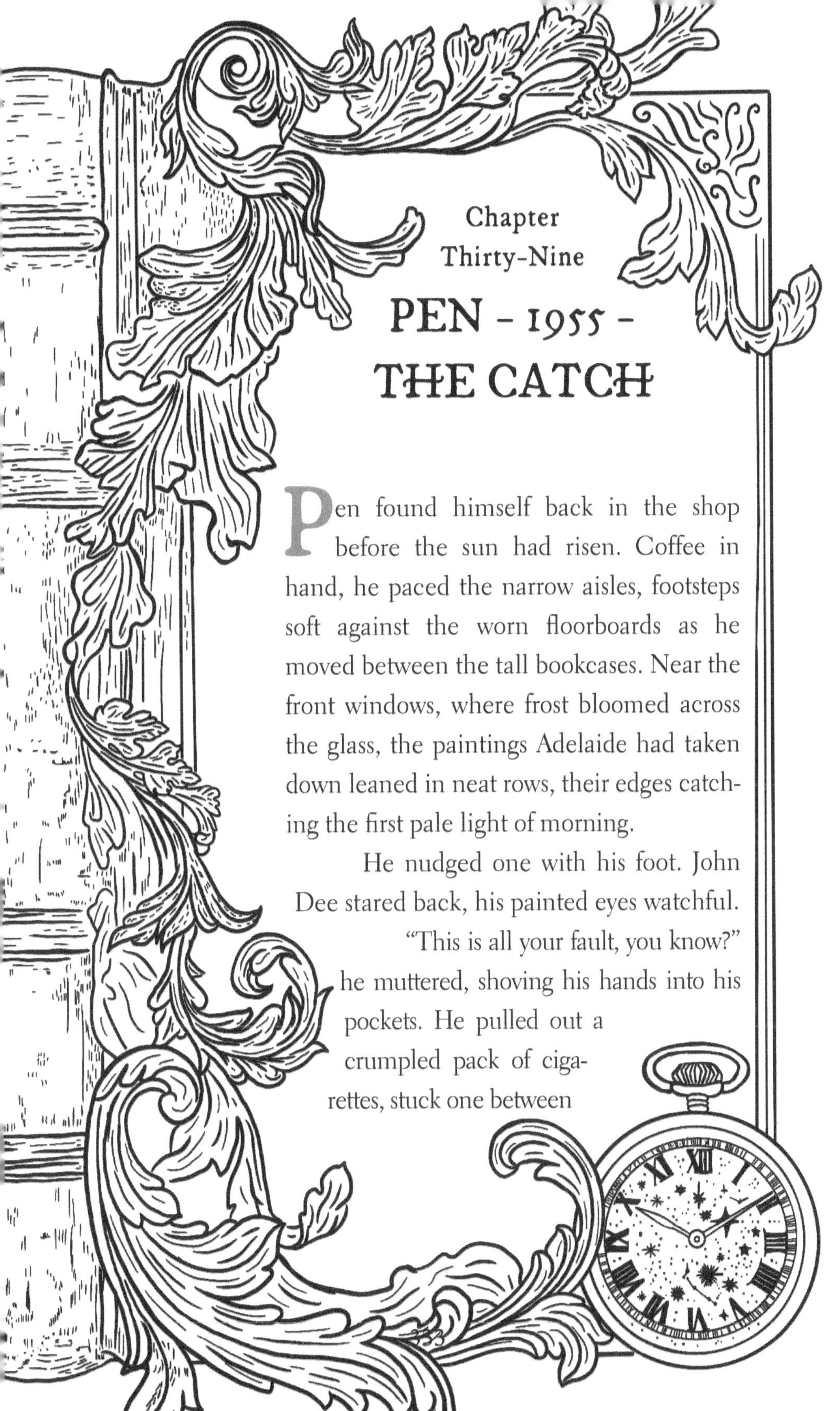

PEN - 1955 -
THE CATCH

Pen found himself back in the shop before the sun had risen. Coffee in hand, he paced the narrow aisles, footsteps soft against the worn floorboards as he moved between the tall bookcases. Near the front windows, where frost bloomed across the glass, the paintings Adelaide had taken down leaned in neat rows, their edges catching the first pale light of morning.

He nudged one with his foot. John Dee stared back, his painted eyes watchful.

"This is all your fault, you know?" he muttered, shoving his hands into his pockets. He pulled out a crumpled pack of cigarettes, stuck one between his lips, and paused. A beat passed. Then he sighed, took it out of his mouth, and slipped it back into the pack. He'd made a decision: no smoking in the shop anymore; old books and fire, even in small amounts, seemed like a bad idea. He didn't want to risk burning the place down. God knew what would happen to him then. But today, he was on edge, and the urge was strong.

His stomach churned. He told himself it was the eggs he'd eaten for breakfast, but he knew better. Beneath everything else, it came down to a single, needling truth. He was waiting for her.

Would she come back today or not?

He hated how that thought sent his emotions into disarray. How could one person unravel him like this? She was a variable, a piece of the puzzle, and possibly the key to his freedom. That was all. That was logical, wasn't it? But logic didn't explain the way the Feather Thorn felt different when she was here, brighter, warmer, less like the mausoleum it had become. Less like a prison.

Pen sank into the worn wingback chair by the window, eyes fixed on the slow wash of dawn spilling over the cobblestones. The world stirred, indifferent to him, to the quiet ache inside him. He hoped, no, prayed, that she'd come back today. Just to feel, for a moment, to feel like part of the real world again.

Frankie jumped up onto his lap, curling into a tight ball, resting his tail over his eyes for a nap. Pen absently stroked the little fox, his thoughts circling the man from the day before. The one who had changed the locks. It wasn't just his looks, though they had clearly caught Adelaide's attention, that had irked Pen more than he cared to admit. No, it was something deeper, an unsettling vibe the man gave off that Pen couldn't shake.

Jealousy? He dismissed the word before it fully formed. That was ridiculous. And yet, the discomfort lingered, growing quietly as sunlight crept over the village, burning away the frost that had veiled the town.

A flash of color moved past the window. Adelaide. Pen sprang up, startling Frankie, who tumbled to the floor with an indignant chitter, clearly not impressed, before darting off toward the back of the shop.

Pen barely noticed. He was already at the front of the shop, just as the door creaked open. Adelaide stepped inside, her cheeks pink from the cold. As she took her coat off, she glanced down at the letterbox and her face lit up when she spotted the edge of the letter peeking out. The smile that appeared could have stopped time if it hadn't already been stopped.

She reached for the note, carefully pulling it free. As she read, her smile widened, and a soft laugh escaped her lips.

When she reached the end, Adelaide folded the letter neatly and slid it into her back pocket, patting it as though to ensure it was safe. Then she turned and made her way toward the staircase wall, where the fresh coat of green paint from the day before stood out in the dim light.

Pen followed, stepping up beside her as she stood studying the wall. The color had darkened slightly as it dried, but it still looked vibrant. She tilted her head, lips pursed in concentration.

"It looks great," he said softly, knowing it was pointless, yet needing to say it all the same. His words dissolved into the silence, unheard.

Adelaide didn't respond, not even a glance in his direction. He was nothing but a ghost to her, and the truth hit hard, leaving him feeling hollow. No matter how much he wished it, she couldn't see him, couldn't hear him. He swallowed it, forcing the emptiness down.

One by one, she began rehanging the paintings. Their bright gold frames stood out in stark contrast to the dark green backdrop, and Pen couldn't help but smile. The green was definitely the right choice. The space felt transformed.

He hovered near her as she reached for the large portrait of

John Dee. She wrapped her arms around the frame, straining slightly as she lifted. Without thinking, Pen reached for it too, his hands closing around the top edge just above hers. He didn't know if it helped. Maybe it didn't matter, but the instinct to steady her, to ease the burden even a little, was stronger than logic.

Together, though she didn't know it, they carried the painting up the stairs. At the top, Adelaide stood on her tiptoes, trying to hook the wire behind the frame onto the nail. She fumbled, the painting wobbling in her hands. Pen let go briefly to adjust the angle of the hook, but a moment was all it took.

A breath. A heartbeat.

Her foot slipped.

Too late, he caught the way her brow furrowed, the way her body pitched back, and he moved before thought could intervene. He lunged, arms outstretched, expecting to pass through her like smoke.

But he didn't.

He caught her. Solid. Warm. Real. Time seemed to stutter. She gasped and caught the railing, then the moment shattered. Pen staggered back, eyes wide, her weight gone from his arms. All that remained was the electric impression of her body, the warmth fading like a dream.

He looked down at his hands. He had touched her. Felt her. How?

Adelaide turned, her gaze sweeping the space, eyes wide. For a breathless instant, Pen thought, hoped, she saw him. But her eyes didn't quite meet his. She looked past him, her focus landing on the wall behind where he stood.

"Thank you," she whispered.

She hadn't seen him, but she had sensed his presence, had known that he'd kept her from falling. Had she felt him as he had felt her?

He sank onto the stairs, limbs trembling. Whatever force had allowed their brief connection had drained him of all his energy. He could still feel the echo of her skin against his, the memory of holding her weight for that one impossible second.

Below, Adelaide moved to the door. She paused and glanced back toward the loft. Her eyes searched the shadows, as if trying to locate someone just out of reach. Then she turned, pulled on her jacket, and left the Feather Thorn.

Pen remained on the step, watching the empty space where she'd stood, the hush of the shop pressing in. But the stillness didn't feel the same. Something was shifting; he could feel it in the air around him. It was as if someone had briefly opened a window and let in some much-needed fresh air.

The energy felt different, and Adelaide was the catalyst.

It took a few minutes for his strength to return. When it did, Pen rose on unsteady legs and made his way down to the hidden room. He lowered himself into the chair in front of the old Underwood typewriter. His gaze scanned the walls, papered in years of frantic thoughts, scribbled notes, sketches, half-baked plans for escape. The sight should have focused his mind, spurred him into action. He should have been strategizing, planning, doing something now that he'd made contact, but all he could think about was the warmth of her, Adelaide, in his arms.

He hadn't realized how much he'd missed it: human touch. The casual brush of a sleeve. The weight of a hand on a shoulder. Even a nod from a passerby. All of it had been absent for so long. And now, for the first time in ages, she had reminded him what it meant to be seen.

He reached for a fresh piece of paper, threaded it into the typewriter and let his fingers hover over the old metal keys. A thousand thoughts surged forward at once, tumbling over each other. He longed to tell her everything, that he was trapped, that he was there with her, just out of reach. He wanted her to know he had saved her and that she had unknowingly saved him too, that her presence had cracked something open inside him that had been sealed shut for decades.

But he knew he couldn't say those things, not yet. She wouldn't believe him, and worse, they might frighten her away. Whatever fragile thread existed between them could snap if he pulled too hard. She had spoken aloud, sensing him in some way. It wasn't much, but it was a start.

The truth would come in time. Slowly. Gently.

The letters, though, she probably assumed had come from someone in the outside world. Where else would she have thought they came from? Surely not some man trapped in time within her bookshop? These little notes were merely a way to bridge the gap, but eventually he would have to tell her his story, but not yet. But perhaps the incident on the stairs was a crack in the door. If he was subtle enough, maybe he could push it open and lead her toward the truth in other ways.

He glanced at the thin leather spine of Rowland's journal, picked it up, and ran a finger across the faded ink on the first page. If she read this, really read it, she might begin to understand.

He returned to the typewriter and typed a short note, brighter than the last, a touch warmer. A test, but also a gift. He promised himself that the next one would be the one where he explained everything.

As the day slipped into evening, Pen crept upstairs with the letter and Rowland's journal in hand. He placed them in the letterbox and stepped back. If she was as curious as he hoped, she'd open the journal. And once she did, the door to the truth would begin to open.

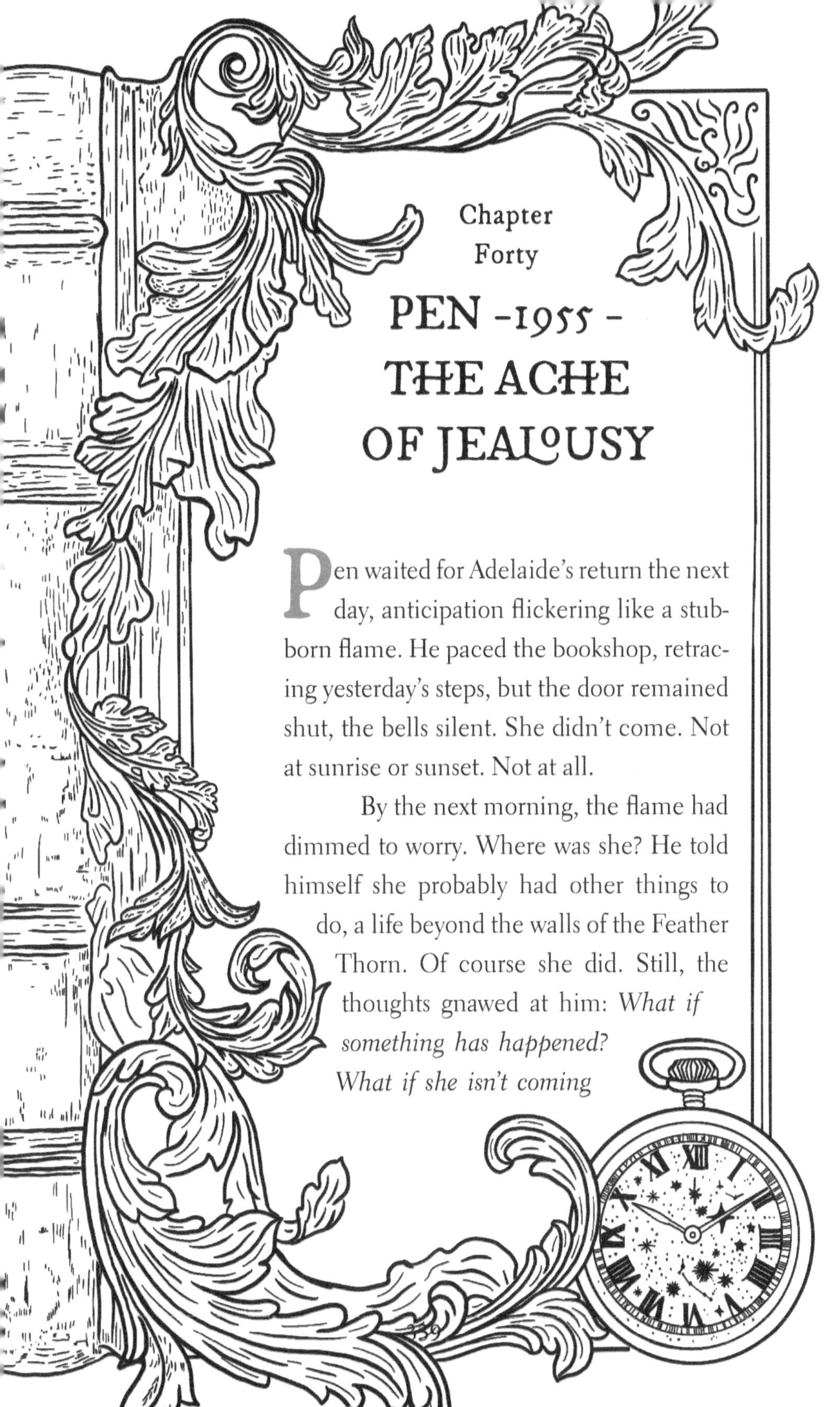

PEN -1955 -
THE ACHE
OF JEALOUSY

Pen waited for Adelaide's return the next day, anticipation flickering like a stubborn flame. He paced the bookshop, retracing yesterday's steps, but the door remained shut, the bells silent. She didn't come. Not at sunrise or sunset. Not at all.

By the next morning, the flame had dimmed to worry. Where was she? He told himself she probably had other things to do, a life beyond the walls of the Feather Thorn. Of course she did. Still, the thoughts gnawed at him: *What if something has happened? What if she isn't coming back? What if, God forbid, time has spun away again?* He stood at the window, flipping his lucky penny over and over in his fingers, his wingtip shoe tapping a restless rhythm against the floorboards. He felt pathetic, waiting for someone he couldn't even speak to. It felt a little too close to stalking, and maybe it was. Still, it wasn't like he had a better use for his time.

It was in this state that it dawned on him: he hadn't picked up a book or dusted a shelf or moved a single display in well over a week. Adelaide had become his orbit, and everything else had fallen away.

With a heavy sigh, he turned on his heel and went to the back room, returning with his feather duster. He made his way to the Religion & Theology section. Dusting had become a ritual of sorts, a way to occupy his time and keep his mind from spiraling. Just a week of neglect had allowed a fine layer of dust to settle across the shelves; just one week, and things were already slipping.

At the end of the bookcase, something caught his eye. Tucked into the corner, half-shrouded in shadow, was a spinning wheel, the kind used to spin wool into yarn.

A spinning wheel? Where had it come from?

He approached slowly. It hadn't been there before, he was certain of that. Adelaide hadn't brought it in; he would have seen.

The wood was old, worn smooth in places, polished by generations past. He reached out to touch it, but pulled back as soon as his fingers skimmed its surface. It felt… wrong. Wrong in a way he couldn't explain.

He crouched to get a better look when a sound broke the silence: the turn of a key in the front door. He stood quickly, just as Adelaide stepped inside. Relief swept over him, but it didn't last.

The lock guy was with her again. He watched them make

their way into the main space, toward the freshly painted wall. Adelaide didn't even glance at the letterbox.

He followed them, skirting the edges of the bookcases, moving like a shadow beside them.

"Here it is! Even though you've seen it through the windows, it looks even better up close, don't you think?" Adelaide's voice was light, flirty even. She gestured toward the painted wall with one hand while the other slipped into the pocket of her jeans. A slight rocking on her toes betrayed her nerves.

Pen caught the way the man hesitated before flashing a practiced grin.

"It looks great! I did a pretty good job mixing that paint." He nudged her shoulder playfully.

She turned and smiled, and Pen's heart deep-dived into his stomach. What he would have given to have her look at him in that way.

"So, what's next on your list?" the man asked, reaching out and straightening a slightly crooked picture.

"I'm thinking about tackling the children's corner next, and then the reading nook upstairs," Adelaide replied, curling a piece of hair around her finger.

"Show me the nook, it sounds cozy," he said, adding a wink.

Adelaide's cheeks blushed a soft shade of pink, and she motioned for him to follow. As they ascended the stairs, Adelaide went first. Pen's gaze followed them. The man's eyes were fixed on her backside, lingering there as they made their way up. Pen clenched his jaw. What kind of man just... stares like that? Sure, she had a beautiful figure, but gawking like that was so blatantly disrespectful. Crude.

Pen stayed at the base of the stairs, hands fisting in the fabric of his trousers. He should turn back. Give them space. Be decent. But instead, he followed, up to the loft, toward the warmth of laughter, unable to resist the low thrum of his own rising jealousy.

As he reached the top of the stairs, the low, seductive voice of the man echoed off the ceiling. "How about a repeat of last night?"

As Pen rounded the corner, Adelaide was leaning against the wall, cheeks flushed, the man towering over her, one arm braced above her head, the other wrapped firmly around her waist, pulling her closer.

Pen's breath hitched, and his chest tightened like a vice. Heat surged to his cheeks as his heart pounded, the rush of blood roaring in his ears. Never in his life had he felt anything like it. Raw, fierce, and unexpected. He couldn't look away. Couldn't stop the spiral. And when she kissed him, Pen felt the air leave his lungs, a slow twisting pain coiling through his insides.

He turned sharply, willing himself to retreat, to escape the ache clawing at his ribs. The sound of their kissing chased him back across the loft, an undeniable rage boiling in his veins. He kicked the side table by the stairs, sharp, quick, not even thinking. A release for his building frustration. The small framed sign—*Shhhhhh I'm reading*—crashed to the floor. The glass shattered with a crack that echoed.

What had he just done? This wasn't him; it was his father. The outburst, the loss of control. It wasn't who he was, and it wasn't who he wanted to become. But the feelings were too much: jealousy, grief, powerlessness, all of it rising too fast, too heavy. And it spilled out before he could hold it back.

He crouched, reaching for the broken shards, when he heard footsteps.

"What the hell was that?" the man asked.

Pen's hand hovered over the mess. Moments later, Adelaide and the man were standing there, staring down at the glass. Were they seeing this? Were they seeing the scattered glass?

He was certain he hadn't touched the picture before. Not once. Hadn't even been near it the day he trapped himself in time. So how had this happen?

There was no denying it now. Something was shifting; his presence was somehow bleeding through.

Adelaide tilted her head, brow furrowed. "Not sure how that happened," she said. "I'll grab a broom and clean this up. I'll be right back, Ewan." She disappeared down the stairs.

Like the light switch. Like the moment on the stairs. He was reaching through, his actions somehow rippling through the veil.

"So, you want to go out for a pint?" the man, Ewan, apparently, asked casually when she returned, broom and dustpan in hand, as she knelt to sweep up the shards. *He* didn't offer to help.

Adelaide dumped the glass into the bin and looked up. "I would like to, but I probably should get to doing a bit more work here. Plus, I promised Camie I would meet her later."

Ewan waved it off. "Oh, come on. This place isn't going anywhere, and it's not like you've got a day job. It's my day off. Let's go have some fun, Camie can wait."

He stepped closer to her, arms sliding around her waist. Another kiss.

The casual way Ewan touched her, spoke to her, like she was a prize to be claimed, not a person to be respected, it made Pen's skin crawl. There was no softness in it. No wonder. Just expectation. As if everything about her existence was about fulfilling his desires.

Adelaide didn't seem to notice. Or maybe she didn't mind.

She leaned into him briefly, then pulled back with a smile. "I guess you're right. I can take a day off."

"That's my girl," Ewan said with a smirk, giving her butt a playful smack. "Now let's go get steaming." He grabbed Adelaide's hand and practically dragged her down the stairs.

Desperately trying to cool his nerves, Pen stood in the loft, gaze sweeping the room, then landing on the suspended ship, next to the model plane. He had once imagined a life here. A future. Now he was a ghost watching from the rafters, a prisoner in his own creation. Watching the woman who made the Feather Thorn feel like home fall for someone else. And if that wasn't the definition of hell, then he didn't know what was.

THE HIDDEN JOURNAL OF JOHN DEE

December 9, 1582

Edward Kelley has returned, and the moment I had been anticipating has come to pass. He began his scrying session this afternoon, his gaze fixed on the obsidian disc, his voice soft as he began his incantations. As the minutes passed, I could sense the energy shift in the room, a subtle tension hanging in the air. Then it happened, Kelley's eyes rolled back in his head, and a voice that was not his own spoke through him. It was deep, resonant, and filled with a power that shook me down to my very bones.

The voice, *it was not human*, I am certain of it, told me what I had feared: the ritual had not fixed the rip permanently. The work we did was only a temporary bandage, a fleeting solution that would not withstand the ravages of time. The being told me that the Astral Synchronum, if it is to keep the tear in time from widening, must not remain where the rip first began but near a line of energy in the ground. To my surprise, and dismay, their revelation did not point to Dunblane Cathedral, where we had so carefully performed the ritual, but to a small village near Gare Loch, in Scotland. There, it must be kept bound in a building, sealed away, and never again used or moved. If it is disturbed, the seal that we placed on it might fail, causing the rip to grow larger, the consequences even more dire.

The divine being, through Kelley's lips, made it clear that the consequences of our actions would echo far beyond my own lifetime, as it was my idea originally. My name and bloodline would be forever tied to this task, punished for disrupting the natural order of time. A weight, a dreadful burden, pressed upon my soul in that moment. I begged the being to tell me a way to permanently fix it, saying I was willing to sacrifice my own life if it meant I could seal the rip. It laughed a dark and foreboding sound that seemed to resonate into the walls of the small kitchen where we sat. It said the only hope of permanent repair lies in a being of mixed blood, one who is neither fully human nor fully divine.

Before I could question the being further, Kelley's body gave a violent shudder, and the voice that had spoken through him withdrew, leaving its words hanging heavy in the room around us. Kelley collapsed, his breathing shallow and labored, as though he had expended all of his energy in that brief moment of divine communion. We sat in silence for several minutes, the reality of what had been said sinking in. There is no answer yet, only more questions, and no certainty in the path forward. But one thing is clear: our work is far from over, and the task before us has grown infinitely more complicated.

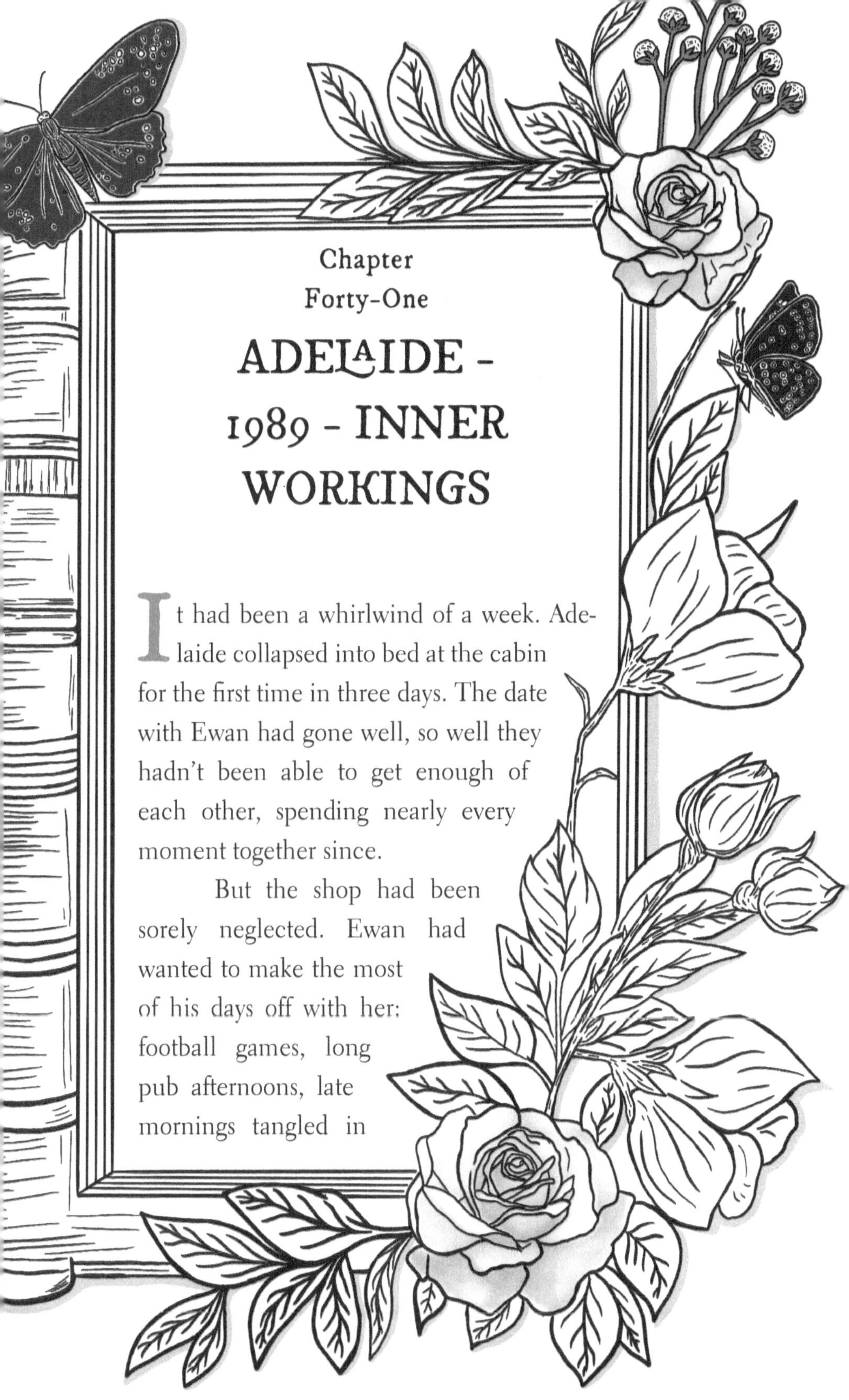

ADELAIDE – 1989 – INNER WORKINGS

I t had been a whirlwind of a week. Adelaide collapsed into bed at the cabin for the first time in three days. The date with Ewan had gone well, so well they hadn't been able to get enough of each other, spending nearly every moment together since.

But the shop had been sorely neglected. Ewan had wanted to make the most of his days off with her: football games, long pub afternoons, late mornings tangled in bedsheets. It was fun. Easy. But already she could feel the slide. Another man, another rhythm she didn't set. Was it the men she chose, or was it her? Maybe the problem lay in how easily she let them take the lead, falling in step without asserting herself. That wasn't what she wanted anymore. She couldn't let her relationship with Ewan become a mirror of her time with Jeff. No, next time they met up, she'd tell him what *she* wanted to do.

Thankfully, Ewan was working tomorrow. She needed space. Needed to get back to focusing on the Feather Thorn if she had any hope of opening before the end of November. The Christmas season loomed, one of the busiest times in retail, and if she was going to make any money, the shop had to be ready for holiday shoppers.

Tomorrow, she'd tackle the kids' corner and place an order for new stock, whatever she could with what little remained of her savings. Camie had promised to take her to a few secondhand shops outside Glasgow later in the week, ones that sold home goods. The bookshop needed new rugs to replace the threadbare ones. Maybe a few extra reading chairs. A small table-and-chairs set for the kids' area. She wanted the space to feel welcoming, a place where people could settle in, lose track of time, and breathe in the quiet comfort of books.

Her mind slowed as exhaustion weighed her down, heavy as the blankets she barely managed to pull over herself. Her limbs ached. Her eyelids sagged. She hadn't slept properly in days, not at Ewan's, and her body was crying out for rest.

Sleep came as soon as her eyes closed. But it wasn't the peaceful kind. Dreams overtook her, strange and vivid. Unsettling.

She stood in the loft at the Feather Thorn, gazing down at the forest of stories below, when she noticed a man dusting the shelves in the history section. He was whistling, a soft, wandering tune that stirred a buried memory. Her grandfather used to hum it when she was little, though she couldn't quite place the melody now. The man moved toward the window, the soft rays of morning light spilling across his features. He was handsome in an old-fashioned way, with dark wavy hair neatly brushed back, clean-shaven, but with a face that seemed etched with sorrow.

There was something about him, something that pulled at her heart. He stood there, gazing out the window, a deep sadness shadowing his expression, as if he were waiting for someone he knew would never come. She felt an urge to reach him. To offer him comfort.

She started down the stairs.

But before she could get close, he vanished. His form dissipating like smoke on a breeze. All that remained was the faint trace of cologne, the same one she'd smelled countless times in the shop.

His absence, so sudden, struck her. Grief welled in her chest. She found herself wandering the rows of books, searching for him even though she knew he was gone. Tears pricked her eyes. Then, just before they began to fall, a gentle hand touched her shoulder. She turned quickly, heart surging with hope, but as she spun around, the dream unraveled.

The shrill beeping of her radio alarm clock pulled her back. Adelaide jolted upright, and the dream slipped away like sand through her fingers, leaving only an ache, as though she'd lost someone dear.

She sat for a moment, tried to rationalize it; perhaps it was an echo of Carolyn and Rowland's story, imprinted in her mind like an old photograph. A memory never lived, but still carried.

Rolling out of bed, she stood and wrapped her arms around herself. The chill of the cabin bit through her flannel pajamas. She shuffled to the fireplace and added the last of the logs from the dwindling pile. Enough for one more night, maybe. It was clear now; she'd have to move into the Feather Thorn sooner than anticipated, likely by tomorrow.

Adelaide packed a few things into boxes before heading to the bookshop. Not much, just clothes, essentials. A toothbrush. A handful of books. She straightened and looked at the pile. This was it. Everything that had survived the wreckage of her old life. A pair of jeans with frayed cuffs, three T-shirts. The only things that were truly hers were the picture of her parents and a few dog-eared paperbacks. The rest had come secondhand or from Carolyn. Maybe it was better this way. No sharp-edged reminders. No echoes of Jeff.

Still, he crept in. Even with Ewan, laughing at the pub, pressed close at the football match, Jeff still lurked in the corners of her mind. His betrayal lingered like a bruise, tender and slow to fade. The bitterness returned, sharp as ever. Had he even thought of her since she'd left? Or had he been perfectly content, moving on with his new life with Stephanie? Pouring her coffee, holding her hand the same way, telling her all the same stories. Tears came without warning, and she let them fall. She knew she needed to call the lawyer. The thought hovered, annoying and insistent. But not today.

She wiped her face on her sleeve. No more spiraling. The Feather Thorn needed her. The November deadline was fast approaching. There was no room for distractions, none at all. Not Jeff. Not even Ewan. He was handsome, yes, magnetic, definitely, and she'd had more fun with him than she'd had in ages. But the shape of her days had begun to curve around him, and that was too familiar. Boundaries needed to be set. She couldn't afford to lose herself in another man, especially not now.

Outside, the wind bit at the windowpanes. Winter had begun to lick at autumn's heels. Too cold to walk into town today. So, she took her things to her car, started the engine, and made her way toward the village. Rooftops blurred past in muted grays and browns. People talked in towns like this, across counters, over fences, between sips of tea. She had no doubt her name and Ewan's had made the rounds. And though she tried not to care, part of her couldn't help wondering what, exactly, they were saying.

She'd take a break for lunch later and visit Carolyn. The last time they'd sat down together was over veggie pie. Her aunt would want an update, and if there was any news flying around, Carolyn would surely tell her.

So much had shifted in such a short span of time. Ewan had swept in without warning. She'd let herself be pulled into the newness of it all, intoxicated by the getting-to-know-you stage of the relationship.

Relationship? No, that was the wrong word. She frowned, knuckles whitening around the steering wheel. They were just having fun, weren't they? That was all. No expectations, no labels. She wasn't ready for anything more.

The shop appeared ahead. She pulled into her parking spot beside the building and shut off the engine, breath fogging in the cold air as she stepped outside. Not quite ready to begin her tasks at the Feather Thorn, she crossed the street to the Marbled Clover to grab a little fuel for the day.

Warmth greeted her as the door swung open. Butter and cinnamon wrapped around her like a shawl, and the cold quickly disappeared into the cozy atmosphere of the bakery.

"Adelaide!" Dottie's voice rose from behind the counter. "So nice to see you, sweetie. How's it going over there?"

"Good," Adelaide replied. "I'm about to go paint another wall today, but I thought I'd stop in here for a few snacks to keep my energy up."

"Good idea," a man's voice called from the back room. Iain emerged, balancing a tray of steaming apple turnovers. The scent of spiced apples and caramelized sugar rolled into the room.

"Those look dangerous!" Adelaide said, her mouth watering.

Iain grinned. "You better believe it. And they taste as good as they look." He set the tray down.

"I don't doubt it," Adelaide agreed. "I'll take a couple of those, and how about some of the apple cinnamon donuts, too? I bet they'll go great together." She looked down at the display case where golden rings of dough dusted with sugar and spice waited invitingly.

"You got it," Dottie said, reaching for a box and filling it up. "So," she added, folding down the lid, "do you have any idea when you'll be reopening the shop?"

Adelaide glanced back over her shoulder toward the Feather Thorn. "Hopefully in a few weeks. I want to have it up and running for Christmas."

"Smart," Iain replied. "People are already talking about it reopening, and they'll be eager to support it."

Dottie passed the box over the counter to Adelaide. "Here you go, love."

"Let me grab you a fresh cup of coffee to go with that," Iain offered as he walked into the back.

Dottie leaned in a little. "So, I'm assuming you told your aunt about the shop?"

Adelaide gave a short laugh. "Yeah, and you were right, it

didn't go down well at first. But I think she's coming around to the idea. Mostly because she knows I'm not going to back down."

"Well, she can't blame you there. You sound just like her, stubborn to a fault."

"Really?" Adelaide asked, the comparison catching her off guard. "How so?"

"I mean, look at her. She never married, and if you ask me, I don't think she ever gave up looking for Rowland."

"Why do you think she never gave up looking?"

"Well, for years she pestered the police to keep the case open. Wouldn't let it go. Rumor is, once they finally closed it, she hired a private investigator. Then came the tarot cards, tea leaves… that sort of thing. She was grasping for answers."

Adelaide's stomach flipped. That kind of heartache, sprawling out over years, latching onto anything that might bring him back, was hard to fathom.

"Did she ever talk to you about it?" Adelaide asked softly. "You two seem like friends."

Dottie shook her head slowly. "We're friends, as much as Carolyn lets anyone be. She's a very guarded person, doesn't let people get too close. It's rather sad, actually. Tends to stick to herself mostly. I think she was part of a book club once, years ago, but it didn't last. Some old friend from town dragged her into it, trying to get her out more."

The kitchen door opened again, and Iain came out with a small coffee decanter.

"I bet you'll need more than one cup if you plan to stay over there working all day," he said, handing it to her. "Take this, and when you're done, bring it back tomorrow, and I'll give you a refill." He winked as she took it.

"Thank you. You two are the best!" She handed a pound to Dottie and gathered her things. As she turned toward the door, her gaze snagged on the photo above it. The Feather Thorn in its heyday, fresh paint, flowers in the window box, people lingering on the steps.

"I hope I can bring her back to this," she murmured.

"You will," Iain stated, wrapping an arm around Dottie. "You're almost there, and by the sounds of it, it's going to be even better than it was."

"Pen would be proud," Dottie added, her smile tinged with something sad.

Adelaide nodded, then stepped outside into the brisk morning air. Just as her feet touched the cobblestones, a moth fluttered past her and toward the Feather Thorn's shop window. It brushed the windowpane and hovered there, wings quivering. She looked up. In the second-floor window, something shifted. A shadow, faint but unmistakable, moved across the dim interior.

Her heart skipped. But she didn't flinch. She'd seen it before, that shape, that presence just beyond the glass. She'd told herself it was just her imagination. A trick of the light. Not anymore. There was something inside the Feather Thorn.

The ghost stories, the whispers about the place, they weren't just old wives' tales. The shadow in the window had a weight now, a presence that curled in the corners like breath on cold glass. It felt like someone. Another soul lingering in the mists, between her reality and the beyond. She began to wonder if, just maybe, it was Rowland. And that perhaps Carolyn had been right all along.

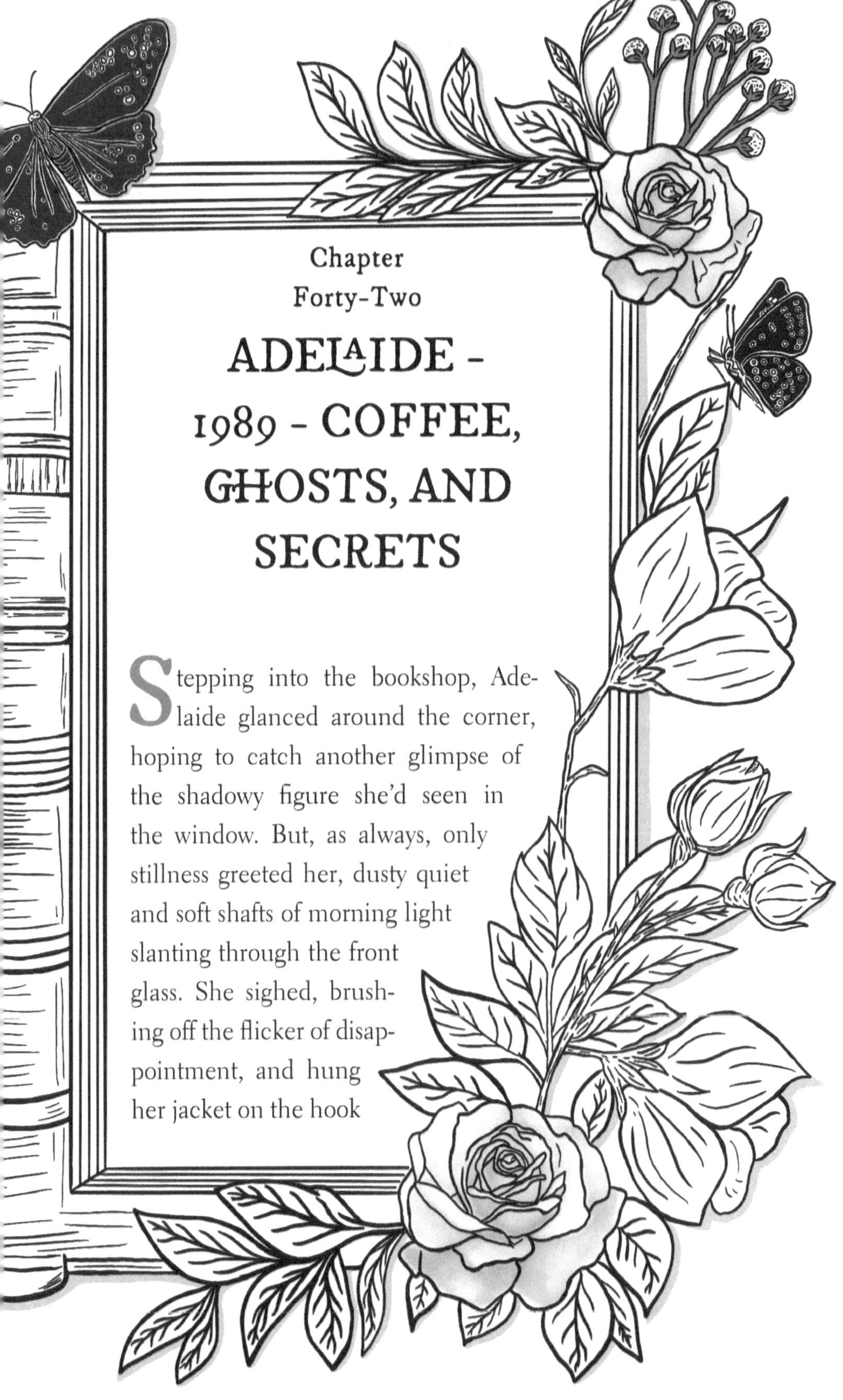

Chapter Forty-Two

ADELAIDE – 1989 – COFFEE, GHOSTS, AND SECRETS

Stepping into the bookshop, Adelaide glanced around the corner, hoping to catch another glimpse of the shadowy figure she'd seen in the window. But, as always, only stillness greeted her, dusty quiet and soft shafts of morning light slanting through the front glass. She sighed, brushing off the flicker of disappointment, and hung her jacket on the hook near the door.

That's when she noticed it: a new letter, its corner poking through the tarnished copper flap of the letterbox. Her heart fluttered. Lifting the lid, she found not just a letter, but a thin leather-bound book tucked beside it. She drew them both out and unfolded the sheet of paper.

The familiar typewritten script stared back at her as she smoothed it out. She read the words aloud, her voice echoing softly in the empty shop.

"Seeing how the bookshop is yours now, I thought you might want to know a little bit about its past while creating its future. I think you're just what it needs. This place seems to sing with you in it."

A smile touched her lips. She folded the letter back up carefully and tucked it into her back pocket, planning to add it to the growing collection stored in a box at the cabin. There was something about Ewan's letters, something that didn't quite match with the man she'd spent late nights laughing with over chips and pints. On paper, he reached her in a way his spoken words never had. Perhaps it was the romance of it all, the clandestine charm of finding typed notes in a creaky old letterbox, as if plucked from another time. She wanted to ask him about them, but was afraid that if she did, it might break the enchantment of it all.

It was the sweetness that surprised her. But she understood. Some people only revealed their true selves through ink. She'd seen it before, with her mother.

After her father's death, the house had fallen into silence. Her mother had packed away her grief like a set of fragile teacups, tucked out of sight, too delicate to touch. As a girl, Adelaide hadn't understood. She'd wanted to know his stories, his favorite songs, how they met, something from before she existed. But nothing ever came.

It wasn't until after her mother's passing that the truth began to surface. In drawers, behind old sweaters, buried beneath years of silence, she found the letters. Piles of them. Pages softened by time and stained with tears. Her mother had written to the man she'd lost, again and again. Adelaide had spent her childhood thinking her mother had never let herself feel it. But she had felt it, all of it. She'd just hidden it away, kept it secret, tucked deep where Adelaide wouldn't see. She'd done it to be strong. For her.

A sadness crept over her at the thought of her mother's heartache, and she pushed the sorrow to the back of her mind. With a deep breath, she walked over to the wingback chair near the window with the book in hand and sat. The leather was cold against her legs as she curled into it, the book resting on her lap.

She opened the cover. It wasn't just any book. It was a journal. The first page was dated September 12th, 1931, with a name, Rowland, scribed at the bottom.

Her heart sank into her stomach. This was Rowland's journal. She ran a hand over the edge of the page, a strange reverence stirring. *How did Ewan come to have this?* But that question could wait. She turned to the next page.

The early entries were scatterings of thoughts and sketches, plans to turn the building his uncle had left him into a bookshop. He wrote with warmth about his childhood love of books, how he used to imagine a life spent surrounded by them. That was the dream, and this place would be it, his own literary haven.

Further in, the entries became more detailed. Floor plans, shelving ideas, notes about window light. He wrote about meeting a man named Roger, who had helped him find a book dealer in London. The purchase of all the books has cost him his inheritance. "I've never felt poorer in coin," one entry read, "but richer in purpose."

She ran her finger over that line. This place had been built with love.

As she turned the pages, things began to get more interesting, more personal. Rowland began writing about a woman who had opened a small tea shop across the way. Adelaide didn't need a name to know who he meant. The way he described her, *her smile as radiant as the summer sun, a glance that could undo a day's weariness*, left no doubt. Carolyn.

The sweetness of it pulled at something inside her. She had only ever known Carolyn, shaped by loss, by grief, by years lived alone. But here was a version of her that shimmered with youth, light, and laughter.

Rowland hadn't found the courage to introduce himself to Carolyn, not yet. Instead, he'd just been admiring her from afar, tiptoeing toward the edge of something precious. She turned the page to the next entry. December 19th, 1931.

The last several weeks have been spent alone, and I feel more isolated than I have in a long time. I had hoped that moving to Scotland and opening the bookshop would help me connect with new people, especially after losing so many friends during the war. But even surrounded by customers, I feel utterly alone.

I've tried to build up the courage to ask Carolyn if she would like to go out with me, but I feel as though she is out of my league. Such a beautiful woman wouldn't be interested in a man like me, broken from the war, with a limp that never fully healed and scars that run deeper than the ones on my body.

She closed the journal and set it aside on the windowsill. She felt like an intruder. Rowland hadn't just shared his thoughts, he'd laid bare his pain. She wasn't sure she had the right to read more.

Had Ewan read this? Did he know about Rowland's grief and war-haunted sorrow? If there were deeper, more intimate confessions hidden within those pages, she wasn't sure it was meant for anyone else to read. And how had he come by the journal at all? Had he found it here, in the shop?

She moved to the counter, her thoughts now clouded by unsettling questions when they should've been focused on the task at hand. She picked up the coffee decanter Iain had given her and poured herself a cup into one of the mugs she'd borrowed from the shop and took a slow sip. She reached for the box of donuts. It was open. Had it been like that when she set it down earlier?

Her gaze flickered to the far corners of the shop, then back at the box, then she smiled. Had it been the ghost?

She was all but convinced now. The Feather Thorn was indeed haunted. And the stories around town didn't seem far-fetched anymore. Odd happenings, vanishing shadows; it was the only explanation that made sense. Yet, the idea didn't scare her.

If anything, it felt… reassuring. Like Rowland was still here, watching over the place he'd built. She chuckled to herself. Her very own Casper the Friendly Ghost.

"Help yourself to a donut," she said to the empty room, taking one from the box. She broke it in half, dipped it into the steaming coffee, and took a bite.

Still, the journal occupied her thoughts. It sat on the windowsill like a beacon. Her conscience tugged one way, her curiosity the other.

No, she decided, *I need to focus.* She turned her back on it and found the phone book she'd borrowed from Carolyn. *Time to get back to work.* Flipping through its thin yellowed pages, she found the number for the book dealer in Edinburgh and placed an order. A mix of children's titles: *The Polar Express, Chicka Chicka Boom Boom, Anne of Green Gables,* and a few adult titles that she'd loved that summer, purchased for the library in Glastonbury: *The Remains of the Day, The Bonfire of the Vanities, Lonesome Dove.* With luck, they'd arrive before she opened at the end of November.

She turned her attention back to the children's section. The layout might have worked thirty years ago, but nowadays, children need space to sprawl, to play, to be loud. She pictured a reading rug, a few low chairs in the corner, maybe a basket of wooden toys for restless hands while parents browsed.

The corner wall wrapping around the door had always felt dim, a pocket of gloom at the edge of the shop. Not a place for children. She'd chosen a mint green, reminiscent of frost-covered ivy, the perfect pick-me-up for the area.

Pulling her paint supplies over to the corner, she took down the old portrait of a wood duck that would not be going back up, and two small tapestries so worn and grimy, their patterns had all but disappeared. Those, too, she set aside for the bin. She stirred the paint, poured it into the tray, and rolled out the first stripe. The wall brightened with each stroke of the pale green, transforming the dark space into something more cheerful.

As she worked, she began to sing, "Just What I Needed" by The Cars. Fitting, really. The Feather Thorn had been just what

she needed, a project, a purpose to pull herself out of the depths of
sorrow and self-pity.

The paneled wall gleamed by the time she was done. The
nook had taken on a new life, fresh, soft, and inviting. A perfect spot
for a mother to curl up with a book and a giggling child.

Satisfied, she cleaned her brushes, packed away the paint,
and poured herself another cup of coffee. Ian had been right; it was
definitely more than a-two-cup kinda day. As she perched on the
edge of the counter, nibbling on an apple turnover, her gaze kept
drifting back to the windowsill.

There was no use fighting it. She'd tried to resist, but the
pull hadn't gone away. If anything, it had grown stronger. Maybe
there were answers in those pages, about Rowland, about the shop,
about whatever lingered within its walls. Maybe that was reason
enough to read on.

She stood, crossed to the wingback chair, and settled into
the worn leather seat. Then she opened the journal and began to
read.

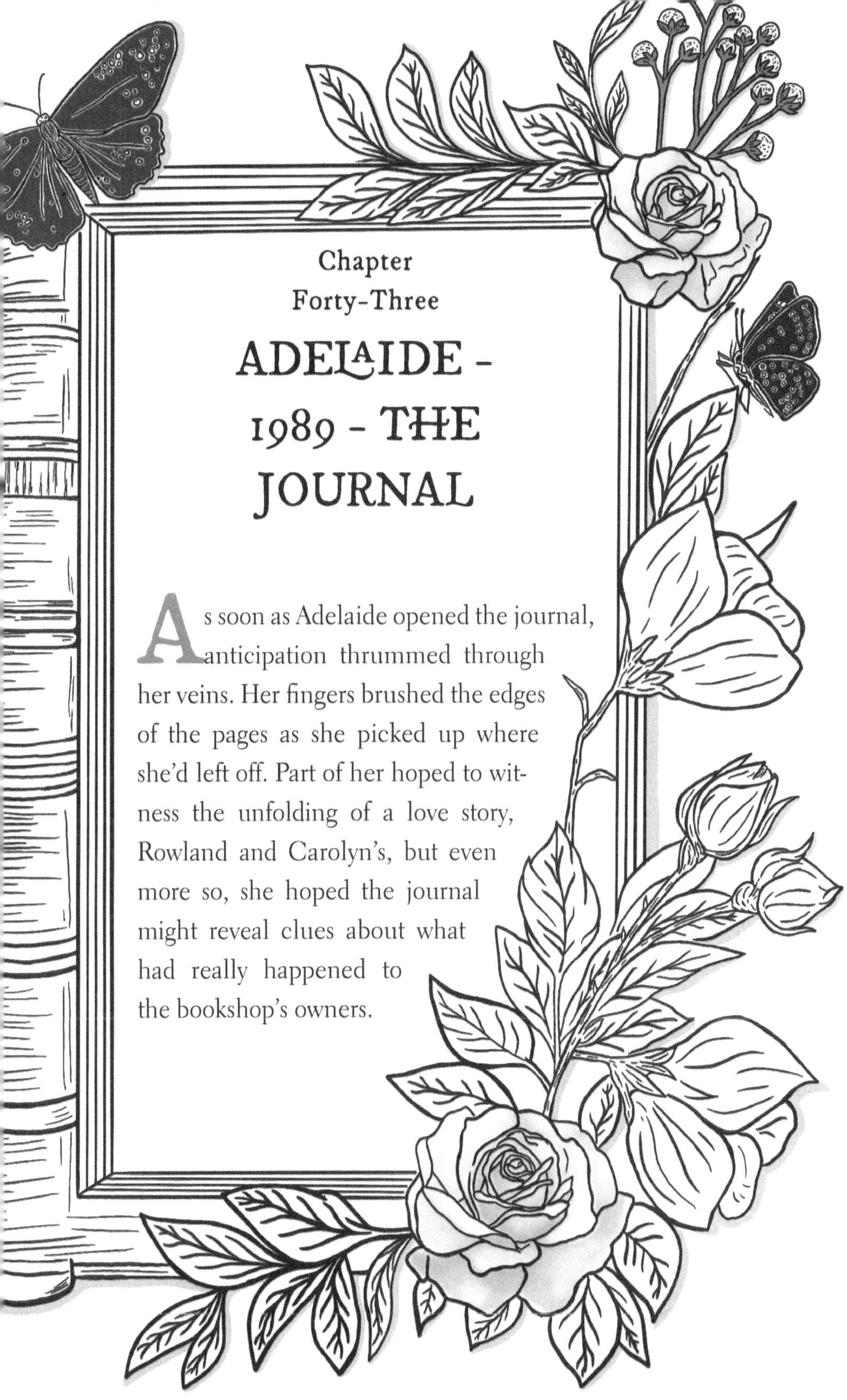

Chapter
Forty-Three

ADELAIDE –
1989 – THE
JOURNAL

As soon as Adelaide opened the journal, anticipation thrummed through her veins. Her fingers brushed the edges of the pages as she picked up where she'd left off. Part of her hoped to witness the unfolding of a love story, Rowland and Carolyn's, but even more so, she hoped the journal might reveal clues about what had really happened to the bookshop's owners.

December 28th, 1931

It's hard to believe that just a few days ago, my spirits were so low. Now, I feel as though I am walking on clouds. Carolyn surprised me on Christmas Eve with a basket full of homemade biscuits and teas. I invited her in, and we spent hours sitting in front of the windows, talking as we indulged in her festive treats. From that day on, we've found it nearly impossible to be apart, and I find myself thinking of her every spare minute of my days. I am glad that she found the courage to speak to me, as I am not sure how long it would have taken me to gather the nerve, being as shy as I am.

She made the conversation so easy, and there seems to be an endless number of things for us to talk about. I've planned a dinner for us the day after tomorrow, and I plan to kiss her for the first time. My heart leaps at the thought of it, though my nerves are set to flight.

Adelaide smiled. There was a sweetness in his words that felt almost too pure for this world. No wonder Carolyn had been so smitten. Rowland was gentle, thoughtful, kind; they sure didn't make them like him these days. She turned the page, expecting more of the same, but what came next was entirely different.

January 15, 1932

It's strange, the way things have shifted these past few weeks. Carolyn and I have settled into a quiet sort of harmony. Dinner together each night, reading side by side in the evenings. There's a peace in that, something I didn't realize I was missing. But last night, last night, something changed.

As she was gathering her things to leave, I heard them, chimes. At first, I thought it was just the wind, or perhaps something from the street outside. Then, when they persisted, I looked at Carolyn, at the small watch she wore on her wrist. I asked her if she could hear the chiming, and when she answered no, I knew. It was "the chimes." I'd heard the stories, of course, Uncle Roger's warnings, the strange family legend we all grew up with. But to hear it for myself unsettled me to my core.

When Uncle Roger died, he made it clear that if I ever heard those chimes, I was to ignore them. Ignore them? How could I? They're here, and they're real. And now that I've heard them, I can't seem to shake the feeling that something is about to change. The stories say the watch has the power to bend time itself, a gift and a curse that our ancestor John Dee left behind. A power that, if misused, could unravel everything.

I never thought I'd hear them. I thought I was safe, that the stories were just that, old tales told to keep us cautious. But now I know that the watch is real, my curiosity awakened, and I have begun searching for it in the shop. Yet, everywhere I look, it turns up empty. I know this might be unwise, but I feel as if they are calling to me.

Adelaide stopped reading, her breath catching in her throat as the hairs on her arms stood on end. Was this the artifact Carolyn had spoken of? Could a simple watch, an heirloom, truly be the cause of Rowland's disappearance? It seemed he hadn't believed in his family's legend until the day he heard the chimes.

Another chill coursed through her, and she instinctively glanced over her shoulder. Nothing. As always, the room lay empty. The thought that Rowland might be the ghost haunting the Feather Thorn settled heavy in her mind. Strangely, the idea didn't feel absurd at all now.

She turned back to the journal and read on, entry after entry, scanning for another mention of the watch. Page after page offered glimpses of Rowland's quiet courtship with Carolyn. He wrote of picnics by the river, quiet evenings in the bookshop, and their shared laughter echoing through the town's cobbled streets. But no mention of the chimes. Not until the very end.

May 30th, 1932

It was a quarter past six when the last customer departed the shop, and I secured the doors for the night. The day had been a blur, busy enough that the hours slipped away unnoticed. As I conducted my final inspection of the premises, ensuring all was in order, I heard them again, the chimes.

Months had passed since their first haunting toll, and until this evening, they had remained silent. My efforts to locate the source of the sound had been entirely fruitless. I could not fathom where they might originate, for I had personally overseen the cleaning and remodeling of the shop and had discovered nothing that could explain their existence.

Yet, once more, they rang out, seemingly from somewhere within the shop. I froze, my senses straining to discern their source. Then it struck me, they were emanating from beneath my feet. But the Feather Thorn had no cellar. Or so I had believed.

Following the sound, I made my way to the back of the shop. I tapped the floorboards with the tip of my shoe, listening intently. My pulse quickened as I detected it, the unmistakable hollow resonance of an empty space below. Dropping to my knees, I knocked with my knuckles, confirming the void beneath the boards.

Without hesitation, I pried them up one by one, revealing a narrow staircase descending into shadows. A damp, earthy smell rose to meet me, sending a shiver down my spine as the chimes grew deafening like a caged bird finally set free.

I lit a candle and descended into the cold dark space. At the bottom, I found a small stone chamber. It was empty, save for layers of cobwebs and grime. Yet, the chimes persisted, echoing through the space, making it hard to determine their direction.

Closing my eyes, I focused solely on the sound. When I opened them again, I knew where to look. A section of the wall stood out, a single stone, slightly misaligned, leaving a narrow crack just wide enough to slip a finger through. My hand trembled as I pulled the stone free, revealing a small wooden box and a leather-bound book tucked away in the hidden recess of the wall.

Back in the light and warmth of the shop, I opened the box. Inside, nestled in its center, lay a small gold pocket watch. The chimes had ceased as soon as I plucked it from its hiding place, as though the artifact's purpose had been fulfilled. But the air around it seemed charged, the weight of its presence heavy like a storm. I dared not touch it. The power emanating from the watch was unnerving, and the legends I had dismissed as bedtime stories suddenly felt terrifyingly real. Stories of what might happen if one were to tamper with the watch, its destructive nature, and how it was said to bend reality. I was seized by regret for having unearthed it.

With great care, I returned the watch to its hiding place. Yet, even now, as I commit this account to paper, its presence lingers, unshakable, pulling at my thoughts. There is something about its power that refuses to let me go.

Instead, I have turned my attention to the leather-bound book I found alongside it. The journal appears to have belonged to John Dee himself. My hands itch to uncover its secrets, to understand the true nature of the artifact hidden beneath the Feather Thorn.

Adelaide blinked, eyes sore from reading. Outside, the sky faded into an inky blue, the last of the light slipping away. The shop had grown dim without her noticing. She leaned back in the chair, gaze drifting to the floorboards.

Rowland had found the watch, here, beneath her feet. A secret staircase, a hidden chamber. Rising from her chair, she absently tapped on the floorboards as she walked toward the front counter, ears straining for that telltale hollow sound. Yet, despite her efforts, she found nothing.

Could it really be true? That somewhere within these walls, a watch capable of bending time was hidden? That the ghost she suspected haunted the Feather Thorn was Rowland?

The thought seemed absurd on the surface, yet as she stood there, alone in the quiet shop, a seed of belief began to take root.

THE HIDDEN JOURNAL OF JOHN DEE

December 12, 1582

The past few days have been filled with a strange mix of dread and hope, tempered by the weight of what we must now face. Edward Kelley is recovering his strength after the scrying session. His body drained, the divine connection having tapped into his very life force. Even though he wants to try and speak with the divine again right away, I have insisted he rest for now. We need him to be at full strength to be able to hold the being long enough to gain the information we need from it.

Kelley mentioned something that has ignited a flicker of hope within me, though it brings with it a new layer of uncertainty. The divine spoke to Kelley of the *Nephilim*, the descendants of humans and celestial beings. These beings, according to what we gathered through his divine communion, are the key to permanently sealing the rift in time. I cannot fathom how such a creature might exist in our world, for the Nephilim were said to have been wiped out in the Great Flood, their bloodline lost to history.

The thought both terrifies and fascinates me. If the Nephilim truly still exist, I must find one. But how? Unless Kelley can tap back into the divine again, there would be no determining where such a being might be found, no guidance on how to identify them.

As if this burden were not heavy enough, I have also begun the process of securing a building in the village near Gare Loch, where the line of this energy is said to be. I dare not risk leaving the Astral Synchronum here in our town, where it might reopen the tear at any moment. No, it must be moved and soon.

I have made arrangements to purchase a building there, one that will serve as a permanent sanctuary for the Synchronum, where it can be sealed and protected. The ritual will have to be done there, according to detailed instructions given to Kelley by the being. But we cannot do it without the help of Flora, an acquaintance of Kelley. She resides in a small village outside of Gare Loch and possesses the knowledge and power we need to bind the Synchronum permanently within the building.

There is something undeniably unsettling about seeking the help of, dare I call her a witch? But I must admit, it is a necessary evil. We need her abilities, her knowledge of the arcane, to ensure that the Astral Synchronum will remain sealed away. Without her, I fear that the entire plan will fail. Flora will be the key to completing the ritual and keeping the rift from spreading. I can only hope that her motivations are pure, though I find it difficult to trust someone so entwined with such dangerous powers.

My thoughts return to the Nephilim. If there is any hope of repairing the tear for good, I must find one of these half-angel, half-human. The rip must be sealed, and if the Nephilim are the key to that, I will stop at nothing to find one.

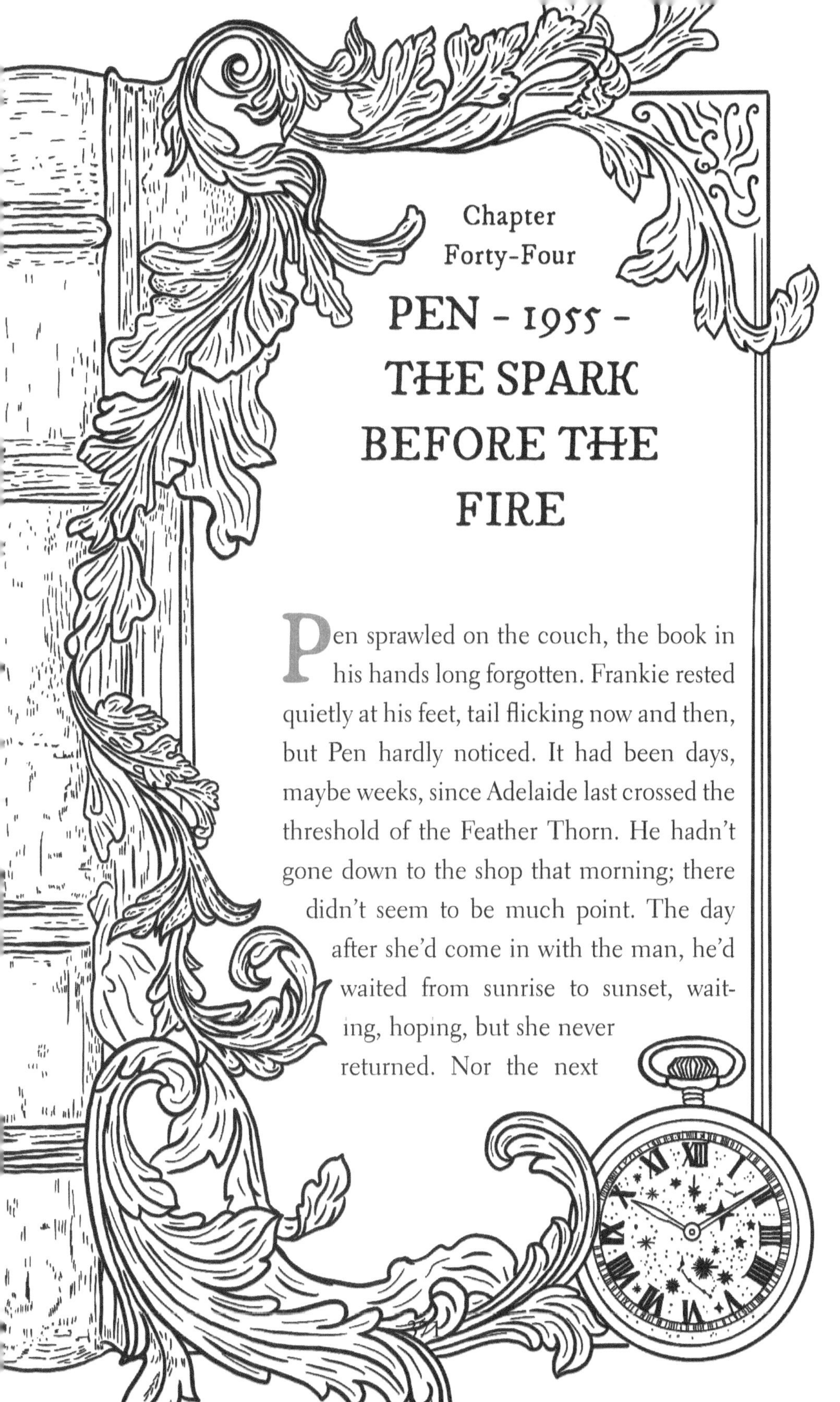

PEN - 1955 - THE SPARK BEFORE THE FIRE

Pen sprawled on the couch, the book in his hands long forgotten. Frankie rested quietly at his feet, tail flicking now and then, but Pen hardly noticed. It had been days, maybe weeks, since Adelaide last crossed the threshold of the Feather Thorn. He hadn't gone down to the shop that morning; there didn't seem to be much point. The day after she'd come in with the man, he'd waited from sunrise to sunset, waiting, hoping, but she never returned. Nor the next day. Nor the one after that. The thought he might have driven her off dug in like a thorn. Worse was the possibility that she simply preferred the company of that man, Ewan, and she'd lost interest in the shop. The weight of it settled low, sinking like a lead weight in his stomach.

He stared down at the open book, but the words swam, sliding off the page like water through fingers. All that remained were thoughts of Adelaide, of her absence, of the quiet, growing fear she might never come back, and what that would mean for him. It wasn't just the idea of being left here forever. It was the thought of never seeing her again. Never hearing her voice. Never feeling the warmth she brought to the room.

Restless, he rose to his feet, setting the book aside. He shut the door quickly, ensuring Frankie didn't slip out. The fox had a knack for disappearing into the shop, and Pen didn't have the heart to chase him out of the stacks again. He needed to move, to do something, anything, to silence the thoughts swirling in his mind. He decided to tackle the back area and dust the shelves he'd neglected the day before.

The shop felt emptier than usual, like it was slowly sinking into a cold, lifeless state. Shadows stretched long and low along the walls, and a chill seemed to settle over the place like a burial shroud. Even the floorboards seemed hesitant beneath his feet, their customary groans muffled, as if the entire space was holding its breath. The further Adelaide drifted from the shop, the more his own life and the shop seemed to wither. Or maybe it was just him, missing her, missing the light she brought to this place.

He rounded the corner and stopped.

Against the dark forest green paint, three new paintings hung, replacing Carolyn's familiar landscapes. The first depicted a carnival, but twisted, nightmarish. Rides askew, grinning faces warped into leers. The second was a mountain range under a sky stained with hues that didn't belong, sickly purples, bruised greens. The last: the silhouette of a man framed against a blazing fire.

These paintings hadn't been here yesterday. Adelaide hadn't been here either. A chill crept up the back of his neck. Where had they come from?

The sadness that had clung to him all morning shifted into unease. Something had changed. Something he hadn't invited in.

He reached for the edge of the first painting, then froze. The sweet jangle of the doorbells rang out, bright and familiar, and his heart kicked up. Turning, he walked fast, nearly running toward the front of the shop.

Please, let it be her. Just Adelaide. Not Ewan.

He couldn't take another one of their necking sessions in the romance section. Not today.

She stood alone, quietly reading the letter he'd left her, and all the worry he felt only seconds before drained from him all at once.

Adelaide's face lit up as she read, her smile curling into a perfect bow. There it was, the smile that set his soul ablaze. And just like that, the shop seemed to breathe again, the warmth coaxed back into the walls.

She tucked the letter into her back pocket. She was saving them, the letters he'd written her. He followed her as she moved to the wingback chair by the window, journal in hand. But her smile faltered. Had something in his letter stirred a memory or thought that saddened her?

He longed to touch her shoulder, to ask, to explain, to assure her he hadn't meant to cause her pain. But all the wishing in the world wouldn't change the fact that he couldn't.

She sat and opened the journal; her eyebrows lifted at the name inside. *Yes, read it.* This was his way in. His plan. To guide her through the past, to help her see the truth without scaring her off.

But his hope was crushed, like a half-burnt cigarette stubbed out on pavement, when she snapped it shut and set it on the windowsill after only reading a few entries. She sat there in silence, staring out the window onto the quiet street.

What had she read? What entry had unsettled her? His mind flipped through the pages he'd skimmed long ago, hunting for anything that might have struck too deep. Then he remembered the entry about Carolyn's illness. How could he have overlooked that? Of course, it would hit hard. It was her aunt. Her family. Had he made a mistake in giving her the journal?

Before he could even step closer, she rose and walked away. Not toward the exit, toward the counter. He followed, confused, until he saw the coffee. And the box. It was from the Marbled Clover. Lifting the lid, he peered inside: apple cinnamon donuts. His favorite. Just the sight of them made his mouth ache with longing. What he would have given to taste just one bite.

Adelaide turned, her gaze landing on the open box. She frowned, puzzled. She could see it. She could see the lid had been lifted. His hand hovered near it, fingers tingling.

"Help yourself to a donut," she said.

Every cell in Pen's body sprang to life at her words. Was she talking to him? He waved his hand in front of her face. Nothing. He glanced over his shoulder, half-expecting someone else to be there, but it was empty.

She'd said it, as if she believed someone unseen was there.

Does she think I'm a ghost?

If she did, the thought didn't seem to frighten her. Pen stared, something slowly dawning. If she believed the Feather Thorn was haunted, it opened up a world of possibilities.

It meant she was open. To him. To this.

His mind raced, turning over a hundred different ways he could reach out to her now, how he could finally tell her the truth. He'd have to ease her into the idea that he wasn't actually dead, just trapped. It would take time. He'd have to be careful. Gentle. But for the first time in forever, hope flickered, soft as candlelight, but steady enough to see through the doubt. Being a ghost might just be the best thing that had happened to him in years.

PEN - 1955 - JUST WHAT I NEEDED

Pen leaned against the doorframe, watching as Adelaide painted the children's corner a soft shade of green. But it wasn't the color that held him. She moved like the room belonged to her. No inhibitions. Hips swaying, brush sweeping in time with a tune she sang, one he had never heard before.

Her voice curled around the lyrics like smoke around candlelight. He still couldn't place the song, but the line "just what I needed" echoed with unnerving precision how he felt every time she stepped into the shop.

And then he felt

it. A spark in his belly, small at first, then rising, growing into a wildfire, heat spreading through his entire body. She stirred something in him that he hadn't known still lived. Yet she had no idea he even existed, apart from thinking him a ghost. But he was fairly certain ghosts didn't feel the kind of desire that was coursing through him like a raging inferno.

When she finished painting, she cleaned the tray, rinsed the brushes, still humming as she worked. She wandered back to the desk, poured herself another coffee, and reached for a donut. He watched as her gaze kept drifting to the journal. Before he could nudge it closer, she'd already picked it up and sat back down in the wingback chair by the window.

She hesitated, thumb brushing the edge of the cover, as if debating whether she should continue reading. But something in her seemed to settle, and with a sigh, she opened its pages and resumed where she'd left off. Pen moved closer, standing just behind her, his gaze shifting between the lines she read and the changes in her expression, brows drawing together, mouth curving faintly.

He could tell exactly when she reached the part about the watch by the way she paused, her shoulders tensing, her gaze lifting as she glanced over her shoulder into the empty shop. It was as though she sensed his presence again. She looked right past him, through him, but it felt like she was getting closer.

She read until twilight settled in, daylight thinning to dusk in the shop. She closed the journal, slow and reluctant, like someone not ready to leave a dream, and as she stood, Pen saw her tap her foot on the floorboards, and he knew exactly where she had left off in the journal. She knew there was a secret room underneath the Feather Thorn. Now, he just needed to wait until she had finished reading, and then he could lead her to it.

She set the journal on the desk, grabbed her jacket, and glanced back over her shoulder one last time before slipping outside into the dark.

He stood there, listening to the echo of the door as it settled shut behind her. The emptiness that followed felt deeper than before, but it didn't crush him. Not this time; this was progress.

Just as he turned to go upstairs, the door chimes rang out again, bright and unexpected. He whirled around. Adelaide had returned, arms full with a box so large she had to shift her weight to balance it. But instead of placing it on the counter, she carried it across the shop and straight toward the stairs, straight toward him.

Cracking the door open with her foot, she nudged it, and Pen pushed it open a bit wider, allowing her to slip through and up the stairs. She climbed slowly, breath catching near the top, and set the box down with a sigh. Reaching for the ornate knob, she opened the apartment door, and just as she did, Frankie darted out into the stairwell.

Adelaide let out a startled scream, stumbling back. But Frankie didn't run far. He stopped two steps down, sat perfectly still, and looked up at Pen with a soft whine. Adelaide stared at the little fox sitting obediently, like a well-trained dog waiting for a treat.

"How did you get in here?" Adelaide muttered, eyeing the fox with a puzzled expression.

Pen raised a hand, silently commanding Frankie to stay. The fox didn't move.

Adelaide took one cautious step toward him, then one more, confusion etched across her face. Pen dropped his hand, and Frankie sprinted down the stairs and into the shop. He'd figured it was better for her to learn that Frankie was a fox instead of some mysterious creature lurking in the dark.

She watched him go, mumbling under her breath. "A fox! Well, that's a bit mad."

Pen couldn't help the low laugh that rumbled out. It *was* mad. All of it. But if this was madness, he'd happily take it, if she were a part of it.

She turned back, picked up the box she'd left at the threshold, and pushed the door fully open. She paused, just briefly. Pen knew exactly what she was thinking. He remembered the first time he'd crossed that very same line, as though he were an intruder in someone else's space.

But whatever doubt there was didn't last long. Adelaide took the box to the small kitchen table and flicked on the light above her. Moving into the living room, she turned on the lamp there too.

The dim glow painted soft amber onto her cheeks and forehead. She looked like she belonged here. Like she was home. The way she moved made his heart thud a little faster. What was she doing? He stayed in the doorway, hands twitching uselessly at his sides, as he watched her pause at the coffee table and pick up *The Great Gatsby*. That book. He'd read it so many times he'd nearly memorized each page. Before the Feather Thorn had become his prison, Gatsby had felt like a kindred spirit, both of them reaching for lives beyond their means, dreams too big to hold. Even the bookstore itself had seemed too good to be true, and in the end, it had been. Like Gatsby, he'd built his own illusion, trapping himself in a place he didn't truly belong.

She flipped through the pages of the book, lips curling as she murmured, "Guy after my own heart," before setting the book back down.

They were nothing, just words, but they lit an electric flutter just beneath his ribs. She loved it too. That story about a dreamer.

Adelaide turned and walked back toward the door. "Well," she said softly, voice trailing into the quiet, "it's just going to be you and me, old girl. And you, Rowland."

Pen froze at her words. She thought he was Rowland. Of course she did. He'd left her that journal, hoping it would help her understand, but all it had done was tangle the truth in a story she thought she already knew. Her eyes roamed the room one last time before she whispered, "I promise I'll take good care of the Feather Thorn. I know what it meant to you, and I'll carry on your dream."

Pen sank into the kitchen chair, raking both hands through his hair. He hadn't meant to deceive her, but how could he possibly explain the truth now? That he wasn't Rowland. That he was trapped here in time, not just some ghost haunting the history section.

His eyes drifted to the box she'd left behind. Whatever was inside tugged at his curiosity. It wasn't his place to look, he knew that, and it was taking everything in him to leave it be. He leaned in slightly, just enough to tempt a glance, then stopped himself. Guilt rose up and pulled him back. It wasn't his to inspect, and invading her privacy wasn't the kind of man he was.

Minutes ticked by. The mystery of its contents gnawed at him until he finally surrendered. With a sigh, he muttered, "So much for the respectable man I used to be." Then reached for the lid.

At first glance, it looked like nothing much, mundane things, a toothbrush, a bright pink bottle of something with a scent he couldn't quite name, a bundle of clothes.

Then the realization struck him. This wasn't just a collection of odds and ends. This wasn't a delivery. It was *her* life in a box, her cardboard suitcase. Adelaide was moving in.

Pen sat back, stunned. She wasn't just passing through. She was here to stay. And just like that, the Feather Thorn, which had been his whole world, was about to become hers, too.

He leaned forward again.

Toward the bottom, there were books. He took them out one by one. *The House of the Spirits* by Isabel Allende, *It* by Stephen King, and *Oranges Are Not the Only Fruit* by Jeanette Winterson. None of the names rang a bell.

At the bottom of the box, his fingers brushed against something familiar. He carefully pulled it free, a copy of *The Great Gatsby*. Dark blue cover, eyes like searchlights staring out from the dusk. It wasn't like his copy, but it still felt like an old friend.

Curiosity piqued, he flipped it open. His breath caught. *Published by Scribner, 1983.*

He checked the others, frantically, as if the truth might change if he looked hard enough. *1982. 1986. 1988.* But it didn't. Book after book whispered the same thing: he had lost decades. Thirty years, maybe more.

His world tilted. Suddenly, the apartment felt too small, the walls pressing in as the weight of time lost settled heavily on his shoulders. He'd known, of course he had, that time had passed. He'd seen Carolyn, older, quieter, her light dimmed. But thinking it and seeing it printed in black and white were two different things.

Pen pinched the bridge of his nose. The life he'd once known, the people, the places, the promises, they were all different now. Gone. He'd lost everything in what had felt like only months. Yet years had spun past, the world shifting and reshaping itself while he remained unchanged.

He wanted to hate it. All of it. The shop. Time. This country that he didn't belong to.

But just as the grief began to rise, another thought broke through.

Helensburgh had been the first place that had welcomed him and seen him for who he was, and not what family he had come from. Here, he had found belonging. No, he couldn't hate this place. It had offered him a glimpse of a future he'd never dared to dream of. It was here that he'd found purpose, his love for books growing into a passion that defined him. He'd wanted to follow in Ward's footsteps, to become a teacher simply because it was easy to mimic someone else's clear path. But the Feather Thorn had enabled him to be more than Ward's shadow. It had given him his own path, and it had made him the version of Pen he wanted to be.

And now, it had brought him Adelaide.

He looked back into the box, his breath steadier now, and caught sight of something tucked at the very bottom. A photograph. Carefully, he lifted it out and turned it over in his hands. A couple stood behind a young girl, all three facing the camera. The child's smile, wide and bright, was unmistakably Adelaide's.

He traced a finger gently along her face. How had she ended up here? Maybe she'd been sent to Helensburgh, just as Ward had once sent him, told to find her place, to figure out who she was meant to be. Or maybe it hadn't been anyone at all who sent her.

Maybe it was fate that had drawn her to the Feather Thorn, quiet and unshakable, the way it always seemed to work when no one was paying attention. Maybe she hadn't come to save the shop. Maybe she'd come to save him.

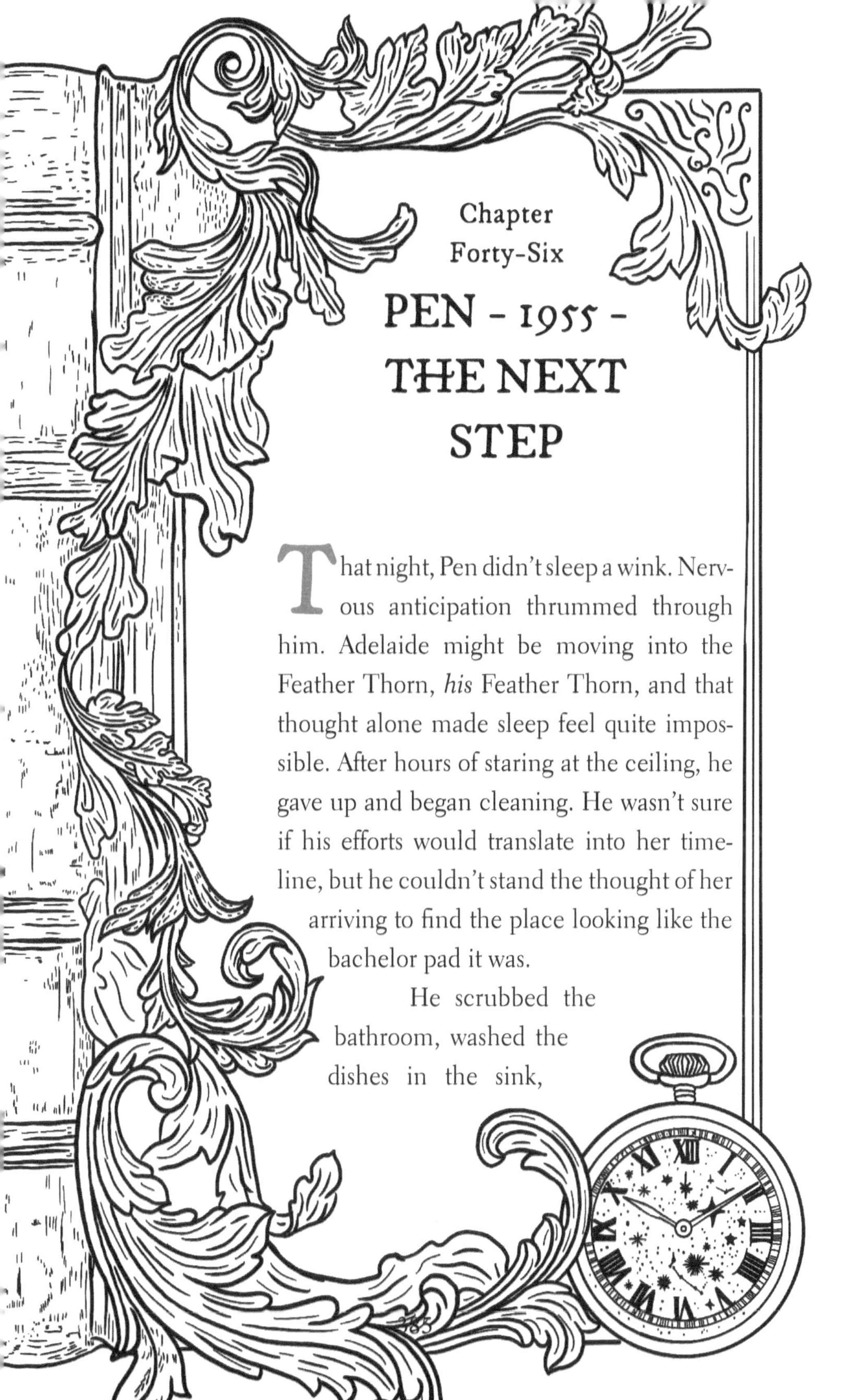

PEN - 1955 -
THE NEXT STEP

That night, Pen didn't sleep a wink. Nervous anticipation thrummed through him. Adelaide might be moving into the Feather Thorn, *his* Feather Thorn, and that thought alone made sleep feel quite impossible. After hours of staring at the ceiling, he gave up and began cleaning. He wasn't sure if his efforts would translate into her timeline, but he couldn't stand the thought of her arriving to find the place looking like the bachelor pad it was.

He scrubbed the bathroom, washed the dishes in the sink,

and tidied every corner. All the while, his mind churned, racing with everything he wanted to tell her, the truths he longed to pour into a letter.

He wanted her to know it was him, not Rowland, who was here with her. That he was trapped in time, not some wandering ghost. He wanted to tell her how her presence had reignited a spark of hope he thought had been extinguished long ago. That he found her captivating, and the sound of her voice was something he could listen to for the rest of his life without ever growing tired of it.

As he descended the stairs into the hidden room, it pulsed with a strange energy, a hum that rose through the floor, raising the hairs on the back of his neck. He knew what was coming before it even began. Moments after he sat at the desk, the watch began to chime. Two quick notes followed by one long, drawn-out tone, then silence.

Each time, the chime was different, but still haunting. Pen had only heard it sound a handful of times since the night it had trapped him, and he still hadn't deciphered what its melodies meant. The only pattern he'd found was celestial: the chimes seemed to correspond with astrological events. Tonight, a full moon aligned with Saturn, a rare dance that he suspected had to do with the watch's song.

Over the years, Pen had become something of an amateur astronomer, pouring himself into the study of the night sky. Charting the stars, tracking planets, and noting alignments had become both a pastime and a lifeline, giving him purpose as he searched for the rhythm of the watch's mysterious tolls, something that might be his key to freedom.

The thought jarred him from his lovestruck stupor. Adelaide wasn't just a beautiful distraction; she was his best hope of escape. But to get there, he needed to keep his wits about him, to focus on the puzzle at hand, not on winning over a woman who couldn't see or hear him. The stakes were too high to let his heart steer him off course now. He had to give her information: dates, times, possibilities, not just longing on a page.

So, instead of drafting another letter, Pen reached for his star ledger and jotted down the date and time of the chime. The simple action steadied him, grounding his thoughts.

He thumbed through his previous entries, looking for patterns he might have missed, a clue that might reveal when the next activation would occur.

He exhaled deeply, running a hand through his wavy hair, frustration mounting as he leaned back in his chair. The back legs wobbled slightly under his weight, mirroring his own heavy thoughts. His feelings for Adelaide had complicated everything.

She wasn't just a means to an end anymore. She had become his anchor. His light. A reminder of all the things he'd once dreamed of. But dreams wouldn't set him free.

He needed focus. He needed clarity and control. He needed her to finish the journal. Pen pulled a blank sheet of paper from the desk drawer and slid it into the typewriter. The metal arms lifted, the keys clacking sharply as he began to type.

Dear Adelaide,

I am glad to see that you are reading Rowland's journal. It explains so much about the origins of the bookshop and the tragic situation Rowland found himself in all those years ago. When I first discovered it, it felt like a lifeline, and I clung to every word, hoping it might shed some light on my own situation.

Pen paused, fingers hovering as he read over the words. He

wanted to tell Adelaide everything, but the time wasn't right. Not yet. But if he waited until she finished the journal, he would be able to confide his own tale, and everything would change.

He took a deep breath, nodded to himself, and typed the closing lines:

When you reach the end, the secrets held within the Feather Thorn will become clear. Until that moment, I will hold off on sending you my next letter.

P.S. The shop is coming back to life again, thanks to the care and dedication you've poured into it.

He pulled the paper out with a snap, folded it neatly, and tucked it into the letterbox before returning to the apartment.

At the top of the stairs, Frankie was perched by the door, chittering away as though scolding him for taking so long.

"Sorry, buddy. Time kinda slipped away," Pen said as he pushed past him. Pale morning light had begun to creep across the apartment walls, tracing long shadows. His heart quickened at the sight of the new day, and the possibility of Adelaide moving in, that his solitude might finally be broken. He made a quick breakfast of scrambled eggs for Frankie before heading to the bathroom to shower and shave.

Freshly washed and wrapped in a towel, he sifted through Rowland's old wardrobe. He wanted to wear something a bit nicer than his normal attire, and Rowland had much more dapper clothing than he did. He settled on a pair of dark tan trousers, a starched white button-down shirt, and a rich brown tweed vest, the color of freshly tilled earth. Back in the bathroom, he slicked his hair back with pomade, the scent conjuring memories of Ward. He swallowed down the sorrow that came with that memory. Staring at his reflection, he let out a soft laugh. "Why are you getting yourself dressed to the nines for a woman who can't even see you?"

His smile faded, slipping into something quieter, something between longing and grief. He stood there, a man dressed for someone who would never see him. Still, he had done it. Fixed his collar, shaved, even smoothed his hair. For her. And somewhere in the middle of it, he realized he wanted to be seen.

Not just looked at. *Seen.*

The ache of it settled low in his chest, strange and sharp. He hadn't felt anything like this, not even before he was trapped. How had he gone so long without ever wanting something like this? Without realizing what he was missing?

There was so much of his life he'd never really lived.

In the kitchen, Frankie was licking the last of the egg from his bowl. The fox flicked his tail and cast him a pointed look, as though unimpressed by his effort to look nice.

"Don't start," Pen warned, clearing away the plate.

Making his way toward the apartment door, he paused, glancing up at the cracked plaster ceiling. "Give me a sign," he whispered. "A sign that I'm at least moving closer to an escape."

And then, as if the heavens themselves answered back, the chimes from the shopfront door jingled, cutting through the silence like music.

THE HIDDEN JOURNAL OF JOHN DEE

December 20, 1582

Today, Kelley and I arrived in the small village near Gare Loch, to inspect the house that will serve as the site for the next phase of our work. Though Kelley has regained some of his strength, he remains too weak to commune with the divine yet. I worry for him as each scrying session seems to drain him not only physically but mentally, and more profoundly than the last. But I need him for the spell, and for now, he must focus on this task.

Giordano is not with us, nor have I shared the truth of our failure with him. He still believes that the ritual we performed has repaired the tear in time, and I will not tell him otherwise. This is my burden to carry. It was my idea, my ambition, that set these events in motion. Though Giordano's calculations and craftsmanship were instrumental in the creation of the Astral Synchronum, the fault is mine, and I will not risk drawing him into this further.

The house we have come to see is a tall two-story structure of gray flagstone. It stands larger than my own home, more suited for a shop or a public house than a private dwelling. Yet, it is exactly what we needed.

Inside, the building was as unwelcoming as its exterior. It was cold and damp. The walls inside were caked with years' worth of grime, and the building's tall windows were dusty and shrouded in shadow, giving the entire place an air of melancholy. We explored the rooms in silence, looking for a place where we might hide the Synchronum.

We found what we needed: an old root cellar beneath the main floor. The space was dark, its walls hewn from stone, and the air was heavy with stillness. It was hidden, secure, and perfectly suited for sealing the Astral Synchronum away.

Flora is someone Kelley knows well, a woman of considerable skill in the craft, though she must keep her talents carefully concealed. Though I have long sought knowledge in the occult, I hold witches with a wary respect; their craft, for all its power, is easily turned to dangerous ends. In these times, their talents must be hidden, for those who are discovered rarely escape the wrath that follows.

Flora, however, from what Kelley tells me of her, is not the sort of woman to be easily intimidated. She has survived, hidden in plain sight, a woman of means who might never be seen as anything more than the quiet merchant's wife. She is cautious, and she must remain so, and we must take every precaution not to be seen here with her. The spell we perform tomorrow must be discreet, and we must ensure that Flora's involvement remains a secret.

I dare not call her a witch aloud, but that is what she is, by all the old ways, by every measure of magic known to those who walk this path. And yet, in this place and time, the word itself is a curse. If we are not careful, she could easily be accused, and if that happens, the consequences will be dire for all of us, for associating with a known witch could bring the eyes of the law too closely upon us.

Tomorrow, we will meet her in the shadows of night, and the spell will be cast. The Synchronum must be sealed, hidden away, and bound by her powers. Only then can we begin to hope that the rip will remain sealed, that time itself will hold steady at least for now until I can find one of these Nephilim to seal the rip permanently.

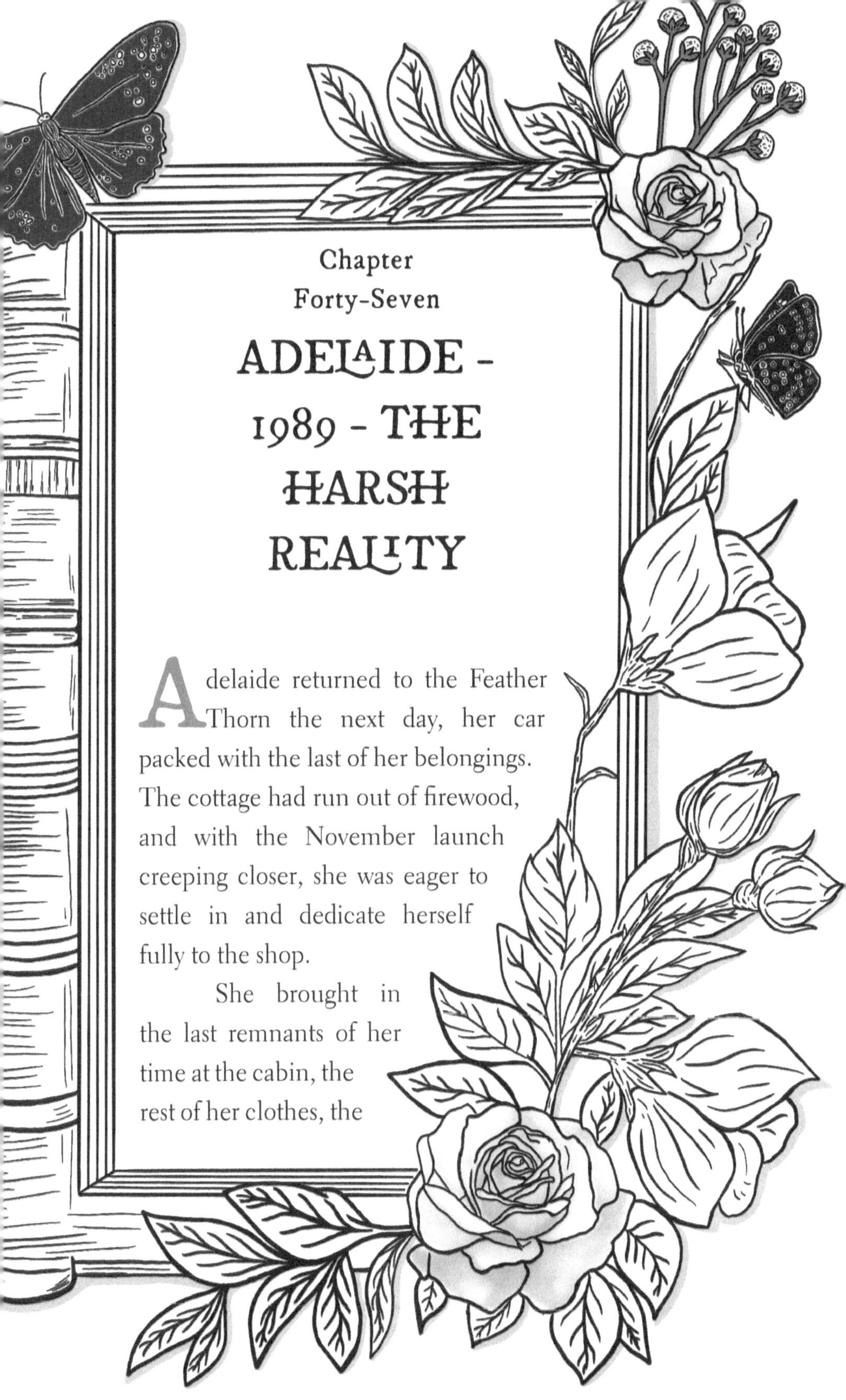

Chapter
Forty-Seven

ADELAIDE –
1989 – THE
HARSH
REALITY

Adelaide returned to the Feather Thorn the next day, her car packed with the last of her belongings. The cottage had run out of firewood, and with the November launch creeping closer, she was eager to settle in and dedicate herself fully to the shop.

She brought in the last remnants of her time at the cabin, the rest of her clothes, the wool tartan blanket, the ugly elephant lamps she'd somehow grown fond of, and the painting that once hung above the mantel.

Gently lifting the canvas from the box, she made her way to the stairwell to the loft, where Carolyn's other paintings formed a hodgepodge gallery along the wall.

Adelaide held it up beside the others, looking for a spot to hang it. The painting was as beautiful as any of Carolyn's pieces. But as she held it up against the rest, something about it felt different, more personal than the others, more intimate, as if it held a piece of Carolyn's heart not meant for public display.

After a moment's hesitation, she turned away from the wall and tucked it back into the box, and cradled it as she climbed the stairs to the flat. At the door, she paused, steadying herself, half-expecting the little fox to dash out again. But the flat was silent. Sunlight poured in through the windows in soft golden ribbons, warming the floorboards and bathing the space in a gentle glow.

The place looked cleaner than she recalled. A small crease formed between her brows. Had she just misremembered it from the murkiness of twilight last night?

She set the box beside the others and drew the painting out again. Turning, she scanned the room until her gaze landed on an empty wall in the living room that seemed to need something to brighten it up. When she approached it, she noticed something odd: a nail, already hammered into the exact spot she'd intended to use. Rising onto her toes, she hung the painting. It fit perfectly, as if it belonged there.

A chill ghosted down her spine. Had Carolyn painted this for Rowland? Had it always been meant for this spot? A thread of unease wove through her thoughts. More and more, she was stumbling upon fragments of her great-aunt's past, fragments she wasn't sure she would have willingly shared. For now, she would keep this one to herself.

Returning to the box, she began unpacking her clothes and stacking them in folded piles on the kitchen table. Once the box was empty, she tossed it toward the door and moved on to the next. Lifting the flaps, she stopped short. The picture of her parents sat on top. She was sure, absolutely sure, she had packed it at the bottom, with her clothes on top. Had someone gone through her things? She glanced over her shoulder.

But she'd change the locks.

Could it have been Ewan? He knew where she kept her spare key. But why? Her gaze shifted toward the bedroom. Could it have been Rowland's ghost? Could ghosts even move things?

She exhaled. The flat now felt less like a refuge and more like a museum, one where ghosts were still rearranging the exhibits. Shoving up her sleeves, she grabbed her notebook and made a note: find a book on spirits. If Rowland's ghost was here, she needed him to know she wasn't trying to replace him. Maybe there was a way to speak to him, or at least show him she meant no harm.

Descending the stairs, she felt the warmth of the morning sun wrap around her. The Feather Thorn always looked best in the first light of day, sunshine streaming through the large shop front windows. She could hardly wait to see what it would be like in the summer months when she could open the door and let in the warm inviting scents of flowers mingling with the sweet harmony of the bakery across the street. The thought made her smile.

As she moved toward the front desk, the scent of men's cologne hit her, but it was much stronger than normal, impossible to ignore. She spun around, scanning the aisles, the corners, the stairwell. Nothing, but she knew there was someone there, just beyond sight.

Down here, she didn't mind the idea of Rowland's ghost so much. The shop didn't feel personal in the way the flat did. If his spirit lingered among the books, she could almost make peace with it. But upstairs was different. Up there, it felt like stepping into someone's bedroom uninvited, and that thought stirred a strange kind of guilt in her. She was here to begin something new. Even if it meant sharing the space with someone unseen, she wanted to do it right.

Approaching the front desk, Adelaide's eyes fell on the journal sitting on its old weathered top. She had meant to grab it the night before, but the chaos with the fox had derailed her. Just as she reached for it, a sliver of cream paper caught her eye, another letter peeking from the letterbox. The journal temporarily forgotten, she pulled the letter free.

Dear Adelaide,

I am glad to see that you are reading Rowland's journal. It explains so much about the origins of the bookshop and the tragic situation Rowland found himself in all those years ago. When I first discovered it, it felt like a lifeline, and I clung to every word, hoping it might shed some light on my own situation.

When you reach the end, the secrets held within the Feather Thorn will become clear. Until that moment, I will hold off on sending you my next letter.

P.S. The shop is coming back to life again, thanks to the care and dedication you've poured into it.

She ran her thumb over the smooth corner of the paper.

There was a gravity to these words that hadn't been there before. This wasn't just another note; it felt like the closing of one Chapter before the next could begin. The implication that the journal held the final piece of Rowland's story made her stomach knot. If Ewan knew this, why hadn't he gone to the authorities or told Carolyn? Why give the journal to her, of all people? Was she meant to pass it on, to carry the weight of its revelations for him?

Her gaze flicked back to the journal, now even more compelling. Ewan hinted at a struggle that mirrored Rowland's, but the details were frustratingly vague, leaving her with more questions than answers.

Grabbing the journal from the counter, she headed for the wingback chair by the window, just as the door chimes rang out.

"I hope you have your roadtrippin' pants on," a familiar voice called out.

Adelaide turned to see Camie in the doorway, swaddled in a bright purple puffer jacket and topped with a wildly out-of-place Western-style hat.

"Road trip?" Adelaide asked.

"Don't tell me you forgot? It's Thursday, remember? Secondhand shopping day!" Camie beamed.

"Oh my gosh, I nearly did."

"Well, it's a good thing I got here early to remind you," Camie said, stepping inside. Her eyes grew wide as she took in the surroundings. "Wow, I've always wanted to come in here. It closed down long before my time."

"Have a look around while I grab my things," Adelaide offered.

Camie meandered in and out of the rows of books while Adelaide took her coat off the hook and retrieved her bag from under the counter.

"This place is fantastic," Camie called out. "Folk'll be buzzing when you open again."

"I hope so. There's still a few bits to sort, but it was in pretty good shape when I bought it. Just needs a bit of updating," Adelaide replied as Camie returned to the front of the shop. "Hence today's shopping trip."

"Well, lucky for you, you've got the queen of secondhand bargains by your side. I've got you covered, and now I have a better idea of the space, so I can really help."

"I need all the help I can get." Adelaide smiled, leading the way out.

Outside, a big brown Ford Transit van idled at the curb.

"Meet Tina!" Camie announced, sweeping an arm like a game show host. "Tina Turn'ya dreams into reality with all this space in the back for all your treasure hunting finds!" She swung the door open and hopped in.

Adelaide laughed, warmth bubbling up. She loved Camie's free spirit, and her energy was infectious. It reminded her of what she'd been missing out on life all these years: friends, spontaneity, a bit of silliness.

For the first leg of the drive, Camie unleashed a torrent of gossip. Adelaide nodded and smiled, though most of the names meant nothing to her. Eventually, the conversation took a turn.

"Okay, spill," Camie said, eyeing her sidelong. "I heard someone spotted you leaving Ewan's place mid-morning. So, unless you two are into breakfast dates, I'm guessing you spent the night."

Adelaide groaned. "I figured someone would see me. Has the gossip mill gone wild?"

"Oh, don't worry about what people in town are saying.

This'll be old news in two days, and they'll have found someone new to talk about."

"Wow, that bad, huh?"

"Never mind about them? I want to know what *you* think about Ewan."

"He's… great. Funny, charming, handsome… and romantic," Adelaide said, trying not to let her smile betray how much she was swooning over him.

Camie arched a brow. "Romantic?"

"Yeah, he's been leaving me these sweet little notes at the shop," Adelaide told her, unable to contain the warm feelings that swelled in her belly when thinking about the letters.

"No way," Camie said sharply, but her tone didn't sound like disbelief; it sounded like fact.

"Seriously, he has."

"I've known Ewan forever, Addie. It's not him sending you those letters. Ewan might be handsome, but he isn't the sharpest tool in the shed. And he's the last person who would be writing love letters…"

"What do you mean?" Adelaide asked, as her smile faltered into a frown.

"Listen, I wanted to see how serious you were about him before saying anything, but you should know, Ewan's a laugh, sure, but that's all he is. He's not someone who's ever going to settle down. I figured he was just a rebound, you know, after your husband. The perfect 'dip-your-toes-back-in' kind of guy. But he's not a romantic, and he's definitely not the one leaving you those notes."

"He is. I mean, it has to be him. Who else would it be?" But even as she said it, doubt crept in. Camie sounded so certain, but who else knew what she was doing inside the shop?

Camie let out a sigh. "Addie, Ewan's seeing three other women right now. I hate to be the one to tell you, but I'd rather you hear it from me before you fall any harder for him. Honestly, I didn't think you'd get serious with him. And believe me, he has zero time for writing love letters with a rotation like that."

Adelaide went still. Cold washed over her, and the world seemed to tip upside down. The feeling was nauseatingly familiar, like the day Jeff left. Her throat tightened. How had she been so naive? She'd tried to stay guarded, but with the letters and their time together, she'd built up this fantasy of who he was.

"Addie, are you okay?" Camie asked, glancing at her, pity in her eyes.

Adelaide hated that look. She'd seen it too often after her father died. Poor little Addie. "I'm fine. I should've seen it coming, I guess."

"I know it stings," Camie replied, "but Ewan's not the end of the road. There's someone out there who's going to be perfect for you. Hell, maybe the mystery guy leaving you those letters is the one."

The line fell flat, and they both knew it.

Adelaide turned to the window, looked out, watching the world blur by. If it wasn't Ewan leaving the letters, then who was?

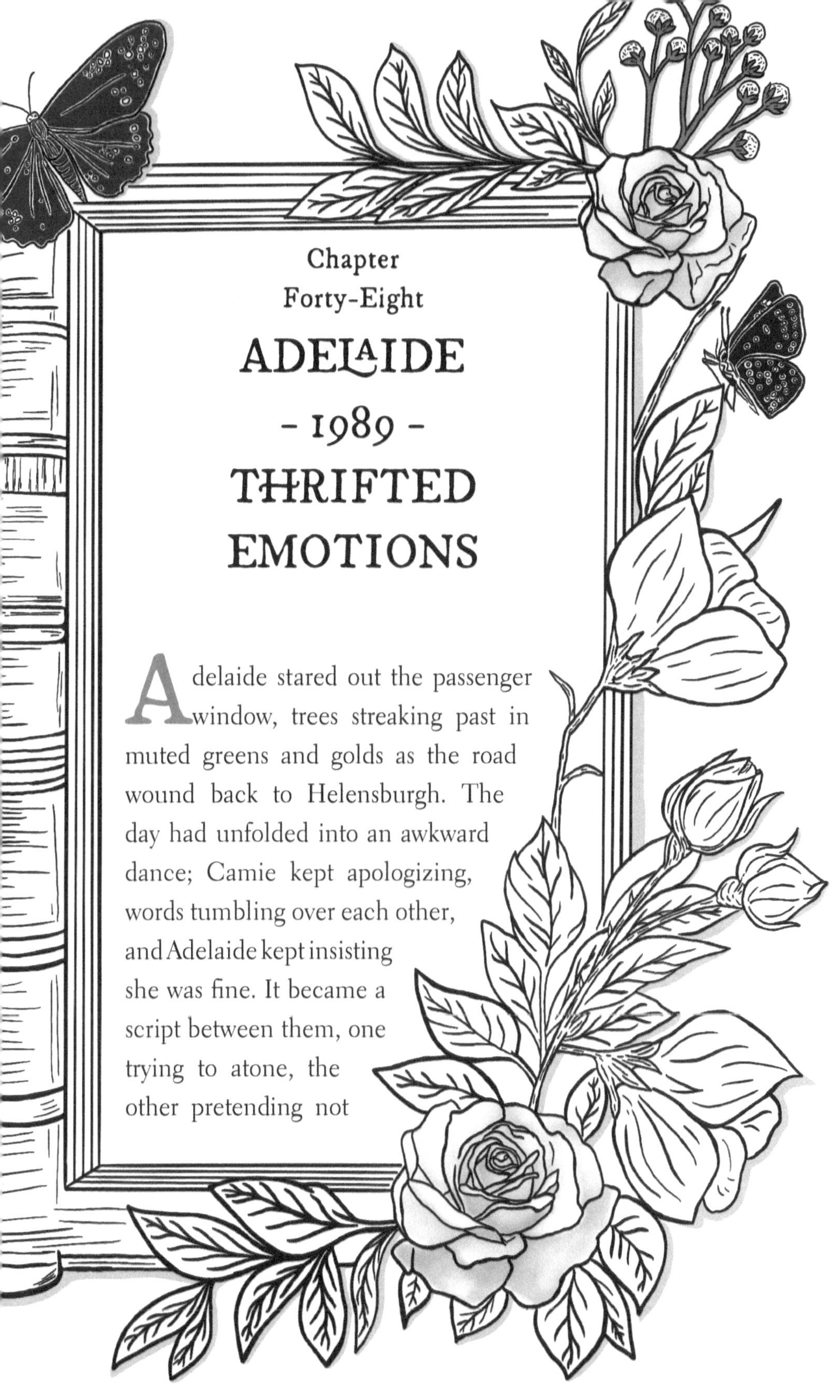

Chapter
Forty-Eight

ADELAIDE

- 1989 -

THRIFTED
EMOTIONS

Adelaide stared out the passenger window, trees streaking past in muted greens and golds as the road wound back to Helensburgh. The day had unfolded into an awkward dance; Camie kept apologizing, words tumbling over each other, and Adelaide kept insisting she was fine. It became a script between them, one trying to atone, the other pretending not to bleed. She told herself she hadn't been that into Ewan. Maybe even believed it a little bit. But her heart still ached. Over the past week, she'd laughed more and felt lighter than she had in a long, long time. Between his cheeky smile and those letters, the carefully constructed wall surrounding her heart had crumbled down.

Still, she needed to be positive: the day hadn't been a complete loss. Glasgow offered the usual big-city chaos, horns and chatter, university students buzzing like bees, but her mood was too heavy to really absorb it all. They'd walked the tangle of Byres Road and Ashton Lane, picking through charity shops and vintage stores, Adelaide trailing behind Camie, hands brushing fabrics and spines, mind a million miles away.

The back of the van now held a mountain of their finds: two rugs, an orange velvet chair for the reading nook, a wobbly table, and mismatched chairs for the children's area. All beautiful pieces, but they hadn't eased the quiet ache pressing against her ribs.

By the time they pulled up outside the Feather Thorn, the sky had deepened to violet. The streetlamp and the van's headlights cast long, crosshatched shadows across the shopfront, like a chessboard. Sitting in the passenger seat, Adelaide felt the harsh truths of the day rush back in full force, leaving her in checkmate. She'd thought the sting of Ewan's betrayal and the ache in her belly might fade with the setting sun, but it hadn't.

"Well," said Camie, glancing over her shoulder, "I think we did a cracking job!"

Adelaide forced a smile. "We did."

She followed her new friend to the back, where the van's double doors creaked open. Camie shoved aside a massive bag of clothes bound for the Common Blue.

"City clobber weighs a ton," she huffed, then dragged the

children's table free with a theatrical grunt.

The evening had turned raw, their breath steaming in the air as they ferried the furniture inside, fingers numb by the time the door clicked shut behind them.

"Camie, thank you for today. I had a great time, and I got everything I needed. If the books I ordered arrive on time, I think I can actually open in a few weeks."

"No bother. It was fun. I don't usually have company on these kinds of trips." Camie gave the velvet chair one final push into a cozy corner of the shop. Then her expression softened. "Hey… I know I've said this a hundred times already today, but I really am sorry I had to be the one to tell you about Ewan."

"It's okay. I'm glad you told me. Better than looking like a complete fool," Adelaide said.

"You're not a fool. He's an ass," Camie scoffed, shaking her head. "And hey, don't forget, there's still someone out there leaving you those sweet letters."

Camie was right. The letters. A strange mix of warmth and unease rippled through her. There was comfort in knowing someone cared enough to encourage her, to offer kind words when she needed them most. But the other side of it, the thought of being watched, that someone knew where to leave them…

She glanced at the darkened window, gaze falling to the letterbox. "If it's not Ewan leaving me those notes, then who do you think it is?"

"No idea. Your guess is as good as mine. I'll keep an ear out, though, see if I can find anything out. You know what people in this town are like." Camie was drifting toward the door. "Well, I better get going. Need to drop off the new clothes before I head home. You up for a pint next week?"

"Yeah, sounds good." Adelaide pulled the door open for her. "Thanks again. For everything."

Camie gave her a warm, genuine smile. "Anytime." Then she was gone, disappearing into the van, its headlights sweeping the cobbles, leaving Adelaide in the doorway of her quiet shop.

This would be her first night here. Alone. The thought lit a bolt of excitement, and a matching jolt of dread. She hadn't told Carolyn face-to-face that she was moving into the Feather Thorn. Instead, she'd taken the coward's way out, scribbling a note and leaving it on her kitchen table. The truth was, she couldn't bear the thought of her great-aunt's worried expression, the questions, the sadness in her eyes. It was easier to avoid it altogether. She scooped up Rowland's journal from the desk and made her way to the flat. Time to settle, time to read. Yet, a prick of apprehension lingered. What if something in the journal made her feel less welcome here? But weariness had dulled her nerves. At this point, if Rowland's ghost burst out of the walls shouting "boo" as she lay in bed, she wasn't sure she'd do anything but roll over and pull up the covers.

Upstairs, the light was on. Adelaide paused, brow furrowing. Had she left it on this morning? She was fairly certain she hadn't. The soft glow spilled onto the landing, comforting, but also not. There was still a faint, unsettling sense that she was in someone else's space, stepping into a room that someone had just stepped out of. It brushed the back of her neck, but before her unease could take root, her stomach growled, a sharp human reminder of her more immediate needs. She hadn't eaten since lunch with Camie, and that had burned away long ago. She should have picked up something for dinner in Glasgow.

She approached the fridge and rested her fingers on the cold metal handle. Had anyone cleared it out after the last owner went missing? Sooner or later, she'd have to face it. She drew in a breath, held it, then pulled. The door released with a faint pop, followed by a burst of cold air to her face. The shelves were bare, except for a lone yellowing box of baking soda slouched in the back. A small mercy. She hadn't known what she was bracing for, but it wasn't that.

"Note to self: get food," she murmured, rubbing her stomach.

She clutched Rowland's journal closer to her chest. The day had stretched her thin, and all she wanted now was a warm bed and the quiet comfort of her new space. A food run would have to wait until tomorrow.

Snatching up the wool blanket from the pile of her things on the table, she padded to the bedroom. Collapsing onto the bed, she braced for a cloud of dust, but none came; instead, the mattress welcomed her with the crisp, faintly floral scent of fresh linens. She inhaled, slowly, suspicious.

Odd, she thought. She leaned over and clicked on the side lamp.

The room blinked into light, and for a split second, Adelaide could have sworn she saw a figure in the doorway. She closed her eyes, opened them and looked again. The space was empty, just the hallway softly lit by the glow from the kitchen. *Rowland?*

She looked around at everything he'd left behind: books stacked on the table, a hairbrush on the dresser still threaded with his hair, clothes waiting in the closet for a man who wasn't coming back. It felt like a time capsule, untouched and deeply personal. What was she supposed to do with it all? She didn't feel right just throwing it away. She would ask Carolyn tomorrow; she would know what to do.

Adelaide turned the journal over in her hands. "I know this is probably an invasion of your privacy," she said softly to the room, "but I'm only reading it to find out what happened to you so I can tell Carolyn and give her some peace."

The journal warmed beneath her fingers. Whoever had been leaving her the letters knew something about the history of this place, something tied to Rowland's past. How had she ever thought it had been Ewan? Camie was right, Ewan was all charm and no substance. When she'd asked him the last thing he'd read, he'd said the TV guide. That should have been her first red flag.

Adelaide snuggled deeper into the blankets, flipping to the last page she'd gotten to. Rowland's words spilled across the paper with the same tenderness and precision she'd come to expect, entries about a trip Rowland had planned to take Carolyn to Rosslyn Chapel. He wrote of it like a pilgrimage, every detail meticulously imagined, his joy palpable at the thought of their first holiday together.

Then abruptly, the tone shifted. The handwriting grew erratic, slanted, the ink pressed harder into the page. Something had gone terribly wrong.

Carolyn had fallen ill. Tuberculosis.

She already knew this part of the story, but through Rowland's eyes, the tragedy felt raw.

He blamed himself for her illness, for taking Carolyn on the trip, knowing that TB was spreading throughout the country; he blamed himself for wanting too much, for stealing time. He wrote of her likely future, of children she wouldn't be able to carry, a truth that seemed to have shattered him into bits of the man he had been.

Adelaide's eyes burned. Now she understood why Carolyn refused to believe he had just abandoned her. Perhaps something had gone wrong, and he had died trying to save her?

Her breath stilled as she turned the page. Only one entry remained.

I have just returned from Carolyn's house, where she lies ill upon her deathbed. The doctor has informed me that if the fever does not break soon, she will not likely survive the night. In a last, desperate attempt to save her, I have taken leave while Susan remains at her side.

I feel I have no choice but to use the one thing that might save her: the Astral Synchronum. If any fortune exists in this dreadful situation, it is that tonight marks a lunar eclipse, an activation point that will allow me to use the device and move back in time, to stop us from ever taking our trip to Rosslyn Chapel.

Over the past week, I have read and reread every entry in John Dee's journal. I know that by activating the watch, I will shatter the centuries-old protection my family guarded, risking reopening the fissure in time. But for Carolyn, my love, my life, it is a risk I must take.

I have promised myself that if I succeed in rewriting history, I will lock the Synchronum away, hidden, so that no one else may find it. No one should ever have to make this awful choice between the fate of time and the life of someone they love.

I pray that God is on my side, and that tomorrow I wake in the arms of my love, alive, well, and that this, all of this, will be but a bad dream.

THE HIDDEN JOURNAL
OF JOHN DEE

December 21, 1582

Under the cover of darkness, we gathered in the root cellar, the damp air thick with the weight of what we were about to undertake as we waited for Flora to arrive. She had insisted upon this night for the spell, explaining that the winter solstice carried a rare power with it. The alignment of the cosmos and the Earth's energies on the shortest day of the year would help aid us in casting a binding spell strong enough to contain the Astral Synchronum's power and keep the rip in time from reopening. A fierce winter storm had spun overhead, and I feared that it might halt the binding if Flora could not make it in the harsh weather. It was as if nature itself was trying to thwart our efforts.

Yet, Flora would not be delayed by the weather. When she arrived, she spoke with Edward briefly about the mechanics of the ritual while I had sat silently, observing. She carried with her a satchel filled with herbs and a roll of twine. On the floor of the cellar, she had arranged candles in a circle around an open wooden box, lighting them one by one.

She instructed us to wait until midnight, the precise moment when the veil between realms would be at its thinnest, amplifying the spell's efficacy. As the clock struck the hour, she directed Edward and I to stand across from one another, arms outstretched, our hands clasping tightly to form a circle above the wooden box.

Flora then placed two iron bowls on the ground, one to each side of us. Into the first, she had added rosemary, mugwort, and sage, explaining that these would protect against malevolent spirits or energies that might seek to interfere with the spell. The second bowl she filled with frankincense and cloves to amplify the binding's strength. As she lit the herbs, the thick, aromatic smoke filled the room, threatening to choke me at first. Slowly, however, the sharpness faded into something almost soothing.

With steady hands, Flora lifted the Astral Synchronum and carefully placed it into the box at the circle's center. She closed the lid and began wrapping it with twine, winding it three times while repeating an incantation at each pass around:

"I knot this rope with the strength of the earth,
The power of water, the steadfastness of wind,
And by the fierceness of fire.
Trap this within time and space,
Hidden forever within this place.
For those who try and use its power,
Trap them within its endless hour.
By the power of three, I bind thee. So mote it be."

With the final words, she picked up a candle and poured

its melted wax over the lid of the box, sealing it. She then instructed us to maintain our grasp on one another's hands until she had extinguished the candles in reverse order from how they had been lit. One by one, the flames had disappeared into the darkness, leaving only a solitary candle near the stairwell lit.

I had expected some grand sign to mark the spell's success, a burst of light or a shifting energy like that which Giordano and I had witnessed when activating the Synchronum in the cathedral. But there had been nothing. The silence had pressed heavily against me, and doubt began to creep in. I questioned Flora, my tone a bit sharper than I had intended, however, she reassured me that this magic was of a different nature, subtle and without fanfare. Satisfied, I had tucked the sealed box into a narrow crevice in the stone wall, hidden from sight, and firmly secured it with a stone to hide it from view. Flora, her task complete, had pulled the hood of her cloak over her head and disappeared into the night without another word.

The energy in the cellar feels lighter, and I believe Flora is correct, the spell has worked, and the Synchronum's dangerous energy is safely contained. Yet, I cannot linger here. Edward and I need to travel back to England at the first light of dawn tomorrow. Our work is not finished, for this binding is but a temporary measure. I have to return and begin my search for Nephilim. The hunt for these beings, said to have been wiped from existence in biblical times, will be my biggest challenge yet.

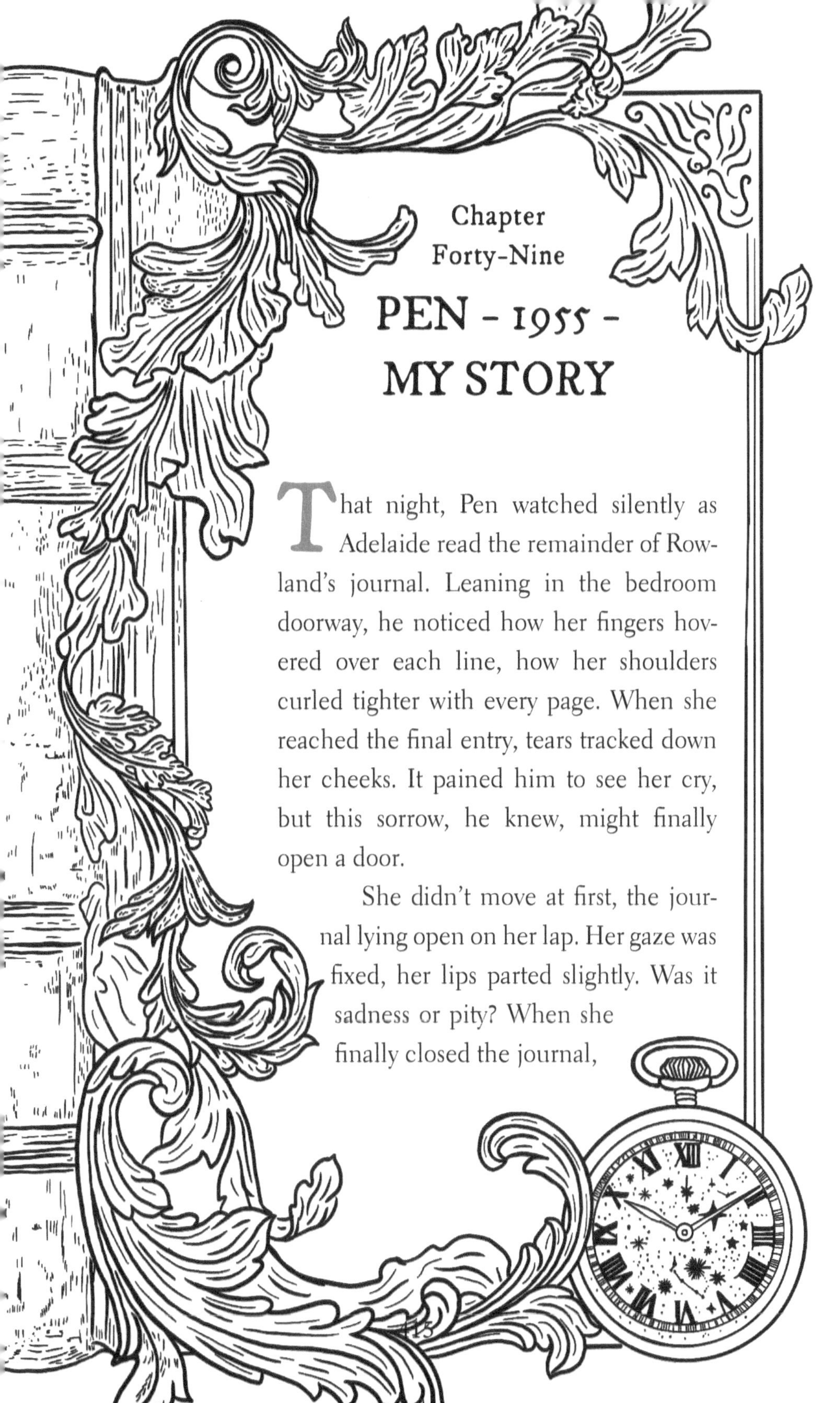

PEN - 1955 -
MY STORY

That night, Pen watched silently as Adelaide read the remainder of Rowland's journal. Leaning in the bedroom doorway, he noticed how her fingers hovered over each line, how her shoulders curled tighter with every page. When she reached the final entry, tears tracked down her cheeks. It pained him to see her cry, but this sorrow, he knew, might finally open a door.

She didn't move at first, the journal lying open on her lap. Her gaze was fixed, her lips parted slightly. Was it sadness or pity? When she finally closed the journal, she spoke softly into the room.

"I'm so sorry, Rowland. Carolyn was lucky to have a man who would risk everything for her… like you did."

But it wasn't Rowland standing in the shadows between the hallway and the bedroom. It was Pen. Trapped between timelines, bound to the space between her world and his. Her eyes almost locked on his, she could sense him there, as if some invisible thread connected them across the unseen divide.

That night, she tossed and turned, throwing the blankets off only to pull them back over herself moments later. Pen remained by her side, keeping silent vigil, watching her thoughts flicker behind shuttered lids. When her body finally stilled and her breathing slowed into a steady rhythm, he slipped away.

The apartment no longer felt like his, and it felt wrong to stay there now. He carried a blanket and pillow down the stairs into the hidden room, and settled beside the Underwood typewriter.

For a long while, he just stared at it. Then, he placed his fingers on the keys.

Dear Adelaide,

As promised, I am writing to tell you the rest of the story now that you have finished reading the journal. Now, with Rowland's story fresh in your mind, mine might not seem so far-fetched.

My name is Pen Turner. I came to the Feather Thorn back in 1955 when the shop was left to me by a man named Ward Richardson, my old neighbor back in West Virginia. His wife, Emily, was Rowland's sister. When Rowland vanished, the deed passed to Emily, then to Ward, and then to me upon his passing.

I wasn't meant to stay. I told myself I'd fix the place up and sell it off, then return home to my brothers, but something about this place just drew me in, and I fell in love with the idea of bringing it back to life. I am not sure how much of those were true feelings and how much was the pull of the magic in this place, and the watch wanting to be found. So, I stayed. I repaired what I could, reopened it that fall, and slowly began to settle into this little corner of the world. For the first time, I thought I might have found a place to belong.

But then I heard the chimes.

I traced the sound to a hidden room, the very one Rowland described in his journal. That's where I found it, the Astral Synchronum, buried among old journals and forgotten relics. I didn't know what it was at the time or what it could do. I only knew it was beautiful and strange. So, I took it upstairs, unaware of the danger I carried with me.

One night, it began to chime again. The sound pulled me from sleep, and in my groggy confusion, I tried to silence it. I must have activated it, though I didn't know how. It was only for a moment. But a moment was all it took to trap me here.

I'm not dead. I'm caught in a loop of time that begins and ends within these walls.

You thought it was Rowland's ghost you felt here in the walls of this place, but it's me. I do not know what happened to Rowland in the end, but I fear his fate might be as mine is, trapped somewhere within time.

I seem to be able to manipulate certain aspects of both our timelines using objects I touched the day I was trapped. One of these is the old Underwood typewriter I'm using to write this letter. I know this must sound impossible. It was to me, too. But I need you to believe me.

I need your help.

For so long, I drifted here, fading into the quiet, thinking this shop would swallow me whole. But then you came with your beautiful light, and it cracked something open. You reminded me of who I was before all of this. Thank you for being the light at the end of this seemingly endless tunnel. For that, I owe you more than words can say.

I hope, somehow, if we work together, that maybe we can find a way to set me free.

Until then, I'll be here with the books.

Pen.

He folded the letter with care, climbed back up the stairs, and paused beside the letterbox. His fingers hovered just above its lid, but the weight of uncertainty held him back. He turned, letter still in hand, and headed back up to the apartment.

Dawn leaked across the mountain tops in pale streaks of burning orange. Pen lingered by the window, watching the light inch forward, hoping the world would offer him some clarity, some sign that this was the right thing to do.

He finally set the letter on the kitchen table, next to her box of things. Then he prepared a pot of coffee. It was a small gesture, an offering of sorts, though he couldn't be certain it would register in her timeline.

As the coffee brewed, the aroma filling the room, Pen leaned on the counter, eyes fixed on the rooftops below and the glowing horizon beyond. A new day had arrived, and with it the jagged edge of uncertainty. The hope he'd clung to while typing that letter now felt brittle. Had he said too much? Revealed his hand too soon? The last thing he wanted to do was frighten her off. But worse still, what if, after all of this, Adelaide didn't believe him? The thought lodged deep in his chest and refused to let go.

Maybe it *was* too soon after the journal, maybe he should give her a few more days. As Pen turned around to retrieve the letter, Adelaide was already there, standing in front of the table, staring down at it. He hadn't heard her come in, too lost in his own thoughts. Sleep still filled her eyes, and she rubbed at them, as if trying to be sure the letter was real. Then her gaze drifted to the coffee pot, and her eyes widened.

It had worked. The coffee had brewed in her timeline. Pen's pulse thundered. Something had shifted. The connection between them felt tangible, as if their energies were feeding off one another, opening a gateway, allowing him to cross the boundary between their worlds in small, unpredictable ways.

Adelaide spun, scanning the apartment like she expected someone to leap out from behind the furniture. But there was no one for her to find, even though Pen stood mere feet away.

She turned back to the coffee, reached for a cup, and filled it to the brim. Then, lifting it toward the empty room with a nod of thanks, she said, "Morning."

Pen swallowed hard.

She moved to the table and picked up the letter. His stomach twisted; this was it, the moment of truth, his one chance. His words would either be the key to his escape or the final lock on this prison.

Adelaide sat down at the table, blew gently on the coffee, and took a slow, careful sip. Then, she began to read.

The cup never reached her lips again as she took the letter in line by line. She leaned in, reading quickly at first, then slowing. Her breath was shallow, and her fingers worked the edge of the paper as she continued to read. Pen watched closely until she finally lowered the page. She didn't move, just stared at it, her thoughts somewhere far beyond her eyes. He couldn't quite read her expression, but something had shifted, a sharpness in her focus, a flicker of understanding. As if the last piece of the puzzle had finally fallen into place. A shape emerging. The truth of what was really happening inside the Feather Thorn.

Slowly, she stood and faced the living room.

"Pen?"

His name on her lips nearly undid him. She believed him, or at least, it seemed that way, enough that she would speak his name out loud. The tension that had knotted his ribs for days began to loosen, unspooling. He stepped closer, aching to meet her gaze, but her eyes moved through him, unseeing. The fragile connection he thought they'd found fell away again, leaving that familiar emptiness behind. He was still invisible.

"If you're here," she whispered, looking around the room, "give me some kind of sign."

Every nerve in his body fired at once. She was reaching for him, and he had to answer, had to do something, anything, to prove he was here, that he was real. His eyes caught the book on John Dee, resting on the side table in the living room. He knew, with certainty, that he could manipulate that.

Striding across the room, Pen reached for it. His grip was unsteady, his heart pounding. The book felt heavier than he remem-

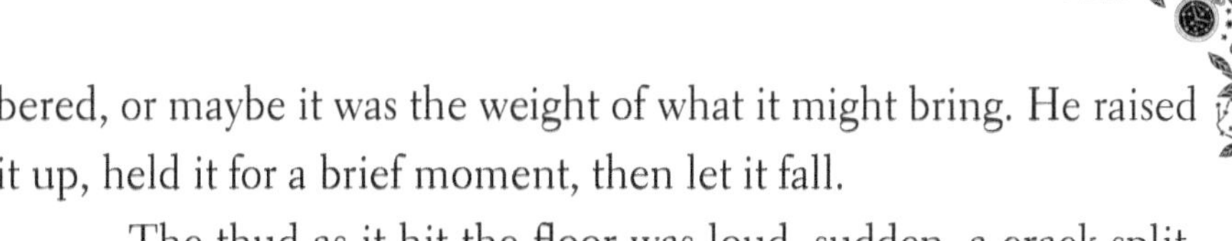

bered, or maybe it was the weight of what it might bring. He raised it up, held it for a brief moment, then let it fall.

The thud as it hit the floor was loud, sudden, a crack splitting the silence in two.

Adelaide jumped, her sharp breath catching in her throat. "Holy shit." She stood frozen, staring at the book on the floor. Then, slowly, she walked over and knelt, fingers trembling as she picked it up. "Is this really happening? Or have I gone completely mad?"

"You're not mad," Pen said. But his words dissolved into the space between their worlds, vanishing before they could reach her.

Adelaide cradled the book, weighing its truth, as though it were both proof and impossibility pressed into paper and ink.

For a moment, Pen felt the ache of being so close to her, yet impossibly far. He longed to comfort her, to say, *This is madness, yes, but it isn't yours.*

THE HIDDEN JOURNAL OF JOHN DEE

January 5, 1583

Weeks have passed since the binding ritual, and the strange distortions in time have ceased. It would seem the spell held, our breach has been sealed. Yet I fear it is no more than a temporary patch, a fragile veil drawn over a wound still festering beneath.

The new year has arrived, and with it, a sense of renewed determination. Edward is finally feeling well enough to attempt another scrying session. His recovery has been slow, but I can see strength returning to him, both in body and mind. I have been waiting for this moment; his connection to the divine will be crucial for us to move forward with the search for a permanent solution to the rip in time. I can only hope that this time, we will uncover the answers we desperately need.

During Edward's recovery, I have spent the last several weeks studying and learning all that I can about the Nephilim. I've spent countless hours in various libraries, digging through old texts. I sought out anything that might shed light on these mysterious creatures. The information was scarce, and some of the texts were difficult to access, so I had to visit several libraries, consulting various priests and scholars who could point me to the right sources.

In my search, I turned once again to the ancient scriptures, especially Genesis 6:1–4, where it speaks of the "sons of God" who took wives from the daughters of men. This passage marks the birth of the Nephilim, beings of extraordinary strength and renown. These giants, it seems, were a product of a union between celestial beings and humans, and they were said to be part of a time of great wickedness before the Flood. According to Josephus in *Antiquities of the Jews* (Book 1, Chapter 3), the Nephilim were destroyed by the deluge, a divine reckoning for their corrupt influence on mankind.

But the story doesn't end there. I found additional details in the *Book of Enoch* (1 Enoch 7:1–6), where the Watchers, celestial beings who once walked the Earth, descended and imparted forbidden knowledge to humanity, and when they lay with the humans, it led to the birth of the Nephilim. Though these beings were destroyed in the Great Flood, their spirits, according to Jubilees 5:1–2, were not entirely banished. Instead, they became demons, lingering in the shadows and continuing to influence mankind in ways unseen.

From what I can gather, the Nephilim are incredibly rare, likely wiped out in the Great Flood as the scriptures tell, but there must be at least one surviving descendant. But how to find them remains a mystery.

Edward has been resting in preparation for his next scrying session, and I pray that it will reveal the next step in our search. If all goes well, I hope to have answers soon, answers that may lead us to one of these beings, and ultimately, a way to destroy the Astral Synchronum for good.

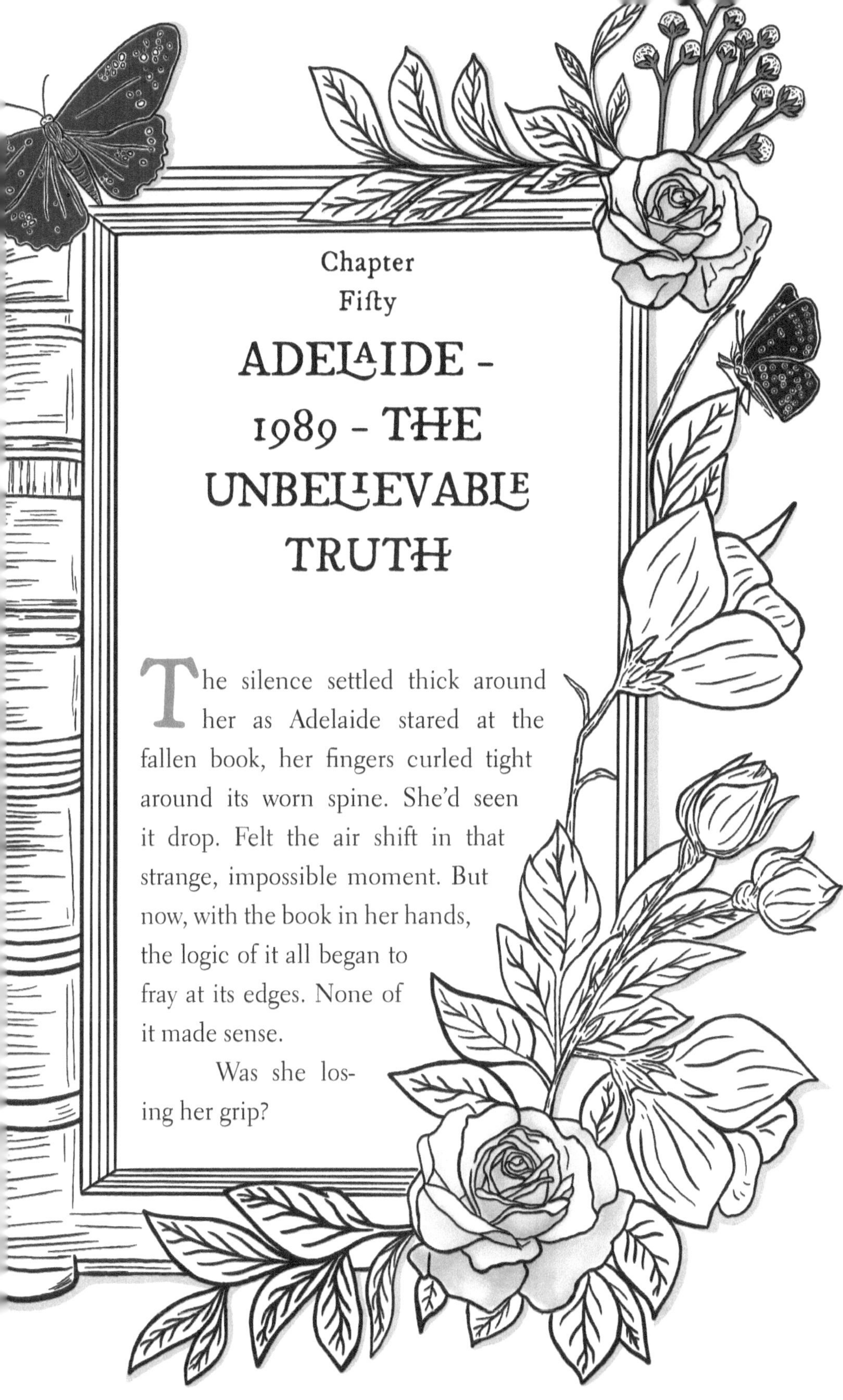

Chapter
Fifty

ADELAIDE – 1989 – THE UNBELIEVABLE TRUTH

The silence settled thick around her as Adelaide stared at the fallen book, her fingers curled tight around its worn spine. She'd seen it drop. Felt the air shift in that strange, impossible moment. But now, with the book in her hands, the logic of it all began to fray at its edges. None of it made sense.

Was she losing her grip?

The question threaded through her thoughts, pulling tighter every time she tried to let it go. She looked around the room, hoping, half-expecting to see someone standing there. Someone real. But there was no one. Just stillness.

A gas leak? Hallucinations? Ewan trying to be clever? She couldn't rule anything out, but none of those explanations fit. It felt impossible. A man trapped in time? Here, in this shop? This wasn't how reality worked. This was the stuff of novels, of dreams. And yet she'd seen the book hang there, suspended, before it dropped, leaving little room for doubt.

She shook her head, trying to clear the fog of disbelief. She'd been so wrapped up in Rowland's story, so convinced it was his ghost lingering in the shadows, that she hadn't considered it might have been the *other* man who had gone missing here.

And yet, if she could believe that Rowland's ghost haunted these walls, then why should this be any less possible?

Then it hit her. The letters, all of them, had been from Pen. Not Ewan.

Pen.

Her heart sank, then skipped a beat, tangled in confusion, awe, and something she didn't yet understand. But she couldn't walk away now. Not from this. Not from him. He was reaching out, asking for her help, and something in her needed to answer that call. But before she could help him, she had to understand how the watch worked, how it had bound him to time, and most of all, why he believed she could be the one to set him free.

"Pen," she called out, a knot tightening in her throat. "I need you to show me where the hidden room is. Please. If I'm going to help you, I need to see the other journals."

She stood there, listening, heart ticking in rhythm with the quiet, counting the seconds. *Come on, give me something, anything.*

Seconds dissolved into minutes, and still nothing.

Her shoulders sagged. Whatever thread that had connected them seconds ago had seemingly vanished, snapped, or frayed; she couldn't tell which.

She turned away, the last trace of hope slipping from her limbs as she crossed back to the table. Her coffee had gone cold, bitter on her tongue, but she barely noticed as her gaze drifted back to the letter.

This is exactly what Carolyn was afraid would happen to me.

The thought struck hard, sparking a chain of questions she couldn't push aside. She was grateful Pen had told her his story when he did. If he hadn't, she might have walked into the apothecary that morning and told Carolyn she believed Rowland's ghost haunted the Feather Thorn. Her aunt would have unraveled. She could see it now, Carolyn's face folding inward, old grief splintering into something fresh and sharp.

But that thought pulled at a deeper thread.

Carolyn had known about the artifact Rowland's family was safeguarding. That much was certain. And if she had believed it had anything to do with his disappearance, how could she not have wondered about Pen too?

Why had she stayed so far from the shop if there was even a chance that Rowland, or Pen, might be trapped inside? No, there was no way she could know the whole story.

None of it added up.

There was more Carolyn wasn't telling her, Adelaide was certain of it, but it wasn't this.

She lingered in the flat, waiting, hoping, for any sign that Pen might return. But the stillness remained, thick and unmoving.

Maybe he's in the bookshop, she thought, pulling on a sweatshirt.

The chill of the stone staircase slinked around her as she descended into the Feather Thorn. When she pushed open the door, warmth greeted her. The clock above the desk struck nine just as the sunlight crowned the tops of the buildings down the street, spilling streaks of gold light across the worn hardwood floors.

She turned toward the staircase leading to the loft. "Pen? Are you here?" she called softly into the stillness.

She waited, listening for any sign, a book falling, a shift in the air, anything that might suggest he was near. But the silence remained unbroken. With a sigh, she climbed the stairs and stood by the railing, looking down over her kingdom of books below. "Pen?" She tried again. Her voice echoed into the empty shop only to be swallowed by the quiet.

Resting her elbows on the railing, she cradled her face, rubbing her temples. This wasn't going to work, calling into empty rooms and hoping that he'd answer. She needed to find a better way to reach him.

Her gaze caught the old ship hanging from the ceiling, a relic from another time. If Pen truly was who she thought was the ghost, then what had happened to Rowland? Had he died trying to use the device, or was he, too, lost in some sliver of time like Pen?

The thought clawed at her. To be stuck, unseen, unheard, with no way back. No one to save you. What an awful fate that would be.

She stood there, hoping the silence might crack, that Pen might find a way through again. But the minutes ticked by, and still, there was nothing.

A flash of movement caught her eye, and her attention was

drawn to the large shop front windows. A young couple emerged from the Marbled Clover, carrying a donut box.

"Dottie," Adelaide said softly to herself, straightening. Dottie hadn't believed Pen returned to America; she thought he'd disappeared, like Rowland. And the way she spoke of him, so fondly, as though he were a dear friend, made Adelaide wonder if Dottie knew something more than she'd let on. Perhaps she knew where the hidden room was. And if Adelaide was going to help Pen, she would need to uncover more about him, to understand who he was, and how to free him.

She walked down the stairs, grabbed her jacket from the coat hook, and stepped out into the crisp morning air, her eyes set on the bakery ahead.

The sweet smell of sugar and spice enveloped her as she opened the door to the Marbled Clover, and the soft melody of the chimes rang out, alerting her arrival. Dottie came around from the back, a wide smile spreading across her lined face.

"Addie, so good to see you, dear! We saw you and Camie unloading a bunch of stuff from her van last night. Looks like the shopping trip went well."

"Yes, it did. I found almost everything I needed. Now I just need to get it all set up and wait for my order of books to arrive."

"Well, if you need a hand, you just say the word. Iain or I would be happy to help."

"Thanks, Dottie, that really means a lot."

"So, what brings you in today?" Dottie asked with a mischievous glint in her eye. "Apple turnovers, or chocolate puffs?"

"Actually, neither." Adelaide hesitated, then leaned in slightly. "I was hoping we could talk for a minute, if you have time. If not, I can come back later."

"Heavens no, now's fine. What is it you want to talk about?" Dottie asked, her curiosity visibly sparked.

"The guy who owned the shop after Rowland."

"Pen?" Dottie's eyes drifted up to the black-and-white photo above the doorway.

Adelaide followed her gaze. She stared at the image, her heart stuttering. That was him. The man behind the letters. One hand tucked casually into the front pocket of his slacks, an air of confidence in his stance. Though the photo lacked color, there was warmth in his eyes, a quiet kindness that transcended time. The idea that this handsome man, thought to be long gone, was still somehow lingering just across the street, trapped between moments in the Feather Thorn. It felt both strange and exciting to her.

"Yeah," Adelaide replied, turning back to face Dottie. "Pen."

"Come here," Dottie said, swinging open a half-door and motioning Adelaide through.

They passed through the bakery kitchen, where Iain was sliding a tray of biscuits into the oven.

"Hey, love," Dottie greeted, brushing his shoulder, "can you watch the front for a moment? I want to show Adelaide something."

"Sure. Hi, Adelaide," Iain said, flashing her his crooked smile as she followed Dottie into another room.

Behind the kitchen of the Marbled Clover, Adelaide stepped into a space that made her pause. It was the most enchanting tearoom she'd ever seen. The walls were half-paneled in a deep navy shiplap, while above, floral wallpaper bloomed in deep greens, oranges, golds, and pale pinks. A long wooden table anchored the center of the room, surrounded by eight walnut chairs. Mint-green metal tea carts stood on either side, topped with polished silver pots and neatly stacked china, adding to the whimsical vintage charm.

"What is this place?" Adelaide asked, her eyes wide as she took in the room.

Dottie giggled. "Oh, this is our hidden gem. It's the Clover Tea Room. We use it for special events and hire it out for parties."

"It's beautiful," Adelaide replied, admiring every detail.

"Wait here a minute." Dottie disappeared and returned moments later with something tucked under her arm.

"Have a seat," she invited, motioning to the chair opposite her. They both sat, and Dottie laid a large book in front of Adelaide.

"Go on. Open it," Dottie insisted, nudging the book closer to her.

Adelaide flipped open the cover. Inside, pages of black-and-white photographs unfolded, candid shots, stiff portraits, playful memories. Dottie reached over and turned to a page marked with a red ribbon.

"This one here," she said, tapping the image, "is Pen."

He looked to be in his late twenties, maybe early thirties, impossibly handsome, with a calm smile and a powdered donut in hand, seated beside Iain on a sunlit bench. In the next photo, he stood at the edge of a wooded trail, caught mid-step as if about to disappear into the trees. Another showed him right here at this very table, cards fanned in his hands, laughter frozen in time. And finally, the same photo as the one framed above the bakery doorway.

"I wish I had more," Dottie added, voice catching, but I had only got the camera a month before he disappeared."

Adelaide studied her, at the sorrow in her expression. "You two were close?"

Dottie nodded. "He was like family. You know when you meet someone and it feels like you've known them your whole life? That's what it was like with Pen. He was easygoing, so sweet, and full of hope. He had a rough upbringing, but inheriting the Feather Thorn meant the world to him, a fresh start."

"How old was he when he went missing?" Adelaide asked, easing into the more difficult questions, like whether or not Dottie knew about the hidden room.

"About your age," Dottie answered, turning the page. "He was only here for six months or so before he vanished."

"What makes you so sure he vanished and didn't go back to America, like Iain seems to think?"

Dottie hesitated, then lowered her voice. "I never told anyone this, but I saw him the night before he disappeared. He was in the flat, cooking dinner, watering his plants. Who does that and then just leaves the next day without a word? It didn't make sense."

A flush touched her cheeks, and Adelaide saw it then. Dottie had harbored a crush on Pen. Married to Iain or not, it was clear. But who could blame her? Pen had that classic, irresistible handsomeness that made women swoon.

"Iain thinks I'm daft, but every now and then, I swear I see his reflection in the windows of the Feather Thorn."

Adelaide's pulse quickened. Had Dottie glimpsed him through a gap in time, or was it just her longing playing tricks with the mind?

"Didn't his family come looking for him or at least reach out to the police?"

"No, not that I know of. Maybe they called MacDuff, but if they did, word never got back to me. That's why Iain's convinced he went back to America. But I just don't think he would've left without saying goodbye. Pen loved that bookstore. He was planning on getting a giant Christmas tree and decorating it with books. You don't dream up things like that if you're about to run away."

Turning to the back of the album, Dottie pulled out two yellowed newspaper clippings and placed them side by side. The first article was about Pen's disappearance, featuring the same smiling photo that Dottie had shown her. The second article, much older, had a photo of a young man, with the headline: *Proprietor of The Feather Thorn Bookshop Missing*.

"Is that Rowland?" Adelaide asked, her throat going dry.

Dottie nodded. "Handsome, wasn't he?"

He was. Tall and slender with a warm smile and sharp, intelligent eyes. After hearing so many stories about him, it was strange seeing his face for the first time.

"Don't you think it's a bit odd?" Dottie asked. "Two men, years apart, both vanished without a trace from the same building?"

Adelaide nodded. Odd didn't even begin to cover it.

"Can I ask you one last question?" said Adelaide. "Did Pen ever tell you about a hidden room in the bookshop?"

Dottie's eyebrows shot up, and her attention snapped back to Adelaide. "No, why? Have you found one?"

"No, but I found an old note about a room that I can't seem to find anywhere in the shop." She knew she couldn't share the truth.

"Well, I highly doubt there's one. If there had been, Pen would have definitely told us about it," Dottie replied, closing the album with a soft thud. "If you don't mind me asking, why did you want to know all this about Pen?"

"Just curious, really. There are a lot of little touches here and there that I can tell were his doing." She was at it again, lying. But she couldn't reveal all she knew. Or what she thought she knew.

"I wish you'd got to meet him, darling. He was a wonderful man, probably one of the kindest, most genuine people I've ever

met. I miss him still."

Well, Dottie's wish might just come true, Adelaide thought. If she could find the hidden room, if she could unlock the secrets Pen left behind, she might not only meet him, she might be the one to set him free.

ADELAIDE

- 1989 -

QUESTIONS

Adelaide crossed the street with a box full of sweets tucked under her arm and her head brimming with everything Dottie had told her. As she stepped through the shop door, she was met by the now-familiar scent of men's cologne mingled with the musty aroma of old books.

"Pen?" she called softly, realizing the scent must be his.

She waited for a reply, but only silence answered.

Setting the box of pastries on the desk, she rounded behind it and perched on the old stool propped against the wall. She stared out into the quiet, hoping to catch a glimpse of him weaving through the shadows, but the room remained still. She opened the box, reached for a chocolate puff, then froze. There was a flicker of movement in the back row of books.

Adelaide sprang to her feet. She hurried through the children's section and into the back aisle.

"Pen?" she called out again.

She came around the end of a bookcase just in time to see the small fox dart between the shelves. It lasted only a heartbeat, a flash of fur and motion, before it vanished into thin air, mid-stride, as if it had slipped through some unseen crack in time.

She gasped.

The fox must be from Pen's timeline.

Heart pounding, she crossed to the spot where it had vanished, dropped to a crouch, and pressed her hands to the floorboards. There was nothing there, no seam, no door, just the dust bunnies that had gathered over time.

Standing there, she rubbed her palms on her jeans. This was getting stranger by the minute. She tapped on the floor, thinking maybe this was where the hidden room lay. But it sounded dense like the rest of the room, not hollow as Rowland had described in his journal. *Not the spot*, she thought as she turned and made her way back to the front of the shop.

Back at the desk, she pulled out an old notepad. If Pen could reach her through letters, maybe she could reach him in the same way.

She chewed on the pen lid, doodling stars at the top of the page as she mulled over what to write. There were so many questions, so many gaps to fill in, but she didn't want to overwhelm him. Instead, she decided to start with the most important ones, the ones that might help her understand how to help him.

Dear Pen,

I hardly know where to begin. There's so much I want to ask you, but I don't want to overwhelm you with questions. Today, I'll start with what feels most important, the things that might help me understand what you're going through and how I can help.

First off, are you okay? How have you been surviving without food?

Do you know where the watch is now? If I'm to help you escape, we'll need it, won't we? Could it be in the secret room, with the other journals? Can you tell me where that room is? I think reading the other journals might help me understand how the watch works.

One more thing, can you always see me, or only when the space between us thins?

Adelaide paused, her pen hovering over the page. Pen's letters had steadied her, encouraged her, softened the edge of her loneliness with the sweetness of his words. The thought of him watching her settle into the life he'd once dreamed of, not with bitterness, but with quiet kindness, twisted something deep inside her. He hadn't tried to scare her away. He'd only ever reached out to her with gentleness.

Thank you for your letters. You have no idea how much I needed those words of encouragement.

I'll be patiently waiting for your next one.

Sincerely,

Adelaide

P.S. That fox, is it from your world or mine?

Setting the pen down, Adelaide stretched her cramped fingers, rubbing the ink-smudged tips against her thigh, then carefully folded the letter. Her eyes drifted to the letterbox. Should she leave it there? Would Pen even see it? She wasn't sure if her note would even transfer to his time. Yet, the letterbox had been the one place where he'd managed to leave them for her, up until today.

Hoping the magic worked both ways, she lifted the lid and slipped the note inside, closing it with a quiet prayer.

She checked the clock: quarter past twelve. The day was dragging on, and the thought of waiting until tomorrow for a response made it feel even slower.

She needed something to keep her mind and her hands busy. She had planned to visit Carolyn at the apothecary today, as it had been a few days since she'd seen her, but she thought better of it. With everything swirling in her mind, seeing Carolyn now felt risky. She might say something she'd regret. No, she needed more time to understand the situation.

When Pen wrote back, maybe then she could decide whether to confide in Carolyn. He might also be able to shed some light on whether she was telling the truth.

Turning away, she wandered over to the pile of furniture from her shopping trip and got to work. She chose one of the new rugs and the little table and chairs and set about finishing up the children's corner.

Once she got started, the day slipped by quickly. Twilight

draped itself across the windows, the golden light dimming to violet. Adelaide remained absorbed in her work until her stomach growled, pulling her back to the present. A glance at the clock, quarter past five, reminded her that if she left now, she could still make it to the market on the edge of town before it closed at six. But going meant passing the hardware store. Ewan would likely be there, and she wasn't ready for that encounter, not today. Now that she knew the kind of man he truly was, whatever flicker of possibility that had existed between them had been snuffed out completely. She wouldn't make the mistake of giving her time, or trust, to someone like that again.

She brushed the dust from her sweater and ran her fingers through her hair. Despite having to pass the hardware store, she knew she needed to go as there was zero food in the flat. She grabbed her jacket and keys and pulled the door closed behind her. Something made her glance back at the shop windows.

For the briefest moment, she thought she saw Pen standing between the rows of books, watching her. But when she blinked, he was gone.

Her feet faltered on the sidewalk out front, and she almost turned back, ready to go and search for him. But hunger won out. She couldn't live on sugar and curiosity alone. She needed some real food, something to keep her clear-headed. The market wouldn't stay open all night, and Pen… well, he wasn't going anywhere.

THE HIDDEN JOURNAL
OF JOHN DEE

January 19, 1583

Today has proven to be monumental, one that may alter the course of our future. For weeks, Edward and I had discussed attempting a scrying session, but he had been too weak and it kept us from moving forward. Now, finally, after much struggle, Edward felt strong enough to try. There was an urgency in his eyes as he suggested it, and I knew that this was no mere suggestion but a final effort to pierce the veil. We settled into the quiet of my study, and Edward removed a large clear crystal from his bag. The gravity of the moment weighed on us both, the room thick with anticipation as we prepared for what we hoped would be our breakthrough.

Edward set the crystal atop a small copper bowl and placed his hand on its top. At first, nothing happened. Minutes stretched into what felt like hours, and I began to lose hope. I feared we might never connect with any divine being again, and if we do not, it might mean that we never get the answers we seek in order to finally destroy the Synchronum.

Just as Edward removed his hand, about to give up, something extraordinary occurred. Within the depths of the crystal, a light began to form, growing stronger until it illuminated the room. A voice emerged with it, not from Edward this time, but from the crystal itself, resonating from its center.

The voice carried with it the power of a god, each word reverberating through the air, sending a shiver down my spine and raising the hair on my neck. It asked us what we sought, and I, with a pounding heart, requested information about where we might find a Nephilim, the only beings who could help us seal the rift in time for good.

The voice responded, acknowledging the problem I had caused, the rift I had created. It assured us that, for now, it had been mended, but the solution would not last forever. It knew why we needed to find one of the Nephilim to destroy the Astral Synchronum and put an end to this danger. The voice spoke of the Nephilim and how only a few had survived the Great Flood and retreated to the highest mountains, hidden away from mankind. Only two had survived beyond that time, and their descendants now walked the Earth, but they were no longer giants, no longer distinguishable from ordinary humans. Most of them unknowing of what they truly were and the power they held within their blood, the power of time itself.

The only way to identify them, the voice explained, was through a birthmark, an ethereal, celestial branding in the shape of the Star of Venus, the Morning Star. It was a mark that identified them as Nephilim, a trace of their ancient, divine lineage.

I asked if the voice could direct me to one of these Nephilim, but I was met with a grave response. The voice could not help us find one directly, saying it was punishment for meddling with the divine. The search would be a quest that might take years, if not lifetimes. It hinted that the search was a burden not meant for me, but for those who would come after. This quest, it said, would likely fall to my descendants in the future.

A chill ran through me at the thought of this. I thought of my son, Arthur, and how I could not bear to leave him with such a responsibility. I could not allow this burden to fall on him, nor on his children. I must find a way to end this, to resolve this matter so that my family will not suffer the consequences of our actions.

And then, as suddenly as it had begun, the communication ended. The crystal returned to its dull, translucent state, and the light faded. Edward sat in stunned silence, clearly astonished. He had never experienced such a clear communication before, and yet there was something unsettling about it. He confessed that, unlike the first encounter with the divine, this being felt less forthcoming, as though it had withheld certain information. He could sense a lingering unease in the air around us.

This revelation has left me with a heavy heart. The search for a Nephilim will be long, and it will not be an easy task. But I cannot let this quest be one that burdens my family for generations to come. I must find a way to end it now, once and for all.

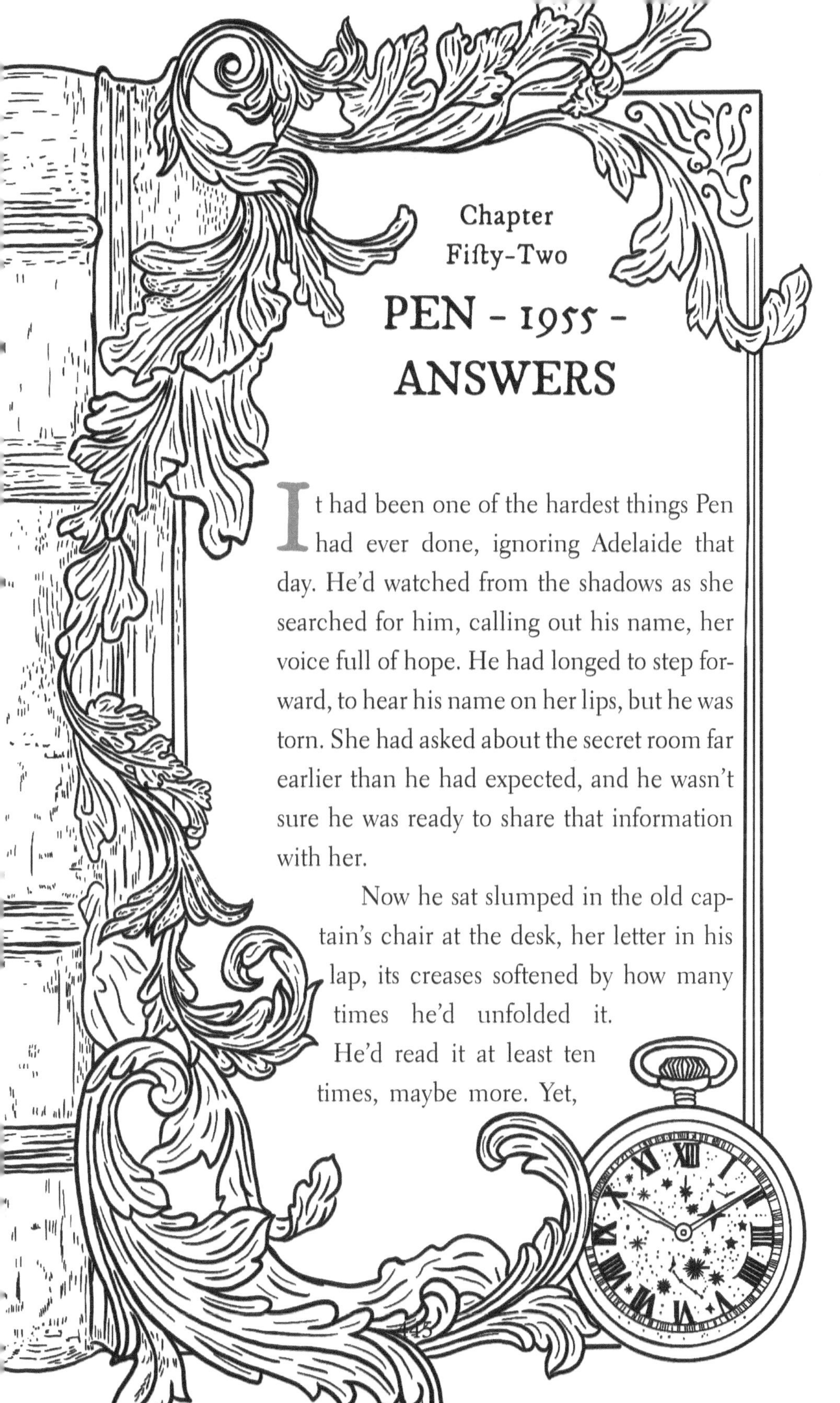

PEN - 1955 -
ANSWERS

I t had been one of the hardest things Pen had ever done, ignoring Adelaide that day. He'd watched from the shadows as she searched for him, calling out his name, her voice full of hope. He had longed to step forward, to hear his name on her lips, but he was torn. She had asked about the secret room far earlier than he had expected, and he wasn't sure he was ready to share that information with her.

Now he sat slumped in the old captain's chair at the desk, her letter in his lap, its creases softened by how many times he'd unfolded it. He'd read it at least ten times, maybe more. Yet, he was still unsure how to respond. He was grateful, even relieved, that Adelaide believed him and was willing to help. But under that relief came a lingering uncertainty. How much could he tell her without putting her at risk? He wanted to tell her everything, about the secret room, the intricacies of the time loop, the years of tangled threads he'd tried to unravel. He could just lay it all out. But something held him back. Some quiet instinct that warned him, *not yet.*

The watch complicated everything. He couldn't risk her touching it without understanding what it was. Its pull wasn't metaphorical; it was physical, real. Once in her hands, she wouldn't be able to resist it. At least the stars were in their favor; the next astrological event was still weeks away. If she found the watch now, it wouldn't have much effect. But the very idea of her getting near it still sent a wave of unease through him.

He spun slowly in the chair, facing his wall of notes, a chaotic constellation of scribbles and string mapping everything he had learned. Years of data layered on top of years of frustration. Lines connecting events, pinpointing the delicate openings in the time rift. He had chased the logic, searched the edges of every theory, but he was no closer to freedom than when he began. It was almost as if something was missing, a piece he didn't have.

But Adelaide did bring him hope.

He turned back to the typewriter, cracked his knuckles, and began to write.

Dearest Adelaide,

I reckon you've got a head full of questions, but first off, I want to thank you. You have no idea what a relief it is to hear that you are willing to help me. I am sure this is strange for you, as it surely isn't the usual way two people correspond, through time and space. I'll do my best to answer what I can, so that you might better understand my situation.

I am well enough. The nature of the time loop is that it is just that, a loop. Each day, everything resets. The apartment, myself, it all stays the same as it was the day I found myself trapped here. So, yes, I do have food, however, I am becoming quite sick of ground beef and eggs.

As for Rowland, I can only guess that he suffered the same fate as me and is trapped somewhere in time, but he isn't here in the Feather Thorn in my timeline.

You were right to think the watch is still hidden safely in the secret room. Yet I hesitate to tell you where. That device is dangerous, Adelaide. I wouldn't wish this fate on anyone, least of all you. Its pull is strong, and without understanding how it works, I fear it could trap you as it did me.

I can see and hear you, though it's like watching through a two-way mirror, as I cannot be seen or heard from my side of time. It is difficult to reach through and manipulate things in your timeline, but it seems that the more time we spend in each other's presence, the more I am able to break through. Why this happens, I'm still unsure. The only things I could influence before you arrived were things I had touched the day I was caught in the time loop. But I was able to turn on the light and steady you on the stairs the day you almost fell.

For now, these letters seem to be the surest way for us to talk. I'm grateful mine have brought you some comfort. What you don't realize is how much light you've brought into this shadowed place. I thought hope had long since abandoned me, but then you arrived.

Your laughter, your voice, it stirred something in me I thought was gone forever. For a moment, I even wondered if you were an angel sent to ease my solitude. But knowing you're real… well, it made my heart remember how to beat again. Tomorrow, speak freely as you work. I'll be listening, and I'll answer you through these letters.

Yours, Pen

P.S. That's Frankie, my pet fox, who seems to have a peculiar ability to bend space and time.

Pen approached the letterbox and slid his note inside, the lid clicking shut. From the apartment above came the soft creak of floorboards, the muffled sounds of Adelaide moving about her day. He stilled, head tilted, listening. Even her footsteps stirred something in him, a pull stronger than he cared to admit.

He longed to go to her, to see what she was doing, to hear her voice, but he stayed rooted, every part of him straining against the knowledge that he couldn't.

He turned to head back into the hidden room, but stopped. At the end of the fiction aisle, where moments ago there had been nothing, now sat an old wooden bench. Its carved legs and high back belonging to another century, its presence wholly out of place. That bench hadn't been there a moment ago, he was sure of that. A chill slid down his spine as he moved closer. The wood was dark with age, its surface worn smooth. He reached out, letting his fingers drift over it. It felt solid, real, but wrong in a way he couldn't explain. Its sudden appearance made no sense. Something was wrong, very wrong.

The changes had begun as whispers: a few missing books, the spinning wheel, and the new paintings on the staircase wall.

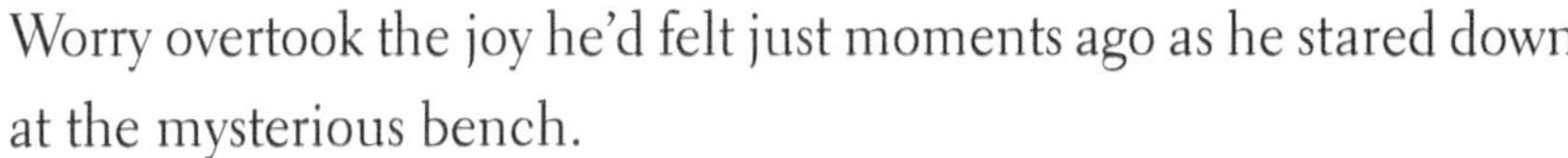

Worry overtook the joy he'd felt just moments ago as he stared down at the mysterious bench.

Its back rested against a section of Jules Verne books, and *From the Earth to the Moon* stared back at him from the shelf, its spine catching the light. *A fitting choice at the moment*, he thought, *when dreams of escape and odd occurrences mingle.*

He'd read that book more times than he could count. In fact, Verne had become one of his favorite authors since he'd been trapped here. For years, the tales had served as a refuge, offering journeys to worlds far beyond the walls of the Feather Thorn. At first, they had worked as an escape for his restless soul. But today their magic felt dulled.

This was no longer fiction.

Verne's words felt hollow, the quests inside the pages distant. There was something far more pressing unfolding here, something that affected both him *and* Adelaide. Something that didn't follow the rules of the time loop.

THE HIDDEN JOURNAL OF JOHN DEE

December 15, 1583

It has now been nearly a year since Edward and I uncovered the information about the Nephilim. Yet, despite our efforts, we are no closer to finding one than we were when we first began. Edward has performed many scrying sessions, and while some have yielded valuable insights into the nature of the angels, none have brought us any closer to our goal. The search for a Nephilim feels like an unreachable challenge. If they blend so seamlessly into human society, unaware of the immense power coursing through their blood, then finding them is like searching for a needle in a haystack.

I fear that the entity we spoke to was right in its ominous prediction, that I may never find a Nephilim in my lifetime. Yet, despite this grim possibility, I cannot bring myself to abandon this search. I will keep trying, even if the odds are against me. The rift cannot be allowed to remain, and the Astral Synchronum must be destroyed. It is a burden I must bear, no matter how long it takes.

Edward, ever the pragmatic one, has advised me to begin documenting everything for my descendants. He believes that, should my efforts fail, they will need to have all the knowledge

I have gathered so that they may continue the work. He has suggested that I leave behind a comprehensive record detailing everything I have done, everything I have checked off in my search, and the steps they must take to seal the rift and destroy the Synchronum.

I agree with him. It is not only my duty to finish what I've started but to ensure that my family is prepared to carry on this mission if I cannot. To that end, I have begun compiling documents, listing every step taken, every lead followed, and every failure we've encountered. I have also written out detailed instructions for the care and upkeep of the property near Loch Gare, to ensure that it remains safe and within the family until the day when the Synchronum is finally destroyed.

Though the strange disruptions have ceased, and the spell appears to have sealed the rift for now, I know it is but a temporary patch. The fabric of time remains weakened. The seal will not hold forever, and should the Synchronum be used again, the rip will open once more. Reality will shift, folding in upon itself in ways no man can predict, and the consequences may ripple far beyond this world.

For now, I must accept the possibility that this task may fall to others. But until that day comes, I will continue my search. I will dedicate the rest of my life to finding a Nephilim, to sealing the rift, and to ending this curse I have placed upon the Earth. Even if it takes me a lifetime, I will not rest.

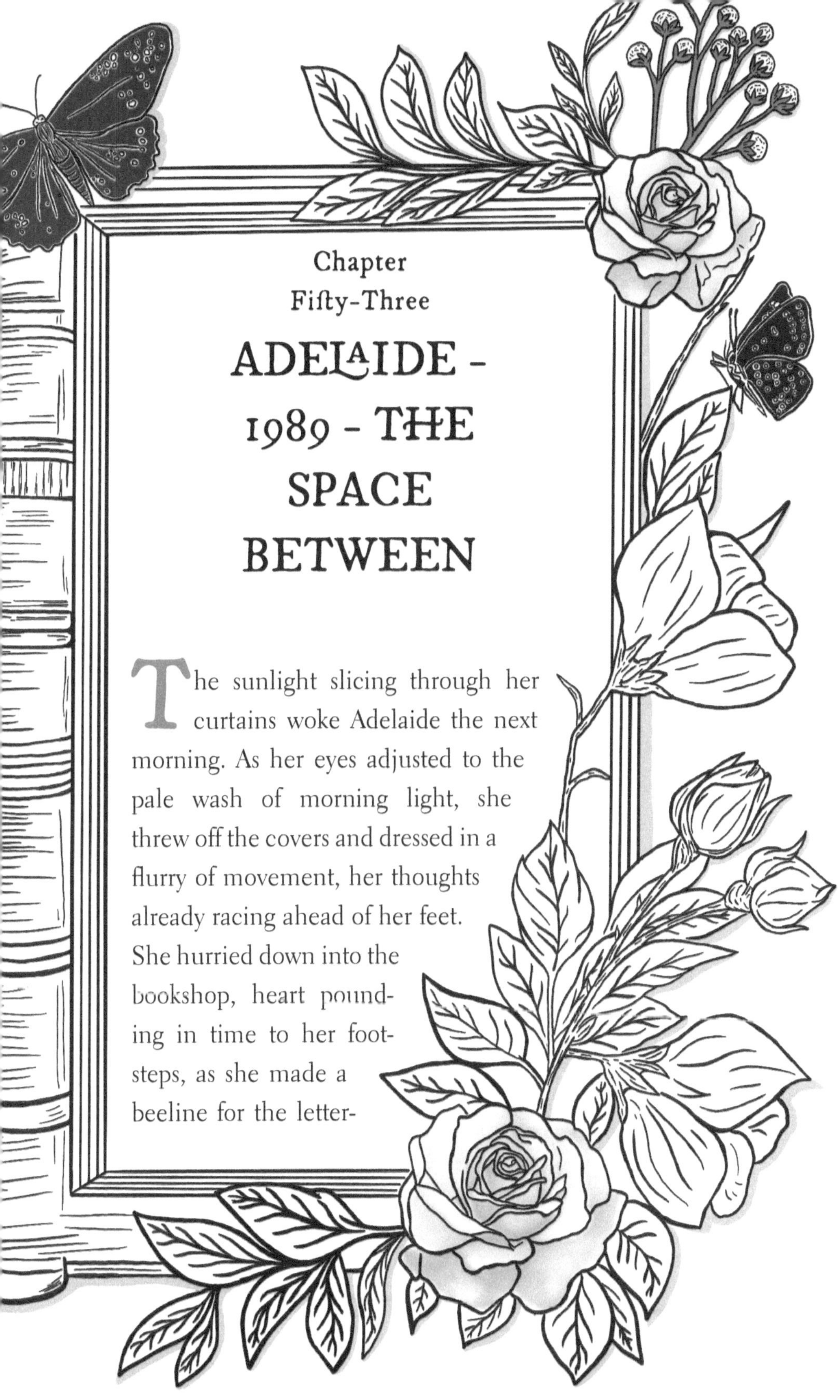

ADELAIDE –
1989 – THE
SPACE
BETWEEN

The sunlight slicing through her curtains woke Adelaide the next morning. As her eyes adjusted to the pale wash of morning light, she threw off the covers and dressed in a flurry of movement, her thoughts already racing ahead of her feet. She hurried down into the bookshop, heart pounding in time to her footsteps, as she made a beeline for the letterbox. When she lifted the lid and saw the folded paper inside, it was as if a swarm of butterflies took flight in her stomach.

Clutching it, she crossed to the wingback chair and sank into its worn embrace, and rubbed the lingering sleep from her eyes. Her fingers fumbled over themselves as she unfolded the paper, her breath catching when she landed on the first line: *Dearest Adelaide*.

Warmth spread through her as she devoured the letter, taking in every word. When she reached the end, she barely paused before starting over, this time slower, lingering over every phrase.

At first, she felt a sting of disappointment. Pen didn't trust her enough to reveal the location of the hidden room. But by the third reading, that feeling gave way to something quieter, more forgiving. She saw the care threaded between his words; he wasn't shutting her out, he was trying to protect her from the device, from the consequences of stepping too close.

Several parts of Pen's letter snagged in her thoughts. The idea that time reset each day; if that were true, then he hadn't aged a day beyond the photographs in Dottie's album. This opened a corridor of questions she wasn't ready to walk down. She forced herself to focus instead on something more immediate.

Rowland.

Pen had said he wasn't here in the bookshop. Which meant Rowland's fate still remained unknown.

But it was the final part of the letter that stayed with her. He'd said that she'd brought him back hope, that her voice had stirred something deep inside him. Adelaide's cheeks flushed with embarrassment as she recalled all the times she'd danced and sung in the shop. But beneath that flush of awkwardness, she felt something else stir, something far more dangerous than mere bashfulness. A flicker of emotion she dared not name, let alone indulge.

Now that she knew he could see and hear her every move, she resolved to be more mindful of how she carried herself inside the Feather Thorn.

She glanced out the window as a thick quilt of dark clouds crawled across the sky, casting a shadow over the rows of books. Then, with a quiet breath, she got to her feet and turned back to the shelves.

"Good morning, Pen. Looks like we're in for a storm today," she said.

She should have been unnerved by the idea of an invisible man roaming the shop, but instead, there was a strange comfort in knowing he was there. The place felt less lonely, the silence less heavy.

She turned to make her way back to the desk, but froze at a loud thud. A book had *fallen* from the gardening section. She quickly crossed the shop and found a book lying face down. Picking it up, she saw it was titled *Morning Glories: A Guide to Planting and Growing*.

A smile tugged at the corner of her mouth. "Clever," she murmured, slipping the book back onto the shelf. Another thump echoed from across the room. She turned and walked briskly toward the sound, stooping to retrieve *The Tempest and the Sunshine* by Mary J. Holmes.

A laugh escaped her lips. "We'll be lucky to see any sunshine today, by the looks of it."

She didn't need to see him to know he was standing near. The hairs on the back of her neck stood up, and she let out a quiet breath, her smile lingering. "Well, I could certainly use some coffee," she continued, pretending to grumble. "Unlike yesterday, no one had it ready for me when I woke up this time." With a playful huff, she crossed to the back of the shop and slipped through the narrow door that led to the stairwell. When she reached the flat and stepped into the living room, she stopped.

There, curled up in the corner, was the little fox. Its russet coat rose and fell with its soft steady breaths. She didn't move, only watched, mesmerized by the impossible.

How did he slip so easily between timelines? Was it his instinct to sense the frayed edges where time wore thin?

She inched forward, the floorboards creaking underfoot. Frankie's ears twitched, and his eyes blinked open, locking onto Adelaide.

In a flash, the fox sprang to its feet, scrambled toward the door, and then vanished into thin air.

Adelaide exhaled slowly. "Thank God I already know what's going on," she said, hand on the doorframe, "otherwise, that would've sent me straight to the loony bin."

But she did know better. And now, she had to focus.

The weight of the day settled on her shoulders as she moved to the kitchen. She filled the kettle, set it to boil, and scooped the fresh grounds into the percolator. Her breakfast was quick and simple, toast and a smear of jam, and with the coffee, it was just enough to shake off the fog of sleep and coax her into motion.

Once finished, she slipped into her old painting clothes, smudged with the previous day's paint, and headed downstairs to tackle the last drab wall in the shop. In the little reading nook, she shifted the chairs and the small end table aside, then unfurled an old sheet to protect the wooden floor.

"You're lucky you're stuck in another time," she called into the quiet, a teasing edge to her voice. "If you weren't, I'd have you painting this wall."

As rain battered the old slate roof of the Feather Thorn, Adelaide spent the day painting, her brush moving steadily as she spoke to Pen. She told him how singing had once been more than comfort, it had been a dream, and that was why he'd heard so much of it lately.

She explained that back in uni, she'd been in a band called The Dusty Brocade, and they'd been good. Good enough to start turning heads. But then she met Jeff. Her voice softened as she shared how her dreams of singing faded, eventually disappearing altogether when she married him, as he didn't like the idea of her out at the pubs, and he was jealous of the guys in the band. He'd told her it wasn't the kind of life a married woman should live, and she'd believed him. She gave it up, thinking it would win her a quieter, steadier kind of happiness. She had wanted to make him happy because when Jeff was content, it was like basking in the warmth of summer. But when he wasn't, it felt like winter had arrived, cold and hollow.

Once she began speaking of Jeff, it was as if a floodgate opened and the words poured out, all the compromises she had made, all the ways she had shrunk herself to become what he wanted. And in the end, it still hadn't been enough.

She continued well into the afternoon, still painting, telling Pen every heartbreaking detail of her life, her relationship, and his betrayal. There was something liberating about talking to someone who could only listen. No interruptions, no judgment, no rush to fix or explain. For the first time since it all unraveled, a lightness came over her, like the last of her hurt had finally drained out of her system.

By the time she stepped back from the wall, brush limp in hand, she was spent, mind a worn thing, and body heavy with a good kind of ache.

"Well, I'm shattered," she said to the dusk-filled shop. "Think I'll grab a bite and turn in."

She was halfway to the stairs when a thud came from the children's section. She veered off course to see what book Pen had left her. Lying face up next to the low shelves was *Goodnight Moon* by Margaret Wise Brown.

A smile curved the corners of her mouth.

"Goodnight, Pen," she whispered into the stillness.

THE HIDDEN JOURNAL
OF JOHN DEE

June 8, 1599

To My Descendants,

I pen this letter as my days are coming to an end, both a confession of my folly and a guide for those who come after me. In my arrogance, I sought to create a bridge to the divine, one that would allow me to commune with celestial forces beyond without the aid of seers like Edward Kelley. I had wished to unlock the heavens by my own hand, to find a path unbound by reliance on others. This ambition led to the creation of the Astral Synchronum.

What I intended as a tool of enlightenment became instead a harbinger of destruction. My understanding of the divine order was inadequate, and in my haste, I tore open a rift in time itself. This wound threatens all, for it is a flaw in the fabric of our existence, one that cannot mend on its own. Even though Edward and I have been able to stop it temporarily, the fix will not hold forever. If the device is not destroyed before it fails, then our reality will collapse, falling into whatever lies beyond.

In my efforts to mend the damage I caused, I sought out the Nephilim, the descendants of the ancient giants born of divine and mortal union, as told in Genesis. Though the Great Flood wiped out most, some survived in secret, their bloodline hidden among us. These modern descendants are marked by a Star of Venus birthmark. They hold the power to help seal the rift and destroy the Synchronum.

I have spent years seeking them. With the favor of the royal court, I scoured the better part of Europe, speaking with priests and scholars, scryers and witches. I pored over ancient texts, from Genesis to the *Book of Enoch*, hoping to understand the Nephilim. I pursued every lead. I examined records from the witch trials, seeking accounts of birthmarks upon those accused. I consulted healers, searching for traces of miraculous bloodlines. One tale from Italy told of a woman who bore the mark and healed others with her touch, but by the time I found her village, she had long since passed, leaving no heirs. Yet in all my travels and searches, I have come up short.

To you, my descendants, I entrust the care of our estate near Gare Loch as the Synchronum is hidden there within its walls. The house itself is spelled to ensure that the Synchronum remains within its boundaries, and it must never fall into the hands of others. Keep the property safe, and never sell or abandon it. This house must remain in our family, for the wards and protections are tied to our bloodline and must stay that way until the Synchronum is destroyed.

I must bid you caution: It will chime during celestial alignments, but only those born within major astrological alignments will hear its call. Should you hear the sound, resist the urge to touch it, for doing so will ensnare you in the flow of time, trapping you within an endless loop.

Edward and I have spoken many times with the divine and have been given detailed instructions on how to go about the destruction of the Astral Synchronum. If a Nephilim is found, you must follow these instructions diligently.

On the winter solstice, under the light of a full moon, place four candles to mark the cardinal directions, North, South, East, and West, and light them in a clockwise motion.

1. Between these points, place copper bowls as follows:
   - Between North and East, place a bowl of lavender to represent the wind, aiding clarity in your spellwork.
   - Between East and South, place a bowl of cinnamon to represent fire, aiding in action and power.
   - Between South and West, place a bowl of chamomile to represent water, offering protection and healing.
   - Between West and North, place a bowl of cedar bark to represent earth, grounding the ritual and stabilizing the energies.

2. Hand the Synchronum to the Nephilim and bid them stand within this circle. They must speak these words thrice: *"With the blood of the angels that*

*courses within my veins, banish this device until noth-
ing remains."*

3. The Nephilim must then spill a drop of their blood
    upon the Synchronum. Only their divine heritage
    can reverse its power and seal the rift, distorting it.

I leave this document to you in the hope that you may one day succeed where I have failed. Should you find the Nephilim and complete the ritual, know that you will have ended the curse. But be wary of the Synchronum, for it is a powerful and dangerous object. It will test your resolve and tempt you to use it for your own purposes, but you must resist.

May you carry the burden with honor, and may you succeed in sealing the rift and restoring balance to the world. If you are ever in doubt, know that you are not alone; those who have come before you have walked this path, and now you must continue it.

My wish is that you succeed where I have failed. The fate of time itself may rest in your hands.

Yours in hope and humility,

John Dee

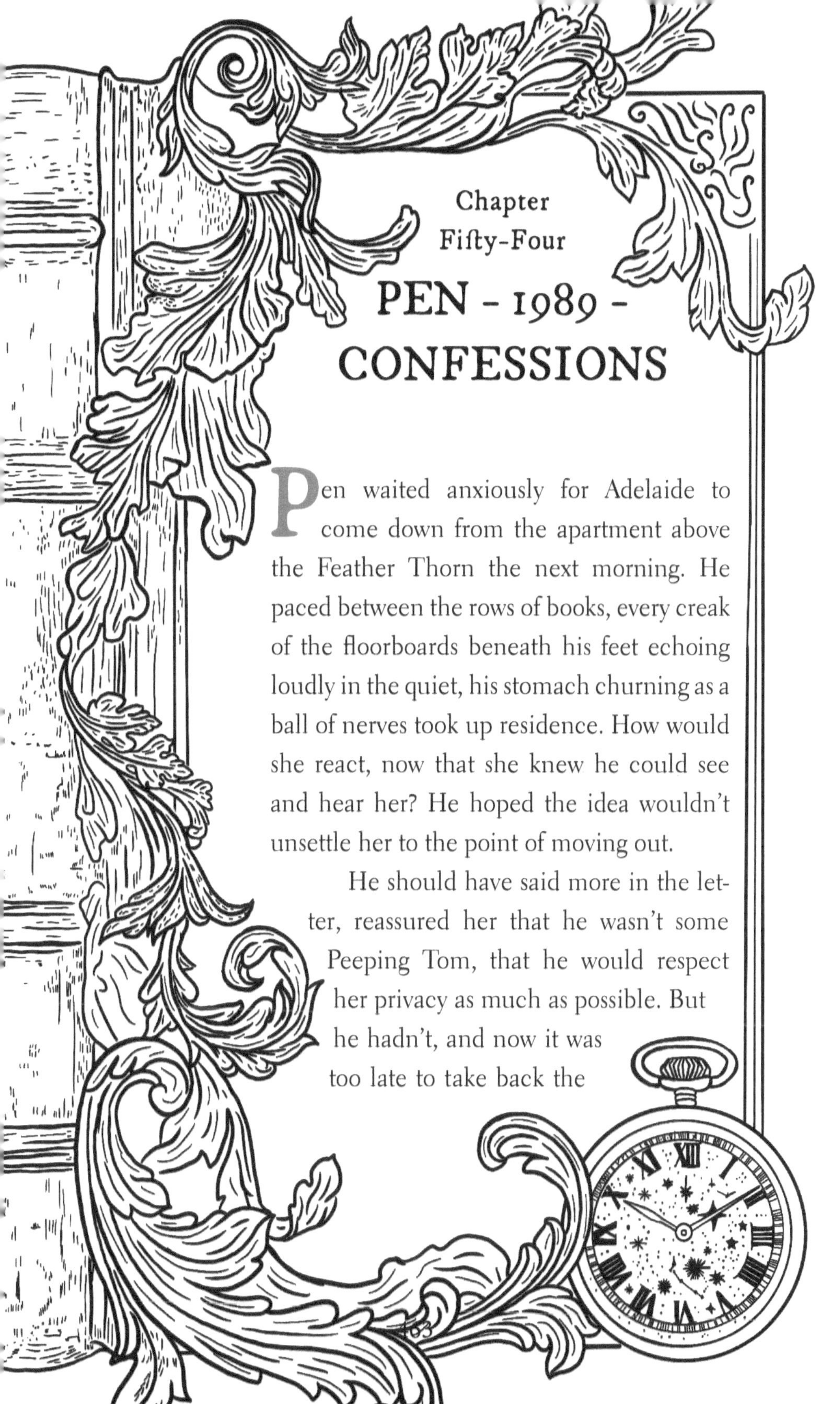

Chapter
Fifty-Four

PEN - 1989 -
CONFESSIONS

Pen waited anxiously for Adelaide to come down from the apartment above the Feather Thorn the next morning. He paced between the rows of books, every creak of the floorboards beneath his feet echoing loudly in the quiet, his stomach churning as a ball of nerves took up residence. How would she react, now that she knew he could see and hear her? He hoped the idea wouldn't unsettle her to the point of moving out.

He should have said more in the letter, reassured her that he wasn't some Peeping Tom, that he would respect her privacy as much as possible. But he hadn't, and now it was too late to take back the silence. The thought of her leaving, of being alone in the shop again, brought back that all-too-familiar hollow ache in his chest.

As the first rays of morning cast their golden glow across the shop, there she was, like the sun itself. Adelaide quickly made her way over to the letterbox and fished out his letter, clutching it like something precious. A smile crossed her features as she carried it to the old wingback chair.

Pen watched as she unfolded it, her fingers slow, almost reverent. She didn't smile right away. Instead, she leaned back in the chair, one knee bouncing absently, eyes scanning the page with quiet intensity. He held his breath as she finished, her gaze drifting toward the window, then returning to the letter. She began reading it over again, slower now, her lips pressing into a thoughtful line. He searched her face for clues, an arched brow, a faint frown, a catch in her breath, but her face stayed emotionless as she read.

Then, finally, her mouth quirked into a smile, and her radiance returned.

After that, he had come up with a clever game of dropping books with titles that said the things he couldn't.

He wished she could see him, to match her smile with one of his own. He leaned against the wall, watching through the veil of time. Her presence anchored him, and he hoped that somehow, he was doing the same for her.

That afternoon, she talked to him as she painted. Told him about her days at university, the band she'd been in. Her voice was steady, companionable, like she was speaking to someone across the room, and her words flowed as easily as the paint she rolled across the walls. But then the conversation took a heavier turn as she began to speak about her husband. As her brush moved in long, even strokes, her truths spilled out too, layer by layer.

Pen's heart sank at her words. Her story was heartbreak-ing, and he ached for her, for everything Jeff had put her through, everything he had taken from her. It was a good thing he was trapped in time, because if he hadn't been, he might've driven straight to Glastonbury, wherever that was, and roughed him up a bit. What kind of man stepped out on a woman like Adelaide? He couldn't fathom it. Things between men and women must have changed quite a bit in the thirty years since his own time.

He saw the sadness in her eyes, the way it dulled their usual spark, and it tore at him. When a single tear slipped down her cheek, he instinctively reached out, wanting to rest his hand on her shoulder. But his hand passed through her like a shadow, meeting only the cool air between them.

She worked long into the afternoon, painting until the light outside turned to dusk. When she finally set her supplies aside and headed for the stairs to the apartment, Pen knocked *Goodnight Moon* onto the floor. The book was one of the newer additions to the shop, a title left behind by the man he'd scared away all those years ago.

Adelaide rounded the corner and bent to pick it up, pausing as her eyes lingered on the title. She smiled, then tucked it neatly back onto the shelf before whispering, "Goodnight, Pen," before she headed upstairs.

"Goodnight, my star," he said, his voice echoing back to him in the stillness of the now-empty shop.

He turned around, intending to find a book and settle in for the night, but something gave him pause.

The back of the shop looked darker than it should have, even with twilight settling in. A shadowy dimness seemed to pool there, as though the light refused to touch it.

Pen frowned, unease settling in his chest like a cold fog. He moved toward it, his steps slow and hesitant. Rounding the corner, he froze.

The window that once overlooked the alleyway was gone. In its place stood a solid wall of stone.

The air felt different here, thicker, heavier. Pen stepped closer, every sense on edge. It wasn't as if the window was just boarded up. It had vanished completely. And the two bookcases that had flanked it were gone too.

The absence of the window hit him like a missing note in a melody he'd known by heart. Pen laid his palm flat against it. Like the bench, there was a wrongness to it, a feeling he couldn't explain, as if the energy threading through it didn't belong to this place.

He let his hand fall away.

"What's happening here?" he murmured, a sinking feeling settling deep in his chest like a stone dropped into still water. The small things, at first, he could have dismissed: Adelaide moving something when he wasn't looking, his memory playing tricks. But this… there was no pushing this aside.

Something was happening here. Something he couldn't explain. And it had all started the day she walked in.

He raked a hand through his hair and reached into his pocket for his lucky penny, flipping it between his fingers as he turned and headed for the front of the shop. The motion steadied him, but not enough.

Dread followed, close and quiet. Something in his timeline was unraveling.

Had the journals said anything about this? He couldn't recall. Most focused on the stars and the planets, detailing how their alignments opened portals to other realms, to the heavens themselves. But there had been no mention of anything like this. Nothing about objects appearing out of nowhere, about rooms rearranging themselves.

Pen dropped into the wingback chair.

The hairs on the back of his neck rose. What if this wasn't random? What if this strange phenomenon could affect him too? What if the same force that erased the window could erase him from this timeline as well?

And if it did, where would he go?

Maybe this was what had happened to Rowland. Had the shop shifted into another plane of reality, taking him with it?

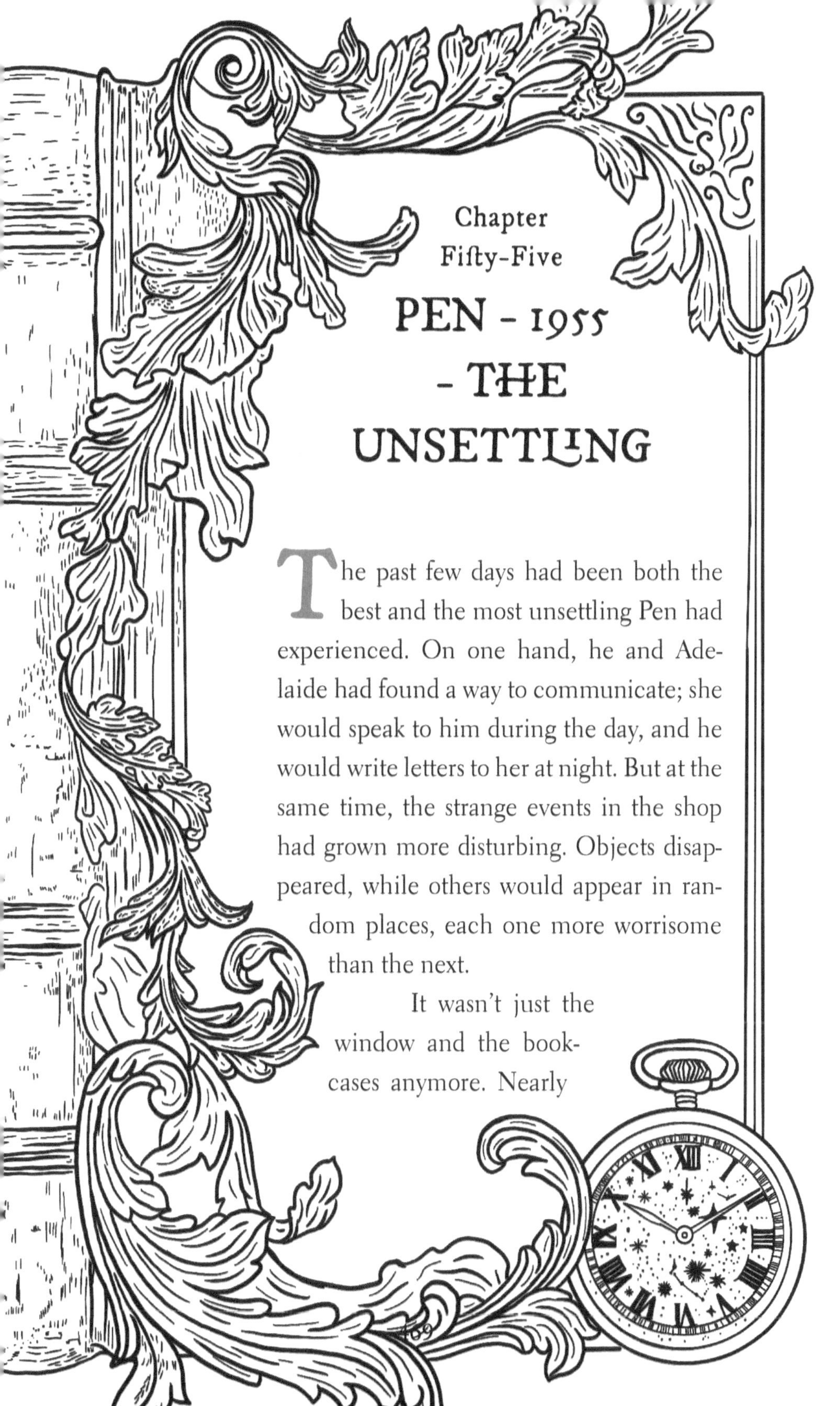

The past few days had been both the best and the most unsettling Pen had experienced. On one hand, he and Adelaide had found a way to communicate; she would speak to him during the day, and he would write letters to her at night. But at the same time, the strange events in the shop had grown more disturbing. Objects disappeared, while others would appear in random places, each one more worrisome than the next.

It wasn't just the window and the bookcases anymore. Nearly

the entire fiction section had disappeared, along with the front counter. In their place stood a battered workbench covered with tools that looked centuries old, possibly from the late sixteenth century. The most troubling addition was a straw-stuffed sack bed now occupying the back corner where the window used to be. Maybe the bookshop was reverting to some older version of itself, back to when the building had first been built.

Now, when Pen wasn't with Adelaide in the bookshop, he spent hours in the hidden room searching for answers. He debated telling her what was happening, but he wanted to make sense of it for himself first. Plus, he didn't want to frighten her, and in truth, there was nothing she could do to help at this point anyway. It would only burden her. They had to wait for the twenty-first, still days away, before the watch could be activated again. He just hoped the Feather Thorn would still be standing by then.

Tonight, Adelaide had gone to the Dark Dagger, a local bar, with Camie, and Pen paced the bookshop, uneasy. Part of him worried she'd run into Ewan, another part couldn't stop thinking about the disconcerting fact that another bookcase had gone missing since she left.

A sudden rustle broke through his thoughts; Frankie sprang out from the shadows, making Pen jump. The little fox darted between his legs, letting out a string of high-pitched chitters as he circled around him in a figure-eight.

"Hungry? Me too," Pen said. "Let's go get some grub."

He did his best to avoid the apartment when Adelaide was home. It had been tricky at first, trying to balance eating and feeding Frankie without disrupting her schedule, but he'd managed. Frankie, however, had not been pleased with the change in his feeding times.

Pen still wasn't used to sharing his space with another person, and several times he'd stumbled across something unexpected. And tonight was one of those times. When he walked into the kitchen, he stopped short; there, draped over the kitchen chair, was a bright red bra. He swallowed hard, looked away, then glanced back. So this was what it was like to live with a woman: bras on chairs, hair brushes on tables, a whole world of private rituals suddenly made visible. He smiled despite himself. If this was it, it wasn't all that bad. He could very easily see himself getting used to it.

Walking over to the table, he reached for her hairbrush to move it aside, but his hand passed through it, just as it had when he'd tried to touch her. He recoiled and stepped back. That had never happened before. In both timelines, he'd always been able to touch things; maybe not move them in Adelaide's world, but in his own, he could at least touch them. He looked down at his hand, hoping it was still solid flesh and bone, and not fading into the abyss like the bookcases had.

He let out a breath, seeing that his hand was indeed still whole.

Frankie chittered at his feet, snapping him back.

"I know, I know, you're starving," he muttered, walking over to the fridge. He pulled out the ground beef again. Frankie didn't seem to mind, but Pen had had enough burgers to last him a lifetime. What he would have done for just a ham and cheese sandwich and a bag of chips.

As the meat sizzled in the pan, unease bubbled up inside him, threatening to overflow. What if the brush was just the beginning? What if he couldn't move anything anymore, couldn't type letters to Adelaide? Or worse, what if the typewriter vanished? He hadn't thought of that until now. If that happened, he would have no way to communicate with her. No way to tell her what was happening. As soon as he set the food down for Frankie, he bolted for the stairs and descended to the secret room. The stone steps chilled his feet, and his breath echoed off the walls as he rounded the corner. A sigh escaped his lips. The Underwood typewriter was still there.

He didn't think he'd ever been so happy to see it. He pulled out the old chair, sat down, fed in a sheet of paper, and rolled it up, ready to type. He decided it best to write Adelaide a letter, let her know what was happening, just in case one of these days he or the typewriter vanished.

He typed quickly, explaining everything, how some objects had vanished while others appeared out of nowhere. How the shop itself felt like it was slipping through a crack in time. And that if he ever stopped writing, at least she would know why.

He didn't want to scare her, and there was still a chance he might figure things out in time. So, instead of leaving the letter in the usual spot, he folded it and decided to put it somewhere she might eventually stumble upon it if he did go missing.

Pen threaded another piece of paper into the old Underwood and began typing again; this one she would find in the morning.

Dearest Adelaide,

Good morning. Despite the overcast weather that seems to hang over this country, you, my dear Adelaide, are like the sun itself, your rays of beauty lighting up every dusty, shadowed corner of this shop. I want you to know that over the past few weeks, your company and conversation have brought me fully back to life. Jeff was a fool to lose someone as wonderful as you, a damn fool.

It looks like the shop is almost ready to open. Just a few more days, and I can only imagine how excited you must be. You've done such a wonderful job bringing color and life back to these walls. I wish so badly I could be there with you, in your timeline, when you open those doors. You will bring smiles to so many people, just as you do for me. The town of Helensburgh was lucky when you arrived. I will be waiting to hear your voice tomorrow and dreaming of it tonight.

Yours,

Pen

Letters in hand, Pen headed up into the shop. He slid the one meant for tomorrow into the letterbox, then tucked the other one into the John Dee book resting on the counter. If he ever went missing, he knew she'd search for answers within its pages, and the letter would be in it, waiting for her. Then, he sat in the quiet, listening to the sounds of a world that might not hold together much longer, and waited for Adelaide to come home.

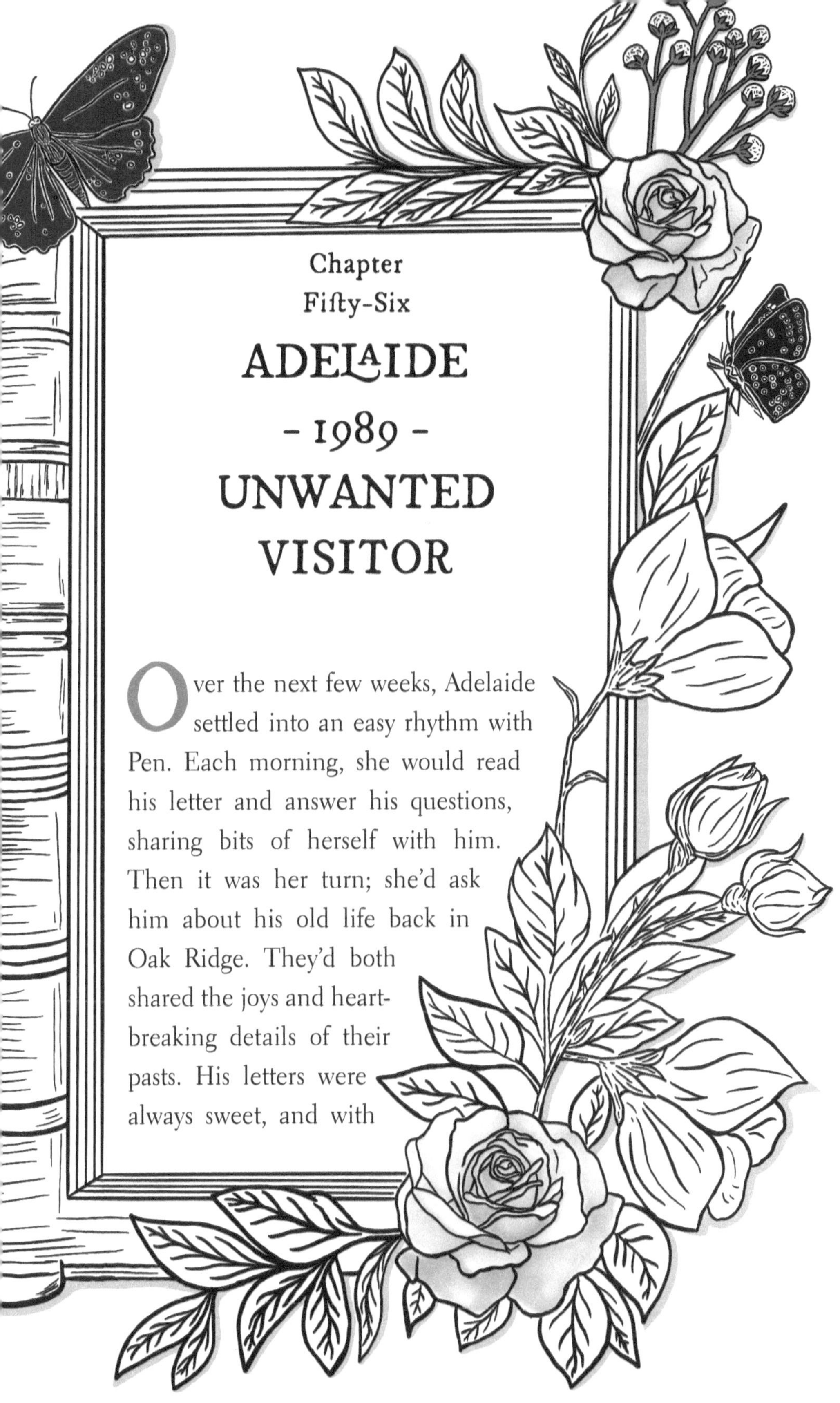

ADELAIDE

- 1989 -

UNWANTED VISITOR

Over the next few weeks, Adelaide settled into an easy rhythm with Pen. Each morning, she would read his letter and answer his questions, sharing bits of herself with him. Then it was her turn; she'd ask him about his old life back in Oak Ridge. They'd both shared the joys and heart-breaking details of their pasts. His letters were always sweet, and with each one her heart fluttered a tiny bit more.

She felt she'd come to know Pen better through letters than she'd ever known Jeff. Their exchanges, though interrupted by the gaps in time, were deeper than any conversation she'd had with her ex. Jeff had never talked about his feelings, claiming it wasn't "manly," but with Pen, his emotions flowed freely on the page. Dottie had been right. There was something different about him. He was everything she'd said and more.

Adelaide was just finishing moving a section of books when the shop's door chimes rang out. Walking to the front, she saw the postman had arrived. Four large boxes sat on the floor.

"Good morning, miss," the man said, holding out a slip and a pen. "Can you just sign this for me?"

"Of course," she replied, signing and handing the paper back to him.

"Sure glad to see you reopening this place. We need a bookstore in town," he told her, tipping his hat as he left.

Adelaide smiled as she lifted the first box onto the counter. She grabbed a pair of scissors and sliced through the tape, peeling back the flaps to reveal the glossy covers of the new children's books she'd ordered. A rush of excitement filled her. If this was how it felt every time a new order of books arrived, she was certain she'd be a bookseller for the rest of her life. It was even better than the thrill of Christmas morning.

She was reaching for the next box, already imagining the treasures inside, when the shop's door chimes rang out again.

However, this time when she looked up, it was Ewan she saw standing in the doorway.

"Let me get that for you," he insisted, taking the box from her and setting it on the counter.

Adelaide folded her arms tightly across her chest. "Ewan, what are you doing here?" A knot formed in her stomach, and heat flushed through her, part anger, part nerves. She hated that he had this effect on her.

"I just wanted to stop by. See how you were doing. Haven't heard from you in a few weeks."

"Oh?" she said. "I figured you'd be too busy, seeing as you have Mary and Kelly to keep you company." Her fingernails pressed crescents into her palms as she fought to quell her emotions.

Ewan stepped closer, unfazed, as if her knowing about the other women didn't even matter. He moved like nothing had changed, like he still had a right to her space as his hands found her waist and he pulled her hips into his.

"Oh, don't be like that," he murmured. "You know how much I like you. Those girls mean nothing."

She shoved him back, hard. "Oh, really? Not sure they'd agree with that."

"Addie, come on. We had fun. You really want to throw that away? What about that night at my place, when you—"

A crash rang out behind him. Ewan flinched, his eyes wide as the crushed velvet chair lay tipped over sideways on the floor.

"What the hell was that?" he asked, staring at the chair.

Adelaide smiled, a cool, quiet grin. "Your cue to get the hell out of here," she said, waving her hand toward the door.

"Babe, come on. It's my day off. Let's just—"

The chair slid violently across the floor, stopping inches from his shins. He stumbled back, eyes wide.

"What the fuck!"

Adelaide crossed to the door and opened it with a flourish. "Like I said, your cue to leave."

He shot her a look, defiance mixed with fear, glanced over his shoulder at the shop, then reluctantly walked out.

She slammed the door behind him with satisfying force, a laugh bubbling up from her chest. It felt *good* telling him to bugger off, and witnessing Pen's theatrics was the cherry on top.

"Oh, Pen," she said, grinning. "That was brilliant. Did you see his face?"

She picked up the chair, pushed it back into its spot, and returned to unboxing the books.

"Well, that was Ewan," she said, knowing Pen was still listening. "My first mistake in the world of being single."

She paused for a moment, her thoughts shooting back to the day in the loft with Ewan.

"Oh, wait, holy shit. It was you, wasn't it? The table in the loft the day he was here. You knocked it over." She laughed, shaking her head. "Wow. Even you knew he was bad news. I guess I was the only one who couldn't see it."

Her smile trailed off, the book order forgotten. She was quiet for a long while as the memory of that day returned. Ewan's voice, his hands, the tension, but then the crash of the table falling, glass shattering. Pen had done that, but why? One word kept surfacing. Jealousy. She almost laughed. It sounded ridiculous. Pen had barely known her then. But maybe that wasn't quite true. She'd been coming to the shop for a little over a week at that point, and he'd been here all that time. He'd known her far longer than she'd known him.

The idea that Pen might have been jealous of Ewan made her heart flutter and flip. There was no denying it: she was crushing hard on the invisible man in her bookshop, as crazy as that sounded.

"Well," she said to the empty room, shaking her head, "the last thing I have to do before we open next week is get these books put away and this new rug down."

She kicked the large rug she'd bought with Camie. She'd avoided laying it down until all the painting was finished, the final touch to her makeover of the space. The rug wasn't perfect, a little worn at the edges, but the color, deep rusts and greens, would bring the whole front of the shop to life. She planned to lay it lengthwise, through the center of the room, along the pathway through the bookshelves leading to the stairs. The old rug there now was worn thin in places, its colors so faded she couldn't even guess what they'd once been.

She rolled up the old one, dragged it to the back door, and hauled it into the alleyway for the bin man to pick up. She paused as she stepped back in. Hadn't the door been navy blue before? Now, a thick stained oak door with a brass handle stood in its place. She'd only used the back door a handful of times; she had to be misremembering.

"Weird," she muttered.

Shrugging it off, she dragged the new rug into position. It was larger than she remembered, stretching farther across the floor than the old one had. That wouldn't have been an issue, except it overlapped with the small rug tucked beneath the stairs.

She let out a sigh and walked over to it, lifting the small table that sat on top and setting it aside. Then she crouched down and tugged at the corner; the rug resisted, snagged on something hidden underneath. She pulled harder. *Must be caught on a nail or splintered floorboard.* When it finally broke free, she stopped. Beneath its edges, the floor looked… wrong. Not damaged, deliberate. There, just under the lip of the stair, was a faint seam in the boards. A ring. Brass, flush with the wood.

Her heart raced; she'd found it, the hidden room from Rowland's journal.

How had she not thought to look here? It had been disguised so perfectly, blending in with the floorboards around it. Hidden in plain sight.

Bending down, she curled her fingers around the cold metal ring, and the old wooden door groaned softly as she pulled it open. Faint, unexpected light flickered from below. A warm orange glow crept up the dark stone stairs, spilling into the shop like a whispered invitation for her to follow it.

She propped the door open, then hesitated, Pen's warning echoing in her mind, his unease about the watch and the danger it carried. For a moment, she stood still, half-expecting him to reach out and stop her. But he didn't.

Taking a deep breath, she descended into the cool, musty space below.

What greeted her sent her pulse into a frantic rhythm. The room was sparse, stone walls pressing in close around a single bookshelf on the far side, holding no more than a handful of aged volumes, and a large oak desk in its center. Its surface was bare except for an old Underwood typewriter. She didn't need to be told. This was it. This was where Pen wrote his letters to her.

Adelaide pulled out the captain's chair, sat at the desk, and ran her fingers over the cold metal typewriter keys, the same keys Pen touched night after night, each letter spelled out with care, with feeling. Her heart ached at the intimacy of it but she quickly pulled herself back. She looked down at the desk drawers and gave one a tug. She tried the next. And the next. But they were all locked. Why were they locked?

"The watch… it's in here, isn't it?" she whispered. "The key. There must be a key. Pen?"

The silence stretched on, but in the stillness, something clicked into place in her memory. The painting.

"John Dee's painting," she said aloud, rising quickly. "The key, taped on the back."

She raced up the stairs to her jacket and rifled through the pockets until her fingers brushed cold metal. Spinning the ring of keys, she spotted the smallest one, no bigger than something meant for a jewelry box. It rested between the key to the Feather Thorn and the one to her old house with Jeff, a slender wedge between all she had left behind and everything she was about to discover.

She swallowed hard, the weight of the moment settling in, then turned and hurried back into the hidden room.

As she rounded the back of the desk, something caught her eye. A piece of paper sticking out of the typewriter. It hadn't been there a second ago.

She sat down, heart pounding, and read the words typed on the crisp white paper: **Be careful.**

"I will," she said. Pen was there with her in the room, his presence was as real as the walls surrounding her.

She slid the key into the first lock and turned it. As the lock clicked open, a rush of nerves flooded through her.

Taking in a deep breath, she opened the drawer. Inside lay a neat stack of journals, just as Pen had described. She lifted one from its resting place, turned it over in her hands, and thumbed through a few pages before setting it back down. The next drawer contained star charts and what looked like some kind of handheld telescope. She glanced at the drawer to her left, the last one she hadn't opened yet, and paused. The watch. It had to be in here.

Doubt crept in like a cold draft. Did she really need to open it? If the watch was locked away, wasn't that safer? Wasn't that better than meddling with it as Pen had advised against?

But curiosity tugged harder. She had to know. She told herself she'd just look, and if the watch was there, she wouldn't touch it.

With a slow breath, she slid the key into the final lock and pulled the drawer open. It was empty, save for a small blue velvet bag.

Her fingers trembled as she lifted it out. The fabric was soft and thick, the weight inside unmistakable. Loosening the drawstrings, she pulled it open, just enough to peer in. Nestled against the rich blue lining was a shiny gold pocket watch. She tried to examine it inside the bag, but it slipped around too easily in its silk lining, its weight shifting with her touch. There was writing on its side, but the bag's shadows obscured the detail.

She knew she shouldn't touch it, but what if reading the inscription helped her understand? What if it held a clue? It might help her figure out how it worked so that when the time came, she could free Pen. Gently, she hooked two fingers inside and edged the watch just far enough to see.

They weren't words. Symbols, sharp and distinct, curled along the edge in a language she didn't recognize.

A chill swept the room, brushing her skin like icy breath. She could feel the energy pouring from it, charging the atmosphere in the room. She flinched, pulled the strings shut, securing the watch back inside the bag. Placing it gently back in the drawer, she pushed it shut, turning the key in a decisive twist.

"That little thing caused all this trouble?" she whispered into the empty room.

The typewriter clacked.

Once.

Twice.

A third time.

The keys clacked again, sudden and sharp, just inches away.

Adelaide froze; a shiver lifted the fine hairs on her arms. Her pulse thundered in her ears. He was here, not just a whisper in the walls or a feeling in the room, but communicating with her in real time.

Her gaze settled on the page, where the words glistened with fresh ink.

One word.

All caps.

YES

"Pen?"

Half of her wanted to laugh, the other half stood frozen. It was one thing to feel his presence, quite another to watch him leave ink on paper, like a ghost. He was here. She didn't know how, but he was here. A cautious smile pulled at her lips.

"I have an idea," she said, nudging the typewriter to the side of the desk, making room. "Let's try talking like this. What do you think?"

The room fell still, then the tapping of keys, and on the paper, the words appeared:

I think you're brilliant.

Adelaide smiled fully and opened the first drawer again, pulling out the journals. Five in total.

"Are these all Rowland's?" she asked, flipping through the pages.

No, also John Dee's, Pen typed.

She studied each journal in turn, thumbing through them slowly.

"Do you know what all of this means?" She looked at the pages filled with what looked like mathematical equations.

Yes. Over the years, I've learned how to read them. In my timeline, I have notes on the wall of this room that connect things from each of the journals with the watch. But it's as if something's missing.

"Like what? Another journal?"

A pause, then the keys clacked again.

I hadn't thought of that. But yes. You're one smart cookie, Adelaide.

She laughed. "You'd better believe it." She reopened the drawer where the journals had been stored. "Are you sure you've checked everywhere?"

I know every inch of this room and the bookshop. If there is another journal, it's not here, Pen typed.

"Hmm, I wonder," she muttered, tapping along the walls and bottom of the drawer. Each knock echoed back the same hollow sound, but she wasn't convinced. She ran her fingers along the edges, pressing gently at each corner, feeling for a catch, a groove, a hidden compartment.

Nothing.

Adelaide frowned, then pulled the entire drawer out and set it on the floor. She leaned over, peering into the dark cavity it had left behind. A whisper of cool air brushed her fingertips as she reached in, her hand groping along the back paneled walls. For a moment, there was nothing, just smooth wood and empty space. Then, her fingers brushed against a firm edge tucked down toward the side, near the base of the second drawer.

Her pulse quickened. She wiggled the object loose, slowly working it free from the narrow gap, and drew it into the golden light of the room. A beat-up leather-bound journal lay in her hands. The cover was cracked, its spine fraying, the surface soft with handling.

"Journal number six," she breathed, setting it on top of the others, her heart still racing.

The keys of the old typewriter clicked once again.

Well, I'll be damned, appeared boldly on the crisp white paper.

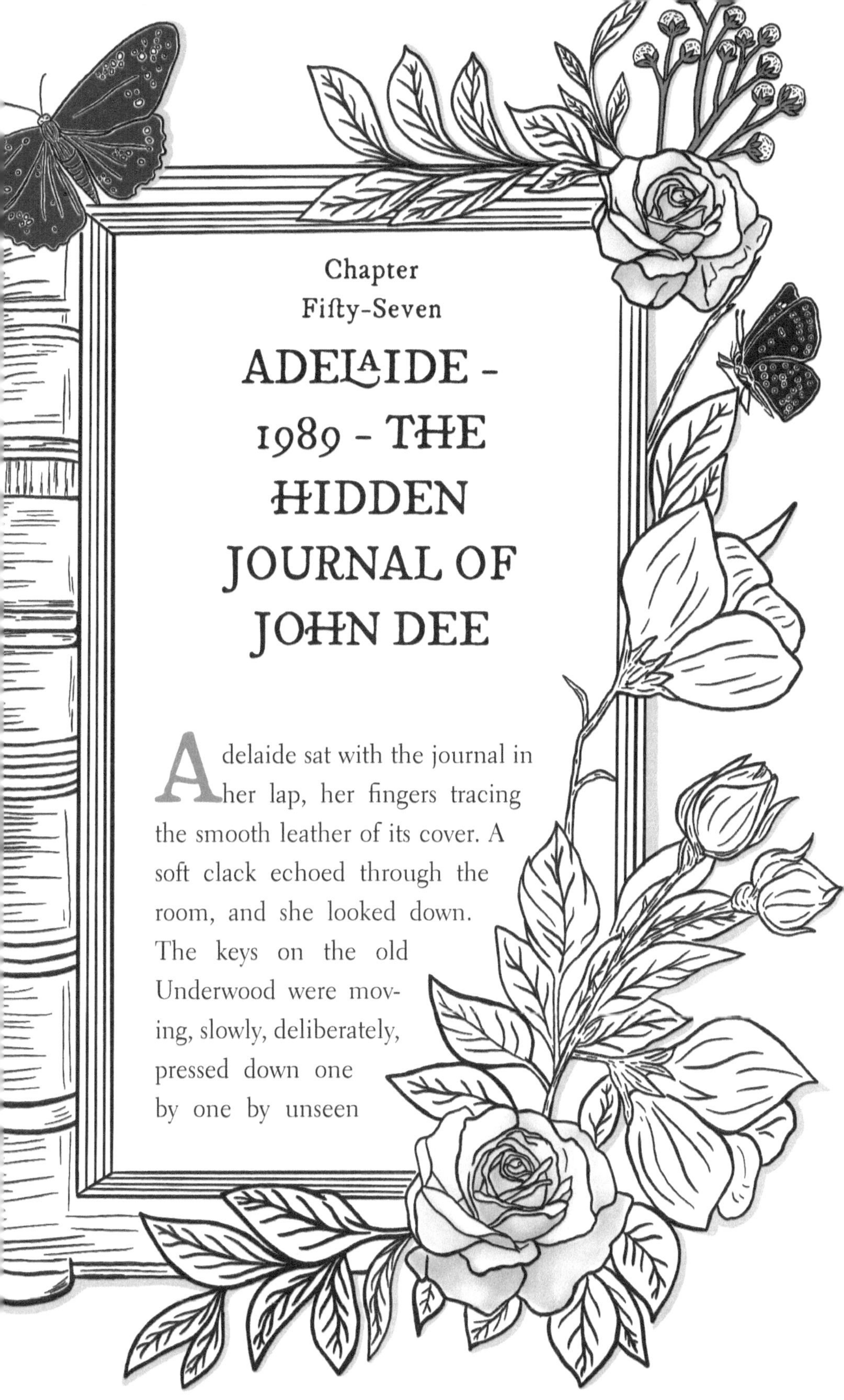

ADELAIDE – 1989 – THE HIDDEN JOURNAL OF JOHN DEE

Adelaide sat with the journal in her lap, her fingers tracing the smooth leather of its cover. A soft clack echoed through the room, and she looked down. The keys on the old Underwood were moving, slowly, deliberately, pressed down one by one by unseen hands. She stared, transfixed, as metal arms struck the ribbon, imprinting letters onto the page.

Open it, Pen had typed.

She hesitated, the air thick with a strange, ancient energy, one that felt both forbidding and powerful. Somehow, the journal felt heavier with the weight of secrets it held. Swallowing her apprehension, she slowly cracked it open. No burst of light, no pull through time. Just parchment the color of old tea and ink faded to a soft brown.

Pen's presence pressed close, stronger than ever. Adelaide could sense him standing just over her shoulder, breath ghosting against her neck, attention fixed on the page.

She cleared her throat and read the first line aloud:

"September 5th, 1582. Today, after a most intense scrying session with Edward, he received word that the device Giordano and I have labored upon these many years must be completed before the Pope enacts his new Gregorian calendar next month."

She turned, speaking over her shoulder to the empty air. "Pen, this is John Dee's actual journal. It's not like the others. Those must have just been field notes."

She didn't need a reply to know he'd heard her. But the keys clacked anyway, the carriage shifting forward with a soft metallic ding.

I think you're right. Maybe it will tell us how the watch operates.

She nodded, flipping the page. "My thoughts exactly."

Together they read on, page after page, absorbed in Dee's words, how he had created the Astral Synchronum, the geometry involved, the lunar timing, the spiritual preparation, its intended purpose. And then came the darker passages, entries inked with urgency, words written by a hand that seemed to tremble on the page. How, when they'd tried to activate it, something had gone terribly wrong. Adelaide's breath caught as she turned to the next entry. But before she could read on, the chimes at the shop's front door rang out, their sound drifting down into the hidden room.

"Did you hear that?" she whispered.

Click. Click. Click.

YES

"Me too. Hold on. I'll be right back. Don't read on without me," she said, jumping to her feet.

She sprinted up the stairs, her heart pounding. Whoever had come in couldn't be allowed to find the trapdoor. As she emerged from the hidden space, she breathed a quiet sigh of relief; the person hadn't wandered in that far yet.

She quickly shut the trapdoor and hurried toward the front of the shop.

"Addie, are you here?" a familiar voice called.

Adelaide stopped in her tracks at the sound of her name. Carolyn. The last person she'd expected. Honestly, she'd figured it would take coaxing, or maybe even bribery, to even get her great-aunt through the door for the grand opening. And here she was, just popping in.

Truthfully, she hadn't seen much of Carolyn since moving into the Feather Thorn, aside from a brief visit to collect a few odds and ends from the cabin. She'd wanted to give her aunt time to adjust, knowing that buying the bookshop had likely stirred up unwelcome memories for her.

"Carolyn? What are you doing here?" Adelaide asked as she rounded the corner. Carolyn stood framed by the doorway, bundled in a puffy leopard-print jacket that nearly grazed the floor. There was a strange look in her eyes, and Adelaide couldn't tell if it was skepticism or old memories.

Adelaide raised an eyebrow. "Nice coat."

"Thank you. It matches my bag," Carolyn said with a grin, swinging the purple leopard-print purse side to side.

Adelaide laughed. "It certainly does."

"Camie found it for me. I've been looking for something like this for years now."

Adelaide blinked. Of course. She'd seen Camie with a leopard-print something tucked into her pile when they'd checked out at one of the secondhand shops in Glasgow.

"She really can find anything," Adelaide teased. "So, what brings you here? Shouldn't you have closed up hours ago?" She glanced at the clock; it read quarter past seven.

"Oh, I had a big tea order to pack up for London. Needs to ship first thing, so I had to stay a bit late." Carolyn sighed. "Plus, I did promise I'd stop in to see what you've done with the place. I thought maybe we could grab a bite to eat after. I don't feel much like cooking tonight, and I haven't seen you in a few days."

Adelaide glanced over her shoulder toward the trapdoor; she'd wanted to spend the rest of the night reading the journal with Pen. To see if there were answers on how to free him, but she couldn't say no to Carolyn.

"Sure. Let me give you a tour first," she offered, flicking on all the overhead lights.

Carolyn followed as Adelaide led her through the shop, pointing out the things she had done. She started with the children's section, then on to the cozy reading nook, and finally to the wall where her paintings hung, each one adding a touch of warmth and color.

"It looks great, lass," Carolyn said, her eyes glued to her paintings. "You've done a wonderful job."

"Thanks, it's coming together nicely. I'm hoping to open next week."

As they made their way back to the front, Carolyn paused mid-step, her head tilting slightly. "Is there someone else here?"

Adelaide tried to keep her expression neutral. "No. Just me. Why?"

"I thought I heard you talking to someone when I came in, that's all." Carolyn glanced toward the back. Her eyes didn't just drift, they searched, like she expected someone to be there.

The silence held too long. Adelaide forced a laugh. "Probably the pipes. Or me talking to myself."

She swallowed hard. Carolyn definitely knew more than she'd let on. She always had. And that look in her eye said she hadn't just heard something, she'd sensed it. Perhaps she knew Pen was here.

"Come on, let's grab that bite to eat," Adelaide said, forcing a casual tone. "I wanted to ask you more about the guy who owned this place before me, Pen Turner." She watched Carolyn closely, searching for any sign of hesitation.

Carolyn's expression barely shifted. "Pen? Well, not sure I'll have much to tell you. I didn't really know him well."

"Oh? Dottie said you two were friends," Adelaide countered, pressing gently.

"We knew each other, sure, but I wouldn't say we were friends." Carolyn's gaze flickered, betraying a hint of discomfort. "He gave me a book once, and I painted the sign out front. That's about it."

Adelaide nodded slowly. "Oh really, what book?"

Carolyn waved a hand, too quickly. "Oh, I don't know. Something old. It's in my guest room somewhere, buried under layers of dust, I'm sure."

And there it was, the flicker again. A too-fast answer, eyes that didn't quite meet hers. Adelaide held her smile, but her mind was already turning. The locked guest room. The shadow she'd seen under the door. There was something in there, something Carolyn was hiding. And she could feel it deep in her bones; whatever it was, it had to do with Rowland, Pen and this shop, and she was going to find out exactly what.

"Well," Carolyn said briskly, turning toward the door, "we'd better go if we want to get into the Royal Mantle before the kitchen closes." But before stepping out, she glanced over her shoulder one last time, her eyes scanning the rows of books.

"Let me just grab my things. I'll meet you at the car," Adelaide replied, watching as Carolyn disappeared into the chilly night air outside.

As the door shut, she spun on her heel and sprinted back to the trapdoor. Lifting it just enough, she whispered down to Pen, "I'll be back. Wait for me."

Then, letting it close, she grabbed her jacket and stepped outside into the cold. Tonight, she would try her best to get Carolyn to slip, to say something, anything, that would reveal just how much she really knew. And if that didn't work, well, she wasn't above pulling a James Bond and sneaking into that locked guest room herself.

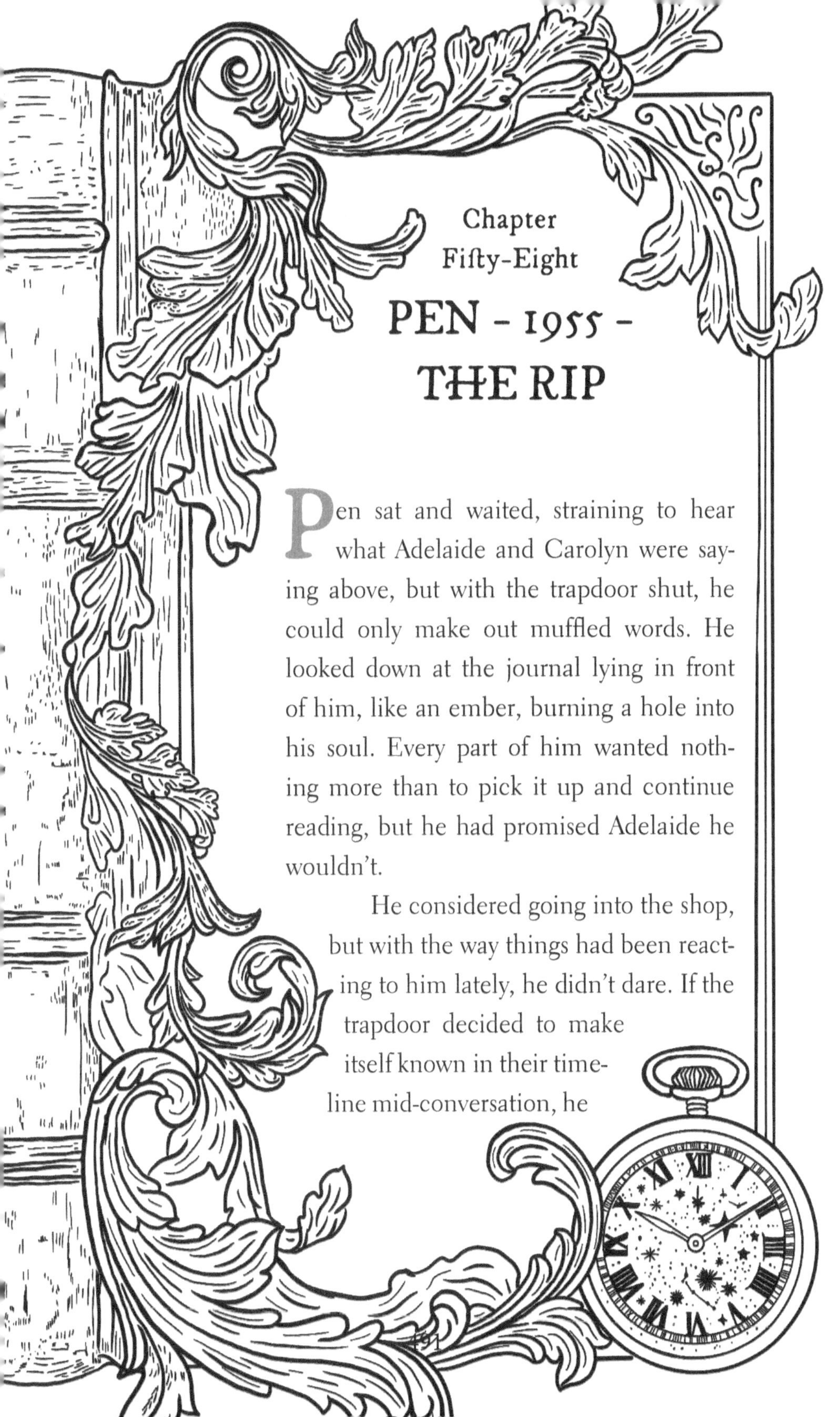

PEN - 1955 -
THE RIP

Pen sat and waited, straining to hear what Adelaide and Carolyn were saying above, but with the trapdoor shut, he could only make out muffled words. He looked down at the journal lying in front of him, like an ember, burning a hole into his soul. Every part of him wanted nothing more than to pick it up and continue reading, but he had promised Adelaide he wouldn't.

He considered going into the shop, but with the way things had been reacting to him lately, he didn't dare. If the trapdoor decided to make itself known in their time-line mid-conversation, he might do more than just startle Carolyn. So, he waited.

When the front door finally closed behind them, he headed back to the apartment to make himself and Frankie some supper.

It felt strange, coming into the apartment now. For years, it had been both his home and his prison, but now it belonged to Adelaide, and she had begun to leave her mark on it. He didn't mind, though; he actually liked the little things she'd brought with her. The painting above the sofa, the cozy blankets, and the framed photos. Even the clutter of her mismatched mugs. All of it softened the place. Well, all except for that god-awful elephant lamp she'd placed on the side table in the living room. He could have done without that.

He opened the fridge, reaching for the ground beef, when a strange flicker, sharp and quick, caught his eye through the window. Was it lightning? A storm approaching?

He turned and crossed to the window, peering out over the quiet town. It couldn't have been lightning; the sky was clear, the moon bright overhead. His gaze swept the street. The apothecary glowed under the orange wash of the streetlamps. As his focus shifted farther down… he froze.

The bakery was gone.

So were the shops beside it.

In their place stood a long stone wall, moss-covered and ancient, running alongside a narrow road that weaved past a cluster of tall oak trees that stretched out into the countryside. Beyond that, the moon lit up a mountain range he didn't recognize. It looked nothing like what had been there before, as if it were an entirely different place altogether.

Pen's gut twisted. He blinked hard, hoping it was some trick of the light. But the dark stretch where the buildings had been didn't change. Nothing moved. Nothing existed there anymore.

The air thickened, as if the pressure had dropped and the shop was bracing for something. Not a storm outside, but one curling just beneath the surface of reality. It was the same wrongness he'd felt the night the window vanished, when the shelves disappeared. But this time, it wasn't just a flicker. It had settled in, rooted deep, like something had taken hold and wasn't letting go.

The fear that had been humming beneath the surface began to swell. This wasn't just about being trapped anymore. Something far worse was taking hold; his timeline was being rewritten into something new, something wrong.

"What the hell is going on?" he muttered, staring at the street, half of it still Helensburgh, the other half twisted into something he didn't recognize.

Fear flooded through him. This wasn't just some missing bookcases anymore. It was something far beyond that now; something was beginning to fracture his reality, pulling parts of this place away and adding things that didn't belong. He was glad it seemed to be confined to his timeline, since Adelaide hadn't mentioned anything strange happening in hers. That was a small comfort. But he still needed to figure it out, and fast.

"Frankie," he called, already moving toward the door. "Come on, boy." He didn't wait for the fox to follow. He sprinted down into the bookshop and over to the trapdoor, yanked it open, and descended into the secret room beneath the shop.

What had shifted tonight to push everything over the edge? It always came back to the watch. That damn watch. Tonight, Adelaide touched it, and now, it seemed the thread holding everything together had started to completely unravel. Why? It didn't make any sense. There was no astrological event, no reason her touching it should've triggered anything. Yet it had.

Pen reached the desk and turned to the journal still lying on its top; his fingers tracing the edges of the worn pages. He'd promised Adelaide he wouldn't continue without her, but after what he'd just seen, how could he not? The answers were right here, and the world was crumbling around him.

He sat down in the old captain's chair, and it groaned its welcome. "Sorry, Adelaide," he whispered into the stillness as he lit a cigarette, the smoke curling from it as he clenched it between his fingers.

Flipping to the last page they'd read, his eyes raced, scanning the next several pages. Symbols, diagrams, and a warning. A single line stared up at him, the ink darker, messier, written in haste. He read it once, then again, aloud:

"A week has passed since that night in Dunblane, and at first, life appeared to carry on as normal. But now, subtle discrepancies have begun to emerge, each one hinting at a fissure in reality as we know it. The clock in my study, a trusted companion for years, chimed out thirteen times at midnight. This I could have dismissed as a malfunction or overwinding, perhaps. But when I stepped outside to observe the stars, I noticed that one of my most reliable fixed points, a star I often used for navigation, had shifted. It no longer aligned with the constellation it had anchored for centuries, as though the heavens themselves had been rearranged."

John Dee had seen it too. All those years ago, he'd experienced the same unsettling phenomena. When he and Giordano created the Astral Synchronum, they had unknowingly caused a rip in time itself.

Pen read on. Dee and Giordano had tried to mend the tear, weaving together a makeshift patch, a desperate attempt to hold their timeline steady. But the solution had come with a warning: once sealed, the device was never to be used again. Another activation, and the stitch wouldn't hold. The tear would rip open again. The delicate fix they'd managed would unravel completely, and this time, the damage might be irreversible.

Pen's fingers tightened on the edge of the journal.

Rowland had used the watch, desperate to save Carolyn, and in doing so, he'd peeled back the fragile patch John Dee and Giordano had stitched over the rip in time. Then Pen, in his ignorance, had activated it again, loosening it even further. And now, with every passing moment, it was unraveling, the last fragile threads barely holding it together.

Even Adelaide merely touching it seemed to have caused more strings to break.

He felt it then, the quiet give of something beginning to slip. The world he knew was thinning. Not all at once, but inch by inch. And the replacement was a reality he didn't recognize. This was no longer about escaping a time loop. If he didn't find a way to stop the tear, to fix the patch, there might not be a reality to escape to.

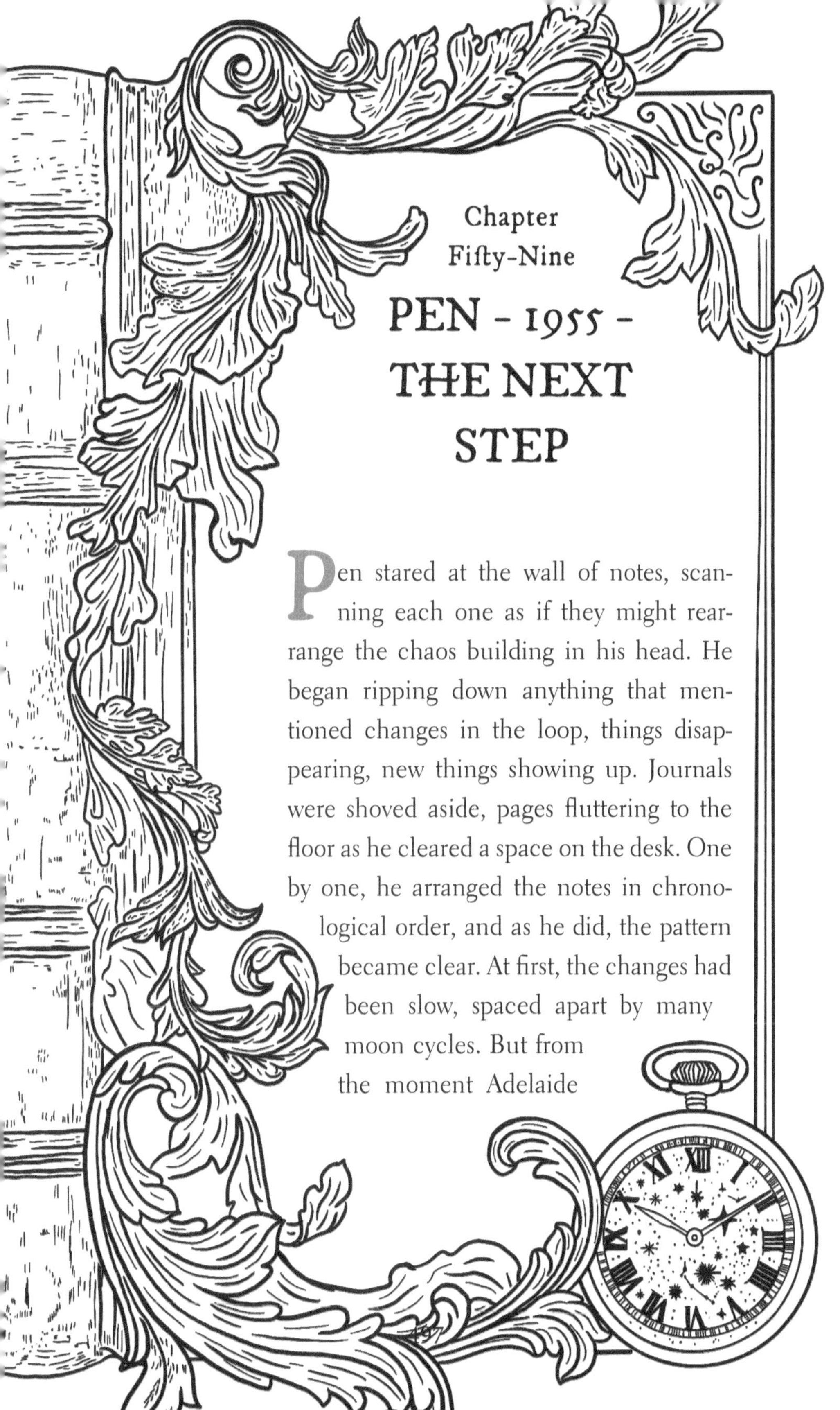

Chapter
Fifty-Nine

PEN - 1955 - THE NEXT STEP

Pen stared at the wall of notes, scanning each one as if they might rearrange the chaos building in his head. He began ripping down anything that mentioned changes in the loop, things disappearing, new things showing up. Journals were shoved aside, pages fluttering to the floor as he cleared a space on the desk. One by one, he arranged the notes in chronological order, and as he did, the pattern became clear. At first, the changes had been slow, spaced apart by many moon cycles. But from the moment Adelaide arrived, the pace had accelerated. He'd known this, sensed it, but seeing it mapped out in front of him hit him like cold water: the loop was unraveling.

Gone were the days of missing books and mysterious scraps of paper. Now, half the shop's bookcases had vanished, and the northeast side of town was simply gone, replaced by a landscape he didn't recognize.

He leaned on the edge of the desk, breathing through the tightness in his chest. The more he looked, the more his impending fate became impossible to ignore. If things continued at this pace, he feared that the next astrological event, on the twenty-first, might be too late.

A cold fear coiled inside him, threatening to strike at his usual calm. Then, the shop door chimes rang out, their sweet, familiar melody breaking him free of his dark thoughts.

"Adelaide," he whispered. Just her name on his lips eased his mind, but the next sound shattered any relief: her scream, sharp and panicked.

"Adelaide?" he shouted, already halfway to the stairs. He took them two at a time, shoes thudding up the narrow passage. His shoulder grazed the frame of the trapdoor as he vaulted through, palms planted on the wooden edge, the momentum carrying him into the shop.

He stopped. Dead in his tracks.

Right in the middle of the bookshop stood a post, thick as a tree trunk, rising from the floorboards to the ceiling. And tied to it with a coarse rope was a goat. Its amber eyes blinked at him slowly, chewing something with the kind of unbothered calm only animals seemed to manage, even in the middle of something utterly impossible. It let out a single long, loud bleat that rang across the shelves, grounding him in the reality of the moment.

It wasn't the sight of the goat that startled him most. It was the fact that Adelaide was seeing it too, in her timeline. This wasn't just about losing himself anymore; it was about losing her, losing everything they knew.

"Pen!" Adelaide's voice jolted him back to movement. He knocked a book off the nearest shelf, the heavy thud letting her know he was there.

"Pen, what's going on?" she asked, her voice trembling.

He walked to the trapdoor and slammed it as hard as he could, hoping the sound would carry through to her side. She flinched and turned toward him. Knowing his meaning, she hurried down into the hidden room.

Pen moved to the typewriter, fingers hovering briefly before he slid a fresh sheet of paper in, and the Underwood rattled to life.

Go upstairs and look in the John Dee book on the counter.

Adelaide was up the stairs in a heartbeat. Pen listened as she moved across the shop to the front counter, pausing where the book lay. A moment later, her footsteps echoed above, then she reappeared in the hidden room, letter in hand.

She rounded the desk and sat, unfolding the letter with shaking hands. He watched her read the words he'd written only days ago, when the first cracks had widened into something he could no longer ignore. The muscles in her face tightened as she finished.

"Pen… why didn't you tell me sooner?" she whispered as she set the letter down, the color draining from her face.

He let his hands speak for him again.

I didn't want to scare you. I thought it was only happening to me. I didn't know your world was changing too.

She swallowed hard. "It's been happening for a while now.

I should have said something, but I thought I was just… forgetting things, misremembering things. I couldn't remember the color of the back door, or where I'd placed a book." She shook her head. "I kept blaming myself, thought I was losing it, but this—" She gestured toward the shop above them. "A giant post and a goat? That's not just me being forgetful."

Pen hesitated. Then, he carefully responded through the keys.

Don't be mad, but I read ahead in the journal. After seeing half of Helensburgh was missing in my timeline, I had to know what was happening. Read the next three entries.

She picked up the journal and turned to the entry she had left off on. As she scanned the pages, her expression shifted with every word. Her fingers tightened on the book, and when she finally closed it, she looked straight to where he stood.

She couldn't see him, but she could sense him. He could feel it. Twice now, her gaze had landed right where he was, as if she could almost see the shape of him in the air. The divide between them was thinning. He didn't know what it meant yet, only that their connection seemed to be getting stronger.

"The watch… it ripped a hole in time," Adelaide mumbled. "And when Rowland used it to save Carolyn, it broke the mend John Dee placed on it."

Yes, Pen clicked.

Adelaide's fingers hovered over the journal, her brow drawn tight. "Pen, this isn't good. We need to figure out how to stop this."

He pressed the keys in slow, deliberate strokes, each one heavy with what he already feared.

Rowland must have known the risks. He was the one who hid the journal. He knew the whole story and what could happen

if the watch was ever used again. He risked time itself to save her.

She didn't answer right away. Instead, she bit her thumbnail, a far-off look in her eyes, before she finally spoke. "I think Carolyn knows something. She's hiding something from me… something about you and Rowland." Then she leaned forward and picked up a scrap of paper from the desk, its surface covered in scribbled dates. "What are these?"

Pen's breath caught.

You can see my notes?

That wasn't possible, was it? Other than Frankie and his letters to her, nothing physical from his timeline had ever crossed through the veil. Everything from his world had always remained locked away with him.

"Yes… What are they?"

I've been tracking everything. I wrote down everything that disappeared or suddenly appeared in my timeline.

Adelaide nodded, flipping through them. "Smart." Her hand stopped on one marked September 8th. "That's around the time I bought the Feather Thorn. Looks like things started happening more often after that."

They did. I don't know why, though.

She rubbed her forehead, a slow, weary motion. "Pen, we need to finish reading this journal. And… I need to get into Carolyn's guest room. She's keeping something in there that's connected to this place, I just know it. It might help us."

Pen hesitated. Her face was pale, the dim light catching the shimmer of sweat on her temple.

She winced as each clack of the typewriter echoed in the quiet room.

Are you okay?

"I'm fine… just a headache, that's all."

There was a hollow beneath her eyes that hadn't been there earlier. Then, as she leaned forward, a single drop of blood slipped from her nose and fell onto one of his notes, leaving a bloom of red.

Adelaide… your nose.

She wiped it with the back of her hand, eyes widening as she stared at the red streak across her knuckles. "God, I haven't had a nosebleed since I was a kid."

Panic tightened in his chest.

GO TO BED.

You need to rest.

We can pick this up in the morning.

Adelaide sighed, folding her arms. "Okay, fine. But… what am I supposed to do about the goat?" A small, weak laugh escaped her. "I can't believe I'm even asking that question."

Just let it out the back. It'll wander over to the field, and I'm sure some farmer will be glad to find it roaming around in the morning.

"Good idea," she said, already rising. She reached the foot of the stairs, then stopped, glancing back over her shoulder.

"Pen… will you come up and sleep on the couch tonight?"

Three soft clicks sounded from the old Underwood, but she didn't turn around to see what he'd written. She just smiled, knowing the answer, and walked up the stairs.

Pen stood still for a breath, the lamplight flickering over the desk where her blood stained the edge of his note, a small, vivid mark that should've been impossible. But it was there. Real.

Proof that the barrier between their worlds was thinning.

It should've felt like a breakthrough. A sign they were getting closer. But instead, it knotted up something deep inside him.

The more the veil thinned, the wider the tear grew between their realities, letting in a world that was neither hers nor his.

He moved toward the stairs, toward her. The space between them had never felt so close. Or so dangerous.

They were running out of time. Not just to save him, but to save her. To save everything.

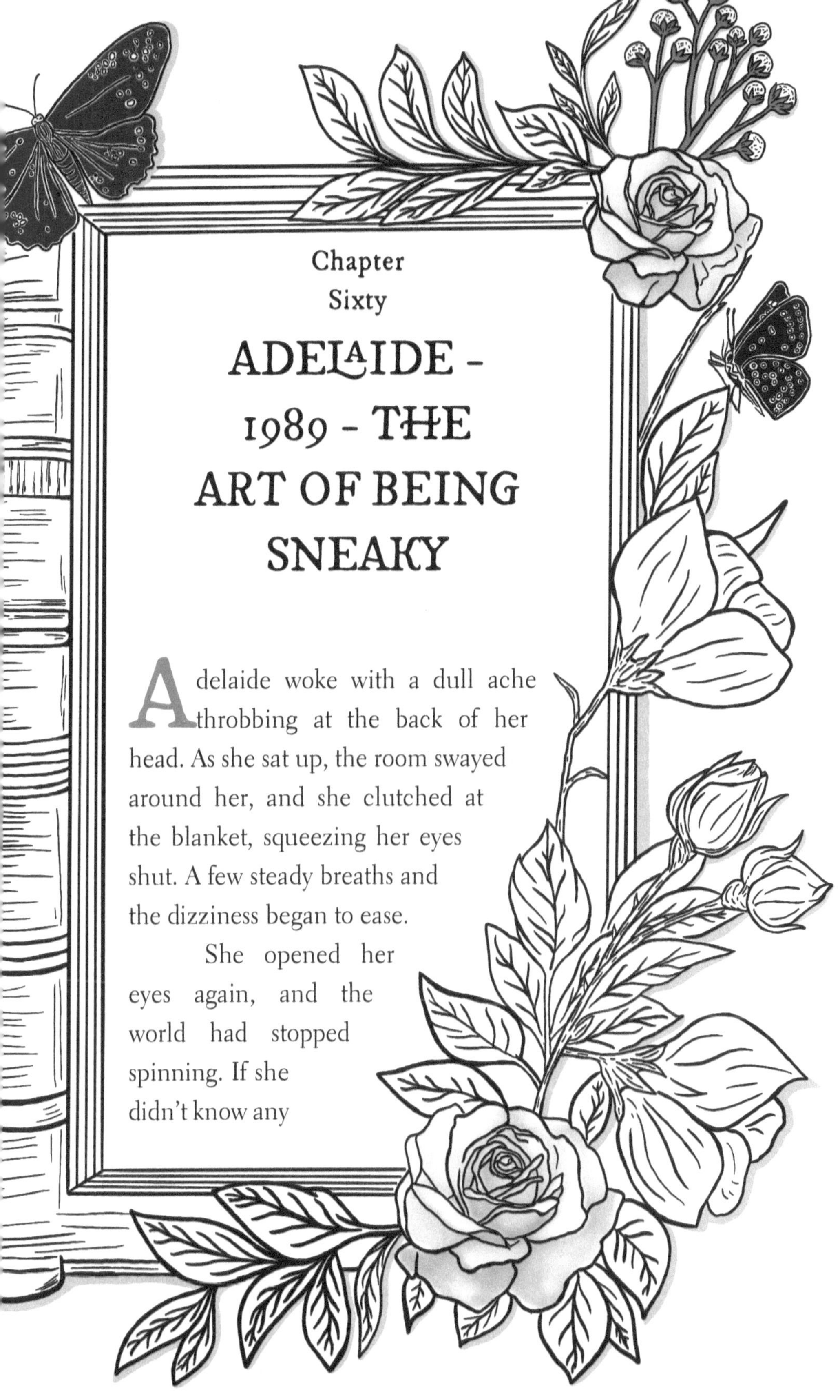

ADELAIDE – 1989 – THE ART OF BEING SNEAKY

Adelaide woke with a dull ache throbbing at the back of her head. As she sat up, the room swayed around her, and she clutched at the blanket, squeezing her eyes shut. A few steady breaths and the dizziness began to ease.

She opened her eyes again, and the world had stopped spinning. If she didn't know any better, she'd have sworn she was nursing a hangover, but the last drink she'd had was at the pub with Camie a few nights ago.

Pulling on her old cardigan, she made her way to the bathroom. Turning on the tap, she splashed cold water on her face, then glanced up at her reflection and flinched. Two dark circles clung beneath her eyes, and her skin was pale, almost paper-white. She looked awful.

"I've overworked myself," she said, trying to shake off the unease.

The smell of fresh coffee tugged her into the kitchen, and she smiled. Pen had stayed the night in the flat, just as she'd asked.

By the percolator, a folded letter rested against her favorite mug. Her smile deepened, and for a moment, the ache in her head and the weight of her worries lifted. She poured herself a cup, carried it to the table, and sat.

Blowing gently on her coffee, she took a cautious sip, then unfolded the letter.

My Dearest Adelaide,

I hope this coffee finds you in your timeline and that you are feeling better this morning. I am worried about you and think you should take a few days to rest. It pains me to see you unwell. What I wouldn't give to hold you, to comfort you there in your time. Please take it easy today, and when you read this, tell me how you are. I'll be sitting on the sofa with Frankie.

Yours,

Pen

When she finished reading, she looked over at the sofa, her

heart swelling. What she wouldn't give to feel his arms around her, to feel his presence beyond ink and paper.

She stood and moved over to the sofa, sensing the shape of him there, the way the air felt subtly warmer, the quiet more meaningful, and she sat down beside that feeling.

"Good morning, Pen. Thank you for staying last night, I feel better this morning," she said, though her voice caught a little on the last word. It wasn't quite a lie; the headache was beginning to subside, but the exhaustion was bone-deep, and she hoped he couldn't tell.

The flat remained silent, and she wished she'd brought the typewriter up here, though she wasn't sure if it would work outside the hidden room.

"I wish you were really here," she whispered into the stillness, "in my time, with me."

As the words left her lips, something moved beside her, a flicker, like a candle flame in a breeze. Out of nowhere, Frankie appeared, curled up in a tiny red ball right next to her thigh.

The little fox cracked one sleepy eye open, tail flicking lazily. He didn't run this time; he stayed nestled beside her, his warm fur brushing against her side.

She stared at him, hardly daring to move, then slowly, she reached out, her fingers grazing the soft fur between his ears. She expected him to dart away, to vanish back into Pen's timeline, but he didn't. He just leaned into her touch, pressing his head into her hand as if to say, *Don't stop.*

She smiled and looked up toward the space where she knew Pen must be watching. "He's finally warming up to me."

For a little while, the loneliness quieted as she stayed with him, stroking the fox's soft fur. Then she blinked and just like that, he was gone.

This is madness, the whole thing, she thought, staring at the empty spot on the sofa, the cushion still faintly indented, the fabric still warm from where Frankie had been only moments before. The room felt too quiet now.

She sighed and lifted her mug. The coffee had gone cold, but she drank anyway, then walked to the window, tugging her cardigan tighter around her shoulders.

"Pen, we have some sleuthing to do today," she said, gazing outside. "As soon as Carolyn arrives at the apothecary, I'm going to her house and I'm getting into that guest room. She was tight-lipped at dinner, but I know she's hiding something important in there, I can feel it in my bones."

She could feel Pen beside her now, in the way the air shifted, like a presence brushing just out of reach. Her thoughts drifted to the fractured world he had described, how from this very window, half of Helensburgh no longer existed in his reality.

"I wish you could tell me if things have got worse in your timeline," she murmured.

A faint cloud of breath appeared on the windowpane, as if the glass itself had exhaled. Then, slowly, the word **SAME** emerged, traced into the fog.

Stunned, she stepped back, the coffee mug in her hand tilting, a thin stream slipping over the rim as she set it down without looking. It was as if everything stilled, the air, the light, even her breath, and she could feel the veil thin as he broke through. How was Pen doing this?

"Pen," she whispered. She reached out with tentative fingers, brushing the still-damp glass. "The same, that's good." She smiled. "Well, looks like we don't need to bring the Underwood up here after all. "We're learning, aren't we? Little by little."

However, her smile was replaced by a frown when her eyes flickered to the living room. One of the side tables was now missing.

"Pen, I think you should keep reading John Dee's journal while I'm gone. We need to double down and figure this out. It's still days from the twenty-first, and we don't know how much more time we have."

Another wisp of fog curled across the glass. **AGREE**

She nodded. "Good. Okay, I'm going to get ready. Keep an eye out for Carolyn for me, okay?"

She made her way to the bedroom, the cardigan slipping off her shoulders as she gathered her clothes. In the bathroom, she shut the door and twisted the shower tap; the water hummed through the pipes, and steam began to fill the room. She peeled off her nightshirt and winced. Her shoulder ached, no, burned. It was sharp, raw, like she'd been scalded. Turning, she strained to see her reflection in the mirror, but the steam had already fogged up the glass.

"You in here?" she whispered.

She thought of his voice in the letters, the gentleness of his concern. The way he wrote *Dearest Adelaide*, like she was something precious in a world coming undone. For a fleeting moment, she wondered if Pen was the gentleman he seemed to be, or if he was in the bathroom now, watching her. The thought should have unsettled her, a man she couldn't see, couldn't touch, possibly standing just a breath away, but instead, it sent a warmth racing through her body.

"It's okay if you are," she murmured to the fog, trailing her finger through its mist.

Her eyes stayed fixed on the mirror, willing the words *I'm here* to appear, but none came. Of course he was the gentleman she believed him to be.

Smiling to herself, she stepped into the shower and let the hot water soak through her hair, stream down her aching spine, pour over the blistered skin of her shoulder. It stung, but she didn't pull away; she turned into it, letting the heat push the tension from her muscles, letting it wake her fully.

By the time she stepped into the kitchen again, she felt more like herself, at least on the outside. Dressed, makeup on, hair crimped, and bangs curled into place. She'd taken her time getting ready today, and she knew why. She wanted to look good for him. For Pen.

At the window, she spotted the *Custom Teas* sign out on the pavement in front of the apothecary.

"Was it Carolyn or Jen who opened today?"

A soft breath fogged the glass. **Carolyn**

"Perfect," she said, grinning. "Okay, I'm heading over. That should give me a few hours before she comes home for lunch."

A fresh swirl of fog formed. **OK**... then another... **Good Luck!**

"Thanks. You too. I hope those last few pages give us something useful. And if I'm lucky, maybe I'll find something that will help us too," she said, grabbing her bag and heading for the door.

Stepping out into the crisp morning air, Adelaide zipped up her coat and walked toward her car. Out of the corner of her eye, she caught sight of Dottie. Heart racing, she quickly slipped into the driver's seat, started the engine, and pulled away before Dottie could wave her down. Guilt stabbed at her. Dottie didn't deserve to be dodged like that, but she couldn't afford questions right now. Time was limited, and if she was lucky, she had just over two hours, maybe less, to snoop around before Carolyn came home for lunch.

As she drove out of town, her eyes caught something off in the distance. She slowed the car, squinting through the windshield. A giant barn off to the right, standing alone in a field of wheat. She slammed on the brakes. That had been a forest the day before. "What the hell?" She gripped the steering wheel tighter. Things in her timeline seemed to be catching up with Pen's now.

Her stomach was a ball of nerves, and her mind was filling with an overwhelming number of questions. Reality was fraying at its edges, but she couldn't stop thinking about Carolyn. About what she might be hiding. There was no reason to keep secrets unless those secrets meant something bad.

She wasn't sure she could handle much more. The fact that both her and Pen's timelines were rapidly shifting into something different, *somewhere* different, was worrisome enough.

She pulled into the driveway, parking in line with the path to the stone cabin. If Carolyn returned early, she'd claim she'd forgotten something, a book, a scarf, anything.

Flipping over the pot of dead chrysanthemums by the door, she retrieved the spare key and let herself inside.

The familiar scent of herbs and woodsmoke greeted her, and she bit her lip, guilt creeping in. Sneaking around like this felt wrong, but when time itself was unraveling, unusual measures were necessary.

She kicked off her shoes and hurried up the stairs. She tried the guest room door, but just like before, it was locked. With a sigh, she went to Carolyn's bedroom. Everything looked just as it had the last time: bed neatly made, not a cushion out of place. It was a room preserved, unused, oddly impersonal. It had the look you'd expect from an old woman's room, all flowery fabrics and lace trim, but it was a far cry from the cluttered, eccentric charm of downstairs.

A wave of guilt washed over her as she began rummaging through drawers in search of the key to the guest room. However, each one came up empty.

"Where is it?" she muttered, massaging the dull throb at her temple.

Then she remembered what Carolyn had said about the beams in the house being good hiding spots. She turned, stepped out of Carolyn's room, and walked straight to the one beside the guest room's doorframe. Running her fingers along the backside of the rough, aged wood, she felt something cold beneath her touch.

A small brass key slipped from its hiding place and landed in her hand.

"Bingo."

She slid the key into the guest room's lock and turned. With a soft click, the door swung open, and what she saw inside stopped her cold.

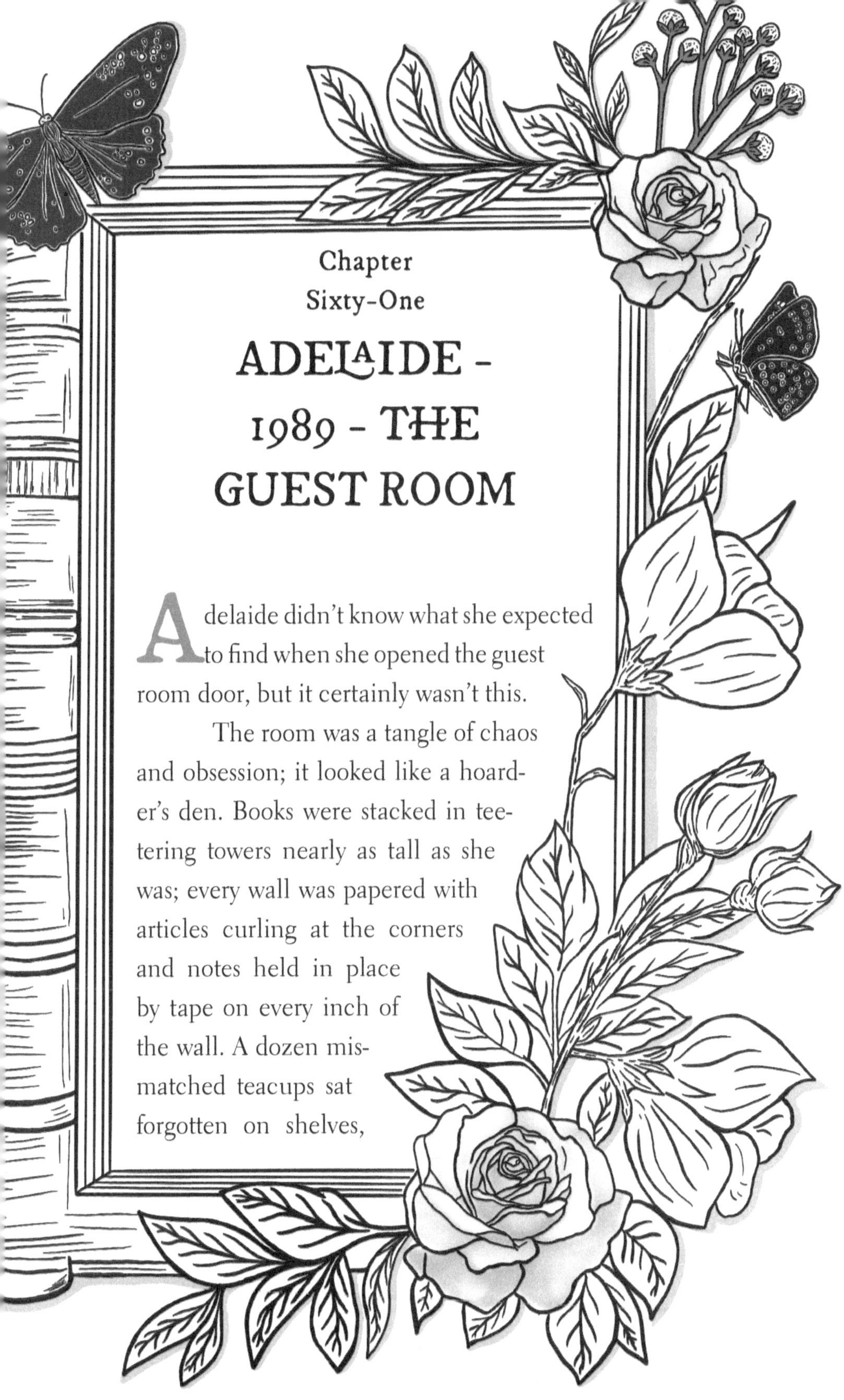

ADELAIDE – 1989 – THE GUEST ROOM

Adelaide didn't know what she expected to find when she opened the guest room door, but it certainly wasn't this.

The room was a tangle of chaos and obsession; it looked like a hoarder's den. Books were stacked in teetering towers nearly as tall as she was; every wall was papered with articles curling at the corners and notes held in place by tape on every inch of the wall. A dozen mismatched teacups sat forgotten on shelves, the windowsill, the floor, most stained with dried rings, some still half-full and growing a skin. Plastic milk crates lined one wall, stuffed with papers and notepads, like makeshift filing cabinets.

The air smelled thick with burned incense and something more herbal, like sage. Melted wax pooled across ceramic saucers, candle stubs scattered around the space.

A sense of trespass crept over her. This wasn't a guest room anymore. It looked like something out of an old detective drama, the kind where the cop becomes obsessed with the case.

Her eyes landed on the bed. Unmade. Sheets tangled. Pillows dented. A well-slept-in bed. Unlike the perfectly made one across the hall in Carolyn's room.

"What the hell?" Adelaide whispered.

She stepped in carefully, her foot brushing aside a crumpled leaflet on eclipses. Her gaze moved to the corner, where a towering stack of books had partially collapsed, spilling open texts on astrology and the cosmos. A smaller pile beside it contained various religious texts in English, Latin and something she couldn't place.

Carolyn definitely *knows something.*

She turned toward the wall, now close enough to make out a web of sticky notes. Rows upon rows of them in various colors. Carefully arranged, almost obsessively so. It took a moment, but soon she began to discern their meaning. The blue notes, dates mostly, some circled in red, tracked astrological events, going back a century or more, including 1932. The year Rowland had gone missing.

Next to them in a dense line, the pink notes chronicled verses, fragments of Latin, old English, possibly Gaelic. Some were shorter quotes, others full verses, scrawled in Carolyn's neat hand.

Then she saw the yellow ones. They weren't like the others, and there were fewer than the rest. Her stomach flipped as she began to read.

He pushed the pot over again today.

There was a flicker in the glass, his shadow, I would know it anywhere.

The basket's lid lifted right in front of me.

Adelaide stepped back, her skin prickling.

They were about someone. *Who is the "he" she's writing about? Pen?*

Her eyes skimmed over Carolyn's notes: a shadow in the window, movement in a doorway, unexplained noises. And then. Her breath caught.

March 5th, 1978 – He moved a book off the windowsill in the guest room.

Adelaide's heart thundered in her ears. This wasn't about Pen. Carolyn wasn't talking about Pen at the Feather Thorn. She was talking about Rowland.

Here.

In *this* room.

"Holy shit." She spun, suddenly seeing everything with new eyes. When Carolyn wasn't at the apothecary, she must have been spending all of her time here, with him.

A notepad lay on the bed, its pages turned up with use. She hesitated, then picked it up.

Something has changed in the past few weeks. Rowland hasn't been as active as before. It's as if the veil has thickened, and he can

Adelaide felt like a stone sinking into a deep well. Rowland *was* here. He had been, all this time.

She looked around the chaotic room, at the candles, the constellation maps, the yellowed verses, and her heart twisted.

"Rowland?" she called softly. "I'm Adelaide, Carolyn's great-niece. I need you to try and communicate with me. Are you trapped here, in some kind of time loop?"

She stood still, holding her breath, waiting. The room remained silent as her pulse pounded.

Then, *thud.* A book from a nearby pile toppled to the floor.

Adelaide turned toward the sound. "Rowland… does Carolyn think you're a ghost?"

Another book slid off and landed beside the first.

"How?" Adelaide whispered. "How did you get trapped here? The watch can't leave the bookshop."

This time, there was no reply.

But Adelaide could feel it now, the energy, the weight of something that had been tethered to this world for far too long inside this tiny room.

She bent down, but before her fingers reached the floor, a drop of blood dripped from her nose; swearing under her breath, she twisted her arm and caught it on the sleeve of her jacket.

"Not now," she muttered, wiping the blood away before picking up the first book Rowland had knocked off the pile. It was a well-worn Bible. A deep green silk ribbon marked a page. She opened it there, scanning the passage: purgatory, and the spirits trapped within. A cold shiver ran down her spine as thoughts of Pen and Rowland flooded her mind.

In their own ways, both were trapped. Caught in something neither fully understood. The watch had imprisoned them in their own version of purgatory, separate from the living, tethered to a place, to a moment in time.

She reached for the second book. Not a Bible this time, but something altogether stranger: a heavy clothbound volume filled with spells. The pages crackled as she flipped through them. There were torn scraps of paper tucked inside listing the herbs needed for rituals. The plants named were ones she recognized; almost all of them were plants she'd seen growing in the field near the cabin. It struck her then just how desperate Carolyn had become.

She trembled as she turned another page: spells to send spirits away, to speak with the dead. And then one more: to bring a spirit back to life.

None of it would have worked, though. Because Rowland wasn't dead. He was trapped, just like Pen.

A sharp ache bloomed behind her ribs as she imagined Carolyn alone in this room, year after year, lighting candles, whispering words into the dark, believing she was living with the ghost of the love of her life, holding on to someone who could never answer.

Adelaide wiped at her eyes, and as she did, something caught her attention, a flash of polished wood. She crouched and pulled out a Ouija board from under the bed, the letters worn from use. Carolyn had really tried everything, it seemed.

A car door slammed outside. Startled, she dropped the board, nearly missing a half-drunk cup of tea. She nudged it back under the bed and darted to the window; Carolyn was back early.

Panic surged through her as she bolted from the room, trying not to knock over anything in her wake. Locking it quickly behind her, she rushed to the beam; fingers slick, the key slipped, once, twice, before she finally wedged it back into its hiding place. Her socked feet thudded down the stairs, breath catching in her chest. Each creak of the floorboards sounded like thunder in her ears.

By the time the front door opened, Adelaide was standing in front of the bookshelf, back ramrod straight, notebook in hand, trying desperately to mask her ragged breaths.

"Oh, heaven!" Carolyn gasped, clutching her chest.

Adelaide forced a sheepish smile. "Oh, I'm so sorry! I didn't mean to startle you. I just, well, I wanted to take a look at your romance collection. The shop's section is slim, actually non-existent, so I thought I'd come here and jot down a few titles to order in." She held up a tiny notepad and pen, voice as light as she could make it. "I was going to ask first, but when I looked in the shop window, you were busy. I didn't want to bother you. I figured you wouldn't mind if I let myself in."

Carolyn exhaled, shaking her head with a smile. "Of course not, you just scared me half to death! I saw your car and figured you were at the cabin. I didn't expect to find you sneaking around my steamy reads." She let out a soft laugh. "Find anything good?"

Adelaide nodded quickly, snapping the notebook shut and stuffing it into her back pocket. "Yes, lots. I've got a whole list to give the book dealer on Monday." She really hoped Carolyn couldn't see through her act.

Lying had never been her strong suit. Her mother used to say she wore her guilt on her face. Maybe that had been true when she was a teenager, sneaking out to drink behind the cricket pavilion, but this wasn't a white lie about curfew; this was time itself hanging in the balance.

Carolyn turned toward the kitchen and set a brown paper bag on the counter, and began unpacking it, pulling out a loaf of bread, a block of cheese, and an onion.

"You want to stay for lunch?" she asked, retrieving a cast-iron pan from the cupboard. "Nothing fancy, just cheese and onion toasties."

Adelaide hesitated. The smell of grilled onion and cheese always made her nostalgic for winter evenings, but she couldn't stay. Not with Pen waiting, and everything she had just discovered burning a hole in her thoughts.

"You know those are my favorite, but I can't today," Adelaide told her, forcing a regretful tone. "I promised Camie I'd have lunch with her at the bookshop."

More lies. Smooth on the outside, but she felt every word stick to the roof of her mouth with guilt.

"All right, if you're sure," Carolyn said, already slicing the bread.

"I'm sure. But thanks. And sorry again for scaring you," Adelaide replied, heading toward the door. "Are you going back to the apothecary, or is Jen taking over the afternoon shift?"

"Oh, I'm done for the day. It's been slow, no need for both of us to be there." Carolyn smiled warmly, but Adelaide didn't miss the slight twitch at the corner of her mouth. "I think I might just pull one of those books down and read a little romance this afternoon, now that you've got me thinking about it."

"Sounds like a perfect afternoon."

But Adelaide knew better. She knew that as soon as she walked out that door, Carolyn would be taking her sandwich upstairs into the guest room to be with Rowland.

"I'll stop by and see you at the apothecary tomorrow," Adelaide said, opening the door and stepping into the biting cold.

As she made her way to the car, a prickling sensation crept up her spine; she had the distinct feeling of being watched. She turned slowly, glanced up toward the guest room window, and there, caught between shadow and light, was the unmistakable silhouette of a man.

Rowland, it had been him all along, the shadow and the secret Carolyn had been hiding in her guest room.

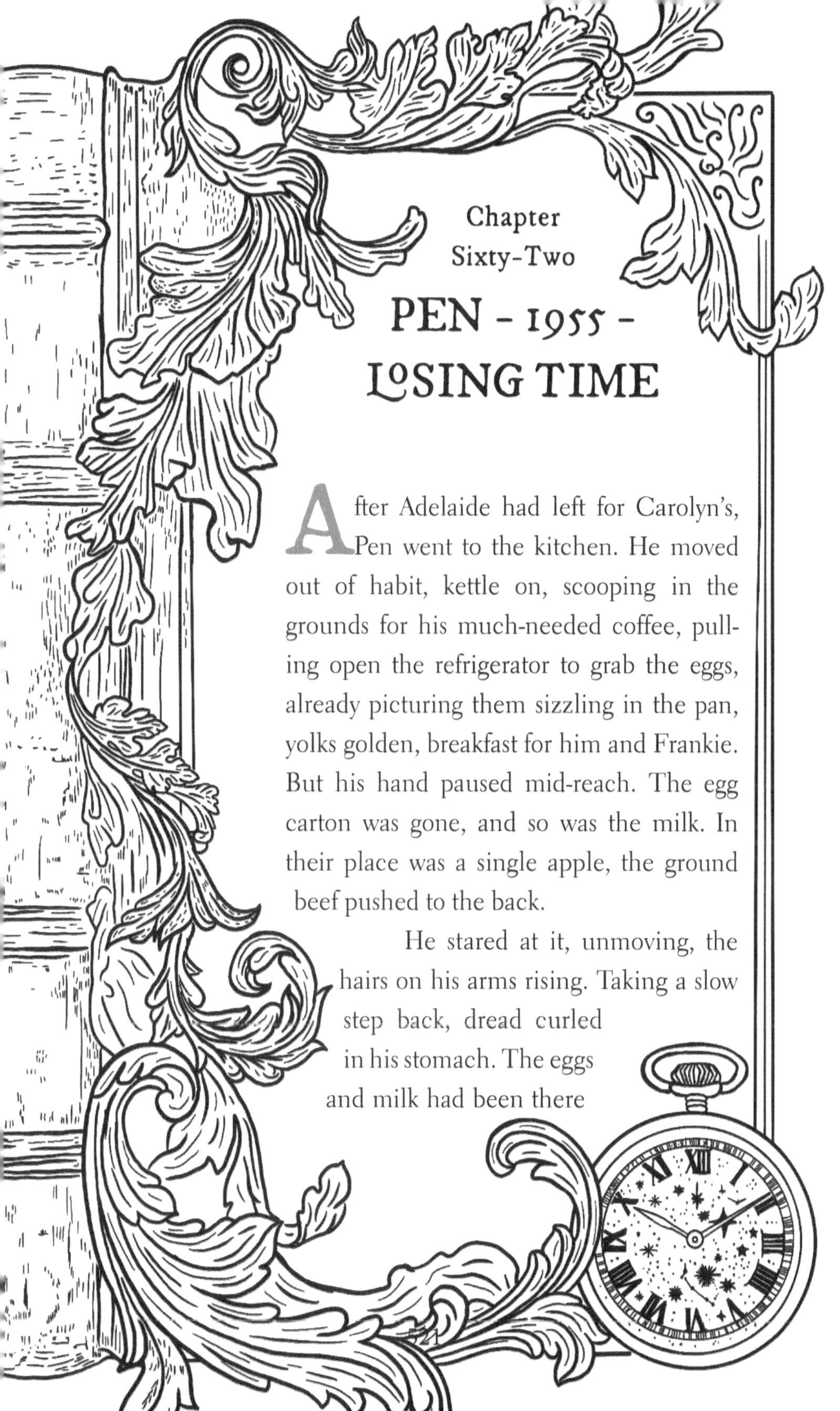

PEN - 1955 - LOSING TIME

After Adelaide had left for Carolyn's, Pen went to the kitchen. He moved out of habit, kettle on, scooping in the grounds for his much-needed coffee, pulling open the refrigerator to grab the eggs, already picturing them sizzling in the pan, yolks golden, breakfast for him and Frankie. But his hand paused mid-reach. The egg carton was gone, and so was the milk. In their place was a single apple, the ground beef pushed to the back.

He stared at it, unmoving, the hairs on his arms rising. Taking a slow step back, dread curled in his stomach. The eggs and milk had been there yesterday, had always been there, every day. They were a staple, part of his routine, until now. A few days ago, he would have welcomed the change; he'd longed for fresh fruit and would have given his left eyebrow to have something different, but now? The apple didn't feel like a gift, and unlike Adam in the Garden of Eden, he had no desire to risk trying it. This was bad. Really bad. He shut the fridge with more force than necessary, the seal sucking closed.

From the bedroom came the soft patter of claws on wood, then Frankie appeared, tail high, weaving frantic loops around Pen's feet, a string of chirps and chitters spilling out, his usual signal that breakfast was overdue.

"Hey, boy," Pen said, bending down to ruffle the fox's silky fur. "No eggs today, burger for breakfast instead, okay?"

Pen opened the fridge again and pulled out the ground beef, breaking off a small portion for Frankie. His own appetite had vanished, his stomach now full with a gnawing unease. What if all the food vanished? Would he and Frankie starve here, trapped in this unraveling pocket of time?

He placed Frankie's bowl on the floor and wrapped his hands around a warm mug of coffee, more for comfort than anything else. His mind moved back to the journal, the one John Dee had left behind, filled with accounts of the same kind of blips in reality that Pen was now witnessing firsthand.

His gaze swept around the apartment. At a glance, nothing else had changed. And yet, there was an uneasy energy in the air, pulling at him. Drawn to the window, he walked over, hesitant to look but too afraid not to.

The view in full daylight was worse than he remembered. More unsettling than it had been in the twilight hush of early morning, or even under last night's eerie moon. The colors outside were oversaturated, unnaturally vivid; the sky an unfamiliar shade of blue, too deep, too pure, almost electric. It was like nothing Pen had ever seen before, either in real life or in the countless books he'd pored over at the Feather Thorn. It was foreign in a way that made his skin crawl.

What he'd taken for oak trees in the moonlight now revealed themselves as something else entirely, strange hybrids, part evergreen, part birch. And he knew that no tree in this world looked like that. He'd read *The Complete Encyclopedia of Trees* cover to cover four times during his arborist phase, and nothing in those pages came anywhere close.

John Dee had believed he was seeing into another reality, and from what Pen was looking at right now, he would have to agree. Dee had written that once the tear in time was mended, the world returned to what it had been. If he could perform the same ritual, perhaps it would be enough that things would return to normal. And maybe this time, the patch would hold. He was holding onto that idea as the alternative was grim.

Turning away from the window and its unsettling view, Pen glanced down to find Frankie sitting at his feet, gazing up at him with his big, bright eyes.

"Done?" he asked, following the fox's glance to the empty bowl. "Okay, then, let's head down into the shop."

Pen walked down the stairs and into the bookshop, Frankie close behind, his bushy tail swishing lightly against Pen's leg. Lately, he'd been more clingy, as if he, too, could sense that their timeline was growing unstable.

He slipped open the trapdoor and headed down the stone stairs. But as Pen stepped into the hidden room, he froze, foot still on the last step.

The bookshelf was gone. And all the books that had once lined it. His eyes snapped to the desk. *Please still be there.* Relief flooded him as he spotted the typewriter, exactly where it should be, still perched atop the old oak desk like a silent sentinel.

But his breath caught again when he looked closer. The journals. There had been six. Now only four remained.

Pen crossed the room in three strides and began flipping through them, fingers fumbling in urgency. Rowland's journal was there, along with two of the astronomy notebooks. And at the bottom of the stack, thankfully, was John Dee's journal.

The missing ones, he realized, were the volumes filled with astrological notes and mathematical equations. Crucial, yes, but ones he had read so many times he could almost recite them from memory. He eased into the captain's chair, the tightness in his shoulders giving way. At least they still had the most important one, Dee's journal.

He picked it up and turned to the page he'd left off, deciding to finish reading it now and take detailed notes, just in case it was the next thing to vanish. They couldn't afford to lose anything that might point the way forward. For all he knew, this book might be the only thing that would help them figure out what to do next.

There was a little under a quarter of the journal that remained unread, and given his current sense of urgency, he figured he would finish it before Adelaide returned from Carolyn's.

As he read, he scribbled notes onto an old yellowed pad of paper. According to Dee, Edward Kelley claimed to have spoken with the divine and learned that the only true way to repair the rip in time was through the help of a Nephilim, some kind of human-angel hybrid.

Pen paused at that. If he weren't living through this madness himself, he might have scoffed. A pocket watch that could open a portal to the heavens and manipulate time, beings descended from angels with the power to mend fractures in reality. It sounded like something torn from the pages of a science fiction novel.

And yet, here he was, living within those pages.

The Nephilim, according to Dee, looked just like ordinary humans. The only way to identify one was by a birthmark, in the shape of the Star of Venus.

How the heck were they supposed to find someone like that? It felt like searching for a ghost in a hall of mirrors. Or worse, like trying to find a particular grain of sand in a desert where the dunes kept shifting.

On the final page, Dee had written a letter addressed to his descendants. His tone had shifted here, less scientific, more urgent. He begged them to safeguard the Astral Synchronum, calling it their birthright and warning them never to let it fall into the hands of anyone outside their family. Whether it was used for good or evil, he said, it would reopen the rip in time. Worse, if it did, it might not ever be closed again.

The letter ended with one final plea: that his descendants continue the search for the Nephilim, and should one ever be found, follow the instructions included to destroy the device for good.

A knot formed in his stomach. After all of these years, not a single person, including John Dee himself, had managed to even come close to finding one of the Nephilim. So how on earth was he supposed to?

Doing the only thing he could in the moment, Pen copied the instructions into his notes, then rolled a fresh sheet into the typewriter and began transcribing them for Adelaide. Having two copies felt like a small act of control in a world quickly slipping beyond it.

This problem had seemed challenging, but now, it bordered on downright impossible. How were they supposed to find a biblical creature from before the time of Christ? The thought pressed down on him. The hope he'd once clung to was fading fast, not in a slow receding tide, but a dramatic crash. And in its place surged a dizzying fear of what would happen if they failed to stop the rip.

What the hell had Rowland been thinking? Then, Pen thought of Adelaide, her voice, her laugh, the way she filled a room with light, and the question twisted back on him. If she were the one slipping away, wouldn't he have done the same? Wouldn't he have risked everything to save her, just as Rowland had done for Carolyn?

Pulling the paper from the typewriter with a swift flick of the bar, he replaced it with a fresh one and began typing again, this time a letter. He worked slowly, carefully breaking down everything he'd learned from the last part of the journal, trying to cram in all the crucial details. As he neared the end, he hesitated. There was one more thing he needed to say. He didn't know if it was too soon, if it would frighten her, or confuse her, or come out wrong. But none of that mattered. Not now. If this place was unraveling, she had to know. He couldn't leave it unsaid.

If I disappear tomorrow, I wouldn't change a thing. The watch may have been my prison, but it also brought me to you, and I would give up a thousand timelines just to see you and hear your voice here. You have been my savior, my angel, my love.

With a final flick of the bar, he pulled the letter free and gathered it along with the copied instructions, two slim pages, but they carried the weight of everything. Holding them tightly, he made his way upstairs, whispering a silent prayer that when Adelaide returned, the bookshop would still be waiting here in her timeline.

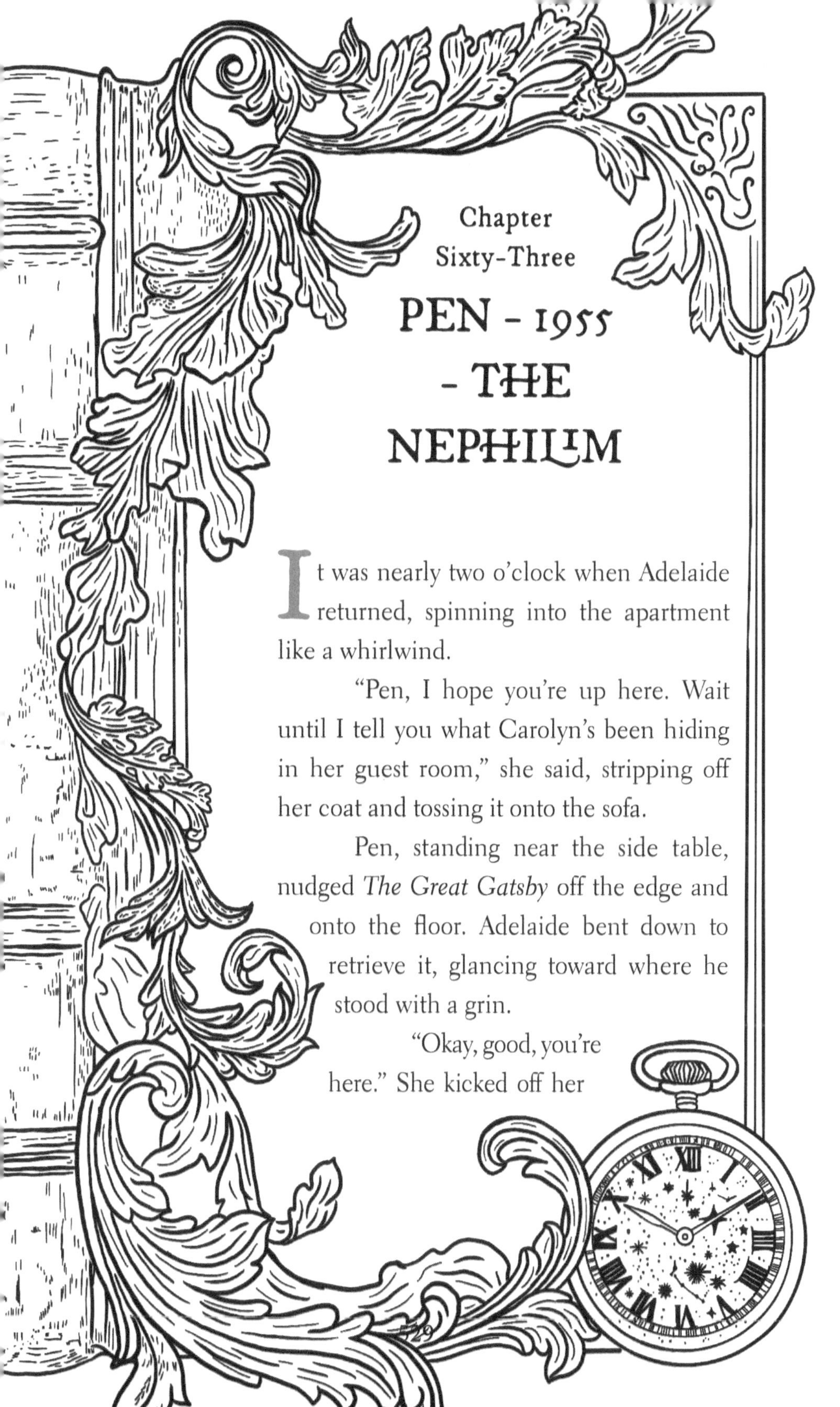

PEN - 1955 - THE NEPHILIM

It was nearly two o'clock when Adelaide returned, spinning into the apartment like a whirlwind.

"Pen, I hope you're up here. Wait until I tell you what Carolyn's been hiding in her guest room," she said, stripping off her coat and tossing it onto the sofa.

Pen, standing near the side table, nudged *The Great Gatsby* off the edge and onto the floor. Adelaide bent down to retrieve it, glancing toward where he stood with a grin.

"Okay, good, you're here." She kicked off her

shoes. "Wait until you hear this. So, I got into the guest room, and when I unlocked the door…" She took a deep breath, words tumbling out as if she'd been holding them in for hours. Pen had never seen her so flushed with adrenaline, so bright-eyed and animated before.

"Carolyn's been living in there. I mean, really living in there. There were piles of books about astronomy, Bibles from around the world, spell books, and dozens of notes taped to the walls. She's been trying to piece it all together, connect the dots on what happened to Rowland."

Pen moved to the window, exhaled onto the glass, and traced two words into the fogged pane: **She knows**

Adelaide caught the message and hurried to his side. "Well, kinda. But get this, she wasn't just hoarding books and journals in there. Rowland is there, Pen. He's in that room!"

Pen's mouth went dry. *Rowland? There? But how?* He blew another patch of mist onto the glass and wrote: **Are you sure?**

"I'm positive. I asked if he was there, and he knocked over a book, just like you did when you were trying to get my attention." Her expression shifted, the thrill of discovery giving way to troubled curiosity. "The thing is, Carolyn thinks he's a ghost. She's been trying to help him *move on,* cross over to the other side, which isn't going to happen, is it? He's not dead, Pen, he's trapped, just like you. But how is he trapped there?"

Pen stared at her. **My question exactly**

Adelaide rubbed her arms. "The journal said the watch couldn't leave this building, so how is he trapped at Carolyn's? How is that even possible?" She didn't expect him to have the answer; he could see that, but her question hung in the air like an echo of something much bigger.

"On my way home, I crossed a bridge over a small winding

river," Adelaide said with breathless disbelief. "Which sounds completely normal… if it had been there *this morning*." She paused, voice softening. "And that's not all. A large barn and field have appeared where the forest used to be on the outskirts of the village. Things are changing, fast."

Her eyes clouded with unease as she stared into the distance. "We need to try to fix this sooner rather than later."

Look on the table, Pen wrote in a fresh puff of breath on the glass.

Adelaide turned. She saw the papers on the table and moved toward them, sitting down slowly. "You read the rest of the journal?"

Yes

She reached for the first page, the instructions for destroying the watch, reading through them carefully, brow furrowing as it always did when she was concentrating.

"This is good news," she murmured. "Now we know how to destroy it. But…" Her voice tightened. "What is a Nephilim and how do we find one?"

I don't know

Read on

She picked up the second page, his letter. He'd come so close to not writing that final paragraph. Now, as she read it, he could only watch.

He watched as her eyes moved steadily over the words, slowing as she reached the end. She lingered there, reading the last lines again and again.

The silence stretched so long, it felt unbearable, until Pen thought he might break from it.

Then, finally, her voice came. "First," she said, "this just got a lot more complicated. Finding some mythological creature seems…

impossible." She folded the letter in her lap and looked up, voice barely above a whisper. "Secondly… me too."

Her eyes shimmered. "As crazy as it sounds to have fallen for someone I can't even see, it's happened, and I wouldn't change it for the world. I'm glad Jeff left me. I'm glad I ran away to Aunt Carolyn's. I'm glad I followed that moth to the Feather Thorn, because they all led me to you."

A tear slipped down her cheek, and Pen's whole being ached to reach across the space between them, to wipe it away, to hold her even for one second.

"And even if this is all we ever get," she whispered, "it's better than anything I've ever had before."

She was right. If this was all they had, then it was enough. He drew a heart on the glass.

She smiled through the tears and wiped her cheeks. "So," she said, blinking hard, "what do we do now?" Her gaze fell back to the letter. "I think it's safe to say we're not going to find one of these Nephilim before the twenty-first, it's only a few days away."

We research

"You're right." She stood, resolve sharpening her features. "Let's go downstairs and pull out anything we can find on these Nephilim."

Pen followed her down into the bookshop. She moved quickly, heading straight to the religious section at the back. He was relieved to see the tall bookcase still standing in this timeline, one of the few that remained untouched.

"Let's start on opposite ends and work toward the middle," Adelaide suggested, already tugging down an old thick Bible bound in rich burgundy leather. "If you find anything that mentions the Nephilim, drop it to the floor, and I'll add it to the stack."

They spent the latter part of the day poring over every religious text on the shelf, and by the time the sun began to set, a small stack of books had gathered near Adelaide's feet.

"I think this is it," she said, picking them up and walking over to the reading corner. "Okay, let's split the stacks. If you find anything that might help, write it down and then type it up for me to read."

She opened the book, already immersed.

Pen liked this new assertiveness in her, direct, with purpose. Just when he thought she couldn't be more attractive.

He worked through three books in his stack, scanning indexes, pages filled with vague mentions and translations. The final volume was no better. Like the others, it referenced the Nephilim only in passing, offering nothing of real consequence.

Just as he closed the book, Adelaide's voice broke the hours-long silence.

"The Nephilim," she read aloud, fingers tracing the words. "The children born of the sons of God and the daughters of men. They were giants, both mighty and terrible. In their strength, they walked among humanity, their very presence a force to be reckoned with. Some were said to be heroes, legends of old, beings of incredible power, revered by mortals, almost like demigods. But most…" She paused, eyes scanning ahead. "Most were something darker."

The fire in her tone dimmed as she continued on.

"These beings, born of divine and earthly blood, were cursed. For their very existence was an affront to the natural order. Though some performed great deeds, many turned to violence, corruption, and sin, bringing ruin to Earth. And when they died, they did not ascend to the heavens as mortals do. No, their spirits were condemned to remain here, trapped between realms, their souls twisted and forsaken. These spirits, the Bible called them demons. Their cursed presence lingers still, the remnants of what they once were, fallen, lost, and forever bound to Earth."

Adelaide closed the book, her gaze drifting to the fading light outside. "What we call demons… are we dealing with demons?" she questioned, just as a drop of red splattered onto the cover of the book. She touched her nose. "Damn, another nosebleed?" She walked to the front desk and pulled a tissue from the box, pressing a wad up into her nose.

When she returned, Pen was already writing on the window near where they'd been reading.

Rest. It can wait till tomorrow

"But can it?"

Yes

He hoped she'd listen. The timeline shifts seemed to be affecting her physically now, and that made him nervous.

"It's not even six yet," she said stubbornly. "I'll never fall asleep this early."

Relax and Read

She smiled. "Okay, but only if you promise me one thing: you'll join me. Let's read upstairs together."

He scrawled back quickly, **OK**

"I'll be right back," she said, standing and walking toward the hidden room.

She returned minutes later with John Dee's journal in hand. "I figure I might as well read it all the way through. Maybe I'll spot something you missed, a loophole. Seeing we got nowhere with these." She pointed at the stack of books by the chair.

Pen followed her back upstairs and into the apartment, grabbing *The Great Gatsby* off the side table as they passed. He trailed behind her to the bedroom, pausing for the briefest of moments in the doorway before stepping inside.

Adelaide set the journal on the nightstand and shrugged off her cardigan, tossing it onto the dresser. With her back to him, she slowly unbuttoned her shirt, the fabric falling open, revealing one bare shoulder.

"Pen," she whispered.

The way his name fell from her lips struck him like lightning, lighting up every part of him, waking something deeper.

"Stay," she said into the empty room, letting the shirt slide from her shoulders completely and pool onto the floor at her feet.

He stood only feet away, yet lifetimes apart, timelines layered like glass panes, separating him from the one thing he wanted most. His heart pounded with the ache of it, with the ferocity of his longing. If he could break time, he would, just to be with her for even a single moment.

He watched as she reached behind her back and unhooked her bra. It slipped from her body, and something inside him clenched. Every sense, every nerve ending, lit up at once. He stepped behind her, so close he swore he could feel the warmth radiating from her skin.

He longed to reach out, to touch her, to feel her, soft and real beneath his fingertips. To kiss her. To be with her.

He lifted his hand, expecting the familiar resistance of absence, the way his fingers usually passed through her world like fog. But this time...

Warmth.

He was touching her, really touching her.

A jolt of heat surged through him as their reality shifted.

As he brushed her hair aside, she drew in a breath, her body stilling beneath his touch. He lowered his lips to her neck and kissed her, softly, testing the boundary between what he longed for and what was real. Her skin was warm, tasting faintly of salt and something sweeter, like summer heat ripened into nectar.

She gasped and leaned into him. It was all the permission he needed. He pressed his mouth to her skin again, trailing kisses down the delicate slope of her neck, his hands moving instinctively, reverently, fingers tracing the shape of her arms, her skin like silk on their tips.

He hadn't touched another soul in decades. And even then never like this. Not skin to skin, heartbeat to heartbeat. Not with the weight of longing blooming into something exquisitely tender.

"Adelaide," he whispered, her name falling from his lips like a vow.

She turned her head slightly as she answered. "Pen." The sound of his name trembled between them, as fragile and undeniable as the moment itself.

This has to be a dream, he thought, as he wrapped his arms around her from behind, drawing her into him, her back to his chest, her presence anchoring him like gravity. For a moment, just a moment, it felt like time was finally working in their favor, that it had opened a door, and let them step through, together.

But then…

As if some cruel trick had been played, his hands passed through her like mist dispersing at sunrise, the warmth gone in an instant.

He staggered back, breath unsteady, desire still coursing through him even as the weight of her absence sank in. And then he saw it. Just beneath her cascade of hair, where his hand had only brushed seconds ago, was a birthmark.

A birthmark in the shape of the Star of Venus.

The mark of a Nephilim.

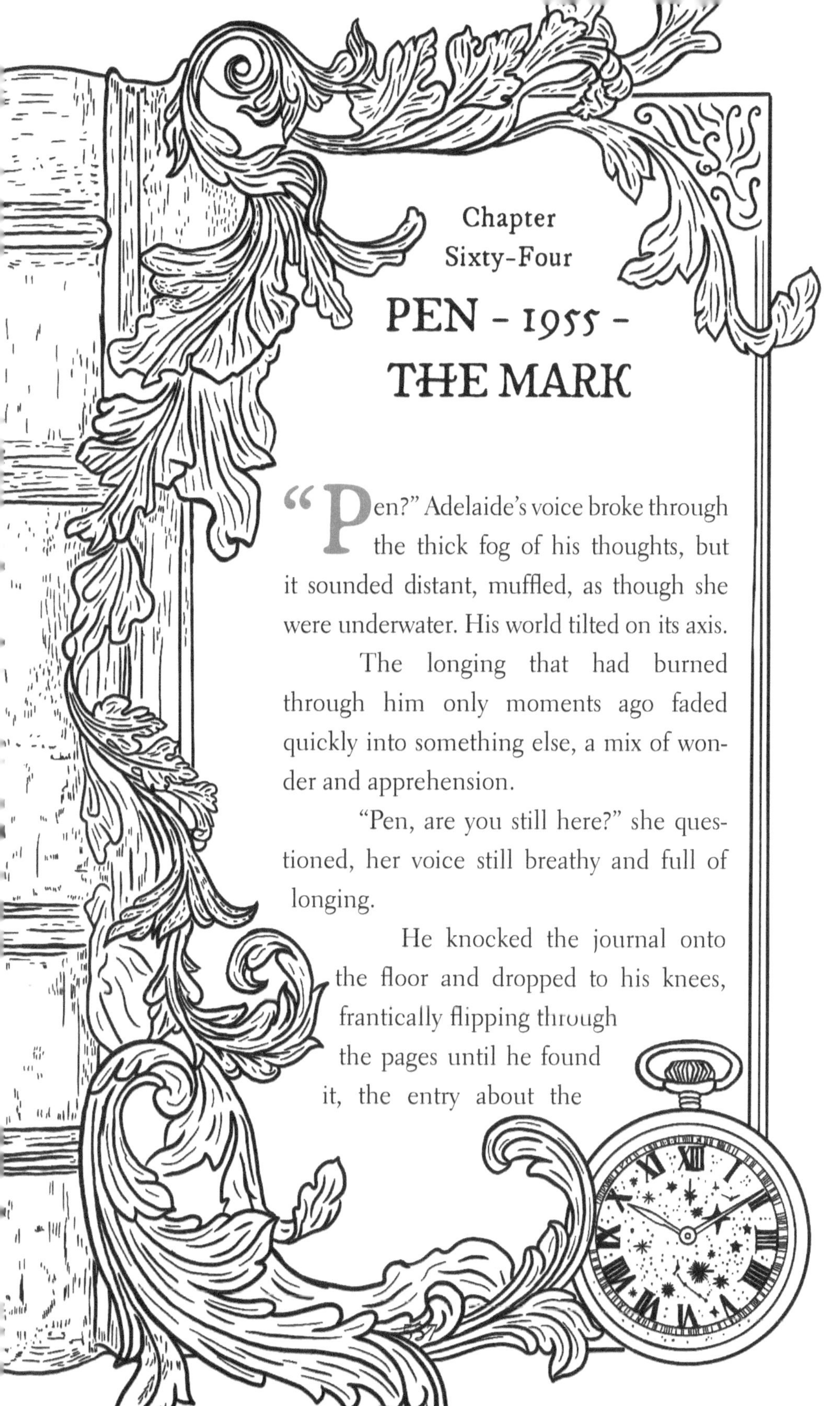

Chapter
Sixty-Four

PEN - 1955 -
THE MARK

"Pen?" Adelaide's voice broke through the thick fog of his thoughts, but it sounded distant, muffled, as though she were underwater. His world tilted on its axis.

The longing that had burned through him only moments ago faded quickly into something else, a mix of wonder and apprehension.

"Pen, are you still here?" she questioned, her voice still breathy and full of longing.

He knocked the journal onto the floor and dropped to his knees, frantically flipping through the pages until he found it, the entry about the

Nephilim and the birthmark.

The only way to identify them, the journal read, *is through a birthmark, an ethereal, celestial branding in the shape of the Star of Venus, the Morning Star. This mark signified their heritage, a trace of their ancient, divine lineage.*

His knees wobbled, the floor suddenly unsteady. How could this be happening?

Pen looked over as Adelaide pulled on her sweater. She reached down to pick up the journal, but Pen pressed his hand firmly against it, pinning it to the floor.

Her brow furrowed, tugging at the journal again. "What's going on?" she asked, her voice edging into frustration.

He pressed down harder, trying to get her to pause, to understand.

"Do you want me to read this page?" she asked, her tone now carrying a hint of annoyance.

Pen let go.

She scooped up the journal and sat on the edge of the bed. He watched as she began to read, her expression shifting subtly as she worked her way through the passage. When she finished, she looked up, her brow still knitted in confusion.

"I don't understand."

She doesn't know. She doesn't realize what she is.

How could he tell her? How could he make her see that she bore the mark, that she was the very thing they'd needed to find? That she was the key. The one who could destroy the watch. The one who could mend the tear in time.

His gaze dropped back to the journal, to the line that haunted him: *Most of them live unaware of what they truly are, oblivious to the power held within their blood, the power of time itself.*

It all made sense now. Her presence, her effect on the time-line. The growing connection between them. And it explained why the unraveling of reality had accelerated; the watch must have been reacting to her proximity.

He wanted to be relieved that they didn't have to search for a mythical being after all, but relief was also crushing. How could he tell her that the fate of this reality, of time itself, rested within the blood in her veins? Telling her she was the one, the one who could stop all this, meant handing her the fate of the world, and maybe that was more than she could bear.

Pen hurried into the kitchen, *The Great Gatsby* still in his hand. He let it fall with a deliberate thud, the sound echoing through the apartment. Within moments, Adelaide appeared, her expression taut with concern.

"Pen, what's going on?" she asked again.

He turned to the window, exhaled on the cold glass and wrote the words: **Hidden room**

"I hate this," Adelaide said, her voice sharp and raw. "I hate that I can't see you. I want to see you!"

Her words cracked through the air like a command, power-ful and absolute, like the voice of a god.

Then, something shifted. She blinked, stared, and for the first time, her gaze didn't slide past him or settle near him. She looked directly into his eyes.

"Pen," she breathed, voice full of disbelief. "I can see you. I can *see* you!"

She rushed toward him, joy lighting up her face, but as she got closer, her expression faltered. The smile faded, her steps slowed, and disappointment crept in.

What had just happened? Had he broken into her timeline,

or had she slipped into his? Either way, her powers were manifesting, even if she wasn't aware of it.

Pen breathed onto the window again, scrawling the words **Hidden room** once more.

She nodded, the light in her eyes now a tangle of confusion, her brows drawn tight. She turned and led the way out of the apartment, down through the bookshop, and into the hidden room.

Pen went straight to the typewriter, fingers trembling as he began to write:

Adelaide, this is going to be hard for you to take in, so please sit down. Tonight, when you took your shirt off, I noticed something on your shoulder, a birthmark.

"Pen, I don't have any birthmarks."

But then, a flicker of realization crossed her face. "Was it my right shoulder?"

Yes.

She ran her fingers over the spot, wincing. "This morning, when I was getting into the shower, my shoulder hurt; it felt like it was on fire, like I'd burned it." She shrugged the sweater off her shoulder, twisting awkwardly to try to see the spot. "What does it look like?" Her voice was quieter now, worry filling in the spaces between her words.

Pen stared at the mark, the Star of Venus, shimmering faintly as though her skin were lit from beneath, a window letting out her inner light.

His fingers hovered over the typewriter keys as he searched his mind for a way to tell her. Then he began to type.

The Morning Star. Look in the dark brown journal and turn to the fourth page.

She pulled the journal from the stack and opened it, her

hands steady, but her breath no longer so. On the fourth page, drawn in intricate black ink, was the symbol, five points interwoven. Below it, a line of delicate script.

The Star of Venus signifies divine guidance and the merging of earthly and celestial realms.

Adelaide stood motionless, and Pen saw her chest rise, saw her swallow, saw the exact second the truth began to bloom behind her eyes.

Without a word, she turned and left the room. He followed. Her steps grew faster, more purposeful as she climbed back into the bookshop, then into the apartment. She made her way into the bedroom and over to the journal that still lay open on the bed.

She snatched it up, her eyes darting over the page. And then she went pale, the color draining from her face in an instant. A thin line of crimson trickled from her nose, traced a line over her lip. She wiped it away absently with her sleeve, her expression lost somewhere far away.

Her eyes glazed over, and she simply sat there, silent and unmoving. Pen sat beside her, instinctively reaching out to offer comfort. But his hand passed straight through, as if she were made of light and vapor, not blood and bone. The ache twisted deeper. How badly he wanted to hold her, just to let her know she wasn't alone with this, whatever this really was.

"No," she whispered. "It can't be. It can't be!"

Then, to his surprise, it was like an idea struck her, then a smile. She tossed the journal aside and sprang to her feet. She bolted from the room and out the door, and Pen followed, struggling to keep up.

"Adelaide!" he called after her, but his voice didn't so much echo as evaporate, no weight, no sound, nothing real.

She fled down the stairs, into the bookshop, over to the front desk. The air had shifted, thickened, as if time itself had grown heavy, swollen with a coming storm. The shadows on the floor dragged unnaturally behind her, flickering like they were caught in the wake of something unseen.

She tore open her bag, yanked out a ring of keys and sprinted back into the hidden room.

Pen was right behind her, dread curling through him like smoke in his lungs. She couldn't… she wouldn't… it wasn't safe…

Her steps were sure, urgent. She went straight to the desk drawer, the one that housed the watch. The key slid in and turned with a click.

Pen lunged for the typewriter.

No.

NO!

Please.

But it was already too late.

He watched helplessly as the watch slipped from the bag and into her hands. The moment it touched her skin, the room went still. Time held its breath. Then the world detonated, like a shockwave, and a surge of ancient power unfurled.

Light exploded outward, not from the watch, but from her, a raw, searing light that poured from her skin like a supernova. Her hair lifted, caught in a wind that wasn't there, and her eyes blazed in a molten gold. Symbols, unfamiliar, intricate, seemed to shimmer just beneath her skin, glowing patterns tattooed in fire, shifting and reshaping across her collarbone, her arms, as though her soul had been etched in forgotten ink, as if she held an ancient text within her.

Pen was forced back, arm raised against the brilliance, his

vision fracturing at the edges. She was too bright, too fierce, like looking at the truth with naked eyes.

"Adelaide, no!" he yelled, voice ragged with fear. He prayed the sound would somehow reach her, pierce through whatever trance had taken hold.

But she didn't hear him.

She stood still, her eyes distant, and her expression blank. Her lips moved, but the voice that emerged wasn't hers. It was deeper, resonant, echoing from every corner of the room, carrying the weight of something far older than either of them.

"I command you to bring forth this time loop and merge it back into the line of time from which it came. Cease the separation and make two become one again."

Her words crackled in the air, each syllable warping the space around her. The walls groaned, the ceiling shivered, the bookcases in the shop rattled like brittle bones above. Around her, a vortex of light and shadow spun into being, drawing everything into its center.

And then, silence.

The glow began to fade, and the room fell into shadows once more. For a heartbeat, silence reigned.

Then the jolt came. A burst of pure light surged from her and then imploded back in on itself, sucking the air from the room. Pen's lungs seized. For a moment, he stood there, fearing the light might consume them both, turn them to nothing more than a pile of ash.

But the light ebbed, the vortex collapsed, and stillness returned.

Adelaide stood at the center of it, in human form again, the watch slipping from her fingers and falling to the desk.

Her shoulders sagged, her knees buckled, and her body crumpled toward the unforgiving stone floor. Pen dove forward, and this time, he caught her. Not mist. Not shadow. Her. Flesh and bone.

His arms wrapped around her as she folded into him, solid and trembling. Her eyes fluttered open, and for the briefest of instants, they locked on his.

She looked at him, *really* looked at him, as if she saw not just him, but everything. Past. Present. Future. All the strands of time.

Then, as quickly as it happened, her consciousness slipped away. Her body fell limp against his, and Pen held her there, torn between awe and terror, between love and the impossible truth of what she was.

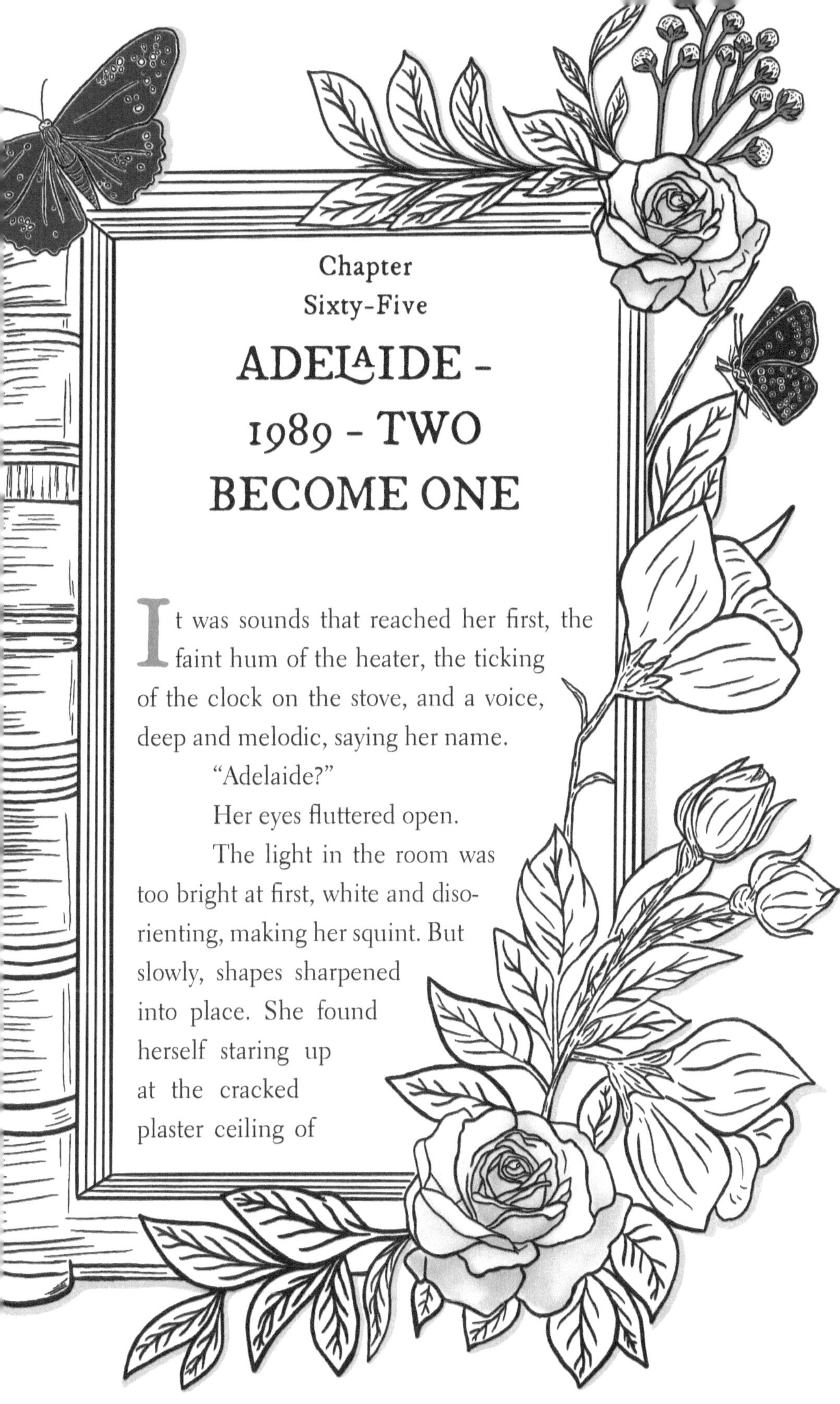

It was sounds that reached her first, the faint hum of the heater, the ticking of the clock on the stove, and a voice, deep and melodic, saying her name.

"Adelaide?"

Her eyes fluttered open.

The light in the room was too bright at first, white and disorienting, making her squint. But slowly, shapes sharpened into place. She found herself staring up at the cracked plaster ceiling of the bedroom in the flat above the Feather Thorn. She would have recognized it anywhere: the lightning-bolt fracture that ran the length of the room, splitting it clean in two. Blinking a few times, she tried to wipe the lingering sleep from her eyes.

She didn't remember falling asleep here last night; her mind felt foggy and slow, like it was slogging through water. Then, like a dam breaking, the memories came. The journal, Pen's touch, the birthmark. The terrifying realization that she was one of these biblical monsters. But then, cutting through the swirl, was the feeling of his arms catching her as she fell.

She bolted upright, and the room swayed around her.

"Whoa there, take it easy," the voice said, smooth and warm, with a lilting cadence that belonged to another era. There was something old-fashioned about the way he spoke, gentle, composed, a formality of a time long past.

She turned, and he was there. Pen. Not a flicker, not a shadow, not a scrawl on fogged glass. Him. Sitting beside her in the bed, rubbing her back with quiet familiarity.

But how?

She blinked again, her mind skipping. She remembered the watch, the feeling of it in her hands, but the rest was only fragments, like pieces of a broken mirror, shards of light and motion. And then Pen's face, his hands, catching her before the dark took over.

"Pen?" she breathed, as though saying his name might break the spell.

He nodded, smiling. That smile… he was the most handsome man she'd ever laid eyes on, not because of the angles of his face or the way the sunlight haloed his hair, but because she'd seen who he was inside long before she ever saw his face. He was dashing, yes, but it was his soul that made him beautiful.

Joy spread across her face, sudden and wide, and she dove at him, her arms wrapping around him, burying herself in his warmth with a fierce, grateful hug.

He caught her effortlessly, cradling her against his chest, his grip firm yet gentle. She breathed him in, pine, citrus, the trace of worn cologne she'd come to associate with corners of the bookshop. A hint of cinnamon, too, like home, baked into the scent of him.

He was here. Warm, solid, real. He was here, with her, in her time.

"But how?" she asked, tilting her face up to his, disbelief softening into wonder.

"It was you," he said simply. "Everything changed the moment you took the watch out of the bag. There was this rush of wind, a bright light. Then I was there, catching you as you fell."

His voice was music to her ears, smooth and rich, and she drank it in, letting it steady her.

"I don't remember," she murmured.

"I'm not sure you were fully there," he admitted. "It was as if something had taken over your body and you were in a kind of trance." His gaze flickered to the nightstand, where the journal of John Dee rested, a closed question waiting to be answered.

She followed his eyes, then reached for the book, flipping to the page about the Nephilim.

"So… am I one of these creatures?" she asked. "One of these demons?" Her voice cracked.

Pen reached out and gently took the journal from her hands, setting it aside. "No," he said firmly. "You are most certainly not a demon or any kind of creature. I think you must be a distant descendant of one, yes. That you must carry the divine magic of the angels in your blood." He looked at her, eyes shining. "But know this, you're human. And whatever power brought me here, it wasn't darkness, it was you. How else would I be sitting here with you right now?"

She looked down at her hands, flexing her fingers as if they might reveal some hidden truth. Then she met his gaze again.

"Did I fix it?" she asked. "Did I destroy the watch? Did I mend the rip in time?"

Pen's expression darkened, shadows flickered behind his eyes, and he didn't answer right away. His gaze drifted past her, into the hallway.

"No," he said at last, his voice quiet. "But you ended the time loop for me. You brought me back."

He wore a smile, but there was something behind it, a weight of something unspoken. Still, he squeezed her hand, holding on as if grounding himself in the moment.

"And for that," he continued, his voice turning softer, "I will forever be grateful. Because this, right here, you, were worth all the years of solitude."

As she looked at him, the world itself seemed to hush; even time, that fickle companion, held its breath as if it, too, had been waiting for this very moment. She had dreamed of this: the warmth of his arms, the sound of his voice, the voice she had longed to hear so many times. For the sheer wonder of being together, two souls sharing the same space in the same reality.

The moment hung between them, stretched thin, fragile as spun glass. Adelaide met his gaze, and the world beyond them blurred, lost to the pull of something far greater than time or circumstance.

She reached for him, fingertips brushing the line of his

jaw, then sliding into the soft waves of his hair. He leaned into her touch, and the way he did, like it steadied him, like he needed it, made something deep inside her twist with need.

She searched his eyes, not lost in their color but in the soul behind them. The man who had waited. The man who had endured. Then she drew him in, her lips finding his. A slow, burning heat unfurled inside her, more than just passion. It was nothing like she'd felt before, not the longing or lusting of a first kiss, but one born of return. A reunion of what had always belonged.

He had felt it too; she knew in the way he trembled against her touch, in the sigh that escaped him when their mouths met, in the reverence with which he touched her. The way his hands moved over her like he was committing the shape of her to memory, not just her body, but her presence, her being. He pulled her closer, breath catching at her temple. "I've dreamed of this…" he whispered.

His fingers traced the curve of her back, and she shivered, not from cold but from the warmth of him, the way his fingertips brushed her skin, leaving sparks in their wake. She sighed against his lips, drinking him in like something holy.

"You deserve nothing less than worship," he murmured in her ear, and the words struck so deep she nearly wept. His lips traveled lower, mapping her neck with quiet devotion, as if painting her into his memory for a lifetime to come.

"I'm yours, Pen," she whispered.

She saw the fire light in his eyes, felt it in the way he stilled for half a heartbeat. "And I'm yours," he said, voice hoarse.

He kissed her then, fiercely, hungrily, as longing gave way to fire. Layers slipped away, buttons undone, fabric falling to the floor until there was nothing between them but the warmth of their skin and the unspoken ache of something sacred.

A golden shimmer pulsed through the room, flickering light at the edges of her vision as he laid her back softly on the bed. She swore she could feel the universe tilt, shifting to make space for them.

And when they came together, their bodies entwined, souls blazing, lost within each other, it was as if the world itself folded back. The flickering light surged, rising a brilliance so pure it could have been the opening of the heavens.

For one breathless instant, as they reached their peak, they slipped free of time. There was no before, no after, just this: two beings bound together in love, in magic, in something deeper than flesh. The beginning of a love that burned like a star being born.

When the light faded, leaving them tangled in the hush of the aftermath, she lay nestled in his arms, pressing a hand to his chest, feeling the steady beat of his heart beneath her palm.

He was real. Here. Hers.

She thought of what she was, a creature between worlds, neither wholly human nor fully angelic. A being shaped by fate, by blood, by forces beyond her understanding. And yet, if being a Nephilim had led her here, if it had given her the power to bring him back, then she would have chosen to be one a thousand times over.

She was no longer afraid of what she was.

She was his.

And he was free.

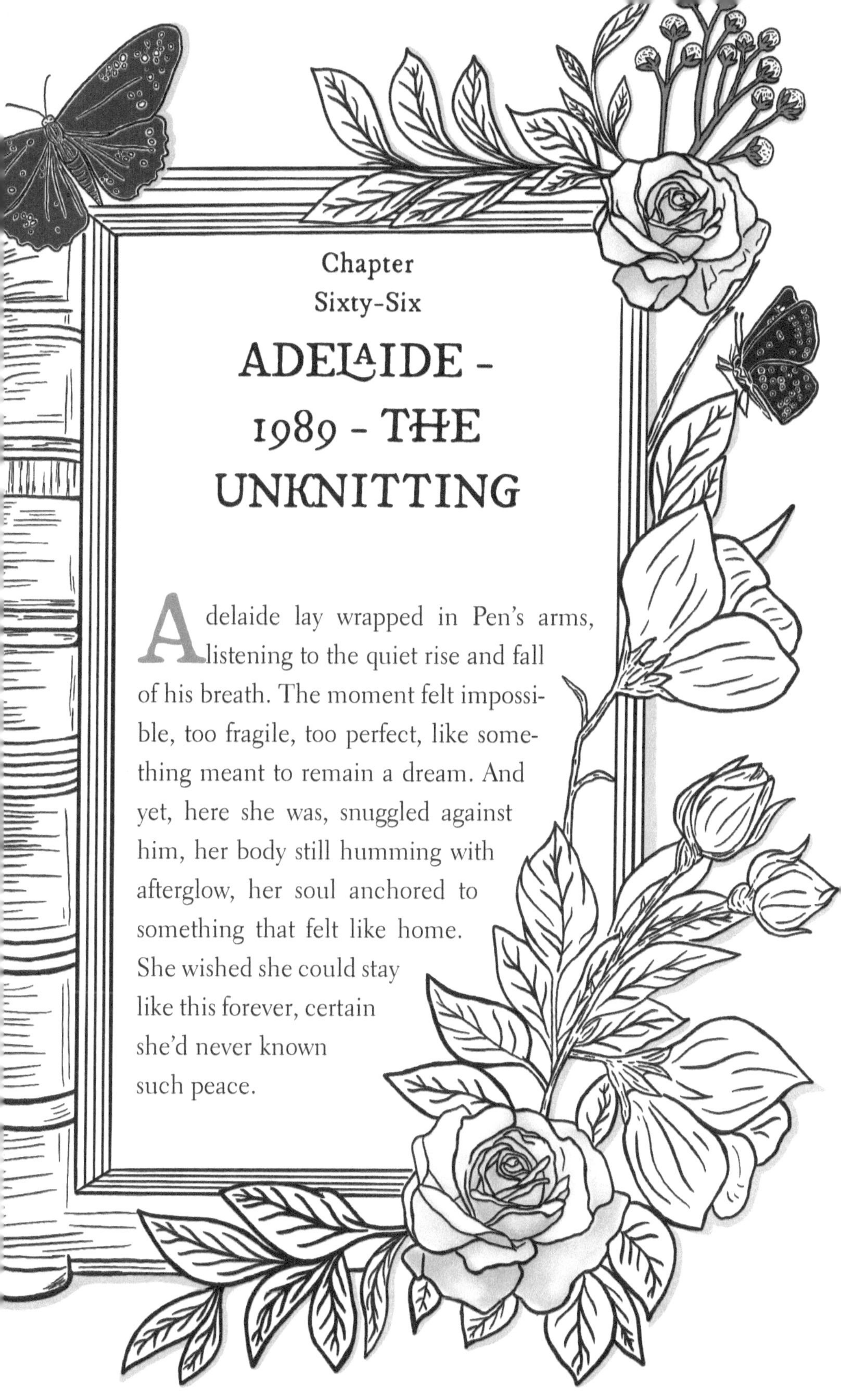

ADELAIDE –
1989 – THE
UNKNITTING

Adelaide lay wrapped in Pen's arms, listening to the quiet rise and fall of his breath. The moment felt impossible, too fragile, too perfect, like something meant to remain a dream. And yet, here she was, snuggled against him, her body still humming with afterglow, her soul anchored to something that felt like home. She wished she could stay like this forever, certain she'd never known such peace.

She let herself sink into the stillness, willing her mind to follow. But it wouldn't. Though her pulse had begun to slow, her thoughts had already begun to race, stirring up a whole new world of questions.

"Pen," she said, lifting her head from his chest. "Do you think when I pulled you from the loop, it also ended the loop for Rowland?"

"To be honest, I had the same thought just a moment ago."

"Maybe we should go over to Carolyn's," she said, sitting up. Suddenly, lying still felt unbearable. The quiet had passed, a crack had opened, and the questions kept pouring in. She swung her legs over the side of the bed and pulled on her clothes.

"Leaving so soon?" Pen teased.

"I don't plan to be gone long, just long enough to make us some coffee," she said with a smile.

He shot up in bed, tension creeping into his posture.

"Wait, don't go in there—"

It only took her two steps into the hallway to understand why. The flat, or what had once been the flat, was gone. In its place stood what looked like the upper loft of an old barn. Wide wooden beams arched above her, the floor beneath her feet was raw and unfinished, and light spilled in through tall, unglassed windows, casting long bars of morning sun across the space.

"I was going to tell you," Pen said softly from behind.

She didn't turn. Her stomach plummeted, and her head spun, trying to stitch sense into the unraveling sight in front of her.

"When did this happen?" she asked, voice barely above a whisper.

"Right after you freed me from the loop."

Adelaide took a tentative step forward. The air was thick with the scent of fresh timber and hay. The flat hadn't just changed, it had reverted, as if the building had been peeled back to its original form.

She could tell it was the same place, just laid bare.

She rushed to the windows. The street was still there, but not as she remembered it. The bakery was gone, and the cheerful sign that had once hung over its door was nothing but weathered wood.

Adelaide turned to Pen, her teeth biting at her thumbnail. "What about Dottie and Iain? What happened to them?"

"I don't know," he admitted, stepping closer and resting a hand on her shoulder.

This wasn't just a problem anymore; it wasn't something that could be patched or reversed with a ritual; their reality was folding in on itself, piece by piece, and if they didn't act soon, their world would be replaced entirely.

Frankie skittered into the room, his small paws barely making a sound against the unfinished wood floor. He paused, nose twitching, looking around, then let out a soft chitter as he trotted over to Pen.

"No breakfast today, buddy. I'm sorry," Pen murmured, bending down and stroking the little fox's head.

Adelaide exhaled sharply. "What are we going to do? The solstice isn't until tomorrow." She glanced down at Frankie, who blinked up at her with wide, uncertain eyes.

"First, we need to see what else has changed. Why don't you get dressed and head over to the apothecary to see Carolyn? I'm not sure I should be seen just yet. Showing up looking like I did back in 1955 might stir up more questions than we want to answer."

"Okay," she said, nodding. "I guess you're right. And if Carolyn is there, that gives us time to sneak over and see if Rowland is back in our timeline."

"Good thinking."

Adelaide cast one last look out the window. The town beyond no longer looked solid. It was as if two versions of it, two realities, were bleeding into one another, one melting over the other, swallowing up the familiar and replacing it with something twisted. The trees were wrong, the buildings, too. Even the horizon bent in an unnatural way. Everything that was coming into focus from the other reality was distorted, colors too sharp or too dull, proportions off, almost like a dream painted from a memory and blurred by time.

Below, people were on the street; some walked on, oblivious, their routines undisturbed, but others seemed dazed, expressions clouded with confusion and despair. It was clear now. Some were already caught in the shift, and others hadn't fully crossed over.

She turned away and reached for the door, but Pen caught her hand, fingers curling around hers, spinning her back toward him.

"I don't want you to be surprised by the bookshop," he said. There was something in his voice, and a crease between his brows that hadn't been there before. "It's different."

"How different?" she asked.

He hesitated, and that hesitation told her everything.

"It's not the Feather Thorn anymore," he told her, eyes dimmed with something heavier than sadness.

A shiver worked its way down her body. The shop she'd poured herself into, the hours spent painting, restoring, dreaming, was gone in the blink of an eye. Not just altered, not broken. Gone. She swallowed hard, pushing down the tears. Would she ever see it again? Would she ever get the chance to run her bookshop the way she'd imagined?

"Be careful," he added, pulling her into a kiss.

She kissed him back, letting the moment press into her skin. Everything melted away, the worry, the questions, the unraveling world. There was only Pen. She wished she could freeze time and slip back into the loop with him. As their lips parted, reality crashed down around her once more. She did her best to give him a reassuring smile before she opened the door and walked out.

"I'll be back soon," she promised, as she stepped out into the unknown.

She descended the stairs with cautious steps, the stone stairwell still its usual damp. When she walked through the door that should have led into the Feather Thorn, it wasn't old books or Pen's cologne she smelled, it was iron, smoke, hot metal. The air shimmered with heat, the scent of scorched leather and fire saturating it like incense of times past.

A steady hammering echoed through the space, metal on metal. She rounded the corner, each step slower than the last.

Pen had tried to prepare her, but now, staring into the furnace-lit room, it felt like her dreams had been burned to ash. The bookshop was gone, completely gone.

In its place stood a forge, massive and glowing with firelight. Where the children's corner had once been, iron tools now hung. Where the register had sat, an anvil glistened with fresh sparks. A man stood, hunched over it, hammering a long glowing strip of metal, each strike sending a shower of sparks flaring. His face was shadowed, and he didn't look up.

She didn't know what to do. He was right there, directly in her line of sight, yet his eyes never lifted to her. It was as if she didn't exist, as if she were nothing more than a ghost.

She turned slowly, hand brushing the doorframe as she whispered to the empty air, "This must've been how Pen felt."

As she slipped outside, Adelaide braced for the familiar bite of winter, but it never came. Instead, a warm breeze brushed her skin, carrying the sweet scent of freshly cut grass and blooming flowers. The seasons had shifted, just as the town had.

Then she looked up. The sky… it looked wrong.

It was the wrong kind of blue, almost periwinkle, and scattered across it, faint but unmistakable, were stars. Stars, in daylight. Stars that didn't belong.

Head down, she hurried down the street, trying not to look at the sky again.

The chimes over the apothecary door jingled as she entered, and the familiar scent of herbs and spices curled around her. The counter was empty, but from the back room came the sounds of movement and a gentle humming.

"Carolyn?" she called, keeping her voice soft, not wanting to startle her.

"Just a moment," came the reply, followed by the clatter of tins.

When Carolyn appeared in the doorway, dusting her hands on her apron, she paused and looked at Adelaide. There was no spark of recognition, no warmth of familiarity. "Can I help you?" she asked, and Adelaide's heart sank.

Adelaide just stood there. She sounded right, she even looked right, mostly. Same kind eyes, same calm presence, but the blue of those eyes skewed slightly green, and her hair, once silver and white, now shimmered auburn, the white only just beginning to creep in. She looked younger. By at least ten or fifteen years.

Adelaide turned, glancing around the shop. The jars lining the walls were the wrong shape, square instead of round. The dried herbs that once hung in loose wreaths now dangled in neat bundles, bound tightly with twine. Things looked… almost right, but not quite.

"Are you all right, dear?" Carolyn asked, her voice kind but wary.

Adelaide forced herself to nod. "Yes. Sorry. I'm just passing through." She swallowed. "Can you tell me the name of this town?"

Carolyn smiled, the same sweet smile Adelaide had known for

years. "Welcome to Leymark."

Her stomach twisted. "Thank you," she murmured, turning to leave.

"Have a blessed day," Carolyn called.

The door shut behind her with a gentle click, and Adelaide stood motionless on the street, her breath catching as panic clawed its way up her throat. This wasn't Helensburgh, not anymore.

She turned. The hardware store, Ewan's shop, was gone, replaced by an old stone church, its roof sagging under a carpet of moss, the walls cracked and covered in lichen. Had Ewan vanished too? It was then she thought of Camie, Camie and the Common Blue. Had they been swallowed up by this new reality too?

Or maybe she and Pen had simply fallen all the way through? Was this what it meant to be on the other side of the tear?

In front of her, another building appeared, one that hadn't been there minutes ago. Her stomach twisted with worry, and she tore back to the Feather Thorn, shoes thudding over cobbles, heart pounding harder with each step. *Please still be there. Please still be there.* She burst through the Feather Thorn's door and up the stairwell into the flat. And there he was, still there, waiting for her.

"How did it go?" he asked, eagerness filling his voice.

"Not good," she replied, trying to catch her breath as she collapsed onto the bed, biting at her thumbnail. From what she could tell, this room was the only part of their old world that remained. "It's gone. All of it."

"What do you mean?" Pen asked, frowning. "I saw you walk into the Purple Thorn." He sat beside her.

"That's just it," she said, looking over at him. "It looked like the apothecary, but it wasn't the one I knew, and it wasn't my Carolyn. She didn't even recognize me, Pen. It was like I was a stranger to her."

Adelaide's eyes blurred with tears, the ache rising too fast to swallow.

Pen's brows knit together, confusion flickering across his face, but then he reached for her, gently taking her hand in his, his thumb brushing her knuckle. "Are you sure?"

"She called the town Leymark." She turned to him. "I did this," she whispered, the guilt rising to her throat. "In my rush to free you, I didn't stop to think what touching the watch might do." Her voice cracked as she dropped her face into her hands. "I was selfish. I just wanted you here with me."

Pen brushed a tear from her cheek and pulled her into his arms, holding her tight. She let herself sink into the warmth of him, his embrace a shelter from the biting reality, but it was temporary. They didn't have time for all of this, not now; they needed answers.

"We have to go to Carolyn's," Pen said, his voice steady now. "If Rowland's out of the loop, maybe he knows something that can help us."

Adelaide nodded.

Pen let out a sharp whistle, and Frankie darted out from a corner, his ears perked. "We'd better take him with us." He scooped the little fox into his arms as they headed for the door.

As they moved through what used to be the bookshop, Pen stuck his arm out, stopping Adelaide before she stepped into view of the man who was still hammering away at the anvil. "We don't know how these people might react to us," Pen whispered, peeking around the corner.

"I don't think he can see us," Adelaide said. "When I came down earlier, he looked right at me, but it was like I wasn't even there."

"But Carolyn saw you?" Pen asked.

"Yes, but maybe that's because she knew me in another reality. This guy," she nodded toward the metalsmith, "he's never seen me before. I don't know, Pen. I'm as clueless about the rules of this as you are."

They slipped past the man and stepped outside. As they walked in front of the Feather Thorn, Adelaide saw Pen look back, his eyes wide as they roamed around. She'd almost forgotten that he hadn't been outside in nearly thirty years. How strange it must be to feel the breeze on his skin again and the sun on his face.

As they made their way toward the alley, she sent up a silent prayer: *Let it be there. Let just one thing still be the same.* She hadn't seen a single vehicle on the streets, and she wondered if they even existed in this timeline. Her chest squeezed when she rounded the corner and spotted her car, still there. Her battered little Volkswagen Golf was exactly where she left it yesterday.

As they drove in silence toward Carolyn's, Adelaide noticed the road signs had changed, along with parts of the landscape. The world was slowly rewriting itself, trees where there had been meadows, hills where there had been farms.

She turned to say something to Pen about it, but stopped. He was studying the dashboard, fingers hovering over the different knobs, tracing the dials to the radio. She'd almost forgotten that this was all new to him. He hadn't been beyond those bookshop walls since 1955. But this wasn't the world she'd hoped to show him; it was as new and strange to her as it was to him.

Relief washed over her when they pulled into Carolyn's driveway. The house stood just as it always had, the garage door closed, flower beds wild and full.

"Things look the same," she said, reassuring Pen as much as herself.

"Maybe the rip has only affected the center of town where the watch is," Pen suggested.

"Let's hope so," she said.

At the front door she lifted the pot with a dead chrysanthemum. The key was still tucked beneath, another small mercy.

Inside, the house exhaled the same scent as yesterday, lavender oil, sun-warmed wood, and the faintest trace of cinnamon. Nothing seemed out of place or changed in any way.

"Follow me," she instructed, heading toward the stairs. Pen set Frankie down, removed his wingtips, and followed her up.

"One second," she said, reaching behind the beam and pulling the key free of its hiding spot. She paused for a moment, wondering what they would find when she unlocked the door. Would it be the same, or would Rowland be there, whole and present in this new reality?

Holding her breath, she turned the key. The door gave a soft groan as it opened. The room was exactly the same. Stacks of books, curled notes, a mess with meaning, but no Rowland.

"Well," she said, turning back to face Pen. "I guess it didn't work."

But he wasn't looking at her. He was smiling. Not vaguely, not politely, but a full, wide, almost incredulous smile, like he'd just seen the impossible.

Adelaide followed his gaze, but there was nothing there. Nothing she could see. "Pen? What are you looking at?"

Pen tore his eyes away and looked at her, almost in disbelief. "Can't you see him?"

"Who?"

"Rowland."

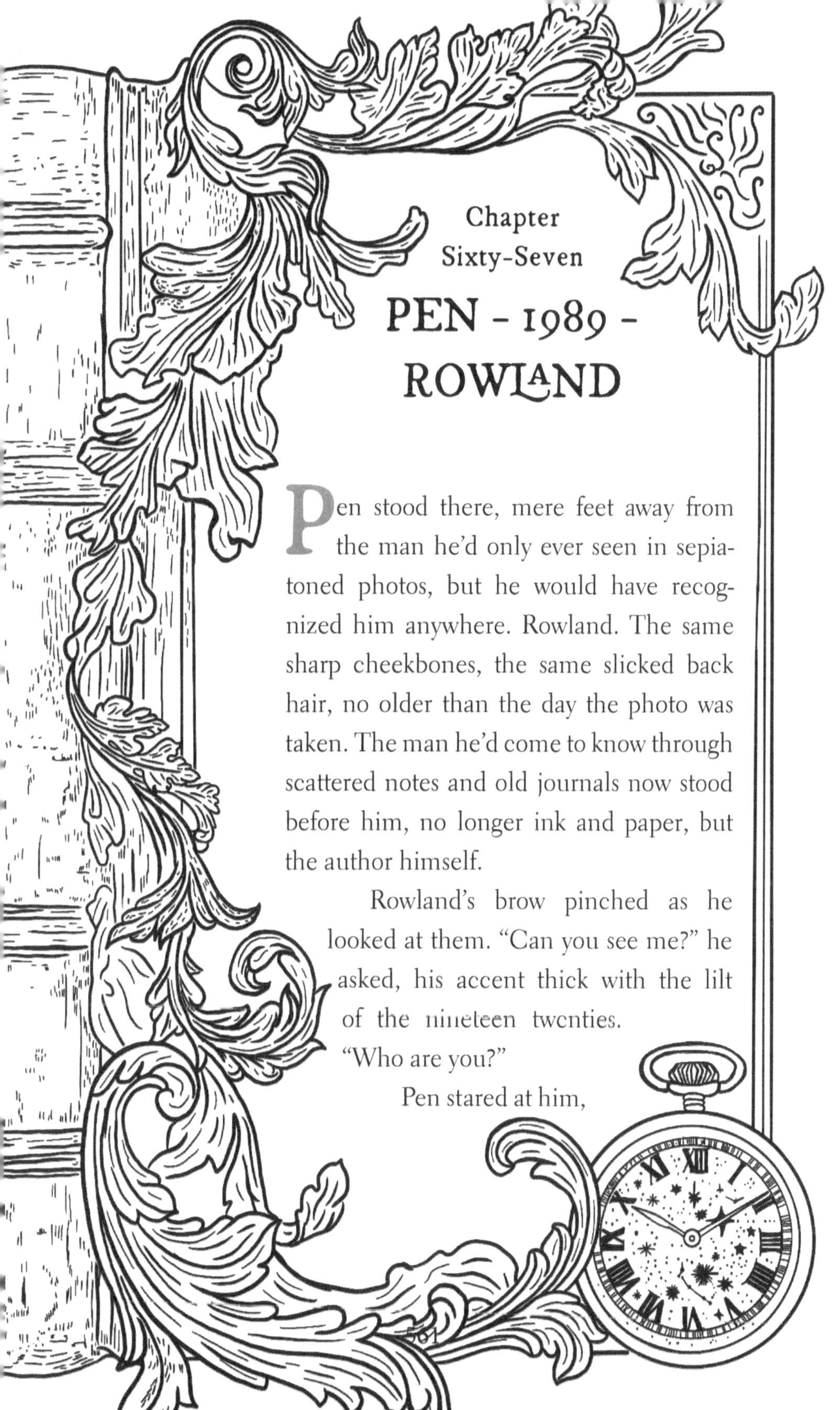

PEN - 1989 - ROWLAND

Pen stood there, mere feet away from the man he'd only ever seen in sepia-toned photos, but he would have recognized him anywhere. Rowland. The same sharp cheekbones, the same slicked back hair, no older than the day the photo was taken. The man he'd come to know through scattered notes and old journals now stood before him, no longer ink and paper, but the author himself.

Rowland's brow pinched as he looked at them. "Can you see me?" he asked, his accent thick with the lilt of the nineteen twenties. "Who are you?"

Pen stared at him,

then took a breath. "Pen Turner," he said, stepping forward and extending a hand. "Nice to meet you."

Rowland's grip was firm, and Pen's mind reeled with questions. How was this possible? Why could he see Rowland but Adelaide couldn't?

As if reading his thoughts, Rowland said, "How can this be? No one has seen me since I got trapped here."

"To be honest, I'm not sure," Pen said, looking over to Adelaide, who was standing by the door, eyes sweeping the room, searching for a man just out of sight.

Rowland followed Pen's gaze, then his eyes narrowed. "That's Carolyn's niece," he said. "She was here the other day. I tried to reach her."

"Yes, she told me," Pen replied, "she said you knocked over some books. Even though she couldn't see you, she knew you were in here."

"But she obviously still can't see me. How is it that you can?"

Pen paused, wading through his thoughts, but none of them were clear. "Maybe because I was also trapped in a time loop by the watch."

Rowland's eyes widened, and he stepped closer, a flicker of hope sparking in his gaze. "You got out? But how?" he pressed, voice now edged. "How did you even get hold of the watch?"

Pen walked over to a stack of books, trailing his fingers over the worn spines. "I found it in a hidden room beneath the Feather Thorn." He recounted his story in pieces: the slow fade of the shop into abandonment, Emily's passing, inheriting the shop from Ward, and the strange pull that made him stay, determined to restore it to its former glory. The journals. The watch. The moment time buckled.

Rowland listened without interruption, face tightening in places, then going still as Pen described the ripple effect that followed.

As Pen finished, he turned to Rowland and asked him the question that had been weighing heavily on his thoughts. "If you knew using the watch would cause the patch John Dee placed on the rip in time to fray, why did you risk it?"

Silence stretched, and Rowland's shoulders dropped as if the weight he carried had just grown heavier. When he finally spoke, his voice was raw with regret. "I had to, for her," he answered, pausing for a moment. "You have to understand. She got sick, so sick, and the doctor told me to say my goodbyes…" Rowland's voice broke, and he swallowed hard. "I couldn't. I couldn't just let her die."

He blinked hard, the sheen in his eyes betraying the sorrow sitting on the surface even after all these years.

"She was everything to me. I thought… if I could stop us from ever taking that trip, I might be able to save her. I had to try, had to reverse what had happened." His gaze drifted to the window, voice just above a whisper. "There was a full moon that night, with Saturn in alignment. I'd read Dee's notes enough times to know what that meant. I waited for the chimes, and when they came, I activated the watch."

Rowland paced the room, weaving in and out of the clutter on the floor. "John Dee hadn't meant for the Astral Synchronum to open portals through time. That was an accident, something that happened after their failed attempt to activate it. No one had ever meant to use it for time travel. But I was desperate. I had run out of options; all I had was a hope and a prayer it would work. So when the first chime rang out, I wound the watch backward, to the exact date and time I needed. When the chimes stopped, it was like a hurricane had blasted through the room. And I knew. I knew then that it had worked."

Pen listened, a dozen questions rising all at once, but one question slipped past the rest. "How did you end up trapped here? The watch can't leave the Feather Thorn, right?" He glanced at Adelaide, who stood quietly, watching but only hearing one side of the conversation.

Rowland nodded. "You're right. It couldn't leave the shop. That's why I had to turn back time there, instead of where I should have been, here with her. As far as I knew, there were only two rules to how it worked. First, when your past and present selves share the same space, the danger isn't in your proximity; it's in knowing. If you both become aware of each other, the tether weakens. And when that breaks, so does reality. Second, the number of chimes determines how many hours the portal stays open. It only chimed three times. Three hours. What I *didn't* know then was that if I didn't make it back before the last hour of the final chime… I'd be stuck, wherever I was when the portal closed." He exhaled sharply, gesturing to the guest room. "For me, that was here."

Pen frowned. "But there's no food in here, no water. How have you survived?"

Rowland let out a humorless chuckle and nodded toward a wicker basket tucked in the corner. "Lucky for me, I showed up on just the right day, at just the right time. I arrived at Carolyn's house just as *I*, my other self, was pulling up to take her on our trip. I waited for myself to go inside, then stole the crank from the car."

Pen's eyebrows lifted. "You *stole* from yourself?"

Rowland smirked. "I did what I had to. When they came out and the car wouldn't start, I slipped into the house, up to this very room. I had to hide the crank somewhere we might find it again later, not somewhere too obvious, and the guest room seemed as good a place as any."

His expression darkened. "I watched them trying to work out what had happened. My watch was ticking down the minutes, and I realized I hadn't thought things through. I couldn't leave the room without passing them. And if my past self saw me…" He shook his head. "I couldn't risk it. I would have destroyed both my reality and theirs. So, I paced the floor, desperate to find a way back to the Feather Thorn. I wasn't paying attention and knocked over a potted plant sitting on the dresser near the window." His voice grew weary as he went on. "I heard her footsteps first… then my own. And I panicked. I slid under the bed, holding my breath as they stepped into the room."

Rowland's gaze turned distant, memory taking over. "She saw the plant on the floor, set down the picnic basket she was carrying, and started cleaning up the mess. I can still hear her voice: *What in God's green earth happened here?*"

His lips turned up into a half-smile, though his eyes held only sadness. "And that's when my past self decided that if they weren't going on holiday, they might as well *make the most* of their time at home, if you catch my meaning."

Pen smiled, then laughed. "Are you telling me you got stuck in time because of…"

"Yes. Because of *exactly* what you're thinking. I stayed under the bed the whole time," Rowland said, "as my last chance of escape ticked by. Later, as Carolyn was getting dressed, she spotted the crank. I watched as she walked out, crank in hand, down to the car. By then, my time had long since run out. The final hour had passed. When I tried to leave, it was like an invisible barrier had sealed me inside the room." He turned back to Pen. "That was the

long-winded way of saying Carolyn left the picnic basket behind.
I've been surviving on Scotch eggs and meat pies ever since."

Pen rubbed a hand over his jaw, struggling to find words.
"How long before Carolyn started believing your spirit was here?
That you were a ghost?"

Rowland moved to the window, staring out at something
only he could see. "Time's a funny thing in here. I'm not exactly
sure how long. I failed to stop us from taking the trip, but somehow,
she survived the fever. By the time she was better, the *past* Rowland
had caught up to my timeline and became me, and she thought I'd
left her." His voice grew heavier. "She cried for days. And knowing *I*
was the cause of her pain… it was unbearable. So, I found a way to
let her know I was here. I knocked over the plant again. And again
and again. After the fourth or fifth time, she finally realized it was
me." He hesitated, his voice breaking slightly. "But she thought I
was a ghost. She believed I had died."

Pen remained silent, as the weight of the story settled over
him.

"She became obsessed with figuring out what had happened
to me," Rowland continued. "She knew about the watch and our
family's promise to protect it, but the journals were hidden away in
the secret room, so she never knew the truth behind it. She searched
for years, notes, books, anything she thought might hold an answer.
But she was chasing the wrong thing." He turned back to Pen, eyes
misted. "I watched her grow old. She never married. Never moved
on. Just faded, became a ghost herself." He swallowed hard. "She's
spent her whole life searching for answers to a problem that didn't
even exist, and there was nothing I could do. I've tried to reach her,
Lord knows I have. But all I can move in both our timelines is that
damn potted plant and a few books."

Pen exhaled sharply, rubbing the back of his neck. "I'm sorry you had to endure that." He pictured Adelaide following the same path. It would be an awful thing to witness, to live with.

Rowland nodded. "Now you must answer my question. How did *you* escape the time loop?"

Pen glanced at Adelaide, a slow smile tugging at the corner of his lips. "Her."

Rowland frowned. "What do you mean?"

"She's a Nephilim."

The blood drained from Rowland's face. "No," he whispered, shaking his head. "I thought they were just a myth, a story meant to keep us on our toes." He ran a hand through his hair, pacing again, hope flaring in his eyes. "Can she free me?"

Pen hesitated. "I don't know. To be honest, she doesn't know how she broke me out."

Adelaide stepped forward, gaze fixed on an empty space near Pen. "If I *could* free you, Rowland, I would. But I have no idea how to without the watch."

Rowland's face fell.

"There's something else you need to know," Pen said. "When you used the watch to try to save Carolyn all those years ago, you weakened the seal John Dee placed on the rip in time. Then, when *I* touched and trapped myself, I made it worse; it unraveled even further." He glanced at Adelaide. "As soon as Adelaide got near it, being what she is, she accelerated the unraveling." He inhaled deeply before delivering the final blow. "Our reality is already being taken over by another."

Rowland's face turned ashen. "How bad is it? How much is left?"

"The town's already gone, but the outskirts, this house, seem untouched for now."

Rowland rocked back on his heels, hands shoved into his pockets. He was quiet for a long while before he finally spoke. "If she is what you say she is, then she *can* stop this. She can destroy the watch."

"Yes," Pen agreed. "But not until the solstice. Not until tomorrow night."

"Then we'd better pray that what's left of Dee's patchwork will hold," Rowland said firmly. "And if she is the cause of the acceleration, then you need to keep her far away from the watch."

Pen turned to Adelaide, standing on the edge of it all, watching him, unaware of the full conversation, but likely understanding the gist. He nodded. "You're right. We need to distance her from it, just one more day, and when tomorrow comes, we can destroy it for good."

Rowland studied him, something unreadable in his expression. Then he exhaled, shaking his head. "You love her. I can see the way you look at her. It's the same way I looked at Carolyn. The way I still do."

Pen didn't answer. He didn't need to.

Rowland's voice turned somber. "There's something you need to understand. When she destroys the watch… it will erase the entire timeline it created."

Pen's stomach dropped. "What are you saying?"

"If that watch never exists… *you* never get trapped in time. And if you're never trapped in time…" His voice softened, laced with quiet sorrow. "You two will never meet."

Pen looked over to Adelaide, as a sick sense of impending grief flooded every inch of him.

"You will lose her," Rowland added quietly, "forever."

Pen's jaw clenched. "What other choice do we have? What's the alternative?" he snapped, sharper than he intended.

Rowland held his gaze. "There isn't one. You *don't* have another choice. Once the watch is destroyed, all the timelines will realign as they were meant to be. I don't know what that means for me either; maybe I'll never meet Carolyn, maybe the Feather Thorn will never exist. But it's the only way I will ever be free." He paused. "Carolyn is growing older, and soon it will just be me trapped here alone for all of eternity."

Pen couldn't breathe. The future he'd barely begun to imagine, the one with Adelaide at his side, was slipping away.

He couldn't tell her.

If she knew, she would never agree to destroy the watch.

A part of him dared to hope. That maybe they could find a way to stay here, in this broken sliver of reality. Patch together something new. Build a life in the ruins. But he knew better.

It wasn't just about them or their love.

The timeline was too fragile, too many lives hanging in the balance. Rowland's eternal imprisonment, the destruction of everything they knew… it was too much to sacrifice just to keep her by his side.

No. Things had to be set right. The watch had to be destroyed.

Even if it meant losing her. Even if it meant forgetting.

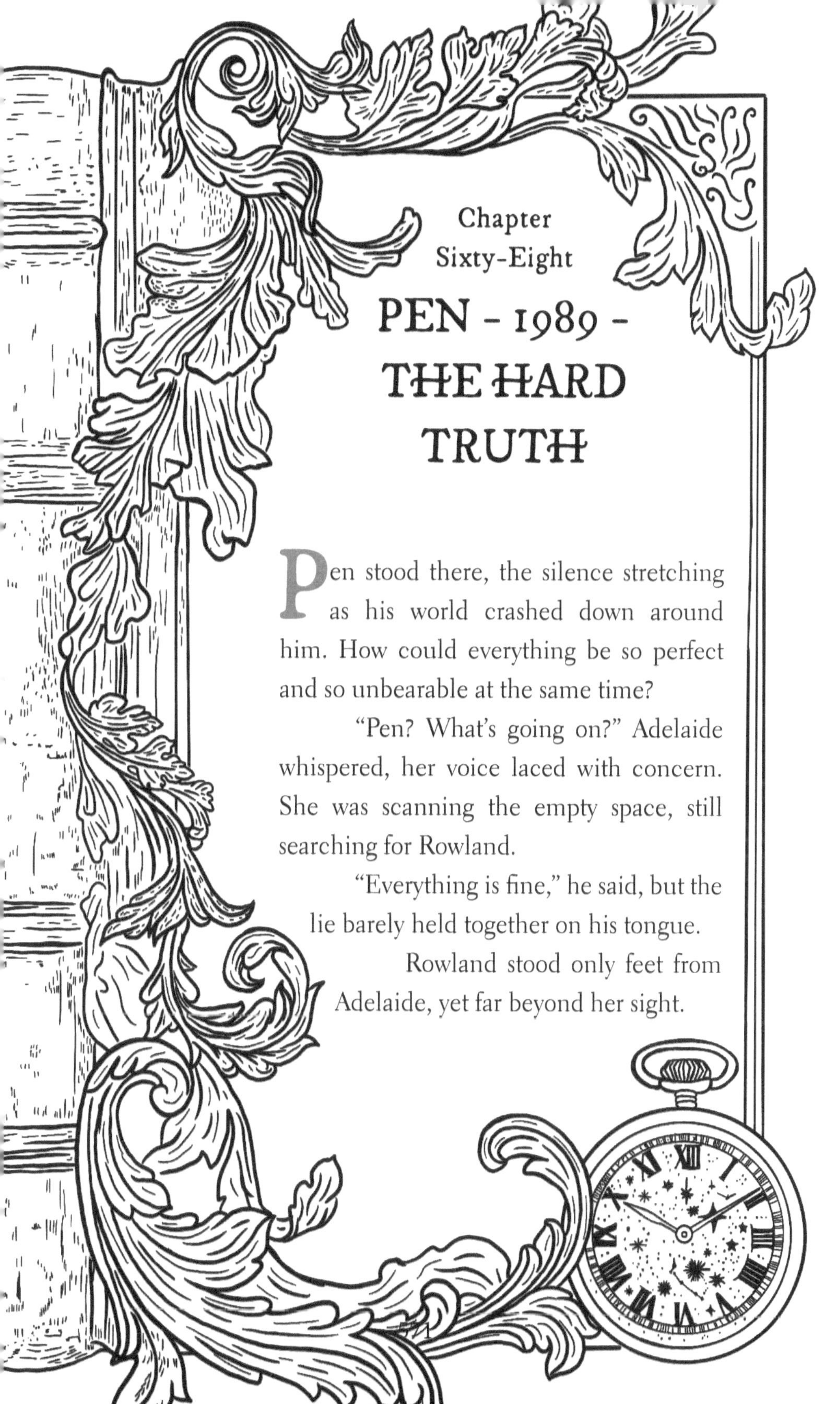

Chapter
Sixty-Eight

PEN - 1989 - THE HARD TRUTH

Pen stood there, the silence stretching as his world crashed down around him. How could everything be so perfect and so unbearable at the same time?

"Pen? What's going on?" Adelaide whispered, her voice laced with concern. She was scanning the empty space, still searching for Rowland.

"Everything is fine," he said, but the lie barely held together on his tongue.

Rowland stood only feet from Adelaide, yet far beyond her sight.

"You still have a day with her," Rowland said gently. "Go and enjoy it. Then do what needs to be done."

Pen swallowed hard, nodding before turning back to Adelaide. "Rowland's right," he agreed. "We need to keep you away from the watch, which means staying clear of the Feather Thorn until tomorrow."

Adelaide's expression slackened, and she hesitated. "What? I don't understand."

"He thinks your proximity to the watch is causing the rip to worsen, and I think he's right," Pen said, walking toward her. "Do you think we could stay at the cabin without alerting Carolyn?"

Adelaide paused, chewing her lip. "Yes, yes, I think so," she said. "But we'll need supplies, some extra blankets and candles."

"Then let's get what we need and head over before she gets home," Pen said, motioning toward the bedroom door.

Adelaide nodded and slipped past him, her footsteps fading down the stairs.

Pen turned back to Rowland. "Will we remember any of this?"

Rowland's reply came quiet and sure. "No."

The finality of the single word struck Pen like a bullet.

"I hope you have better fortune in your next chance at this life," Pen said as he walked out of the room.

Behind him, Rowland said, "You as well."

Downstairs, Pen found Adelaide at the linen closet, arms full of folded blankets.

"Look in that first cupboard there," she said, pointing to a tall, narrow door beside the refrigerator. "The candles should be in there."

He opened it, surprised by the assortment of items inside: candles of every shape and size, tins of oil, jars of herbs, soup bowls, and an impressive variety of liquor bottles.

"Think she'd miss this?" he asked, lifting a bottle of red wine and holding it up for Adelaide to see.

She gave a mischievous grin. "I think we can get away with it. Put it in the basket, along with a few candles and a box of matches."

He packed them into the reed basket on the table that looked just like the handful of others hanging from the kitchen beams.

Adelaide was rummaging through the cupboards and refrigerator, muttering to herself as she searched.

"What are you looking for?" Pen asked.

"Just a few essentials for tonight. We can't go hungry," she said, holding up a block of cheese and a crusty loaf of homemade bread.

His stomach gave a hopeful twist at the prospect of something other than ground beef and eggs for the first time in decades.

"I know it's here somewhere," she said, leaning deeper into the fridge. "Where did she hide it?"

He stepped closer, watching as she shifted things around until she let out a triumphant "Voilà," and held up a Tupperware container.

"What is it?" he asked.

"You'll see," she teased, tucking it into the basket with a smug smile. Then, straightening, she glanced toward the door. "Okay, we'd better go before she gets back. Remember, Carolyn doesn't remember me, and if she finds us here, it'll be hard to explain."

"You're right. I'd almost forgotten," Pen said, grabbing the blankets and hoisting the basket off the table.

Pen whistled into the stillness of the house, and a rustle sounded from the far corner. Frankie bounded out. "Come on, boy," he said. And with one last glance around, the three of them headed to the door.

The cold met him as they stepped outside, sharp and bitter. Frost laced the grass, and a thick bank of cloud dulled what remained of the daylight. Here, the air felt truer to the season, brisk and biting, not like the eerie warmth they'd left behind in the village. Pen tightened his coat, fingers already beginning to numb.

He drew in a long breath. After so long sealed inside the bookshop, he'd forgotten how fresh air tasted. How the wind slid over his skin, how the trees whispered, and the ground smelled of damp leaves and moss. He hadn't realized how much he'd missed it all.

But something felt different. The world seemed darker, more ominous than he remembered. Maybe it was the weight of what he knew, the fate that loomed ahead. Or maybe, somehow, he could sense the rip in time, slowly creeping toward them, like a storm building on the horizon.

"Okay," Adelaide said, shaking him from his thoughts. "Let's move the car up the road. We can't leave it out here for Carolyn to spot."

They loaded their pilfered goods into the back of the car, and Adelaide pulled onto the road, stopping just beyond a curve where the trees would shield it from view. She pulled into a small turnout and shut off the engine.

"I know a shortcut from here," she told him, stepping out and shutting the door behind her.

Pen followed, carrying their supplies as they trudged through a field of knee-high wheatgrass, Frankie at his heels.

"There it is," Adelaide said, pointing toward the outline of a stone cabin nestled at the edge of the woods. She glanced back at him with a smile. "Almost there."

Suddenly, Frankie sprinted off after something through the tall grass.

"Frankie!" Pen called, whistling low and long. His voice carried through the field, but the fox didn't come; instead, he bounded through the underbrush, leaping and pouncing, still on the chase, his red coat flickering like fire between the tall stalks.

Pen took a step to follow, but Adelaide gently caught his hand, holding him still. "He's free now too," she said softly.

The words hit hard. He looked down at her hand in his, warm and certain. She was right. Frankie was never meant to be a pet, never meant to be caged as he had been all these years. He was a wild creature, and he deserved to be free in nature where he belonged.

Adelaide gave his hand a soft squeeze, her eyes full of understanding. "Come on," she said with a soft smile, motioning for them to keep walking.

Pen paused, just a second, scanning the field for one last glimpse. Then, as if summoned, Frankie's head popped up through the grass. Their eyes met, and Pen could see the happiness there. Then the fox dashed off again, vanishing into the thick wheatgrass.

He bit the inside of his cheek and forced down the tightness rising in his throat, the sorrow at seeing his companion for the last time, then he turned back to Adelaide and followed her down the path.

At the cabin, Adelaide pulled a set of keys from her pocket and unlocked the door. "Glad I didn't give these back to Carolyn this week like I planned," she said as they stepped inside.

The door creaked open, and cold air rushed out to meet them. The thick stone walls held the chill like a tomb.

"We're going to need firewood," Pen said, stepping in. "It's freezing."

"Yeah, this place is an icebox. We'll have to sneak back and grab some logs from Carolyn's woodpile."

They set their things on the table and stepped back outside, following the narrow path through the frost-tinted field. Pen
glanced around, hoping for a final glimpse of Frankie, but the little
fox was gone, and the emptiness at his heels made his heart ache.

Ahead of him, Adelaide moved easily, hair swaying from
side to side with each step. She glanced over her shoulder and
smiled. For one gut-wrenching moment, he wished he could
freeze time, to stop everything right here, with her, in this quiet
moment of peace.

Time had once been his prison, an endless loop of solitude
and waiting. And now? Now he would have gladly taken that cage
again if it meant getting to see her every day. Still, he knew how that
ended; his fate would mirror Rowland's eventually. Alone. Watching the person he loved grow old and die.

They had to destroy the watch.

What crushed him, though, wasn't just the loss. It was knowing he wouldn't remember any of it. Not her laugh, not the way her
eyes met his, the way her body felt against his. And she wouldn't
remember him.

He ran a hand through his hair, palm dragging down the
back of his neck. *Focus. Be here. Make these last moments count.*
But his mind wouldn't cooperate. No matter how hard he tried, it
kept circling back to the ache in his chest, the inevitable loss waiting just ahead.

They returned with armfuls of firewood, and Pen lit a fire in
the hearth while Adelaide laid out a picnic on the floor in front of
it. The flames crackled, filling the small stone cabin with warmth,
chasing away the lingering chill. Shadows flickered along the walls,
stretching and swaying like silent witnesses to the night unfolding
before them.

Pen watched her as she poured the wine, her eyes sparkling in the firelight as she told him a story about her childhood. He let himself drift into the moment, into her voice, into the comfort of something that felt heartbreakingly right. For a while, it was easy to forget.

Adelaide leaned back on her elbows, her eyes finding his. "Can I tell you something?" she said.

"Of course."

She hesitated, fingertips grazing the rim of her wine glass. "It was your letters," she said finally, her voice quiet. "The ones you left in the old letterbox. You don't know what they meant to me." Pen stayed quiet, watching her. "When I first got here, I felt completely adrift. I hadn't done anything on my own in… I don't even know how long. And then I found the bookshop. But I felt like maybe I wouldn't be able to do it. Until I found one of your letters. You told me I was doing a great job. That the Feather Thorn was coming back to life because of me. You made me believe it was possible. You kept me going when I couldn't see the end."

Pen's heart clenched, his throat tightening around words he couldn't say. She didn't know that tomorrow, none of this would exist. That their story would be unwritten, their memories erased. He would become a stranger to her, and she to him, and everything they had would be nothing but dust in the wind.

He forced a small smile. "I just… wanted you to know what I saw. You were bringing something beautiful back into the world, and I thought you should hear it."

Adelaide reached for his hand, lacing her fingers with his. "It was more than that, Pen. You helped me believe in myself again. You reminded me I was capable of being more than just someone's wife. That I could make a life here for myself."

The words hit him like a punch to the chest. He looked down at their hands, his thumb brushing over hers. "When I came to Helensburgh all those years ago, I wanted to be someone different, someone better than the poor kid from Oak Ridge. I thought if I could make something of myself, then maybe it would mean I mattered. But being here… being *with you*… it's made me realize I don't have to be anyone else." He paused, swallowing the ache rising in his chest. "*You* made me see that."

Adelaide's expression softened. "You've always been enough, Pen. Today and forever in my eyes."

Pen tightened his grip on her hand, memorizing the feel of it, the shape of her knuckles, the curve of her palm. *By tomorrow, you won't even remember me*, he thought, and the thought nearly broke him.

All those years trapped inside the Feather Thorn, he'd dreamed of freedom, of what his future might look like if he ever got out of the loop. Now that he had, the future felt like a curse. He couldn't bear to look ahead, not when every step meant leaving her behind.

So he stayed here. In the moment.

He pulled her close, wrapping her in his arms and kissed her with the urgency of someone whose time was running out. "You gave me more than you'll ever know," he whispered as they sank back onto the makeshift bed on the floor and made love once more.

Later, as the fire burned low and the cabin filled with the soft rhythm of their breaths, she curled against him, into his arms like she belonged there, and drifted off to sleep.

He held her tight. The thought of letting go, of giving her up, felt impossible.

"I love you," he breathed into her hair, so softly she wouldn't hear. "Always."

He didn't sleep that night. He couldn't. He didn't want to miss a single second with her.

Instead, he watched her breathe, watched the firelight trace the curves of her face like a memory he didn't want to lose. He burned every detail into his mind, desperate to hold on to it, even knowing it would slip through his fingers like sand tomorrow. But tonight, tonight he would let himself dream, dream of what life might have been like if things had gone differently. If this had been their beginning instead of their end.

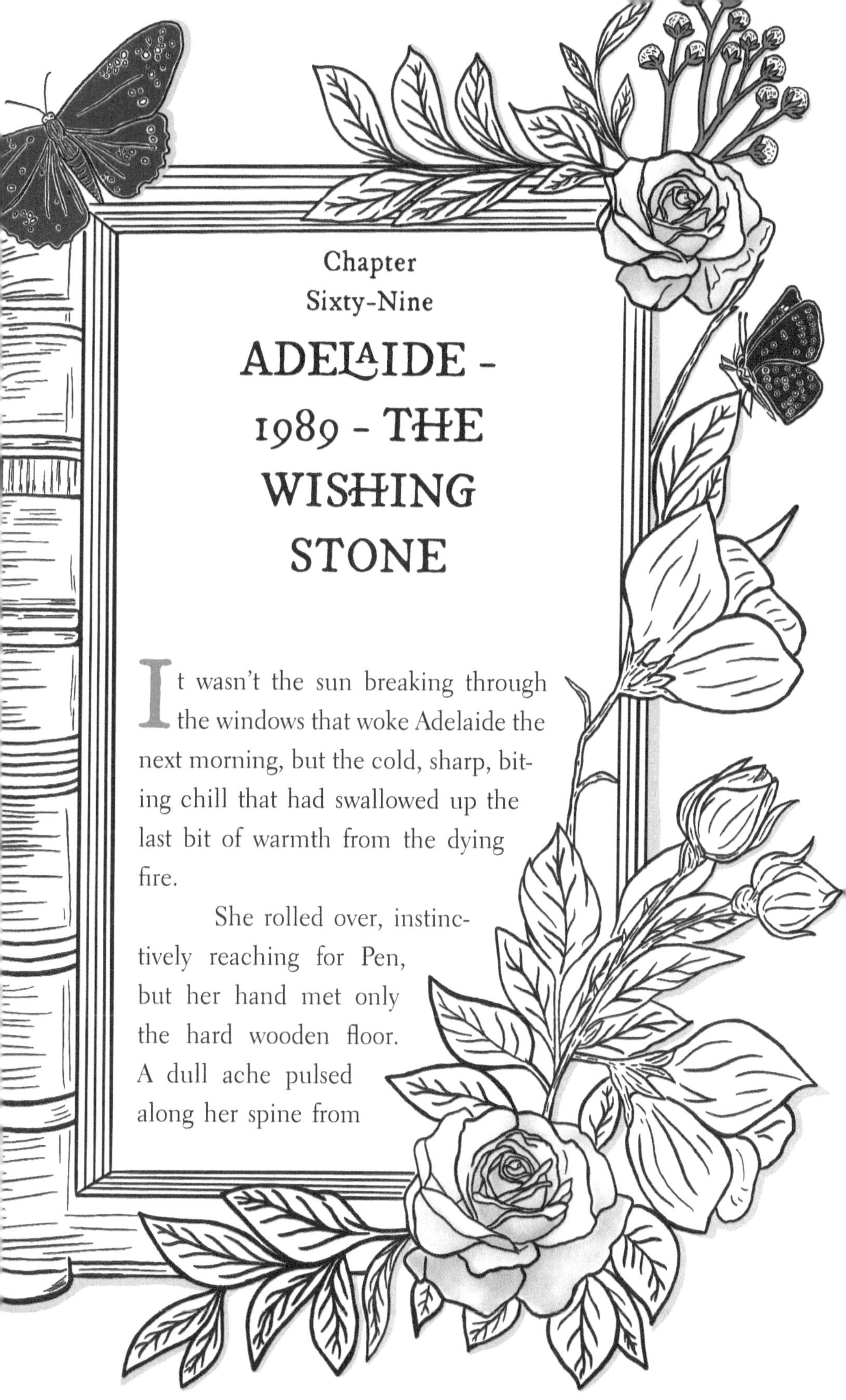

ADELAIDE – 1989 – THE WISHING STONE

It wasn't the sun breaking through the windows that woke Adelaide the next morning, but the cold, sharp, biting chill that had swallowed up the last bit of warmth from the dying fire.

She rolled over, instinctively reaching for Pen, but her hand met only the hard wooden floor. A dull ache pulsed along her spine from the night spent sleeping there. They hadn't made it to the bed, but being wrapped up in Pen was all she'd needed for comfort then.

The air felt different. A stale tang of cigarette smoke clung to the room, unfamiliar and out of place. A sudden fear surged through her, her pulse hammering in her veins. Had it happened? Had the other reality slipped past the edge of town and stolen Pen away from her?

She sat up fast, scanning the small space.

Empty.

Throwing off the blanket, she pulled on her clothes, barely registering the stiffness in her limbs as she hurried to the bathroom, hope clashing against dread. Pressing a hand against the door, she knocked.

No answer.

She pushed it open, but still she found nothing, only the stillness of an undisturbed room and an orb spider that had spun a web in the corner.

Panic clawed at her throat, mixing with the sourness of too much wine from the night before. She leaned against the sink, forcing herself to breathe.

"Is anything different?" she whispered, scanning the space with careful eyes.

But everything was just as she'd left it the day she moved out. Nothing had changed. Nothing had been added or erased. It seemed for now, the rip hadn't made it this far.

Her breath hitched. Was she losing her mind? Had any of it been real?

She was on the verge of questioning her own sanity when footsteps creaked across the front porch. She rushed to the window, peeked outside, and a wave of relief flooded over her.

Pen. With an armful of firewood stacked against his chest, his coat peppered with sawdust.

She threw the door open before he could reach for the handle, and a gust of air followed him in, warm and unsettling against her skin, making her nerves stand on edge.

"Good morning," Pen greeted cheerfully, moving past her to the fireplace. He knelt and stacked the wood, brushing stray bits of bark from his sleeves.

"Not sure I needed to grab this, though," he mused, glancing over his shoulder at her with a crooked smile. "Feels like it's heating up outside. Strange how it's still so cold in here."

Adelaide knew why. The other reality was creeping toward them like an advancing tide. But she didn't want to start their day with the impending doom that waited just beyond sight.

"These stone cabins hold the cold," she said instead, offering a small smile.

Pen returned it, but the spark was gone from his eyes. He knew the truth too, but neither wanted to be the first to admit it, to speak that truth out loud. Not while time still allowed them to pretend.

"How long have you been up?" she asked, stepping into the small kitchenette.

"A while now," he answered, pulling off his jacket.

She reached into the basket and pulled out the Tupperware container she'd taken the night before. "Now you get to see what I snuck into the basket," she told him, opening the lid with a pop. The rich scent of freshly ground coffee filled the air.

Pen grinned. "Now that's my girl," he said, stepping behind her and wrapping his arms around her waist as she scooped the coffee into the filter and set the pot to brew.

She turned in his embrace, sliding her arms around his neck and pulling him into a slow, lingering kiss. She could have melted into him, lost herself in the warmth of his touch, the steady beat of his heart against hers. If she let herself, she might never let go.

But as their lips parted, the weight of the day ahead crashed down on her like that tide breaking against the shore. She pulled away and moved her attention back to the steady drip of the coffee pot, as if it could hold back the inevitable.

"When should we go back to the Feather Thorn?" she asked, knowing they couldn't avoid the conversation much longer.

"Not until close to dark," Pen said. "We don't know how far the rip has progressed, but judging by the shift in the weather, I fear it's spreading, whether you're there or not." Concern darkened his features.

"I think you're right," she admitted, trying to mask her exhaustion with a smile. But Pen wouldn't be fooled.

"Listen," he said, catching her hand and pulling her back toward him. "This is what we're going to do today. We're going to spend time together, like it's just a normal day, like we're any other couple. And then, just before dusk, we'll figure out our plan. Okay?"

He kissed her again, as if sealing the promise.

When the coffee was ready, they carried their mugs to the fire and curled up on their makeshift bed, sitting in comfortable silence as they drank.

Adelaide traced the rim of her mug and looked up. "I have an idea," she said. "There's a place Carolyn used to take me when I was young, just beyond the woods behind the cabin. She called it Fairy Grove. There's a stone there, if you whisper to it, they say, it listens. Maybe we should try it, wish on the wishing stone, for luck."

Pen smiled, warmth returning to his eyes. "Sounds like something out of a fairy tale, but I think that sounds like the perfect way to spend the afternoon."

Adelaide tilted her head. "It's still hours until the afternoon. What are we going to do until then?"

As soon as the words left her lips, Pen was kissing them away, and she knew exactly what they would be doing.

But the kiss wasn't full of desire or heat; it was sorrowful and tender. It felt deliberate, steeped in something unspoken. Like he wasn't just kissing her, but trying to hold on, to carve the moment into memory, as if this might be the last time he'd ever get the chance.

She pulled back, just a fraction, enough to search his face. "Is everything okay?"

His gaze met hers, the blue of his eyes darker than she remembered, shadowed with something he was trying to mask.

"What is it?" she asked again, her fingers brushing lightly against his cheek, grazing the faint stubble there.

"Nothing," he said, forcing a small smile. "I just wish we could have met in a different way."

She huffed a soft laugh, trying to lighten the mood. "If we had, you'd be an old man by now."

"I suppose you're right," he said, playing along. "Would you still have said yes if I'd asked you out, old man and all?"

She shrugged. "Depends. Would you have looked this dashing as an old man?"

That earned her a real laugh, the tension in his shoulders visibly softening. She leaned in again, cutting off whatever he was about to say. This kiss was different. The hesitation melted away, and they lost themselves in it, then in each other. They moved together as they had the night before, as if the space between them had grown unbearable, knowing the morning light could not last forever.

The sun had climbed higher by the time they surfaced, limbs tangled in the blankets, wrapped in the heat of one another, the fire now a faint ember.

Adelaide lay nestled against his chest, her fingers lazily tracing shapes along his arm. "If we don't move soon, we'll fall asleep and miss the whole solstice thing tonight," she murmured. "Let's go for that walk now."

"You're probably right," he teased, running his thumb across her jawline before pulling her into one last, lingering kiss.

She pulled away, arching a brow. "If I didn't know better, I'd think you were trying to tire me out, Mr. Turner."

He grinned. "And if I was?"

She let out a playful scoff as she sat up, the blanket slipping off her shoulders. "Not going to happen. Get your arse off the floor and get dressed," she waggled a mock-stern finger at him.

With an exaggerated groan, he sat up and began pulling on his clothes.

"I promise," she said, lacing up her trainers, "tomorrow we can stay in bed all day in the flat. And the next day. And the next. Until you're sick of me."

The teasing warmth in his expression faded, replaced by something softer, sadder. He reached for her hand. "I could never tire of you, my sweet Adelaide," he murmured.

Her heart skipped at the words, not just because it was something she had longed to hear, but because she *believed* him. He meant it, every word.

For the first time in what felt like forever, the future looked brighter.

They were only hours away from destroying the watch, only hours away from being done with this once and for all. If John Dee's predictions were right, the rip would cease to exist, and the world would settle back into place.

But what if he hadn't been right? What if the fracture didn't heal and the world didn't right itself?

What if the damage was already done, if the other reality had taken hold, weaving itself into their existence too tightly to be unraveled? Would the ritual still work? Would any of it?

There were no answers, no promises, only the looming unknown, with no certainty until they stepped into the moment that would decide everything.

All she could do was hope.

"Okay, ready to go?" Pen's voice nudged her from her thoughts.

She blinked, pushing the questions aside, looked up at him and smiled. "Yes."

She walked to the door and swung it open. A warm summer breeze rushed past her, spilling into the cool cabin.

As they stepped outside, though, something shifted in the air, a wrongness she hadn't noticed before. It was subtle, a single out-of-tune note in an otherwise perfect song. A shimmer of something threading through the trees, the same wrongness that had blanketed the town after everything had changed. The tear was getting closer.

Pen looked up, and Adelaide's gaze followed skyward. The blue above was thickening to something almost purple, and faint stars had begun to form, too early, too wrong, pinpricks in a painted veil.

"It's happening," she said, head still tilted toward the heavens.

"It is," Pen murmured, slipping his hand into hers, lacing their fingers together. She held on tighter, as if pressure alone could anchor them in what was real. "There's nothing we can do about any of this until tonight," he added, his voice steady. "So let's just try to enjoy the beautiful, warm day while we still can."

"You're absolutely right," she agreed. "Follow me."

She led him through Carolyn's field, where golden wheat-grass bowed in the breeze and wildflowers tilted their faces toward the strange sky. At the edge of the woods, a massive oak tree stood, its sprawling branches creating a natural archway, a tunnel of shade, a doorway into another world.

"This way," she called over her shoulder. She stepped through first, the air instantly cooler, the dense canopy overhead allowing only patches of dappled light to spill onto the forest floor. Pine needles softened the path bordered by lush ferns, and the air smelled of damp earth, pine, and the faint, familiar scent of fall leaves.

The forest hadn't changed. Not yet. It welcomed her like an old friend.

When the trail reached a clearing, the trees parted just enough to let a column of golden light spill onto the earth. At the center of it, bathed in the glow as if on a stage, was a large rock, covered in moss.

"Here it is, Big Rock," Adelaide said with a nostalgic smile. "Or as Carolyn calls it, *Fairy Grove*. She always told me this was a wishing stone. Like a well, but instead of tossing in a coin, you make an offering and a wish."

They stepped onto the soft, moss-covered ground, a plush carpet beneath their feet. Trinkets dotted the floor, offerings from other years: a ceramic mug, smooth stones and crystals, buttons, a thimble, a tiny glass flower. And nestled into a deep groove in the rock's surface was a small heart-shaped necklace.

"Look," she said, pointing to it. "I put that there when I was little."

Pen turned to her, curiosity flickering in his eyes. "What did you wish for?"

She hesitated, then smiled. "Normally, I wouldn't be able to tell you, or it wouldn't come true. But seeing as it already has, I suppose it's safe."

She rose onto her tiptoes, lips brushing his ear. "You." Then she kissed him.

It was slow and sure, full of things she hadn't yet had the courage to say and might never get another chance to. When she pulled away, she let out a soft, breathless laugh, and placed her palm to his chest.

"This," she whispered. "This is what I wished for."

Pen's expression softened, and for a moment, the world outside the forest didn't exist.

"Alright," she said, breaking the spell, "now the question is, do you have something to give the stone? Something to make a wish with?"

Pen stood still for only a second before reaching into his pocket. He pulled out a shiny penny and stepped up to the rock.

Adelaide watched as he stared at the coin in his palm, lips moving silently, then he placed it gently onto the mossy surface and stepped back.

"What about you?" he asked. "Are you going to make a wish?"

She shook her head, smiling. "Nah. Mine already came true. Best not to push my luck."

PEN - 1989 - THE NORTH STAR

Night fell sooner than Pen had wanted.

By the time they emerged from the forest, the sky had already turned, a heavy charcoal blue, dense with the weight of a storm about to break. They walked back to the cabin mostly in silence, fingers laced together, both lost in thoughts of what lay ahead.

Pen couldn't stop replaying something Adelaide had said earlier: that tomorrow, they could stay in bed all day. And the next. And the next, until he was sick of her.

She had no idea.

No idea there wouldn't be a tomorrow for them.

If the ritual were successful, if the watch were destroyed, then time would reset. The rip would close, but time would pull them apart, back to wherever they were meant to be if the watch had never existed.

He should tell her. She deserved the truth.

But how could he take that hope from her? That hope, fragile as it was, was all she had left to hold on to. How could he tell her that the future she saw for them was nothing but an illusion?

As they stepped into the cabin, a wall of heat wrapped around them. The fire still smoldered in the hearth, and with the rising temperatures outside, the space felt stifling.

"What if we get there and it's too late, what if everything's already gone?" Adelaide asked, breaking the silence. "What if the watch is gone?"

Pen exhaled. "I don't think that could happen. The watch is the cause of all this. It has to exist both here and in the other reality."

She nodded but didn't look convinced. "We'll find out soon enough, I suppose." She reached for a glass, poured herself some water, fingers tightening around it. "When should we leave?"

Pen glanced out the window at the darkening sky. "We should go now," Pen said. "The sun will be fully down within the hour."

She hesitated. "And we need to stop by the apothecary before it closes, for the herbs."

"Good thinking. Let's move."

They left behind the blankets and supplies they'd taken from Carolyn's and headed to Adelaide's car.

The drive back to the Feather Thorn passed in silence. Adelaide kept her eyes on the road, and Pen kept his eyes on her. He still didn't know whether to tell her or let her believe they had more time.

Because this time, there would be no letters slipped into the old letterbox. No messages in fogged-up windows or echoed through typewriter keys. This time, it would be final.

Why did this have to happen? Maybe he was cursed. Maybe this was penance for some forgotten sin in another life. Like standing at the gates of Heaven, told he could step inside but only to look around, to see its glory, before being turned away.

As they pulled into Helensburgh, the town was unrecognizable.

The familiar outline of the Feather Thorn stood in its normal place, the apothecary, along with a few of the homes that lined the street. But everything else had shifted, like a town rebuilt from a faded photograph, familiar in shape, but wrong in all the details. Roofs shaped at odd angles, lampposts flickered with candlelight, and entire buildings appeared warped, reshaped into forms that didn't quite belong to this century or ones past. The sky was streaked with strange blues and purples twisting like ink spilled in water, speckled with too many stars, like they were looking up at another galaxy altogether, and maybe they were.

They passed a few people, cloaked in what looked like seventeenth-century attire, tricorn hats, long coats, lace at the collar. Two of them turned and stared as they drove by, their expressions flickering with surprise, while the rest carried on as though moving through some dream, unaware of the world beyond their own shifting.

Two stone buildings stood ahead, buildings that hadn't been there the day before. One looked to be a butcher's, the other a cobbler's, though Pen couldn't make sense of the signs hanging in the windows. They weren't written in English, or any language he recognized, just jagged lines and looping symbols.

As Adelaide pulled up beside the shop, unease curled in Pen's gut. The blue trim was gone. The sign, too. The Feather Thorn no longer looked as it had. But it wasn't just the paint or the missing name. It was something deeper. An uncanny wrongness that made the building seem like a bad translation of itself. Like a fish gasping on land, still a fish, still recognizable, but stripped of what made it whole.

"We need the journals, if we're going to make sure we are doing this right," Adelaide said as she shut off the engine.

"You're right." Pen reached for the door, following her out and into the Feather Thorn.

The once cozy space lined with bookshelves was gone; the hot forge loomed in its place. The man was still there, sweeping the floor as the forge's embers faded to a dull glow. Just like before, they were still ghosts to him.

Adelaide moved toward the stairs. And there, just as it had been in the real Feather Thorn, was the trapdoor. She exhaled, hope returning to her eyes. She pulled on the ring, and the door opened. Pen followed her down, but when they arrived at the bottom of the stairs, it wasn't the hidden room they knew waiting for them.

No desk. No books. No typewriter. No journals.

Just a single oil lamp casting shadows over sacks of grain and potatoes.

"Shit!" Adelaide spun, eyes wide and frantic. "What happened to everything? The watch, the journals, Pen, are we stuck here?"

"I don't know?" he said, fighting to keep his voice calm. "But we will figure this out." His mind played back everything he had read, piecing together every detail from Dee's notes. Then it came to him. John Dee's hiding place. A loose stone in the wall. He'd mentioned it only once, but still, if the building had been rewound, maybe it was still here.

Pen stepped up to the cold stone and ran his hands along the wall.

"What are you doing?" Adelaide asked as she watched.

He didn't answer, just kept feeling the damp stones, silently praying. *Please, let it be here.*

Then, a stone shifted beneath his touch, only slightly, but enough. "It's loose," he said, as he wiggled it free.

Behind it, tucked in the dark hollow, lay the journal and a leather bag.

"Oh, thank God," Adelaide said as he pulled them free.

"We should keep these with us now. No more chances," Pen said, handing the items to Adelaide and pushing the stone back into place.

She nodded, still pale. "We need to get over to the apothecary soon."

Adelaide passed the journal to him, and Pen opened it, turning to the last page.

"Okay, we need lavender, chamomile, cedar, and cinnamon," he read aloud.

"Got it." Adelaide checked her jacket pocket and pulled out a few coins. "Let's hope this place still takes pounds. If they're trading in goat's teeth or salt stones, we're in trouble." She offered him a tight smile, but the tension remained, heavy as they made their way back up the stairs and outside.

Across the road, the Purple Thorn glowed soft under the altered sky. Just as they approached, the door opened; Carolyn stepped outside, taking in her tea shop's sign for the night.

"Pen, do you think she should see you? What if she freaks out?" Adelaide shot a whisper to him over her shoulder and slowed.

"She isn't the same Carolyn as our version, remember. If she doesn't know you, she certainly won't remember me." He gave her a slight nudge. "Let's keep moving."

"Excuse me, are you still open?" Adelaide asked.

Carolyn looked up, catching the streetlamp's glow in her crystal-blue eyes. "Yes, come in," she said, holding the door wide. "I was just getting ready to close up for the day, but you're more than welcome to browse for a few minutes."

Pen followed Adelaide inside, doing his best to act natural, though being this close to her made his blood run cold. He'd seen her from the bookshop window, white hair, an aged face weathered by sorrow, but now, standing just a few feet away, she looked only slightly older than when they'd met in 1955. It unsettled him. As if time itself were flipping a coin.

As he stepped past her into the shop, she studied him, tilting her head slightly. "Do I know you?" she asked, curiosity flickering in her gaze.

Pen felt his stomach drop. She was looking at him too closely. "No, I don't think so," he said, forcing an easy smile. "We're not from around here."

Not a complete lie. But still, a lie.

Carolyn narrowed her eyes. "You look an awful lot like my tailor over on Copper Lane. Pen Turner. You wouldn't happen to be related to him, would you?"

Pen Turner. His name. His heart stopped. Adelaide spun around, her eyes wide.

How? How did *this* version of Carolyn know his name? Did *he* exist in this reality? Had another version of him lived a full life here in Scotland?

For a heartbeat, hope rose. If another version of him was here, did that mean there was a chance, however small, that he could find his way back, that some part of him *belonged* here, that there was a version of his story that didn't end tonight?

But then Rowland's warning slammed into him.

When your past and present selves share the same space, the danger isn't in your proximity; it's in knowing. If you both become aware of each other, the tether weakens. And when that breaks, so does reality.

"No, I'm sorry," Pen said quickly.

Carolyn studied him for a beat longer before giving a small, thoughtful nod. "Strange, you look like you could be his son."

She moved to the windows, shutting them one by one, the faint warmth of the dusk breeze slipping away with each latch.

"You can feel the seasons changing," she said with a wistful smile, returning to the counter. "So, what is it you two are looking for?" she asked, though Pen could still feel her eyes on him, curious, assessing, not quite convinced.

"We actually just need a few things. Lavender, cinnamon, cedar, and chamomile," Adelaide said.

Carolyn arched a brow. "I have all of those. Now, either you're making a soothing bedtime brew, *or* you're planning to destroy something." She gave a small chuckle as she turned and pulled the jars down from the shelves.

Adelaide shot Pen a glance, half-smile, half-grimace, then busied herself inspecting the jars while Carolyn worked.

Once everything was measured and bundled, Carolyn rang them up behind the counter. "That'll be one pound."

Relief washed over Adelaide's face at the familiar currency, and she quickly pulled the coin from her pocket, placing it on the counter.

"Thank you," she said, accepting the small bag offered. "It was really kind of you to stay open a few minutes longer for us."

"No trouble at all, my dear," Carolyn said with a warm smile, the same smile Pen remembered from all those years ago, but also different at the same time.

Adelaide turned toward the door, but Pen remained where he stood, still caught in the strangeness of it all.

Carolyn met his gaze one last time, then, without another word, she turned and disappeared into the back room.

Back out on the cobbled street, Adelaide turned to Pen, eyes wide. "Holy shit, how did she recognize you? She didn't even know who I was, and *I'm* her niece."

"I have no idea," Pen said, his voice tight. "But if there's another version of me out there… We should get out of sight before anyone else sees us."

He didn't wait for her reply. His pace quickened as they crossed the street and ducked back through the Feather Thorn's entrance, slipping past the blacksmith once again.

Upstairs, the attic greeted them with its stark emptiness, the ghost of a life once lived.

"How much time do we have?" Adelaide asked.

Pen walked to the window and peered out. The sky was darker now, but still *wrong*. He squinted, searching for stars he'd memorized over countless years, but the constellations were fragmented, scattered, as if a celestial hand had shaken the night sky and left the pieces to fall out of place. His stomach twisted. The North Star was missing.

It had always been his constant, the first to appear, fixed in its position, a quiet reassurance that some things never changed. But now? It was gone.

"What's wrong?" Adelaide asked, moving to his side.

"I can't find it," he said, voice strained. He kept scanning the sky, willing it to appear. "The North Star, it's not there."

"Are you sure?" She leaned forward, gaze following his.

Fear rushed through him, thick and suffocating. What if they were wrong about the solstice? What if the timeline had already drifted too far off course? They'd seen it rewrite the seasons. Summer had taken hold when it should have been winter. Had they missed their window here in this reality?

He swallowed hard, trying to calculate and map the sky. Hoping that the rip hadn't spread past the borders of town, that there was still more of *his* world left than this one. If that were the case, the ritual could still work.

"Look, there!" Adelaide pointed toward the distant mountains. His gaze followed.

Tucked into the crook of the peaks, just rising from the horizon, a single star glimmered, brighter than all the others in the sky.

"Yes," he breathed, gripping her hand. He squeezed it for just a second before stepping back. "The North Star is out," he said. "Which means we can start whenever we're ready."

"Great. Let's gather the rest of what we need," Adelaide said, opening the journal and flipping to the list. "We have the herbs, now we just need a few bowls and a knife." She glanced around the empty space. "The bowls…" She sighed. "We don't have any. God, I wish I had thought about that when we were still at the cabin." Her lips pressed into a thin line as she looked around.

Pen thought for a moment, then walked back to the window. He scanned the town below, sweeping over the darkened streets. Just a few doors down from the apothecary, a house sat with four small pots perched on the windowsill, tiny green sprouts pushing through the soil.

"I have an idea," he told her, turning from the window. "I'll be right back."

Before Adelaide could question him, he went into the bedroom and grabbed Rowland's old paperboy hat off the back of the door, then slipped out the door, moving quickly down the stairs and onto the street.

The silence outside pressed in like fog.

He looked both ways, making sure no one was watching, then sprinted toward the house. At the windowsill, he quickly dumped the dirt unceremoniously onto the cobbles, stacked the pots, and tucked them into his coat.

But as he turned to run back, footsteps echoed down the lane.

A figure appeared; Pen froze.

His pulse pounded in his ears, louder than the wind that stirred the leaves around him. Instinct made him duck his head, shoulders drawn tight as he tried to shrink into nothing, hoping, no, wishing that he was invisible to him, just as he was to the man in the forge.

He knew, *knew*, he shouldn't look, just in case it was his alternate self. Because if what Rowland had said was true, and two versions of the same person became aware of each other, then this moment could tear apart the last fragile seam holding everything together.

But… he couldn't help himself. He was like a moth to a flame.

A chill passed through him, something unseen curling around his spine, an invisible thread drawing his gaze upward like a string being pulled.

His eyes lifted for just a second, but it was long enough.

Long enough to see the man walking toward him, trench coat flaring around his boots, his face half lost in shadow. But Pen didn't need the light to know who it was.

Because it was *him*.

Chapter
Seventy-One

PEN &
ADELAIDE -
1989 - THE
SOLSTICE

Pen's eyes shot down instantly, his pulse hammering in his ears. He yanked the brim of his paperboy hat lower, hiding his face as he quickened his pace. Crossing the street, he veered away from his alternate self, who, thankfully didn't even seem to notice him.

The moment they passed, he felt it, an invisible snap in the air, like static catching on skin. A crackling energy, sharp and electric, making the hairs on the back of his neck stand on end.

Then…

A deafening crack of thunder tore across the sky, echoing off the buildings and through the fractured night.

Pen bolted, the stolen pots clattering inside his jacket as he sprinted through the strange town. He didn't stop until he crashed through the Feather Thorn's doors, barreled up the stairs, and into the attic apartment.

Adelaide spun from the window, her eyes widening. "Pen!" she gasped, taking in his winded, hunched-over form.

"Did you see him?" he asked between ragged breaths. "Did you see the man on the street?"

Her brows knitted together. "Man? What man?"

"The one who walked past me," he said, straightening. "In the long coat. He looked, he looked—"

"No. I was watching the whole time. I didn't see *any* man."

"What do you mean you didn't see him?"

"I didn't see anyone," she repeated, turning back toward the window. "I only saw you. You grabbed the pots, brilliant idea, by the way, and then ran back here. There was no one else."

"What about the thunder?" he pressed, striding toward the window and scanning the empty street.

Adelaide chewed at her thumbnail, a worried look pulling at her face. She shook her head. "I didn't hear any thunder, Pen."

That couldn't be right. He'd *heard* it. He'd *felt* it. A heavy silence stretched between them as he kept his eyes locked on the horizon, his chest rising and falling with uneven breaths.

"Tell me you can see this," he said, his voice barely above a whisper, his gaze fixed on something in the distance.

Adelaide stepped beside him, following his line of sight. At first there was only cloud and shadow, then the skyline rippled, and the illusion peeled back. Her lips parted. "What is that?"

Pen turned toward her, hope sparking in his eyes. "You see it too?" She gave a small nod, still staring. "Yes, I don't understand."

Where there should have been sky, there was *something else.* Something vast that had risen, gleaming spires, unfamiliar architecture, a skyline etched in steel.

"A *city*?" Adelaide asked, her voice growing more unsteady by the second.

"Yes." Pen didn't take his eyes off it. "I think it's another reality breaking through. The rip is spreading, not just through time, but through *other* realities now." His expression darkened. "This is much worse than we thought."

Adelaide tore her focus away and looked at Pen. "The man you saw, who was he?"

Pen swallowed hard. "It was me. An *older* me. The age I'd be now if I'd never been trapped."

His eyes widened, as a thought struck, sharp and sudden.

"Oh, no," he murmured. "It must have been our proximity. Two versions of me existing in the same space, too close. I thought he didn't see me, but he must have. That's what caused the tear to expand. That boom, it wasn't thunder, it was the rip growing wider." He turned fully to her, urgency flaring in his voice. "Adelaide, we need to do the ritual *now*, before this spreads any further."

But even as the words left his mouth, a deeper truth clenched in his chest. He couldn't let her go through with this, not without knowing what it would cost. She deserved to know the truth, even if it was heartbreaking. He stepped closer and took her hands in his.

"There's something I need to tell you first."

Adelaide's pulse kicked up. She saw the warning in his eyes before he even spoke, knew she wasn't going to like what he had to say, and her stomach somersaulted.

"Adelaide, you need to understand something," he said carefully. "When you destroy the watch, you destroy its entire timeline."

The words landed hard, and she froze, air catching in her throat as if the wind had been knocked from her. It wasn't the ground that gave way, it was everything she'd built inside. Each hope, each fragile belief that she'd dared to hold, collapsing inward like burned paper folding to ash.

"Does that mean… none of this would have existed?" she whispered. Tears pooled, clinging to her lashes, warping the world into a watery blur.

It didn't make sense. How could this be happening now, just when she'd begun to feel whole again? She'd dragged herself out of the grief, out of that hollow, aching place Jeff had left her in. Pen had felt like a reward. A sign that the pain she'd gone through had meant something. That surviving it had earned her something beautiful, Pen's love.

But maybe it wasn't a reward at all, maybe it had been a punishment.

The Bible called the Nephilim abominations, hunted by flood and fire, wiped from the Earth by God himself. What if Pen's love was never meant to be a blessing? What if it was given only so it could be taken away? A consequence, a punishment of being born a creature of the in between.

She looked up just as Pen exhaled slowly, seemingly trying to find his words.

"Yes. If the watch never exists, I never get trapped in time. And if I never get trapped… we never meet."

A sound tore from her lips, raw and broken. "No." The first tear slipped free, and then a cascade. "No, that can't be!" She shook her head, as if denying it would change the truth.

Pen reached for her, pulling her into his arms. "Rowland told me."

She stiffened. Then, realization hit her like a knife to the ribs. "You've *known* this whole time?" She shoved him away, her voice breaking. "*And you didn't tell me?*"

Pen's expression crumbled. "I didn't want to hurt you."

"So you lied?"

"I thought… if you didn't know, it might be easier on you." His voice was quiet, pleading. "And… I didn't think you'd go through with it if you knew."

Her breath came fast and uneven, thoughts crashing against each other.

"But I couldn't let you do this *without* knowing first," he finished, his voice raw. "You have the right to know everything, even if it's hard. The right to walk into this knowing what it will truly cost."

For a moment, neither of them spoke, nor did they move. The silence was full, not empty, dragging with it the sacrifice they were being forced to make.

"How selfish do you think I am?" Adelaide's voice rose, anger sharpening her words. "Did you really think I would let the whole world *fall apart* just so we could have a happily ever after?"

"No, of course not," he said, his voice low. "But if it came down to choosing what I wanted instead of what was right…" He met her eyes. "I just know that if *I* had the power to destroy the watch, I don't think I could do it. I don't think I could lose you."

Tears streamed down her face as she stepped toward him, and without hesitation, he pulled her into his arms, holding her tightly as his own tears fell silently against her hair.

"I will always love you," she whispered against his chest. "No matter the time, no matter the place… I will find you."

She looked up at him then, her blue eyes full of certainty, full of love, and the faith that he didn't feel he deserved.

He couldn't say it, he couldn't tell her this truth. Couldn't tell her that in a matter of minutes, she wouldn't even *remember* him. Not his name, not his face, not the time they had shared. He couldn't take that last lingering hope from her.

His heart ached in a way he had never known before. "You will always be my one true love, Adelaide," he said, his voice thick.

He reached instinctively into his pocket for his lucky penny, needing the smooth, comforting surface on his fingertips. He'd forgotten it was gone, left as a token for his wish. He prayed in that moment that his wish would come true, that he wouldn't forget her, that he could hold onto the memory of her even after the watch had been destroyed.

Without warning, a crack of thunder split the air, real and violent, shaking the walls and the floor. Adelaide flinched. This time, she *did* hear it.

Their heads snapped toward the window. Off in the distance, where the earth met the sky, a thin line of gold stretched across the mountains, the first light of dawn.

But the sun had only just set.

"No," Pen breathed, the word clawing out of him. "It's too

soon. It can't be dawn already. *We need to do this now!*"

Adelaide was already moving. She opened the journal with shaking hands, flipping to the page they'd marked. Pen dropped to his knees beside her, pulling out his pocket knife. The blade bit into the old floor as he carved the four cardinal points, North, South, East, West, into the wood.

There was no time left for hesitation. No more space for their grief. No more questions, no more confessions. The time Pen once had in abundance was now nothing more than fleeting moments.

They both knew what had to be done would break them. Still, they moved forward, not to hold on, but to let go. For something greater than either of them.

Adelaide, followed close behind, placing the clay pots at the points he'd marked. Her movements were careful, as if she were trying to make peace with what was coming.

Together, one by one, they placed the herbs where they belonged.

Between North and East, **lavender**.

Between East and South, **cinnamon**.

Between South and West, **chamomile**.

Between West and North, **cedar**.

Pen pulled the leather bag from his pocket, his hands shaking as he walked over to Adelaide.

He lifted his hands, cupping her face, memorizing the feel of her skin, and he kissed her. Drinking her in one last time. It was deep, desperate, full of every unspoken word, every lost moment, every stolen second they had left. The world around them faded, the chaos, the fear, none of it mattered.

"I love you," he whispered, wiping the tears from her cheeks. "It's all going to be okay."

"I love you, too," Adelaide whispered back, pressing one final kiss to his lips. When she stepped into the center of the circle, a moth fluttered in through the window, looping around her in wide, searching arcs, as if she were the light it had been seeking all along. In that moment, it felt right, as though everything had come full circle, and she was exactly where she'd always meant to be. Maybe this was her true purpose. Maybe this was why she'd been called to the Feather Thorn.

To destroy the watch.

Pen handed her the bag, his fingers lingering against hers for the briefest moment before stepping back, out of the ritual's boundary. His chest tightened as their eyes met. He wanted to say something, *anything*, but the words caught in his throat.

What could he possibly say?

He could have poured every ounce of love into words, shouted them through the gathering storm, but it wouldn't matter. In minutes, none of it would have ever existed.

And his heart ached beneath the weight of that truth, a grief too vast for breath.

Another crack split through the air, louder this time, and the floor beneath them fractured like porcelain, jagged lines spidering toward the circle that protected them. The old slate roof above them shook, sending down a scatter of wood splinters and dust. The world outside the window had now bent and morphed into something neither of them recognized.

"Adelaide, now!" he urged, eyes locked on the breach inching closer. If it reached the circle, if it shattered the boundary, everything would be lost.

Adelaide clutched the journal, her hands trembling as she read, eyes darting over the instructions of the ritual. Her pulse thundered in her ears.

She was to be the savior of this world and the destroyer of her own.

Her fingernails dug into the soft flesh of her palm as she fought to stay strong, even though she felt like she might shatter into a million pieces.

She looked at him once more. And in his look was everything.

How can I go through with this?

The floor creaked again, louder this time, the sound like bone breaking. Adelaide blinked hard, tore her gaze away from his, and lowered her head to read. She would do it. Even if it broke her. Even if it shattered the only happiness either of them would ever know. Because this wasn't about them. It never had been. It was about every fractured sky, every veering timeline, every life touched and untouched by the device. And putting an end to it for good.

"Pen, I need your pocket knife," she said, her voice tight but steady.

He stepped forward just as the ground shook again, pressing the hilt of the knife into her palm.

Adelaide drew a breath, reached into the leather bag, and pulled out the Astral Synchronum. The golden surface caught the dim light, gleaming with a terrible, ancient beauty.

The moment her fingers wrapped around it, the room exploded with light, turning night into day. Brilliant white beams shot from her body, illuminating every crack, every corner, every shadow. Symbols, intricate and angelic, bloomed beneath her skin, glowing fiercely before fading again, as if something long-dormant had awakened within her.

Pen shielded his eyes, heart pounding.

Adelaide didn't flinch. She stood there, calm and resolute.

When she spoke, her voice rang out clear and unwavering, resonating with a power far older than her own.

"With the blood of the angels that courses within my veins, banish this device until nothing remains."

The words hung in the air like a command from the heavens. Then, she dragged the blade across her palm. Blood welled in a thin line of crimson, glowing faintly in the light. She pressed the watch into it, its golden surface soaking in her blood like ink on parchment.

The reaction was immediate. The air trembled, vibrating with raw energy, and the symbols beneath her skin flared once more, brighter than ever. The walls shook violently, dust and stone rained down, and the building groaned as if it, too, might crumble just as their old world outside the windows had.

Pen fought the urge to run to her; he wanted to be there, holding her hand as the watch's timeline shattered, but the ritual's boundary held firm. All he could do was stand helpless, and watching her.

Adelaide's eyes never left his, and in them he saw everything: grief, courage, and her love for him. She repeated the incantation twice more, each word striking the air like a bell tolling fate.

On the final utterance, a surge of light burst from her chest, spiraling around the Astral Synchronum until it glowed molten. The watch gave a final keening chime, its gears spinning wildly, faster and faster.

Pen saw her mouth the words *I love you*—

And then, before he could even breathe the words back…

A white-hot explosion of light consumed everything. The room. The town. The sky. Brighter than a supernova.

Then—

Nothing.

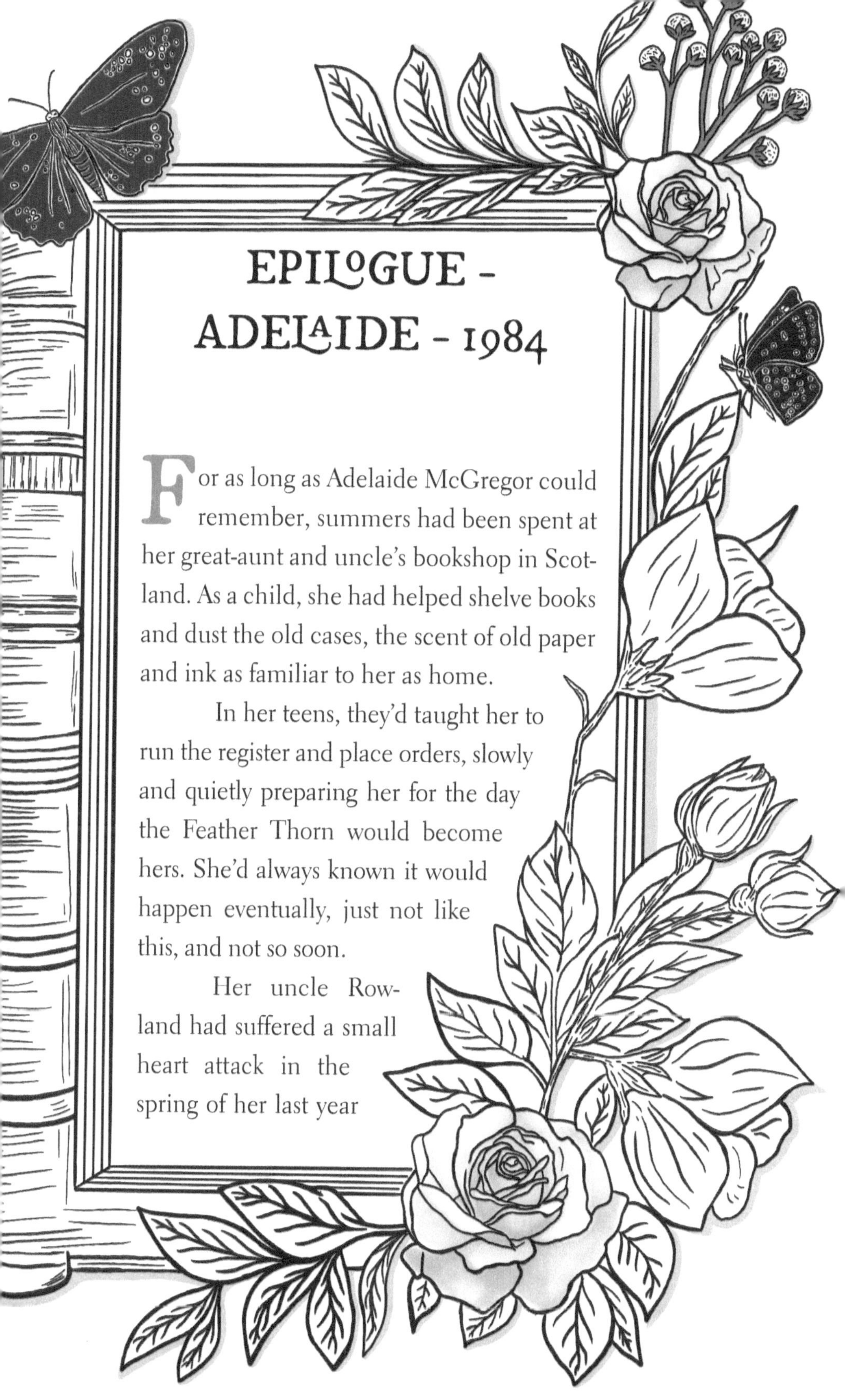

EPILOGUE – ADELAIDE – 1984

For as long as Adelaide McGregor could remember, summers had been spent at her great-aunt and uncle's bookshop in Scotland. As a child, she had helped shelve books and dust the old cases, the scent of old paper and ink as familiar to her as home.

In her teens, they'd taught her to run the register and place orders, slowly and quietly preparing her for the day the Feather Thorn would become hers. She'd always known it would happen eventually, just not like this, and not so soon.

Her uncle Rowland had suffered a small heart attack in the spring of her last year at uni, and Carolyn stubbornly refused to let him return to run the shop.

And so, one day, just as she arrived back at her dorm from a long but interesting lecture on John Dee, the royal occultist, she found a letter waiting for her.

It read: *Addie, it's time. If you want it, the bookshop is yours now. Love, Carolyn.*

Of course she'd said yes.

Her father had been thrilled, mostly because it gave him an excuse to visit Scotland more often. Her mother, on the other hand, had been quietly heartbroken that she wouldn't be coming back to England.

She was only weeks away from finishing her Cultural Studies degree at Edinburgh University, which had a heavy focus on music and its influence on literature. Her mother had called it a useless degree, and maybe it was. But none of that mattered now, because her true dream, the one that had always been waiting for her, was finally within reach.

She left it all behind after graduation, packed her things, ended it with Jeff, a guy she'd been going out with for the past year, who'd been more habit than heart, and set off for Leymark.

It had always felt like she was meant to be there. She couldn't explain it, not even to herself. But something about Leymark, about the Feather Thorn, called to her. As if her path had already been laid out, written in the stars.

That was nearly four years ago, Adelaide thought, turning the heavy bolt lock and pushing open the door. She propped it in place with an old iron owl, a gift from Dottie, who owned the bakery across the street. She'd given it to Adelaide the day she took over the Feather Thorn, a small token of luck for her new Chapter ahead.

Adelaide stepped onto the small walkway leading to the cobbled street and secured the Open flag in its post. A warm breeze drifted past, carrying the promise of summer and the scent of Dottie's fresh scones, which set her stomach groaning. Spring had always been her favorite season, a time of fresh starts and new beginnings.

She waved to Dottie and her husband, Iain, who stood in the bakery window, watching the quiet town wake up for the day.

Just as she turned to head back inside, a large moth, nearly the size of her hand, swooped down and darted through the open door.

"Oh no you don't!" she called, rushing in after it.

The last thing she needed was a book-eating moth wreaking havoc. Did moths even eat books? She wasn't sure, but she wasn't about to take any chances.

She chased it as it fluttered between shelves, weaving through the bookshop, before veering toward the wall of paintings. It landed delicately on the edge of one of Carolyn's canvases, the one of the field behind her house.

Adelaide smiled. Carolyn had once told her the story, how she and Rowland had planned a trip to Rosslyn Chapel, only for a storm to roll in, trapping them inside for the weekend. Rather than sulk over their ruined plans, Carolyn had set up her easel and painted the view from the guest bedroom window.

The contrast of bright wildflowers against the storm-darkened sky had always made it one of Adelaide's favorites.

She stepped forward, cupping her hands, ready to catch the moth, when a voice behind her made her jump.

"Don't touch it, or it won't be able to fly again," a man said, his accent unmistakably American.

Adelaide turned to see a handsome man, around her age,

standing at the bottom of the stairs, looking up at her, one hand resting on the newel post.

"They have a light coating on their wings, some people think it's dust, but it's actually tiny scales called chitin," he explained. "If you touch it, it can weaken the wings, and they won't be able to fly again."

"Well, thanks for the science lesson," she said, with a touch of sarcasm, stepping away from the painting. "But how do I get it out of here?"

"Time," he said with a small smile. "You know, moths are called 'messengers of magic'; it's good luck to have one fly through your door."

She frowned, descending the stairs toward him. "They can deliver whatever message they want, as long as they don't eat my books."

He laughed. "Moths don't eat books."

Adelaide raised an eyebrow. "And I'm meant to just take your word for it? Are you some kind of moth expert?"

"No, not really." He grinned, extending his hand. "But if I were you, I'd be more concerned about bookworms, with all these old books."

She shook his hand, his grip warm. "Thanks, I think I've got that covered. I'm Adelaide."

"My name's Pen."

There was something oddly familiar about him, though she couldn't quite place it.

"So, Pen," she said, turning to the front of the shop, gesturing for him to follow, "what brings you to the Feather Thorn? Looking for anything in particular?"

"I'm actually just stopping in to see the place. It's kind of a weird story," he said with a small chuckle.

"Oh, really? Do tell." Adelaide crossed her arms and leaned against one of the bookshelves.

He smiled awkwardly, hesitating before going on.

"I graduated from Bates last year and started a postgraduate research position in astronomy at the University of Edinburgh. Ever since I arrived, I've been having this recurring dream about a wishing rock, a bookshop, and something to do with a feather." He ran a finger along the spine of a nearby book, his eyes drifting over the shelves. "A colleague suggested it might be this little shop in Leymark. So, I finally decided to drive up this weekend and see it for myself."

"And?" Adelaide asked, her curiosity sparked.

He glanced back at her, his expression caught somewhere between disbelief and wonder. "It's the exact bookshop from my dream. Same layout, same smell, even the chime on the door." He shook his head slightly. "Weird, right?"

"Weird might be an understatement," Adelaide joked. "You know, I've read about that kind of thing happening. Some people say it's echoes from another lifetime."

"Maybe. Not sure I believe in all that, but somehow this place found me in my dreams."

Pen looked up at her, and for a long moment, they simply held each other's gaze.

Adelaide felt her heart drop, a strange sensation rippling through her, something she'd never experienced before. It was as if something inside her had broken free, flooding her with a warmth she couldn't explain.

"How long are you in town?" she asked, the words spilling out before she could stop them.

"Just the weekend." He flashed a smile that only intensified the feeling surging inside her.

"Well," she said, glancing at the moth, fluttering past the history section, "if you're not busy tomorrow, maybe you can stop by and check if my winged messenger is still hanging around. Being an expert and all, I might need your help getting it back outside, without damaging its wings, of course." She paused, then added, "I'll repay you by buying you lunch."

He laughed. "I'll bring a butterfly net. They can be tricky to catch. Kind of like time. Slips past you before you even realize it." He turned toward the door.

"See you tomorrow, then," she said, watching him go.

"Until tomorrow." He waved and stepped out into the sunlight.

The door remained open, a warm breeze drifting through, carrying the scent of spring, scones, and something else: the beginning of something new.

DEAR READER,

You might have noticed the theme of moths woven throughout this book. The idea for *The Messengers of Magic* came to me one day out of the blue, when I overheard a man talking about how moths were once known as messengers of magic. That single phrase sparked something in me, and from it, this entire story bloomed.

If you've read my other books, you probably know I love tucking in little Easter eggs, those hidden details that reveal themselves on the second or even third read. This book is no different. Now that you've reached the end, I can finally share one of my favorite hidden gems I have ever tucked away inside a book: every business name in the story, including the name of Adelaide's band, and the street the Feather Thorn is on, were inspired by real moths found in Scotland.

The idea came to me early in the writing process, when I ordered a field guide on British moths for inspiration. (Which took nearly three weeks to arrive from Scotland.) As I wrote, I would flip through that book, looking for names that felt like they belonged in the world I was building. *The Feather Thorn* was the first and most important name I chose. The rest bloomed from there.

Here's a list of the names you might recognize, along with the real-life moths and butterflies that inspired them:

- **The Feather Thorn** — *Feathered Thorn (Colotois pennaria)* A rust-brown moth with feathery antennae, often seen fluttering in autumn twilight.

- **The Marbled Clover Bakery** — *Marbled Clover (Heliothis viriplaca)* A rare summer visitor in the UK, this pale green moth feeds on wild clover and thistles.

- **The Purple Thorn Apothecary** — *Purple Thorn (Selenia tetralunaria)* A beautifully shaped moth with angular wings and dusky purple hues, most active in spring.

- **Clifden Motter Lodge** — *Clifden Nonpareil (Blue Underwing) (Catocala fraxini)* Once thought extinct in the UK, this striking moth has vivid blue underwings hidden beneath gray-brown forewings.

- **The Dotted Chestnut Diner** — *Dotted Chestnut (Conistra rubiginea)* A soft orange-brown moth that flies in late autumn and overwinters as an adult—rare in Scotland but a lovely name.

- **Emperor Moth Inn** — *Emperor Moth (Saturnia pavonia)* The UK's only native silk moth, with large eye spots on its wings to scare off predators.

- **Camberwell Street** — *Camberwell Beauty (Nymphalis antiopa)* A rare but showstopping butterfly with deep

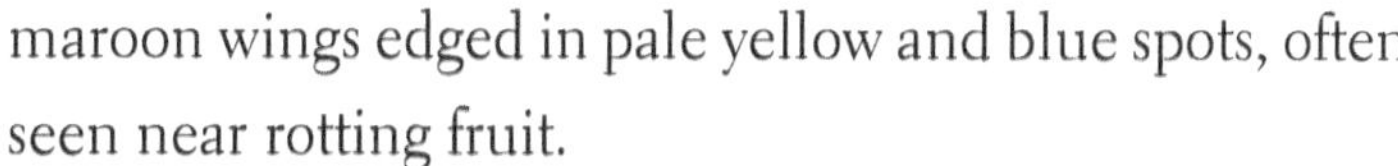

maroon wings edged in pale yellow and blue spots, often seen near rotting fruit.

- **Bloxworth Hardware** — *Bloxworth Snout (Hypena obsitalis)* First recorded in Bloxworth, Dorset—this subtly colored moth is rare and elusive.

- **The Common Blue** — *Common Blue (Polyommatus icarus)* A dainty butterfly found in grassy meadows, its males flash brilliant blue when the sun hits just right.

- **The Dark Dagger Bar** — *Dark Dagger (Acronicta tridens)* A cryptic gray moth with dark dagger-like markings; its caterpillar is just as fierce-looking.

- **The Royal Mantle Restaurant** — *Royal Mantle (Catarhoe cuculata)* Delicate and rarely seen, with a regal blend of deep purple and cream on its wings.

- **The Dusty Brocade** *(Adelaide's band)* — *Dusty Brocade (Apamea remissa)* A subtly patterned moth with dusky gray wings, often seen near hedgerows and wildflowers.

Thank you for reading this book and being part of the magic in the worlds I create. Without readers like you, I'd be wandering them alone.

Yours,

Jessica Dodge

ABOUT THE AUTHOR

Jessica Dodge is a native Vermonter with a deep passion for storytelling. With a degree in motion picture direction and over a decade as a visual artist, she now brings her worlds to life on the page with a cinematic flair. Her bestselling series, *The Triquatra Chronicles*, has captured the hearts of readers who love magic, mystery, and Celtic folklore.

When she's not writing, Jessica enjoys spending time outdoors with her family and four beloved dogs. The forest is her sanctuary, rivaled only by the misty highlands of Scotland. She's a lover of all things vintage and never turns down a good treasure hunt through a thrift store for old, forgotten things. She has an impressive collection of baseball caps and vintage journals. You might find her collecting rocks by a stream or curled up on the couch with a good book and a pup (or three) nestled at her side. Writing is her magic, and she's grateful to share that magic with the world.